SILK

Heart of India Series

Silk
Under Eastern Stars
Kingscote

The Great Northwest Series

Empire Builders
Winds of Allegiance

Royal Pavilion Series

Swords and Scimitars
Golden Palaces

SILK

LINDA CHAIKIN

BETHANY HOUSE PUBLISHERS
MINNEAPOLIS, MINNESOTA 55438

Cover illustration by Joe Nordstrom

Copyright © 1993
Linda Chaikin
All Rights Reserved

Published by Bethany House Publishers
A Ministry of Bethany Fellowship, Inc.
6820 Auto Club Road, Minneapolis, Minnesota 55438

Printed in the United States of America

Library of Congress Cataloging-in-Publication Data

Chaikin, Linda.   Silk/ Linda Chaikin.
    p. cm.

    1. British—India—History—18th century—Fiction.
I. Title.
PS3553.H2427X54   1993
813'.54—dc20   92–46506
ISBN 1–55661–248–6   CIP

This first book of *Silk*
is dedicated to
Sharon Madison,
along with the words of Psalm 20:1–5.

LINDA CHAIKIN is a full-time writer and has two books published in the Christian market. She graduated from Multnomah School of the Bible and is working on a degree with Moody Bible Institute. She and her husband, Steve, are involved with a church-planting mission among Hindus in Kerala, India. They make their home in San Jose, California.

Prologue

KINGSCOTE SILK PLANTATION, NORTHEAST INDIA

JUNE 1793

The gilded clock in the Long Gallery of the Kendall mansion chimed the hour of ten. Through the open verandah the familiar jungle sounds from the Kingscote Plantation drifted on the humid air into Coral's bedroom. The screech of a night bird pierced the darkness, followed by an eerie cackle. Leaves and vines rustled, and if she fed her imagination, she could distinguish the low grumble of a Bengal tiger.

Dressed in a white peignoir, Coral, newly turned sixteen, left her bedroom and hurried down the hall. Her deep green eyes shining with excitement in the candlelight, and her golden hair falling about her shoulders, she descended the winding mahogany staircase intending to speak with her mother about the following morning's event.

Coral paused in the shadows at the sound of low, anxious voices in the gallery below.

Clutching her candle as close as she dared, Coral peered over the banister into the Great Hall. She was greeted by the sight of her stalwart father, Sir Hampton Kendall, standing near the door in a boot-length riding cloak. Her mother retrieved his tricorn hat from off the table as he belted on his scabbard.

Whatever would goad her father to ride out at this hour?

His deep voice reached her on the stairs. "Major Jace Buckley best be sending some of his sepoys to track this tiger, or the commissioner will hear my complaint. A half-dozen kills along the river alone! Aye, the brute's the worst man-eater seen in many a year."

"Must you ride to the outpost tonight?" Coral's mother questioned him. "Tomorrow's ceremony means so much to Coral. This will be her first time out of sickbed in months."

"Aye, I'm not forgetting that, Liza."

"She expects you to be there. She is already disappointed her sisters are still in Calcutta."

Her father's voice lowered, and Coral strained to catch his words. ". . . is it wise? The ritual could provoke the ghazis . . ."

"On Kingscote?"

"To be certain, this is not the raja's palace at Sibsagar, and yet . . ."

"We've always respected their beliefs, as they have ours."

"Tales of abductions, of druggings permanently affecting the mind, are not exaggerations. First converts from among their own are oft times murdered by the ghazis. It is their way of discouraging any from abandoning the caste system."

"Surely you do not think anything so dark could happen here?"

"With the maharaja asking the East India Company for military help against Burma, I discount nothing. Major Buckley arrived a few weeks ago, and more sepoys are on the way from the Calcutta garrison. Resentment over the Company grows."

"But it was the maharaja who sent emissaries to Calcutta asking for help."

"Aye, yet not all in the royal family are pleased with his move."

"They fear another annexation by England?"

"This time the province of Assam. Distrust of the Company's motives in sending troops cannot benefit Kingscote. And a Christian baptism of a Hindu taking place here will only increase the tension among the workers."

Her mother's voice lowered: "You are right about mounting tension. Even Rajiv wonders if he did the correct thing in giving Jemani permission. If we hadn't promised—"

"You spoke to him?"

"He came by this afternoon hoping to talk to you. He told me you promised him your support. Your presence as the *burra-sahib** of Kingscote would lend credibility before the other workers."

He groaned. "Ah, Liza, I did promise him . . . little Coral talked me into it. But that was before the drums of war beat so loudly."

Elizabeth Kendall laughed with soft affection and rested her forehead against his strong arm. "And you tell me I am too lenient with her."

"Are we both not spoiling her? Yet this long struggle with her illness . . ." Her father sighed. "But there

*See p. 347 for a glossary of Indian terms.

11

is little I can do about keeping my promise now. This ugly matter of the tiger must be taken care of. The beast will soon be stalking Kingscote if we do not stop him! With twenty new children arriving to work in the silk hatcheries, the tiger must be killed."

He laid his hands on her shoulders and kissed her forehead. "Explain the matter to Coral."

"Yes, but what of Rajiv?"

He frowned. "I will stop by the bungalow before I leave. Another warning is wise. Should anything happen, I do not want these hands of mine tainted with their blood."

"Hampton! Do not say that. May God give us peace."

"Aye, and you and Coral best be getting to your prayers as soon as possible."

"You will encourage him?" she asked as he embraced her.

"I will," came his rugged voice. "I already vowed to stand with him. But—I am not comfortable with this. I was against this Christian ritual from the moment Coral came to me with it."

"I know, dear, but it is not as if we are sounding a trumpet before us. It will only be the four of us at the river."

He sighed.

"Darling, we did promise," she insisted. "Coral has been so ill . . . and this is the one bright moment she has known in a year. It is not as though she deliberately pressed Jemani to be baptized."

"I know, Liza, I know. But the words of those books have been burned into Coral's soul. I dare say they've kindled thoughts of bold exploits."

She hesitated. "Yes, the books . . . I sent for them from the shop in London. . . . Men like Brainerd and Wesley are worthy of study. And she enjoys them so."

"Goodly men, all. But this past year, with naught else to do but read and study them, she has changed from the girl we raised."

"She is joyful now, whereas in the past she was melancholy."

"It is only that she is so young to have brought the Indian girl to faith in the Blessed Christ. And she worries me a little." He frowned. "Will she ever want to mind the matter of marriage and children?"

"Of course she will. Give her time, dear."

"Does she not spend too much time with the workers? If she is lacking friends, perhaps it is time to send her to school in London."

"You sound so European!" Elizabeth chided in a teasing voice. "It was you who laughed at my colonial attitude when I arrived here as your bride, so naive of India. But Coral was born here! She feels none of that. Is it any wonder she has developed this kinship with the land and its people?"

"Aye, and I am proud of her. She is naught like her sisters. But is it not time she also meet the lords and ladies at Roxbury House in London? Her sister Kathleen is enough trouble . . . worming her way out of marrying her honorable Scottish cousin! Coral should be married soon—"

"Oh, Hampton, she is much too frail! Please, you promised me we would wait!"

He swiftly embraced her, his strong hand awkwardly patting her lustrous dark hair. "Now, now, my sweet dove, do not be upset . . . we will wait . . ."

There was a moment of silence, then Elizabeth's voice came again: "Hampton? About Jemani . . . you must admit that she is worthy of Coral's friendship. She is an excellent teacher of the Hindi language. And with Coral leading her into the Christian belief, it is not so surprising the two have formed a bond."

"And what is wrong with her two blood sisters?"

"You know very well Kathleen and Marianna are still in Calcutta. Besides, they do not share the same interests Coral has developed."

"In that, she is like you," came his tender voice. "I will not begrudge her the faith that makes you so strong."

They held each other until Elizabeth spoke. "But I do wonder sometimes about Jemani."

"In what way, Liza?"

"She is so gracious, so intelligent for being an untouchable." Elizabeth's voice lowered. "The other day she was reading Indian poetry to Coral."

"Is that so surprising?"

Elizabeth's voice remained quiet: "It was written in Sanskrit."

"Sanskrit! Now how would she be knowing the language of the ruling caste of brahmins?"

"I don't know, Hampton, I have often wondered. . . . Did Rajiv ever explain who their families were?"

"Nay. They were hungry and exhausted when I found them by the river. Jemani ill and expecting the child. Rajiv mentioned Rajasthan. They wandered here, looking for work, he said. I saw no reason to pry. Are you asking me to?"

"No, no, not now. I would not wish to alarm them by your questions. They risk enough already."

"Whatever Rajasthan meant in their past, it will not matter to Kingscote. If trouble confronts us, it will come from the meddling of the East India Company in Assam! I blame my brother-in-law for it. Sir Hugo is at Jorhat now. And I have little doubt he is promising the maharaja protection from Burma."

14

"Let us not discuss Hugo. . . . I would delay the baptism until you return, dear, but in Jemani's condition I think it best we do not. The baby is due in eight weeks."

He sighed. "Do as you will, Liza. I shall return as quickly as I can settle matters about the tiger with Major Buckley."

"Isn't he Colonel Warbeck's son?"

"Aye, and a friend of our son. Buckley's a good-looking devil, a rogue and a gentleman all in one. Good blood, too, and a strong wit. I suspect he'd produce me some strong grandsons—"

"Hampton!"

Coral had not moved from the shadows on the staircase, nor did she now. Her legs felt weak from being confined to bed for so many months with tropical fever. With one hand gripping the banister, and the other holding tightly to the candle-holder, she watched her father bend to kiss her mother goodbye, then leave by way of the heavy wooden door. Coral's excitement died like an extinguished flame. *Ghazis* . . .

Unwilling that her mother know she had overheard, she rose and silently retraced her steps up the stairway to her bedroom. A movement below in the shadows of the open library door caught her eye. Without a sound, the door shut. Someone else had been listening. *One of the house servants?*

She waited until her mother had left the Great Hall for the kitchen to give the nightly orders to the *kansamah;* then, bolstering her courage, Coral went quietly down the stairs and crossed the marble floor to the library door. Taking hold of the door latch, she opened it wide.

The library was in semidarkness. She stood in the doorway with the light from the hall behind her, still

15

holding her candle. Books lined the walls from floor to ceiling and filled her nostrils with the rich smell of leather. During her year of illness these precious books had been her only friends.

"Who is in here?"

Silence greeted her, and so did a breath of the hot, muggy night air coming in through the split-cane window shades. Coral stood there for a moment longer, then went to close the window. She peered out into the garden, but saw no one. Had she imagined seeing the door shut? Was her ongoing fever playing tricks with her mind again? She pulled the window shut and latched it.

Exiting the library, she slowly climbed the staircase, pausing at each landing to glance back.

Once in her room, Coral stood in the shadows, her gaze fixed on the small whitish flame of her candle. She tried to shake off the feeling of unease, but the words of her father burned within her mind:

"The first converts from among their own are oft times murdered by the ghazis."

Had not her mother said there were no fanatics on Kingscote?

Coral knew the Hindu caste system was strictly adhered to, and there were times when there was trouble in the village. But the Hindus that were part of Coral's world—men and women like Natine, Mera, Rosa, and a host of others—were all people whom she had known and grown up with as a part of her life on Kingscote. They were always friendly to her, and she held a deep affection for them. But it was true that her beliefs and theirs had not yet collided. Would Jemani's baptism change all this?

Some of her first memories were of her gray-haired *ayah*, Mera, rocking her in a split-cane chair in

16

the nursery, humming some ancient Indian song while Coral's older sister, Kathleen, played with wooden blocks on the ishafan rug. Mera had been their ayah until the birth of Marianna and the arrival of the younger Burmese woman, Jan-Lee. Coral's childhood memories were all pleasant, like the many times she and her sisters had crept into the kitchen to beg sweet *barfis*—milk cakes made with coconut—from Rosa. While her brows would scowl down at them, Rosa's dark eyes were always full of mirth.

No . . . these dear people were not the Indian fanatics known as ghazis. She would never believe that they could act in violence. Yet what did she truly know about their ancient religion? Except for the Hindu festivals when the juggernauts—huge, extravagantly decorated temple boxes—were dragged through the streets, she knew little.

In spite of Coral's efforts to dismiss her unease, her father's words brought a prickle to her skin. It was true that permission for Jemani's baptism had been nearly impossible to obtain from Rajiv.

Coral smiled to herself as she recalled how Jemani had retained her demeanor when arriving last week for the daily language lesson. No sooner were they alone, than she rushed to Coral with the news that her husband Rajiv had changed his mind. After three months of firm refusal, Rajiv finally agreed to permit his wife's baptism in the holy river before the baby was born. They had thrown their arms about each other and laughed when Jemani's extended womb hindered the embrace.

"You were right! Our God has heard my prayer!" Jemani then lowered her voice to a whisper. "Do not say a word to anyone, but Rajiv is also showing interest in the Christian teaching. Last night as we lay in

17

our bed, he asked me important questions about the Christ of your Book."

Thinking back over that moment of spiritual joy brought Coral new resolve. No, she had not been wrong in showing Jemani the gift that Grandmother Victoria Roxbury had sent to her on the Christmas of 1791. The Bible was bound with embossed leather, the pages edged in gold, and Coral's name had been inscribed on the cover leaf along with the Roxbury coat of arms.

What had happened to Jemani after that was more an act of God than a plan instigated by Coral. She had asked Jemani to transcribe some of the verses in the gospel of Saint John into Hindi. And within five months, after much secret discussion between them, Jemani had declared that she wanted to become a Christian.

Now, as Coral lay in the dark, sleep remained elusive. She convinced herself the reason was that her father had ridden to the military outpost at Jorhat while a man-eating tiger was roaming the jungle. Watching the mosquito net that encircled her bed flutter lazily in the light breeze, Coral soon found herself drifting off.

By morning, the ghosts of the night before had evaporated with the sweltering Indian heat. At the still waters of the glittering Brahmaputra River, Coral slipped the ankle-length tunic over the head of the lovely young Indian woman, and let it fall into place.

Jemani smiled, her warm brown eyes shining and a tinge of rose showing beneath her copper skin.

"Rajiv will come with the memsahib," she told Coral, speaking of Elizabeth Kendall. Jemani glanced through the mango trees in the direction of the dirt road and her gaze took on a far-distant look. "My Rajiv is a prince. There is no one better among men. He shall be a goodly father."

Coral strained to hear the *ghari* coming down the narrow road. Instead she heard the familiar cackle of mynah birds in the branches. To ease the building tension, she tried to coax a smile from Jemani. "You are right about not wanting to wait. If we delayed any longer, instead of an oversized tunic, you would need to don a *shamianah*," she said, speaking of a large Indian tent.

Jemani gave a nervous giggle, then sobered, running her palms over her protruding womb. "Both I and my child will be baptized together. Rajiv knew I wanted this."

Coral picked up the skirts of the simple muslin dress that she had donned for the wet and muddy occasion and hurried toward the bank, feeling the dried elephant grass brush her pantaloons. She stooped, letting the warm water trickle through her fingers. Her gaze scanned the river. There were no crocodiles, nor any sign of the one-horned black rhino. A few disinterested monkeys swung through the green branches along the bank, and fruit bats enjoyed the mangoes.

"The temperature is fine," Coral called over her shoulder. "Mother said the water will not hurt your condition."

"The memsahib is wise. I feel at peace knowing she will deliver my son."

"Son?" teased Coral. "My, but you are in a positive mood. I will take a girl any day."

She expected to hear another laugh, and when there was silence, Coral turned her head to discover the reason. Jemani had walked toward her, her dark eyes searching Coral's face.

"If my baby is a girl, Rajiv and I will name her Coral. Son or daughter, you will protect my child?"

Coral stared up at her. The idea that any child would need protection on the Kendall silk plantation brought immediate anxiety. A realization of her own responsibility over Jemani's public confession deepened Coral's resolve to protect her friend.

"Say you will, Coral." Jemani stooped down beside her, anxiously searching her eyes.

Coral rested a hand on her shoulder. "The Kendall family has produced silk on this land for nearly a hundred years. Our men have fought soldiers from Rangoon and warriors from Sikkim. Neither my father nor my brothers will run away from danger, Jemani. And neither will I."

"Your father is honorable, and brave."

Coral felt a rush of pride. "Yes, he is all that. And he will not permit hostility toward you and Rajiv as long as you live on Kingscote. Your baby will be safe."

Coral felt Jemani take hold of her hand and place the palm against her womb. She whispered intently: "You and the memsahib are my only friends. Now the true Holy Man—Jesus—has washed me clean. He has done what the holy Ganges cannot do. Today my heart can laugh and sing. For the first time I do not fear death, for a thousand rebirths do not await me, rather eternal life. But there are things you do not know, Coral. Things I cannot—must not—tell you."

Coral felt uncomfortable. *What things?* she wanted to ask, but Jemani continued. "Is not memsahib a godmother to your cousin in Calcutta?"

Coral thought of her spoiled cousin Belinda Roxbury. Her two sisters were visiting her now.

"Yes, and my aunt and uncle are my godparents. Why do you ask?"

Jemani's expression was intense. "And this you do in the church?"

"Yes . . . I suppose you might say that."

Jemani drew in a breath. "I know we are different. You are from England and I—"

"I too was born in India," Coral interrupted.

"Yes, that is so. Then please, will you consider becoming godmother to my child?"

Coral stared at her, wondering if she had heard correctly.

"Rajiv told me to ask you before the baptism."

Coral felt her throat constrict. She had never seen Jemani this earnest before. For Coral to make such a promise without her parents' permission was unthinkable, and yet . . . she felt a gentle pressure from within that bid her to risk something of herself, since Jemani was risking so much.

Coral looked into the trusting eyes of her friend and found that it was easy for her emotions to let the request take root in her soul. During the year of her illness, she had lain in bed listening to her mother reading from the autobiography of the great colonial missionary to the American Indians, David Brainerd. His dedication to Christ, and his love for the people he served, had often brought tears to her eyes, and it was easy to imagine herself following in his steps.

Her sister Kathleen insisted that Coral felt too deeply, and reacted impulsively, but Coral could not help herself. Strong emotion came easily. And now, the urgent request made by her first convert lit a small flame in her heart. As she stared into Jemani's dark eyes, she could feel the heartbeat of the child touching her palm.

21

"Yes, Jemani."

Jemani's eyes glistened. "You are more than a friend. You are as close to me as my sister was."

"Was?"

"She is dead."

Coral stared at her, but the creak of ghari wheels and the plod of horse hooves on the road caused Jemani to loosen Coral's hand, and she stood, drawing Coral up with her.

Coral squinted beneath her raised hand. "It is my mother, and your husband is with her."

With a pleased cry, Jemani hurried to meet him.

Coral watched as the dark, handsome Rajiv stepped from the ghari and assisted her mother down to the ground.

Elizabeth Kendall, carrying her Bible, greeted Jemani with a palm to her cheek, then walked to Coral. "I am proud of you, dear."

Coral slipped her arm about her mother's slim waist.

Minutes later, Coral stood on the bank, holding the blanket and a cloth to dry with. Her heart thumped as she watched her mother leading Jemani by the arm into the river. A quick glance at Rajiv showed an immobile face. What was churning within his mind Coral could only guess. She looked back to see Jemani standing before her mother, nearly waist deep in the water. Coral squeezed back her tears.

Thank you, God, for this privilege. I thought my life was wasting away on a sickbed. Yet out of my weakness, you have brought life everlasting.

She heard her mother speaking, and the words came enriched with new meaning to Coral.

"Jemani, you have taken Jesus the Son of God to be your Savior and Lord. And because you have confessed your new faith, I now baptize you in the name of the Father, the Son, and the Holy Ghost. Amen."

A gentle swoosh filled the hot morning. Water rippled, and Jemani came up sopping wet, her ebony hair sticking to the sides of her face. Elizabeth opened her arms, and Jemani stepped into them.

Coral watched them standing there in an embrace that transcended nationality.

Yes, Jemani had been right. They were truly sisters.

Rajiv broke the emotional intensity. He stepped into the river, reaching out both hands to help the two women back onto dry ground, and then holding his wife, he murmured something in Hindi. She smiled up at him, and he brushed his fingers across her cheeks, wiping away the tears. He kissed his fingers, then touched Jemani's lips. Coral turned away from the intimate scene.

Coral heard a sound behind her, coming from the thick jungle growth. A sweeping glance along the fringe of trees revealed nothing. *The wind?* she wondered. *Perhaps a bird or a monkey.*

She was turning back toward the river when the unmistakable flash of a white *puggari* disappeared into the thick green. Someone had been crouching behind the bushes. Watching. Someone who did not want to be seen. No doubt he had only been curious, and yet fearful to show himself, not wanting to associate with the condemned act.

Just then, several overripe figs plopped to the dirt from the branch above Coral's head. She looked up into the gnarled tree, shading her eyes. Eight-year-old Yanna straddled the limb, her black pigtails swinging. The girl swung down and landed gracefully on sandaled feet.

Coral let out a nervous breath. "Yanna, were you up there all that time?"

Yanna ran toward her, wearing dusty white. She murmured in Hindi: "Burra-sahib warn me to stay away. But Jemani is my friend."

The title of burra-sahib—the "great man"—was used on Kingscote for Sir Hampton Kendall. But her father was away at the military outpost in Jorhat. Had he spoken to the child before he left late last night, or was Yanna speaking of someone else?

Her mother's voice interrupted her thoughts.

"Coral, come along dear, we must get back."

"Yes, Mother, I'm coming."

"You too, Yanna," called Elizabeth. "You can ride on the driver's seat with Rajiv."

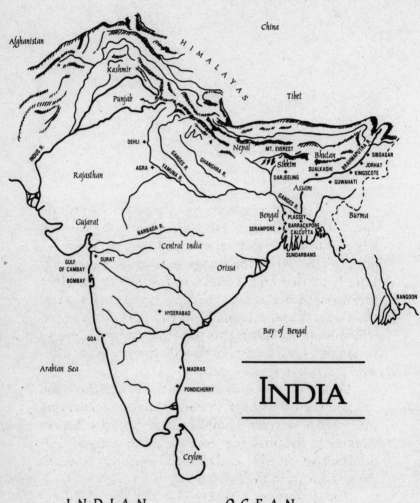

Afghanistan

China

HIMALAYAS

Kashmir

Tibet

Punjab

INDUS R.

DEHLI

Nepal

MT. EVEREST

Bhutan

SIBSAGAR

GANGES R.

Sikkim

SUALKASHI

BRAHMAPUTRA R.

JORHAT

Rajasthan

AGRA

YAMUNA R.

GHANGHRA R.

DARJEELING

KINGSCOTE

Assam

GUWAHATI

GANGES R.

Gujarat

NARBADA R.

Bengal

PLASSEY

Burma

Central India

SERAMPORE

BARRACKPORE

CALCUTTA

GULF
OF CAMBAY

SURAT

Orissa

SUNDARBANS

BOMBAY

HYDERABAD

Bay of Bengal

RANGOON

GOA

Arabian Sea

MADRAS

PONDICHERRY

INDIA

Ceylon

INDIAN   OCEAN

1

Coral stared anxiously from her bedroom verandah at the jungle perimeter surrounding the Kendall silk plantation. Silence permeated the rosy dusk. No elephant feet raised the dust along the road where they usually carried huge bundles of raw silk to the river. In season, the flat wooden barges would set off toward the Ganges, and eventually to the port of Calcutta, where ships belonging to the East India Company would sail for the ports of the silk-hungry West: Venice, Cadiz, Lyons, and London.

Coral's eyes were riveted on the road, where the twilight seeped through the branches of intertwining trees. There were no sounds coming from the Indian workers in the huts, nor from the newly arrived children being trained to feed chopped mulberry leaves to the silkworms in the hatcheries.

Coral tensed. Thinking about the children brought her concerns back to Jemani and the dilemma confronting her. Rajiv was missing! Jemani, distraught by the news, had gone into premature labor. If she gave birth now, the baby would be born six weeks early.

Her hands tightened on the wrought-iron railing. Perhaps the news that Jemani's husband was missing would prove to be nothing serious, and he would return unharmed. But even if he did, the crisis now facing Coral would remain.

Unaware of Rajiv's disappearance and its effect on Jemani, Coral's mother had left before dawn to deliver medicine to the nearby village. With the tiger scare holding Kingscote captive, her father had accompanied her, bringing several armed workers with him. Even her two sisters were away; not that they would be much help, she thought dourly. Kathleen would balk at the idea of delivering a baby, and Marianna would swoon!

Unless her mother returned soon, she would need to deliver the baby alone. Coral's heart gave a nervous flutter. . . . Suppose she forgot something important? Suppose she froze at the sights and sounds of Jemani's suffering?

No, she must be strong. She had promised Jemani that she would not forsake her. Coral took in a deep breath and tried to relax, but her efforts brought no relief. Her heart thudded. She had previously accompanied her mother to assist during the birthing process of other workers on Kingscote, but never had she delivered a baby by herself. She closed her eyes and tried to remember everything her mother did, but anxiety left gaps in her memory.

If it had not been for my prolonged struggle with tropical fever, I would not be facing this emergency, she thought. How simple matters would be if she were with her sisters in Calcutta visiting her aunt and cousin, with nothing more important to do than attend a round of elegant balls and picnics in the escort of young British officers.

Of course! she thought. She could turn to Jan-Lee! The Burmese woman who had been her devoted ayah could deliver the baby. She whirled to leave the verandah, but stopped. Her delicate brows came together. No, she could not! Jan-Lee would not be in any condition to aid her as midwife, since she had given birth to her own child only days ago.

Frightened, Coral stared out across the sloping lawn that led to the low banks of the Brahmaputra. The eastern sun deepened into shades of orange above the river, and thread-legged cranes gathered to drink and lift their eyes to the distant clouds.

If only her mother would arrive in the boat! Not a whisper of wind stirred her flaxen tresses that were plaited in thick braids at the nape of her neck. She was dressed as one would expect on a plantation that produced some of the finest silk in the East—in a cool and loose-fitting silk tunic—a practical style of dress bearing little resemblance to the yards of skirts, crinolines, and hoops that she would be expected to wear at Roxbury House when she arrived in London to visit her grandmother.

The leaves on the trees were painted with dust, and her mother's garden of purple bougainvillea lay withered and thirsty in the sun's heat. Coral had lived through many dry seasons where all life was poised with expectation, waiting for the first grumble of thunder, the first fat drops of water to splat against the powdery dust. The insatiable thirst of the giant land awaited brief fulfillment in the flood that would wash all things clean and fill the rivers. At the moment, Coral's prayer broke like an India flood upon her soul:

Lord, please help Mother get here in time!

Cutting through the afternoon stillness, frantic voices shouted from the direction of the river, followed by the trumpeting of an elephant.

Coral shaded her eyes, hoping that her prayer only moments before had indeed been answered.

Coral stared toward the *ghat*, where stone steps led down to the small boats. Two white-clad barge workers, called *manjis*, ran toward the mansion. Another rode the back of a gray elephant, its ears flapping like tents.

Natine, who was her father's *kotwal* over the other servants on Kingscote, left the front porch to meet them on the lawn. He stood with dignity in a white puggari and a long blue shirt over white baggy trousers. The manjis spoke rapidly in Hindi, but Coral could not hear what they were saying. They seemed overly excited for the mere arrival of her mother. *Something is wrong.*

Natine hurried back up the lawn toward the house, and Coral grasped the railing and leaned over.

"Natine! What is it? News from my mother and father?"

The turbaned head lifted in her direction. His walnut-skinned face was grave. "No, miss-sahiba. They are still in the village."

Her father had returned a week earlier from the British outpost near Jorhat. Only yesterday, he had warned them that it was a Royal Bengal tiger—ten feet long, male, aggressive, and white-ruffed. Tigers, of course, were not unusual around Kingscote, and Coral had seen many. This one, however, was a maneater. Since her father had ridden to the outpost, the tiger had attacked two fishermen, mauling one and eating the other. The tiger proved to be cunning, avoiding the traps, terrorizing the village, and now holding Kingscote captive.

"What did the manjis say? Is it the tiger?"

"Major Buckley sent a message: The tiger is on Kingscote. He says the workers must be on guard. The women and children are not to venture out."

Her father had already told her that a patrol belonging to the 21st Light Cavalry in command of the native *sowars* had been on the lookout for days.

Her stomach muscles tightened. She had no choice but to disobey the major's orders. Did Natine know about Jemani, that she must deliver the baby? She guessed that he did, but his expression had not softened.

From the kitchen below, she heard the pleasant sounds of dinner being prepared. Mera's voice floated up to her on the verandah, rebuking the two Indian children who had done something wrong. Faithful, loving Mera . . . but there was no use ordering her to assist in the delivery; the head female servant of the household would vow that she preferred death to breaking caste with an untouchable.

"Any news about Rajiv?" she called down.

Natine hesitated. "Not yet. With the news of the tiger, I must call off the search."

He turned away and began to issue orders to the two workers. Coral felt queasy. *Where is Jemani's husband?*

She remained at the rail looking down. The workers listened to Natine as though he were the burra-sahib. Recently, she had become aware of how all the *nauker-log* jumped to obey his commands. Natine was both respected and feared. She had once

31

asked her father about Natine's background, and discovered that he was of the *rajputs* from Moghul country in Rajasthan, central India. The rajputs were said to be born in the warrior caste of the Hindu system, only one rank below the priestly *brahmins*. One thing was certain; Natine did not permit the nauker-log to forget.

A distant rumble reverberated. She tensed. The tiger? No—she blinked as a brilliant flash of dry lightning zigzagged across the murky sky, heralding the monsoon. The sullen grumble echoed its warning as movement drew her eyes in the direction of the silk workers' huts. Yanna raced across the dusty field toward the house, her willowlike body lost in the flapping white sari. Coral's heart began to pound. No. . . .

She had sent Yanna to stay with Jemani early that morning after the news of Rajiv's disappearance, and she knew the child was bringing her the words she did not want to hear.

Yanna stood barefoot in the dust. "Missy Coral! Missy Coral! Must bring memsahib and come quick!"

Coral's hands turned clammy. Her own calm voice surprised her. She leaned over the rail. "Wait for me, Yanna. I will be down in a minute!"

The girl nodded, her small hand clamped across her mouth, her round dark eyes frightened.

Natine was still standing below in the stone courtyard adjacent to the lawn. She noted the rigid shoulders that shouted his resentment over her involvement. Except for his common garb, he could have passed for some Moghul king from the glorious Indian past, disdainful of the English influence. She called out, ignoring his displeasure: "Natine! I will need

Mera to help me. Call her at once."

For a moment he remained immobile, like a deaf mute staring up at her. At last, he brought his fingers together at his forehead in *namaste*. He went up the porch steps into the house and headed toward the back of the mansion.

Coral whirled, ran from the bedroom verandah, and snatched up her mother's medical bag that waited by the door. She lifted her tunic and rushed down the flight of stairs, ignoring the weakness in her knees. Whether it was due to fear or illness, she could not be certain. She paused at the bottom and caught her breath, feeling her heart thumping. With dignity that far surpassed her sixteen years, she walked past silent servants who pretended to know nothing of the emergency. In the hall, she stopped and looked toward the back of the house. "Natine? Mera!"

The mansion walled her in with silence. From outside she could hear the distant shouts of *mahouts* riding away on their elephants to warn the silk workers of the tiger.

Had Natine delivered her message? "Mera!" She set the bag down and ran back into the kitchen. Only the male kansamah was there, his brown hands dusted white with flour. He looked up, the usually good-natured face impassive.

"Harish! Where is Mera?"

"I do not know, Miss Coral."

"Where is Natine?"

"He went to warn the workers of the tiger."

So. Natine had ignored her instructions. Well, there was nothing to be done about it now. She spun around and hurried out.

On the verandah steps, she paused to look out

across the wide lawn toward the river, still hoping to see the barge bringing her mother.

The white-clad manjis, leaving their work on the Kendall boats, ran along the bank shouting to the other fishermen to take heed.

"Tyger! Tyger!"

"Kahbahdar! Tyger! Kahbahdar! Tyger!"

Coral dared not think about the ten-foot Bengal tiger. She hurried after Yanna, who ran ahead across the field in the direction of the road, dust rising beneath her soles. Every so often Yanna stopped to cast an anxious glance over her shoulder to make sure Coral was following.

What will I do when I get there? thought Coral, feeling the sweat trickle down her ribs. With her mother's bag in hand, she hurried on. "Lord, please be with me. . . ."

Again she tried to remember everything her mother had taught her about delivering a baby. Months of illness left her gasping as she ran behind Yanna, the dirt encasing itself inside her slippers. Fatigue assailed her. Her brain spun dizzily.

Yanna waited near the road. Here they would cut across the shadowy acres of mulberry trees to the whitewashed hut.

"Wait," Coral cried breathlessly, forced to pause beneath an arch of trees. She leaned against the trunk trying to catch her breath. There was no wind, insects droned, the jungle smelled hot and dry, and the sounds of the tropics were magnified in the stillness: "Monsoon, monsoon," they seemed to murmur.

Yanna stood watching Coral, her large dark eyes tense. She impatiently brushed the gnats from her cheek.

A sound coming from farther down the road caused Coral to straighten, and she gazed down the avenue of trees. Horse hooves raised the distant dust, followed by a faint jangle of metal.

"Soldiers, Missy." Yanna ran back and stood shyly behind Coral's skirt.

Relieved, Coral stepped into the road. Her older brother, Michael, would be riding with them.

A small patrol belonging to the regiment of the 21st Bengal Light Cavalry rode around the bend, and encountering Coral, reined in their horses. She caught a flash of dusty black and silver uniforms from the six British soldiers and two officers. Behind rode a dozen Indian sowars, who drew up on sweating horses and waited.

Coral's eyes scanned the faces of the British soldiers, looking for Michael, but he was not among them. Inadvertently she met the confronting gaze of the officer in command. His physical good looks were indisputable. He was strongly built and wore the uniform well. His hair was very dark; his eyes, a penetrating bluish black beneath dark lashes. His chiseled features, streaked with dust and sweat, betrayed that he had ridden hard for some distance.

Unsmiling, his gaze swept Coral with eyes that revealed nothing. He rested his gloved hands on the saddle in front of him.

"Miss, I sent orders that no women or children were to venture out."

His tone was official, immediately putting her on the defense. Coral's lips closed mutely.

"I suppose you are one of the Kendall daughters?" His voice suggested that he already knew who she was, and that he expected a confrontation with this spoiled silk heiress, who would add to his frustration after a disagreeable day of tiger tracking.

Coral considered herself anything but spoiled, and said too sedately: "I am Miss Coral Kendall, if that is the intent of your question, Captain."

"Major," he corrected with a faint smile. "Major Jace Buckley."

Coral's emotions retreated behind a dignified shield. She did not trust men who were either too good-looking or too self-confident.

She felt unusually stiff, and tore her eyes away, giving a touch to her thick braids. She saw an older man with a reddish gray beard and heavy brows and felt more comfortable. There was something familiar about him. She had seen him before, but where?

"Now, lassie, to be sure, we be knowin' who ye are," he said with a thick Scottish brogue. "Did ye not get the warnin'? The tiger's been spotted nearby. Ye best not be aboot."

She raised her arm and pointed in the direction of the silkworm hatchery centered in the large mulberry orchards. "I'm not going far. I have urgent business to attend to." She paused for emphasis. "My father *owns* Kingscote."

The uniformed captain smiled kindly. "Aye, lassie, and I be knowin' Sir Hampton Kendall well. 'Tis a fact I'll be workin' for him soon. The name is Seward."

Seward. . . . The name had a pleasant ring to it, and she placed it in her memory. Before her father's marriage to her mother, Lady Elizabeth Roxbury of London, he had sailed to China for trade in tea, jade, silk, and porcelain. That segment of his adventurous life he no longer talked about, for her mother would gently interrupt and change the subject, but Coral recalled that the name Seward was part of that history.

"I believe my father has mentioned you."

Seward grinned. "Aye, lassie. And ye be the prettiest picture of a Kendall that could be!"

Coral was afraid she would blush and glanced back toward the major, who impatiently flapped his reins against his gloved palm.

"I doubt if Sir Hampton would want you wandering around without an escort, Miss Kendall," came his bland interruption. "Is your father about? I have business with him."

"He has gone to the village with my mother. My brother was said to be riding with you, Major. Would you know where Michael Kendall is?"

He did not answer. Captain Seward turned in his saddle to look at him. "Well, Major?"

Coral picked up the tension in their exchanged glances but waited silently for an answer.

The major responded with the lift of a gloved hand, and while his voice was polite, he gave the impression that Seward was to keep silent. His eyes fixed on the child Yanna, then came back to Coral.

"Miss Kendall, I am sorry to report a death on Kingscote. I believe he is one of your father's workers. Michael is seeing to him now."

The major's words came as a sickening blow. Instinctively Coral knew that it was Rajiv. In a gesture of protection she drew Yanna against her skirt.

"The tiger?" she asked, but even as she inquired, she read something unpleasant in his eyes.

"It has not yet been determined." He appeared to take note of the fact that she had drawn the child close to her, and he studied her face. "As Seward said, the tiger was spotted close by. I will have one of my men escort you and the child back to the house. I am sorry, but that is an order."

Coral's frustration mounted. She shook her head. "You do not understand." She picked up her mother's medical bag and said delicately: "Ahh . . . a friend of mine is about to . . . to deliver." She wanted to add, *Possibly the wife of the man you found*, but aware that Yanna clung to her, she did not. Before the long night was over, she must tell Jemani that Rajiv was dead.

Had his death been an accident? A tight feeling restricted her throat. More than ever she felt responsible for Jemani. Did Rajiv's death have anything to do with her baptism?

Major Buckley did not seem the slightest bit bothered about the delicacy of childbearing, although the situation did seem to provoke a spark of irritation.

"She is about to have a baby?"

Coral glanced toward the trees, brushing a stray strand of hair from her throat. "Yes, excuse me, I must hurry."

"Then you will need an escort, Miss Kendall. Where is your friend?"

"Not far." She pointed. "In one of the huts."

He gave her a slanted look. "Those are the silk workers' huts."

Did he think that because she was the daughter of Sir Hampton Kendall that she had no friends among the Indians?

She was about to reply when behind her, coming from the direction of the mansion, the clop of hooves interrupted. Coral whirled with expectation, and with a rush of relief saw her mother driving the pony trap.

Her dark hair was smoothed back into neat braids coiled at the nape of her neck, and she wore a modest muslin working-dress, now splotched with perspiration. Even so, her mother retained an elegance not easily masked. Coral knew that hidden from view near her feet was the rifle her mother always brought with her.

Coral gathered up her skirt and ran to meet her. "Mother!"

Elizabeth Kendall stopped the wagon and reached both arms to clasp her daughter.

"I was afraid you would not come," breathed Coral, taking solace in the familiar fragrance of her mother's sachet. The quiet brown eyes and the gentle touch of her mother's palm to the side of her face told Coral that all was once again in order.

"You were brave to come alone, Coral. But you should not be out of bed."

Coral basked in her mother's compliment. "I had to. It is Jemani! She went into labor!"

Elizabeth frowned. "Yes, Mera told me. Did she fall?"

"No, oh, Mother!" she lowered her voice. "It is Rajiv! He was reported missing last night, and now—"

"What! Last night? But I was not told before I left this morning with your father."

"Natine did not mention it until breakfast. By then you and Papa had already gone! Jemani went into labor, and now the soldiers seem to think that—"

"Oh no! Does Jemani know he is missing?"

"Yes, but it is worse than that. The major has found the body of one of the workers. Michael's looking into the matter now. Mother . . . suppose. . . ?"

Elizabeth's face drained of color, and Coral felt her

mother's fingers tighten about her arm.

Major Buckley had maneuvered his horse up to the side of the wagon, and Coral noted that now he was the precise military gentleman.

"Madam, I regret to report a death. I believe your son may know who he is."

Elizabeth's questioning gaze met his and she gave a guarded glance in Yanna's direction.

"Your fears are justified. Your son is taking care of matters now. I will have Captain Seward notify Sir Hampton."

Her mother sat for a moment in the wagon, stunned, and Coral's thoughts rushed to Jemani. She would have no husband to help raise her child.

"I understand a baby is due. I will have several of the sowars escort you."

"Yes, yes, thank you, Major Buckley. You are very thoughtful."

"Shall I escort your daughter back to the house?"

Coral felt a prickle of exasperation. Now why did he press the matter of her returning to the house?

Elizabeth looked preoccupied with troubling thoughts. "Yes. Perhaps that is best." She turned to Coral. "Dear, maybe you should return with the major."

Coral took hold of her mother's arm. "But I promised Jemani. After what has happened I cannot just go back to my room and wait. Mother, you must let me help, please!"

Elizabeth scanned her daughter's face worriedly. "Are you feeling strong enough? You look a trifle pale, Coral. . . ." Quickly she felt her forehead for a new outbreak of fever. Her dark brows came together. "You know you should not be out of bed. It is much too soon."

"I cannot abandon Jemani at a time like this. It was I who encouraged her baptism, and now Rajiv—"

Coral stopped. Her eyes averted to Major Buckley. He sat listening and watching her, apparently without the slightest qualm at doing so.

Coral managed to retain a practiced dignity that could equal her mother's. "Mother, I feel well enough. Jemani expects me to be there. I would never forgive myself if I were not."

"At least use my *chunni* over your head. The sun is still hot." Elizabeth helped Coral into the wagon and turned toward Yanna, who was already seated in the back. "Yanna dear, hand Missy Coral my chunni. It is in the basket. . . . By the way, Major, will you tell my husband to come for us in the morning? And do stay the night. My husband will see to your comfort."

Major Buckley touched his hat and turned his horse back toward the road. "Your hospitality is received gratefully."

Coral felt his gaze, but stared ahead, her back straight.

The wagon surged forward, and Coral held both hands on the seat as she bounced from side to side.

"The major is the son of Colonel Warbeck in Calcutta?"

"What, dear? Oh . . . yes, Jace Buckley is adopted."

Colonel Warbeck was not familiar to Coral, although she was acquainted with some of the military in the East India Company. Her uncle—Sir Hugo Roxbury, who was married to her mother's younger sister Margaret—was a high official in the civilian service to the governor-general at Calcutta.

"You do not know Colonel Warbeck, but your aunt Margaret knew him when she was a young girl in London. . . . The colonel's a rigid man, very much the soldier, I am told. His son, on the other hand, is somewhat of an adventurer."

"The major is adopted? What happened to his parents?"

"I am not certain anyone knows. I've heard everything from his father having been a corsair, to his mother being a lady in London. One must never listen to gossip. Evidently he was already an orphan when the colonel found him. Somewhere near Darjeeling, I believe. He had been taken into the home of a guru."

A guru! Then was he raised a Hindu? Coral glanced over her shoulder past the two sowars who were riding a discreet distance behind to guard them. The major was talking to Seward. There was a noticeable air of earthiness about Major Buckley that contradicted any notion of mysticism. As Seward turned his horse to ride, the major looked in her direction. Quickly, Coral jerked her head away.

If he were brought up by a guru, then he would possess a clear insight into Hinduism. Was this Eastern religion important to him?

Elizabeth Kendall touched the pony lightly with her whip, and Coral steadied herself as the trap jostled forward across the dusty field. In the distance, the whitewashed huts stood against a darkening backdrop of thick jungle. Chattering monkeys and shrieking birds permeated the branches of the trees above their heads.

"Rajiv's death complicates everything," murmured her mother. "Say nothing to Jemani until the child is born."

Coral nodded. "You do not think it had anything to do with the baptism?"

"The major and your father will discover what has happened." She reached over and squeezed Coral's arm. "Do not feel badly. You did well in instructing Jemani in the Scriptures."

Coral felt anything but victorious. *What about Rajiv?* The hopeless question kept repeating itself in her mind. Yesterday he walked the earth, with a wife and their first child on the way, a man with hopes, with the potential of knowing God. Now, he was dead. It was over. Like a tiny flash of light streaking across the Indian sky. Gone. *Jemani! How can I tell you?*

2

Night was upon them. A shudder of thunder shook the hut. The small earthenware oil lamps cast shadows on the walls of the low, square room, with its floor of smooth-plastered mud and cow dung. Jemani gripped the cloth tightly, biting into it, as Elizabeth Kendall murmured words of courage.

Coral's wrists ached from wringing cotton cloths to swathe the perspiration from Jemani's body. "Get fresh water," she told Yanna.

The child struggled to the door with the earthen gurra, then paused to look back, her round eyes luminous as the thunder growled.

"Hurry, Yanna, be brave."

Coral knelt beside Jemani and gently washed the sweat from her face and throat. Her skin had taken on a puffiness, and dark circles showed beneath her eyes as her suffering continued into the night. Coral did not show her feelings of alarm over childbirth, but inside she cringed. She had witnessed the anguish before, but seeing Jemani suffer so made it more real.

How many times had her mother gone through this? Five times—no! How could she have forgotten even for a moment the death of baby Ranek who had died after only forty-eight hours? That was six months ago. . . . A worried glance at her mother showed that signs of frailty due to that difficult birth were still evident.

The room was empty except for the birthing stool that Jemani was lying on. Her mother had it brought to the hut a week before. It had armrests, a slanting back, and a cutout seat. Elizabeth sat on a low stool, and Coral sat at Jemani's left. Despite the suffocating heat, a fire blazed in the open hearth, where Yanna kept the water boiling.

Coral was exhausted, and her clothing stuck to her skin. Far worse was the frustrating task of trying to keep flies away. When Yanna wasn't busy watching the fire or going for water, Coral had her stand behind Jemani swishing the two large chik fans shaped like elephant ears. Now and then, Coral would get a burst of the refreshing breeze.

Next to her mother was a low rattan table containing yards of white cloth. For the first time, Coral caught a glimpse of the baby clothes that would dress Jemani's new infant. With a blink, she recognized them as having belonged to Ranek Kendall. He had worn them during his brief hours on earth. Her eyes darted to her mother's face, haggard with heat and weariness. Nothing of her mother's generosity truly surprised Coral. Not even her willingness to use the expensive embroidered blanket and infant gown that had been sent by Grandmother Victoria from London. The colorful Roxbury family insignia clashed in the meager hut with its walls blackened by woodsmoke.

A muffled cry brought Coral's attention back to Jemani. She cooled her face with the cloth, her touch reassuring. Coral glimpsed the baby's head, and both excitement and fear welled up inside her. "Soon now, Jemani, go ahead and yell. As loud as you want!"

Sweat mingled with Jemani's tears, and anguish furrowed her young brow. "Coral . . ." Jemani's ragged whisper came. "Not good . . . I . . ."

"Soon, Jemani, soon," and she glanced at her mother. Something new and startling in her mother's face frightened her, and she wondered if she had the right to reassure her. She wanted to cry out, *What is it? What's wrong, Mother?*

Jemani's body tensed in a final push to free the tiny newborn.

"The baby is alive," came Elizabeth's quick voice. "It is a boy, Jemani! He looks healthy!"

Coral watched her mother working quickly now with brown cord, a boiled knife, and an odd assortment of ointments, bottles, jars, and cloths.

Jemani was crying softly, and Coral dribbled water across her cracked and bleeding lips, and smiled down at her bravely, although she suspected that her friend could not see her. "Did you hear, Jemani? A strong, healthy boy! You see? God did hear our prayers! What will you name him?"

"Coral . . ." Jemani's whisper came so weakly that Coral brought her ear close to lips that barely moved. "My baby . . . is not crying . . . he must cry . . ."

Yes, why isn't he crying? Coral wondered with growing alarm. Her mother had said the baby was alive. She watched her mother washing the tiny pink infant in a pewter bowl of wine.

Again Coral tried to smile, wiping Jemani's face, even as perspiration wet her own. "He will."

Jemani's voice was scarcely above a whisper—"My Rajiv . . . any news?"

Coral glanced anxiously at her mother, but Elizabeth shook her head.

All at once Coral heard the infant suck in a breath, sneeze, then let out a hearty wail! Coral laughed and leaned toward Jemani. "Did you hear that? All India is awakened. You will have your hands busy with that one."

But a closer look at Jemani's face wiped the smile from Coral. She was turning a sick-white, with blue splotches beneath her eyes. The wails of the newborn filled the hut, mingling with the thunder. Jemani's lips formed words, but her voice was too weak for Coral to hear. Coral's frightened eyes darted to her mother. Elizabeth's words sliced through the stillness: "Quick, take the baby, Coral."

Coral took the bundle and placed it next to Jemani's side. When she turned back toward her mother, she saw an expression that caused her to freeze. Fear clamped about her insides like iron fingers. Her eyes dropped to the blanket beneath Jemani, and widened. She wanted to gasp, but choked it back, her throat constricted. She stood rigid, staring at the growing pool of bright red blood. Slowly it grew larger in spite of her mother's tireless efforts to stop it. Her mother kept massaging and kneading Jemani's womb, her own face wet with perspiration, her lips moving in silent prayer.

Coral could not move. Yanna let out a tortured sob.

"Outside, Yanna!" Elizabeth choked, but the child stood there, two small hands pressed against her mouth choking back sobs.

"Coral! Put her outside!"

Coral's legs moved as heavily as though weighted down with lead. She stooped, struggled to pick Yanna up, and brought her to the door.

She stepped out into the blackness. A gust of wind struck against her, causing her to lose her breath. Her braids at the back of her neck came undone, and her tunic whipped about her. Lightning stabbed the sky. Yanna clung to her like a frightened cat.

Unexpectedly a man stepped from the night, but she could not see his face.

"Yes?" The calmness of Major Buckley's voice shocked her back to her senses. She pushed the child into his arms, and her voice was muffled in the wind.

"Take her, please! I must get back!"

He must have understood what was happening from the anguish in her voice, for he said something comforting to Yanna, who willingly clung to his neck, sobbing.

Coral turned back, slamming the door against the wind. One look at her mother's face told her what was happening. Helpless, Coral watched her trying to stop the bleeding. Stained cloths were tossed aside one by one as she reached for yet another.

Coral's eyes rimmed with tears. Her throat cramped. She sank back against the door, feeling the wind push against it. *Not Jemani too, Lord! Do not take her, please . . . do not take her. Not with the baby just born. Not with Rajiv gone too.*

But she knew that Jemani was dying, and her mother could do little to save her.

"Coral! Quick! She's asking for you."

Coral rushed to her side and knelt, throwing aside her own fears. "I am here, Jemani," she said, surprised that her voice could sound so calm, so strong. She must not let her know how frightened she was.

"Jemani?" she took her hand. How cold and clammy she felt! She held it between her own, as though by holding tightly she could hold on to her life.

". . . member . . . you . . . promised . . . won't . . . change mind . . . won't forget . . ."

"I remember. I will not change my mind."

". . . so weak . . . cannot face . . . leaving me . . . do not go . . . afraid . . ."

Coral swallowed against the ache in her throat. Hot tears blurred her vision. "Remember the words we read in Hindi? Say them with me in your mind."

Coral struggled to utter the words of Psalm 23 aloud, and slowly the little room was enveloped in a sweet hush. Elizabeth Kendall's voice joined in as she knelt beside Jemani, resting a hand on the young woman's damp hair.

"Yea, though I walk through the valley of the shadow of death, I will fear no evil for thou art with me . . ."

". . . with me . . ." came Jemani's murmur. "With—"

No longer was her face frantic, no longer fearful. Jemani grew quiet. The promise of Scripture came on wings of pleasant breezes, as clear as sunlight shining on crystal water.

"Jesus," whispered Jemani, so sweetly that Coral's breath paused. She watched Jemani's lips move softly into a sigh. "Jesus . . ."

Coral felt Jemani's fingers, heard her whispering, "Take . . . my son. His godmother—you promised—no . . . untouchable . . ."

Coral glanced desperately into her mother's face searching for permission. Elizabeth's face was wet; she hesitated, shutting her eyes and helplessly shaking her head as though tortured by decision. "Dear God in heaven! Whatever shall I do?"

"Mother," rasped Coral, pleading. "Mother, *please!*" Coral's heart felt as though it would burst, and she choked: "This is partly my fault—I—I am the one responsible for what has happened! The baptism, Rajiv—"

She could not go on and laid her wet face on Jemani's chest. She felt Jemani's fingers weakly touch her hair.

"Coral—"

"You may promise," came Elizabeth's whisper.

Coral lifted her face. "Yes, Jemani, yes! I promise."

The young mother let out a soft sigh. The room was wrapped in silence.

Coral shut her eyes, one hand holding Jemani's, the other resting on the baby next to her. She caressed the blanket, feeling the softness of the expensive silk edging from Roxbury House in London and the gentle breathing movements of the baby beneath her hand.

The pressure of Jemani's fingers grew weaker, fading away, until at last Coral felt it no more. She stared down at Jemani's still face, and Coral's expression set with determination. "I promise," she whispered again.

3

The red embers in the hearth were out. Streaks of grayish dawn were breaking in the eastern sky, and outside the hut the first large drops of water made contact with the dust.

The door stood ajar, letting in the damp smell of earth and trees, and the monsoon broke into its full fury. Piercing zigzags of light did a war dance across the sky, and the rains came gushing forth turning dust into mud, the mud into small running streams. Kingscote rejoiced, and the jungle came to life. Coral sat without moving, drained of emotion. She watched her mother wrap the newborn more carefully in the blanket for the wet ride back to the mansion.

Her mother walked toward her with the infant in her arms, and their eyes met in wordless understanding. *She too wants this baby,* thought Coral. *Will he fill a void left by Ranek?*

Coral smiled weakly as her mother's fingers played in her mussed blonde hair. For a moment neither spoke, and Coral rested the side of her face against her mother's breast.

"I feel so ancient."

53

Elizabeth continued stroking her daughter's hair in silent understanding.

Coral lifted her head and scanned her mother's wearied face, searching for answers. Reality came rushing in like a flood.

"What will Father say?"

Elizabeth looked toward the open door as though expecting to find the rugged form of Sir Hampton standing there. The rain hammered so loudly on the small roof that Coral wanted to place her palms over her ears.

Elizabeth was quiet. She raised her hand to push back a wisp of dark brown hair. "I do not know."

Coral knew her father to be a rugged but tender man. There was not the slightest doubt in her mind that after twenty years, he was still deeply in love with her mother. She had seen the way he looked at her at the dinner table after a long, tiring day, and could not mistake the devotion in his gray-green eyes. If anyone could win over the heart of Hampton, it would be her mother.

Elizabeth moved the blanket aside to peer at the baby. The silence lengthened. When she spoke, her voice was a whisper. "He will say . . . it was a fair thing to do, Liza, but an unwise decision where Kingscote is concerned. Especially after Rajiv's death."

Coral shivered, although the monsoon did not cool the air. The hot, dry, dusty weather was now hot, humid, and muggy. She murmured hopefully, "Maybe his death was an accident. Maybe it had nothing to do with Jemani's baptism."

But one look at her mother's expression did little to reinforce her words.

"Your father will know more today," Elizabeth said simply.

54

Coral took Jemani's son into her arms and wondered about the future. "And *then* what will Father say?"

Elizabeth managed a smile. "Then he will say, 'What did you name the lad?' "

Coral felt so completely relieved, yet so exhausted, she laughed and wept at once.

"Gem," Coral said after a moment. "That is his name. Like a jewel, he is the one bright glimmer in all that has happened, born the night of the monsoon, when the earth is quenched and satisfied."

"We will indeed call him Gem. And we shall raise him to serve the Lord of the monsoon, that he may bring new life to his people."

Coral looked toward the open doorway, hearing the crunch of boots. Major Jace Buckley stood there, his hat pulled low to keep the rain out of his eyes. His gaze took in the scene in one glance, then focused on the infant in Coral's arms. His expression remained unreadable, and his resonant voice was directed to Elizabeth.

"You no longer need worry about the tiger, Mrs. Kendall."

Elizabeth gave a deep sigh of relief. "You trapped the beast?"

"I had to shoot him," he stated.

"Yes . . . of course. Thank God it cannot harm anyone else."

Coral busied herself with the infant, refusing to comment, unwilling to meet the gaze of the intriguing officer.

"Yanna is back at the house," he told Coral.

She was obliged to look up at him. "Thank you."

"I left her in the kitchen."

"Yes . . ."

"You have our gratitude, Major," said Elizabeth. She walked toward him. "I am afraid I will need someone to tend to the burial. Your sowars will most likely refuse."

He showed little expression, giving Coral the impression that he knew the Indian mind well. "Seward and I will see to it," he said.

"Thank you."

"There is a ghari waiting to bring you back. Better leave now before the road turns into a riverbed."

"You have been very helpful," she said tiredly. "However, I will stay until after the burial. Has the body of the worker been identified yet?"

"It is Rajiv."

Coral held the baby a little tighter. "How did he die, Major?"

She noted a hard glitter to his eyes. "A dagger through his heart."

A dagger! Coral felt sick. Then his death was not an accident as she had hoped! But who would do such a dreadful thing to Rajiv? Ghazis? Oh, surely not! Not on Kingscote. Someone from the village, she thought . . . yes, that was it. *It has to be.*

Her mother's face was drained of color, and she turned toward Coral as though anxious for her to be safe at the house. "Major Buckley will see you to the ghari, Coral. The baby will need to eat soon. Bring him to Jan-Lee."

"Yes, Mother." Coral lifted the blanket protectively about Gem and walked past Major Buckley into the downpour. The rain was warm on her face and felt sweetly refreshing.

The silk workers were standing in the rain, smiling and celebrating, although furtive glances were cast in her direction by the women. She felt them staring at the bundle in her arms. Coral held him close, looking from face to face, almost challenging any of them to raise a word of opposition. Children played in the mud, squealing. And from the jungle came the distant sound of an elephant trumpeting his delight.

Major Buckley's voice interrupted the moment. "Boy or girl?"

"A boy."

"What did you name him?"

Her eyes rushed to his, and for a moment she was confronted by flecks of hard black within deep blue.

"Gem." And without completely understanding her feelings of determination, or what motivated her to say so, she added, "Gem Ranek—after a baby brother who died some months ago."

He did not reply at first. "A worthy name," he said smoothly.

"So I thought, Major."

The ghari waited with the door open.

"Your brother has said you've been ill with fever. Better get inside. You are dripping wet."

She brushed aside the damp hair that clung to her throat, and allowed him to assist her across the oozing mud. He handed her into the ghari, and Coral settled her wet tunic about her, holding Gem.

Before the major closed the door, he paused. "I commend you for your courage."

Her eyes reluctantly met his steady gaze as she responded, "I have never considered myself especially brave."

"While we are alone, I would like to say something."

She glanced at him cautiously. "Yes?"

"You have me mystified."

"Indeed? I cannot imagine why."

"A silk heiress . . . a white colonial lady taking a servant's baby . . . an Indian baby . . . which makes me wonder if you know what you are doing."

Coral stiffened but made no reply.

She studied him as he stood there, oblivious to the downpour, in a rather arrogant stance. Here was a young man with strong opinions, a man who did not fear voicing them.

"I am sorry that I mystify you," she said lightly.

A dark brow shot up. "May I ask why Jemani and Rajiv's baby should mean anything to you? There must be a hundred other babies about Kingscote."

She busied herself with Gem's blanket. "Not a hundred babies, Major. Perhaps ten or twenty."

He smiled a little. "Granted. Ten to twenty . . . but why *this* baby?"

"For a number of important reasons. I did not consider Jemani a servant. We were friends. During the months of my illness, I was confined to my room—I doubt if a man of your background would understand how lonely and boring prolonged illness can become."

He watched her thoughtfully.

"Jemani taught me Hindi, and I taught her the teachings of the Christian church. Now she is gone . . . and Rajiv is dead. And her child has no friends here among the Indians on Kingscote. I promised her I would protect her baby . . . a godparent, you might say."

He was silent, and Coral felt her face turning warm. There was no sound but the splat of rain hitting the roof of the ghari.

"You will, of course, find an Indian family to take him," he said.

Why is he so interested? she wondered. "No. I intend to keep him."

"I was afraid you would say that." His gaze was sober. "You are making a mistake."

Her lips parted slightly over his temerity, but he went on easily. "I suggest that if you pursue this idea, you will invite trouble. More than you realize."

She was alert. "Why do you say that? What do you mean? And what concern is it of yours?"

"Just this. I knew Rajiv well."

"Oh?" Her breath went out of her all at once. "You knew him? When? Certainly not since he came to Kingscote?"

"No, but I knew he was working here for your father. I've known Rajiv in the past."

His tone was evasive. Was he trying to keep his own past in shadows?

"I know who his family is. They will not want this child raised a Christian."

Coral tensed, and as though expecting him to take Gem from her arms she leaned back a little, holding the baby close to her shoulder. "You are wrong, Major Buckley. Rajiv had no family. Neither did Jemani. They wandered here months ago, escaping a famine in Rajasthan. Rajiv worked with the elephants—he was very good—"

"Yes, he was," came the calm interruption. "Rajiv was a fighter. He led them into battle. We fought together once."

"Truly? You seem to have quite a past of your own, Major."

"Which has nothing to do with our discussion."

She rushed on—"And Jemani came to the house as my personal tutor in the Hindi language. My mother baptized her only a few weeks ago."

"And partly because of that baptism, Rajiv is dead."

Coral wanted to flinch. "You do not know that. You said yourself you had no idea who killed him!"

"No." His jaw set. "Otherwise I would do something about it. But I have a good guess. Whoever put that dagger in his heart knew exactly what he was doing. It was a ritual killing."

Coral felt a pang of nausea.

His voice softened. "I am sorry to be blunt, but it's important you understand what you are getting involved in. I believe someone sent for Rajiv. Someone he trusted. And he went, only to find that trust misplaced."

She recalled what her mother had said about Major Jace Buckley being raised by a guru. Her father had also commented that he was a rogue and a gentleman all in one. Could she trust him? Was he relentless in his attitude because he opposed converting Hindus to what the Indians called a *European* religion?

"Rajiv's uncle is a Raj."

Coral grew still.

"You understand the implications?"

Coral was astounded by his words. "Yes." Her voice was quiet and dull. *But it cannot be true*, she thought.

"Royalty," she stated aloud. "I do not believe it is possible."

"I have heard that the Raj disowned his nephew because he married an untouchable. For a loyal Hindu to break caste is worse than death. Others besides Rajiv have been put to death for doing it."

She whispered: "You think he was killed because he married Jemani?"

"I have no proof of the maharaja's involvement. It may have been someone else in the royal family. Yet I've seen these types of killings before. The Raj rejected his nephew, but if it comes to his attention that Rajiv has a son, and that son is now a ward of an English family who intends to raise him a Christian—well, Miss Kendall, you see my reasoning."

Coral shuddered at the thought of turning Gem over to vindictive relatives. They might throw him to the crocodiles as a sacrifice.

"Jemani entrusted her son to *me*. It was her dying wish. Had she wanted Gem given to Rajiv's family, she would have told me."

His expression was now bland. "You might consider that she had something to hide. Something she never explained to you, even though, as you say, you were friends."

Reluctantly she recalled Jemani's words at the river. *There are things you do not know . . . things I cannot—must not, tell you.*

But Coral would not discuss this with the major. Instead, she said firmly, "I do not believe it. What could she have to hide? Had Rajiv lived long enough, he, too, would have committed Gem to me. They would want him to be raised a Christian, and I intend to see that he is. He is mine now," she stated. "I will not give him up easily."

Even at a time of sobriety and warning, the major could show unlikely amusement, as if her determination alerted his curiosity. He smiled. "The depth of your conviction surprises me. How old are you?"

She blushed. He could be too blunt. She was tempted to exchange years with Kathleen, but instead spoke the truth. "Sixteen."

He looked exasperated. "Sixteen! You are hardly more than a child!"

Child!

"Major! You forget yourself. I am not a child."

61

"Maybe. In my opinion—"

"You are somewhat aggressive in sharing your opinions, Major."

"In my opinion, Miss Kendall, you are too young to get into this kind of dilemma. Therefore, it is my duty to inform your father of the Raj."

She sucked in her breath, and for a moment she visualized her plans in ruin.

"Sir, you will not frighten me," she whispered.

"I am not trying to frighten you, but warn you."

"Gem is *mine!*"

A brow lifted. He looked her up and down. "I am certain a silk heiress can have anything she wants—"

Coral felt her cheeks turning warm. The man was arrogant!

"—but an Indian baby who is the grandnephew of the maharaja? It may prove costly to you . . . *and* to your father's silk plantation."

His suggestion disturbed her more than she was willing to show. "I know exactly what I am doing."

"Do you?"

"Yes." Her eyes refused to yield.

His narrowed a little. The rain ran down the brim of his hat. After a moment he gave a little nod of his head.

"As you wish. But remember that I warned you."

Coral shivered, not knowing if it was from her wet clothing, or the warning in his voice. He started to turn away, and she stretched out a hand in a pleading gesture. "Wait—"

Suddenly she felt bone tired, her emotions spent. He must have noticed. He seemed to notice everything, she thought, troubled.

"I am sorry if I sounded rude," he said. "But I

dislike the idea of a young girl ending up with a broken heart."

Coral gazed down at the baby. How could this infant warming her embrace ever bring her a broken heart?

"Please . . . say nothing to Sir Hampton. I—I am not the only one who wants him," she found herself explaining quietly. "My baby brother died six months ago . . . he was only two days old. My mother . . ." she stopped, feeling as though she were betraying her mother's privacy.

His expression was inscrutable, and she could not tell if his thoughts on the matter had wavered or not. Before she could say anything more, her mother came out of the hut, covering her head with a sari.

"Go on without me, Coral," she called. "Major Buckley is kind enough to see that I give Jemani a Christian burial. Tell your father I will be home soon. We will talk then."

"Yes, Mother."

Coral's eyes swerved back to Major Buckley's, and her dark lashes narrowed a little. "I do not suppose you would change your mind? I suppose you will tell her everything . . . and frighten her."

He folded his arms across his chest. "Neither of you seem to frighten easily," he said flatly.

"She will not believe you any more than I do."

Coral turned her head away as a sowar walked up and saluted the major. There followed a quick exchange in Hindi.

The major spoke fluently, a result of being brought up by the Indian guru, Coral decided. She caught something about Captain Seward reporting back to him at once. The sowar saluted and climbed inside the ghari.

Without another word exchanged between her and the major, he shut the door. A moment later the vehicle moved off toward the Kendall house, the wheels churning through the reddish-brown mud.

Coral turned in her seat to look out the window at the driving rain. Her mother stood next to the major, a fragile figure beside his rugged build. A small black book was in her hand. Coral then glanced across the seat at the sowar. His deep brown face was impassive, his eyes straight ahead. She wondered what he thought of the Christian burial of Jemani, and of the Indian infant in her arms that would be carried inside the Kendall mansion and taken upstairs to the English nursery.

4

Coral awoke from her nap with a start. Rajiv and Jemani were dead . . . and she had taken responsibility of Gem.

Neither her father nor her brother Michael had come to the dinner table earlier that evening. Along with the major, they were still looking into the matter of Rajiv's death. The workers were being questioned about what they might have seen or heard, and her father had talked to Natine alone in the library. Evidently no one knew anything, and Rajiv's death remained unsolved. What effect this might have on the Kendall relationship with the Indian workers was unclear. In the past it had always been pleasant; the men and women who worked for her father were loyal servants. But the ugly death of Rajiv cast a foreboding shadow . . . and now his son slept in the Kendall nursery.

Coral sat up, hearing her father and mother speaking in the hallway. Prompted by her mother's pleading voice, Coral slipped from her four-poster bed and went to the door.

What if Major Buckley had spoken of the maharaja to her father? And what if he refused to let them care for Gem? What would become of the tiny infant? She already knew well enough that no one on Kingscote would raise him. And if he were sent to this unnamed royal family, there was a chance Gem would be slain. Coral had no weapon or resource but prayer.

She rebuked herself for listening to her parents' conversation in the hallway, but having caught the baby's name she could not resist. She stood by the door listening, her heart thudding. Her father's voice was clear:

"The Roxburys will not look upon this easily. I fear Sir Hugo is right. Mutiny is ever a shadow hovering over Kingscote."

"Yet you always told me it was part of the risk of being a *feringhi* in India. And the child will never take the place of your blood grandchildren. As he matures, we can send him away to school in London. If we hesitate to stand by our friends, what will the Hindus think of the church?"

"Now, Liza, I've no thought of abandoning the lad. But I confess to being worried about Coral. You know better than the rest of us that she isn't well. She is only sixteen! She will be going to London soon. How can she mother a child?"

"Coral is more mature than you give her credit for. She is more studious than her sisters. And . . . she wishes to stay at Kingscote instead of going to finishing school in London."

"Aye! Not go to London with her sisters!"

"Now, Hampton! At first I said no, that you would not allow it, but darling, perhaps it is not so terrible an idea. She is hardly strong enough for a five-month voyage. Do let her stay at home with Gem until he is three," she pleaded. "After that, she can journey to

Roxbury House. Gem will be old enough to travel with her, and we'll place him in a good school."

"Whist! Three more years? What of a husband?"

"Hampton . . . she is so lovely. She will have no difficulty . . . and remember your promise. It will give her time to grow stronger. And—well, Coral has suggested she does not wish to marry soon, and—"

"Oh she has, has she?"

"There is time for all that. Girls do not marry as early as they did when we were young. Belinda is all of seventeen, and Margaret and Hugo are quite patient."

He gave a grunt. "Do I not have Kingscote to think of? I need strong heirs, and I am hoping to have many of them. With young Alex interested in music, and Michael restless and wanting to travel, what will Kingscote do if both my sons turn their backs on silk?"

"They will not disappoint you. And yet, shall our sons and daughters be traded in marriage for good blood?"

"Blood, I am not worried about, but grandsons, I am. Coral needs to go to London to get a husband. That young nephew of Sir Hugo's . . . what was his name? Hugo boasts enough of him! The chap has pestered me on the subject for the last two years!"

"Ethan," she explained. "Doctor Ethan Boswell. And I must say, I'm inclined to think he is the correct choice when the time comes. Margaret too has written of Ethan. He is young and gifted. Uncompromising in his interest in tropical diseases. And more importantly, Ethan is Christian. And I'm assured he is willing to wait several years, since he is aware that Coral is ill."

"A physician will make a fitting husband." He gave a laugh. "I dare say she may need one close at hand.

Perhaps we should arrange for her betrothal now."

"Oh, Hampton! Do be serious! Give them both time to meet and become friends. In the meantime, dear, she can pursue her education here. Her interest in languages continues, and there is much I can teach her. Although," she said thoughtfully, "I do think we should insist on at least a year at Lady Anne's Finishing School with her sisters. Hampton—about the child. Jemani died believing we would see to her baby, that he grows up in the church. I shall never forgive myself if I do not see the vow through. And Coral feels as strongly."

"But Coral is so young. Can she handle this?"

"Are you not forgetting me? I will do everything I can to help with the child. The infant is so beautiful."

His voice grew husky with sudden emotion. "So maybe it is you, my love, and not our little Coral who is determined to keep him? Then why did you not say so in the first place?"

Elizabeth's voice rushed on. "I have already spoken to Jan-Lee. She has agreed to nurse him with her own Emerald."

"Oh, Liza, Liza my love, you know well enough that I would do anything to please you. When we first married, I was even willing to turn Kingscote over to Hugo and return to London with you to live the life of a lord. Forbid! It was you who wished to stay, who came to love Kingscote as I. Yes, if you want this Indian baby, then you may have him. And when he is old enough, I shall pay for his schooling in London. But are you certain it is not our own son you have on your heart, and the Indian baby only reminds you of him?"

Elizabeth's voice broke—"God gave me Ranek for such a short time . . . and we will never have another child—"

Inside her room, Coral closed her eyes and leaned against the door, her throat constricting. She knew how her mother ached with loneliness. When did empty arms ever get used to losing a child?

"Liza . . ." Hampton's voice came as a broken whisper.

There was silence.

"Liza, let the child stay . . . and if one day we are sorry for this act, so be it. Let the Good Master who waters Kingscote look to our path."

Coral's heart felt as if it would burst. She could not contain herself and flung open the bedroom door, throwing her arms about her father's strong neck. Her cheeks were wet. "Oh, Papa, Papa, thank you. I will make you proud of him, you will see."

Hampton's gray-green eyes glistened. "What is this?" he pretended to be stern. "Listening behind closed doors? I'd expect as much from Kathleen, but you?"

She laughed up at him. "Dear Papa, I love you."

Elizabeth smiled up at her husband, and her eyes shone with pride. She rested her cheek against his forearm.

"You will both have to stand with me against the outcry certain to come from the Roxburys. Sir Hugo will have a dark expression over this."

"We will stand with you no matter what the rest of the family says," Coral stated.

"Grandmother Victoria will listen to reason," said Elizabeth of her mother. "I will write her at once. Knowing Mother, she will threaten to swoon over an Indian child in the family, but she will soon relent."

"Sounds like war," he said with a wince. "Then so be it. Is not justice and mercy on our side? Kingscote has survived a hundred years, and by God's grace it will continue."

"Why, Papa, you sound like a parson," laughed Coral.

He cleared his throat. "Seward would disagree, having known my nefarious past." He brightened. "Did I tell you? He soon will be out of the military. He's coming to work for me here at Kingscote. I cannot think of a man I can trust more than Seward!"

Unexpectedly he called out to his Indian servant, his voice in good humor. "Natine! What do you mean standing there in the shadows on the stairs? Find Seward and Major Buckley! We shall celebrate with a toast to the future!"

Natine stepped forward, his dark eyes remote. He salaamed. "Celebrate, burra-sahib?"

"Tonight marks the birth of Gem and his entrance into the Kendall household. No, do not look like a croaking toad, my old friend. We will hear no omens of ill news from you." He turned back to Elizabeth. "Who knows? Maybe I will get myself an heir after all." He gave a laugh. "An Indian godchild as committed to silk as I am."

Natine stood masked in shadows. He turned away, turban held high, and went down the stairs.

From the room that joined her own, Coral heard the wail of the infant and hurried back to find Jan-Lee lifting him from the cradle. Holding her own child in one arm and Gem in the other, she sat down in the rattan rocker, and Coral drew near, kneeling beside her.

"One day I will see you rewarded for your kindness, Jan-Lee."

The Burmese woman wore an impenetrable face,

and her dark eyes were solemn. Rain beat against the windows.

"Jemani is gone . . . her husband too. It is sad. I will do my best for you, Miss Coral."

Coral laid a hand on the shoulder of her childhood ayah. "It is not the end for Rajiv and Jemani. It is the beginning. And the beginning for Gem. To the living belong the promises of this life. I want to see that Gem has opportunity to grow up strong, with an education in London, to become all that he can be. It is in my power, the power of the Kendall family, to do this, and we will."

"Your heart is kind, child. But not everyone understands this kindness. Some misunderstand. As if you deliberately step into the Indian flower bed, and crush. For your sake, Miss Coral, walk with light feet."

"I shall try, Jan-Lee."

They listened to the raging monsoon, and the contentment of both infants feeding. One, the daughter of Jan-Lee, an oriental servant; the other to become Coral's godchild, perhaps one of the many future inheritors in the wealthy and powerful silk dynasty that reached from India to London.

5

Recalling Major Buckley's remark that she was little more than a child, Coral chose a blue silk frock that she felt added a touch of maturity to her years. She brushed her hair until it shone like burnished gold, then she drew it back into a neat chignon.

Pausing on the octagonal stairway, she looked below. Golden lamplight flooded down upon the square entrance hall and showered upon the polished redstone floor. At the bottom of the staircase, and to her left, was the ballroom, with its double crystal chandeliers that her mother had shipped from Vienna and the heavy wood furniture with muted-rose velvet cushions. There would be no dancing tonight, so Natine had ordered the servants to leave the plush ivory-colored Afghan rugs on the polished marble floor. Elizabeth's prized paintings from the Roxbury London collection graced the pale walls, including a recent painting of Coral with her pet elephant, *Rani*. There was another painting of her older sister, Kathleen, in a white French lace ball dress, and one of her baby sister, Marianna, with her strawberry hair still in

73

childhood braids, seated in a garden of yellow primroses.

Coral came quickly down the stairs as strains of Mozart began to fill the house. She walked to the archway that led into the ballroom and saw Alex seated before the keyboard, master of his music. His fingers danced across the keys, while every fiber of his lean body consumed the drama of his music. His dark handsomeness hinted of poetic moodiness, with eyes that flashed an internal storm. The familiar shock of dark hair fell across his forehead, and like his character, it forever resisted any attempt toward management.

The guests in the ballroom were attentive as his personalized music style crashed with the violence of lightning and thunder, held its emotional peak for several moments, then eased like a sigh into ocean waves playing across the sand. . . .

Coral glanced across the room until she saw Major Jace Buckley. He was not watching Alex, but her. She turned her head away.

The music ceased. The room was still. Then exuberant applause broke out.

Alex stood, smiled almost shyly, then walked toward Michael and Major Buckley.

A minute later as conversation resumed, her father's strong voice could be heard above the crowd, and she caught glimpses of her mother overseeing the silver trays of refreshment, while a dignified Natine watched the other servants. One mistake, one slip of etiquette in their well-trained behavior meant that he would delegate them to less important jobs in the kitchen.

There were several other young men in uniform with Major Buckley, and Captain Seward was there enjoying a discourse with her father. Michael was speaking with the major, while Alex, newly arrived from his musical studies in Austria, only listened, as though drained by his music.

Coral noted that the major appeared at ease in fashionable surroundings. He was no longer dusty or sweat-stained, and he wore a clean riding cloak. He was assessing the painting on the wall of Coral with her elephant. Rani was kneeling in a circus stunt that she had taught her.

"Coral, come here, I want you to meet Jace."

Michael's voice interrupted her thoughts as her older brother walked toward her, grinning, his arm outstretched.

So Michael was on a first-name basis with him. Had Major Buckley told him that he believed Gem was related to a maharaja?

Her brother showed no concern, however, as he took her arm and led her in the major's direction.

Michael was gifted, as were all the Kendall children, with physical attractiveness. His hair was not as dark as Alex's, and bore the Roxbury tinge of red when seen in the light, and he was strongly built like his father. Unlike Alex who hated the sun, Michael had always thrived outdoors, on adventure—a trait not at all appreciated by his father. Perhaps Michael's cravings for risk would not have been frowned upon had those ambitions been centered on Kingscote silk.

"This is my sister Coral," he was saying to Major Buckley, his strong arm wrapping around her shoulders.

"We've met. Good evening, Miss Kendall."

She could hardly believe that the languid tone and the disarming smile belonged to the same arrogant man who had earlier confronted her about Gem.

"Good evening, Major," she said precisely.

Michael laughed. "Call him Jace. He is not the hardheaded officer he appears. He's more suited for an Indian tunic, buckskin trousers, and a seacap."

Coral smiled politely, but the thought of calling him Jace made her uneasy. She was relieved when the major gestured his glass toward the painting, changing the subject.

"Your elephant?"

"Yes. She is called Rani, a true queen. She was only a baby when I got her."

He murmured smoothly: "The mother was killed, and you adopted her?"

"Yes, she—" Coral hesitated. Her eyes swerved to meet his, her cheeks turning warm. She found a hint of a smile on his lips. He turned back to the painting and seemed to study it with a good deal more interest than was genuine.

"I enjoy collecting orphaned animals," she said with a hint of challenge.

"I commend you. It is not every woman who enjoys the excitement of wild and dangerous pets. I've collected a few myself."

"Indeed?" she sipped her refreshment. "A cobra?"

She was aware that Michael and Alex turned to look at her, surprised by her tone, but she ignored them.

Major Buckley did not appear to be the slightest bit offended and fixed her with a disconcerting smile.

"Actually, a cheetah. . . . I still have her. If I get mauled one day I'll have no one to blame but myself."

Coral glanced away to the painting on the wall, swishing her peacock-feather fan. "A cheetah, you say? How interesting, Major. I collect them."

A dark brow went up.

"Miniatures, that is," she said. "I am searching for one carved in ebony stone. I understand they are rare and hard to come by."

"They are. But they can be found in the right place. You need to know where to look. I will keep your interest in mind in my travels."

What kind of travels had he involved himself in? Aside from the vague description given of him by her mother and father, she knew nothing of Jace Buckley. How had Michael met him?

"You are a collector of rare menagerie?" she asked.

"Only to sell. I've a man in London who collects. I would like to see your collection sometime."

"You travel to exotic locations a good deal, Major?"

"Recently this uniform has kept me on a leash. All that will change soon."

Coral became aware of a rather curious expression worn by her brothers. Michael in particular seemed to enjoy watching Major Buckley.

"I suspect you have Rani eating out of your hand," Major Buckley told her.

"She is outrageously spoiled," agreed Coral. "She wouldn't have posed for me had I not bribed her with more time in the river . . ." She touched her chignon. "Actually, I like things to be free and wild."

"Not a typical Kendall as you can see," said Michael with a smile. "Coral's the only one in the family who would approve of our treks into the Himalayas."

"Have you two known each other long?" she asked.

"For several years. Michael and I met in Darjeeling. Your brother saved my life in an avalanche."

"If I recall correctly, old friend, it was the other way around," Michael countered. "Do not be so generous, Jace." His smile vanished. "Cowardice is not your cup of tea."

"An avalanche!" repeated Coral. "Michael, you never mentioned it."

Michael glanced toward his father, who was in conversation with Seward, and said in a low voice, "You are jesting, of course. You know Father. Any talk of a near-fatal accident, and there would be further opposition to my expeditions."

"A grand idea," quipped Alex dryly, sipping chilled pineapple juice. "What you see in ice, wind, and jagged peaks, I shall never fathom." He grimaced. "Grant me the intoxicating summers on Vienna's Danube any day."

"Ah, I might agree with that. Having felt the wings of death brush against me is quite enough for the present. Jace and I are turning civilized." His expression took on an intensity that Coral had seldom remembered seeing on Michael. "We are entering into a partnership in a tea plantation in Sikkim—perhaps the hill of Darjeeling."

Coral attempted to keep herself from catching her breath in surprise. *Michael and Jace—partners?*

"A tea plantation," mused Alex. "Father will be disappointed."

Michael sobered. "I hope to provoke a bit of excitement in his blood. Jace and I have our plans made. But I will need Father's good graces."

Alex smiled at Major Buckley. "In other words, Michael will need a loan to buy the land from the Raja of Sikkim." He turned his smile on Michael. "I wish you luck, dear brother. You will need it."

Michael pretended to throw a punch at his shoulder. "That, and a brother's moral support to help convince him. You and your music have more persuasive power over Father than anything I could ever do."

Alex's smile disappeared. "My good favor will increase if you provoke Father's displeasure again. He will not like it if you take to sea with the major next year." He added with rueful tone—"Since I am the younger son of the famed Sir Hampton Kendall, I might be able to get by with studying music in Vienna. But you know too well how he has his mind set on you taking over the silk production one day."

"Perhaps we will join the two plantations into one grand enterprise," said Michael lightly. "Silk and Darjeeling tea! What more could the English want?"

"England may smile, but you are forgetting Jace," said Alex. "Half the tea plantation will be his. He may have something to say about merging with the Kendalls."

"Ah, yes, let us toast the famous name of Buckley! Good Queen Bess would have rejoiced to have such a seadog in her service," said Michael, and turned to Jace. "Success, my adventurous friend! Let us salute the fastest clipper yet to sail the seas!"

A tea plantation in Darjeeling, thought Coral, intrigued, but uncertain whether or not she liked the idea of her brother being partners with Jace Buckley. His friendship with Michael meant she would come into future contact with him. The thought brought with it unease, since he shared her secret about Gem. Yet she found herself wanting to earn his admiration. She waited for an opportunity to display her knowledge of Darjeeling, unable to forget that he had called her a child.

"Why Darjeeling, Major?" she asked casually. "If I remember correctly, my father said there was fighting in Sikkim." And to show herself quite grown-up and informed of military matters, she added: "Gurkhas from Nepal, are they not?"

Major Buckley's expression showed both surprise and admiration. "Yes, they gained some territory, but fortunately, the Raja of Sikkim was able to turn them back with the help of Bhutan and China. Fighting goes on, but the area we are interested in is reasonably quiet."

"But whoever heard of tea growing in Darjeeling? I thought it came from China."

"It does. But an Indian friend of mine is certain it grows wild in Darjeeling. I believe he is right. However, we have not found it yet. We plan another expedition soon."

"Did you say *wild* tea?" asked Alex with apparent disbelief.

"A wild tea bush most likely suggests it was first smuggled in from China," said Major Buckley. He smiled slightly. "Perhaps our first 'Indian' tea shares something of a common history with the first silk cocoons brought into Assam."

"Forbid," jested Alex throwing up a slim hand. "Do not let our father hear you say that. He is adamant that silk is native to Assam."

"As well it might be," said Michael. "But do not forget our illustrious but notorious great-grandfather James Kendall settled here after he left Burma and China."

"What?" mocked Alex good-naturedly. "You nurture suspicions he carried silk caterpillars with him? Let us toast the grand memory of Princess Mei Lin Chang!"

Coral was not thinking of silk but of Alex's remark about Michael going to sea with Major Buckley. Her father would not be pleased. There was no secret about the disagreement between Sir Hampton and his two sons over the future of the vast enterprise of Kingscote. Alex had been permitted to his serious study of music in Austria only because he had lapsed into severe depression when first forbidden. Mother and Grandmother Victoria Roxbury in London had convinced their father to permit Alex to pursue his passion. However, Michael, as the firstborn, was another matter.

She hoped her voice did not sound too cautious, "Then you have not told Father of your interest in a tea plantation?"

Michael winced. "After tracking the tiger for two days, I am not in any mood to take on a wounded bear. But I admit Father seems in a good mood tonight." He looked across the room in Hampton's direction. Devotion to his father, despite differences, showed in his dark eyes. "It looks as if the thought of a new baby in the house has been well received. Mother looks radiant too. Perhaps Gem will become the needed balm for the loss of Ranek."

"And his disappointment in his own sons," added Alex.

Michael leaned over and planted a kiss on Coral's cheek. "Congratulations on Gem. Rajiv and Jemani would be pleased if they knew."

As Michael's lips brushed her cheek, Coral's eyes went to Major Buckley, searching for reaction to the remarks about Gem. She noticed that he did not seem to be attentive, but preoccupied by other thoughts as he gazed across the room. She turned her head and saw Natine standing unobtrusively near a window, as much of a fixture in the ballroom as one of the paintings.

Coral's thoughts drifted back to Michael. He had never mentioned Jace Buckley before, and aside from the incident in the Himalayas, she wondered how they had met. Evidently they were trusted friends, since both men were willing to risk partnership. Michael had many friends who were considered to be adventurers, who belonged to another side of his life—a life that he did not bring home to Kingscote.

Major Buckley sampled a dessert of fresh mango and coconut, sprinkled with sugar. She wondered what was meant about Michael going to sea with him, but hesitated to ask, not wishing to show herself too curious about his ventures. Somehow she suspected the major of having too many.

She picked up a small glass of pineapple juice, the cut crystal glimmering.

"Then you are not of a mind to pursue your career in the military, Major Buckley?"

He set his plate down and his eyes followed an Indian who was now offering hot tea and Arabic coffee. Coral motioned for the boy to come.

"As a matter of fact, I will be out of uniform in a few months," he said.

"You sound pleased."

He smiled. "Delighted."

The major took a cup of coffee from the outstretched silver tray and dismissed the boy.

No doubt the military had curtailed his freedom. She thought of what her mother had told her about his upbringing.

"Colonel Warbeck must be disappointed. Usually fathers wish their sons to carry on the family interests."

"Most fathers do," put in Michael, and again glanced toward Sir Hampton. "Excuse me a moment."

He left them, walking in the direction of Sir Hampton and Captain Seward.

"When do you intend to start the tea plantation?" she asked.

"Michael will start without me. I will be away from India for some time. There is the small matter of money before I am able to buy in. I will be taking my clipper to sea. If Michael fails to convince your father, then he will join me. We intend to sail to Macau for tea and jade."

Alex chuckled. "Michael gets nauseous riding an elephant. He will prove little help on board your clipper."

Coral sipped her cool refreshment. "You own a ship?"

"I am buying the *Madras* from the Company. She's at berth in Calcutta right now, anxiously waiting for me to discard my uniform."

"From China, where will you go?" Coral asked.

"Oh, Cadiz, Portugal, other places, then London."

As he spoke of his plans in hauling cargo from China, his restlessness was apparent. Underneath his present facade of discipline, Coral saw a young man without bonds or ties, and she could almost feel the energy straining against its leash.

East India men were away at sea for two years at a time, and sometimes longer. She surmised that he was out to become independent and successful while enjoying the freedom of his own ship. An adventurous sea captain was a man to stay away from, she decided, friend of Michael's or not.

Natine appeared behind them carrying a letter. "A message for you, Major-sahib."

Coral could tell nothing of the contents of the message from the major's expression, but he seemed preoccupied. A moment later he folded the paper and placed it in his jacket. "I must leave tonight."

"Trouble?" Alex asked.

"Another skirmish with Burma near Manipur. Your father, I believe, has also had trouble recently."

Alex sighed. "Kingscote has had trouble with Burma for as far back as any of us can remember. We hire mercenaries to fight with us. Thankfully, matters usually calm down after a skirmish or two."

"I'm wanted back at the outpost."

He turned toward Coral. "If you will excuse me, Miss Kendall, Alex."

She watched as he exchanged polite farewells with her parents, explaining his need to return. He said something to Michael who laughed loudly, then glanced in her direction. Annoyed, she swished her fan to cool her face. In the company of Seward and several other military men, Major Buckley took his hat and gloves from Natine and followed him from the ballroom into the hall.

Coral waited a discreet moment, then slipped away unnoticed.

She found Major Buckley by the front door, alone with Natine. From Natine's expression, she surmised that he did not feel comfortable in the major's presence. Seeing Coral standing behind them, he salaamed and walked away.

Major Buckley turned toward her, and for a moment neither of them spoke. The pelting rain crashed against the window, drowning their silence.

"You did not say anything to my father about Gem."

He gave no direct reply as he slipped on his gloves.

"Why did you remain silent?" she asked.

"Take into consideration what I told you earlier."

"I have. My decision remains the same."

"I thought it would. Then I will leave you to set your own course."

Her voice was soft, hopeful: "Then . . . you are not going to voice your suspicions?"

"Do not ask me why I decided not to speak. I haven't the dimmest notion." He gazed down at her. "Maybe it is the shine in your eyes. Maybe it is your mother's laughter tonight . . . maybe it is the hope I have for the boy. Rajiv was a friend. His son is an orphan, and maybe I'm sentimental. Always a mistake. But with the chance to grow up in the Kendall household as a godchild of Miss Coral Kendall—I find myself hoping it works out for Gem, and you. Perhaps I've decided to believe in the laughter I heard tonight." His lips turned into something of a smile. "You, of course, do believe in impossible dreams?"

Impossible dreams . . . was that what the future held for Gem?

She was touched by his unexpected warmth. "Yes . . . and thank you."

"Do not thank me. I have the distinct feeling I am not helping you at all."

"Oh, but you are."

"I doubt that. In fact, if I had an ounce of good sense I would speak to your father at once."

"But you will not."

He studied her, then reached to open the door. "No. But my silence makes me partly responsible for the future—and that too is a mistake." His gaze became distant. "Goodbye."

He opened the door to step out into the torrent of rain.

A few minutes later, when the sound of horses' hooves had died away, Coral lifted her skirts and made her way up the wide stairway toward the upstairs hall.

Gem was waiting.

6

The Madras, *Diamond Point Harbor, Calcutta*
December 1793

Jace Buckley whistled as he shed his black and silver jacket, shako, and military sabretache. He slipped into the worn buckskin breeches, and rubbed his smooth chin; in a short time he would have a beard. He imagined the colonel's blue eyes turning into icy daggers should he see him looking—not like his disciplined son, but like the illegitimate offspring of the notorious Captain Jarred Buckley.

In the Great Cabin aboard the clipper *Madras,* he was no longer Major of the 21st Light Cavalry, but an independent sea captain on his way to buying his own ship. An interloper, as the Company called them.

Jace's lips thinned into a tight line. Interlopers were better known as China traders. They had betrayed his father, leaving him on the beach of Whampoa in a storm to face angry warlords while they escaped on junks.

Jace stared at the coffee mug in his hand. It had belonged to his father. . . .

Even to this day, he could relive every second of that scene on the beach with the waves crashing in around him, the cold black water tasting of brine, and in his imagination, of blood.

As a boy of eleven, he had clutched to the sharp rocks where he hid, and he could see his father tied hand and foot on the beach, the waves crashing against the shore.

Jace felt his stomach churn with the vivid memory. He could see the Chinese warlord in black, hear the angry words shouted in Chinese, see the curved blade smash against his father's throat, beheading him. As he watched the waves suck back the head, he turned away to vomit, betraying his presence.

Jace Buckley's years as a child-slave to opium dealers began that day. It wasn't until he was in Whampoa at age fourteen that he had managed to escape.

Jace had survived by a strong will—although Seward insisted it was by divine providence. Seward also had a notion that pain over the past prevented Jace from risking emotional involvement with others.

He had escaped China through the caravan route over the Old Silk Road through the Himalayas. In India he was befriended by a guru named Gokul. When the British army sent a patrol into central India to put down a quarrel between ruling Marathi factions, Jace had been discovered by then Captain John Sebastian Warbeck.

Warbeck, who had never married (Jace knew it was because of losing Lady Margaret Roxbury to her family's choice, cousin Hugo), had brought him back to the Company headquarters in Calcutta and, in process of time, had "civilized" him, as the colonel put it.

Jace was sent to the respected military academy

in London, and upon his graduation, had emerged as the cool and restrained young son of the colonel. Jace had returned to military life in Calcutta, out of respect for what the colonel had tried to do for him, and taken his place in the East India Company as expected.

For the first few years, in order to honor the colonel, Jace served the Company well in India—he even won an award for bravery and was eventually promoted to the rank of major. But Jace yearned for freedom and often found himself at odds with the interests he was meant to serve.

The East India Company and the military worked closely together, for the Company was more than trade—it had become part of the British government. The military's purpose was to support Britain's interests in India, interests with which Jace often found fault.

Jace now had his freedom ... but the disagreement between him and the colonel had gone so badly that the colonel had lost his usually restrained temper and ordered Jace out of the house.

Jace's rugged features flushed in anger at the memory. In a gesture of subconscious rebellion, he belted on the scabbard holding the sword that had belonged to his privateer father. Jace then snatched up the urn and sniffed the brew ... if his kansamah had watered down the Arabian coffee again, he would throw him into the harbor. He had warned him twice. A good soaking would do him good. He poured a mug and tasted it. Ah, just the way he liked it: strong and scalding. Jace turned to the small golden langur monkey. "What do you say, Goldfish, are you ready to adopt a life at sea?"

The monkey clapped its palms together, then contentedly munched on sections of coconut. Jace had intentionally given the monkey a name to fit its new life aboard ship.

Jace looked over at Gokul. The old Indian merchant who had befriended him as a youth folded each article of the uniform as carefully as he counted his rupees at the end of a thieve's day at the bazaar. He flecked off a piece of dust. "Ah, sahib, it had its glory." He breathed on the brass buttons, then rubbed them against his sleeve.

Jace lifted a brow. "Sorry, old man. I do not share a glimmer of your sentiment." He then mocked a groan of ecstasy as he slipped into a leather jerkin and calf-length boots. He stretched his muscles.

Gokul chuckled. "Ah, the cheetah, he is free again!"

Apparently caught up in the excitement of the upcoming voyage, Gokul rolled his dark eyes toward the cabin ceiling, holding the sabretache to his protruding belly. "The sea! The wind!"

"Aye, we'll second that," bellowed Seward, ducking through the cabin door, with Michael Kendall just behind, carrying his bags.

Michael dropped them and stood feet apart, hands on hips, looking about the Great Cabin with interest. Just beyond was the Round Room.

"My first voyage to China," said Michael. "You will end up making a seadog out of me yet, Jace."

Jace tossed him and Seward tin mugs, and Gokul poured.

"To freedom," he said with a smile.

Michael laughed. "And the *Madras*!"

"And we best not forget the good clipper's captain," added Seward with a grin. He walked up and grabbed Jace's shoulder with a hearty hand. "There be none better but Jarred Buckley himself—" and he added swiftly, "Christ rest his soul! May the ship's first cargo of tea and porcelain bring ye a step closer to payin' her off."

"Do not forget our Darjeeling project, sahibs," urged Gokul.

A banana skin slapped against Gokul's belly and landed at his sandals. The others laughed when the monkey escaped from the cabin, leaving Gokul muttering with indignation.

———————

The *Madras* set sail from the Bay of Bengal for the Dutch East Indies, taking on spices at Sumatra, Java, and Bali. Aside from some minor disagreements with the Dutch, they continued on their voyage to Singapore, where they harbored for two weeks, then entered the waters of the South China Sea two months after leaving Calcutta.

In February, while nearing the China coast, they made their first contact with foul weather when a typhoon struck. Jace brought the ship to safe harbor at Macau, and they arrived at Canton two weeks later.

The wharves were a babble of ethnic singsong dialects, mingled with the stringent odors of sweaty bodies, stale fish, and feathered ducks—head and webbed feet intact—strung up to dry.

Seward insisted upon going to Heavenly Jade Garden, an open-air bazaar where throngs of peasants gathered in the cool of evening to shop, eat, socialize, and enjoy the traveling magicians.

As always, the Garden was teeming with people. Tiny shops competed for space in the crowded bazaar, their colorful paper lanterns glowing in the darkness. Ornamented arches and floating paper dragons of red and yellow created a ceiling of color.

There were many coolie kitchens in Heavenly Jade Garden, each one sending forth pungent smells of Chinese cooking. Memories of his boyhood came flooding back. Jace felt both anger and pain. He had thought he would be able to handle the sights and sounds of the only face of China he had known, but as it all came rushing back he felt trapped.

Jace found himself amid a throng of people: acrobats, magicians, Flower Drum Song singers, and calligraphers. Men sat puffing from water pipes and drinking tea; still others cracked watermelon seeds between their teeth. Owners of shops, trying to lure in customers, hustled about the ancient boulevard in skull-caps, some had pigtails, others had their heads partially shaven, their silk gowns often threadbare. Jace recognized the brightly dressed minority races from the northwest provinces of China and Mongolia in embroidered red and blue jackets.

He watched Seward striding ahead unintimidated by the foreign culture, his sharp eye sizing up the various coolie kitchens for the evening meal. Jace remembered Michael, and looked behind him. He had stopped to watch an acrobatic family with a black and white Panda bear on a leash.

Jace waited for him, hands on hips. From the empty expression Michael wore, Jace assumed that he had ceased to take in the sights, smells, and the high pitch of the Chinese language. He was about to walk back and take him by the arm when Michael's expression turned to one of amazement.

Now what? thought Jace wearily, and lowered his hat. Michael jerked his head toward him, gesturing at Jace across the Garden. Not wanting to involve himself, Jace scowled and gestured for him to follow, but Michael threw up both hands and again beckoned him to come. Jace sighed, glancing ahead to see where Seward was. His rugged frame was easily spotted among the peasants going into a coolie kitchen.

Jace began making his way back through the crowd to Michael. It took him a minute to get there, for someone was setting off firecrackers, and the sparks and trails of smoke had evoked a crowd. As Jace walked up, Michael grabbed his shoulder.

"I say! Look over there—the man in black is about to lop off an old man's head!"

Jace felt a sickening reminder of the past. Michael's words did not surprise him. Cruelty to slaves and the indifference of the ruling class he knew by experience only too well. The last thing he wanted to do was to look in the direction where Michael pointed. But Michael was persistent. "Is it real? A circus, perhaps?"

Reluctantly, Jace turned in the direction of a myriad of gleaming lanterns strung over an arch constructed of stone blocks, named inappropriately for this particular occasion the Plum Blossom Gate of Good Fortune.

Masking the revulsion he felt inside, he studied what he knew to be a Chinese merchant of some authority, for he was dressed in a black satin jacket that reached to his knees. In his hand he carried a long sword gleaming as fiercely as his black eyes. He glowered down at a wizened old Chinese man with silver pigtails.

"The Manchus are a minority from northeast China," Jace explained. "They've conquered and ruled the Hans for some two hundred years. The old one must be a Han, his master a Manchu. Obviously he is a slave who has annoyed him." His voice revealed none of the kindled emotions churning inside.

Michael whipped his head around to stare at Jace. "Annoyed? Will he be permitted to cut off his head because he is *annoyed*?"

Jace had never told Michael about his father being beheaded on the beach at Whampoa. He could not explain to him how he felt now at seeing the cruelty repeated. Nausea swept over him. He must get away as swiftly as he could. Jace masked his feelings and met Michael's gaze.

"The old one is probably one of a thousand others across China who has died this day for angering some imperial magistrate, or even a merchant of peasant blood. Those who die are the lowliest of slaves. And whoever owns them may do as they wish, including lopping off their heads."

Michael stared at the ongoing scene. Jace looked at the old man sprawled on his face, begging. Jace gave Michael a prod in the opposite direction. Seward was waiting in the coolie kitchen, probably wondering what had happened to them. Besides, he could not stomach seeing the old man losing his head—

"Sha!" shouted the ruler.

Jace hesitated, knowing enough of the language to understand the death threat.

"Most worthless dog! Most vermin-infested piece of flesh! Where is the stone? Find it now in the dust! Creep and crawl and sift with your fingers till you find it or I shall chop you into a hundred pieces for the cauldron! The eye—where is the eye?

"Sha!" The Manchu swung his sword, whipping it over the old man to terrorize him, slicing at his threadbare gown. With a yell, he grabbed the pigtail as though to lop it off, but struck the dust instead. He leaped from his stair, shouting again, landing firmly on two muscled legs. "The stone! Find it!"

The old man was crawling frantically about, sifting handfuls of dust between his thin trembling fingers.

The scene was mostly ignored by the crowd, who hurried about their business with passive faces, too afraid themselves to notice. Hawkers continued pitching their wares—perhaps with louder voices—mule carts plodded by a little faster, and beggars limped away.

Jace unexpectedly found himself pushing his way through the crowd until he stood facing the rich shop owner. The merchant held a miniature black cheetah in his hand, and one of the emerald eyes was missing. Jace was surprised to hear his own voice, calm, almost disinterested, as though he did not care in the least what was happening.

"The cheetah with the missing eye . . . how much?"

The angry man turned to him. "It was worth much until this dog dropped it! The emerald is lost!" He calmed suddenly and bowed. "But I have others to show you. Please! Step inside my despicable and humble shop!"

Jace exchanged bows and said tonelessly: "I seek a cheetah with one eye, Most Honorable Sir."

"One eye?"

"One eye. Two eyes will not do. I will buy this one, or I shall resume my journey through the Heavenly Jade Garden a disappointed wretch."

The merchant's countenance swiftly altered. He gave another bow and murmured: "Step inside my worthless shop. The cheetah with one eye will be yours."

"I shall pay handsomely, but only if this inferior, miserable dog also becomes my property."

Jace withdrew a small leather pouch from inside his tunic and emptied gold coins into the merchant's palm. They glimmered in the lantern light, and the merchant ogled. Even the peasant-slave turned his white head to stare at the dancing glitter.

I must be a sentimental fool, thought Jace, and clamped his jaw as the merchant laid aside his sword to count the coins.

"The one-eyed cheetah and the old dog are mine," said Jace.

The merchant bowed deeply. "The cheetah and the old dog are yours, Most Honorable Sir."

Michael stood with an expression of disbelief. Jace accepted the ebony cheetah, then gestured for him to bring the old man. Jace walked away. Michael and the old slave followed.

They had not gone far when the old one rushed past Jace, stopped a short distance in front of him, and fell to the ground.

"Honorable Master! I am Yeh Jin-Soo, your miserable, wretched dog."

Jace said quietly: "Get up, friend Jin-Soo, you are safe now. You will call me Captain. I hope you don't get seasick. We are on our way to London."

The old one was struck speechless. He stared at him. Then rose to his feet, his thin black kimono dusty. He brushed it with dignity, bowed gravely, then walked behind to follow.

Jace looked askance at the cheetah with one eye, then shoved it inside his tunic. Michael burst out laughing, threw an arm about his shoulder, and they walked on.

They found Seward seated in a coolie kitchen. Jace sat to join him, and although he had no notion of what he was eating, Seward confidently boasted: "It be simmerin' for a day or two in a cauldron. Makes for flavor and tenderness."

Jace was now in a good mood and hungry. He ate while Seward went on to educate Michael on the correct way to eat among the peasants. "To show satisfaction, ye need to be makin' loud slurpin' sounds, smack yer lips, and snap yer chopsticks like so."

During the following days, the *Madras* was loaded with its cargo of tea and prized Chinese wares. A short time later, the crew set sail from Canton, confident about the next leg of the voyage to the port of London. After a year of prosperous and adventurous expeditions, they returned once again to the Indian waters of the Bay of Bengal.

Calcutta remained as Jace had left it, but perhaps even more crowded, with the East India Company thriving. English families had arrived to meet their husbands serving the Company and to take up residence at Fort William.

It was now February 1795, and Jace had not seen Michael in several weeks. Sir Hampton Kendall had arrived from Kingscote to meet with Roxbury about a family matter, and Michael was staying at his uncle's residence near Government-House.

Anxious to return to the shipping business that would secure their tea plantation, Jace had left the bungalow he shared with Seward in the infamous Chowringhee area of Calcutta, and had gone to the East India Company to discover what opportunities were available in shipping. He found nothing that interested him. He could do better as a privateer. As he left the office and crossed the wharf, he heard a loud shout in a familiar voice.

"Buckley! Wait up! I've splendid news!"

It was Michael, riding by in a carriage with Sir Hugo Roxbury's daughter, Belinda. As the driver brought the horses to a stop, Michael jumped out and came toward Jace at a run. He was dressed immaculately, bearing no resemblance to his appearance during his year aboard the *Madras*. He was again a Kendall, an heir to a silk dynasty. Jace looked at Belinda Roxbury. She stared at him, smiling demurely, her lashes lowering.

"The benediction from heaven is upon us!" said Michael.

Jace was skeptical and gave him a slanted look from under his hat.

Michael said victoriously, "You will see I am right. My father is looking to haul a cargo of silk to Cadiz. He asks to meet with you on the ship this afternoon."

A voyage to Spain alerted Jace's interest, for he also had a friend in Cadiz whom he wished to see again, an Arab merchant who handled expensive Moorish heirlooms. Jace had bought items from Hakeem before, and he was looking for the mate to a pair of ivory elephants that the director of the Company in London wanted.

He took paper and pen from his tunic to calculate the profit they would most likely clear from the voyage. It turned out to be nearly double what the Company had just offered him for a run to the Spice Islands.

"Is your father willing to contract with privateers?"

"He is now." Michael pulled Jace out of his cousin's hearing. "Last night he and Roxbury argued over the Company. My uncle's been after him to make a pact with the East India Company to protect Kingscote

98

from Burma, but my father will have none of it. He prefers to do things his way. Independence is in his blood. First thing this morning he told me he'd decided to hire interlopers."

Jace respected Kendall for standing his ground against Roxbury. Partly because he resented the Indiamen for monopolizing shipping. This new knowledge sparked his curiosity about the relationship between the Kendalls and Sir Hugo Roxbury.

"Your father has always hired mercenaries to fight for Kingscote. Why is Roxbury pressuring him to sign a pact with the Company?"

Michael frowned. "The disagreement between them is not new. Even as a boy I remember my father complaining of Hugo's manipulations. The Roxburys of London own a percentage of Kingscote, just as the Kendalls do a portion of the Silk House in London. But Hugo's share in the actual plantation doubled when he married my mother's sister and also inherited her share."

No wonder Roxbury wanted Kingscote under East India Company jurisdiction. Since he was a high official he would benefit from the decisions made, just as he would gain by a marriage between his daughter Belinda and Michael. Sir Hampton had a strong contender for the silk enterprise in his brother-in-law, Sir Hugo. Jace already knew that Michael was interested in his cousin Belinda.

"This is our opportunity, Jace. My father has spoken well of you."

———

That afternoon, Sir Hampton arrived on the *Madras* with Michael. Jace was pleased to see that the disagreement between him and his son over his sailing to China was over. Kendall stood with a hefty arm about Michael's shoulders.

"I admit to having a bit more on my mind where you're concerned, Buckley, than the *Madras* taking on Kingscote silk."

Jace was instantly cautious. He was not certain that he liked the sound of Kendall's voice. "Oh? And what could that be?" But Sir Hampton did not appear anxious to explain. He roamed the Great Cabin, pausing now and then as though recalling pleasant memories of a ship. Kendall picked up the cheetah with one emerald eye.

"Roxbury will return to Kingscote with me, and Michael too," he was saying. "There is to be a family gathering of some importance. It concerns my middle daughter, Coral. I believe you met her when you were a major in the military."

Jace said nothing. He watched Sir Hampton inspect the cheetah.

"What will you take for this?"

Jace thought of Jin-Soo. "It is not for sale."

"A shame. My daughter collects wildlife miniatures."

"Yes. She told me."

"She would like this one."

"It has a missing eye. Even at that I paid an exorbitant price!"

Michael smiled and said to his father, "An interesting tale about that cheetah; I'll explain later. It has become our mascot."

"Mr. Kendall, surely a cheetah for your daughter is not what brought you to my ship."

Sir Hampton smiled. "No. Clever workmanship, though," he said of the miniature. "If you do change your mind, I would like to buy it." He set it down on the desk and turned to fix Jace with his full attention.

Jace leaned back against his desk, his features unreadable. He was determined that Kendall would not rummage through his mind.

"I want to hire you and your ship to bring my silk to Spain. Did Michael explain?"

"He did. And I'm interested."

"Good. As I said, there is something else, Buckley. There is to be an official church ceremony on Kingscote. I came to Calcutta, not only on business, but to bring back the Anglican minister from St. John's. My daughter is adopting Gem as her son. Did Michael tell you? He'll be a new member of the Kendall family. Since Coral is not well enough to make the tedious journey to Calcutta, the bishop has kindly agreed to travel to Kingscote."

Jace wondered if he had heard correctly. The Kendall daughter was *adopting* Gem? And Sir Hampton seemed quite willing to allow her to do so. Had he forgotten what happened to Rajiv? But how could Jace fault Kendall when neither he nor the rest of the family knew the background on Gem? That was due, not only to Coral's silence, but his own. Jace could hardly accuse Sir Hampton of recklessness for allowing Coral to make the child her son—and his heir. A look in Michael's direction showed no concern either. Both were oblivious to the risks involved.

"If you wish to hire the *Madras* to sail to Cadiz, well enough. However, I do not see how else I can be of help to you."

Sir Hampton kept his sharp gaze on Jace. "Both Michael and Seward tell me you are experienced in silk from your years in China."

Jace had not told Michael he had learned silk as a child-slave to the emperor, and he wondered what grand picture Michael might have painted of his years in China to Sir Hampton.

"I would like you to return to Kingscote with me," Hampton said, and he must have seen Jace's surprise, for he added with a chuckle, "Only for a brief duration, Buckley. I need an experienced man to oversee the loading from the hatcheries. I usually do it myself, but I shall be absorbed with the family events surrounding Gem's adoption. I've spoken to Seward, and he insists you are most qualified with hatchery work."

Kendall pulled a five-hundred-pound note from inside his vest, and laid it on the scarred desk. Jace became aware of Michael's look, urging him to accept.

"Another note will follow, upon safe delivery of the silk to Cadiz," Sir Hampton said. "What do you say, Captain Buckley, do we have a bargain?"

Michael coughed. Jace glanced at him. *Darjeeling*, Michael's expression prodded.

"Your offer is hard to resist, Sir Hampton," said Jace.

Sir Hampton laid a heavy hand on his shoulder. "I know a strong captain when I see one. Michael has every confidence in you, and so do I. I have not forgotten your help on Kingscote. You are the manner of man I can trust." He held out his hand. "Then we have us a bargain, Buckley. Say we leave Sunday after the services at St. John's?"

Jace took his hand. "A bargain, Sir Hampton."

"Good. Michael will fill you in on the details. We will need to travel more slowly because of the women. Lady Margaret and her daughter Belinda will accompany us."

Jace watched Sir Hampton and Michael walk to the cabin door, but there was more on his mind.

"About your daughter's adoption of the child,"

Jace said, keeping his voice casual. "This must be quite a celebration for the Roxbury side of the family as well."

A flicker of annoyance showed in Sir Hampton's bronzed face. He masked it swiftly enough and smiled. "Roxbury protested as we expected. But his and Margaret's decision to come to Kingscote to attend the family affair is a healthy sign that he will soon mellow."

Jace did not judge Sir Hugo Roxbury to be a man who mellowed. Showing none of his thoughts, however, Jace went on casually, "Your daughter must be quite pleased."

"Aye, she is indeed." His rugged face softened. "My daughter adores Gem, and so does Mrs. Kendall. And I would be remiss, if I failed to include myself." He gave a brief chuckle, and straightened his hat. "The rascal has won me over without a bit of difficulty."

Jace said pointedly: "I hope his charm equally woos Sir Hugo."

If Kendall caught his insinuation, he chose not to show it. He turned away. "Gem will make a fine Kendall grandson. A strong heir." He gave a swat to Michael's shoulder and pretended to scowl. "With you as slow as your sisters to marry, I best be thanking the good God above for a grandson."

Michael responded with a laugh. "I promise not to disappoint you. As soon as Jace and I buy our tea plantation, I shall consider Cousin Belinda."

"Tea!" came the lightly mocking voice. And he turned to Jace with a helpless expression. "What is wrong with silk, I ask? Tea, bah! 'Tis a curse to swallow the stuff!"

"Jace will agree with you on that much."

"As for your cousin Belinda, she has her eyes on your brother Alex."

"Alex! What does she see in *him*?" he asked fiercely.

"Now, now, enough of your envy. Come, Hugo is waiting for us at Government-House and pacing the floor, to be sure. An odious fellow—but do not tell your mother I said so."

After their footsteps died away, Jace murmured under his breath, "Adoption!"

Absently picking up the cheetah, Jace rubbed his thumb over the smooth carving. From what he knew of Roxbury, he was a ruthless seeker of power in the politics of India. What if he prowled around, asking questions about the boy's parents? If he discovered the child was the grandnephew of a maharaja, there would be harsh political consequences for Kingscote.

I should have spoken to Kendall the night of the monsoon, he thought, and felt a rise of irritation with himself. Why did he allow a sweet, young face with pleading eyes to come between him and wisdom?

7

Although a week had passed since his arrival, Jace had not yet seen Coral. The group's arrival at Kingscote had been met with little fanfare, as the family was immersed in preparations for the adoption ceremony. There was to be music, numerous religious rituals, a gala picnic on the front green with huge amounts of food, and a British military band from Jorhat. News of the elaborate preparations disturbed him, and Jace told himself that he must speak to Coral without further delay.

Upon casual inquiry of her whereabouts to Michael, Jace was informed that Coral was confined to her bedchamber, recovering from a recent attack of fever.

"Uncle Hugo wants her to go to London to seek medical treatment from Ethan," Michael added.

"A physician?"

"Yes, and a cousin. They say he specializes in tropical diseases."

"A Roxbury cousin, no doubt."

"Yes. Hugo's nephew."

Jace assumed that Michael had mentioned his

own presence on Kingscote, and that Coral would find little cheer in knowing that the one who shared her dark secret was here.

When another day went by, and their paths did not meet, he decided he would risk sending her a message by way of the child named Yanna, asking to speak to her alone. If she was strong enough to attend the ceremony, then she could take a ghari to meet him at the hatcheries where he was working.

Jace wrote what he hoped would force her to meet with him:

I must see you alone about Gem.

Captain J. Buckley

Coral's reply was swift in coming. Yanna giggled as she brought the message to him, then turned and ran away to a group of other giggling girls.

I will come down to the river the morning
the elephants haul the silk to the barges.

Miss C. Kendall

Satisfied, Jace went back to work on the river, overseeing the Indian workers preparing the flat-bottom barges for the trip downriver to Guwahati.

———

It was the morning the children working in the hatcheries most anticipated. At least twenty elephants were loaded with bundles of silk cocoons for the circus-like trek down to the river's edge. The manjis would unload the bundles onto the barges for the journey to Guwahati. After the elephants were unloaded, their reward was to be washed and humored by children carrying brushes made of boar bristles. No one

106

on Kingscote was certain who enjoyed the ritual more: the elephants, or the host of orphan children.

The great gray beasts were now coming from the direction of the hatcheries in the mulberry orchard. The first elephant in the long line came around the corner of the dusty road, followed by a host of others trumpeting and flapping their ears. The shouting children, carrying their coveted brushes and rags, ran to the side nearest the thick trees, well out of range of the heavy lumbering feet. The experienced *mahouts* sat low on the elephants' necks, directing them with an ankus. Behind them were the bundles of silk cocoons that the *Madras* would bring to Spain.

Jace stood near the wide gray waters of the Brahmaputra, but his attention was arrested away from the caravan and toward the Kendall mansion. In the carriageway, a two-horse ghari was wending its way down to the river. Once near the road, the ghari-wallah stopped, climbed down from the seat, and came around to open the door.

Jace saw Coral seated alone with a baby boy, who was about a year and a half old. The boy was squealing with excitement and pointing, while she kept a firm hand around his waist to keep him from escaping her lap. The child was the picture of affluence, obviously the object of Coral's doting affection. Gem was a striking child, his handsome features and brown eyes full of innocence and delight.

The scene intensified Jace's dilemma. He watched as the toddler squirmed with joy at each elephant lumbering along the road. Gem threw his arms around her neck, and Coral pointed to where the elephants slowly lowered themselves knees first into the shallow banks for their wash. Their trunks thankfully sucked up the water to squirt over their backs, sometimes spraying the boys attending them. Gem's laughter mingled with theirs.

Coral laughed too, and the musical sound drifted to where Jace stood. His eyes narrowed. She, too, was the image of affluence, and he convinced himself that he did not notice how time had enhanced her attractive appearance. She wore festoons of blue silk, and a straw hat trimmed with white lace covered her blonde tresses.

Jace jerked his hat lower and strode across the road toward the ghari. He stopped in the dust, feeling the heat, his eyes confronting the freshness of her sun-touched beauty. Coral's ability to make an impact on his emotional armor irritated him.

For a moment, she appeared to be so occupied with Gem that he thought she was oblivious to his presence. He rested his hands on his hips, staring at her from beneath his hat. Would she even recognize him without his uniform? At least he had shaved off his beard before he arrived.

"Miss Kendall," Jace said in a voice that was altogether too formal.

Her green eyes, fringed thickly with lashes, met his. The color in her cheeks told him she was not as indifferent to his presence as she made out to be.

"What a pleasant surprise to see you again, Captain. Michael tells me you will soon be sailing for Spain." She rushed on with hardly a pause, "I apologize for the delay in our meeting." She looked away to the river. "I was waiting for the elephants to come today. It gave me an excuse to leave the house and be alone with Gem. I—I thought we could talk during a ride to the hatcheries. I've an excuse to go there. I'm looking for Yanna."

"Do you need an excuse to leave the house?" Jace

responded bluntly. "Or merely one to be seen with me?"

She did not reply. He noted the faint darkness beneath her eyes and thought of her ongoing struggle with the fever. He felt uncomfortable. *Just how ill is she?* He knew of some who had died as a result of tropical fever.

"I take no pleasure in causing you unease, Miss Kendall."

Her eyes came back to search his, and the determination he remembered from the past was visible. Despite frail health, she had a strength of purpose many lacked. It was a spirit Jace admired, even if it did lead her toward trouble.

"You will attend the festivities?" came her breathless question.

Obviously, his presence on Kingscote at this particular time disturbed her, although she was trying to pretend that it did not, that the secret they shared about Gem was of no consequence.

His eyes flickered with wry amusement. "You are inviting me?"

"But of course," came her quick reply. She busied herself with Gem.

"Then I would not miss it, Miss Kendall. Unfortunately, neither would the maharaja—if he knew."

Her eyes widened. "Please! Do not speak of that."

He saw her glance about to make certain no one else was within hearing distance.

"I am sorry, but we must discuss it," he said quietly. "When last we met, you intimated only caring for the child. A godparent, was it not? You said you would send him away to school. I agreed that would be safe enough. But now you are making him a Kendall."

Coral smoothed back Gem's dark curls from his

forehead. "Matters have changed." Her voice began to show her irritation that he had shown up to cast a shadow on her plans. "I have my family's blessing for the adoption. And as I once told you, sir, I am not the only one who wishes to keep him. My mother is very attached to Gem. He has in many ways replaced the baby she lost."

"Yes. You told me . . . I sympathize. I, too, am a friend of sentiment, Miss Kendall, but I also respect your father. And I feel he must know—"

She interrupted. "And my father has great pride in Gem. We want him, Captain," she said firmly. "We all want him."

"Not *all*, Miss Kendall."

Jace was speaking of Sir Hugo Roxbury. Evidently she followed his suggestion, for her expression set with further determination.

So, he thought, *she has already guessed Roxbury might one day be the thorn in her rose garden.*

"A formidable fellow, Roxbury," Jace prodded.

"Yes, but he is a good man, however strongly opinionated," she insisted.

He gave a short laugh. "Sir Hugo? Forgive me if my laughter appears rude, but you will permit me to differ. Colonel Warbeck is well acquainted with Sir Hugo. And, I might add, so am I."

She looked at him thoughtfully. "You?"

Jace said casually, "While an officer in Calcutta, I spent evenings at the Roxbury residence, as did others."

Coral was alert now, and she scanned him, saying nothing.

"No matter how we may try to bend the truth for the sake of politeness, neither of us could go so far as to say Sir Hugo Roxbury is a 'good' man. Clever, yes.

Perhaps even ruthless. His ambition drives him. And it is his nature to disapprove of making an Indian child a Kendall silk heir, especially if that position may contest his own."

Jace could see that his words upset her.

She straightened her hat. "It is true that my uncle has tried to change Father's mind, and mine. He has made his case forcefully."

Jace gave a laugh. "I will wager that he has."

"But my life is not my uncle's to control, Captain." She raised her chin. "Nor anyone else's."

"A polite slap, but well taken. Do you think I enjoy this?"

Her face softened. "I appreciate your concerns . . . however, my mind is made up."

"As well as your heart. You have not changed since that night of the monsoon."

She brought her eyes up to meet his, and Jace noticed how her lashes tilted upward at the edges and made a delicate shadow on her ivory skin.

"Yes, my heart is made up. I could not give him up for all India!"

The silence became uncomfortable. Gem stared up at him with luminous brown eyes, and chubby fingers unexpectedly reached over to latch hold of the cord lacing on the front of his tunic. Jace tried to pry his fingers loose without being rough, but Gem was determined to hold on.

Coral hastened to intervene, looking embarrassed. "Gem, do let go of the captain's tunic."

The boy merely giggled and continued clutching the strings.

Jace smiled. "I have a suspicion you do not mind Miss Coral at all," he told Gem.

"Mummy, Mummy."

Jace realized his mistake. She was not "Miss Coral" to Gem.

Jace untangled himself from the boy.

"I cannot believe you would be so horrid as to come all the way to Kingscote to unmask our little secret," Coral whispered.

"I think you know better than that," he gritted. "As you can see—I am loading Kendall silk."

Jace swung into the ghari, seating himself across from her and calling up to the driver: "The hatcheries!" He shut the door, and the vehicle surged forward.

A strained silence passed before Jace spoke. "He's a pleasant child to behold. He looks like his father," he said. "He's going to be handsome."

"Yes," Coral said proudly, glad to have the course of their conversation altered. "Quite handsome. And he shall travel through all Europe and have the best of education."

Remembering his friend with a dagger through his heart, Jace felt his insides tighten. As he stared at the boy, Gem smiled, suddenly shy now, and buried his face in the folds of her silken skirts.

"I can see why he has won over the affections of your father."

"Captain," she said breathlessly. "You are not going to break your promise to me? That night of the monsoon . . . when you were leaving . . . you said you would say nothing . . . that you would leave me to chart my own course."

"And you have. A word of caution: Watch out for Hugo Roxbury," he stated flatly. "He is clever enough to ask questions better left buried in the past."

She settled her skirts uneasily. "What reason would he have for asking questions?"

"Call it instinct on my part, if you will. But the

fact is his coming here now has deeper motivations than merely attending a family ceremony. I've had a month to study him since leaving Calcutta. There is not a sentimental bone in his body."

His tone softened. "Be cautious. Will you?"

"Yes, of course I will, Captain."

"Thinking back . . . have you any idea who may have sent that message to Rajiv? Someone in the mansion, perhaps?"

She shook her head and closed her eyes, as though trying to remember, yet forget, at the same time.

"No, no one. There has been no trouble since the dreadful incident. Rajiv and Jemani are all but forgotten, except by me."

"Someone else remembers. That someone put a dagger through Rajiv. Two or three years means nothing."

Her hand drew Gem closer. "What are you going to do?"

Both Coral and Gem were watching him. The child was sweetly oblivious to his situation, the Kendall daughter all too aware of the predicament, yet unrelenting.

"I shall tell you what I intended when I came here. I told myself I would speak to you first. That I would make you see I am bound by honor to speak to Sir Hampton." Jace looked at Gem. "But it is obvious, Miss Kendall, that I am two years too late. Whatever I do will bring pain, not only to you but to your family. However, the one question remaining is whose heart shall I risk to my silence?"

She said softly: "I shall forever be in your debt."

His eyes caught and held hers. "Bribery, Miss Kendall?"

She blushed. "I only meant—"

"I know what you meant. But I did not come here to collect favors. Nor do I want to bind you with indebtedness. I respect freedom too much to play games."

"You also respect my father, and I appreciate that, truly I do. It may help you to know that I will not be staying much longer on Kingscote. I am going to Roxbury House in London for schooling. In fact, I'll be returning to Calcutta with my uncle and aunt when they leave here. Belinda and I will join my sisters who are already in London. And Gem will come with me. He will be safe in England. I will place him in a good school there."

"A wise decision. Go as soon as possible."

The ghari stopped at the hatcheries. Jace opened the door, prepared to leave without further discourse.

Her voice interrupted. "Do let me tell you something about the production of silk, Captain Buckley."

His alert gaze swerved to meet hers. He had thought she would be anxious to get away from him. He already knew about silk production . . . but he also knew an invitation when he heard one, even though veiled in the disguise of teaching sericulture. He was certain she only hoped to win him over into keeping silence about Gem. Jace found her ulterior motive amusing.

"As you wish. You have my rapt attention. Suppose you explain to me about the silkworm."

"Caterpillar, actually."

He smiled. "How interesting."

The mulberry orchard stood against the backdrop of the jungle. Normally the outspreading branches were thick, the leaves a dark glossy green, but they were in the process of being stripped by the children, and then pruned by the young men in preparation for next season's crop.

The workers' commune appeared a self-sufficient village, with a few shops and hundreds of small huts. Some were made of woven grasses; others were square, low rooms plastered with mud, dried cow dung comprising the floor. Old men, unable to do the heavy work any longer, waited to accomplish their tasks of carrying trays of dried cocoons. Now they squatted in the shade taking turns puffing on a hookah.

The arrival of their ghari was noted, but the adults went on with their work. The children, however, kept looking over their shoulders, giggling among themselves. They were scampering up and down the mulberry trees gathering leaves. Many of them stared and smiled as Jace strolled with Coral and Gem in the direction of the wooden hatcheries.

"All right. What do we see first?" he asked innocently.

"What would you like to know? I am an expert, you know."

"I must confess. The truth is, I know everything there is about caterpillars."   ·

"You?" she paused, and looked up at him, surprised. "How? I thought you adored tea . . . wild, was it not? Somewhere in Darjeeling?"

He picked up Gem and let him ride on his back.

"I do not exactly adore tea either. But it will become a rich market when the East India Company bans shipments from China."

"How do you know that? About the Company, I mean?"

He did not answer how he knew. "As for caterpillars . . . I spent four years feeding the miserable things

115

by hand in China while you were still crawling around on the nursery rug."

"How ancient and wise you sound, Captain. Let me guess . . . you must be about the same age as Michael."

He said nothing. He was a year younger.

Gem seemed only too happy to ride on his back.

"These Chinese silkworms," she taunted, as they walked slowly toward the buildings, "no doubt they belonged to your father?"

"No. The imperial emperor." He glanced down at her and saw her cover a smile. She did not believe him.

"You were a friend of the emperor?" she asked.

He was about to say—*"No, his slave. One of a thousand, until I escaped by wit and charm. Aren't you proud of me, Coral? The other children either died or are still tending cocoons as men, but I escaped."*

But he caught himself. His past would mean little to her. And he did not wish to share it.

"No, not exactly a friend," he said.

They paused to watch a large group of young boys climbing the trees and gathering the mulberry leaves.

"So you know all about sericulture, do you?" came her challenging voice.

"Try me."

"Very well," came the light, musical voice. Coral looked up at Jace with amused eyes and a bright smile. "I shall bypass all the ordinary information such as gathering the tons of mulberry leaves—almost three hundred and fifty pounds for eight thousand worms."

"You are certain it is eight, and not nine?"

"My father has lectured that point, time and time again at breakfast, since I was five years old."

She walked on, and he followed. Gem insisted on

removing Jace's hat, then replacing it again every ten seconds.

"I shall also omit boring you with the chopping, the spoon-feeding of the new larvae, and the cultivation in their hatcheries known as a 'nursery'—since you know all about it."

Now she paused and looked at him, satisfied.

"Instead, Captain Buckley, I shall ask you a profound question. One you *must* have been taught by the emperor of China."

Jace smiled, amused. "I wait with breathless anticipation, Miss Kendall."

"What is the process for dealing with a newly hatched worm that will not wake up and eat?"

His mouth curved upward. "Naturally you wish a profound answer."

"Naturally."

"Let me consider . . . ah, yes! I was given a chicken feather and sternly commanded to tickle it awake," came the grave reply.

Coral laughed her surprise. "You are right! Then you truly were involved in sericulture in China?"

"Where else? And no barking dogs, crowing roosters, or eating garlic. It upsets the freshly hatched worms, or should we call them babies? And, you must see to it that they eat, devour their meals, and take naps in harmony."

Coral laughed. "I am shocked, Captain. You are as tedious as my father. He has a hundred rules from China and never deviates. I would not have guessed you knew so much about silk. Did you truly serve the emperor?"

"Yes. But I assure you, he was not the slightest bit grateful. A most dour man. He never walked. I used to wonder if he had feet like the rest of the poor human race. He was carried wherever he went, and he always had a blade in his lap, only too anxious to lop off someone's head."

They passed the large group of older children and women who were busy chopping the leaves. The smaller children carried the trays into the hatchery for young women to feed the worms.

"Shall we visit the nursery?" she said with a smile. "Papa has more 'babies' than he knows what to do with. This is only the west wing of the nursery. There are acres more. But whatever you do, do not talk. You will upset them. Do you hear, Gem?"

Inside the hatchery it was quiet and still, except for what Jace believed was the sound of the silkworms actually munching. He had been told it was his imagination, but he was certain he could hear a "fizzing" sound. They were ravenous eaters.

A hundred or so young women, called silkworm "mothers," were spoon-feeding the chopped mulberry leaves to the larvae. Jace stared at the pastel-hued silkworm cocoons, filling tiny dry cubicles set in wooden frames.

"Most of the cocoons are never allowed to hatch," she explained when they emerged from the nursery. "Although some are kept for egg production. The emerging moth damages the cocoon for unreeling, and in silk production the unbroken thread is desired. But then, you no doubt know this."

Jace followed her out across the yard to one of the outbuildings where the children were busy.

Seated on the mud floor, young girls were busy in the traditional method of spinning silk, known as thigh-spinning. The girls looked up as they entered, and fixing their eyes on him, they took to giggling.

Jace stooped down beside a girl to watch, but she

grew clumsy with embarrassment.

"Ah, I see how you do it," said Jace, pretending to be extremely interested. "You pierce the cocoon at one end, then draw the fiber across your leg."

At the mention of "leg," they giggled even louder. The blushing girl dropped the cocoon and covered her face with both palms while she laughed.

"Do you think I could do that?" he teased her.

One bold girl of ten said soberly: "Leg too big. Too much hair, silk get caught."

The hut became one loud giggle. Jace saw not the girls but himself at that age—lost, an orphan, and soon bent on a sinful path of the worst kind.

"Yanna? You will come back to the house with me," Coral told one of the giggling girls.

Gem was determined to play with the cocoons, so Jace scooped him up and walked outside.

Suddenly Jace wanted to be gone from Kingscote as quickly as he could get the barges loaded. During the ride back to the river, he was silent. If she noticed his withdrawal, she did not let on, and when he made his polite goodbye, she extended a gloved hand, her eyes saying what they both knew she could not say in front of Yanna.

He would say nothing to interrupt the adoption.

8

The church ceremony took place without incident. The day was warm and the sky clear as the family gathered on the lawn beneath a blue-fringed canopy.

Jace stood aloof from the others while the Anglican bishop read the church liturgy, and then from the Bible. Pompous documents were laid out on a long table. Coral, Sir Hampton, and Elizabeth Kendall dipped the gold quill into ink and wrote their signatures, followed by the bishop.

Jace was taken with the joy on Coral's face at the end of the ceremony when she took Gem by the hand, and together they walked up to the bishop and stood before him. Private words were spoken between the three of them; then he lifted Gem into his arms and intoned a long prayer. Coral then placed a tiny gold cross on a chain around the child's neck.

A copy of the signed documents were delivered to Sir Hampton, and a second went to the bishop. "I give you Gem Ranek Kendall," his pious voice announced, and Coral turned toward the family with Gem, smiling. Jace walked away.

121

There was an abundance of food, conversation, and laughter as the day wore on into afternoon. Jace did his best to avoid Coral, who sat on the spacious green lawn with her silken skirts spread about her. A young Indian girl shielded her from the sun with a white lace parasol. Coral's Bible lay beside her.

Despite her excitement over the adoption ceremony, he noticed that she did not look well. Beside Coral, seated on cushioned stools, Elizabeth Kendall and Margaret Roxbury chatted together, as two sisters do who have not seen each other in a year, balancing their luncheon plates on their laps.

Some feet away, still dressed in black velvet and white lace, Gem Ranek Kendall romped with rabbits, peacocks, and other fowl, under the watchful eye of an expressionless Burmese ayah. A tiny Burmese girl of about Gem's age romped with him. "No, Emerald," he kept saying as the girl won the attention of the peacock. "My turn. My turn. Obey Gem."

Jace smiled to himself. The boy already knew that a Kendall was to be obeyed.

Jace had no wish for company, even though Michael and Alex stood by him, drinking from tall crystal glasses and discussing the upcoming voyage to Spain. Cousin Belinda Roxbury was flirting outrageously with her cousin Alex, who seemed amused by her. Michael did not look happy.

As Jace looked away from Coral, he caught the intense dark stare that momentarily held his own. Sir Hugo Roxbury evidently did not approve of him looking at his niece. Observing that stare, Jace was reminded that Coral's uncle did not appear pleased with the day's events. No doubt he also disapproved of Michael sailing with him to Spain, and of their plans for a partnership in Darjeeling.

Jace had no inclination to appease Sir Hugo, for he did not like the man. Yet he had no wish for unpleasantness and was turning to leave, intending to prepare for the trip to Guwahati early the next morning, when a pleasant voice called to him—

"Captain Buckley? Do join us! You must eat something." Mrs. Elizabeth Kendall sat shaded beneath a parasol held by a child. She smiled and beckoned him to their low table.

Mrs. Kendall was a gracious woman. Unwilling to excuse himself and thus appear rude, Jace walked over and heard a rustle of silk as the ladies pulled back their skirts to make room for him on the grass. Mrs. Kendall proceeded to fix him a plate, piling on an assortment of English dishes.

"If you are anything like my two sons, you enjoy a hardy appetite," she said.

Jace accepted the plate, although he was not hungry, answering numerous polite questions from both Elizabeth and Margaret about his upcoming voyage to Spain. Coral was silent. When at last the desserts were served on wheeled carts, there was a lull in the questioning, and the ladies discoursed among themselves.

Coral leaned toward him and said quietly, "You are leaving in the morning, Captain?"

"Yes, aren't you relieved?" Jace smiled. "I shall fade back into the Indian sunset." He set the empty plate down and rose to his feet. "You will excuse me. There is work to do before I leave for Guwahati tomorrow. Thank you for the luncheon." He glanced over at Gem who still romped with the Burmese child in the grass. "And may the shine stay in your eyes."

Jace offered his thanks to Mrs. Kendall, shook hands with Sir Hampton, and with a word to Michael about Guwahati, left the celebration without a backward glance.

Coral watched Jace leave, her emotions a jumble of contradictions. She told herself she was glad he was gone. One slip of the tongue about Gem, and she would have swooned for the first time in her life! She had sensed his unease, just as he must have sensed her own. Not once had they exchanged glances, although aware of each other. She had noticed that he forced himself to eat, to sit quietly, to behave the gentleman, when all the while he had wanted to avoid being there at all. Sitting at her feet, as was expected of an attentive suitor, must have been especially irksome to him, she thought. And quite suddenly, Coral wanted to laugh. She restrained herself, knowing that it would most likely come out as an hysterical giggle, convincing her mother and aunt that the day had been too much for her. She closed her eyes against the sun's glare and tried to cool her emotions.

He was gone now. There would be a long, long voyage to Spain and perhaps to other distant ports. Possibly she would never run into him again. Good. Then she would not need to worry about him saying anything to her family about Gem. But then, somehow she had guessed all along that he would not. Perhaps the captain was not as hardheaded and arrogant as he appeared.

The excitement of the morning was ebbing away. Coral realized how tired she felt, and the heat was beginning to drain her of strength. She excused herself from her mother and her aunt, giving them a customary kiss on the cheek, and calling for Jan-Lee to bring Gem and Emerald.

Today Gem is truly my son. A smile flitted across

her face as Coral made her way back to the house. Soon the two of them would journey to London to meet Grandmother Victoria Roxbury . . . and Cousin Ethan Boswell.

9

It was August of 1795, and already late in the season when the *Madras* sailed from Diamond Point Harbor carrying Kingscote silk. They sailed the Bay of Bengal toward the strait between Ceylon and the Indian coast, then went across the Indian Ocean and came to the island of Zanzibar—isle of cloves, wild coffee, and forests of coconut palms. Here, as planned, they took on spices.

" 'Twas yer father's haven," Seward told him.

Jace remembered the hot white sands and glittering blue waters of Zanzibar, where his father had owned a small bungalow on the beach.

The *Madras* dropped anchor, stopped farther down the coast, then sailed around the African horn, making port at the Cape of Good Hope. From there, the voyage brought them along the Gold Coast of Africa—where the devious slave traders abounded—and eventually they came to the port of Tangiers. Staying a short time, they sailed for Spain and arrived at Cadiz late in December of 1796.

The town of Cadiz, dating back to the times of the ancient Phoenicians, was built on a cliff overlooking the sea. The silk was unloaded in the port, the price was good, and the funds were divided between the three of them. With it they intended to buy heirlooms from Moorish Spain, then sell them to the wealthy collectors in London. Jace expected to return to Calcutta by October of the next year, avoiding the monsoon winds of August and September. Everything, it seemed, was going well. He had almost begun to believe Michael's declaration that heaven's benediction was upon them.

Since the weather for sailing in the Atlantic was questionable, Jace was anxious to leave Cadiz within the next three days. The city was a flourishing port, its bazaars crowded with merchants, soldiers, sailors, slave traders, a few pirates, and many scholars. Although he had friends in the ancient city, Jace preferred to walk the lighted arcade alone. He spent the morning at the famous stall of the Booksellers where he found several copies of old writings to add to his collection. Besides owning a copy of the Hindu holy writings, the Vedas, he had acquired a copy of the Muslim Koran and a King James Bible—but not even Seward knew that he was making a comparison of the three main world religions.

Tired of browsing through manuscripts, Jace left the Booksellers and stood on the corner of the arcade with his purchases. Noise, music, and a babble of voices filled the air. He walked to a tavern-inn on the cliff above the sea to wait for Seward and Michael. They would bring Hakeem, the Arab merchant who specialized in prized antiques.

The low-raftered inn was crowded with seamen when Jace arrived. It was damp and cold outside, and a fire burned in the wall-sized hearth. He found an empty place overlooking the western sea, now shrouded with incoming fog, and ordered portions of roasted lamb.

Michael arrived, tense and excited, seating himself opposite Jace. Leaning across the table, he said in a low voice: "After London, we can return to India and start the plantation!"

Jace cast him a caustic smile. "What did you do, rob a temple? It will be three more years—if all goes well."

Michael grinned, undaunted. "Seward found your merchant friend. And wait until you hear the Arab explain."

They both turned toward the door. Seward strode into the common room, and Jace recognized the wealthy Arab beside him, clothed in a flowing robe and smoke-blue silk turban. His short Muslim beard was well-trimmed, his hawklike black eyes snapping with pleasure when they rested on Jace.

"Greetings, son of the great Captain Buckley! I see you are back to the ways of the sea, and free of the infidel uniform." His crafty old eyes gleamed. "Ah, is it not in your stars to become an auspicious explorer like your father?"

Jace stood and greeted the Arab with a smile. "Hakeem! You old Teller of Tales! How good to see you again! So my father was an explorer, was he?" Jace laughed. "You mean pirate, do you not? Better read your stars again, Father of Hypocrites! What do you have this time for the greedy markets of London?"

"Ah!" Hakeem removed the cloth wrapping from a carved ivory elephant, its emerald eyes glittering like green fire. He set it on the table before Jace.

"The East India director will most appreciate the mate to the one you sold him last time. He has sent an inquiry asking for it."

Rawlings, director of the Company in London, had a compelling interest in collecting antiques from the East, as well as a secret maze of informers who delved into intrigue.

"The elephant is the least of the items he offers," Michael interrupted. "Tell him about the heirloom, Hakeem."

"Ah, yes, the alabaster jewel box."

Michael turned to Jace. "It is from twelfth-century Moorish Spain, dating from the Great Count Roger I."

Jace raised a skeptical brow at Hakeem. "The First Crusade?"

"It is so, my friend. It belonged to the family of the Norman Count. It is worth much on the market."

"Rawlings will be impressed," said Jace, then said deliberately: "But our funds are beleaguered."

Michael leaned toward him and said in a low voice, "If we pool our resources, we can buy it."

Jace knew that, but he was experienced in dealing with Hakeem. Michael was right about one thing. An heirloom belonging to the Norman Count would bring enough money to return to India to buy the Darjeeling land.

Michael's dark eyes snapped with excitement. "Gokul says he can hire tea workers from Nepal. Think of it, Jace! You and I—owners of a tea enterprise. In a few years it is possible to become as successful as Kingscote."

Jace knew what financial success could bring him—complete freedom from the colonel.

"I can marry Belinda," continued Michael.

Jace gave an ironic laugh. "You speak like a vagabond. Are you not a silk heir? You can have Roxbury's daughter if you ask for her. But remember—even after we buy the land, it will take a number of years to grow, harvest, and ship the tea."

Jace turned back to Hakeem. "Where is the heirloom? Do you have it?"

Hakeem spread his palms. "It waits in Cordoba."

Seward groaned. "And why did ye not bring it, I ask ye? Cordoba be days of travelin'."

"I can have it for you in two weeks."

"Two weeks? Are you mad with wine? The weather won't hold."

Hakeem looked out the window with a scowl. "Ah, but a treasure from the glorious past is not easy to come by. Despite the risk, it is worth the wait."

"Let it wait, Cunning One, until we come this way next year," replied Jace, pushing back his chair to stand.

"Ah, but your sea chest will bulge with the rich fatness of Moorish Spain. The alabaster jewelry box is so rich a bounty as to be like a beautiful damsel. If you will not embrace her, she will run to embrace another."

"He has something there," Michael told Jace.

Jace said nothing. He bit into the tender roast lamb, aware that Seward watched him with hungry countenance. He pushed the platter over to him.

"We cannot wait," said Jace.

"Then I cannot hold her until you return from London." The Arab's black eyes glinted, and he whispered, "O Great Ones, the heirloom will bring you at least a treasure chest of English pounds."

"We will wait the two weeks," argued Michael.

Jace silently calculated with one eye on the sea.

"This I will do. I will send a message tonight to Cordoba," said Hakeem. "The owner will hasten his journey. Say, five to seven days?"

Jace had traveled to the great city before and knew

this was possible. "We best travel to Cordoba our-selves."

"We can leave tonight," pressed Michael.

Jace looked at Seward, who rubbed his bearded chin.

"I don't know, lad. Ye know I be as committed to Darjeeling as ye and Michael. But ye be right about the season. Yet, I admit a few thousand pounds be worth a delay. But if ye be in favor of sailin' tomorrow, I be with ye. Maybe we best take us a vote."

"You have it, Seward. We will vote," urged Michael. "What do you say, Jace?"

Jace hesitated. After all, he was the captain, and he knew best when to sail his ship.

"The Deuce! Sometimes one must take a risk if he is to win," pressed Michael.

"Then we'll vote. You first."

"I vote for Cordoba," said Michael, and smiled at him.

Seward frowned in the direction of the harbor, then cast an apologetic glance at Jace. "I be tempted to do the same."

"Well, is it yes or no?"

His brows pulled together. "Aye."

Michael laughed and got to his feet, clapping Jace's shoulder. "Do not look so dour. Are you not a worthy seadog? It runs in your blood like your father before you. Seward will vow to that. Is that not so, Seward? Look Jace, if we weathered the South China Sea, you can get the *Madras* safely to London, then home to India. Sit down, old chap, have some Arabian coffee!"

————

Confidence . . . usually Jace had enough to spare.

As dawn broke on their fifth morning at sea from Cadiz, uncertainty nagged at his heart, just as the moist wind tugged at his leather jerkin. He stood on the quarterdeck while his narrowing gaze swept across the iron gray expanse of the Atlantic Ocean. The twelfth-century heirloom was locked inside his sea chest in the Great Cabin, along with the ivory elephant, waiting for their meeting with Rawlings in London. The price paid to the Arab merchant had exhausted their pooled funds, but the London market would be a rich one.

Seward came up beside him, his broad face lacking its good humor. He leaned against the rail, the wind stirring a thatch of chestnut hair tied at the nape of his neck. For a moment he did not speak, and along with Jace watched the murky sunrise color the length of the horizon an amber haze. The ship creaked and groaned.

"I do not like it," breathed Jace.

"Aye . . . I be rememberin' long ago . . .'twas but a lad then. A mere coxswain was I, on one of the meanest slave ships to sail. We come head on with a storm havin' the same feel as this."

Jace stared ahead. "I will agree my father was a blackguard, but he did not trade in slaves. I would remember."

"No need to get riled, lad. I knew Buckley better'n ye did. 'Twas not speakin' of yer father, but another captain, a sure reprobate, that one. A derelict, he was, by the name of Newton. Been doing a lot of thinkin' about him lately."

"I never heard of Newton."

"Ye wouldn't. Was before yer time. We was comin' toward London . . . just like now. Unsuspectin' we were, and before we get there, we run into wind and waves. Ain't seen the likes of it since. Ship was near to be battered to sticks . . . them swells rose, I'd say, near fifty feet. Maybe higher. 'Twas enough to scare a sinner into quick repentance. Worst thing ever been through. Aye, 'twas enough to bring the young captain on his face before the Almighty."

Jace was in an ill mood. "Are you hinting I am neglecting the Almighty?"

"Didn't think I needed to hint. I be includin' myself in that."

"Never mind. Where is Michael?"

"Most likely in his cabin. He's a mite sick. Makes a poor sailor. I be thinkin' we best leave him in India when we take to haulin' our tea."

Jace left Seward and went to Michael's small cabin. He was still thinking about Seward's suggestion that he was not devout enough. That Seward considered himself an Anglican was no secret, but Jace had never seen him practice his faith. He tapped on the door. When there was no answer, he opened it. Michael was sprawled on his cot, pale and sick.

"Ah, poor laddie," Jace mocked. "And no lassie to hold your hand."

Michael slowly turned his head toward the door, opening one eye and groaning. "Get out of here."

"Fine way to speak to your captain. I should have you helping the kansamah gut fish. He's making a savory stew."

Michael groaned again and turned his head to the wall. The ship heaved and sank. "How—much— longer?" he whispered.

Jace folded his arms and smiled. "Oh, another ten days. Maybe longer."

"Ten days! My insides will all be heaved overboard by then!"

"Now, now, old chap, all you need is some liquid down you. I can smell the broth simmering. A few fish heads improve the flavor."

Michael moaned and tried to get up as though to slug him. Jace smiled and sank comfortably into the chair, stretching out his boots, his arms behind his head.

"Cheer up. The worst storm of your life is coming. I thought I should warn you."

Michael fell back to the pillow. "Now you tell me. We should have stayed in Cadiz."

"You mean," gritted Jace for emphasis, "we should have left three weeks ago. I think I already mentioned that and was voted down. Next time I will ignore my tea partners and exercise my right as captain of my own vessel!"

"Yes, yes ... we heard you howling about it a dozen times ... do not sound so injured. At least we got the heirloom. Ah, Darjeeling! I can feel the firm ground beneath my feet now! I can smell the fresh tea leaves gently moving in the breeze, see the white caps of the Himalayas—"

Just then, the ship pitched, Michael groaned, and a Bible and a stack of books tumbled from the table onto the floor and slid to Jace's boots. When the ship steadied again, Jace picked them up. There was an autobiography of the colonial missionary to the American Indians, David Brainerd.

"Brainerd?"

"Coral gave it to me before I left."

There was also a volume by Whitfield, and another by John Wesley. Jace had heard of both reformers while in London. He leafed through them, pausing to see Coral's signature. No doubt she had plenty of time to read during her bouts with tropical fever. He imagined that she could hold quite a discourse on the Reformers. Jace realized, however, that he knew practically nothing about them. Holding the Bible, he tried to get Michael's mind off his misery.

"After we sell the heirloom, we can decide on the style of our residence. I think we should build us a white Georgian mansion."

Michael looked at him. "You once said you detested mansions."

"I have changed my mind. I want it equal to Kingscote. In fact—I want it to rival anything you Kendalls have."

Michael opened one eye. "What for?"

Jace settled more comfortably. "I have never lived in a sparkling white mansion with a blue roof. I just decided I want one. With furniture from France."

Michael ran a hand over his face. "I care not at all, dear fellow . . . I have had my fill of mansions and French furniture. All I want is a humble bunk that does not buck."

Jace leaned his head back against the chair and stared at the ceiling, absently running his thumb over the leather binding of the Bible. "Maybe I will order Persian silk coverlets for my bed."

Michael grunted.

"I will have one of those mattresses that are stuffed with goose feathers, and a hundred servants to wait on me." His eyes glinted with amusement as he looked at Michael. "What do you think?"

"I think you sound like Solomon," came his dull voice.

"I did not say female servants," Jace corrected. "Solomon—the wisest man on earth, yet he took a thousand wives." He laughed softly.

Michael lifted his head and looked at him. "You

know about his wives and concubines?"

"Do you take me to be completely ignorant?"

Michael waved a hand. "No offense, Captain. I simply did not know you had read the Scriptures."

"A most interesting tale how that particular Bible came my way."

"I have always thought you believed in Christ."

Jace scrutinized him. He could not see Michael's expression, for he had one arm across his face, and the other across his stomach.

Actually, Jace had read the entire Bible through, to compare it with the Vedas and the Koran. He had found the person of Christ without fault—more than a mere man. A true Master, but one who demanded all. Jace was not willing to surrender all to anyone.

"About Darjeeling," he said, changing the subject. "Once in Calcutta, we will make an expedition to see the Raja of Sikkim. He will be delighted to see our gold. By the time we get back, Seward and Gokul will have a roof over our heads to protect us from the monsoon." He smiled. "Our Georgian mansion can wait a few years."

"Superb thought . . . land. I cannot say I want to go through this again."

"The upcoming storm will be treacherous. Stay below. Tie yourself to your bunk."

Michael gave a short laugh. "Do not worry, Captain. The only thing that will tempt me from my cot is a sinking ship. May God forbid."

"A sober thought. Where do you want these?" Jace was still holding the books.

"In that drawer. Unless you care to read them."

"Brainerd looks interesting . . . well, maybe I will read them all. I like to discover what goes on in the mind of a man who gives up everything to preach to a bunch of naked savages," he said of Brainerd, "or those who argue church doctrine on the streets of London amid hawkers of fish and posies. The mind of someone who would lie in bed for a month and read them is also curious."

"I do not know the answer to any of their minds. I have yet to reach the spiritual summit of Brainerd, or for that matter, my dear little sister. But one thing is clear . . . Brainerd found the American Indians to be more than naked savages."

Jace handed Michael his Bible. "Ever heard of Newton?"

"No. Why?"

"Never mind. Read Psalms. You need some cheering up. I suggest number 107. Verses 23 to 30."

Michael seemed curious enough to get his mind off his stomach, and began searching through his Bible.

Jace was ready to duck out the cabin door when Michael said, "I suppose Brainerd found in Christ everything he gave up, and more." He paused. "I do not know if I could give up a tea plantation to tell savages of their Creator."

Jace looked at him. "Excuse me, noble Rector, but you do not have one yet to toss to the flames of divine call. Read. I have business with the pilot . . . if you want to see either India or London again."

Michael managed a sick grin, and tried to focus on the words of the psalm. "Ah! It is about a ship! Listen to this—'So he bringeth them unto their desired haven,' " he quoted. "Ah . . . I like that; peace and rest."

———

Desired haven, thought Jace, as a strong blast of

wind struck him and sea spray wet his face. He walked
to the ladder, pausing to squint at the sky. It was an
ugly hue, with fierce clouds. The *Madras* rolled and
pitched, and a hissing spatter was carried along the
deck.

Desired haven. . . . Jace was not ignorant of the
claims of Christ. Yielding to His Lordship would mean
giving up control of his own plans. The last thing Jace
wanted was to be vulnerable. He knew enough of what
was in the Book to understand that Christ would not
settle for anything less than his surrender. Jace did
not like the word surrender . . . the times that he had
laid bare his emotions to others only brought memories of rejection. He knew that Christ was not a hard
taskmaster, and yet—what would He demand of him?
To give up his ambitions? His ship? Perhaps to become
an Anglican minister walking about in a robe—

"Captain!" shouted Jin-Soo. "Ginseng tea answer
to all things!"

Jace turned. The beloved old man was determined
to serve Jace personally. He stood in a baggy knee-
length black kimono holding a bronze urn and cup, a
smile on his crinkled face. The wind whipped at his
white pigtail as he bowed low at the waist.

"Jin-Soo! You know better than to be on deck
when it's pitching like this. Go below, now!"

"I go, Captain, but you drink tea first. Need much
strength. Dragon-devils stir up sea, spew waves instead of fire. You up all night, yes?"

The Chinese miracle brew was the last thing Jace
wanted now. "Where is my coffee? I want it black and
scalding. And do not bring it up to me. I'll send the
coxswain."

"Captain is very stubborn." He added in labored
English: "Arabic coffee is no good. It is very bad. Chi-

nese tea is very good. Captain needs a woman to look after him. Jin-Soo fail. Yes, I go, I go!" he shouted above the rising wind as Jace glowered. Turning, the old one struggled back down the steps.

The deck, deserted now by all but the best of his experienced seamen, heaved up and sank again beneath Jace's boots. The *Madras* shuddered its complaint and groaned, while the wind doubled its velocity.

"Cap'n!"

"What is it, lad?"

The coxswain was pasty white as he clung tenaciously to one of the shrouds. "Pilot say 'e dinnae 'no what 'e to do. Cannae pilot 'elm. Say 'e done lied aboot sailin' Indian Ocean in monsoon—"

"Lied? Of course he lied. Did he think I believed him? But I will have his head if he leaves the helm now!"

"Aye, Cap'n, I tell 'im."

"Where's Seward!"

"Methinks 'e be below, Cap'n!"

No doubt checking on Michael, Jace thought.

Below at the bottom companionway steps, Jace took a moment to shrug into his oilskins, shouting at the same time, "Seward!"

Jin-Soo thrust his head out a cabin door. "Seward is not here, Captain. He went to Great Cabin looking for you. You want coffee now?"

"Later, Jin-Soo, and keep an eye on Michael. He is sick."

"But—"

Jace turned heel without another word. He imagined his ship a piece of driftwood tossed on the waves, being sucked toward the open jaws of a hungry behemoth. It took an experienced seaman to maneuver down the passage; he leaned into one wall, then the other, as the ship pitched and rolled. As skilled as he was, it took longer than usual to climb the narrow wood steps leading topside. Jace threw open the companionway door and ducked out into the roaring squall, intending to go to the helm.

The thrashing wind took his breath away, and he held to the door, his boots planted squarely apart to avoid stumbling crazily across the heaving deck. Black swells of seawater washed over the rail onto the main deck, lashing up about his calf-length boots like snarling dogs. Torrents of rain struck against his face. The daylight had darkened to twilight. For a second he stared ahead of him, disbelieving what he saw.

Impossible! Michael had vowed he would not come up on deck!

Yet there he was!—grasping the rail and staring into the mountainous swells as though in a trance. Had he gone mad?

Jace moved toward him, then saw the danger coming—a dark swell rising above the side of the ship like a breaking black avalanche.

"Michael! Hold on!"

But the wind sucked his words into a cavern of noise and silenced them. The monstrous wave swooped over the railing onto the deck, instantly burying everything in its flood. The icy force slammed Jace back, knocking him off his feet. Half-blinded by stinging salt, his mind shouted: *Michael!*

Jace caught sight of him in the seawater that rushed down the ship's tilting deck. He heard Michael yell, caught a glimpse of his attempt to grab a shroud line, and saw his hand touch nothing but air.

Jace hurled himself after him, lunging to grasp the back of Michael's collar before he was washed overboard. Jace grabbed his drenched hair instead, and held relentlessly to the line with his other hand while the sucking wash tried to rip them apart. The sea engaged Jace and Michael in a tug-of-war, demanding to fish them both overboard into its watery net. There was little between them and the mountainous dark swells. *God! Not Michael—*

The ship heaved portside, throwing Jace against the railing. Pain stabbed through his body like red-hot daggers as he felt his ribs crack. Weakness assailed him, and only after the water rushed back to sea did the ugly realization rip through his mind. He no longer had hold of Michael! He had lost him!

Still grasping the rail, Jace leaned over the side of the ship and searched the swelling dark caverns. "Michael!" he shouted, but his voice mocked his feeble effort. "Michael!"

Despair flooded his soul, then rage.

"Filthy curse!" he screamed at the sea.

The *Madras* vaulted. Jace slid across the deck like a slippery fish on its belly. He slammed into the ladder that led to the quarterdeck and the Great Cabin. Unable to move, pain from his cracked ribs made it difficult to breathe. His numb fingers touched a rung, fumbled, then wrapped about the wood. Struggling to his knees, Jace gritted his teeth against the pain. A second surge of water flooded after him, wrapping about his legs like a viper trying to snatch him back. Jace crawled up the ladder and clung there between the two decks trying to gain his breath.

"Captain!" shouted his first-mate.

Jace yelled his orders, though he knew it was too late. "Man overboard! Sound an alarm! See if you can spot him!"

Like a drunken man, the first-mate staggered

across the afterdeck, shouting as he went.

The ship rolled, and Jace stumbled onto the deck, leaning against the rail for support while edging his way toward the captain's cabin.

The open door slammed back and forth on its hinges, and Jace stumbled inside, grasping hold of his desk. The storm made the cabin as dark as evening.

God, why? Why! "Why did you not take me instead!" Jace gritted into the silence. *You know he was worth two of me!*

The emotional loss stabbed at him with a retching pain far worse than his cracked ribs.

Jace fumbled to remove the oilskins, and then his jerkin, but could not. His body sprawled over the desk.

"Jace!"

Seward ducked his head under the doorway, knocking off his tricorn, taking in the scene with a glance. "Ye be hurt!"

"Michael's overboard. I lost him."

Seward's voice sucked in, then snapped with emotion. "Aye!" He stood there in shock.

"I gave orders to search for him, but . . ."

The ship rolled, and too weak to balance himself Jace fell against the chest of drawers. Pain brought a moment of blackness, but he fought against it.

Seward grabbed him and lowered him onto the floor. Quickly he lit the swaying oil lantern above the desk.

"Bind my ribs and get me to the helm."

Seward glowered over him, wild with fury. "Nay, lad! Will I lose ye also? I vowed to Captain Jarred Buckley I'd be yer surety! Ye'll not leave the cabin!"

"Pull yourself together! Do as I say, Seward!"

Jace tried to raise himself to an elbow, but Seward's big hands slammed him back to the floor, and

143

pain lashed through his ribs. He glimpsed Seward's wild expression, the lank hair hanging in his eyes.

"Ye be goin' nowheres, laddie."

"Don't be a fool! I'm captain of this ship! Now get me to the helm, that's an order!"

As though struck with an icy blast, Seward blinked, and slowly his hold loosened.

"Aye," he growled darkly. "I be hearin' ye. Captain, eh? Better ye stayed in uniform! And would to God I'd never let Hampton's son come!" He turned away, smashing his fist against the wall. "Now the only son of Jarred Buckley be followin' his drownin'. 'Tis the devil's storm out there!"

"Snap out of it! You speak to me of God! Where is He? Is it the Devil or your Christ who commands the wind and sea?"

Seward sobered. His ice-blue eyes narrowed as he knelt beside Jace. He removed Jace's oilskins, and used his knife to slit open the leather jerkin, exposing his chest.

"Well said. It be the Almighty's storm all right, and there be a message in it for us all. Ye be as stubborn as yer father was, nay—worse, ye are!"

"Stop your grumbling and do something!"

Seward glared down at him. With strips of cloth he bound Jace tightly.

"Ow!—easy, you grizzly! You want to crack the rest?"

Seward grunted and stood unsteadily. "Nay a bad idea if it keep ye safe." He pulled Jace onto his boots. For a moment Jace's brain spun and nausea gripped him.

"Ye be standin'. Walk alone, Captain, or ye'll not be goin' to the helm!"

"Then I will get there alone. If the *Madras* sinks,

this captain's going with her!"

Jace swayed toward the door, but was so dizzy that he slammed into the wall. He tried again.

Seward winced, mumbling under his breath; then throwing a hefty arm about his shoulders, he turned him toward the cabin door.

"Like yer pirate father ye be. Damnation awaits ye!"

"Silence your cursed tongue!"

"Nay! Damnation awaits us both! Do ye think 'twas a mistake that the Almighty took a goodly lad, and left the stubborn, rebellious son of a pirate?"

Jace swung his fist, but he was too exhausted, and it missed as Seward ducked. Blackness swirled in Jace's brain, and he stumbled, crashing upon his desk and into unconsciousness.

Seward grabbed him. "Ah, lad! I didn't mean it! God forgive me, I didn't mean it!"

The coxswain appeared, sopping wet and shaking, bracing himself with both hands in the doorway. Seeing his captain unconscious, and Seward weeping, he too broke into a bawl.

"God 'ave mercy on us, Cap'n! Christ 'ave mercy! Dinnae find no Master Kendall! And 'elmsman 'e ran, and 'e too done gone overboard! Cap'n—"

"Silence, boy!" Seward thundered. "Get yerself in here! Take care of the captain. He be unconscious, do ye hear?"

"Aye, sir!"

Seward grasped the boy by the scruff of his tunic, lifting him up off his heels, his eyes blazing. "And if ye show yerself above, I'll throw ye to the sea myself!"

He dropped the coxswain, who fell to the cabin floor. "Aye, Mister Seward, I 'ear ye!"

Seward stumbled toward the door. "May the mercies of the God of Jonah be upon the filthy lot of us!"

10

Kingscote
July 1796

Coral laughed as she leaned over the small bed in the upstairs nursery, Gem's arms holding tightly to her neck. The large brown eyes ringed with dark lashes stared up at her and he giggled, refusing to let go.

"Kiss me again, Mummy."

"There—on the forehead."

"Nuther one."

"Time for bed. You must be rested if you are going to ride with me on the elephant tomorrow."

"Not sleepy."

"Not sleepy, indeed," Coral teased, giving him a squeeze. "You can hardly keep your eyes open—why, you are even making me sleepy. . . ." and Coral pretended to yawn.

Gem smiled, and a tiny dimple formed at the corner of his mouth. "Sleep here, Mummy."

"Mummy must sleep in her own big bed, but I will sit with you until you are asleep. Are you ready to give thanks to God for the day we have had together? You got to see your great-uncle Hugo today, and Great-aunt Margaret."

Gem nodded and shut his eyes so tightly that his nose wrinkled. "Thank you, Lord Jesus. Amen."

Coral smiled and covered him lightly with a blue cotton sheet. "Good night, Gem."

"Night, Mummy . . . Mummy? Ride baby elephant tomorrow?"

"Yes, I think so. Go to sleep now."

She dimmed the light on the table beside the bed until only a golden glow shone in the nursery. Dolls, blocks, and other toys were neatly stacked in their blue-painted bin. She drew the mosquito net about his bed, then walked to the open verandah.

Before going to her room down the hall, she stepped out into the darkness, breathing the scents coming from the garden. From the silk workers' huts near the distant hatcheries came the smell of wood-smoke.

Alone, and without the sharp eyes of Jan-Lee scrutinizing her for signs that she had overextended herself, Coral took advantage of the solitude to lean wearily against the verandah rail and draw a long breath. She did not dare tell them how exhausted she felt! Would she ever be strong again? There were so many activities she wanted to experience with Gem, but could not because her strength failed her. Fever and weakness, the result of tropical illness—her second relapse since the birth of Gem—had left her thin and tired. Even simple tasks, like bathing and dressing Gem, she had been forced to leave for Jan-Lee.

Her delicate brows came together. She had promised to ride with Gem on the elephant, but would she even have the strength? *I must go to bed,* she thought. *I must get some sleep.*

Later that night, the air was full of jungle sounds seeping in through the net gathered around her bed. Coral tossed restlessly, slowly coming awake.

She strained to hear what had awakened her, but heard little except the thump of her heart. Then, the thud of horses' hooves and shouting voices stabbed the night. One of the voices belonged to her father!

Coral flung the covers aside and pushed her way through the mosquito net. Scurrying across the floor to the verandah, she peered below. Male servants ran in all directions while Sir Hampton shouted orders.

"Father, what is it?"

Coral could not see his face as he looked up at her, rifle in hand. "Stay inside, Coral. Marauders! They appear to be sepoys. The swine set the mulberry grove on fire."

Fire! Horrified, Coral looked off in the direction of the jungle. Faintly, through the thick darkness of the trees, she could see the orange-red piercing through the blackness of branches. On the breeze came the foul odor of smoke. *Marauders!* Her father had said they looked like armed sepoys—the Indian infantry. Were these renegades who had mutinied against their commander?

A scream came from below, and she caught a glimpse of Mera and Rosa running from the house.

"Fire!" Hampton shouted in Hindi. "The silkworm hatcheries are in danger!"

The children! thought Coral with trepidation. *Who will get the untouchables out of the huts?*

Natine ran from the stables bringing two horses. Hampton swung himself onto the saddle.

"Hampton, wait for Hugo! Do not go alone!" Elizabeth Kendall shouted from the front doorway.

"Father!" Coral shouted over the rail. "The children!"

"Hugo is coming now!"

Other workers on horseback galloped toward Hampton. The war cry of trumpeting elephants shrieked through the blackness and Coral covered her ears. The trained mahouts arrived, prepared to lead them into battle. Her father galloped toward the hatcheries with Sir Hugo Roxbury, and the yard was left in silence except for the anxious dialogue of her mother and Natine. Coral watched flames leaping up from distant branches.

A fire, she thought, dazed. *Why would there be a fire here? Did the enemies come from Burma?*

Still stricken, Coral glanced below. Her mother now stood with Margaret and the female servants, staring after the galloping horses. But Natine was looking up toward the mansion, past Coral, in the direction of the nursery.

The nursery was safe from the fire, of course—Coral froze with sudden horror. Fear gripped her like iron bands. She whirled, and like a mad woman, she screamed, running and stumbling from her room. "Gem! Gem! Come to me! Quick, Gem!"

Coral stumbled down the hall, her shift clinging about her ankles. Grabbing the silk and pulling it to her knees, Coral ran down the hall, whispering, "Lord, protect my son!"

She reached the nursery door, flung it open and burst inside. "Gem!"

She stopped, a scream dying in her throat. Jan-Lee lay on the floor, unconscious. Coral's eyes darted to the small bed. *Empty.* She went weak. Her gaze sought the verandah and met the glittering black eyes of a sepoy in a soiled brown puggari. He clutched Gem under his arm, one leg already swung over the verandah.

"Stop! Stop!"

"Mummy, Mummy, Mummy—!"

Gem's hysterical screams thrust Coral in his direction. Reaching the verandah, she clawed the sepoy's face as he grabbed for a rope to make his escape.

"Let go of my baby!" she screamed as the man slapped her backward. Coral stumbled to her feet, grabbed the heavy pot from the floor and hurled it at his back. Whirling, his fist smashed into Coral's face, sending her crashing to the floor.

———

Coral had no recollection of how many weeks had lapsed since the abduction of Gem. Now and then, she would awaken from a fever-induced delirium to see her mother beside her bed, haggard from lack of sleep. Sometimes it was Aunt Margaret who answered her tormented cries. Other times it was Jan-Lee murmuring sighs as she wiped Coral down with cool cloths, her dark eyes saddened.

When Coral's eyes did open to a greater awareness of her surroundings, she realized that she was in bed and so weak she could hardly turn her head. The room was in shadows, with the sunblinds drawn, and one small golden lamp burned on a table. Silence surrounded her, and the chair beside her bed was empty. Somewhere in the distance she could hear the wheels of a horse-drawn wagon nearing the front yard. From below, came voices.

Coral tried to speak—"Mother. . . ?"

The feebleness of her voice alarmed her. It was not Elizabeth who responded, but Jan-Lee who came swiftly from the shadows and bent over her with serious eyes searching her face.

"Hush, hush. You must sleep. Miss Elizabeth will be back soon."

"W-what . . . is all that . . . that noise? Tiger—"

"There is no tiger. You dream."

"Noise . . . I hear . . . voices—"

Jan-Lee wrung the water from a cloth and wiped Coral's face. "Do not worry yourself. Your mother will come soon."

"Gem . . . any news—"

As Coral tried to focus her gaze, she saw that Jan-Lee's face twisted with grief.

"Miss Coral . . . there is something I—" she paused, then turned toward the door. She left Coral's side and spoke in a low voice to someone, but Coral could not make out her words. She struggled to raise herself to her elbow; never had she felt this weak. *Maybe I am dying* . . . she thought, and strangely she felt no alarm.

Coral heard a rustle of skirts, and her mother came toward her, pale and drawn in black satin. "Coral, dear." Elizabeth reached a cool palm to the side of Coral's face.

Coral's eyes absorbed her mother's stiff black funeral dress and ankle-length veil. She saw the black prayer book with the embossed gold cross and the white handkerchief. Her gaze darted back to her mother's face. All at once the truth stabbed. She choked back a wrenching sob, her cold fingers flying to her mouth.

"Gem!" A horrid cry escaped Coral's lips.

Elizabeth fell beside her, her eyes swimming with tears, her face contorted with grief, and Coral felt her mother's sobs even as she gathered her into her arms.

"I am so sorry, darling, so sorry. They found him by the river—"

"No!" Coral clutched her mother, her fingers digging into her flesh with uncontrollable rage. "No! It is not fair!"

Elizabeth Kendall held Coral against her breast, her trembling hand stroking the tangled hair as she rocked her tormented daughter.

"Lord," whispered her mother. "Give us your grace. You have promised—comfort my daughter."

Coral stiffened and cried: "They killed him! Jace was right! Oh, my poor baby! What did they do to you, what did they do—"

She sobbed deeply until her lungs could no longer inhale. Her heart thundered in her ears, sending the blood pounding in her head until she felt it would explode.

Her mother continued to hold her, rocking her as though she were an infant. Coral could feel her mother's tears mingling with her own. Horrid images of the abductor plunging a dagger into Gem's heart burned within her mind. She could hear his last words begging her—the hysterical screams, *Mummy, Mummy, Mummy!* brought convulsions of pain. Coral wept until her throat ached and burned, and she was numb with pain.

"Why, Mama?" she choked into Elizabeth's breast.

"Only God has the answer," came her mother's whisper.

"But why did God take him from *me*—I . . . I was

teaching him Bible stories, I was helping him to memorize Scripture verses—I taught him to love Jesus—why, Mama? Why did God take him from *me*?"

Elizabeth shook her head, her eyes welling with tears. "I do not know—" and her voice broke—"I asked Him that when He took Ranek—"

They held to each other in silent grief. "His steps cannot always be traced, my darling. He wants us to trust Him in the dark, and in the howling storm."

Elizabeth continued to rock Coral, speaking softly through her tears. "We may never understand in this life why bitter things happen to us, why God permits pain and loss. But He is perfectly wise, and His tender mercies endure forever."

She tilted Coral's face toward hers, brushing away the tears with her handkerchief, scented with lavender. "If we cannot understand the wisdom of His actions, then let us draw near to the rich bounty of His consolation.

"Go ahead, dear, cry all you wish, and I shall cry with you, it is necessary. But we sorrow not as those who have no hope." She smiled through her own tears. "Christ is our hope. Today we buried Gem with the words of Christ: 'I am the resurrection and the life; he that believeth in me, though he were dead, yet shall he live: and whosoever liveth and believeth in me shall never die.'

"Today, the Almighty has given us a cup of gall to drink. But even in this, let us find thanks. For He would not give it to us to drink if there were not some good within. We can find the sweet taste of peace in that. Gem is safe now, my darling. Nothing can ever hurt him again."

Nothing can ever hurt him again. . . . Slowly Coral's sobbing ceased, and a deep weariness settled over her. Her eyes were swollen and her mind heavy with sleep. Elizabeth brought a cool glass of water to her lips. Coral drank and could feel nothing but her mother's heart thumping beneath her ear.

In the weeks following, Coral's emotions were dazed, while her health had taken a swift turn for the worse. She recalled only snatches of what had taken place during those days. They had found Gem, Coral was told, dead in the river. The details were not given, and Coral did not want to hear them, yet. She knew of the crocodiles. Her mother explained that the silk hatcheries had been saved. The untouchables were not hurt. The fire turned out to be smaller than first suspected, and when Hampton and Sir Hugo had arrived on the scene with armed workers, the marauders had already withdrawn and disappeared into the thick jungle.

It was clear to Coral that the attack on Kingscote had been only a ruse to lure them from the house, with the abduction of Gem being the primary motivation. Jace Buckley had been right. *Jace!* If only she could see him now and talk to him. If only he were still in the military and stationed at Jorhat! But he was on the other side of the world. Gone. Like Gem. Everything was gone.

When six weeks had passed and Coral showed no sign of improving, a hastened family gathering was called for in the library, and a decision was made. Coral would make the voyage to London.

155

"Your cousin Ethan is an expert on tropical diseases," her mother explained. "According to your uncle, Ethan studied the illness while spending time with the Company in Rangoon. We have expectations for your recovery. It is worth a try, dear. We cannot go on like this—" Unexpectedly her voice broke, and Coral felt her mother's damp cheek against her own. "Will I lose you, also?"

"I will be all right, Mother," but Coral wondered if she spoke only to cheer her. "But . . . I don't wish to go . . . I'm so tired . . ."

"It is a risk to send you on the voyage now, but your father and I agree it's a far greater one to keep you here."

"But—"

"Hush, darling. I will journey with you as far as Calcutta. And Uncle Hugo and Aunt Margaret will care for you aboard the ship. Your father and I agree this is the best decision we can make. We could ask Cousin Ethan to come here, but it would take a year. This way, you will be in London in half the time."

Caught amid illness and the need for her grief to heal, Coral's feeble efforts to thwart the family decision met with failure. Her sisters were already enrolled at school and writing for her to join them. And Grandmother Victoria was anxious for Coral to come and stay at the family estate. If the treatment was successful, she would have private tutors, and perhaps in the future, a year at Lady Anne's Finishing School.

But Gem! She would never have her baby to embrace again.

The Madras, *off the coast of London*
February 1797

The storm raged on for several days. When the wind exhausted itself into periodic gusts, and the rain dwindled to scattered squalls, the coast of England emerged from the gray wisps of fog to beckon with open arms the storm-battered ship. The seasoned crew of English and Indians, interspersed with a few haggard but expectant Malaysians, responded with a shout as the dawn broke on the London estuary. The East India port waited, a safe haven.

A roar of voices sprang up in a familiar English lymeric:

"Ohhh—the King 'e loves 'is bottle, me lads,
The King 'e loves 'is ale!
An betwix 'is bottle and 'is lass,
'e'll drink us all to 'ell!"

Captain Jace Buckley watched the gray swells ease before the ship, his bronzed features fatigued from lack of sleep. He supposed his ribs were healing well enough, but his soul was not. He tried to mask his moodiness. No one must guess how badly he hurt. Jace would not easily recover from what had happened to Michael.

Nagging thoughts plagued him: *If we had sailed two weeks sooner . . . if we had not gone to Cordoba . . . we would have missed the storm, and Michael would be alive. If . . .*

Jace did not wish to discuss his feelings. He only knew that he was in a black mood, and his relationship with Seward was none the better for it.

He blames me for his death, Jace thought grimly.

157

And maybe he is right. I was the captain. I should not have listened and stayed at Cadiz. I knew better. But I gave in to Michael. Michael was a novice . . . he did not know, he could not have guessed the seasons. But I knew. Yet I stayed. And I let him down. I failed them both.

The sense of infinite loss that he had experienced when first realizing that Michael had slipped from his grasp haunted him. How would he be able to explain to the Kendalls?

His hands tightened on the rail, his eyes narrowing. It made no difference that Michael had disobeyed orders and gone topside. The result was the same. He was dead.

Jace tried to shed the nagging feeling that the alabaster heirloom was tainted with the blood of the eldest Kendall son. He could not.

What of the Darjeeling tea plantation? Should he set it aside, or pursue it? At the moment, it did not seem to matter. There were few people he had truly cared about. Seward was one, Michael another. The loss only gave Jace excuse to further harden his heart. If he learned to care about some thing or someone, it was ripped away. *No more,* he thought. *Never again.*

Seagulls screamed and wheeled above the churning wake, and shifting his gaze from the coastline, he observed the two boatswain mates who swung like monkeys above him, inching their way along the wooden yards to unfurl the main sail. Overhead, the canvas flexed and snapped to the salt-laden wind, while foam splashed over the bow.

The crew became alert as the sound of his boots on the oak ladder preceded the captain's arrival onto the deck.

His leather jerkin, breeches, and calf-length boots

differed little from those of his crew. His coloring from the sun was as golden as his Indian kansamah's, causing the blue-black of his eyes to become piercing. His long hair and scraggly beard made him hardly recognizable from the once polished and ceremonious Major Jace Buckley of the 21st Light Bengal Cavalry.

Greeted by a grinning crew happy to be coming into port, Jace knew that the loss of Michael meant little to them. He had been only a stranger, just another English civilian. The loss of the helmsman had been forgotten in a day. The crew had weathered the bleak storm without damage to the ship, the cargo was safe—and they would be paid. The crew was satisfied. Now the brawling alehouses on the wharves awaited their celebration.

Jace passed by his jubilant crew members and entered the Great Cabin with its dark overhead beams, throwing back the shutters on the stern windows. A shaft of sunlight fell across the scarred oak desk, where Goldfish jumped up and down and performed cartwheels for his dreary master. Jace scooted the monkey aside.

"Go ahead. Keep it up. And as soon as we dock, I'll exchange you for a parrot."

Apparently undisturbed by his master's idle threat, Goldfish grabbed the oil lantern swaying over the center desk and sailed happily across the compartment, landing on a chest of drawers as though home in the Indian jungle.

"Useless creature," Jace murmured, sinking into the chair behind his desk. Every bone in his body complained at the harsh treatment of the last ten days. His eyes ached from lack of sleep, and his brain buzzed. He squinted at his sea chest. Within it were a number of precious items, and safely stashed away at the bottom was the heirloom from the Norman kingdom of Sicily.

Jace yielded to frustration and smashed his boot against the sea chest, sending it across the wooden floor.

Opening the desk drawer, his eyes fell on the small black Bible that had belonged to Michael. Jace hesitated, then opened the cover, once again reading the delicate inscription:

May 1795, Kingscote
To my dearest brother, Michael
May His words grant wisdom, peace, and life everlasting. A special thanks for your support in the matter of Gem's adoption.

Your sister, Coral

His jaw tense, Jace leafed through the delicate pages. He had gone back to Michael's cabin to pack his belongings and found the Bible. He opened it to Psalm 107 and discovered Michael had taken time to underline the verses that Jace had mentioned to him before going on deck. Jace read them:

They that go down to the sea in ships, that do business in great waters;
These see the works of the LORD, and his wonders in the deep.
For he commandeth, and raiseth the stormy wind, which lifteth up the waves thereof.
They mount up to the heavens, they go down again to the depths: their soul is melted because of trouble.
They reel to and fro, and stagger like a drunken man, and are at their wit's end.

Then they cry unto the LORD in their trouble, and
 he bringeth them out of their distresses.
He maketh the storm a calm, so that the waves
 thereof are still.
Then are they glad because they be quiet; so he
 bringeth them unto their desired haven.

How long he stared at the words he did not know.
That nagging phrase stuck in his brain again—*desired
haven.*

At last Jace closed the Bible and placed it with
the three volumes of Brainerd, Whitfield, and Wesley.
Out of memory and affection for Michael, he would
read them. Then he would return the books to the Kendall family with the rest of his belongings. When that
would be, he did not know. He would be in London
until June. Seward was writing a letter to Sir Hampton Kendall now, explaining his son's death. Jace too,
as captain of the ship, would write his explanation and
condolences. But the news of Michael's death would
not reach Kingscote for months. Again, he looked at
the inscription in the Bible. Someday, he would also
return the Book to Coral.

The next day they anchored in the London port.
Early morning discord echoed on the wharves of the
East India docks where the *Madras* was moored in its
narrow berth. The London estuary swarmed with men
of various nationalities and dress, a fisherman's pie of
alien tongues mingled with rough English.

Jace was standing with Seward when he heard
Jin-Soo and turned to see the old Chinese man hurrying toward him.

"Captain receive message. Expected to eat dinner
tonight with Sir Rawlings at company headquarters.

Dinner at seven. I will ready the bath, Captain. I will lay out your garment."

A fleet schooner eased itself beside the *Madras*. Dock workers began to unload the treasures stashed in its massive hold. On the docks below, horses strained to pull the overloaded drays, while men sweated to stack barrels and crates.

Later, as Jace soaked in the wooden tub, he watched Seward pace. Now and then he would stop, pull a timepiece from a deep pocket in his waistcoat, scowl, then begin his pacing again.

"You prowl like a caged cheetah," said Jace. "And the sound of your boots is grating to my nerves."

Seward glanced awry in his direction. "The hour be awastin', lad. Cannot ye soak another day?"

Jin-Soo poured another bucket of water over Jace's head. "Hand me the shears, Jin-Soo. The disgruntled Mister Seward is about to starve. The side of mutton he devoured this morning was not enough. He awaits roast goose at Rawlings' table."

Unintimidated by the irritated twist to Seward's lips, Jin-Soo laughed with merriment in memory of Seward's noted appetite.

Jace tossed the shears to Seward, and Jin-Soo held a mirror for Jace's approval.

"I be doing me some hard thinkin'," said Seward. "The death of Michael be a lastin' grief to me. Won't be easy goin' back to Kingscote, facin' Sir Hampton and Miss Elizabeth. And I be doin' some thinkin' about Captain Jarred Buckley's son, too. While we be waitin' to sail, I've decided to stay in Olney."

Olney! Seward's news took him by surprise, and Jace fixed the mirror on him, looking at Seward over his shoulder. The grave expression was a familiar one in recent days. Neither of them was in a pleasant mood. The tea plantation in Darjeeling had not been mentioned once in their conversation, nor had the Moorish heirloom. And even though Michael had not been Seward's charge, and Sir Hampton had approved of the voyage, Seward felt responsible.

"I did not know you had family in Olney," said Jace.

Seward scrutinized Jace's thick dark hair and chopped the curling tendrils to the nape of his neck. Jin-Soo swept them up. "Aye, ye be right, I don't. They be in Aberdeen—what be left of them. 'Tis a man in Olney I wish to season with." His sharp eyes met Jace's in the looking glass. "Truth is, I be wantin' us both to call on the captain."

Jace became alert. "A sea captain?"

Seward's expression darkened as though memories of his own past bore him trouble. "A shipmaster of a slave ship. Long ago. I hear he be in Olney. Time I looked him up."

"The one you told me about, the one in the storm?" Jace felt uncomfortable. Evidently a horrendous storm at sea had wrought some manner of spiritual change in the culprit's life.

"Aye, 'tis the man. Captain John Newton be his name. 'Twas a vile bloke back in me youth. Be a man ye ought to meet while here in London."

Jace said nothing and ran his fingers through his hair, satisfied. Unlike the present style of long hair, he preferred it short. "I gather this Captain Newton is a minister?"

"Aye, so it be said. He was the rector at Olney for some time. Still might be. Be interestin' to hear what happened to him."

Jace was noncommittal. "You go stay with this captain friend of yours, Seward. It will do you good, and like you say, we won't be sailing until spring."

He felt Seward's gaze.

"Be hopin' ye might come. Good to escape the *Madras* awhile."

Jace was unreadable. "I have work to do."

Seward's silence pricked at his insides, but he did not like to be cornered.

"Like I said, if I get a chance, I may come and meet Newton. But do not count on it. I will be busy while in London. You know how Rawlings is. He will have work for me to do at the Company. There is also repair to be done aboard ship."

Seward grunted. "Ye be makin' an excuse."

Were they excuses? Why should he be uneasy about meeting this man Newton? And yet he was. . . .

Jace changed the subject. "Jin-Soo, hand me the razor." He touched his short beard. Except for a mustache he had worn in the military, he preferred to be clean-shaven. When Seward took out his watchpiece for the second time, however, he relented, sighed, and reached for the towel in Jin-Soo's hand. "What is this?" he asked him, squinting at a floral tin that Jin-Soo offered.

Jin-Soo smiled widely. "Sweet powder, Captain. Heavenly Lotus Blossom. You like, yes?"

"I like, no. One would think I was calling on a damsel instead of the cheroot-smoking, burly-headed Rawlings."

"Consider makin' time for Olney, lad. If for no reason except I be askin' ye."

Jace turned and scanned him, then went to his bunk where Jin-Soo had laid out the garments that had been packed away. Systematically, Jace eliminated what he did not like, using deft fingers to toss aside a silk shirt with ruffles about the cuffs, the lacy jabot, and the smoke-blue silk waistcoat that matched the narrow breeches that were much too tight. Instead, ignoring Jin-Soo's protestations, he unlocked his sea chest, then removed a cream Holland shirt with full gathered sleeves that tightened about the cuffs and a V neck that laced below the throat. Next came a pair of black light woolen trousers, the calf-length boots coming up over them. He belted on his scabbard and grabbed his dark cloak, then paused—

Jin-Soo stood extending the Moorish heirloom wrapped in a cloth. "Prize to buy us tea plantation, Captain. Jin-Soo will work very hard there, with Gokul and Mister Seward."

Jace was aware of Seward's penetrating stare. He did not need to be reminded of its cost in blood. Without a word, he took it from Jin-Soo, placed it back within the chest, turned the key, snatched up the carved ivory elephant, and wrapped it in a handkerchief. He stopped when he saw Jin-Soo's expression of bewilderment.

"Another time, old friend." Jace walked out.

Seward gave an affectionate tug at Jin-Soo's pigtail as he strode toward the cabin door. "Keep the captain out of mischief till I return. Feed him much Ginseng tea."

Jin-Soo grinned and bowed low at the waist. He attempted to quip Mister Seward's jargon: "Sooo long, Mister Seward. You take it easy."

Jace expected a comment on leaving the heirloom

in his trunk, but he was grateful when Seward seemed to understand and said nothing. There needed to be a time of healing before either of them could face it.

With the setting sun, the London night had turned damp and chilly, with tendrils of fog wrapping about the district's warehouses and buildings.

Jace turned up the collar of his cloak as he strode with Seward down the creaking quays. Beyond, tiny clapboard rooms and houses built atop the buildings leaned precariously toward the littered street. Barefoot waifs were out begging, and sharp of eye, caught sight of Jace and Seward, receiving a coin. The old and sick slept in the dark alleyways. Acrid smoke curled from chimneys as home fires were stoked against the seaborne chill. Soot mixed with the driblets of misty fog covered every surface. An echo of horse hooves announced the coming of a cabby, and Jace whistled for the driver.

A plump man with scraggy white hair drooping from beneath his hat pulled up and leaned down from the driver's seat to unhitch the door. "Aye, gov'na, where to?"

"Leadenhall. East India Company."

Jace climbed in, Seward after him, dragging the door shut behind him. The coach lurched ahead and rounded a narrow corner.

"What about Olney?" Seward pressed.

Jace leaned his head back against the seat, lowering his hat as if to snooze. "You never give up, do you?"

"I promised yer father before he died I'd take good care of ye. Done a poor job."

"Thanks. But I believe I am doing well enough. Salve your conscience. I am no one's problem but my own. You have been a friend. That is all I've ever wanted."

"Then humor an ol' friend with gray in his hair. Come to Olney before we sail."

Jace raised his hat to squint at him. "Perhaps. But I'll not vow to it. Understood?"

"Aye, lad, 'tis enough." Seward settled back in the leather seat, suddenly relaxed and pleased. After a moment, he asked: "Did ye say ol' Rawlings was servin' roast goose?"

11

Known affectionately by many as the "old converted sea captain," John Newton was no longer the curate at the church in Olney in 1797. He had retired, and Walter Scott was minister, but Seward had located the house Newton shared with his wife of many years and the hymn writer William Cowper.

"Master Cowper be best known for his hymn, 'There Be a Fountain Filled with Blood, Drawn from Emmanuel's Veins,' " Seward told him, and started to bellow forth a stanza.

Seeing the glitter of black in Jace's otherwise blue eyes, Seward stopped, shrugging his heavy shoulders. "Admit a frog sounds a wee better, lad. But remember 'tis the words that count."

"I am not altogether dense, Seward. You need not explain."

It had been with uncertainty that Jace gave in to Seward and accompanied him to Newton's house one rainy night in March. Jace told himself that he could endure the old captain's tale of heaven's intervention. After all, it was not as though he himself were a heathen. If he chose to, he could debate theology with the best of them.

But hours later, when John Newton left the cottage room to get a book from his study for the "young Buckley," Jace used the opportunity to turn on Seward. "You vowed—'no sermon.' He has discussed everything from Calvin to the pope!"

"God forbid I should seek to silence the man. 'Tis no fault of me own if he wishes to share his fair words shown him by the grace of God."

"Not your fault!" Jace scoffed. "He has been preaching for three hours!"

"Easy, man, 'tis not preachin', but 'talk.' "

His eyes narrowed. "Call it as you wish. I call it sermonizing."

Seward's sharp eyes riveted on him. "One would think ye faced the bars of Newgate Gaol, instead of fair company with a saint of God."

"Never mind," Jace gritted. "Just keep your tongue silent, will you? If you would stop asking a hundred questions, I could make an excuse to leave."

Seward obstinately folded his arms across his broad chest and leaned back in the chair, his gaze narrowing. "I be apologizin' for no such thing. A bit of goodly news be balm for yer conscience and mine." He suddenly smiled broadly beneath his reddish mustache. "Just sit awhile, lad. 'Twill do ye good. Ye be as fidgety as Goldfish."

"Now look here—"

Jace stopped and cast a glance toward the door leading into the kitchen. Seward followed his look, then rose awkwardly to his feet, clearing his throat.

The silver-haired and plump Mrs. Mary Newton entered with tea and sweet biscuits. Jace too stood and with little effort displayed his most charming manners, helping her with the tray.

"Your kindness is appreciated, Mrs. Newton," he said smoothly. "I cannot recall the last time Seward and I have enjoyed freshly baked sweetbreads. I am afraid my kansamah aboard the *Madras* has settled for cooking with mold and seawater."

He looked at Seward, waiting for a perfunctory reply to the offered tea and cookies. When Seward only shifted his stance, Jace quipped, "Is that not right, Seward? You like tea and biscuits."

"Oh, aye, aye, 'tis so, Madame . . . er . . . we thank ye much," and he leaned over the tray, taking several of the tiny biscuits into his big hand.

"Use a plate, Seward," said Jace dryly.

"I beg yer pardon, Madame."

Jace managed a charming smile as he accepted the detestable cup of tea, watching in mute horror as she added a heaping spoonful of honey.

Newton had returned with not one book for Jace to take back with him on the *Madras*, but two. Jace gravely accepted them, saying something about how he had read Brainerd and Whitfield, and was well into John Wesley.

He immediately saw his mistake. Newton admitted that he had been greatly influenced by George Whitfield and the Wesley brothers, then launched into a discussion of Whitfield's belief in predestination, versus Wesley's belief in free will.

Jace bit into a biscuit. What would have been instantly devoured aboard ship felt dry and tasteless in his mouth. He glanced at Seward, who was clinging like a drowning man to every word, prolonging the discourse by asking questions that even Jace was able to answer.

The rain continued to pelt against the window,

and the fire leaped and danced in the hearth as if pleased that Jace had to sit and listen. He wanted to take off his coat and loosen his cravat, although logic told him that the room was not too warm. In fact, the expansive cottage room was pleasant and nicely decorated. But somehow Jace was sure he would feel more comfortable in his own tiny cabin on the *Madras.*

There was a moment of silence. Jace did not like the quiet. He quickly opened the *Olney Hymns*, published in 1779. The hymns were written by Newton and William Cowper, a member of his congregation. According to Seward, Cowper had been invited to take up residence with the Newtons due to periods of deep depression. It seemed that William Cowper had once tried to commit suicide.

"Yes, it is true," began Newton. "One day Brother Cowper ordered the coachman to bring him to the London Bridge where he intended to jump off and end it all. The trip took longer than necessary, and when it seemed to him that they should have arrived, Cowper impatiently halted the coach and got off—only to find himself at his front door! They had gone in circles for an hour."

"Blest be God!" said Seward, deeply moved.

"The coachman blamed the mistake on the fog, but Cowper knew the hand of God had spared his life that night. He has since written hymns that lift the depressed soul heavenward."

Jace said nothing. The thought that the Almighty might be so personally involved in the affairs of men could be intimidating to one who wished to escape.

Together William Cowper and John Newton had published the *Olney Hymns*, now used by many Christian groups meeting in homes or in small free churches throughout London.

Jace casually leafed through the hymnal, his tanned, rugged expression refusing to show anything. If he were honest with himself, he would admit that the incorrigible slave trader turned parish curate had baited his curiosity. It was amazing indeed that a man of Newton's background could write such tender words about Christ.

In spite of himself, Jace listened, moved by Newton's description of his youth, for there was much in his tale with which he could associate.

Newton's father, like Jace's, had been a sea captain. But unlike himself, Newton had known his mother during early childhood, and she had proved herself to be a devoted Christian who prayed, as mothers often do, that her son would grow up to become a preacher.

Jace, on the contrary, had never seen his mother. He did not even know who she was. She might have been a tart from some exotic port, or as Seward said, a lady; although the latter seemed quite improbable. And he was certain that no woman had ever prayed for him.

"My mother died when I was a young boy, and I followed my sea captain father to a sailor's life," said Newton. "I soon joined the Royal Navy, but loathed the discipline."

Jace thought of his own dislike of the military. He set his tea cup down, then picked it back up again, drinking the stuff for lack of something to do. Again he leafed through the hymnal.

Newton told of deserting the ship, of being caught and flogged, and eventually discharged.

Jace thought of his brevet of courage earned in Rangoon. There was a difference.

"I then headed for regions where I could sin freely,

and ended up on the west coast of Africa, working for a slave trader," said Newton.

There, Newton had been treated roughly by the trader and was soon engulfed in a life of wretchedness.

"I was a horrid-looking man, toiling in a plantation of lemon trees on the Island of Plantains . . . my clothes became rags, I had no shelter, and was begging for unhealthy roots to allay my hunger."

He had managed to escape the island, he told Jace and Seward, "And in the following year my ship was battered by a treacherous storm . . . I had been reading *The Imitation of Christ*—aye, I fell upon my knees crying out to God for mercy. I was a wretch who found amazing grace."

Jace paused. *Amazing Grace.* The words caught his attention. *That song . . . those words*—he had heard them before. Where? He turned to that hymn in the book he held, and now the words stared up at Jace as Newton's voice went on glorying in the grace of God.

> *Amazing grace, how sweet the sound,*
> *   That saved a wretch like me!*
> *I once was lost, but now am found,*
> *   Was blind but now I see.*
> *'Twas grace that taught my heart to fear,*
> *   And grace my fears relieved;*
> *How precious did that grace appear,*
> *   The hour I first believed.*
> *When we've been there ten thousand years,*
> *   Bright shining as the sun,*
> *We've no less days to sing God's praise,*
> *   Than when we'd first begun.*

Jace felt the rain in his memory, could feel it on his face, could hear the sweet voice of a woman singing.

He closed his eyes as it came back to him. The monsoon on Kingscote. The little whitewashed hut where the Kendall daughter and her mother had delivered the Indian girl's baby . . . it was the funeral. Mrs. Kendall had sung that song.

"Aye, I remember that storm aboard ship," Seward was saying darkly. "I didn't believe the change in ye would last. Thought it was born of the hellish night. Now I've seen and heard ye, and I be knowin' for a surety." He shook his head. "I believe in this Christ, and yet—there be no assurance, naught but the fear of damnation. I be sure of nothin'."

Jace closed the hymnbook with a soft thud, scanning one man and then the other. This was getting out of control. He started to speak, but Newton looked concerned and leaned toward Seward, resting a firm hand on his broad shoulder.

"Wesley, too, feared damnation. He found no peace in the liturgy of the church. Scriptural faith is a very different thing from a rational assent to the gospel."

"Michael had that faith," said Seward, and unexpectedly his eyes filled with tears.

Jace sat in stunned silence, watching the tears run down Seward's creased face. A big man, a strong man, weeping like a child! It frightened him, for it meant that a man could lose control, could become vulnerable—

Newton was speaking to Seward now in a gentle tone, almost a whisper, "Faith in your Savior, Seward. That's the assurance."

Jace felt his heart wrench. *I must get out of here!*

Suddenly, he found his own voice interrupting, sounding cynical, challenging: "You speak of faith! What *is* faith? It is merely what a man wants to believe it is, and nothing more. I have seen a Hindu carve his flesh into bloody ribbons to appease Kali. I have seen a Muslim with his forehead flattened from bowing on stone toward Mecca. I have seen those devoted to Rome weeping, their knees bloody as they crawl to beg mercies of the Madonna. And I have seen Protestants baptize by the edge of the sword and destroy one another for differences in interpretation. They *all* claim they are motivated by faith."

He had thought he might anger Newton, but the man was not disturbed at all—and that disturbed Jace.

"What others may describe as faith is not so at all, my friend. It is human activity engaged to please the god of their religion, usually a god of terror.

"This is Christian faith: a renouncing of everything we are apt to call our own, and relying wholly upon the blood, righteousness, and intercession of Jesus. You see, there is a wide chasm between a religion of works and the Christian's faith in a finished work accomplished by God himself in Christ."

Jace was silenced. Whatever frustration had motivated his outburst was gone. But an internal struggle ensued, one he had been desperate to avoid. God wooing, convicting. It was gentle, yet painful, and Jace felt his will striving to retain its lordship.

As though being burned upon his soul, the words rang through his mind—*"You must yield every area of your life to the Captain of your soul."*

Abruptly, Jace stood to his feet with books in hand, surprised at his reaction. "I have found our discussion interesting, sir, but I must be going. Books are hard to come by, and expensive. Perhaps it is best if I did not take them."

Newton looked at him. Jace felt transparent. *He*

knows . . . he understands what I am feeling. For the first time in his life, his self-confidence was cracking. *Danger.*

"No need for that. You can return them to me the next time you are in London."

It sounded like a challenge, one that Jace could not bring himself to back away from. As their eyes locked, Jace heard himself saying calmly, "Very well. I shall be back one day."

"Good." Newton smiled and stood to his feet. "You are welcome here, any time. Next time you must tell me about yourself, Captain Buckley. Seward has shared a little of your upbringing in India, and I am most interested. I would like to hear more."

Somehow Jace managed to retain his outward indifference. He shook Newton's hand, thanked him, made the correct compliment about Mrs. Newton's tea and biscuits, then turned toward Seward with a challenging gaze, though his voice was casual. "Coming?"

Seward cleared his throat and stood. "Aye. One thing more—" he turned to Newton.

Jace sighed within.

"They say ye retired for ill health and be failin' in memory, but there be no evidence of it tonight."

"My memory is nearly gone, but I remember two things: that I am a great sinner and that Christ is a great Savior!"

Jace opened the cottage door and escaped into the rainy darkness, unnerved to discover that the tenderness and strength of Christ was like a sword, able to slash through his bulwark. He felt exposed. Vulnerable. He was not sufficient in and of himself. He had known that, of course; but tonight, quite by accident, he had tasted it.

A stiff wind sent the droplets of rain against his

face, cooling him. He would not go back. He would send the books to Newton.

Jace had prided himself in his ability to avoid emotional entanglements of any sort. Was he vulnerable after all? The thought was disturbing. Where would it lead? What strange, winding paths were these that he had no control over? Like William Cowper and his eerie ride in the fog, would divine providence lead him back to where he must grapple with the infinite—and yield?

To believe, to trust, meant removing his armor and laying bare his heart for scrutiny. No hands other than his own must touch the bruises that were there.

Irritated by this new feeling of weakness, he fumbled with the two books belonging to Newton, trying to protect them from getting wet by placing them beneath his coat, yet feeling as though they were pricks in his side. Now he had the responsibility of seeing them safely returned.

Jace doubted if he would ever find the time, or the desire, to read through *The Imitation of Christ*, even though he was a little curious about the book that had made such an impression on a man like Newton. And as for the *Olney Hymns*—it might be pleasant to read, but he hoped Seward did not find the book a necessary cause to start bellowing out hymns aboard the ship!

Jace knew his irritation with Seward was greater than the situation warranted, but at the moment he did not care. It was Seward who had entangled him in this dilemma.

Jace started down the cobbled street toward town without Seward, lowering his hat against the rain. Despite his nettled mood, the words of Newton echoed through his brain, and he could not silence them, though he tried.

"This is faith: a renouncing of everything we are apt to call our own, and relying wholly upon the blood, righteousness, and intercession of Jesus."

The water on the darkened cobbles glistened under the street lamps, and his boots echoed in the otherwise silent night.

A few minutes later he heard Seward hurrying to catch up with him, but he did not speak as they walked along beside each other, and Seward, as though he understood his mood, wisely remained silent, increasing his stride to catch up.

After twenty minutes, Seward began to whistle "Amazing Grace," stuffing his big hands into his coat pockets, his boots making crunching sounds on the cobbles.

He is quite pleased with himself, Jace thought irritably.

12

Roxbury House, London
June 1797

The shiny black coach boasting the Roxbury coat of arms brought Coral, Margaret, and Sir Hugo through the wrought-iron gate and up the cobbled carriageway. Coral's gaze was fixed ahead upon a green rise with a backdrop of elms, where Roxbury House dominated the English countryside.

So this was her mother's home: the imposing estate where she had been born and raised until her marriage to a maverick Kendall cousin named Hampton.

The three-story gray stone baronial mansion reminded Coral of a castle. The building was heavily turreted, and flaunted some forty rooms of state with elaborate artisan friezework and marble.

In 1660, Aunt Margaret explained, Charles II had awarded the estate to Great-grandfather William, the first Earl of Roxbury, along with the estate's lands and a summer house built on the fashionable London Strand.

"This was during the Reconstruction after the

rule of Oliver Cromwell."

Coral found herself greeted at the heavy wooden mansion doors by Simms, a gaunt-faced butler in spotless black, who escorted the three of them through the massive, chandeliered hallway into the parlor.

Coral decided that Grandmother Lady Victoria, the grand matriarch of the family, was as imposing as the mansion. Her skin had not seen a day of sun in her seventy years, leaving it porcelain clear, and her sharp blue eyes did not apologize for an appraisal that made Coral imagine herself a slave on the auction block. Family jewels glittered on Lady Victoria's earlobes, her throat, her fingers; and the handle of her walking stick flashed with emeralds.

Behind Grandmother stood Simms, who now held the leash of three small, shaggy white dogs with diamond collars. Simms wore a frozen expression that looked dour upon everyone except the matriarch.

However, Coral had underestimated the depth of her grandmother. Lady Victoria's imperious facade melted when she unexpectedly embraced Coral. "My dear grandchild, how precious to have you here. A pity your sisters couldn't be here to greet you, but of course they are away at Lady Anne's. However, Ethan will be pleased."

Ethan will be pleased. . . . Coral felt the pressure of family unity wrap about her like a python. They had already assumed she would marry him. At twenty, she was considered too old to delay marriage much longer.

Sir Hugo's voice interrupted her thoughts: "Coral, this is your cousin, Doctor Ethan Boswell. Ethan, Coral Kendall."

Coral turned toward her cousin and paused,

swallowing back a start of surprise. A tall, handsome man with ash-blond hair and drowsy gray eyes walked up. Evidently he had just been out riding, for he wore a fashionable tweed jacket and brown breeches. He smiled down at her, and tossing his horsewhip to a groom, bent to brush his lips against her forehead.

"Cousin Coral, welcome to Roxbury House."

"Yes, thank you . . . Cousin Ethan."

He continued to smile. "In a few months I will have you well enough for Grandmother to introduce you to London society."

"Yes, yes," Lady Victoria responded, "but first, my dear Coral, I believe a tour of Roxbury House would be in order."

Grandmother Victoria took pride in showing Coral the house, especially what she called the *Royal Hall*. Here, Coral found an elaborate collection of silk tapestries depicting the kings and queens of England. But Coral's favorite room was the all-yellow Morning Room, warmed by the rising sun over the Thames. From here she could step outdoors onto a flagstone court and wander the gardens, which surrounded a large diamond-shaped courtyard.

It was several days later, when Coral was alone in her suite of rooms, that she found the courage to unlock the small cloisonne box that her mother had given to her before she sailed. Inside were the mementos she had asked for, which had belonged to Gem.

"The Lord gave, and the Lord hath taken away. Blessed be the name of the Lord," Coral quoted. She found needed solace in knowing that her little lamb had passed through the gate into the presence of the Great Shepherd.

Inside the box, Coral saw the adoption papers signed by the Anglican bishop, and smiled in memory of that long-awaited day.

She picked up the carved elephant that Michael had made for Gem. It was a miniature of her pet, Rani. Fingering it gently, she remembered how Gem had carried it with him everywhere.

There was something else she was looking for now, the object that had caused her to open the treasure box. She leafed through the mementos, but it was not there. Where was the tiny gold cross that she had placed around Gem's neck on the day of his adoption? She emptied the box on her bed and sorted quickly through the other objects. It was gone! Or had her mother forgotten to place it there?

Coral frowned . . . and then she saw a small red silk pocket embroidered with a Burmese dragon. She smiled.

Jan-Lee had wanted to give her something . . . the cross? No doubt. Had she not been the one to ready Gem for burial?

Quickly she reached her fingers inside, expecting to feel the cold metal, but felt only a small piece of paper. She drew it out and smoothed it open, reading:

September 1796
I do not want to burden your soul, Miss Coral. I do not want to light false candles of hope when it is best to put yesterday far from us. But I find no rest and must write these words. I feared to tell you what I thought when you were so ill. I also fear for the lives of everyone on Kingscote if I rekindle coals of trouble. I fear the fire will destroy the hatcheries, maybe take your life too. I could not bear that.

By now you are safe in London. I will tell you what is on my heart. It was I, Jan-Lee, who readied the child for Christian burial. I wondered why there was no cross on Gem. It was on him when the sepoy stole him from me. It is important that you know the child I readied for burial was badly injured beyond description. But I keep thinking why no cross? One thing is very important. The child had a scar on his heel. I do not remember that Gem had a scar. Maybe you will remember.

Jan-Lee

Coral sank to the bed, so weak that she could not move. She stared at Jan-Lee's letter, unable to even think. *Scar . . . did Gem have a scar?* No! No! She would have remembered! Or had such a thing escaped her? No, that could not be, she would remember if Gem had injured his foot! "Oh, dearest God," she whispered. "What does this mean? What could this possibly mean?"

She ran a trembling hand across her forehead when a rap sounded on her bedroom door. Coral jumped to her feet. "Yes?" she called shakily.

"It is your uncle. May I come in?"

Coral stuffed the letter into her bodice. Before she could answer, the door opened and he stood there, an imperial figure in black broadcloth and a white frilled shirt. His lively dark eyes studied her, then fixed upon the treasure box with its spilled contents.

In three brief strides he was beside her, a hand on her shoulder. Drawing a white handkerchief from his pocket, he commanded, "Blow your nose like a brave girl and wipe your eyes. You are much too ill to torment yourself like this."

Before she could find the strength to react, he

gathered the mementos scattered on the bed, along with the adoption certificate, and placed them back into the box, snapping the lid shut.

"Ethan has suggested the need to wait awhile. Your emotions are highstrung."

Coral made a sudden move to retrieve the box, but Sir Hugo caught her, his brows furrowing with annoyance.

"As I feared. You're becoming obsessed with this loss. You must go back to bed at once. I will call Ethan."

"Uncle!" Coral's voice was indignant. "I am quite all right! Give me the box!"

Footsteps interrupted from the hallway. Margaret Roxbury came into the room, her eyes taking in first Coral, then her husband holding the small box. Her expression tensed.

"Hugo, what are you doing?"

Coral did not miss the sharp glance exchanged between them. But Hugo offered a somewhat mocking smile. "Never mind, darling. I wouldn't want to interrupt your letter writing. The colonel will be expecting *your* response."

Coral was shocked at Hugo's inflicted barb. Her aunt Margaret's cheeks turned pink, and her brown eyes grew distant. She tilted her head to the side with recovered dignity.

"On the contrary, *darling*, I was writing Elizabeth. I have no reason to answer Colonel Warbeck's letter. It was addressed to you, was it not?"

"So it was, my pet." He lifted the box. "She has been looking at the child's toys. It has upset her. Who is responsible for giving her this box now?"

"It must have been Mother. Oh, Coral—it is too soon. You should have waited."

"I will send for Ethan. A sleeping powder will make her rest until morning."

"Do not call Ethan!" Coral protested, her voice becoming shrill with exasperation. "I am fine, and the box belongs to *me*."

Without a backward glance, Sir Hugo left Coral's room, holding the box beneath his arm.

"Whatever are you doing to that child?" snapped Grandmother Victoria from the corridor. Hugo said something quietly, then walked on, and a moment later she came into the bedroom.

"Margaret, good heavens!"

"Mother, she is crying over Gem again, and—"

"Well of course she is going to cry. It is only natural." Her sharp blue eyes snapped with impatience as she rustled across the room and took hold of Coral's arm, easing her to the side of the bed. "When Henry died I wept incessantly for months! I cannot tell you how weary I became of those forbidding it. It did me a world of good. And when the tears stopped, my sorrow was over. Margaret, if you do not wish to see the child cry, then remove your presence from her room. I will sit with her."

"Mother! I was not scolding her for crying over Gem. It—"

"Uncle has taken my treasure box with Gem's mementos," cried Coral. "The adoption certificate—"

"Tsk! Well! I shall get it back at once," Lady Victoria said crisply. "Margaret may find him intimidating, but I do not."

Margaret placed hands on hips and looked toward the ceiling with exasperation. "Mother, I do not find my husband 'intimidating.' "

"Where is he?"

Margaret sighed and threw up her hands. "Downstairs. He is sending for Ethan."

"Good. Coral needs to sleep. In the meantime, I will get your treasure box back," she assured Coral.

Grandmother swept toward the door, and Margaret followed her. "Mother, please do not create a scene."

"Why should I? Hugo is reasonable, is he not?"

Coral sat weakly and watched them disappear from her room, hearing their voices rise and fall as they went down the hall. *Thank God for Granny V!* Coral realized that she had one tower of strength in the house, and if she was to share her hope about Gem being alive to anyone, it would be her grandmother.

True to her word, the cloisonne box was returned. Ethan arrived and handed it to her with a sympathetic smile.

Coral emptied the contents on the bed. Everything was there. Including the adoption certificate.

"Everything in order?" he asked soothingly.

Coral nodded. "Yes—I am sorry about the ruckus."

He smiled, stirring the powder that he had mixed in a glass of water. "No need to apologize." His eyes held hers, and Coral glanced away, busying herself with the box.

"You will feel stronger in the morning. Here, I know you do not approve of this, but do drink it. In time, you will notice marked improvement in your fever."

Ethan handed the glass to her, then sat in one of the tapestry-covered mahogany armchairs. "Uncle is overbearing, but he means no harm. He is concerned, as we all are. If ever you are to get well, Coral, you must give your mind and body time to rest and heal."

Coral knew that and was irritated at being treated like a child.

Ethan stayed until she drank the medication, then excused himself. When he had gone, Coral fought against the drugged sleep for as long as her mind allowed.

No cross on Gem. What does it mean? Anything at all? Could Gem's abductor have removed it and tossed it away? Perhaps her mother had taken it and simply forgotten to include it with the other items. But the scar . . . Gem had no scar—or did he? She would have noticed! And Jan-Lee bathed him—

Coral struggled between dashed hopes and rising excitement. Could the child they had buried on Kingscote be an untouchable? Made to look as though he were Gem?

Coral removed Jan-Lee's letter from her bodice and tried to read it again, but her eyes could not focus clearly as sleep weighed heavily. Her hand too felt heavy, and before the powder made her completely inept, she struggled out of bed and placed both the letter and the adoption certificate—not in the cloisonne box—but in the drawer with her undergarments. She stumbled back into bed, exhausted.

"Thank you, Lord," Coral murmured drowsily. A small candle now flickered with the light of hope in a sea of darkness. But she reminded herself that she was in London, and if Gem were alive and being held by his abductors, he was trapped somewhere in India. What could she possibly do?

"I will write home tomorrow," she thought sleepily. "And also to Jan-Lee. I will tell Grandmother too."

And Jace Buckley—should she risk trying to contact him?

Coral fell asleep with the name of Director Rawlings on her mind. Rawlings, of the East India Company. Her father knew and trusted him. She could trust him too.

———

The weather was warm for a London June, and Coral had been at Roxbury House for a week. She walked with her grandmother across the green toward the small lake created for the estate. Tame ducks and white swans paddled, but a black swan held Coral's attention. The sweet smell of cherry blossoms from the nearby orchard infused the breeze that ruffled the gold curls beneath her sun hat. Still frail from months of illness in India, she remained under the medical supervision of her cousin.

Grandmother sat down on the bench, holding the jeweled handle of her cane, while Coral wandered to the edge of the lake to feed the ducks bread crumbs from the basket on her arm.

There will be no more journeys into the valley of depression, she told herself. The question of why the Lord had permitted the loss of Gem remained obscure. Perhaps she would never understand. She reminded herself of what Job had confessed when losing all that was dear to him. *The Lord gave . . . the Lord took away . . . blessed be His name . . .*

Ahead was the cherry orchard, where the extensive stables awaited her growing desire to ride the well-bred line of horses. Ethan had suggested they go riding together soon in order to show her the rest of the estate grounds.

"What do you think of Ethan?" Grandmother asked bluntly.

Coral laughed. "Really, Granny V, do you expect

190

me to fall in love so easily?"

Grandmother did not blanch. "Tsk, tsk, dear, I did not ask you if you were in love, did I?"

"No," Coral admitted, "but—"

Grandmother Victoria wore a triumphant expression. "However, since you have brought the matter up, I shall offer my opinion."

Coral tried to lure the black swan to come near. "I am sure you would offer your advice regardless," she said with a little smile.

Grandmother did not appear the least bit disturbed. "You are quite right. I shall. Ethan is possibly the best match the family could make for you, considering your health, and the noteworthy fact that he is Sir Hugo's only nephew."

"Uncle Hugo does agree that his nephew is noteworthy," said Coral in a humorous tone. "Nevertheless, I shall not be rushed into anything as important as marriage. I hope the family does not intend to pressure either of us. Cousin Ethan seems quite engrossed in his medical research." She glanced sideways at her grandmother. "And I too want to begin my studies as soon as possible." Coral was thinking of a linguist who taught Hindi, but she doubted that anyone in all of London could be found. There was also her interest in the music of Charles Wesley, and the new hymns of the Dissenter Movement, which were placing a new emphasis on congregational singing, something that was frowned upon as strange by the state church.

"No one is going to demand that you marry Ethan, child. Unlike Hugo, I happen to agree with your mother and Margaret on the matter. A woman ought to love a man before she is expected to vow her fidelity to his name. Nonetheless, I cannot stress strongly enough the importance of marriage within the family.

We cannot trust the fate of the Roxbury/Kendall dynasty to the greedy appetites of strangers. Heavens! With four granddaughters to arrange for, and a hundred penniless scamps running about with titles who are only too anxious to please an heiress, the family must be careful indeed. You do see the difficulty facing us, do you not? Coral! Do pay attention when I speak to you."

Grandmother Victoria's voice cut through the dark memories that had momentarily held Coral in their grip, making her shiver with coldness and reminding her that she was now in London to begin a new life. The words of her grandmother pressed along the same theme that she had heard from Sir Hugo on the voyage from Calcutta, and now, as then, they made little impression.

"Yes, Granny V, I am sorry. My mind wandered."

"Whatever were you thinking of, child? Are you still grieving over the Indian boy?"

Coral turned, her feelings evident on her face. "Oh, Granny V! You should have seen Gem! He was such a winsome boy, so bright, so beautiful, you would have loved him. I should have had his portrait painted—" She paused for a moment, unable to go on. She walked over to her grandmother and sat down beside her. "If I had his portrait, I would at least have something to look at."

The black swan wandered onto the grass nearby and Coral tossed more crumbs. "Gem adored Bible stories. He could repeat them in perfect English. Everything was going so well until the night of the fire—" Her voice faltered.

Grandmother leaned over and placed her thin veined hand on Coral's. There was a moment of silence while Coral brought her emotions under control. She squeezed her grandmother's hand.

"Poor child. Sir Hugo is right. You have traversed a wretched path. I did not mean to upset you like this. Well, you say you taught the boy well," she concluded lamely. "There is that consolation to enhearten you."

"Yes, and if Gem is dead—I have every confidence he is in the state of the blessed."

Coral felt her grandmother's piercing gaze.

"Life is plagued by 'ifs' my child, but I cannot understand why you would question the fact of the boy's death?"

Coral met her gaze. "Grandmother, there is a possibility Gem is alive . . . that the child found was not my son, but one of the untouchables working in the hatcheries."

Coral wanted to squirm under her grandmother's scrutiny.

"Good heavens! Hugo told me you might—" She stopped, and for the first time appeared unable to cope with the situation.

Afraid she would lose her support, Coral rushed to explain about Jan-Lee's letter.

Grandmother's eyes brightened a little. "You have the letter?"

"Yes. I will show it to you before I write Director Rawlings. You might as well know that I have decided to hire mercenaries to try to locate Gem."

"Mercenaries! Forbid! I could never allow such a thing. Whatever will Elizabeth say if I permit you to make contact with the seamy side of London?"

"Sir Rawlings is a gentleman and quite respectable."

"The director of the East India Company? Posh! He is a knave if there ever was one."

"He is a friend of my father," Coral soothed.

"Oh, and indeed! Hampton was a knave himself, in the old days, until Elizabeth settled him down. I will have no scandal surrounding your stay in London."

"There will be no scandal, Grandmother, I promise. I will do it in secret. No one will even know."

"Tsk, tsk, no scandal you say. It was scandal enough that you were permitted to adopt an Indian child. Have you any notion the gossip Lady Vivian has sown about London?"

Coral glanced at her uneasily. "No, but I do not particularly care."

"The precise reaction I would expect from a granddaughter being raised in a raw and heathen environment like India! If I had my way you would never be permitted to return to that land. And that goes for your sisters as well. I shall tell you what the gossip is saying."

"Granny V—"

"It is said the child belonged to Michael or Alex."

"You do not mean—"

"I most certainly do. And the Indian woman is believed to be a concubine on the plantation. Why else, they say, would Sir Hampton Kendall allow his adoption?"

Coral jumped to her feet. "Jemani was my friend, and I made a vow to her that I would look after Gem." Coral's cheeks were flushed with indignation. "The English can be positively—pigheaded!"

If she expected Grandmother to become upset at that, she showed no alarm.

"You are quite right," she said. "But since such goings-on do take place in London royalty, as well as among those working for the East India Company, well, you can see the natural path to which the feet of men do run."

"I will not listen to their gossip, and I am certainly not going to let it upset me further. If they want to believe he is the offspring of a Kendall son—then let them. They will believe it regardless of my denials."

"That is true. However, I must say that I, for one, do not believe it. Knowing how Elizabeth and you feel about Christian matters, I do not find it all that surprising that you took the boy in. But child, you must be reasonable about your feelings. Regardless of his parentage, hiring mercenaries will do nothing to bring him back."

Grandmother snatched bread crumbs from the basket and tossed them to a fat white goose that had waddled from the cherry orchard. "This is most upsetting."

Coral felt a new tide of weariness and sat down, her outburst leaving her more subdued. The last thing she wanted was to lose her grandmother's support.

"I am sorry, Granny V. I did not mean to alarm you."

"I want nothing more than to see you happy, Coral, but—" and she sighed. "While I dislike admitting this, I suspect that Hugo may be right after all."

Coral felt a rise of uneasiness. "About what?"

Grandmother glanced at her, her pale eyes troubled. "About your inability to adjust to the boy's death. Grief is one thing, and I think I have made it clear you need not go into a closet to have a good cry. But this matter of Gem being alive, of this letter . . . your thinking is not quite . . ." she halted, "what shall we say—stable? I am not blaming you," she hastened. "It was not a pretty thing to come upon that wretched savage in the process of stealing Gem from the nursery. Ethan

195

is convinced that such an experience can leave a mother scarred indefinitely. He is quite sympathetic toward your position."

Coral stared at her, confused. Is that what the family thought? That she was beside herself?

Coral steadied the frustration rising within her, then began calmly, "I admit the fever does cause nightmares, even hallucinations, but I am over that now. There is nothing wrong with my thinking. Did Uncle Hugo tell you there was?"

Grandmother looked pained. "It was a mistake to have allowed you to adopt the baby. You were too young and impressionable. Naturally you grew attached, and his loss has done this to you. I do not blame you at all. I blame Hampton. He should have known the trouble it would cause you, and Kingscote, not to mention Elizabeth. I suppose he did it because of baby Ranek, but I fear Hugo is right."

Hugo . . . Hugo. It appeared the entire family believed him.

"Uncle Hugo means well; however, he is wrong about Gem, and about me. I know he thinks I am unstable, but it is not true, Grandmother. I have the letter from my ayah. My conviction that Gem is alive has nothing to do with grief. And if he is, he is in the hands of his abductors. I intend to continue the search in India."

Coral stood, looking down at her grandmother, her eyes pleading. "Granny V, please understand how I feel. I cannot rest until I know what happened to him." She felt hurt by the alarm in her grandmother's eyes. She bent and planted a kiss on her forehead. "I love you, Granny V. Do change your mind about Director Rawlings. Do you not see? I must write him. I need your support. You will help me?"

Lady Victoria said nothing. Coral waited for a moment, but when her grandmother remained silent, Coral gathered up her skirts, turned, and left.

13

Grandmother Victoria watched Coral walk across the green toward the mansion, removing her hat as she went. She was a determined young woman, so much like Elizabeth. She had lost Elizabeth by refusing to understand her love for Hampton Kendall, and her determination to go to India. She must not make the same mistake with Coral's devotion to the Indian boy.

I have already lost my daughters. I will not give up my granddaughters too. One of them should belong to me, to London, and to Roxbury Silk House. If I cannot have Coral—then I will have Kathleen, Marianna, or Belinda. Why should India take them all?

Using her cane, Lady Victoria stood to her feet, staring thoughtfully after Coral. It might be wiser to sanction Coral's mission to write Director Rawlings, even though Hugo would resist. Giving her granddaughter moral support would win her devotion. How splendid if she could manage to keep Coral and Ethan in London!

Coral believed the boy was alive. But that was impossible. Margaret had explained to her that the child's body had been found a few days after his abduction, but if it would make her granddaughter happy, then why not allow Director Rawlings to look into the matter?

She emptied the remaining bread crumbs from the basket onto the lawn. She had no reason to doubt Margaret's assessment of what had happened that night on Kingscote. After all, she and Hugo had been there in full control of their senses, while her granddaughter's health had taken a dire turn for the worse.

She sighed. It was painful to see Elizabeth's daughter this distraught.

There must be something Ethan can do to make her well again, she thought. *And I will tell her this afternoon to go ahead and write Director Rawlings.*

Satisfied, Grandmother Victoria looked up, surprised to see Sir Hugo standing a few feet away in a dark riding cloak. He stood under an elm tree staring after Coral.

"Good heavens, Hugo, you startled me," she snapped.

"Oh, did I? My apology."

She cast him a tiresome look. "How long have you been there?"

"Not long. I was out riding with Ethan. I decided to come back early."

He walked the short distance from the path to where she stood, his dark eyes empty of expression. "You must not tire yourself, Victoria," he said solicitously. "You know what Ethan told you about your heart. Let me help you back to the house."

"I am quite all right. Stop fussing over me. By the by—Margaret wishes to see you. She is waiting in her room. You have been neglecting her something beastly."

"This dreadful business at Parliament has kept me busy. I'll make it up to her."

"Men, such insensitive creatures. They forever deceive themselves into thinking yesterday can be 'made up for.' It is you, she wants—though heaven knows I don't know why," she said.

Hugo laughed as they strolled across the velvety grass. "Dearest Victoria, how your honesty bears the sting of briars. But what your daughter may want might surprise you."

She cast him a guarded glance. But he said, "You are wrong. One day I will make up lost time with Margaret. But for now, perhaps a month or two at the house on the Strand will help. I was also thinking that it might be good for Coral to come with us."

Lady Victoria looked at him, askance. "This is rather unexpected, is it not? And if it is Margaret you're thinking of, whyever do you wish to bring Coral?"

"Coral's illness and the loss of the boy has been quite hard on her," he said smoothly. "I worry about her. Margaret can help."

"Are you insinuating that her grandmother cannot?"

"Now, now, Victoria, I would be the last to question the diligence you invest in your granddaughters. Belinda can attest to that."

Victoria looked at her son-in-law, feeling somewhat guilty. Belinda had come to her room in tears the night before. It seemed she was in love with her cousin Alex Kendall, but Hugo insisted she marry Sir Arlen George in Calcutta, a distant relative of the governor-general.

"Belinda wishes to marry young Alex. Do not be so hard-nosed about it, Hugo. Sir George is old enough to be her father. Is it not your own ambitions you are thinking of? Margaret tells me you spend too much time with the governor-general."

"Nonsense. My position demands time with the governor."

"Perhaps, but that does not help Belinda."

"Belinda has a head for every handsome young rascal that comes along. Arlen George will be good for her frivolous nature. He is not the jealous sort. A few flings, and he will look the other way."

"You are odious."

"Belinda and Sir George will announce their engagement when we return to Calcutta."

"And Alex? He has nothing to say about this?"

"My dear Victoria," he said wearily. "Alex Kendall is passionately in love with his music. Belinda does not exist in his world. She would never be happy."

"Posh. Alex is interested in more than music, I dare say. Elizabeth mentioned some girl in Vienna. The daughter of his music instructor."

"Which is my second point. Alex, too, is wild, and perhaps too much like Belinda. Tensely emotional. Any marriage between them would provoke temper tantrums. Now, about Coral—it was Ethan who suggested that she come with Margaret and me to the summer house."

The fact that it was Ethan's idea mollified her. He was like a son, and she trusted Ethan when she wondered about Hugo. But when had Hugo and Ethan discussed a two-month stay for Coral at the summer house? Grandmother Victoria felt nettled. Would the family forever persist in making plans without consulting her?

Hugo looked toward the mansion, his face grim. "Coral was distraught at breakfast."

"I did not notice," Victoria said crisply. "Coral insists she feels well enough. Perhaps she would improve if we simply left her alone to adjust on her own. She is quite religious, and finds strength in that."

"Ethan is concerned that she imagines things. He spoke to me a short time ago."

Victoria glanced at the side of his face, noting the square cut to his jaw, the ruggedly handsome features, the spartan look to his lips. Yet he lacked the masculine sensitivity Margaret needed.

She should have married John Warbeck. Another of my sins, Lady Victoria thought unhappily. Aloud, she said: "Did he? He said nothing to me. When did you see Ethan?"

"This morning at the stables. He mentioned the possibility of placing her back on the powders."

Lady Victoria paused, remembering that Coral had mentioned a letter about the boy from her ayah in India. Had she imagined it?

"Coral does not approve of those Eastern powders Ethan is prescribing—or are they your drugs?"

"Mine! Since when would I meddle with drugs?"

"Oh, come, come. Anyway, she claims they keep her mind confused."

"Rubbish. It is her mind that is confusing her, not Ethan's medicine. Stop fussing, Victoria. He's a physician! He knows what he is doing."

"So you wish to take her to the summer house?"

"Ethan believes it may help her. He will keep her entertained with carriage rides, picnics, and boat trips on the Thames. It is a healthy idea. She is becoming morbid."

Victoria studied his sympathetic expression. "She insists there is a letter from her ayah questioning the boy's death. Coral believes Gem is alive."

"Sorrow often creates delusion," came his quick reply.

"Coral does not seem the dramatic sort."

"On the contrary, her strong will makes her quite dramatic. Hampton and Elizabeth sent Coral here specifically to be turned over to Ethan's medical care. We can trust his decisions."

"About this letter. She insists it was in the small cloisonne box you took from her."

"Ah. That again? If I recall, you stormed after me, snatching it away. There was no letter. I would have noticed it at once. There were only mementos. Sentimental objects to send her into fits of tears. Why anyone wishes to keep such things I do not know. Death ends this existence. Why prolong the memory by suffering?"

"You sound positively heathen! I suppose you sympathize with those gurus who spout reincarnation? Posh! Coming back a hundred times as this creature or that, or some ancient tyrant! No wonder Margaret has lost the sparkle in her eyes. I should never have allowed it. I should have agreed to that young buck Warbeck."

"Lady Victoria, your tongue knows the venom of a viper, however well-bred."

"Indeed. I shall report your heretical beliefs to Bishop Canterbury," she said tartly.

Sir Hugo gave a laugh.

"Curse the day my daughters sailed East on Company ships. . . . By the by . . . I nearly forgot—there is a letter waiting for you from a Captain Buckley. It was delivered this morning. You look surprised. Do you know him?"

"Quite well, as a matter of fact. Colonel Warbeck is his father."

Lady Victoria walked on. "Then he did eventually marry. I did not think he would after—"

"No," came the smooth interruption. "He adopted Buckley. The young man is insolent. But I admit he is an excellent swordsman, and knows his way about India. He could be a valuable man to the Company if he were not so independent."

"What could he want with you?"

"I am sure I do not know. But Michael is aboard his ship, which is docked here in London. They intend to open a tea enterprise in Darjeeling."

"Not another plantation in India! You say Michael is aboard his ship? Why am I not told these matters? My grandson is in London, and he has not yet come to Roxbury House?"

"Give him time. Perhaps they have only just arrived."

"Strange that he would leave it to Captain Buckley to get in touch with us. Well, no matter. Coral will be cheered to see her brother."

"Say nothing yet, Victoria. Let me handle this matter, and see what Buckley wants. It may have nothing to do with Michael."

"Very well. I left the letter on the library table. My memory is getting terrible these days. Tell Simms that Michael must bring Captain Buckley with him for dinner. I want to meet this adopted son of John Warbeck."

14

After leaving her grandmother at the pond, Coral walked across the lawn, entered the house, and stood thoughtfully midway up the staircase.

Contacting Director Rawlings and writing home to Kingscote would raise the ugly issue of deceit, and cause untold upheaval for her parents. If Gem was alive, then some other poor child had died, and someone in the village had done this dastardly thing to make them believe it was Gem. Unearthing the scheme and digging into the motives could mean further risk for everyone. Yet she had an obligation to Gem, and to the truth. She would find him. Whatever the cost.

Jan-Lee had understood the risk involved. That was the reason she had been cautious in making known her suspicions to the family. But had she done so immediately, the problems now facing Coral might have been solved with less heartbreak. As it was, she could not ignore Jan-Lee's letter.

Coral thought of Sir Hugo and the cloisonne box. The letter . . . thankfully she had been wise enough to place it inside her bodice before he entered her room. Had she not done so, he would have found it. *But what am I thinking about my uncle!*

"Perhaps I *am* a trifle overwrought," she mumbled to herself.

The house was silent, the servants busy elsewhere, and she slipped into the library with its towering walls of books, crossing the rose carpet to the door that led into a small office. It was a rigid sort of room, crowded with dark furniture, and the drapes were pulled shut. The smell of sweet tobacco clung to the air.

Coral sat down at the desk and proceeded to write two letters: the first to her father, and the second to Director Rawlings at the East India Company on Leadenhall Street.

A short time later, she heard a soft tread in the outer library, followed by a rustle of paper. She stood, again placing the letters inside her bodice, and walked to the door.

Uncle Hugo stood before the window with his broad back toward her. She best let him know of her presence, but before she could, he seemed to sense that someone stood there, for he turned toward her.

His dark beard always made it difficult for her to judge the expression on his face. There was astute silence, growing more tense by the moment. Then his voice came quietly:

"Were you looking for this, my dear?"

Confused, her eyes dropped to his hand. He held up a torn envelope and a sheet of paper.

"I found it on the library table," he said. "It is from Captain Buckley."

Coral's heart began to pound. The captain! But why would he write a letter to Sir Hugo?

Confused, she said, "*Jace* Buckley?"

Sir Hugo stared at her, as though deep in thought, and when he spoke his voice was surprisingly kind.

"Sit down. Alas, we have another tragedy to be borne."

Another . . .

Her mind jumped to the possibilities of disaster. Jace was dead. His ship had sunk. No! Not if he wrote the letter—"What is it?"

"I fear the adventurous Buckley has been derelict in his duty as captain of the *Madras*. It is something I might have told Michael had I thought him willing to listen."

Derelict in his duty? She envisioned him as he was when they had first met—the precise and disciplined major—and her mind struggled with the conflict her uncle's words brought. She could not conceive of Jace Buckley ever being derelict. What was her uncle saying? What had happened?

"His license should be revoked," Hugo insisted. And as she watched him, bewildered, he ripped up the letter in apparent rage and flung it into the small hearth. "The Devil to pay!"

"Uncle!" She hurried toward him, taking his arm. Dark eyes stared down at her.

"I can only believe the worst."

"The worst?" cried Coral. "About the captain? But why would you need to? Tell me what's wrong!"

"A clear mind is needed to captain a ship," he was saying. "The young scoundrel ought to be hung!"

Coral's icy hand fell from his arm, his rage frightening her.

"Michael is dead," he announced. "He was washed overboard in a storm. The captain was not at his post, but drunk in his cabin."

Coral stared up at her uncle as though she'd not heard a word he had spoken. *Impossible.* Her brother was not dead. No, not Michael too! And Captain Buckley would not have been drunk . . . would he? But what did she know about him, really? The Lord would not take Michael so soon after taking Gem. No. It was not true. Dead? Michael? No.

Coral shook her head. Dark waves rolled over her mind, each sending Sir Hugo farther and farther away. His sharp words seemed to repeat themselves in her mind: *Michael is dead . . . Michael is dead—*

"—he ought to be hung!"

15

The gilded clock in the Long Gallery chimed five times. In the library, Doctor Ethan Boswell watched from the rectangular window as the big man named Seward left Roxbury House, shouldering his way into the waiting coach, which rumbled out of sight into the London fog. He had delivered a detailed report of Michael Kendall's death to Sir Hugo, but at the moment, it was not his cousin's death that disturbed Ethan. It was the letter from Captain Buckley addressed to Coral.

Ethan let the red velvet drape fall into place, and with his jaw set, looked across the library at his uncle.

Sir Hugo sat with his head resting against the winged-back leather chair, staring up at the high ceiling. He drew deeply on the tube connected to the side of a long-necked clay pot. With veiled distaste, Ethan watched him exhale a cloud of dark smoke. Hugo's heavily lidded black eyes came to rest on him. The water pipe used in India, known as a hookah, gurgled as he drew on it again.

Hugo exhaled, then spoke between his teeth: "Never mind Buckley. I shall take care of the matter.

211

Do you have Coral's letter to Rawlings?"

Ethan hesitated. He had no reason to question his uncle's account of the boy's death, but the fact remained that his patient believed otherwise. Accepting the letter Coral had written to the Director of the East India Company on the pretext of delivering it left him feeling uncomfortable.

"I have it," he admitted. "Victoria gave it to me. She wants me to deliver it to Director Rawlings. She supports Coral's decision in this."

Ethan felt his uncle's heavy gaze boring through him.

"Come, come, Ethan. The letter." He held out his hand, a ruby winking in the firelight. "The last thing the family needs is a pack of mercenary jackals prowling about Kingscote sniffing out trouble. Victoria means well but is wrong. The boy is dead."

Ethan went to warm himself at the hearth, where a fire crackled.

His uncle continued. "Did you make that fact clear to Coral before you put her to sleep?"

"She understands the facts. She refuses to believe them."

"She's hallucinating again. As her physician, it is your responsibility to see that she recovers from her delusion."

Ethan's expression hardened. "You can be certain I will do everything in my power to see Coral well." He added, looking at his uncle evenly: "Something else. She insists there was a letter from her ayah, and now it's missing."

"There was no letter in the box. Am I accused of thievery?" he asked sarcastically.

"Assuredly not. She may believe that the child is alive, but she will come out of this unreality soon. Her grief over Michael has worsened matters. Two deaths in so short a time would leave anyone in her frail health somewhat erratic. We must be patient."

Sir Hugo tapped his fingers on the arm of the leather chair and watched him evenly. "Remember one thing, Ethan. The silk dynasty is not in business to adopt Indian orphans. A letter to Rawlings will do little except increase the problems on Kingscote. As her guardian in London, I cannot permit it. The boy is gone. So is Michael. You are right, however. This unfortunate loss can only reinforce her instability. Perhaps if you explain the powders are necessary until her mind accepts reality, she will be more inclined to accept the truth."

Ethan looked away from his uncle to the fire. "I was thinking a letter from Sir Hampton might also help. He saw the child for himself, did he not?"

"A letter? To eliminate *her* doubts, or yours?"

"Of course I do not doubt you. Why should I?"

"Just remember, Ethan. You have as much reason to see Kingscote flourish as I. If you want that research lab on the plantation, you will need a silk heiress for a wife."

Ethan flushed angrily, and he shoved his balled fists into his trouser pockets. "I have more interest in Coral than the finances to start a lab."

"I do not doubt that at all," Hugo soothed. He drew on the hookah, closed his eyes, and leaned his head back.

Ethan watched him coldly, but there was little he could do to thwart his uncle.

"I know Rawlings," Hugo went on. "He has two avid interests: collecting antiques, and meddling in Eastern intrigue. He will try to make something of her overwrought suspicions, and I can't allow that. I must

213

do what is best—not only for Coral but for the silk. The boy was slain by angry Hindus over the Christian adoption. I warned Hampton, but he wouldn't listen. Matters are quiet again now . . . rekindling the ugly incident will stir up flames. Hampton and Elizabeth will insist whoever's to blame be brought to justice."

"Entirely just! Let them hang!" snapped Ethan. "If it was a conspiracy, Sir Hampton does well to seek them out. Killing a child! A despicable act!"

"Must you think as a sentimental fool? Will you have Kingscote a smoking rubble?"

"But surely—"

"Stay out of the cobra's den, Ethan, lest you also be bitten and die!"

Ethan stood rigid, understanding the veiled threat. He stared at his uncle. *Uncle.* . . . There was always some question of his being Sir Hugo's nephew. When a child, Ethan had once overheard the filthy talk of two servants saying he was Hugo's illegitimate off-spring. The idea that Hugo may actually be his father did little to soothe him.

"With Burma invading Assam, the last thing we need is a Hindu mutiny on the plantation," Hugo continued. "If there is another fire, this time the hatch-eries will go up!"

"But if the boy *was* murdered—" Ethan insisted.

"Rubbish. What to us is murder is to them mere religious ritual."

"Them? Who is 'them?' "

"My dear fellow, you know India!" yelled Hugo. "Ghazis, of course! The English may tamper with many things, but India's culture must be left alone. If not, we will have a mutiny on our hands, and the Company will lose all rights to trade. We cannot handle further uprisings instigated by discontented maharajas and holy men. The Company has already crossed swords with Burma. There is trouble with Nepal—Bhutan in Sikkim. The last thing we need is Bengal!"

That his uncle could be ruthless, Ethan knew. He had been a boy when Sir Hugo had first become his guardian. He knew little about his mother. He had a vague recollection of a woman's death, a woman with golden tresses and soft gray eyes.

Soon after that, Hugo had arrived in a carriage and took him away from another young woman who had cursed and spit at him. Hugo had calmly shoved her away from him, and Ethan remembered crying when she landed in the mud.

Hugo had been named his legal guardian by a family barrister. Presently they had come to Roxbury House where his attractiveness, and early interest in medicine, had made him his grandmother's darling, and his uncle's heir.

Sir Hugo was a man driven by his ambitions, but Ethan respected his mind. He told himself that however callous his decisions may appear, it was for the good of the family, and therefore, to contest him was unnecessary. And, Hugo was right about one thing: If Ethan married into the Kendall side of the family, the resources he needed for his research would be available with the stroke of a pen. No longer would he need to please Grandmother Victoria, or Uncle Hugo. He would be in control of his own destiny.

The thought of possessing the freedom to open a lab on Kingscote made his heart pound. After all . . . his passion was unselfish. The long years he had dedicated to medicine, years of utter self-denial, were beneficial to humanity. Think of the thousands suffering from tropical diseases across India and Burma that he could help. Was he not helping Coral now? She would get well and strong. He would see to that! Why should he not cooperate with his uncle? Besides, cousin Coral was a lovely girl and would make a perfect wife.

Ethan's fingers thoughtlessly ran along his gold-colored silk doublet and frilled shirt. The chocolate-brown cravat about his throat was meticulously pressed, as were the fawn-colored jacket and matching trousers.

"Well?"

Ethan came back to the moment. He walked up to where Sir Hugo sat calmly in the chair. The hookah gurgled its disgusting sound again. He reached inside his jacket and removed the letter addressed to Director Rawlings.

"As her physician," stated Hugo, "I am certain you will agree a long stay at the summer house will do medical wonders. Say—two months?"

Ethan's jaw tightened. "Only if I accompany her. She will need close supervision under the powders."

"Of course. My next suggestion."

Ethan handed him the letter.

There came a quick tap on the door, and it opened wide. Grandmother Victoria stood there, her silver hair immaculate, her blue eyes going immediately to Ethan.

"It's Coral. Meg says the poor child is having a most dreadful time. She is crying out in her sleep. I do so detest seeing her this way!"

"Yes, Grandmother. I am on my way to her room now." He glanced at Sir Hugo, who had gone to the hearth and was facing the flames. Ethan's gaze dropped to see the letter curling into white ash.

"I certainly hope so, Ethan," Grandmother said in a half-scolding voice, as though he had been neglecting his duty. "Are you certain this trip into London will not be too much for her after the news of Michael? This relapse is unexpected."

"She's on the medication, Grandmother. She will be getting better soon."

Lady Victoria hesitated. "I was thinking I should accompany her."

Ethan was about to agree when Sir Hugo's steady voice interrupted. "Do not forget your promise to the Duchess of Sandhurst."

"Oh posh! My memory again. Then it appears as if I shall be visiting Sandhurst for a few weeks. She will be offended if I do not."

Her satin skirts rustled stiffly as she turned and left with only a glance toward Sir Hugo's back.

Meg, the upstairs maid, waited nervously on the upper landing, one hand holding the banister, the other tugging at her crisp white dustcap.

She curtsied quickly. "Begging your pardon, Doctor. I know it's near your dinner and all, but I can't seem to waken her from the nightmare."

"The nightmare again?"

"A very bad one, sir!"

The woman hurried to lead the way down the hallway to Coral's room. "She's thrashing about something awful, sir, and her nightclothes are sopping wet. She keeps calling the Indian child, and I didn't know what to say or do, and—"

"Yes, Meg, no need to apologize. I was on my way up anyway. You can go down to the kitchen and have a cup of tea, dear. I will send for you later this evening."

Meg curtsied, her face flushed gratefully. "Yessir, thank you, sir."

Downstairs in the library, Sir Hugo removed a second letter, this one from his jacket. He tore it open and read:

June 20, 1797
Miss Kendall:
I received your letter of inquiry into Michael's death today. I will try to excuse your rude questioning about my loathsome and damnable drinking habits. I understand Michael's death is a grave loss to you. I have some books and the Bible that belonged to him. I could have sent them with Seward, but prefer to give them to you in person, as well as my explanation of what happened that day at sea. I will be sailing to Calcutta on June 22, and wish to speak with you before I sail. If you are willing to see me, and to listen without hurling false accusations, send a message to the Madras *at the East India Docks.*

> *Respectfully,*
> *Captain J. Buckley*

Sir Hugo stared at the letter. So Coral had sent an inquiry.

Hugo intended to leave for the summer house tomorrow. It was best that any relationship with Colonel Warbeck's son be put to a stop before it began.

He dropped the letter onto the glowing coals.

The House on the Strand
July

Was she hallucinating? Coral drifted in and out of sleep in her bedchamber, which faced the London estuary. In the shadows of her room she saw Sir Hugo hovering near her bedstand, arranging her medications.

Coral's head felt swollen and painful, and thinking was too hard . . . she must sleep.

Gem—she tossed restlessly, soaked with sweat. No, she must not think of him now. It would hurt too

218

much in the dark. Everything hurt worse at night. She must get strong! She was a prisoner of her own frailty!

Disjointed thoughts came tumbling through her mind. The family insisted her baby was dead. *He* was alive. It was Michael who was dead—buried at sea.

Coral let out a cry, visualizing fish with jagged teeth eating his flesh. No godly burial for her beloved brother! He was cast upon the angry sea, his cries for help smothered by dark brine, his clutching hands grasping at seaweed. Jace Buckley did it! He let her brother die. His screams for help went unattended while Jace drank himself into oblivion in his cabin!

Sobbing, Coral drifted in and out of nightmarish sleep. She could sleep for hours, or was it days? She must be alert to think, to plan her return to India, to pray, to fight; yet inevitably she grew weaker and more helpless. Sleep would come, though she fought against the effect of the medicine, and with sleep came the blackest vision of all—

As if akin to the storm blowing in from the London estuary, the nightmare that had plagued Coral during the worst month of her illness in India came sweeping through her soul.

Loss smothered her heart in the humid Indian night. Once more she slipped out from under the mosquito net encircling her bed. The tender soles of her feet brushed against the mat rugs. She floated to the open verandah. Humid darkness no longer surrounded her. It was dawn.

She leaned over the rail where the emerald lawn ran down to the Brahmaputra River. The clear lemon light touched the quiet water where the wooden barges were being loaded with raw silk. She turned her attention away from the river to the thick jungle, hearing the happy voices of the children working in the hatcheries.

The whimsical voice of a particular child reached out and gripped her heart. Her pulse quickened—Gem! He was in danger! She tried to scream. Her voice became a mocking whisper, "Gem, come back!"

Again she was running as she had in a hundred dreams, searching for the child that remained just ahead but out of sight.

The soft innocent laughter echoed in her soul. Where had he gone to? Why was he hiding from her? Gem never ran away. He always came running to meet her, his soft brown eyes shining under long dark lashes, his shy smile greeting her with the trust between mother and child.

"Gem, my baby, come back!"

She raced down the well-worn path in the direction of the thatch huts belonging to the silk workers.

The workers seemed to scowl at her; then they reached out to stop her. She fought her way through the mob and ran on.

Instinctively she knew that sorrow awaited her behind the thick trees, yet she felt compelled to take the path that she had trod a hundred times in her memory.

At that moment she came to a clearing in the jungle. The stark scene enveloped her in despair. Gone! The huts were all in flames. She whirled to look off in the direction of the Kendall house for help, but it too was burning!

Her hair clung to the sweat on her neck. She stumbled forward, her skirts snagging on thorny bushes. Vines wrapped their tentacles about her ankles to thwart her progress. Foolishly she looked for Gem under a shrub and then behind the charred rubble of a hut. In dismay she dropped to her knees and *gazed up into the heated sky of whitish haze.*

Gem's voice played in the branches of mulberry trees like wind whispering through the leaves, singing the rhyme she had taught him,

"Shepherd, Shepherd, where be your little lambs?
Don't you know the tiger roams the land?"
"Softly, little lamb, softly. I AM always here.
My rod is your protection, My arm will hold you
    near."

Coral bolted awake with a gasp. A dim lamp burned on the table beside her bed, and Ethan leaned over her. "It's all right now, dear, it's all right. It was only a nightmare."

She sank against the damp pillow, struggling for composure. "Oh, Ethan, it is always the same . . . as though Gem is trying to call me—" her voice broke off, her fingers gripping his hand. "Maybe he *is* calling me! I cannot stand thinking about it. Ethan—suppose he thinks I deliberately abandoned him, that I do not love him anymore? Who knows the tormenting thoughts of a child ripped from the safety of his nursery? Suppose they mistreat him, suppose—"

"Coral." His voice was firm, sounding a warning.

She took in a deep breath, exhaling slowly, as he had taught her to do.

After a moment, she relaxed a little. She thought of the letter she had given to Simms to deliver to the *Madras*. Had Captain Buckley received it?

"H-has any letter come for me?"

Ethan smiled. "You know it takes five months for mail to arrive from India. Maybe by Christmas."

"N-nothing else?"

His smile vanished. "Were you expecting a letter

from someone in London?"

"Yes, I wrote Captain Buckley before I left Roxbury House. I wanted to ask him about Michael."

Was it her imagination, or did he grow cool?

"The *Madras* sailed for India in June. This is July. It is no wonder he did not answer you. If he has any conscience at all, he knows guilt over Michael's death."

Coral turned her head away. *July.* Had she been in bed, drugged with medication, for six weeks? She tried to reject her disappointment that Jace Buckley had refused to answer her letter. She would not have thought the cool and restrained major would become a derelict sea captain, but it was known that he was an adventurer who sailed the wicked ports of the East. And did not her mother once tell her that his father had been a pirate?

I will not think of him, she decided, her fingers tightening on Ethan's comforting hand.

"Ethan? The letter to Director Rawlings . . . Grandmother said she gave it to you before we left the estate. Did you deliver it?"

She felt the pressure of his fingers tighten about hers.

"Let's wait and discuss the matter when you are feeling stronger," he said softly.

Coral's eyes pleaded. "No, Ethan, now."

His gaze held tenderness, and she warmed to it. She had felt so alone. Scripture reading had proven impossible, and prayers died on her lips unspoken as sleep took control of her mind.

"I am trying to help you. I want you to trust me, Coral."

She moistened her lips. "I want to trust you. I believe I can."

He smiled. "Then listen to me now with your mind and not your heart."

"I will try."

"If you persist in tormenting yourself about Gem, you may never get well enough to go home to India. Michael's death is wrenching! I understand that, but we must leave them both to God. The matter of the boy is settled."

"It cannot be settled until I get him back. Gem was abducted by the maharaja. Who else could it have been?"

"What raja do you speak of?"

"I—I do not know."

He looked dubious.

"But I am certain!"

"But you do not know who this raja is?"

"No. The major kno—" she stopped. She would not think of him. "Director Rawlings may be able to help me."

He sighed. "The letter was useless. It could only stir up trouble for your father and Kingscote."

"Useless!" She tried to sit up. "But Ethan, I just told you that the director may be able to help."

He studied her with sober gaze, and Coral felt uneasy.

"Gem's body was found two days after his abduction. Sir Hugo told me everything."

"But I told you, Ethan! Jan-Lee doubts that it was his body. The body they found had a scar."

"But there is no letter from this ayah of which you speak."

"I tell you there was a letter! It is missing! It was with the adoption certificate. I put them away before the news about Michael. Uncle Hugo took it, he—"

Coral stopped when Ethan simply patted her

hand. She wanted to wince. He was humoring her. She stiffened. "It should have been there. But I have been too drugged to keep watch—"

His hands held hers tightly, and his eyes were troubled. "Coral. Good heavens! Do you think we are your enemies? You must calm yourself. Listen to me. Even if there was a letter, and your ayah mentioned a scar, it proves nothing."

"It proves the child was not Gem."

"You were ill much of the time during his first years. He could have hurt himself, and you might know nothing about it."

"But Jan-Lee bathed him! She would know. It was she who asked me about the scar. I must write her—"

"Listen. Your mother also cared for him. It could have happened during that time."

Coral paused. She frowned. Her heart sank. She felt the knifelike pain of crushed hopes. "Yes . . . yes."

"Dearest . . . then there were times when the ayah did not have Gem in her care. And more importantly, Hugo was there when they found him."

Sickened, she could only stare at him, clutching the bed covers with trembling fingers. "I remember everything that happened that night—the fire, the sepoy in the nursery, Jan-Lee on the floor—Gem calling for me—" she stopped, aware of his gaze, and it caused her unease.

"Do you remember what happened in the days immediately following his abduction?"

She swallowed, plucking at the cover. "I do not remember them as clearly. I was not well before his abduction, and afterward I had taken to bed." She stopped, her eyes coming to his. "My mother said only that he was found by the river, and I never asked for more details." She thought of the crocodiles. "I was not ready to hear them. I expected the worst."

"Coral, we cannot ignore the fact Hugo was there that night. Do you remember that?"

"Y-yes, he and Margaret were there for the adoption ceremony. And there was something about his meeting with the ruling family at Sibsagar about trouble with Burma."

He looked hopeful. "You are right. He is here in London for the same reason. Uncle is a witness of Gem's death. According to him, your father did tell you the details that night, but even then you refused to listen. It was only then that you became so ill and for weeks were delirious with fever. That could account for your lapse of memory."

Coral felt the cold tentacles of fear. *Had she forgotten? Was there something wrong with her mind?*

Ethan squeezed her hand gently. "Perhaps you have permitted yourself to forget reality because it is too painful."

It cannot be!—Or was it? Was it possible that they had told her, but like Ethan suggested, her memory had rejected reality? Perhaps she had only been too feverish to remember. But the letter from Jan-Lee. She could not have imagined that.

"Ethan, I feel so confused. It is the powders. I do not want to take them again. I—I want to talk to Uncle Hugo. I want to hear what happened to Gem from him."

"Coral, not now. You must rest. You can speak to him in the morning. I will stay beside your bed tonight. Then there will be no nightmares."

"No, *now*, Ethan. I want to talk to him now. I want to hear it from him."

He studied her face, and she knew she must look agitated, even a little wild. He drew in a breath. After a moment, he nodded gravely. "Then you shall. I will ask him to come."

16

Coral sat up, trying to compose her features as the two men entered her chamber a short time later. Suddenly she wished that she had asked Aunt Margaret to come too. Strange . . . she had not seen her aunt in weeks. Was she even at the summer house?

Sir Hugo stood there for a moment in silence, as though analyzing her emotional state. He came to the side of the bed, and she rejected the feeling of being intimidated. His bearded face was masked in shadows. Coral found herself feeling like a child ready to be scolded by a stern father. She must be cautious.

"Good evening, Uncle. I have not seen you in several weeks. Not since we arrived on the Strand."

"I feared to impose upon you, child. I asked Ethan to keep you sedated. Your emotional state is so delicate at present."

She looked at Ethan. Uncle Hugo had asked him to keep her sedated?

Coral showed no alarm under Hugo's steady gaze and made room for him to sit on the bed beside her. She was grateful for one thing: She had known many strong-willed men. Her father, Seward, Michael, and

227

now her uncle. She refused to cower.

"I have not seen Aunt Margaret."

"It was necessary for her to return to the estate soon after we arrived. Your cousin Belinda came home from school and has taken to bed for a week."

"Nothing serious I hope?"

He smiled. "You are the one we are concerned about. Margaret will be here by week's end. She will bring your cousin. You will enjoy that?"

"Yes. I am beginning to feel a prisoner."

"Ah, as soon as you are well, Ethan will have you out at the seasonal balls."

The very thought of waltzing sent her mind spinning and her stomach churning. She must get off the medicine.

"Ethan tells me you wish to discuss the death of Gem. Do you think it wise at the present?" His sober look made her uneasy. Did he expect her to snap like an autumn twig?

"I want to discuss it, Uncle. You must not worry about me. I am no longer grieving over Michael. I know his Christian experience was genuine."

"If your faith enables you to be at peace, so much the better."

She knew that her uncle was not a religious man, but it was disturbing to hear him dismiss the Christian hope as a comforting fancy.

"You feel certain you wish to discuss the death of Gem?" he asked.

The death of Gem. How certain he made it sound. "You—do not recall a letter from Jan-Lee? I kept it inside a red silk pocket. Just before the news arrived about Michael, I put it in a drawer in my room at Roxbury House with the adoption certificate."

He patted her hand. "No, my dear. I have seen no

such letter. I am not in the habit of sneaking about searching through bureau drawers." He smiled, obviously trying to lighten the moment.

"It is missing."

"You are certain it existed?"

Ethan sat down on the other side of the bed and took her hand. The gentle squeeze he gave her was reassuring.

"I am certain."

"Then perhaps it will yet turn up at Roxbury House."

"Uncle—I think Gem may be alive and in danger."

He said nothing but looked knowingly at Ethan.

Coral tensed, looking from one to the other. "I want to hire mercenaries to try to locate him. You will help me? I want to visit Director Rawlings."

Sir Hugo sighed. "Coral, I wish I could help you. I do not want to sound cruel, but I am forced to be blunt in the matter. I know you loved the child, and his loss is a grief to you. Margaret and I understand. So does your grandmother and Ethan. But the boy is gone. He has been dead for over a year. I and your father were both there the night he was found. Try to remember!"

Her heart thudded . . ."You—found him?"

She felt his probing gaze.

"No. It was not I."

Would she have less reason to doubt Gem's death if it had been someone other than Hugo who found him? She wondered if he realized the turmoil of her thoughts.

"Then, who?"

"We were all out looking that night. Your father went in one direction, taking workers with him, and I in another. We arranged to sound an alarm if we found anything. Those in my company had the misfortune of coming upon him by the river."

Coral restrained her emotions. She said, surprised by her calm voice: "You are certain it was Gem?"

"I had no reason to doubt it."

"If *you* did not find his . . . body, then who did?"

"There was confusion among the workers and much carrying on, as one would expect. I believe it was the man named Natine."

Natine. Coral tried to remember what it was about Natine that had upset her the night of the fire.

"Then how—how did you know it was Gem?"

"I saw him. But I did not know for certain; I only knew it was a child of the same age."

"Then there is the possibility—"

"It was Natine who first identified him. But I wanted to be positive. So I sounded the alarm for Hampton."

Her hopes crashed. *Father!*

"Then we all returned to the house to wait for him. Neither I nor Margaret said anything to your mother. Margaret thought it best to let Hampton tell her."

Coral had heard nothing yet to discount Jan-Lee's suspicions.

"But it could have been another child," she insisted. "Whoever abducted Gem did not want us to search for him. What better way than to make us all think he was dead?"

"I would be inclined to agree if Hampton had not identified him."

"My father looked at him?" she asked weakly.

"I, of course, would not take so serious a responsibility upon myself. You do not remember Elizabeth coming to your room and telling you?"

Coral searched her memory. "No," she whispered,

and despite her efforts, successful until now, her voice cracked. "I do not remember, Uncle. I remember nothing but awaking the day of the funeral when she came to my room."

Sir Hugo showed none of his normal constraint or dislike of tears, and his arm went about her shoulders. "There, there, my dear."

How could she forget anything so painful and vivid as this?

"Perhaps there is a solution to this whole matter. Ethan has suggested I write to Hampton. If you have difficulty believing your uncle, surely you will believe your own father."

She did doubt him, but how could she possibly say so?

"It is not that I do not wish to believe you, Uncle, but why do I not remember? And the letter—"

"Ethan suggests it is due to the shock of discovering the sepoy in the process of abducting the boy. He believes it will all come to you in time. Through the dream itself perhaps." He stood. "I will write Hampton tonight. But you must promise to let the matter of Gem rest in silence until you hear from your father."

"Uncle is right," urged Ethan. "You must put all your thoughts into getting well again. If you do, I will try taking you off the powders."

No more medication! She looked at him gratefully. "Yes, I will wait to hear from my father."

"Good," said Sir Hugo, standing. "That should be time enough to see you on your feet and pursuing your education."

When Hugo and Ethan left, Coral lay in her bed, disturbed. Her uncertainty about her uncle was growing, despite her reluctance to mistrust him. *I too shall write Father again . . . just to make sure the first letter was mailed.*

The next few weeks remained difficult ones. True to his promise, Ethan had taken her off the powders, and within a couple of weeks she was strong enough to get out of bed for short periods. Everyone seemed pleased with her progress, and quite unexpectedly Sir Hugo decided they should return to Roxbury House. Coral wisely spoke no more of the missing letter from Jan-Lee or of Gem for fear that her family would think her ill again. Whatever she did in the future, she would need to do on her own. And that meant getting well.

Restricted as she was to the boundaries of the Roxbury estate, Coral was eagerly anticipating the beginning of her studies and getting Gem off her mind.

Now that midsummer was upon them, and her sisters and cousin were home, life picked up its tempo to include a whirlwind of gala balls, dinners, and outings. Marianna was considered too young for the balls but was allowed to attend the picnics. Coral was not strong enough to begin her social debut.

As they sat in the garden having luncheon with Grandmother and Margaret, Coral's sisters and cousin were discussing the upcoming ball to be given by the Duchess of Sandhurst, and Kathleen's amber eyes sparkled. "I am going to design my own ball dress. I showed my idea to Aunt Margaret, and she approves."

"It is quite nice, Kathleen. I think you have talent," Margaret agreed.

Kathleen reached up and gave an unconscious touch to her chestnut-colored hair and exchanged a glance with Grandmother. "And, I am going to stay in London when I graduate Lady Anne's. I shall become a couturiere at the Silk House."

Coral noticed the arched brow of Aunt Margaret as she turned toward her mother. "Will Elizabeth permit Kathleen to stay?"

Grandmother Victoria looked undisturbed. She said in a defensive tone: "With you and Elizabeth in India, the Silk House needs the blood of a Roxbury woman. Kathleen is the eldest. And with her interest in design, it is appropriate that she should stay. I am going to write Elizabeth and Hampton."

"Unlike Coral, I have no desire to go back to India," said Kathleen quickly.

"Oh, but you must, Sissy," breathed Marianna, wide-eyed. "Papa wants the three of us to marry and live on Kingscote."

Marianna, the youngest of the Kendall daughters, had recently turned fifteen. She was the only one to have blue eyes and strawberry hair, taking after Grandmother's side of the family, and her tiny frame and heart-shaped face suggested fragility. Coral knew that her younger sister had not yet been able to get over separation from their mother and that Marianna was anxious to return to Kingscote.

"Papa said you must marry Captain McKay."

Kathleen gave her baby sister a wearied look. "For your information, Father's mind can be changed. Grandmother will see to that."

Cousin Belinda Roxbury frowned, and looked up from her soup to her mother. "I, too, wish to stay in London with Grandmother." She looked at her mother hopefully. "Have you spoken to Father? The idea of marrying Sir George is ghastly! Why, he is all of thirty-five! He shall die before I ever have a gray hair in my locks."

Margaret pushed her plate away, as though her appetite were gone, and took in a small breath. "I said we would not discuss your engagement to Sir George at the luncheon table."

Belinda's dark eyes fell, and she dipped her silver spoon into the mushroom broth without tasting it. "Yes, Mother."

For the first time, Coral noticed how much her cousin looked like her father, Hugo. She had the same striking black hair, the flashing dark eyes, and a certain look that attracted men, despite Margaret's vigil.

Coral knew that her cousin wanted to marry Alex, but engagement to Sir Arlen George was all but certain and would be publicly announced in Calcutta when Sir Hugo and his family returned to the East India Company.

Coral became aware of a pause in conversation and cleared her voice. She had been waiting for this moment.

"Granny V, now that I am well enough to have private tutors in September, I have decided on a music instructor. Anne Peddington's brother, Charles."

"Peddington?" asked Grandmother Victoria as if tasting the name. "Never heard of the man. How did you learn of him?"

"Um . . . at church, Grandmother."

The mention of church did not go over well. The family was strict Anglican, and Coral had been attending a small nonconformist group connected with John Wesley's Methodist movement.

"Anne Peddington's father is a minister. Charles is very gifted with music and has a waiting list for students. But Anne assured me he would make room for me in September."

Grandmother lifted her diamond-studded lorgnette to look at her suspiciously. "I do hope you are not becoming too seriously involved with the Dissenters."

Coral felt the eyes of all those seated at the luncheon table. There was a puzzled look from Cousin Belinda, who vigorously avoided attending any religious services.

"The group is quite respectable, and . . . Ethan has been accompanying me."

Coral felt the prick of her conscience for using Ethan to try to persuade her grandmother. He could do no wrong in Lady Victoria's eyes. Yet this time, even the mention of Ethan did not satisfy her.

"Lady Villary has recommended Mr. Latimer. He teaches her daughter Frances."

"Charles Peddington is an excellent teacher," Coral pressed. "And he knows William Cowper. They sometimes work together on music."

"Cooper?"

"Cowper."

"Am I supposed to know the man?" asked Grandmother. "Goodness knows I have been forgetting things."

"No, you have not met him, but he has a growing reputation as one of London's leading new poets."

"Heavens! Poetry. Not another Charles Wesley?"

"He has met both Wesley brothers, Charles and John. Mr. Cowper works with a minister named John Newton. Mr. Newton wrote 'Amazing Grace' and—"

"Tsk, tsk, dear Coral, these names mean nothing to me. Let us not get carried away with the nonconformists, it only makes for conflict."

"Mr. Newton is an Anglican," said Coral quickly. "He was the rector in Olney."

Cousin Belinda exchanged glances with Kathleen. Coral ignored them. They found her interest in spiritual matters dull and could not understand why she did not put up a terrible fuss about not being allowed to attend the balls. *"You are so pretty, Coral, but you never flirt,"* Cousin Belinda had told her. *"You are no fun at all!"*

With relief, Coral heard Margaret coming to her defense. "Now, Mother, if Mr. Peddington is a good music instructor, what does it matter? As ill as she was, we should be grateful she can even begin her studies. And Elizabeth did make it clear to me when Hugo and I left Kingscote that Coral could choose her own instructors."

Grandmother looked guilty. "Elizabeth told you that? Well, you are right about one thing. We should all be grateful Coral is up and about again. Ethan's done so well by you, Coral. There is new color in your cheeks, and you are gaining your weight back."

"I know you will like Mr. Peddington," said Coral.

"I do doubt that, child, but very well, if you truly want this Dissenter, I shall see to it this afternoon."

Coral breathed a sigh of relief.

17

Roxbury Silk House, London

"Legend tells us that silk was introduced into India by a Chinese princess who smuggled caterpillar eggs into Hotan," Margaret told Coral as they wandered through the salon. Margaret stopped before an intricately embroidered map showing the routes of the silk caravans traveling from the Orient into Persia and Spain, called The Old Silk Road.

"Father insists the caterpillar is native to northern India," said Coral.

Margaret smiled. "He may be right. I suppose we will never know."

Already acquainted with the family history in sericulture, Coral was nevertheless surprised by the elegance of the Silk House with its white-veined marble floors, French chandeliers, and floor-to-ceiling mirrors. The walls of the grand showroom were draped with silk tapestry panels, brocaded with gold on a background of red.

Coral was visiting the Silk House in order to choose the colors and textures for the new garments

Grandmother had promised. While they waited for the head couturier to arrive, she found herself intrigued with the five hundred doll miniatures that were on display in the showroom.

Margaret's eyes flashed with excitement, and a warm blush tinted her flawless skin. "Many of the dolls date back to the rule of King James I. They all wear an original costume designed by Roxbury women."

Margaret took her arm and swept Coral away in the opposite direction. "Wait till you see the silk room."

With rustling skirts, Coral quickened her steps to keep up with her aunt, surprised over the sparkle in her eyes and the joy in her step.

This is her passion, thought Coral. *She loves this facet of silk the way Papa is devoted to the hatcheries.*

As Coral followed after her, stepping through the draperies into the silk room, she paused. The September breeze that came through the open court gently touched the mannequins on display. Cascades of silk quivered and sent a whisper through the atelier belonging to the couturier.

"Soft as a baby's sigh," said Margaret. "Look at these colors. They represent the success of the combined efforts of the family in London and India."

Since Kingscote silk was harvested from muga caterpillars that thrived in the humidity of the Assam valley, it produced a unique, shimmering golden variety, lovely in its natural form. And the silk from the muga bleached and dyed more easily than did the silk from the tussa caterpillar of China.

"Look at this one—coral pink. I think you can guess who Granny V named this after?"

Coral smiled with pleasure and ran her palm

across the slippery variety called satin-silk.

"And these . . ." Margaret swirled the material of a half-dozen new shades. "Sumatra orange, blue-green jade, amber gold, and ivory snow."

"They sound splendid enough to eat for dessert," Coral said with a laugh.

Margaret's eyes shone. "The Duchess of Sandhurst has ordered a new ball dress in each of the new shades for her daughter. Imagine!" She laughed. "Please, do not tell Belinda! She has the notion that being a silk heiress entitles her to keep up with royalty."

Margaret then introduced Coral to the new textures of crisp brocades woven with threads of gold, silk-velvets, paisleys, and taffetas. Coral wandered through the aisles, dazed. "How will I ever decide on the colors for my wardrobe? Why, look—the material looks alive," whispered Coral.

"It is the triangular shape of the silk fibers—see how it reflects the light like prisms?"

Margaret chose a bolt of a golden hue, and draped the silken yards over a mannequin. "Protein gives it a pearly sheen. It moves . . . I know exactly how the material will react to the cut and needle." She ran her fingers beneath it, then let it fall softly.

"Look how perfectly it would match your flaxen tresses and golden coloring!" Margaret sighed with pleasure. "Just being here makes me want to do something with it."

Aunt Margaret held it toward Coral, and then toward the windows, letting the light show its luster. She swirled the yards of shimmering fabric onto the mannequin. "Look how it suggests its own design." She gave the material a few twists and folds, then let it fall. "What do you think?"

Coral was watching Aunt Margaret—she, too, appeared surprisingly beautiful. Was this a reflection of Margaret Roxbury at twenty?

"I think it reminds me of a summer gown in a garden of lilacs," breathed Coral. "Oh, Aunt Margaret! You are so experienced in this. Uncle Hugo should insist you work here for at least part of the year."

The September breeze picked up its intensity, and Margaret closed the French doors. On the way back, she paused to gather up some velvet, touching it to her cheek. Her mood altered like a mist moving across a sunlit sky, and Coral suddenly wished that she had not mentioned Hugo.

"I thought he might stay and run for Parliament. It appears as if we will return to Calcutta sooner than expected. The governor-general has elevated him to a new position in the Company."

Coral masked her surprise. "He must be pleased. I know how much the East India Company means to him. What will his position be?"

Margaret touched the velvet absently. "Hugo is not certain. He will meet with the governor-general when we get back. I confess, Coral, I am frightened."

"Afraid?" Coral said, startled. "Of what, Aunt Margaret? Certainly not of—" She stopped.

Margaret's eyes softened as they came back from her thoughts, and aware once again of Coral, she smiled. "Afraid of Hugo? Is that what you wanted to ask?" she laughed. "No, darling, not in the way you may think. Oh, I know what Grandmother says about being fearful of standing up for my ideas, but it is not so. He has always been gentle with me. Does that surprise you?"

"Well, I . . ." Coral stammered, and did not know what to say. It was obvious from Margaret's smile that she understood her embarrassment.

"Your uncle can be hard. We both know that. He is a complex man and has his dark moods, but I knew that when I married him. Perhaps it is the energy that can drive him to the edge that makes me worry. And then there is Belinda." She turned back to straighten a bolt of silk. "Now that she has graduated Lady Anne's, she will return with us. As you know, her engagement to Sir George will be announced next year. Her disappointment is no secret to anyone, including Sir George."

Coral thought of Belinda's vow to not marry him and wondered how she could possibly thwart Sir Hugo's will. Belinda's hope for a relationship with Alex rested in Margaret's willingness to talk to Hugo. Perhaps this is what worried her—the inevitable conflict that would arise.

Margaret brightened and changed the subject. "Grandmother has not told Kathleen yet, but for her birthday next month she has arranged for your sister to train here with Jacques Robillaird!"

"The head couturier?"

"An exceptional man. He will do your wardrobe."

Coral wondered what her parents would say of Kathleen's interest in design. That Granny V was scheming to keep Kathleen in London came as no surprise, and like her cousin Belinda, Kathleen's engagement to Captain McKay was all but announced. Captain Gavin McKay was from her father's side of the family and was serving in the British military at the Calcutta garrison. Their father took pride in his Scottish ancestry, although he had not been in Scotland since a boy, and he took pleasure in Gavin, the son of his cousin.

Coral understood that it was to Kathleen's benefit that the young Captain McKay was not anxious to marry. Had he wished to do so, he could have pressed the issue of marriage to Hampton, and Kathleen would be forced to marry, since she was a year older than Coral. But Gavin McKay was somewhat of a maverick and seemed more amused with Kathleen's maneuverings to avoid him than he was determined that they marry.

Sometimes Coral thought that Captain McKay was in love with Kathleen but was waiting for her to admit her feelings for him. But Kathleen was adamant. She wanted a career at the Silk House in London. Granny V was just as determined to see that she had her opportunity.

"We will sail for Bengal in May," Aunt Margaret was saying.

Coral felt a tingle of excitement as she realized that she would be free from Uncle Hugo's watchful eye. Her thoughts of Director Rawlings were interrupted by a deep French accent:

"Ah, Madame Roxbury!"

They turned. Coral expected to see a slight man with gray hair. Instead, a robust man in his thirties stood holding a silk ball dress.

"You have come to see, to feel, to smell the silk, that is so?"

"Jacques, how well you know me," Margaret said with a smile. "And to decide on a wardrobe for my niece." She turned to Coral. "This is the man I boasted about in the carriage. May I present Paris couturier Jacques Robillaird, Roxbury's most talented designer. Grandmother 'stole' him from the French Huguenots in Spitafields," she said, speaking of the silk district in London.

Jacques smiled down at Coral. "We Protestants who escaped the fiery stake came to London and brought our knowledge of silk weaving with us."

"For which we are thankful," said Margaret. "Jacques will work with you on your wardrobe, Coral. Jacques—my niece, Lady Coral Kendall."

"Mademoiselle, a pleasure. I have met your sister, Mademoiselle Kathleen."

"Monsieur," Coral greeted with a small curtsy. "I am sure my sister will be pleased to be working with you in the months ahead."

"And now, we have much work to do," he said. "Madame Roxbury has previously told me of your hair and skin coloring. And there must be something grandiose to wear to the Octoberfest Ball given by the Earl and Duchess of Sandhurst."

He drew aside a curtain, and Coral gave a cry of delight.

Fed by her enthusiasm, his hawkish eyes became tender. "I am pleased you approve."

The ball dress was made of billowing watered-jade silk with numerous flounces and gathered up at the left with clusters of amber silk fringe. The shoulders were bare except for tiny puffed sleeves of sheer silk over amber glacé. There were matching gloves that came just below the elbow, a headdress of lace and September mums sprinkled with jade stones, and matching jeweled slippers.

"It is stunning," said Coral, imagining herself at the earl's ball. "It is almost too lovely to wear."

"*You* shall be its life," Jacques replied. "And the rest of your trousseau shall be equally inspiring."

Fall came, was lost to winter winds, and Coral joined in the family festivity of strewing Christmas evergreens and red plaid ribbon along the fireplace mantels, archways, and banisters at Roxbury House.

Outside the rectangular window in the music room, snow flittered onto the holly bushes where red and green peeped through the bed of white.

Today was her last music lesson until after the holiday festival, and she left the window, humming Charles Wesley's Christmas hymn. Charles Peddington was already forty-five minutes late, and she sat down at the piano waiting to hear his carriage. Usually prompt, she attributed his delay to the snow.

Her fingers practiced on the ivory piano keys as she sang the first verse of the hymn:

"Hark! the herald angels sing,
'Glory to the newborn King;
Peace on earth, and mercy mild;
God and sinners reconciled!'
Joyful, all ye nations rise,
Join the triumph of the skies;
With the angelic hosts proclaim,
'Christ is born in Bethlehem.'
Hark! the herald angels sing,
'Glory to the newborn King!' "

Coral's hands fell silent. She sat, her eyes fixed upon the keys . . . remembering Gem. Where was he now? Was he alive?

By now her father had received her inquiry into Uncle Hugo's account of Gem's death, and of Jan-Lee's suspicions, and she expected to hear from Kingscote sometime in late spring. There had been several letters from home since she had sailed from Calcutta in 1796, and a package from Elizabeth. By now the news of Michael's death at sea had arrived on Kingscote. She bowed her head, praying for comfort and strength for her parents, and for Alex.

How would her brother accept this loss? Despite the difference in their personalities, he had been close to Michael.

The rattle of carriage wheels and horse hooves sent Coral to the window. Charles Peddington alighted from the coach, paid the cabby, and came bounding up the steps to the door.

A minute later she heard Simms let him into the hallway, taking his worn cloak and cap, with Charles apologizing for tracking in snow.

Coral smiled to herself as she turned from the window to greet him. Charles seemed anything but a learned music instructor. He was, in fact, but a year her senior, and his youth was couched in boyish exuberance for the music of Wesley, Cowper, and Newton. The singing of hymns was far from being endorsed by the clergy, and still banished by many churches, but Charles insisted the birth of the golden age of hymns would eventually change the worship service.

He came rushing into the music room, out of breath, his brown eyes alert to the fact that he was an hour late. His round face was tinged pink from the biting cold. He brushed back a shock of unruly brown hair from his forehead and shifted his stance, heaving a parcel that he carried under his arm.

"Sorry I am late, Coral . . . it was Anne. You know how she loves books of all sorts. Well," and he heaved a sigh, "my sister came across an old copy of the Olney hymnbook by Newton and Cowper at the book shop, and she wanted me to bring it to you for a Christmas present." Almost shyly he held it out to her. "We wish it were new and leather-bound."

"An Olney hymnbook! Oh, Charles!"

"I fear it is a trifle scarred up."

"As if that makes any difference. I could not have a better gift."

He looked pleased as she took the package from him and brought the book to the piano. "Let's sing!"

She sat down and played several hymns, while Charles joined in. Inevitably she was drawn to "Amazing Grace." When at last they lapsed into reflective quiet, Simms brought hot mulled tea and Christmas cakes. She smiled at Charles and walked to a table where several Christmas packages were wrapped and stacked neatly in a basket. There was a new greatcoat, a hat, and a dashing cape for Charles; a Paris hat, a muff, and a fur-lined cape for Anne; and a number of presents for their rector father: butter cakes, plum and raisin puddings, tins of French chocolates, English toffees, and cookies from the Roxbury kitchen.

"You and Anne are coming to the Christmas Ball next week? Grandmother hopes to meet your father."

Charles blushed. "I am sorry to say he is unable . . . that is, well, our father is somewhat puritanical. He disapproves of balls . . . but," he hastened, "he has no set rule for Anne and me. He has left it up to us, as he has with the meetings at Clapham."

Coral had been attending the meetings at Clapham for several months. The fashionable suburb was three miles outside London where a number of wealthy Dissenters had their homes.

The group of Christian laymen under the godly leadership of their rector, John Venn, was meeting in the great oval library of the banker Henry Thornton.

It was here, amid great books of learning, that Coral's love for the greatest of all books was awakened into something fresh and personal. Coral listened to such great men as the chairman of the East India Company, Charles Grant, speak zealously for the support of missions in the American colonies. And William Wilberforce proved to be not only a fighter for emancipation, but a profound scholar on biblical teaching.

"Are you coming tonight with Doctor Boswell?"

"Ethan is on medical call."

Charles hesitated as though concerned. "I should warn you that Mr. Wilberforce will be there again tonight."

Coral was aware that Wilberforce's debates in Parliament over the abolition of slavery in England had earned Uncle Hugo's disfavor. *"His self-righteous meddling is not to be borne,"* he had stated at the dinner table. While courts had made the ownership of slaves illegal, Wilberforce, and men like John Newton, were striving to try to get Parliament to pass a law that also banned Englishmen from participating in the slave trade.

"Sir Hugo has a meeting at the East India Company."

That night, she went to Clapham in a Roxbury carriage with Charles, and they laughed and sang as the snow flittered down.

The Clapham meetings stressed a practical expression of Christianity, gained not through church liturgy, but fanned to flame through personal involvement in Scripture study and what were now labeled "seasons of intercession."

Although raised an Anglican, and steeped in tradition and ritual, Coral had learned to pray and study the Bible on her own through the many years of illness that had kept her confined to bed. But the meetings in Henry Thornton's library had become a pivotal turning point in her relationship with Christ, and had engendered in her a new awareness of the need for evangelizing the heathen.

It was of interest to Coral that the chairman of

the Company, Charles Grant, attended the meetings, and that the head of the colonial office gave a large amount of aid to the missionaries working in the American colonies. *What would Uncle Hugo think of that?* she wondered with a faint smile.

The meetings stressed the interest of God in the nations. The heathen were people of His desire, not objects of human sympathy; souls whose value to Him was far more costly than silk and rubies, whose liberty from satanic bondage had already been bought by the extreme value of His suffering and death. They were precious trophies to be won and given to the Glorious King.

She thought of Jemani's conversion and wondered how many others on Kingscote might learn of Christ if her father had a small chapel built on the plantation. But then she remembered Rajiv and shuddered. Who would dare come? And at what cost?

Coral decided that the idea of a chapel, like a momentary flame, was best left to flicker and fade.

———

"I cannot understand it," Charles commented to Coral a month later. "Even though God knows I am grateful to teach music, I feel there is something more I want to do." He shrugged. "And yet . . . I see no possibilities."

"Maybe you should enter the ministry, like your father," Coral suggested.

"I have already prayed about that. I feel the need of some work outside England." He smiled ruefully. "I am easily swayed, I fear. I have been reading Brainerd and now have little on my mind but the savages."

"Perhaps you should speak about your concerns with Mr. Wilberforce, or Mr. Thornton."

"I have, and they arranged a meeting with Andrew Fuller of the Baptist Missionary Society. Who knows? Perhaps each of those steps will bring me to a new door."

For Coral, a new door opened a week later, when she learned of a growing Christian movement for children on the London streets called the Sunday School Movement, established in 1780 in some of the free churches.

The Sunday School Movement, made popular by Robert Raikes, not only emphasized the teaching of Scripture to children, but also instruction in reading, writing, and simple arithmetic. The concept had seized her interest at once, and upon mentioning it to Ethan, he offered to take her to observe the meetings.

"Anything, if it brings a smile to your face," he said, and took her gloved hands into his. "Coral, you are looking so well. My hopes for your complete recovery soar like an eagle!"

She smiled up at him. "I have so much to be grateful for, Ethan. The Lord is truly good. And I believe he has blessed you with wise medical knowledge. How good of you to look at Billy Morley today. He is an orphan, you know."

"I did it for you. I like to see you smile."

"There are so many like him on the streets who need a doctor. If only something could be done."

"For me, Coral, it is enough to see you well and strong again. The color is back in your cheeks, and your eyes dance."

She laughed and looped her arm through his as they walked from the small church built in the slums of London. "It is because it is spring."

"So it is." Ethan paused, and stooping to the ground, unexpectedly came up holding a bluebell in his hand.

"For you. The first bluebell of spring. Even the seamy side of London celebrates the good fortune of having Miss Coral Kendall walk her cobbles."

Coral smiled and took the small flower. Her eyes faltered under his intense gaze.

"I am indebted to you, Ethan."

His hand tightened about hers. "You are not well yet. But I will confess my selfishness. I like to hear you say I am the cause behind your smile."

"You are far from being selfish. No one could convince me otherwise."

"I want you to be indebted to me," he said lightly as they walked along toward the carriage.

Coral cast him a glance, laughing, but he was not smiling.

He stopped and turned to gaze down at her, his gray eyes bright and warm in the sunshine.

"I want you in my favor so you will not be able to refuse my marriage proposal. No—do not look alarmed. I am not proposing . . . yet." Ethan smiled. "I am willing to wait as long as necessary. But I will be sorely disappointed if you will not become my betrothed before you return to India."

Coral looked down at the bluebell, feeling the breeze touch her bonnet, and his fingers tighten on her wrist. Betrothed to Ethan . . .

"You know the entire family expects us to marry."

"Yes."

"I will be pleased enough to have you as my wife, Coral. Yet, I want it to be your wish also."

Her voice came with poise: "I will be truthful. Until now I was more concerned with discovering the extent of your Christian faith than anything else."

"And now?"

Coral had to admit Cousin Ethan's behavior was

250

above reproach. She had only to mention a meeting, and if he were not on medical call, he would show up with his carriage. The mention of London waifs being taught in the Sunday school, and the sickness of some of the children, had prompted him to come today to treat them as best he could. *"I have always considered John Wesley's free dispensary in London a godsend,"* he had said. *"There ought to be more."*

Coral had no justification to doubt his Christian faith. And he was stable. Reckless adventure was the furthest thing from his mind. She respected all of this.

"I . . . I am growing fond of you, Ethan."

His hand squeezed hers. "I am more than delighted. I will be wise and say no more now." His voice became cautious. "Then there is no one else?"

"Oh no," Coral rushed to reply.

He smiled. "As long as you say that, I will try to be patient."

"Oh!" A sudden gust sent her blonde curls and bonnet flapping in the wind, and the bluebell in her palm scattered its petals across the dirty London street.

"Come, I will buy you an armful of roses," he said with a laugh and swept her across to the waiting carriage.

Coral, laughing too, glanced back to where the bluebell now lay strewn on the cobbles, and somehow her laughter died.

———

Spring of 1798 came to London with the nodding heads of many bluebells and the delicate scent of lilacs; and Uncle Hugo, Margaret, and Belinda departed on an East Indiaman, bound for Calcutta. Coral stood with Ethan, Grandmother Victoria, and her sisters on the East India dock, watching the ship leaving the harbor. She felt the crisp sea breeze on her face and lifted a gloved hand to wave goodbye.

The outward-bound East India Fleet paraded down the English Channel. The nautical sight took her breath away. She counted at least twenty great three-masters in double line, escorted by proud Royal Navy frigates. The East Indiamen crested through the choppy sea with flags billowing triumphantly from their mastheads, the white canvas swelling out like clouds against the gray-blue sky.

A diverse collection of passengers lined the rail on every ship for a final glimpse of England. Coral could make out soldiers on their way to join the Company's army in Calcutta or Bombay, women seeking husbands, Company officials—like Sir Hugo—and their families taking up a new post, and undoubtedly, adventurers out to seek their fortunes in the East.

"It is the first convoy of the season to be sailing to the Orient," Ethan told her.

Thinking of ships sailing in the Atlantic brought Coral's mind to Michael and inevitably to the derelict young adventurer who was responsible for his death.

"We will see them again in Calcutta," Ethan said in her ear.

Coral looked at him. He was smiling, his gaze sympathetic, and she understood that he had mistaken her gravity for sadness over her family's departure. She smiled at him, then looked back toward the departing ship.

Now I am free to seek Director Rawlings.

18

June 1798

The letter from Sir Hampton arrived in June. Wishing to be alone with its contents, Coral slipped away from the others and went upstairs to her room in Roxbury House.

After shutting the door behind her, Coral tore the envelope open, and with shaking fingers, read her father's scrawling hand:

Kingscote, November 1797
Dearest daughter Coral,

Your mother and I have received a double sorrow. A letter from Captain Buckley arrived last week. By now you also know that Michael was lost at sea. Your mother has taken his death well, yet Alex is most grieved, and we do not know what to do. He has turned uncontrollable, angry with God and man. Remember to pray for him, for this is a sore tribulation for your mother and me.

As for little Gem . . . God rest his soul. It grieves me to the core that Sir Hugo told you the circumstances surrounding his death. He has written ex-

253

plaining the reasons why he was forced to do so. Your mother and I were worried about your health. It seemed best to us at the time to spare you these details.

Yes, your uncle was with me that dreadful night when many from Kingscote were out searching for Gem. As Hugo said, it was Natine who found him washed up from the river. But it was I who identified the little one—what was left of him. He'd been attacked by the crocodiles and was beyond recognition. However, it was Gem, despite your convictions to the contrary. He wore the nightclothes he had on when he was stolen from the nursery, with his name embroidered on the bedshirt, and the tiny gold cross was yet about his neck where you placed it at the time of his adoption. I have enclosed it within this envelope for you to have. Proof, dear daughter, that our heart's wishes cannot change what is the will of the Almighty.

I am sorry to write you these dark words, but you wished to know, and I could not keep them back any longer. I was concerned with shielding you from the ugliness of his death. While there is no evidence as to who is responsible for this wicked deed, I am sure it is the work of someone on Kingscote—or in the village—someone resentful of his Christian adoption.

May God's peace keep your heart. If you love your father, you will not let this loss shroud your future with continued unhappiness and ill health. You must choose to get on with your life, and look forward to marriage with your cousin Ethan, your own children, and a future on Kingscote."

> *Always with love, your father,*
> *Sir Hampton Kendall*

With blurred vision, Coral stared at the tiny gold

cross resting in her palm. Her heart swelled with renewed grief. It seemed only yesterday that she had placed it around Gem's neck.

She walked to the velvet settee and sat down. Attacked by crocodiles . . . beyond recognition. . . . Her mind wrestled with a dim possibility. Was Jan-Lee correct? Was she being unrealistic, groping at illusive bubbles? It dawned on Coral that her father had not mentioned her ayah, or the scar that Coral had inquired about on the heel of the child. Perhaps Jan-Lee would write.

Coral struggled to keep a firm hand on her racing emotions. Suppose the abductors had done this hideous thing to convince Hampton to stop the search? It would be simple enough for them to have exchanged garments.

Her decision came calmly enough and brought new resolve. *I will not be able to get on with the future until the questions about the past are settled in my heart. I owe it not only to Gem, and to myself, but to Ethan.*

At the East India Company, the odor of ink, paper, and lamp oil beset her nostrils as Coral was announced and ushered through the heavy oak door of the director's suite. The first thing that greeted her was a large desk on which lay an open leather case holding a menagerie of exotic safari miniatures: Bengal tigers, cheetahs, monkeys, birds, and even crocodiles. Coral was immediately intrigued.

Sir Edward Rawlings, director of the company, had an oil lamp pulled close to his silver head while looking through a magnifying eyepiece. He was so engrossed that Coral wondered if he knew she was there. She saw that he was evaluating a carved ivory elephant, and what appeared to be its mate sat before him. Were the green eyes made of jade or emerald? Her father had spoken of his old acquaintance as a shrewd man, and the affable English gentleman before her was not what she had expected of Sir Rawlings. In reality, he was a key figure in a network of varied individuals who dappled in the dark and dangerous world of Eastern intrigue. The network was one of several working against each other for various causes. "A delightful surprise to meet a daughter of Hampton."

His voice broke the silence, and startled her. He did not look up but went on with his examination of the elephant. "Do have a chair, Miss Kendall, and tell me what brings you here. I suppose your uncle has sailed for Calcutta by now?"

She did not know why she was surprised that he would mention the departure of Sir Hugo. Naturally, as director of the Company, Rawlings would know what Hugo Roxbury was doing.

"My uncle and his family sailed last week. The governor-general has given him a new position, although I know little of what it is. I believe it has something to do with Burma."

Rawlings looked up for the first time, his sharp gray eyes analyzing her. "You are aware that the king in Assam has signed a treaty with the Company? Thankfully, war has nearly ceased. You say there was an attack on Kingscote a couple of years ago?"

"Yes, that is why I am here. My child was abducted. However, the attackers were not Burmese, but Indian. They were sepoys."

Rawlings looked horrified. "What! Sir Hugo said nothing of the abduction of a European child!"

Coral hastened, "Gem is of Indian blood." Seeing his disinterested expression she added firmly, "He is

256

adopted, possessing the same rights and privileges as any child born into the Kendall family."

A shaggy white brow arched with understanding, but surprise. "I see . . . sepoys abducted him you say?"

"Yes, I entered the nursery as Gem was being carried out onto the verandah . . . I tried to stop the sepoy, but to no avail. I caught a good look at him. He was definitely of East Indian blood. I am here, Mr. Rawlings, because I believe Gem is alive, even though I was informed of his death."

"And what exactly is it you wish of me?"

"My father has spoken of you. I . . . understand you are acquainted with many adventurers in India and Burma. I wish to hire a mercenary to try to discover my son's whereabouts. I want to know for certain if he is alive or . . . dead. And if he is alive I want to get him back. I will pay handsomely for any information."

Rawlings ceased to examine the carved elephant and turned instead to study her, as if pondering whether the determination of such an unworldly young woman should be taken seriously. He looked down, inspected the elephant again for another long moment, then spoke.

"The governor-general in Calcutta has already been in touch with Hampton about the attack on Kingscote. Officially, the Company can do little more, except send word to the raja asking his cooperation in turning up any new information on the boy's abduction. All that, I am sure, has already been taken care of by Hampton."

"And unofficially? Are there not other doors to knock at?"

Rawlings set the elephant aside and scrutinized her again. "Quite . . . but as a friend of Hampton, my dear, I hesitate to involve his young daughter without his prior knowledge. Hampton is not likely to approve of your dabbling in intrigue, and if he wished to use those doors himself, he could."

"He has not done so because he is convinced Gem is dead. My father can be a stubborn man, Mr. Rawlings. He loved my son, and feels his loss. If I can get some glimmer of hope proving Gem is alive . . . I am sure he will listen to me and pursue the matter on his own. But my uncle has convinced him that my determination to find Gem is born of ill health."

"Sir Hugo?"

"Yes."

The older man drummed his fingers, watching her, and Coral was sure she would fail in her endeavor when suddenly he reached for a pen and ink.

"I can give you the name of a man in India who may be able to help you. He knows the area well and has contact with Indian and Burmese spies." He looked up, his sharp eyes meeting hers evenly. "Without apology, I warn you now that this will cost you."

Coral's heart thudded with excitement. "I shall do all I can to meet the price."

"A mercenary risks his life. They do not work cheaply. His contacts also expect to be paid for their risks."

Coral had no money except her allowance while in London, but she pushed that from her mind for the present. "I understand." She must also wait until she arrived back in Calcutta . . . but to have even the name of a mercenary was a start. Suddenly she felt elated. Was the Lord going to answer her prayers after all?

Rawlings folded the paper and placed it in the envelope. "I take it you are not returning to India for a time."

"I am afraid not. There is some schooling to attend, and I am under a physician's care for tropical fever."

"Nasty business, the fever . . . had it myself in younger years." Rawlings paused a moment, studying the young lady before him. "Miss Kendall, I need not tell you to guard this name carefully. Do not banter it about. When you arrive in Calcutta, contact him at the address given in this envelope. I have given you his pseudo name. As I said, it is a risky business."

"Yes, I understand." Coral placed the envelope in her bag with trembling fingers. "Thank you. You have been very helpful, Mr. Rawlings, very kind." She smiled. "My father was right about you. You are a friend, indeed."

Rawlings stood, smiling, and held out his hand. "Let us hope Hampton still thinks so when he discovers just how I have helped his daughter."

———

Besides the Clapham meetings in the library of Henry Thornton, Charles Peddington was also attending what was known as the Exeter Hall group.

Here in the hall in London, where most of the missionary societies held their annual gatherings, the debates were having so strong an influence on the nonconformist community that the government was being swayed to act favorably on missionary matters.

"Especially the notion of white settlers and traders exploiting the natives in the colonies for gain," Charles told Coral.

Charles had just come from one of the meetings, and Coral noticed that he appeared more excited than usual. "I met Andrew Fuller tonight, from the Baptist Missionary Society. He told me about William Carey, and I knew at once that you would be interested."

"William Carey?"

"He sailed to Bengal in 1793. Mr. Fuller has said that Carey intends to translate the Scriptures into every language of India!"

"India!" Coral cried with delight.

"It was Master Carey who first founded the Baptist Missionary Society. Doctor John Thomas came from Calcutta in 1792 and spoke to the group at Kettering, and Master Carey was there. Thomas spoke of the poverty and superstition, and of three brahmins who sent him a letter pleading for help. The Society accepted Doctor John Thomas as their representative. But that is not all. As Thomas spoke to the missionary gathering in Kettering in 1793, he pleaded for others to aid him in the colossal undertaking. It was Master William Carey who stood to his feet and volunteered to go to India with him. Look—I have brought you Master Carey's treatise on world missions. They say it is a literary masterpiece, a charter for the church."

Coral took the pamphlet and read the long and laborious title:

"An Enquiry into the Obligations of Christians to Use Means for the Conversion of Heathen in which the Religious State of the Indifferent Nations of the World, the Success of Former Undertakings, and the Practical Ability of Further Undertakings Are Considered."

"Andrew Fuller was there the night Doctor Thomas spoke at Kettering," Charles went on. "He knows William Carey well. He said that when Carey got up to speak, he vowed right then and there to go with Thomas. Thomas then jumped to his feet, and falling on Master Carey's neck, wept with joy.

"Andrew Fuller said, 'There's a gold mine in India,

but it's as deep as the center of the earth.' He asked, 'Who will venture to explore it?' and Master Carey said, 'I will venture to go down, but you must hold the rope.'"

Coral was moved and sat staring at the pamphlet.

Charles laid a hand on hers. "And Coral—I vowed to the Lord tonight at Exeter Hall."

Her eyes rushed to meet his. "You?" she whispered.

"I do not know what the Lord may have for me, but . . . hearing about India from Andrew Fuller was all I needed to convince me to join my brother Franklin. He is at Calcutta working for the East India Company. I hope to find William Carey and Doctor Thomas."

"Oh, Charles . . . when will you go?"

"Soon. In fact, I am going to tell my father and sister tonight. Franklin has been after me for years to join him. But it was not until talking to Andrew Fuller about Doctor Thomas and Master Carey that I knew what I wanted to do." He took her hand. "Now I know why the Lord brought you into my life, Coral. You have showed me the heart of a nation called India. Through your eyes I have seen her need, her pain, and her beauty. It is where I belong."

Coral's eyes welled with tears.

"And, our friendship can continue after you go home," he said. "I will be able to visit you and your sisters at Kingscote."

In her bedroom, Coral prepared for the night, situating herself beneath the satin covers, pillows fluffed behind her back. With the lantern lit on the stand beside her, she began reading the eighty-seven pages of William Carey's pamphlet—the work of eight years.

Carey's knowledge of world geography, of the racial and religious conditions of the heathen, and of the profound difficulties in bringing the gospel to the world was remarkable. Coral was awed.

Having come from India, she could easily relate to Carey's zeal and compassion for the lost. Her heart knew a sudden excitement as she read how God had filled his mind and soul with the command to go into all the world and proclaim the gospel.

And now he is there, she thought. *He is in* my *India!*

Coral read in the pamphlet that the command to go, and the promise of His companionship, was not simply to the apostolic church, but to all Christians of every generation.

When she finished reading, she laid the pamphlet aside, picked up her King James Bible, and turned to Isaiah 54:2–3, the scripture reference that Charles had written down from William Carey's sermon to the Baptist Missionary Society.

> *Enlarge the place of thy tent, and let them stretch forth the curtains of thine habitations: spare not, lengthen thy cords, and strengthen thy stakes; For thou shalt break forth on the right hand and on the left. . . .*

The words pulsated with holy passion as she imagined Carey preaching on them at the meeting in Nottingham on May 30, 1792. The words of his message became burning coals from the divine altar as though they had been winged her way by seraphim. She visualized not a simple shoe cobbler turned village preacher, but a flaming minister of fire, who with silver sword unsheathed, challenged the slumbering to wakefulness.

"Onward! Outward! Does not His soul thirst for the

thousands, yea millions languishing in Satan's domain, uncontested by His soldiers? Loose the bars, break the chains asunder, proclaim liberty to the captive, offer sight to the spiritually blind; why do you slumber with sword in sheath, and armor set aside? Awake O sleeper!"

For Coral, it was as if God had picked up a quill and began to sketch His will upon her mind. Kingscote sprang up before her, and she saw the hundred Indian children working in the hatcheries.

Sing thou barren who bearest not, break forth and cry thou who travailest not, for the unmarried woman hath many more children than she who hath a husband!

The Scripture verse leaped from the page and demanded her attention.

These, Coral thought, *these children forgotten by all but God are* my *children. It is these that I must go back to Kingscote to save.*

The illusive child she sought in her dream represented more than Gem. The child became many bronze babies; the distant laughter of Gem became the voice of a hundred children calling her to rise up to their need.

Coral's heart pounded. *Oh, Lord, is it possible?* Would He allow her, in the memory of Gem, to reach the untouchables?

But how could I help a hundred children?

Robert Raikes and the Sunday School Movement came to her mind. A school . . . of course. Teach them to read, to write . . . teach them Bible stories and help them to memorize Scripture. What nobler cause is there than this?

Coral remembered how well she had taught Gem. Even though a small child, he had been able to repeat part of John 3:16. If she could teach one, she could teach many. If she could love one child, then God's bountiful love flowing through her could love a hundred, yea a thousand.

Lord, I have prayed so long for guidance . . . is this your Spirit speaking to me? A school? But, how? Coral's pragmatic nature asked.

Her eyes fell on the challenging statement of William Carey that Charles had written across the pamphlet—

"Expect great things from God; Attempt great things for God!"

"Lord, if you make me well enough to go home to Kingscote, I will try to start a school to reach the little children. In your name, I will touch the untouchables."

Late that night, Coral sat at the desk and wrote her mother about William Carey and his work in India. She explained her desire to build a small school on Kingscote and concluded with the verses in Matthew 19:13–14:

> *Then were there brought unto him little children, that he should put his hands on them, and pray: and the disciples rebuked them. But Jesus said, "Suffer little children, and forbid them not, to come unto me; for of such is the kingdom of heaven."*

19

May 17, 1799

Coral's trembling hand held the letter and she slowly sank onto the velvet ottoman in the parlor. Kathleen and Marianna knelt beside her, looking over her shoulder to read the letter for themselves.

Coral struggled to keep her voice calm as she read aloud to her sisters, while Grandmother Victoria stood nearby without moving, her handkerchief knotted in her hand.

Kingscote, October 1798
Daughters,
Circumstances on Kingscote require the three of you to interrupt your stay in London and make arrangements to come home without delay. I will soon be in touch with Seward, who is in Darjeeling. After the death of Michael, he offered his services should I ever need them, and I have no doubt I can depend upon him now. I anticipate his presence in Calcutta to see you safely home by safari. I wrote to Alex in Austria last month. By the time you receive this letter he will have already caught ship and should arrive

at Kingscote ahead of you.

Sir Hugo and Margaret are in Calcutta. They will work with Seward to see to your care. I expect you to be there for some weeks until matters are securely arranged for the journey. Aunt Margaret will explain in detail the circumstances requiring you to come home.

With deepest love, your father,
Sir Hampton Kendall

Coral sat there unable to speak. She heard Marianna's voice catch with emotion. "It is Mama! I know it is! Something has happened to her!"

Grandmother came to her swiftly, and Marianna went into her arms. "Child, we do not know that. Oh, drat that Hampton! He should have explained more! He might have known the tumult he would cause!"

"Surely he has written to you, Grandmother, explaining everything," said Coral. "No doubt Father sent both letters at the same time, but yours somehow got delayed." She added quickly, "That *must* be it."

"This means I will never get to work at the Silk House," cried Kathleen. "I do not want to return to India!" She rushed to her grandmother. "Granny V, do something, anything! You promised me! You said Jacques is going to turn me into the finest couturiere!" Her golden-brown eyes pleaded, and Grandmother looked distraught.

Marianna lifted her heart-shaped face, her cheeks wet. "Sissy, how can you even think about yourself at a time like this?" she accused, her tone suggesting that Kathleen was betraying their mother and father.

"We do not know if anything has happened to

Mama!" Kathleen retorted. "You always think the worst."

"Stop it, both of you," ordered Grandmother Victoria. "Heavens! This is no time to be attacking each other like two cats. Simms!" she called, banging her cane on the floor several times. "Simms!"

"Here, Madame!"

"Call Ethan. Tell him to come at once. I do not care what he is doing, tell him I want him now."

"Yes, Madame."

Coral stood slowly to her feet, still clutching the letter, struggling to keep her fears hidden. "Maybe Kathleen is right. We do not know the circumstances behind Father's request for our return. If . . . if anything did happen to Mother, he would have told us."

"Unless it was like you first said," argued Marianna. "That a letter to Granny V giving details has not arrived yet."

"But there could be an entirely different reason why he has sent for us," insisted Coral.

"Then why did Papa not mention Mother in his letter?"

Coral pushed back her alarm. It would be a long voyage to Calcutta. And Marianna's insecurity would not make it easy. "I do not know . . . but Father has written us other letters without mentioning her."

"That is true," said Grandmother hopefully. "And we did receive a letter from Elizabeth only last month."

"Yes, but she wrote it six months ago," whimpered Marianna.

Coral's attention turned from the others to Kathleen. She had walked to the window and stood with her back toward them. Coral could sympathize with her desire to stay and continue her work with Jacques, but what could she expect Grandmother to do? Their father had made his request clear.

Coral walked up behind her sister, noting the familiar stance that announced one of her difficult moods. Kathleen could be stubborn, and when she was, no one could control her except Grandmother.

"I am sorry, Kathleen," she said softly.

Kathleen made a helpless sound and only shook her head, fingering the brocaded drape and reminding Coral that there was nothing she could say to soothe her disappointment. Still, she tried.

"I understand how disappointed you feel—"

Kathleen turned, her emotions breaking like a flood. "No, you do not. No one understands but Grandmother." Her amber eyes flashed. "No one cares anything about who I am. I am simply expected to do whatever I am told . . . and smile prettily."

Ashamed to release her tears in front of them, Kathleen's jaw clamped, and she brushed past Coral and walked swiftly from the room, banging the door behind her.

Grandmother lowered herself into a chair, her own disappointment etched on her face. "India," she breathed. "Cursed place."

Coral looked up from the letter to meet the piercing blue eyes of her grandmother.

"I want to speak to you later this evening in my room," said Grandmother. "Ethan will be here soon. As much as I deplore doing so, we will need to make immediate arrangements for passage to Calcutta."

"Yes, Granny V."

Grandmother Victoria raised herself to her feet with her walking stick. "This is not the end of matters. If necessary, I shall one day journey to India myself to convince Hampton that Kathleen belongs in London with me."

That evening, Coral entered her grandmother's chambers.

"Ethan has arranged everything," said Coral. "We shall set sail Thursday on the *Red Dragon*."

"Oh dear, so it has come to this moment, has it?"

"Do not cry, Grandmother, I will not be able to bear it if you do." Coral swallowed back the ache in her throat as she embraced the strong-willed, but frail elderly woman, and for a moment they clung to each other.

"I shall miss you, Granny V. Know that I have appreciated everything you have done for me. I will always love you, and I will be back someday . . . wait and see. And Kathleen and Marianna too."

"That is not why I asked you here," came the hushed, tearful voice. "I want you to have this."

Coral's eyes widened as Grandmother Victoria removed from her finger the family signet ring, studded with heavy rubies and diamonds.

"Grandmother, I could not—"

"Nonsense, I will see it with no one else but you. There is Kathleen, of course, but I am leaving her some other things. This ring I want you to have. It has been in the Roxbury family for generations. It is worth a king's ransom."

"Grandmother, I—"

"Here, take it. I have also left you a sizable inheritance in my will. Say nothing to the others."

"But Granny V—"

"Hush." Her eyes twinkled mischievously. "I shudder to think of Sir Hugo's reaction, however . . . I am certain you can use this more than the others."

Coral was moved by her grandmother's trust. She enclosed the family ring in her palm, her eyes moist. "Thank you. Perhaps someday I shall bring Gem here to Roxbury House."

Grandmother searched her face, then smiled knowingly. "You went to see Director Rawlings?"

Coral's eyes glimmered with determination. "Yes. I am going to hire someone to search for Gem."

"A word of advice: Say nothing about this to the other members of the family, especially your uncle Hugo."

"I do not intend to."

"Listen, my child, if you change your mind about India, you can always come home to Roxbury House. . . . which reminds me, Ethan is disappointed you are leaving. Do you not think you should settle matters between the two of you first?"

"I—I cannot, Granny V. I have other plans that are more pressing now." Coral hastened, "I'm sure Ethan understands. He has said he is willing to wait."

Grandmother looked dubious. "What plans do you speak of?"

Coral took her grandmother's hand into her own. "A Christian school on Kingscote for the Indian children," she stated quietly.

Grandmother said nothing for a minute and only stared into Coral's eyes. Then a sigh escaped her lips. "In memory of the boy? Well, you will not likely get the family's support, but I can see that the notion means a great deal to you. You are quite independent when it comes to planning your future. But Hampton and Elizabeth will have something to say about it. Tsk! Enough said. If they agree, I too, will support you. And if you find this Indian child—I want to see him."

Coral threw her arms about her, laughing and crying all at once. "I knew I could depend on you! May God make it so, Grandmother."

20

Calcutta, India
October 1799

Jace Buckley strode through the bazaar, ignoring the excuses of his Indian friend and financial partner, Gokul. At the moment it looked as if they were out of business.

Gokul, huffing in order to keep up with the purposeful stride, held palms against his rounded belly protruding beneath his white tunic and hurried along.

"But, sahib," he objected, spreading his hands, "it was not my blame! Would I lease the *Madras* to John Company if knowing what their cargo would be?"

Jace ignored him. His chiseled features were set beneath his trimmed beard—which he still intended to get rid of—and his dark blue eyes reflected a hardness contrary to his age. He wore buckskin trousers and a loose-fitting black Indian tunic, with his prized toledo sword belted comfortably around his hips; it was a blade that belonged, one used with skill.

Jace stopped abruptly and stared down at the little man. "We both know what John Company is. You leased *my* ship to China traders, knowing full well what the cargo would be and the risk to the *Madras*."

"Ah, sahib!" Gokul corrected. "Patience, patience. It is *our* ship. We are partners, you and I, is it not so? We are as they say—'compatriots.' " Gokul gave a placating smile, but it died under Jace's narrowed gaze.

"*Our* ship, unfortunately," Jace relented. "But I am the captain."

"The best captain to ever sail the sea!" Gokul quickly agreed, his white teeth gleaming beneath his gray mustache.

Jace strode forward with Gokul hurrying after him. They owned half of the ship; the rest was debt. Gokul's weakness of taking risks to win the bigger prize was always the thorn between them, but this time Jace was furious. Having sold the Moorish heirloom to Rawlings on his last trip to London, he and Seward had invested the money in Darjeeling, intending to give Michael's share to his younger brother, Alex, though the matter had not yet been worked out. He had not seen the younger Kendall son since sailing with Michael. Seward had told him that Alex was in Vienna.

Gokul winced. "Sahib, what was I to do? We had only a dozen rupees left in fund. Payment from the China traders would buy us clipper."

Jace groaned at the thought. "Another run to London and I would have had the finances to pay her off. You botched up everything, Gokul! I just signed on with the Company to sail. Now? Nothing! We do not even *have* a ship."

He did not want to hear the excuses again. Thanks to Gokul, his hard-earned clipper had been leased to scheming smugglers in the John Company. Jace strode ahead. He had arrived in Calcutta that morning from

Darjeeling expecting to meet Seward and to ready the clipper for the voyage to the Spice Islands. Seward had sent a message from the residence of Sir Hugo Roxbury explaining that he would not be sailing this time. Out of dedication to the Kendall family, he had gone ahead and accepted a temporary position with Sir Hampton to escort his daughters home to Kingscote.

Not that it matters now, Jace thought grimly. *There will be no voyage.* The *Madras* was tied up in harbor at Singapore, impounded by the authorities for carrying a cargo of illegal opium! To free his "first love," Jace had to come up with a great deal of money; money that he and Gokul did not have. Jace feared he may lose the *Madras.*

Gokul scurried after him, nearly colliding with a cart of coconuts. "Wait, sahib!" The golden monkey clinging to his back squealed his displeasure. Goldfish decided to abandon his ride and leap ahead to his master, lightly zipping his way across several carts and onto Jace's back, clutching his black cap.

Gokul stopped breathlessly and threw up his hands, watching until Jace disappeared into the throng. Even Goldfish had turned his back on him. He sighed dejectedly and turned to go back to the small booking office near the harbormaster at the East India dock. Sahib would never forgive him, and did he blame him? It had been a foolish thing to do.

His brows curved downward over eyes the color of midnight. Jace had not yet heard the worst. Burra-sahib Colonel Warbeck had heard about the fate of the *Madras* and was most anxious to use the dilemma to bring his son back under the British military. Warbeck would not be content until his son was back at his side in the uniform of the 21st Light Cavalry. Jace would most likely strangle poor Gokul when he returned to the house they shared in the Chowringhee area and found the letter from Colonel Warbeck.

Gokul sighed. *Nashudani!* he thought of his own actions. Good for nothing!

———

Coral stood with Kathleen and Marianna amid the noisy throng, waiting for Seward to arrive with a dak-ghari. The carriage would bring them to the honorable East India Company, known as Fort William, and to the Roxbury residence of Sir Hugo and Margaret.

The first thing Coral and her sisters did after disembarking the *Red Dragon* was to turn to Seward with worried, questioning faces, their voices interrupting each other:

"Is Mother well?" rushed Coral.

"Is she dead?" quavered Marianna.

"Why did Father not explain why he sent for us?" demanded Kathleen.

"Now, little lassies, of course Miss Elizabeth be alive."

"You see, Miss Pessimist!" Kathleen said to Marianna. "All your fretting during the five-month voyage was a waste."

"But yer dear mother be ill with the fever," continued Seward.

"Oh no," came the echo of alarm.

"Aye, 'tis so. And Mister Hampton, he be wantin' all of his children home on Kingscote."

"Is Alex home now?" asked Coral, hoping her father had her brother's support.

"Aye, he arrived before ye, and he be helping yer father."

The news of her mother coming down with the fever alarmed Coral, and now, as she and her sisters waited for Seward to arrive with the ghari, she wondered just how ill Mother might be. She said nothing to her sisters, but she could not imagine their father insisting they all come home as soon as possible if her health was not seriously deteriorating.

Coral squinted. After growing accustomed to the misty gray of London, the stark white heat and dust of Calcutta was suffocating. The sun glared down, and the crowd of people in the bazaar reminded her of a swarm of locusts. Providing an annoying background hum was the persistent drone of gnats enjoying the overripe mangoes stashed on the cluttered fruit stalls. Everywhere, insects.

Coral smoothed back a stray curl from her face, then felt Marianna's hand on her arm. "Look, Sissy, everything from coconuts to jade and silk." Marianna peered excitedly about the bazaar.

The sight of throngs of people in various costumes identifying their castes was always intriguing to Coral. She was especially interested in the women who covered themselves from head to toe in what was called a *bourka*, a garment with only two slits in the veil to see through.

"At least they do not need to worry about flies," quipped Kathleen, swishing her peacock fan in front of her face. "Oh, where is Seward?" She turned to fix Coral with a scrutinizing look.

Coral saw the apprehension in her sister's face, and guessed that Kathleen noticed the faint shadows reappearing under her eyes. *They must not know how exhausted I feel.*

Kathleen eyed her suspiciously. "How will you manage the safari to Kingscote? Perhaps we should stay in Calcutta with Aunt Margaret until Father himself comes for us."

Coral was not about to delay the journey and forced a bright smile from under her wide-brimmed straw hat.

"Do not worry about me. Why, I could not feel better. Besides, we have several weeks to recuperate before Seward can arrange the safari. I would trust Seward with my life, anywhere."

"And," said Marianna wistfully, "the journey will seem short knowing Mama waits for us."

"It will be dreadful," stated Kathleen wrinkling her nose. "And furthermore—"

Coral was not listening. Her attention was diverted from her sisters to the dusty road where a group of thin walnut-skinned children clothed in soiled loincloths gave up looking for food in the gutters, and gathered near a silver-haired guru seated beneath a large spreading banyan tree.

The bewildered expression on the little faces, the haunted look of hopelessness in their large dark eyes arrested her emotions. The children were listening to the guru's every word, watching his every action.

Coral shielded her eyes and peered across the street. "Look over there. What on earth. . . ?" The guru's cobra now began to sway to the dismal music of its charmer.

There was a cloud of dust, and with it came the sound of squealing children. The squeals were a mixture of fright and pleasure as they gathered closer around the old man and his lethal toy.

"No doubt the guru has convinced them he can talk to animals," said Coral, irritated by the deception.

"Stay out of it, Coral," warned Kathleen. "Seward will be here any minute."

"Wait here," Coral said, her determined voice allowing for no argument.

"Coral Kendall! Come back here this minute!"

Coral ignored Kathleen's warning, pushing her way through the throng.

"Coral!"

Kathleen's protest was buried in the din. Coral stopped before the stall selling *jellabies*, fried sweets made of a honey batter, and handed the man in a dusty white turban several Indian coins, or "pice."

"Jai ram," she greeted the man in Hindi.

He offered a namaste by bringing his palms together to touch his forehead. Coral filled a basket with the goodies and set out toward the children gathered about the guru.

Jace strode purposefully through the bazaar, shouldering his way past the stalls. Somehow he had to come up with the money to free the *Madras*. He would not accept failure.

A black crow swept in front of him and landed uninvited upon a cart of fast-spoiling fruits. With practiced thievery it managed to fly away with a section of juicy mango. Jace's gaze followed the bird to the branch of a large banyan tree across the dirt road. Beneath the branches sat a wrinkled old guru.

The crow promptly dropped its treat into his master's lap.

Jace watched with irony. The guru had trained his crow well—and there were more. At least a dozen perched in the tree. Meanwhile a crowd of children gathered around the holy man. The sight was a familiar one, and Jace was about to walk on when he glimpsed someone passing by that should not have been part of that foul-smelling crowd.

A young English woman, alone. She was wearing a dark blue silk dress with puffed sleeves and white silk ribbons and was holding on to a broad-rimmed straw hat. Her skin was like ivory amidst a sea of black, her mass of golden curls cascading about her shoulders. The vision was balm to a wound, shade from the white-hot sun. And like the tea plantation and his clipper, Jace momentarily savored the thought of possessing the beautiful damsel.

His eyes narrowed a little. Walking to the edge of the street, he lowered his black dusty hat against the glare of heat rising from the ground and strained to see where this vision had evaporated to.

Half-naked children played in the dust, soon joined by an old gray elephant longing for azure waters. Finding none, the lumbering animal contented himself with a shower of dust on his back.

No, the sun had not gotten to his brains, Jace decided. Nor had she melted in the heat. She was real. The woman stood in the midst of the bone-dry road with a basket of goodies on her arm, a fragile contrast to the harsh and brutal background of dust and sweat.

Jace frowned as he followed her gaze to the children. *Do not tell me she is going to hand out treats? She will be mobbed in seconds!*

He glanced about. Where was her father? There was not an Englishman in sight.

By her sympathetic reaction to the children, Jace judged her to have recently arrived from London, fresh from English tea parties. There were many such ladies who came to the Company to join their fathers or to marry. Like the others who came, he supposed that this damsel also felt compelled to hand out treats to the starving children of Calcutta.

Jace smirked. The "blossom" would soon wilt and

retreat to the refuge of the East India Company, sheltering the like-minded wives and daughters of the military. India could not be won so easily.

The old guru sat on a raised earth platform held in place by some stones. His legs were crossed under him, and his rheumy eyes stared ahead, ignoring the sun. His arms lay still at his sides; not a muscle stirred to interrupt his trance, despite the crawling flies. The only clothing he wore was a soiled loincloth, and his bronzed skin was wrinkled, thin, and hardly sufficient to cover his bones. His white hair was long and snarled; a dirty gray beard rested on his sunken chest cavity.

The woman's voice reached Jace through the noisy din about him. He listened intently, for she spoke Bengali as fluently as he did. Strange . . .

"Children, over here! See? Look what miss-sahiba has for you. You would like some, would you not?"

Jace Buckley stood with hands on hips watching. As if she needed to ask! In a moment they would be on her like an army of war ants.

The children had not heard her invitation, so intent were they on the Guru's cobra.

Jace left the stalls and stepped into the road. He moved toward her, pausing a few feet behind.

"Someone needs to warn you that you are asking for trouble."

She whirled. From beneath the large straw hat he felt the impact of bright green eyes under heavy lashes, an alluring face that left little room for his cynical emotions. He paused—

Where have I seen her before? But if he had, she did not recognize him.

He gestured his head toward the basket on her

arm. "Hand out those and you will be mobbed. Where is your father?"

He saw the distinct glimmer of annoyance at the word "father." It amused him.

"I admit the plight of beggars and orphans is unnerving to ladies from London," he continued flatly. Folding his arms across his chest, he scanned her. "But you will get used to it. They all do."

Little of his own feelings at having been an orphan were revealed in his tone. He knew well what it felt like to go days without food. But his armor was in place—where he intended to keep it. Vulnerability was not an asset for survival. He intended to survive, and he was not about to let his guarded emotions suddenly stumble over an alluring face.

Her expression, he noted, suddenly became a mask of anything she might have felt, although a tinge of color had crept into her cheeks. Her eyes tore themselves from his to fix upon Goldfish chattering at her from Jace's shoulder.

"I was born in India, sir. And I do not intend to grow callous to human misery."

He smiled slightly, and a brow shot up. "I stand rebuked for my unsympathetic ways."

She gestured toward the guru. "And he is deceiving the children. They ought to be warned."

Jace realized that there was much more to the fragile blossom than scent. And while the faint dark shadows beneath her eyes said that she might wilt in time, there was something of steel in her convictions. He said calmly, testing her resolve: "Better watch that cobra."

Appearing undisturbed, she turned her head to study the guru. "Obviously," she countered evenly, "it is defanged."

No swooning damsel, this. She also knew the tricks of some of the fakirs. He glanced at her exquisite frock with its ribbons. "You should not wander about alone."

"He is beguiling them. He cannot talk to animals," she said with growing frustration.

"Half the world is deceived."

She stared at him, her lashes narrowing. His mouth moved into a smile. "My apology. Let me put it another way. If you interrupt the guru, you will get nothing for your pains but that trained flock of crows in the tree. See them?"

She glanced up, squinting against the sunlight at a dozen black shadows perched amid the branches of the banyan tree.

"I am not afraid of crows."

Jace did not know what to make of her. He lowered his hat, arched a brow, and unexpectedly turned to walk away, whistling. "Anything you say."

Coral cast a narrowing glance at him over her shoulder as he crossed the street. There was something familiar about him—the way he talked, the way he handled himself. His dress and brash attitude told her that he was an adventurer, but she could not recall having met one while in London, or for that matter, in India. As such, he was a man to avoid.

She noted that he wore an Indian tunic, but an English cap that looked rather arrogant rested jauntily on his dark head. Was he as cynical as he looked? One thing was certain: the man was conceited, she decided. His beard was well-trimmed, and of the latest fashion, and his hair fit the style of a spoiled cavalier. *Like Absalom*, she thought.

Coral watched him stop before one of the stalls, completely ignoring her, and buy some fruit for the golden monkey, which was jumping up and down and doing cartwheels.

Whatever his faults, there was no mistaking the man's knowledge of India. She respected that. So many of those who came from England to serve in the Company knew next to nothing of the heartbeat that belonged to the land and its people.

She dismissed the handsome stranger and turned away. Holding to her hat, Coral walked in the direction of the tree, speaking to the children.

"Stay away from the munshi," she called in Bengali. "He cannot talk to animals. It is a trick."

The children glanced around, puzzled by the voice. "No trick! No, holy man he has ways, you see!"

"It is a trick," she insisted. "The munshi cannot talk to animals."

Coral held out a sweet bread and smiled. Luminous dark eyes widened and grins spread across dirty little faces. A shout went up like the sound of a battle charge, and a surge of midget troops rushed toward her, jumping up and down, pushing at each other to be first, and snatching at the basket. In a moment it was knocked to the dirt at her feet, and they crawled about her like ants. Within seconds the sweet treats were devoured, and the swarming children cried for more.

"Missy-sahiba, missy-sahiba, hungry!"

"No mother! No father!"

Annoyed at losing his audience, the guru raised his head and mumbled something. Suddenly a circle of black crows swooped down from the tree, the breeze from their flapping wings reaching Coral's face. Children's laughter and cries subsided into oppressive silence. Bird claws dug into her hair and pecked at her shoulders. Flapping black wings blinded her vision while deafening caws crashed against her ears. Coral slapped frantically at them, trying to back away.

The vicious whip of a bullet glancing the air scattered the crows as quickly as they had descended.

Coral was still trembling with fright when the adventurer she had shunned propelled her away, leaving the guru with his rheumy eyes fixed north toward the Himalayas.

"Oooh—I feel as if there is bird lice in my hair . . ." Coral reached a trembling hand to straighten her hat. It was missing. She looked back to see the children running off with it. She began plucking the feathers off her silk dress. "He . . . he just made a noise and they came swooping down on me."

"The crows are trained."

"Thank you . . . for shooting your pistol. I . . . ah . . ." she stopped, finding his gaze disconcerting.

"We have met somewhere," he said.

Coral hesitated, reluctant to agree. "I don't believe so," she said, turning away. "Excuse me. I must go now."

"Next time you take on a guru, make sure he does not have a nest of trained cobras instead of crows. They are not always defanged. And you will not have my gallant presence to come to your rescue."

Her eyes dropped to his scabbard, looking for the hidden pistol.

"I will remember that."

"I am certain we have met before. Cadiz?"

"No . . . excuse me . . . I must go—"

"Paris."

She could not help but smile, turning her head away as she did and looking in the direction where she had left her sisters. "I hardly think so. I have never been to Paris."

"A pity. You would fit so well. Where is your father? As I said, you should not be wandering around alone."

"I am not alone, sir."

They were interrupted by an Indian in baggy white trousers who ran up and salaamed.

"I come for you miss-sahiba. Dak-ghari wait now. Follow please? Missies very upset."

"Yes, yes of course." She could imagine how angry Kathleen was. Coral turned to Jace. He watched her, his hat pulled low over his eyes. "Good day, and . . . ah . . . thank you," she said.

"My pleasure."

Jace stood watching until she disappeared with the ghari-wallah into the throng. "Goldfish, I forgot to get her name."

The monkey covered his eyes with his thin furry hands.

"Yes, I quite agree."

21

"Why, being born a silk heiress is positively dangerous," declared Marianna, her strawberry curls bouncing beneath her blue lace bonnet as the ghari jostled down the crowded, dusty street. "Who was that man, Coral? And how could you be so bold as to talk to him like that? If Aunt Margaret finds out, you will be scolded again."

"I do not know his name," admitted Coral, "but he saved me from that pack of crows."

Marianna pressed on. "Granny V said we must be on guard against all manner of fortune-hunting men." Her expression turned dreamy. "We may get as many as a dozen marriage proposals. Just think. We will always wonder whether our husbands married us for love, or silkworms!"

Kathleen made a face. "What a horrid thought . . . competition from a caterpillar . . ."

Marianna sighed wistfully. "I wonder who I shall marry."

"I do not care if I ever marry," announced Kathleen, looking out the ghari window. "In fact, if I were free to do as I wished, I would stay single and be quite content in London working at the Silk House. Granny V has already written Mama and Papa about my return."

Kathleen looked back at her sisters excitedly. "Imagine—Granny V said someday I could oversee the entire Silk House. I may even open a new one in Lyons, France—perhaps I shall go there on my own!"

Marianna's eyes widened. "Why, Sissy, how can you say anything so scandalous? If a girl does not marry and bear children, simply *everyone* gossips about her. How could you endure it?"

"I could bear most anything to oversee the Silk House," said Kathleen, her amber eyes gleaming.

"Your dreams are so strange. All I want is to get married soon, have children, and live happily on Kingscote. But, Sissy—you know Papa will insist that you marry Captain McKay."

"That rogue!"

"He is bound to be at the ball," said Marianna.

"Then I shall avoid him."

Marianna turned an imploring gaze on Coral. "Sissy, what about your ball dress?

"Hmm?" said Coral absently. She had been wondering why Seward had not showed up with the dakghari. The ghari-wallah had explained only that Seward had been intercepted by a sepoy and had gone to see Colonel Warbeck at the garrison.

The mention of the colonel had jarred a memory of something her mother had once told her, that Jace Buckley was the colonel's adopted son. Thinking of him brought a pang of grief as Michael's smiling face flashed across her mind.

"You are not listening!"

Coral turned her head to look at her younger sister. "Can I wear the blue silk ball dress tomorrow night?" begged Marianna. "You said it was a little small for you, and it is so much prettier than my own, and so much more grown-up."

Coral smiled indulgently. "Yes, you can wear it. It will suit you."

"Coral, you spoil Marianna," said Kathleen. "You look so nice in the blue. You are much too generous. I realize Cousin Ethan will not be there, but—"

"But blue is *my* color," pouted Marianna. "And Coral looks good in any color. You said so yourself. So did Jacques."

Coral was no longer listening. Thinking back to their arrival that morning at Diamond Point, she recalled that Seward had manifested little of his usual cheerfulness. She had first thought that his behavior must have something to do with their mother, but now she wondered. Had he been expecting the sepoy? Why would he go to see the colonel?

The ghari turned under the branches of the gold mohur tree at the entrance to the carriageway, and the Roxbury residence came into view.

Double-storied and painted white, it sprawled lazily in the cool shadows of thick trees growing along the bank of the Hooghly River. Coral suddenly felt a rise of pleasure at being back in India.

The familiar cackle of mynahs and the shrill call of peacocks filled the sunny afternoon, flooding her memory with happy thoughts of Kingscote. While in Calcutta, she would see the Indian mercenary about Gem, and in two months or so, Coral would be home on Kingscote, running up the staircase to her mother's bedroom, bringing the needed medication from cousin Ethan.

Between the colonnades on the verandah one could see the harbor and the ships belonging to the traders. Red flagstones encircled the verandah, and purple bougainvillea twined the columns, adding an artist's splash of color against the stark white stone.

The excitement grew as the ghari neared the front entrance. Coral scanned the host of servants who were waiting. Sir Hugo had more servants than good taste allowed, she decided. Each one was dressed in the customary attire: white trousers and long shirts for the male servants, and the women wore their colorful chunnis over straight, ankle-length tunics.

The ghari door opened, and Coral was the first to step down onto the drive. She smiled at the small Indian boy who proudly presented her with a pink parasol. Under her smile, his shy dark eyes faltered downward to gaze at his bare feet.

From the verandah someone called out, "The missy-sahibas have come."

Aunt Margaret and cousin Belinda swept across the lawn in their afternoon dresses, amid the armada of Indian servants carrying parasols. Indian sun was considered the worst of evils to English women. Even their children were not allowed outside without a large hat.

Coral masked her weariness. She felt the familiar wave of the dizziness that continued to plague her. She would not mind staying home tonight and going to bed early, except that she had promised Ann Peddington to deliver a package to Charles, who was now working at Master Carey's mission station. Coral had been told that Charles Peddington would be at the ball because of his brother Franklin's position in Government-House.

Amid embraces and laughter, the barrage of greetings and questions swelled together into a crescendo.

"Did you have a good voyage? Any storms? Oh,

that is quite too bad! But here you are. . . . Coral! How worn you look. I hope this has not been too much for you. . . . Did Ethan see to your medicine before you left? Thank goodness for that. . . ."

Coral walked beside Aunt Margaret as the small entourage made its way toward the shadowed veran- dah. The heat outdoors was left behind as they entered a hall bordering a colonnade. Water trickled over a fountain, and vines with blossoms trailed over the screened roof. The temperature was surprisingly cooler, reminding Coral of Kingscote with its acres of mulberry trees.

Her sisters and cousin climbed the wide flight of stairs toward the bedrooms, talking of the ball and Belinda's upcoming engagement, but Coral lingered to speak with Margaret alone.

"Girls," Margaret called up the stairs. "I under- stand you have much to talk about, but lunch will be served in an hour. Then you must separate for the af- ternoon and nap until the ball tonight." Belinda turned to look down at Coral, her dark eyes flashing with anticipation. "I was explaining that the ball is going to be even more splendid than we thought. Coral! It is going to be a state ball held at Government- House! Father says most everyone is coming, including the military."

As the trio disappeared down the hall, Margaret looked after her daughter, and Coral noticed the trou- bled expression. Cousin Belinda had written that her engagement to Sir Arlen George was to be publicly announced this Christmas holiday at the round of fes- tivities at Barrackpore, despite her best effort to thwart her father's wishes. And Coral suspected that Aunt Margaret was concerned over Belinda's obvious disinterest in Sir George.

"She cannot wait to get your sisters alone to press them about what Alex is doing," said Margaret wearily.

What Alex may have thought of his cousin, Coral did not know. The one woman he did mention was Katarina Fredricks, the daughter of his music instructor in Vienna.

"Elizabeth wrote me several months ago about Alex's interest in a Miss Fredricks."

"Does Belinda know?"

"Yes. He has written Belinda about her, although Belinda claims Alex thinks of her only as a friend. I admit that I am quite concerned. Her engagement is to be announced this Christmas."

Coral knew little of her brother's romantic life while in Vienna. "He has not mentioned Katarina in his letters to me, but then, Alex is closed when it comes to discussing his feelings about marriage."

"I wish Belinda were a little more like you," said Margaret as they climbed slowly up the staircase. "You have always been sober-minded, so much like Elizabeth. I am afraid Belinda takes after me. I, too, was a trifle frivolous at her age."

"I cannot imagine you ever being flirtatious," said Coral in surprise.

"Not exactly flirtatious, but I thought I knew what I wanted in a man, and was determined to have my way, until . . ."

Until what? Coral wondered, but did not press when her aunt said nothing more. Had there been someone else other than Sir Hugo? She reminded herself again that she would exercise great caution when it came to her own marriage.

"She is young," said Coral graciously. "Belinda will settle down once she marries Sir George."

Margaret smiled ruefully. "Belinda is only six months younger than you are. If Alex was not at Kingscote, I could wish to send her home with you."

"I am sure Belinda would find my life unexciting," said Coral with a little smile, thinking of her cousin's busy social life.

"I am not so sure about that. You will stir up a hornets' nest if you insist on your idea of a school for the untouchables."

Coral looked at her with surprise. "Who told you about the school?"

"Elizabeth mentioned it in her recent letter."

"Mother has not even responded to my request yet. I am surprised she would write you about it. What did she say?"

"Very little. I do not think she has told Hampton yet. And now that she is so ill, she is not likely to. I must say, however, that your uncle is upset about the idea of the mission school."

That did not surprise Coral. He had opposed the adoption of Gem and had manifested little sorrow over his abduction. She knew that she must move with caution.

"Granny V thought there were possibilities for the school," said Coral. "I discussed it with her before I left."

Margaret smiled. "Mother would, of course. She has always encouraged young women with conviction. But she is limited in her understanding of India. Especially of the risks involved to the silk enterprise should the natives become offended with the English presence. Hugo is convinced we must keep our religious beliefs to ourselves."

Margaret's brown eyes flickered with uneasiness and she paused on the stairs. "I hope you will reconsider bringing the matter up, especially with Elizabeth so ill, not to mention your own health. I doubt if Ethan will approve of putting yourself at risk."

Coral drew in a breath. Now did not seem the appropriate time to promote her cause. "At the moment, all I want is to get home to Kingscote."

"Yes, I understand your concern for Elizabeth. But your uncle thinks the school is the reason for your return. I told him that he must not be too hasty, but you know Hugo."

Yes, she did know him. Coral tried to smile. "I did not realize my arrival had caused such a stir. One would think my plans for a school would put an end to the East India Company itself."

Margaret smiled. "At times it does appear a tempest in a teapot, as they say, but after the fire on Kingscote the night Gem was abducted, you can understand the family concern. Sericulture is a family enterprise, and anything you wish to do on your own, such as starting a Christian school, will require approval from all of us." She looked at Coral with sympathy. "I understand your loss over Gem. But a school will not fill that void. Marriage, and your own children, will." She laid a hand on Coral's arm. "I hope you will not upset your uncle. He has been difficult to get along with recently. All that trouble in the north with Burma has him on edge."

Coral chose not to reply, although she disagreed with Uncle Hugo's views. Kingscote was owned by the Kendall family, and if her parents permitted her to build a school, Sir Hugo had no right to throw obstacles in her path. *I must leave all this to the Lord,* she thought. *Only He can make a way.*

"I have been thinking about that fire, Aunt Margaret. I believe it was merely a diversion and not intended to destroy the silk hatcheries."

Margaret hesitated. "I thought of that."

Coral looked at her in surprise. Aunt Margaret had never talked much about that night on Kingscote.

"But, Coral, it is best to forget the entire matter. Why stir up more trouble? Anyway, dear, Hugo is concerned that teaching Christianity may bring down a mutiny upon our heads. He fears that even the Company may be put at risk to the zealots if we give them cause to resent our presence."

"Nonsense, Aunt Margaret. He is overreacting."

Margaret chuckled. "Oh, dear. Do not say that to your uncle. He claims the zealots wish to expel the English from India. And after all we have done for India, too."

A slight flush crept up Coral's cheeks. "Some would say that the Company has done precious little except to use the culture to support its financial pursuits."

"Missionaries would say that, of course. The Company insists they are meddlesome extremists. I have not formed an opinion either way."

Coral made no comment as they made their way up the last round of steps, lifting their skirts as they went. The silence grew awkward. The bearer named Pandy—back and head erect, his blue turban spotless—led the way, making certain that he did not outdistance their slow procession. At the landing he turned to wait for them.

"I understand Charles Peddington will be at the ball tonight," Coral said, intentionally changing the subject.

"Peddington? Oh, the young music instructor you had in London."

"I promised to deliver him a package from his sister."

"Perhaps Pandy can deliver it for you."

"I would rather give it to Charles myself. I thought perhaps he might attend the ball, since he has an older brother who works for the governor-general. A Mister Franklin Peddington."

"Franklin! Of course! I had forgotten Charles was his brother. The two men are so different. Then yes, I suppose he will come. Franklin is secretary to the governor-general. An important position. Too bad about Charles," Margaret said as they reached the landing. "I would think that an industrious man like Franklin would speak to his brother about supporting William Carey's work."

"Oh! Then you know of Master Carey?"

"Only indirectly. The Company is concerned about his printing press, although he does have a friend in Governor-General Wellesley, who appointed him to the staff of Fort William College. But most in the Company oppose missionaries. The other day there was a near riot by brahmins because of some sort of leaflet being distributed on the streets of Calcutta. Do you know this missionary?"

"I have read his work on evangelizing the heathen. Charles is supporting his work. But, honestly, I cannot imagine Master Carey deliberately affronting the brahmins. There must be a mistake."

Coral hoped to visit Master Carey and see his work before returning to Kingscote. From Aunt Margaret's reaction, she could see that this would prove difficult without upsetting the family.

"I am certain Master Carey would be wise enough to not hand out printed matter attacking the Hindus," continued Coral. "He has a genuine respect and love for the people and understands the grave difficulties of introducing Christianity in this culture."

"There are those in the Company who say he and the other missionaries should be deported to London."

"Deported! The East India Company has no right to do that."

Margaret gave her a measured look.

"I mean," said Coral, hesitating, "it would not be a just action. William Carey is a Bible translator. As such, he would not be out stirring up the Hindus. That is not his purpose. I know this, because there are a number of Hindus working with him on the Bengali language. They do not feel threatened by his beliefs. Why should the Company?"

"Well, I know little about the translation of the Scriptures, dear, but your uncle insists that it is bound to stir up trouble eventually. And he is not alone in his belief."

Coral said no more. Neither the Kendalls nor the Roxburys were known for their Christian zeal, although they did attend the Anglican church on holidays, at births, and at funerals. The need for the translation of the Scriptures into the Indian languages was not an important priority on their minds. If she had anyone to turn to in the immediate family, it would be her mother. Coral felt tense. Just how ill was her mother?

As they reached the door to Coral's room, Pandy left them. Through the open doorway, the mahogany floor gleamed with polish, and lace curtains fluttered beneath the ceiling fan called a *punkah*. Made of canvas stretched on a wooden frame, it was pulled vigorously by a small shirtless boy in short white pants to make a breeze. She recognized him as the child who had handed her a parasol upon leaving the ghari.

"You can go now, Jay," said Margaret.

Coral smiled at him as he grinned, salaamed, and ran out.

"They are all darlings. Another untouchable . . . they are everywhere." Margaret sighed. "I will send one of the girls to fill the tub and lay out your ball dress." She scanned Coral's face, evidently noticing the fatigue. "I will have your lunch sent up. That way you will have several hours to nap."

"I would like that. I am tired."

Pandy reappeared with a tray bearing a tall glass of cool lemon water. "For Missy," he said.

Coral smiled. "Marvelous, Pandy, thank you."

When he had gone, Margaret lingered at the door. Coral began removing her gloves, anxious for a cool bath.

"Coral, forgive me for having put this on you the moment you arrive, but . . ." She cast her niece a nervous glance.

"No need to apologize," Coral insisted.

"Hugo and I think a great deal of you."

"Oh, Margaret, I know that. You need not explain." Margaret continued to linger as though feeling the need to convince her about Hugo.

"Your uncle has always had an ongoing interest in your education and future. More so than for Kathleen. It may seem we intrude a little too much." She smiled, and the inner tension showed. "He is so hopeful of your marriage to Ethan. That would almost make you his daughter-in-law."

"I realize Uncle Hugo looks on him as a son, but I would rather not discuss my involvement with Ethan now."

"Yes. And Coral, you will not upset your uncle by mentioning your interest in a school for the untouchables? At the moment, politics in India are unsettling; more so than when you left. You will be careful?"

Coral was weary and anxious to rest. She smiled and gave her aunt a kiss on the cheek. "Do not worry. I shall be discreet. For your sake."

Margaret gently touched Coral's cheek with her palm. "I knew I could depend on you. Hugo and I are already strained over Belinda's upcoming engagement. I should hate to make more tension between us by needing to defend your school."

Coral felt uneasy. The last thing she wanted was to cause more trouble in the family.

"Better get some rest now. With such a pretty face there will be a dozen soldiers wishing to dance with you."

Margaret opened the door, but Coral's question stopped her.

"The ghari-wallah told me that Seward went to see Colonel Warbeck. Do you know why?"

Margaret hesitated. "I did not wish to alarm you so soon after the war with Burma, but one of the military wives mentioned that her husband had news of several sepoys arriving last night from the military outpost at Jorhat."

Jorhat was not too many miles from Kingscote.

"Seward went to see the colonel to discover what information the sepoys may have brought."

Coral was suspicious. "I was told that it was the colonel who called for Seward."

"Yes, that may be. John—" she stopped and a tint of color came to her cheeks. "Ah, the colonel will want to make sure the area is safe for your travel. But I would not worry. The ball is still scheduled, so I suspect the news cannot be all that serious. Perhaps another border skirmish with Burma."

Coral had grown up on the northern frontier amid the tension with Burma. It was not unusual to be seated at the breakfast table and hear her father discussing the fighting between soldiers of the Maharajah of Assam and Burmese infiltrators. War had broken out in 1792, and the East India Company had signed a treaty with Assam to protect them. The war was mostly over now, but there were, as her aunt had said, incidents along the border. It was true that life on the silk plantation was a pleasant one; but the Kendalls were under no illusions. Their subculture in India could crumble with slight provocation. She must not allow anything to keep her from getting home.

The door closed behind her. Coral fell across the cool white sheet and sipped the lemon water while listening to the Indian girl fill the tub.

There came a tap on the door, and Marianna tiptoed in. Her strawberry curls framed her small face, now flushed with excitement. She looked around for Coral's trunk.

"Coral, you promised I could wear the indigo."

Coral smiled wearily and pointed toward her trunk. "Yes, you had better hang it up."

"Oh, Coral, thank you. You *are* going, aren't you?"

Coral yawned. "Yes . . . I need to bring Anne's package to Charles Peddington."

"What will you wear?"

"Oh, I do not know . . . maybe the jade."

"You look good in green. It matches your eyes. You can wear my jade earbobs and combs if you like."

Under Marianna's prodding, the Indian girl had opened the trunk, and the shimmering indigo silk was brought out. Marianna embraced the multitude of folds to her cheek.

"I am going to waltz and waltz until the sun comes up!"

Coral watched her younger sister leave the room, anxious to show off her prize.

She swallowed a teaspoon of the bitter medicine that Ethan had prescribed and quickly took a mouthful of the cool lemon drink.

"And you, Miss Coral? So many pretty dresses!"

The girl carefully emptied the trunk, hanging the frocks in the wardrobe.

"Um . . ." said Coral sleepily, setting her glass down on the rattan table beside the bed. "Silk . . . and from a humble caterpillar . . . the ways of God are mysterious and breathtaking." She could hardly keep her eyes open. "I will wear the green."

"Oh, very pretty!"

As the girl shook out the dress and hung it up, Coral watched the breeze from the verandah lift the yards of the skirt and billow it outward. Jacques' design would be lovely, the jade-green reminding her of the soft richness of the tropics. Coral's eyes closed while she imagined hearing the songfest of birds in bright plumage in the jungle around Kingscote . . . she could almost hear the distant rumble of a Bengal tiger . . . and that made her think of a certain golden monkey that she had seen dangling on the back of the handsome adventurer at the bazaar.

22

Stars were white against the ebony sky. The heat remained oppressive even though a light breeze from off the Hooghly River touched his face. Jace was in a reflective mood. He would have his first meeting in almost seven years with the man who had raised him after his father's death—Colonel John Sebastian Warbeck. It promised to be uncomfortable.

"Ye be lookin' like ye did in the old days," Seward commented as they climbed into the rickshaw that would take them to the East India Company. He cocked his head to scan Jace approvingly. "Maybe not quite. Ye be lackin' the uniform."

Having shed his worn buckskin trousers, Jace felt a stranger in the black broadcloth, the spotless white frilled shirt that tightened at the wrists, and the blue sash. His boots were polished, his sword gleamed, and as Seward said, he looked again like the prized son of the burra-sahib, the colonel. Jace had even shaved his beard and cut his hair.

"I will not be staying for the ball," Jace stated, as though Seward intended to chain him there for the night. "I do not like these gatherings. I never did. I am

303

to meet with the colonel. That is all."

Ahead, Jace could see the familiar outline of Fort William, which housed the Company and its large contingency of workers, families, and soldiers. It was built on the river's bank, surrounded by a strong wall with gates. He had been a boy when he first arrived here with Warbeck. The Company had ended up being his home until after his graduation from military school.

As the rickshaw left the outlying districts of Calcutta and entered the fort, the houses of the English and other Europeans came into view—some of them very fine, even extravagant, and boasting lush botanical gardens.

"Old memories stir like ghosts, do they not, lad?" remarked Seward. "I be thinkin' of the time we served together on the frontier under the colonel."

Jace smiled grimly as he followed Seward's gaze. The lamps outside the quarter guard of the 19th Bengal Native Infantry were bright; the sepoy sentries stood guard in red coats and shakos. His own regiment, the 21st Light Cavalry, was still on duty at the outpost in Jorhat on the northern frontier.

The court buildings and jail loomed ominously against the night sky. At the north end of Maidan Square, the lights burned brightly in Government-House and fell softly across the grass and shrubs of the garden. Near the gate pillars, a half-dozen sepoys stood guard, swords at their sides.

Jace watched the affluent symbols of the honorable East India Company pass by, as though regiments on parade. As the adopted son of Colonel Warbeck, he was an heir to its spirit and ambitions, but Jace had shed his uniform and allegiance to the Company to forge his own way. Now, that gate of freedom, through Gokul's rash actions, had been barred shut.

Jace had been born in and of that empire, but still he was not sure that he agreed with the power created by the Company, which had made itself lord of the maharajas. Two centuries had passed since the first envoys had come to Agra and convinced the great Moghul king to let them build a small trading post beside the Bay of Bengal. Now the Company's authority over India had so expanded that the presidency of Bengal alone ran from Calcutta to Assam.

Someday, thought Jace, English control would most likely sweep across Burma and Afghanistan. Today there were independent provinces yet remaining to the rajas; however, most of these states were forbidden to make treaties with each other or with any foreign power.

The Company, which had begun as a humble trading corporation, was now a colonial lord. The governor-general made treaties with maharajas, enforced the peace, sent out its own tax gatherers—and made war from the Bay of Bengal to the borders of Sikkim. The trouble that brought Jace here tonight was in the region of the northeast, and the man who was England's chief representative in India, the governor-general, had unlimited power in India. Jace knew that when he spoke, a formidable army would move in obedience to the supreme authority in England, His Majesty King George.

In fact, the governor-general controlled the troops of the presidencies in Calcutta and Bombay in the south. Some 200,000 Indian sepoys and sowars serving under British officers in regiments controlled by the East India Company moved at his command, as did the king's 15,000 all-British troops.

Jace found his resentment toward the Company an odd thing to define. He owed his survival as a boy to Colonel Warbeck. His military education, his success in the Company—all had been made possible by the colonel. In return, the colonel demanded his dedication to the cause of the Company. For a time Jace had cooperated; he had even told himself that he wanted nothing else but to serve the Company's ambitions. But later he found himself at odds with many of England's goals in India. When he could no longer follow the leadership, he shed his uniform to chart his own course. Now Jace was once again under the colonel's command.

"I see the Government-House be still in the process of completion. A wee bit like Kedleston Hall in Derbyshire, England, do ye not think, lad?"

"It is the habit of an Englishman," said Jace dryly, "to take their home with them wherever they go."

Seward chuckled. "One would think your blood be less than pure English, talkin' that way. Don't forget, I was a friend of yer father when you was still in knee pants. A truer Englishman ye'll not be findin' anywhere, not even in Oxford."

Jace might have smiled at that bit of rhetoric. However infamous his father's reputation as a China trader in John Company, he was said to have been the younger son of a renowned Buckley family in London. Jace had often tried to recall memories of England; yet he could remember only the rough deck of the ship beneath his feet, the smell of tea, spices, and the dialects of strange ports like Cadiz in Spain, or Malaysia in the East. When a boy, Seward had once suggested to him that his mother had been the deceased Lady Anne Wimbleton, whose father had been stationed at the Company in Bombay. At the time Jace had been naive enough to believe it.

Jace turned toward the Hooghly River. In the dark

were the shadowed hulls of ships and the sound of water lapping against wood.

"No use thinkin' of the clipper, lad. Unless ye go along with the colonel and put yer uniform back on, ye won't likely be seein' the beauty again."

Jace knew that. His stepfather was not a man known to be given over to sentiment, even when it came to his son. Colonel Warbeck was as tough and demanding as the empire he helped to rule. He wanted his son back in uniform beside him, and he would not give up until Jace relented.

He would not relent.

Jace interlocked his fingers behind his head and continued to gaze up at a black sky laced with white pearls. "I was remembering the feel of the deck of the *Madras* beneath my feet; the cool foamy spray wetting my face, the salty taste touching my lips, the sound of gulls—"

Seward moaned. "Hush, lad, the sea still pounds its waves in me own blood."

Both the clipper and the lush cool tea plantation in Darjeeling were fast slipping through Jace's fingers. Like the sands in an hourglass filling its world with tiny grains of white, he too would soon find himself buried in the grip of the Company.

Jace fingered the letter from the colonel beneath his jacket. Seward jumped down from the rickshaw, a ruddy man in a battered tricorn hat and buckskin coat, his even white teeth showing in a grin beneath the wide bushy mustache. "Good luck, lad. I be leavin' ye here. I've business with Sir Hugo Roxbury aboot the trek to Kingscote."

Jace watched Seward disappear through the shadows in the direction of the commissioner's office, then he turned his attention back to the great hall of

Government-House. The state ball was under way. He sighed again, and his boots crunched across the gravel. Chinese lanterns were brightly lit along the front verandah, and orchestra music drifted through the open doors and windows. Jace would not stay long; he was in no mood for festivity.

He went up the steps and entered the wide hall. Through the arch he could look into the huge ballroom, its floor recently polished to a glassy sheen. Lights dazzled from the ceiling, chains of flowers and greenery were strung for decoration along the high walls, giving a palatial effect. The guests were already waltzing, and for a moment he watched the blur of swirling ball dresses amid a floral garden of colors, mingling with the spotless dress-uniforms of familiar regiments and fine civilian clothing of the men serving in the governor-general's council. Indian servants, in white turbans and knee-length coats with red sashes, walked about with silver trays. Across the large ballroom, an orchestra sat on an elevated platform and played the popular waltzes from Vienna.

" . . . I say! Our safari after tiger—"

A voice blurred with the drone of others about the room as Jace began to maneuver slowly through the guests. Colonel Warbeck was nowhere in sight. A woman was coming toward him, and he recognized her as the granddaughter of retired officer Henry Tilliton.

"Why, it is Major Buckley, isn't it?" said Mrs. Marcia Tilliton, swishing her fan, her eyes suggesting they waltz. "Conway was remiss in letting us know you were back in Calcutta," she said, her smile turning to a demure pout.

Bowing a little, Jace acknowledged her greeting, all the while wondering how he could escape. At the same time he met the gaze of Miss Cynthia Daws, who flushed with pleasure. She leaned toward the dowager who sat beside her and said something. Immediately, the dowager looked at Jace and beamed, then struggled to her feet.

Jace turned to flee only to find Marcia Tilliton still at his elbow. Just then a young man in the white and scarlet uniform of the 88th came up, tapped his program, and said cheerfully, "By golly! Number three—this waltz is mine, I do believe, Mrs. Tilliton?"

"Oh my, yes, so it is, I had nearly forgotten!" She turned to Jace apologetically.

"My loss," murmured Jace gravely.

He disliked dancing and moved quickly toward the verandah where he could avoid the guests but safely spot the colonel.

It was sultry for October. Usually the weather had begun to cool by now. Not even the light breeze coming through the windows brought much relief. He stepped aside as a couple left the darkened verandah and passed by him on their way toward the dance floor.

His gaze swept the ballroom, searching for the colonel. Then Jace saw her, and paused. Her expression appeared oblivious to the festivities about her. She stood alone, midway up the winding staircase, while ladies made their way up to refresh themselves in one of the guest rooms. She was holding a package, and glancing about as if expecting someone. But of course, she would be.

She was wearing shimmering silk the color of jade, over an enormous billow of crinoline, with three deep flounces at the left side gathered up with white lace. Her golden tresses were swept up into a mass of French curls and decorated with jade combs, and exquisite jade ornaments dangled from dainty ears.

Ah . . . the beautiful damsel he had seen at the bazaar . . . the woman rattled off Bengali like a native and was not shy about confronting a guru and his crows.

Jace studied her appreciatively for a moment, then as her eyes made a full sweep of the ballroom, they passed him, paused, then quickly looked away, only to come back to him with surprise.

Obviously she remembered him from the bazaar, he thought. But no, he had shaved and cut his hair . . . then—? He, too, hesitated. All at once something in her demeanor opened a door from the past, and he remembered.

Kingscote. So, this was the girl of the monsoon who had carried an Indian baby off to the Kendall mansion so many years ago . . . that boy was now dead. How had she accepted the tragedy?

As they stared at each other, remembering, neither making any approach, he thought of the letter she had written to him about Michael. *She believes me guilty of his death.* He noticed an unexpected stiffening of her stance, and a look of coolness masked her features as she quickly turned her head away.

Just then, a young man, slender and somewhat unassuming, walked toward her from the other side of the room.

"Coral! How grand to see you here in Calcutta!"

"Charles!"

Jace watched her talking to the young man she had addressed as Charles, then Jace glanced about for a form he could pretend was his program. He saw a slip of paper on a table and picked it up. Recklessly he filled in her name for the evening. He was bound to get one of them. She was too polite to refuse him a waltz. After all, they had something in common to talk about. Michael was a good beginning.

An Indian servant appeared at his side and whispered, "Captain-sahib? Colonel Warbeck waits for you in the billiard room."

23

Colonel Warbeck stood in spotless black and white, the golden braid of his jacket reflecting the light of a chandelier. With concentrated precision, he leaned over the far end of the billiard table and made a smooth shot. Jace's entrance coincided with the loud smack of the billiard balls that rolled successfully into the various pockets.

"By the cock's eye!" blared General Basil, his shaggy white brows jerking together. His stubby hand, fitted with too many Indian rings, patted his portly belly. "A lucky shot, Colonel!"

Smiling, the colonel looked up to see his adopted son. "Not at all, General. A matter of calculation."

Jace wondered how much calculation had gone into his summons to see the colonel.

The colonel straightened. For an awkward moment, neither of them spoke. Jace was unreadable and tried to ignore the tug within.

A major, whom Jace did not recognize, left his place near the billiard table and came up behind him and closed the doors, shutting out the strains of the waltz.

"Jace," the colonel greeted, and gestured him with a wave of his hand to a winged chair near the open verandah.

He spoke with the voice of an oracle, a tone which Jace had automatically rebelled against in his youth after the easy rearing of his blood father. After military academy, however, he had come to expect the strong and clear commands of the British army.

Jace crossed the faded red carpet toward the cooler verandah, but did not sit. He scanned his father, noting that the years had not changed him, but then why should they? The colonel was too disciplined to change, or to grow flabby and indolent in India's heat.

Looking at his stepfather, Jace shielded his emotions. He could almost believe that they had never parted company, that the time span which had passed between them had not been years, but merely the length of a waltz about the dance floor at one of the many balls or dinners. The only thing missing for Jace was his own uniform.

Colonel John Sebastian Warbeck was a strong, handsome figure in his early forties, taller than Jace and pounds heavier, but solidly built and able to move with alert grace. His eyes were ice blue and glinted as keenly as sunlight on a frozen lake. Jace felt his eyes flicker over him, but they showed nothing.

His own words were abrupt but appropriate to the meeting. "You asked to see me?"

Colonel Warbeck said nothing for a moment, then set his game piece down and walked out onto the verandah. Jace followed, but remained in the shadows behind him. The colonel, holding the rail with large strong hands, gazed across the spacious courtyard where the colored-glass lanterns cast their light through the leaves of the golden mohur trees. Along the Hooghly River the breeze was a trifle more pleasant. Boats wound their way in both directions, their lights shining upon the water to warn of crocodiles. Palms grew thick along the bank, and the music from the orchestra filtered up to them from the ballroom below.

"A tea plantation," he mused. "You are serious about this?"

Jace was somewhat surprised, but he should not have been. Gokul had told him that his father kept informed of his ventures.

"Gokul was born in the area of Darjeeling. His claim of tea growing wild proved accurate. It can be cultivated and looks to be equal to anything grown in China. I intend to make Darjeeling tea a name known in London."

The colonel remained silent for a moment. "Too bad about your partner. A Kendall son, was it not?"

"Yes. Michael. Who told you?"

"Sir Hugo Roxbury. He did not mince words."

Jace gave him a measured look. "Meaning?"

"Only that as Michael's uncle, he finds it disturbing that he was lost aboard your ship."

Jace found his anger rising. He thought again of the letter that the Kendall daughter had written to him before he sailed from London. Had it been Roxbury who suggested to her that he had been drunk?

"Michael was like a brother. I explained what happened to the Kendall family. They have accepted my explanation. Who is Roxbury to question me?"

"It is best if you do not confront him now. He is a powerful man in Calcutta. A friend of the governor-general. There is a younger brother who Roxbury says is bitter toward you."

Jace thought of Alex. *Does he believe me responsible?*

"If Roxbury has anything to say of my behavior as captain of the *Madras,* he can say it to me."

"I did not call you here to question your behavior as captain, any more than I questioned your leadership when you were in the military. I suspect they are both above reproach."

"Thank you," Jace said flatly.

The colonel said nothing for a minute and Jace walked over to the rail.

"Roxbury insists the Kendalls have no interest beyond silk. Why would Michael have been interested in tea?"

"Sir Hampton is a born master of the regal caterpillar, but Michael wanted to branch out on his own."

"It is the way of sons to disown the paths of their fathers. As though disdain wins them their accolade."

Jace knew that he did not speak only of Michael but of himself. "You know how I feel about the Company. We debated the subject before I left, and came to no understanding." He folded his arms. "Why should I not be interested in a tea plantation? The trading routes into the East may become less rich and fat. Instead of the port of Canton, the Company's ships could be loaded with tea grown here in India. Our beloved King George is screaming for new markets."

The colonel smiled unexpectedly. "We will not argue. Tea it is, and I wish you luck."

Jace was taken off guard. Again, he measured his father, who continued to smile. He offered Jace a cheroot. Jace shook his head, and watched the colonel take out his pipe.

"I have a proposition for you," said the colonel.

Caution . . . He is laying a trap, thought Jace.

His father faced him squarely as his hand played with the hilt of his saber.

"I will be brief. Burma is a smoldering coal on a bed of dry wood. The war went well enough for us, but it is my opinion Assam will never be at rest until we enter Rangoon. A recent raid was made on the outpost near Jorhat."

Jace tensed a little. His friend Major Selwyn was now the commander of his old 21st Light Cavalry. Jace also knew the royal family of the King Gaurianath Singh, in Sibsagar, who had ruled Assam during the Burmese war of 1792. Assam was now a princely state. The raja had long been in disagreement with Burma over who owned the territory and had signed a treaty with the Company. Further trouble in the north could also affect Jace's holdings in Darjeeling, a mountainous region near the Himalayas. His personal treaty with the king of Sikkim giving rights to the hill of Darjeeling hung in delicate balance. The colonel was clever enough to understand that.

The colonel bit on the empty pipe. "You knew Major Selwyn?"

Jace's concern mounted. He did. They had gone to military school in London at the same time. The colonel's use of the past tense prepared the way for dark news. "Selwyn took my position when I left the outpost."

"Hmm . . ." the colonel sucked on the pipe. "A good man. Not as precise as you, but dependable for the sensitive position of Jorhat. Matters with Burma have quieted. You understand what could happen if Burmese are to blame for the attack on the outpost?"

War could begin again. "You do not sound as if you think they were involved."

"The dewan insists they were Burmese."

A *dewan* was the chief Indian minister. This one, Jace assumed, served the Maharaja of Assam.

"Roxbury backs him up," said the colonel. "And Major Selwyn was assassinated in the raid. Sorry."

The colonel turned away for a moment. "Roxbury blames Burma. I doubt it. They have denied it. You have friends in Rangoon who serve the ruling warlord. Have you heard anything about an attack on the British?"

"No. And I am inclined to agree with you. Burma is not ready to begin the war again."

"Selwyn's assassination could not have been instigated by Burma."

"That leaves the maharaja . . . or members of his family. Not all agree with his treaty with the Company."

His father's features hardened, and he glanced toward the billiard room. "Or someone closer to home. The question is, for what reason?"

Jace considered. He would not put anything past certain ambitious men in the Company in Calcutta. But what would they gain?

The colonel bit his pipe. "It is the motive that bewilders me. Why would anyone from headquarters want renewed trouble in the north?"

"To further personal aims perhaps."

"Before I can go to the governor-general, I need something I can get my hands on." He looked at him. "I think Major Selwyn discovered something and was silenced for it. I want you to find out what it was. How well do you know the royal family at Sibsagar?"

Jace hesitated. Selwyn's death prompted his interest in the incident, but he remained cautious. He knew his father was determined to involve him.

"The present raja is a clever ruler and a cunning warrior," said Jace. He thought of Rajiv, the husband of Jemani . . . "I knew his nephew. He is dead now. But he has another nephew, a prince—the Rajkumar Sunil."

Jace was not anxious to run into Rajiv's brother, Sunil. It was said by spies that Sunil intended to use a scimitar on his head. Jace had no doubt that he could protect himself, but he was far from desirous to do battle with him.

"Sunil blames me for a raid on a Hindu temple. A jeweled idol of Kali was stolen before I left the outpost. It was my name that was brought to the maharaja," explained Jace.

The colonel appeared alert, as though he might know something that he was not willing to share with Jace at the moment.

"You have heard of the stolen idol?" Jace prodded.

"Hmm . . . word of such matters travels swiftly. One of the soldiers involved in the raid on the outpost was captured. He is Burmese but has suggested the men he fought with were mercenaries, that they did not serve the warlord in Rangoon."

"Paid mercenaries. Interesting. Did he mention anyone hiring them from the Company?"

The colonel measured him. "No. That is why I called for you. He has asked to speak with you about it. He will not cooperate with anyone there."

Jace arched a brow. "He knows me?"

"He said only that he has heard of you in Rangoon."

Jace was silent. He had secret contacts in Burma.

The colonel passed over his silence and went on smoothly, "I expect your friendship with both the royal family and the Burmese warlord may be able to get to the bottom of what is going on. Your Indian shipping partner, Gokul, should also prove helpful since he is from the area. I want this ugly business swept clean before it erupts into another war. We cannot have our outpost attacked at whim and have the murder of our commanding officers go unpunished. If others see that we do nothing, it will open the door for any who wish to see the British out of Bengal."

"Now wait a minute. I did not agree to become involved—"

The colonel interrupted with a smile and a wave of his hand. "There is one other small matter . . . your clipper—the *Madras*, isn't it? You will be pleasantly surprised to learn that she will soon be at anchor in Diamond Harbor."

In Calcutta? My ship?

"Go to Jorhat. Discover the answer to what is going on, and the clipper is yours. Debt free. You will go, of course, in uniform. You will be reinstated as Major."

. . . *Debt free* . . . Jace stared at his father, then said flatly, "This is no less than extortion."

The colonel was undisturbed. He replaced his pipe inside his jacket. "I prefer to call it something different. Say—*confidence* in your military abilities. You have contacts in the Indian world that I do not. Find out what is going on, deliver the culprit behind this plot, and the clipper is yours. You shall soon be raising tea in Darjeeling."

As Jace watched, surprised, the colonel reached inside his jacket, producing a white envelope. He smiled. "The bill of sale. The impound fee is paid, and the charges of opium smuggling have been dropped."

Jace groaned within. He heard the prison bars of military life clanging about him.

The colonel would never be satisfied until his son

made the army his career, and Jace knew it. It was on the tip of his tongue to turn down the offer and walk out.

He bit back the words and for a moment was silent, not trusting his speech. He tried to remind himself that there was a man behind the spotless uniform, his adoptive father, and that the colonel's game of high stakes, however unfair from his vantage point, were played not in a spirit of revenge for his son leaving the military, but to bring him back.

"Major Selwyn was your friend. I would think you would want to discover his assassin and bring him to justice."

The colonel had touched a second chord of response. Along with the *Madras*, the death of Major Selwyn had all but sealed him back in uniform. The colonel's own plot was progressing as planned.

"I do not need to wear the Company's uniform to find out who killed Selwyn. I can do that on my own. In fact, I could do it better."

The colonel affected indifference. "Ah yes, I nearly forgot . . . there is one other small matter. You will also take up command of the post for two years. Use your discretion to execute the governor-general's policy at Jorhat. The arrangements for your travel are already in force. Papers authorizing you to take command of the prisoner will be given to you. Take the Infantry Company of the 16th with you."

So, his father had risked everything on the gamble that he would not be able to resist.

The colonel tapped the white envelope against his palm. There was a slight smile on the bronzed face and a melting of the hard blue glint. "Welcome back, Jace."

Jace looked from his father's face to the white envelope, and in his mind's eye he saw instead the white canvas of the *Madras* billowing in the warm trade winds. He could pay off Gokul for his small share of the clipper. No more John Company, no more hiring her out to pay bills. He envisioned the fair ship docked in the Calcutta harbor, all his own, and ready to haul Darjeeling tea. . . .

Colonel John Warbeck quietly laid the envelope on the rattan table and walked away.

Jace watched the breeze lift the edge of the white envelope. He sighed. *Major Jace Buckley Warbeck, reporting for duty.*

24

Coral was seated on a teakwood ottoman near the entrance of the verandah with her yards of jade silk gathered about her slippers. She sipped from a tall glass of sweet lemon sharbat, finding it cool and tangy. Across from her, Charles Peddington sat in a chair, exuberant over the Scripture commentary that his sister Anne had sent through Coral.

They sat away from the festivities, and Coral hardly noticed the glittering chandelier and the array of waltzing couples moving across the wide polished floor. The strains of the orchestra danced on the warm night air, and mingled with laughter and voices, but it was the surprise of seeing Jace Buckley that still held her attention.

He was in Calcutta! Did she dare question him about Michael? He had not answered her letter, and she could only conclude that he was ashamed.

God demands we forgive others as He forgives us, she thought, troubled. How could she find the strength to forgive a man responsible for her brother's death? *His grace is sufficient,* she told herself, but continued to wrestle with her emotions.

Another thought raced through her mind. Did he know about the abduction of Gem? Questions whizzed like passing arrows in the night. It was inconceivable that Seward had not told him. Her heart thumped. Would he be able to tell her anything about where Gem might be held? But that would mean forgetting about Michael. . . .

Coral had watched the Indian servant call Captain Buckley away from the ballroom where he had entered the billiard room. A discreet inquiry by Charles had given her the information that Colonel Warbeck was meeting there with some military friends. She sat now with a subtle eye on that closed door. Had he recognized her? He must have. Jace Buckley masked his thoughts too well. One thing was certain. He did not look guilty about the past.

"Coral? Are you feeling well? The journey must have been trying for you," said Charles.

Coral rebuked herself for not paying attention, for she really was interested in what he was telling her.

"Yes, you were describing William Carey's translation work at the compound in Serampore." She also noted that Charles looked ill. He had told her that he was leaving to join his brother Franklin in working for Government-House. *He does not look well at all*, she thought.

"I have been battling this wretched disease for two years now . . . and Mister Carey buried a colleague not long ago."

"From the fever?" inquired Coral worriedly, thinking of her mother.

"Afraid so. His name was John Fountain."

"Oh no, not John!"

Charles turned to her with surprise. "You knew him?"

324

"Not well enough, but he was an acquaintance. A fine man. He was to marry Miss Tibbs. I met him at the Mission Society in London. I knew he was going to join Mister Carey. Does Miss Tibbs know?"

"Yes. She arrived with the Marshmans and Mr. Ward, the printer. Mr. Grant also passed away . . . the fever, I think."

"This is sad news for the mission work. Mr. Carey needs every man he can get."

Charles fumbled with his napkin. "Yes. Well, the ways of the Lord are oft past finding out. But I find myself wondering. Are these trials from the Lord that we might learn to trust Him in hard circumstances, or attacks from Satan?"

Coral shivered. "The powers of darkness cannot take the lives of Christians."

"But the warfare can be oppressive. I should tell you the work is not going as well as William expected. So far there are no converts and a great deal of opposition from unlikely sources." Charles lowered his voice. "I speak of the East India Company, even though Governor-General Wellesley is a fair man. But when he retires, the mission will be in a strait. And Mrs. Carey is having a time of it. Her mind hangs in a delicate balance."

Coral saw his strain. She could not help but notice how much he had changed. No longer was he the gentle, boyish music instructor, but nervous and thin. His hand jerked now and then, nearly spilling his glass of sharbat.

"Mrs. Carey was ill again when I left the mission station at Serampore," he said.

"She grows worse?"

"It grows worse indeed. Lack of finances, food, and shelter have all taken their toll."

"But how did it happen? They say she appeared well enough when they left London with her sister Kitty and Doctor Thomas."

"There may have been something troubling her mind all along, and coming to face the tribulations here in India only brought the matter to the surface."

Coral wondered . . . she remembered something her father had once said about "druggings that permanently affect the mind."

"The death of little Peter did not help, and she was ill in the jungle near the Sunderbans before they came to Serampore."

"Peter? A child?" she repeated.

"He died of fever and dysentery . . . he was the brightest of the Carey children. Even at five he could speak very good Bengali. Mrs. Carey's mental faculties broke with his death, and Master Carey was sick then, too. They could not find anyone to bury Peter."

Coral knew that the Hindus would not break caste.

"Mrs. Carey must be kept in her room. Her meals have to be sent up. There are times when the poor woman rants and raves so that nothing can be done to still her."

"How dreadful."

"It is yet another trial for William, but the work goes on."

Mrs. Carey's loss of Peter brought Coral's mind to Gem. Gem had been just three when he was taken from her. She knew the familiar pang in her heart.

"She did not want to come to India," said Charles.

"No wonder she is ill. She's been through so much. How has Master Carey managed?"

"He is a noble man, Coral. Very dedicated to his work, and to India. While his wife is ill in the next room, William is bent busily over his desk laboring on the Bengali translation. It is the sufficient grace of Christ; what else could it be? He is but flesh and blood as we are, yet he plods ahead doggedly."

Charles lifted his glass to drink, and his hand was shaking.

"Is not Serampore a Danish settlement?" Coral asked.

"Yes, and an open door from the Lord. The move down the Hooghly River has secured our lot. Thankfully, William was able to buy two acres of land from the funds he had earned while running the indigo farm in Mudnabutty. Matters have much improved, but new problems arise from the East India Company."

Coral remembered what Aunt Margaret had told her about the Company's resentment of the missionaries.

Charles hesitated as if he did not care to discuss the opposition now that he was to begin working for the Company. "The British authorities are opposed to missionary work of any sort, fearful of offending the brahmins, although Lord Wellesley has allowed some open-air preaching in Calcutta."

"What of the translation work?"

"It proceeds well, now that Mr. Ward has arrived from London, and we have a printing press. It is by the grace of God that Mr. Bie, governor of Serampore, shows favor toward the task, and even attends the Sunday preaching, bringing other friends of the European community. But the British authorities threatened to send the Marshmans and Mr. Ward back to London when they arrived to work with William. It was Governor Bie's intervention that saved them in the end. Thank God for Denmark!"

"I dare say the Company would hinder the work

in the district altogether if they could get by with it," Coral agreed, feeling troubled. "But they cannot do that, can they, Charles?"

"Carey fears anything might happen after the governor-general retires. They have already threatened to close down the printing press."

"But they cannot do that," she insisted.

"They can, indeed. The East India Company is the law in India. They have no jurisdiction in Serampore; it is Dutch controlled. But if they side with France in the war, that will give the Company reason to enter Serampore and claim control over the mission station and what it prints."

"Let us pray that it does not happen."

He looked unhappy. "My work with Franklin will prevent me from helping Master Carey. But Mr. Ward is doing a splendid job, and he has a wonderful relationship with Mr. Carey's boys, especially Felix. He is like a second father." He hesitated. "I should say, I am not working for Franklin but for your uncle, Sir Hugo Roxbury."

Surprised, she said nothing. No wonder Charles appeared so tense. He walked a tightrope, and Indian crocodiles swam the river beneath.

There was silence. Suddenly the festive color of the evening turned drab, the tang of her lemon refreshment tasted flat, a mosquito buzzing about her ear became loud. Seeing Charles give up his work in exchange for a position with Sir Hugo—even if it was for health reasons—was discouraging. No, disappointing. Charles no longer looked like the zealous young man to whom she had waved goodbye when his ship sailed from London. He was sick and defeated. It seemed that the spiritual enemy had won the first battle.

What would the Company's opposition to the mission work mean for William Carey? And what of Sir Hugo's antagonism toward her plans on Kingscote? How could she possibly think that she could stand?

"You look a bit tired, Charles. Maybe you should retire early this evening."

"Yes, so I was thinking." He smiled. "Perhaps we could discuss the work another time. How long will you be staying with your uncle?"

"Not long. Perhaps only two or three weeks. It is important I return home to Kingscote as soon as possible. My mother, as well, is ill. And I wish to see my father."

"About the mission school?"

"Yes . . . and other matters. I have been away for nearly four years, and I am anxious to see my family." Charles's eyes brightened. "Two to three weeks will give you time to visit Master Carey at Serampore. I can show you about before I go, and Mrs. Marshman can give you some sound advice on your school. She runs the Carey school very well indeed."

Coral measured the consequences of Sir Hugo's displeasure against her desire to visit, and decided his scowl must be risked. She hoped to receive portions of Scripture in Hindi to use with the children, especially the Christmas story.

"I would like that, Charles. I will try to arrange it. In a day or two?"

"Let me know. I will send a ghari to pick you up. You will need to take a small boat up the Hooghly to reach us." He stood. "I have not been the best of company tonight, I fear."

"You will feel better in the morning. Just exactly what is your new post in Calcutta?"

"I shall aid my brother Franklin as secretary to

the governor-general. Sir Hugo convinced me that with my health as it is, I was not using my talents to the fullest at Serampore."

"I dare say, any investment in the work of Master Carey is hardly a waste."

"Yes . . . well, we agree there. As for the Company, it is against making proselytes from the religious sects in India. My work will be strictly business."

"Any uprising would threaten the success of trade," said Coral with a trace of sarcasm.

"I am sorry to admit it, but that is exactly the Company's motive. With my health failing at times due to the climate, I decided to accept Sir Hugo's offer. At least I shall work with my brother. In time, when the Carey school grows, I am hoping to teach music there." He paused. "I thought I had made my plans so well. How soon the wind sends them scurrying like dead leaves."

"You sound weary, Charles. Surely the Lord knows the end from the beginning. Our plans are always on hold for His approval. Once you get well again you can always go back to Serampore."

"Your faith encourages me. You are so much like Anne."

"You have done your best, and you are a champion. But me? I have only begun. How can I turn back before I start?" said Coral.

"You will not. I can see the determination in your eyes. Whatever God has for you, Coral, He will see it through to the end. You believe in what you are going to do. That is half the battle."

Charles Peddington was ill, a wounded soldier on the battlefield of the Lord. And Mr. Carey? Even wounded, he continued to plod his course.

"The merchants of London have turned into

greedy lords, caring not for the souls of men but their access to Indian treasure!" she said.

"Do you speak of Kingscote silk when you speak of Indian treasure, my dear?" came the well-modulated voice from behind her.

She saw Charles Peddington flush beneath his tanned cheeks, his gaze fixed on the man who had spoken.

Coral gathered up her skirts and stood, turning to face her uncle.

Sir Hugo Roxbury, swarthy of face and stern of eye, nevertheless smiled down at her. For a moment she thought he would say more, but he changed the subject. "Well, little niece, how pleasant to have you with us in Calcutta!"

"Hello, Uncle."

He gestured his head, with bushy black locks, toward the embarrassed Charles Peddington. "I am pleased to see you two have renewed old friendships. Did I hear you discussing Carey?"

Coral spoke first to alleviate Charles's predicament. "Is it true that translation of the Scriptures into Bengali is not permitted in Calcutta?"

"You need not concern yourself, my dear. I understand Carey is doing well at Serampore under the protective cloak of Governor Bie. I have nothing against the distribution of Scripture to the heathen, but the Company is not here to legislate Western beliefs upon the brahmin."

Western beliefs. . . . Coral wanted to wince.

"The Company is here to trade. We make no apology for that. It is good for England; it is good for the merchants and shippers."

Coral felt affronted. "But is it good for the people?"

He laughed. "The rulers of India want us here. If they did not, they would send us packing. They outnumber us at least ten to one." He placed a strong arm about her shoulders as though he were the protective, indulgent uncle. Even though he was smiling, she found his dark gaze troubling.

"I hope your concern for the Indians does not goad Hampton into risking the silk production. You are quite a young politician, Coral. One would think you would be on the floor waltzing, sending the hearts of young soldiers pounding. Instead you debate Company policy with Charles!"

His veiled attempt to make light of her concerns was typical, and she tried not to let his mockery embarrass her.

"There is such a thing as the practical side to any matter," he went on. "All Europe praises the quality of silk that Hampton is now producing. Soon we shall clothe Napoleon himself!"

Sir Hugo gave a pinch to her chin as though she were a child engaging herself in matters too adult for her reasoning powers. Coral was furious, but only turned her head away.

"My dear, remember, meddling with the beliefs of the Indian people will cause nothing but dissension and riot."

Charles Peddington quickly gathered his books under his arm, looking troubled. "I regret that I must leave early. Good night, Miss Kendall, Sir Hugo." But before he could get away, they were interrupted by Margaret and Belinda.

"There you are, Coral," Margaret said, smiling. "I wondered who had swept you away. Was that not Captain Buckley who arrived a few minutes ago? Why, hullo Charles. Is Franklin about? I do believe he has forgotten his number," she suggested, looking at Belinda's program.

Belinda looked bored, and swished her peacock-feather fan, obviously not thinking of Franklin Peddington, or Sir Arlen George, who was engaged in a discussion with several military gentlemen across the room.

"Good evening, Lady Margaret, Miss Roxbury," Charles acknowledged politely, blushing as Belinda scanned him. "How good to see you both again. Franklin is across the room talking to Dr. Harvey. If you will excuse me, ladies, I shall remind him of his remiss."

Belinda pursed her lips and looked unhappy, but not so much so that she failed to cast a smile at one of the officers walking past. She leaned toward Coral and whispered behind her fan, "Where did Jace go?"

Jace? Was Belinda on a first-name basis with him? Coral recalled how her mother had told her that the colonel and his son were often guests in the Roxbury home. "I do not know," said Coral tonelessly, and turned in time to see Sir Hugo walk toward the handsome figure in uniform who had just entered from the billiard room. The man with a touch of silver at his temples was watching Margaret Roxbury escort her daughter into the ballroom.

"Evening, Colonel," said Sir Hugo. "You have enjoyed your success in getting your son back into the military, I hope?"

The colonel smiled faintly, taking a glass from off a tray as an Indian servant strolled past. "One of my more difficult tasks, Hugo."

So this is the colonel . . . thought Coral curiously, watching him intently from a distance.

"Miss Kendall, I believe this next waltz is mine."

At the resonant voice coming from behind her, Coral turned, surprised. Her gaze confronted the deep blue eyes of Jace Buckley studying her intently.

25

"Good evening, Captain Buckley," she said politely. But as Michael rushed to mind, she felt her cheeks grow warm and was about to excuse herself.

"Your servant, Miss Kendall."

She doubted that, but his words were the pinnacle of chivalry. He offered a precise bow. "I was certain we had met when I saw you at the bazaar . . . but then, it has been over five years."

For a confused moment her mind darted back to that afternoon. The man before her was not the cocky young adventurer whom she had met; and yet . . . beneath the proper bearing, perhaps he was. She recalled the beard, the long hair, the wild, rugged demeanor. No wonder she had not recognized him. He appeared once again as she remembered him at Kingscote: disciplined, a gentleman of the highest order. All that was missing was the silver and black uniform, the impenetrable militaristic facade that shielded— what? A derelict sea captain? It hardly became him and seemed impossible. The words came before she could think to hold them back.

"What other masquerades do you have stored

away in your sea chest, Captain?"

"Surely your imagination can come up with a few things, Miss Kendall. A uniform, the trappings of an Indian guru, a pirate's cudgel, a bottle of rum, perhaps?"

"No. But I did think the monkey on your shoulder rather cute. If you will excuse me—" she tried to brush past.

"I left him with Gokul, much to his displeasure. He was having a tantrum when I left. By the way, you might offer a finishing-school smile. We are being observed by many curious eyes."

Coral gave a casual glance about her. "I doubt if it matters to you what others think."

"It matters to me what you think. I also doubt that you will walk off and leave me standing on the floor alone. You are much too cultured for that, even without Lady Anne's Finishing School."

Yes, he was still the brash young man that she had met years earlier . . . "Perhaps. But I think you are mistaken," she replied demurely.

"About what?"

Coral looked pointedly at the program in his hand. "This waltz. My aunt thought I would be too weary after the journey, so she did not sign me up."

He smiled slightly and tossed the paper aside, meeting her gaze evenly. "What luck. Then I need not share the evening with any other officers."

Coral did everything she could to keep her poise. What good was a finishing school? All *savoir-faire* failed the moment you needed it. "I . . . ah . . . thought I might retire early after a long day's travel."

"I was not drunk the day Michael was lost."

His bluntness took her off guard. Her eyes came reluctantly back to his.

"I will not let you walk away until I explain," he stated.

The waltz was beginning, and Jace offered his hand, his eyes flickering with amused challenge. "You would not refuse, would you? A precocious young lady who fears neither guru nor crows? Whereas, I am completely harmless—and sober. You believe in fairness, of course?"

She *did* want to waltz with him, perhaps a bit more than she would admit even to herself. "Well . . . I suppose . . ."

The lilting strains of the waltz filled the elegant ballroom of Government-House.

If I miss a step I will feel a fool, she thought as they began to move about the dance floor.

"Somehow I thought better of you," he said, one hand gently resting on her back, the other encircling her own petite hand.

Thought better of *her*! Coral's eyes lifted to his. No, there was no amusement to be found in their depths, only challenge. "A change of opinion regarding character is supposed to be my prerogative," she said.

"You wrote me an accusatory letter. A very *nasty* one, actually. Then you refused to see me to let me defend my honor. That is hardly the epitome of fairness. And it is not the memory I had of you from Kingscote."

"But, sir, I did not refuse to see you."

"But, *madam*, you did not respond to my letter."

Letter? Coral lifted her head, then looked away again. "What letter, Captain Buckley?"

"The letter, Miss Kendall, that I sent in reply to yours. I gave it to Seward to deliver to Roxbury House, and he assured me that he did."

"You answered my letter?"

"Of course."

"But—I did not receive it," she said in a small voice. "I was waiting for it, I hoped—" she stopped. Then what had happened to it? And what had happened to Jan-Lee's letter?

"I asked to see you before the *Madras* sailed, to explain about Michael. I do not know where you came up with the idea that I was derelict in my duty, but I find it offensive to everything I believe in."

Coral's step fumbled, her shock showing through in her lack of concentration. "Oh! Excuse me. Did I step on your foot?"

"Think nothing of it. Then you did not receive my letter?"

Coral drew in a small breath as they swirled about the ballroom. Two letters were missing. One from Jan-Lee, the other from Jace. But she was hesitant to tell him so, for fear he would confront her uncle. *I cannot risk Uncle Hugo's wrath, yet.*

"I was ill for some months . . . my grandmother has a faltering memory, and perhaps she forgot to tell me about it."

His expression displayed obvious disbelief. "Let us not fault your grandmother. I think we both know with whom the blame rests. But for the moment, I will let it slip by. I would like to tell you about Michael. We hit a storm off England. One of the worst I have been in. I had him in my grasp . . . but a wave tore us apart. I will never forgive myself for what happened, but I can assure you of one thing. I did not lose him because I was drunk in my cabin. I cannot understand why you would think I was!"

Coral kept her gaze averted. He had tried to save Michael! But naturally he would, since he was with him, and evidently he had not been in his cabin. Her own guilt was sharp. Why had she believed Uncle Hugo? The truth was, she had doubted him, and that was what had motivated her to write the letter. But when he did not answer . . .

She glanced across the ballroom floor toward her uncle. He was still in conversation with Colonel Warbeck. *Why would he benefit from deceiving me?*

Coral tried to remember back to what had happened after the episode in the library with her uncle and could not recall the details clearly. She had vague recollections of the carriage ride to the summer house on the London Strand, followed by weeks of illness away from the family. She stopped—was it not then, after her mind had cleared, that she discovered the letter from Jan-Lee was gone? Had the entire stay at the summer house simply afforded her uncle opportunity to destroy the letter and gain her cooperation in altering her plans to see Director Rawlings?

Coral wrestled with gnawing doubt. She wanted to trust her uncle, despite their differences. And yet, Coral found her trust shifting to the man before her.

She said a trifle breathlessly, "The waltz is so lovely, Captain. And I do not think Michael would approve of our ruining the entire evening by mourning his death. Oh, please! Will you forget what I said in my letter? I see now that I was wrong. Can you forgive me?"

Was his grave expression a pretense?

"Well . . ."

"Oh, please!"

"I will give serious consideration to your request, say, during the next five waltzes?"

Coral laughed. "Anything to make up for my rudeness." *And to keep you away from Uncle,* she thought, and hurriedly went on: "It was inexcusable of me to jump to such odious conclusions."

He smiled a little and his eyes twinkled merrily. "You will need to be exceptionally nice to me all evening to make up for your trespass. Otherwise, I may need to speak to Sir Hugo about what happened to the letter I sent you."

Coral's eyes swiftly met his. *He must not incur my uncle's wrath!* "Uncle Hugo would have nothing to do with the letter not reaching me."

"No?"

"I am sure it was my grandmother, Lady Victoria. She forgets matters very easily. No doubt she merely mislaid the letter. . . ."

The flecks of black hardened in his eyes. "Perhaps. But she did not tell you the captain of the *Madras* was drunk in his cabin. And I do not believe you would come to that conclusion unless someone suggested it. Which leads me to believe that your uncle filled your mind with deliberate lies about me."

His eyes held hers, and Coral spoke quietly, "Please, will you not forget all that?"

"Yes, as long as you no longer believe it."

"I do not," she said quickly, noting the humor behind his eyes. *He looks as though he is enjoying this,* Coral thought, a bit flustered.

"Good." He smiled. "Then shall we put the past behind us and enjoy the evening?"

"Yes, I think so, Captain. And the waltz has stopped."

"Ah, but the next is just beginning."

EPILOGUE

Coral awoke to the sounds of birds cooing, whistling, and scolding. Half asleep under the satin coverlet with a film of mosquito netting drawn around the bed, her brain, dull from lack of sleep, wondered if Aunt Margaret had erected a bird aviary beneath the window. . . .

Suddenly, images of last night's ball burst like daylight into her subconscious. *Jace Buckley* . . . Coral's eyes flew open.

She smiled, having thoroughly enjoyed the evening. There was an energy, an excitement about him, and because she found him so, Coral reminded herself that she must regard him with caution. Ethan would not like the adventurous sea captain. However, in fairness to Captain Buckley, he had behaved the gallant gentleman—or at least, he had gone out of his way to don the role.

Coral only now realized that she had learned very little about him or his plans, whereas he had managed to learn a great deal about her stay in London, her illness, and Ethan. What they had not discussed was her plans to start the school for the untouchables, and

Gem. Somehow the gaiety of the ball and the whirling waltzes had not permitted serious subjects. All that would come later.

Coral seized the pearl-handled mirror from the nightstand and gazed critically at her face. Despite the late hour she had gone to bed, she felt only a little tired, and a closer inspection showed that the faint shadows beneath her eyes had not darkened.

She threw aside the coverlet and slipped into the ankle-length peignoir lying across the foot of the bed. Pushing aside the veil, Coral crossed the room to the window with its drawn-up bamboo sunshade. The early morning still held the night's whisper of coolness. Along the bank of the Hooghly River, the trees were teeming with a rainbow of color as parakeets fought for landing space.

Coral's thoughts jumped ahead to the upcoming safari that would bring her home to Kingscote. Remembering what Margaret had told her about Jorhat, she frowned a little. "I should have used the opportunity last night to ask Captain Buckley about the trouble at the outpost," she murmured aloud. There was Seward to ask of course, and she intended to speak with him today if possible and discuss the journey. Nothing must be allowed to delay her travel plans, not even political unrest. Yet even the safari home must wait a few weeks—there was something more critical she must do while in Calcutta.

A surge of expectation sent her heartbeat racing. Staying in Calcutta permitted her to pursue the clandestine meeting between her and the Indian mercenary who would search for Gem!

But how could she slip away unseen? She must plan painstakingly.

From downstairs came the morning sounds of the

servants preparing the Roxbury household for the main breakfast in the dining room, and a steaming urn of tea and platters of fresh fruit arrived at her bedroom by a servant and the small Indian child she had met the day before. Jay smiled shyly as he arranged the platter on Coral's rattan table, then lingered. She followed his gaze to a white ceramic dog with a rhinestone collar. The servant gave him a stern look and the boy turned and hurried out.

As Coral chose a wedge of orange mango, she heard Aunt Margaret coming down the hallway. Her aunt looked in through the open doorway, already dressed, her thick dark hair plaited and a smile on her attractive face. But Coral noted a certain tenseness in her eyes, as though other thoughts were troubling her.

"Good morning." She smiled at Coral. "You are looking well. I was afraid Captain Buckley kept you up too late."

Coral smiled in return and took a sip from her teacup. It seemed every woman at the ball had noticed that Jace had not troubled to waltz with anyone else. In a way, she had found it embarrassing, but at the same time she was flattered that he had even stayed at the ball, for she knew that he hadn't intended to. He danced well, and his looks were indisputably intriguing. She recalled the envious glances from Cousin Belinda.

"You do not have much time before breakfast. We have a rule: no one is permitted to straggle in for meals. We eat as a family, and everyone is to be fully dressed. You have thirty minutes."

The door shut, leaving her alone. *Thirty minutes!* If she wanted to send a message to her contact, there was no time to waste.

Coral waited until the sound of her aunt's footsteps died away, then she hurried to the desk. She wrote quickly in Bengali on a sheet of paper:

Saturday, October 13
Huzoor! Javed Kasam:
I am willing to pay a worthy price for important information. Needless to say, our meeting must be kept in the strictest confidence. My ghari will be parked by the Armenian church in the Chowringhee district next Saturday, October 20.

Signed,

Coral paused, tapping the end of the pen with uncertainty. Suppose he sent an inquiry to Sir Hugo? Uncle would then put a guard on her for the rest of her stay in Calcutta. Quickly she signed, *Ayub Khan.*

Coral slipped from her room into the hall, her heart racing. If Sir Hugo saw her . . .

The hallway remained empty while the others busied themselves dressing. She sped to the banister and leaned over. The Indian child was carrying a jug of water up the stairs. She waited for him, then motioned for him to follow her into her chamber. Coral shut the door without a sound and, kneeling, took hold of his tiny shoulders. She smiled to ease the curiosity in his large brown eyes, and whispered in Bengali: "Find me a big boy. One who can deliver a secret message. I will pay him a fistful of rupees. If you do this quickly, unseen, missy-sahiba will have a present for you."

Coral pointed to the ceramic dog she had bought in London.

Jay grinned, caught on swiftly, and whispered, "Big brother, he go, he go for fistful rupees!"

"Hurry then. Find him. Tell your brother what I said. If he agrees, come back to my room."

The boy darted out and, moving as silently as a cat, disappeared.

Coral paced, keeping the door open a crack to watch for his return. Within ten minutes he was back, casting a glance over his shoulder. She drew him inside. "Yes?"

"Big brother in yard behind kitchen. He will go now, missy-sahiba."

"Good boy, Jay." Coral stuffed the sealed envelope inside his tunic, then handed him the dog. He grinned, salaamed, and backed out into the hall.

With relief, Coral sank against the door.

The way was now open to gain the precious information she needed to locate Gem's whereabouts. She would get the money to pay the mercenary, and if her son was alive as she suspected, somehow she would buy Gem's release from his captor.

As Coral hurried to dress for breakfast, she hummed the refrain of a waltz she had danced in the arms of Jace Buckley.

Yes, she was going to enjoy the brief stay in Calcutta. . . .

She reached a hand to touch her Bible on the dressing table, opening it to the presentation page. In her mother's hand was written:

It is never so dark that God cannot deliver.

Hope beat strong in her heart, for she believed the Lord had already heard her prayers, and in His timing, in His own way, He would return the joy of her heart. Coral smiled and left her room to go downstairs, still humming.

GLOSSARY

ASSAM: Northeast India, location of Kingscote.

AYAH: A child's nurse.

BRAHMIN: Highest Hindu caste.

BOURKA: A one-piece garment, usually white cotton, covering the female from head to foot, with a small square of coarse net or slits to see through.

BURRA-SAHIB: A great man.

CHUNNI: A light head-covering; a scarf.

DAK: A resting house for travelers.

DEWAN: The chief minister of an Indian ruler.

GHARI: A horse-drawn vehicle; a carriage.

GHAT: Steps or a platform on the river; also where the Hindu dead are cremated.

GHAZI: A fanatic; usually with religious overtones, but also referring to political beliefs.

HOOKAH: A water pipe for tobacco; also used for smoking other types of drugs.

JAI RAM: A Hindu greeting.

JOHN COMPANY: Another name for the East India Company, usually hinting at its clandestine activities (i.e., opium running).

KANSAMAH: A cook.

KOTWAL: A headman.

MAHARAJA: A Hindu king.

MAHOUT: An elephant driver.

MAIDAN: A large expanse of lawn; a parade ground.

MANJI: A boatman.

NAMASTE: A respectful gesture of fingers to the forehead with palms together.

NAUKER-LOG: Servants.

PUGGARI: A turban.

PUNKAH: A fan made of heavy matting or canvas, sometimes wet, and pulled by a rope to make a breeze.

RAJA: A king.

RAJPUTS: A warrior caste of the Hindus, a rank below the *brahmins*.

RANI: A queen.

SEPOY: An infantry soldier.

SHARBAT: Iced lemonade

SOWAR: A cavalry trooper.

UNTOUCHABLE: One that is below the Hindu caste system, condemned as unclean in this life.

VEDAS: Ancient Hindu sacred writings; their orthodox scriptures.

UNDER EASTERN STARS

HEART OF INDIA SERIES

Silk
Under Eastern Stars
Kingscote

THE GREAT NORTHWEST SERIES

Empire Builders

UNDER EASTERN STARS

LINDA CHAIKIN

BETHANY HOUSE PUBLISHERS
MINNEAPOLIS, MINNESOTA 55438

Cover illustration by Joe Nordstrom

Published by Bethany House Publishers
A Ministry of Bethany Fellowship, Inc.
11300 Hampshire Avenue South
Minneapolis, Minnesota 55438

Printed in the United States of America

Library of Congress Cataloging-in-Publication Data

Chaikin, Linda.
    Under eastern stars / Linda Chaikin.
       p. cm.
    Sequel to: Silk.

    1. British—India—History—18th century—Fiction.
2. Women—India—History—18th century—Fiction.
I. Title.
PS3553.H2427U5   1993
813'.54—dc20   93–25160
ISBN 1–55661–366–0   CIP

July 19th, 1993

This second book of the *Heart of India Series*
is dedicated in memory of my beloved mother who is
now . . . "forever with the Lord."

LINDA CHAIKIN is a full-time writer and has two books published in the Christian market. She graduated from Multnomah School of the Bible and is working on a degree with Moody Bible Institute. She and her husband, Steve, are involved with a church-planting mission among Hindus in Kerala, India. They make their home in San Jose, California.

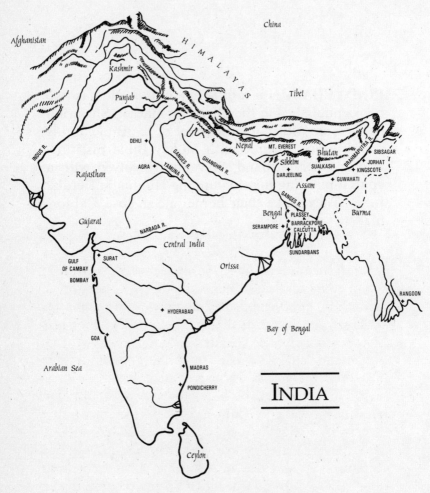

1

Calcutta, India
1799

Jace Buckley scowled a little and ran his hand through his dark hair. His blue-black eyes narrowed under his lashes as he studied the ancient map. Wearing an Indian tunic and worn buckskin trousers, he lounged comfortably on cushions beside a low rattan table. The small private room was divided from the common area by a curtain of wooden beads. The eatery, offering some of the finest Mughlai cuisine in Calcutta, was owned by an Indian family with whom he had close ties.

As Jace waited for his servant-companion, Gokul, to bring the meal and join him, he concentrated on the map given to him by his deceased father, Captain Jarred Buckley. With a calculating eye, he traced the little-known trails crisscrossing the northeastern frontier of India along its precarious border with Burma. *The ruling warlord may be able to offer information on the attack at the British outpost of Jorhat.*

His thoughts were interrupted as the wooden beads parted with dull clacking sounds. He looked up. Gokul

9

stood there, out of breath, one hand on his protruding belly, his marble-black eyes agitated.

Jace rolled the map and placed it within his black woolen tunic. "What is it?"

"I try to stop him, but he ran like a cheetah!"

"Who ran like a cheetah?"

"Indian boy! Maybe fourteen. He disappeared in crowd. Left a message."

Jace stood. "For me?"

Gokul glanced backward over his shoulder. "Best you read it for yourself. The boy knew enough to bring this to Chowringhee address." He reached inside his sleeve and handed Jace a sealed envelope.

There was no handwriting. A letter delivered to him here was suspect. "Did he say anything?"

"He whispered a name."

Jace met his gaze. "What name?"

"Javed Kasam."

The name struck like a blow, but he did not visibly react.

"He sneak in and ask for me. When I came he whispered the name, then ran. There was no time for anything else."

Saturday, October 13
Huzoor! Javed Kasam:
I am willing to pay a worthy price for important information. Needless to say, our meeting must be kept in the strictest confidence. My ghari* will be parked by the Armenian church in the Chowringhee district next Saturday, October 20.

Signed,
Ayub Khan

*A glossary of Indian words is at the back of the book.

Jace frowned. It had been over three years since he had worked under the name of Javed Kasam. Who but a foe would know enough about this side of his life to send him a message at Chowringhee?

Gokul watched him with intense dark eyes. "Trouble?"

"Ever heard of Ayub Khan?"

Gokul pursed his lips. "The son of the Burmese warlord?"

"Yes. But Khan is dead. Someone is using his name."

"This Ayub Khan wishes to meet with you?"

Jace handed him the letter, then retrieved his scabbard, strapping it on. "Ask around the bazaars. I want to know who is masquerading as Khan, and why."

Gokul handed him the letter, his face grave. "Sahib, think well of what you do. This could be a trap."

Jace was thinking of the stolen Hindu idol, Kali. Did this Khan think Jace had it? His jaw set. "I shall meet with him."

"Suppose Ayub Khan comes in disguise? There may be spies waiting by the church. Do not go alone."

Jace had understood the dangers when he entered the complicated world of Eastern intrigue years earlier. His first involvement was quite by accident, the result of bumping into a sticky web of deceit and assassination in northeastern India, and becoming entangled in a plot to steal the jeweled idol of Kali from a Hindu temple, and the death of a much-venerated holy man. He had escaped by posing as an Indian guru by the name of Javed Kasam. Who had killed the holy man, or gotten away with the idol, he did not know, but there were those who believed him responsible. Since that time, he had participated in the art of intrigue on various occasions. Once for a friend; a few times for pay. It was a dangerous way of life, one he wanted to leave behind. Javed Kasam had enemies.

Gokul, who worked the bazaars, knew many informers in the south and north and had kept Jace informed, but the name Kasam had not been spoken in three or four years. Those who knew Jace Buckley to be Javed were few. Gokul was one, and the two fighters from the warrior caste—Faridul and Arif. But these were men he could count on. That only left Rawlings in London, whom he had worked for on two occasions, and the Burmese warlord. Jace had not paid Rawlings a visit since selling him the matching ivory elephant for his collection; and he knew of no one to whom Rawlings might give his name, nor did he believe that the warlord had sent someone masquerading as his slain son, Ayub Khan.

That left only an enemy. Perhaps a man hired by the royal family over the matter of the stolen idol.

"Have Faridul meet the ghari in the churchyard on Saturday. When the carriage leaves, watch to see if it's being followed. If Khan comes alone, I will ride to meet him outside Calcutta near the dak-bungalow. If we stay on the move, there can be no trap. It is I who shall trap Ayub Khan. Go at once."

———

Coral Kendall came down the stairs of her uncle's Roxbury residence in Calcutta. Her green eyes shone beneath a fringe of lashes and her golden curls fell about her shoulders. *How can I sneak out to meet with Javed Kasam?*

She hoped her tension did not show as she saw her sister Kathleen in the entrance hall. Her other sister, Marianna, and Aunt Margaret were waiting on the porch. *If only they would leave for Mrs. Waterman's garden party,* she thought. Even now there was a possibility that she would be late for her meeting with the Indian mercenary.

The customary garden party was being held that afternoon, but Coral had managed to decline the invitation. She tried to smile pleasantly as she carried down her pink fringed shawl for Kathleen to wear with her afternoon garden dress.

"The color will flatter your chestnut curls," said Coral.

Kathleen's amber eyes shone with anything but pleasure. "I would rather not go," she said, taking the shawl. "But Aunt Margaret insisted. I would much rather work on my designs than listen to prattle."

She might have felt sympathy for her older sister, but Coral knew she *must* get her out of the house. She thought of the scrapbook that she had recently seen Kathleen carrying about in her satchel. She had shown Coral some of her clothing sketches, and Coral had been impressed with the intricate work. The dresses were organized under afternoon and evening wear, according to the seasons.

"Why not take your book with you? You might get some ideas. Just think of all those ladies wearing their afternoon dresses. Maybe you could sketch some of them for fun, then see how you can redesign them to best flatter each figure."

"Why, Coral, what a grand idea! I should have thought of that myself!"

With shawl in hand, Kathleen rushed for the stairs. "I will get my things. Everyone will be so busy milling about they will not even notice me sketching!"

Coral smiled. It was good to see Kathleen enthusiastic. Her sister had still not gotten over her disappointment over leaving the Silk House in London.

A short time later, Coral followed the others onto the lower verandah, where the carriage waited to drive them to the Waterman house. It was a bright morning, alive with sunshine and bird song, but a taste of autumn was in the air.

"Goodbye, dear. We will be home before dinner," Margaret told Coral. "Rest up from that nasty fever for the picnic next week. It is the last outdoor social of the season and will last all day and into the night."

Coral watched from the verandah and gave a wave as the white-clad servant assisted her sisters and aunt into the carriage. When the vehicle disappeared around the corner, she picked up her skirts and sped back into the house. She must hurry!

She felt a bit guilty over her secret plans for the afternoon but relieved that her family had left. She was now free for the day.

"If the family finds out what I am about to do, I shall never hear the end of it," murmured Coral nervously. She was not one to mislead, but when it came to Gem, nothing would stop her. She owed her family love and loyalty, but surely she could not be blamed for doing everything within her power to locate information on her son.

As it did so often, Gem's face appeared in her memory, and so did the haunting scream of "Mummy, Mummy, Mummy" that had pierced her heart the night of his abduction. Forever that sight would conjure up a torrent of mixed emotions. She had a fear that her family was right—Gem was dead—but also a fierce determination to find him again . . . at whatever cost.

She had one ally in the house to assist her, however small. Jay.

"I stop ghari-wallah on the street for you, missy. He there now," whispered the little servant-boy Jay.

Coral brushed a thank-you against his dark head, then rushed up the stairs to her room and changed quickly into the clothes that she had prepared for the secret meeting. She scanned herself in the mirror, frowning a little. She might be able to hide her hair color beneath the Indian head covering, but her eyes would give her away.

No matter. Once I meet Javed Kasam in person, I can explain my need for secrecy.

Coral hurried to her wardrobe and took out the traditional full-trousered Indian suit worn by Punjabi women, this one trimmed with silver ribbon. She quickly pulled on the loose-fitting trousers, over which she slipped on a *kameez*, a knee-length smock that flared out at the bottom. The long *chunni*, or head covering, was black silk highlighted with small silver bangles that tinkled. Carefully, she shielded her hair so that her tresses would not show, then wrapped the Roxbury ring tightly in a lace handkerchief and placed it in her beaded bag.

Misgivings flooded in, and Coral shut her eyes. "Forgive me, Grandmother Victoria, but my Gem is worth the family heirloom. . . ."

While Jay kept watch, prepared to whistle if any of the servants loyal to her uncle, Sir Hugo, appeared, Coral slipped from the house by a side door and through the garden.

Jay ran ahead, shimmied up the trunk of a big tree, and straddled a high branch like a leopard. All was clear. Silently as a cat, Coral made her escape from the boundaries of the house.

On the massive open park of green surrounding Fort William, she looked for the rented ghari. The driver was waiting for her, and Coral boarded the carriage. On the western side of the fort was the Hooghly River and the area called Chowringhee, with jungle paths and crowded bazaars. It was to this seamy side of Calcutta that Coral had sent her inquiry to Javed Kasam.

At the northeastern corner of the park, the ghari passed the hawkers, the sweet and tea shops, then moved toward the Old China Bazaar, housing the thriving, mysterious oriental culture. She had a glimpse of coolies wearing triangular chip-straw hats and short pants, and of black doors with red and gold markings, before the horse turned to plod on toward an even older Armenian sector of Calcutta.

Coral's eyes searched for the Armenian Church, built in 1724, and tensed as it came into view. The carriage came to a stop near the church cemetery, and Coral waited, seeing no sign of any Indian that she might take for Javed Kasam. She left the ghari door ajar for his approach and felt the dry wind stir her head covering, jingling the silver bangles. She adjusted it to shield her curls from clear view, her heart thudding.

Several minutes crept by. Her eyes scanned the church grounds and the cemetery beyond. Then she saw him. A big, bearded Indian soldier whom she guessed to be a *rajput* from the military caste of the Hindus. Immaculately dressed in warrior's garb and wearing a sword, he stepped from behind some greenery to walk toward the open door of the ghari.

Coral leaned back into the seat as he blocked the door with his frame, hand on sword hilt. She said nothing as the handsome dark eyes swept the inside of the ghari, coming to rest on the empty seat opposite her.

"Where is Ayub Khan?"

"I am Ayub Khan. . . . Are you Javed Kasam?"

His eyes, hard and black, swerved to confront hers. They narrowed, and Coral tried not to wince. She hoped she had not offended him by using the male name, and tried to explain. "You see, I did not want you to contact members of my family, and—"

The rajput said something to the driver, then before she could respond, he swung his heavy frame into the seat, slammed the door, and the carriage lurched forward, leaving the old church behind.

"Sir! I wish to speak here! Where are you taking me?"

He did not speak and was concentrating on the road behind them. Coral felt panic rising up.

"Javed Kasam, I should like—"

"Silence, sahiba."

She watched him, her alarm growing. He seemed intent on making sure no one followed them. The carriage was moving at a fast clip now, the hoofs of the horse stirring up dust. Coral held her chunni against her nose and mouth. Looking out the window, she saw that they were headed away from Calcutta.

"Where are you taking me!"

"I shall bring you to Javed Kasam."

Then he is only a contact. She relaxed a little. "Is it far?"

"Not far."

The pitted road was inches deep in fine brown dust, and thorn bushes stood as prickly guards on Coral's side of the carriage, keeping her penned. Was she a prisoner? The rajput's promise of *"not far"* turned into an hour's ride, and Coral was relieved to finally hear him order the driver to stop the vehicle.

The rajput guard exited, then commanded the irritated ghari-wallah to keep silent, assuring him that he would be paid well enough for his services.

Coral was not only furious at her treatment but nervous. Just what sort of renegade was this Javed Kasam to hurry off his prospective clients as though they were thieves out to steal from him?

The thud of hoofs sounded, and she turned in her seat to look out the window. Had he come at last? Before she knew what was happening, the ghari lurched forward again and started off at a good clip just as a man swung himself in, slamming the door after him. As he turned to confront her, Coral froze.

2

"Javed Kasam" wore a black Indian tunic belted with a silver chain. The sword was one of those curved, deadly blades called a *tulwar* that Coral had seen on Kingscote among the Indian guards. The turban, too, was black, but it was the man's eyes and handsome features that were becoming all too familiar in the guise of several different men, reminding her that if she did not know Javed Kasam, neither did she truly know the disciplined Major Buckley, nor the adventurer with the monkey on his shoulder who had rescued her at the bazaar.

Coral stared at him. He leaned over and swept aside her chunni, unmasking her golden-colored curls. The blue-black of his eyes glittered. He sank back, and she heard him mutter something in a breath of exasperation.

"But . . . *you* cannot be Javed Kasam."

He fixed her with a narrowed gaze. "And surely, madam, you are not Ayub Khan."

Coral did not know why, but she flushed. "I once heard my father speak of him."

"Which is not quite the same thing. Besides, Khan is dead."

"Oh. Actually, I was afraid you would—I mean—that

19

Javed Kasam would go to Sir Hugo with my name."

"Hardly. I would be blowing the trumpet on my own disguise."

Coral pulled off her chunni and drew in a breath. "You must understand, sir, I am rather new at this vice."

"Vice?"

Aware of whom she was talking with, and knowing how desperately she needed his help, she hastened, "I suppose that is not the proper word. Intrigue would be better."

He watched her.

This is not going the way I intended. She busied herself with the chunni, smoothing the silk with the palm of her hand.

"I must say it is a charming masquerade," came the smooth voice, and Coral looked up. He made a handsome Indian warrior.

"Imagine, an Indian woman of high fashion bearing the masculine name of a Muslim ruling prince," he said. "Do you make a practice of this, Miss Kendall—or should I call you Madam Khan?"

She could not afford to nettle him, and bridled her own irritation. "Speaking of masquerades, just who is it I am addressing? A sea captain, a military major, or Javed Kasam?"

"That depends." He smiled. "You may call me Jace."

Well, I asked for that one. Jace was the last thing she would call him, being too familiar, which of course he knew.

"I would like to know how you got hold of the name." His expression was grave again, and she felt comfortable with the safe distance between them.

"On my word, sir, I intend to explain everything."

"You do realize that there are some matters we simply do not discuss, and one is the true identity of Javed Kasam," he said quietly. "It was a risk for me to meet you like this. I prefer my head where it is. Before we part, you will swear silence to ever having known this Indian scoundrel."

Coral felt uneasy knowing she had brought him some risk. "Of course," she said quickly. "But would you tell me why you are in danger?"

"Since you have requested to see me, I will be the one to ask questions. First, who told you about me?"

She settled back against the seat and met his gaze evenly. "Director Rawlings of the East India Company. I went to see him in his office in London and he gave me your name."

At the mention of Rawlings, she noticed a perceptible glimmer of relief in his gaze.

"Who told you about Rawlings?"

"No one told me outright. I once overheard my father discussing him."

He looked surprised. "Hampton involved in the clandestine?"

Coral said nothing. She knew little of her father's contacts.

"It is not surprising, I suppose. The location of Kingscote would demand contacts in India and Burma. And the man with whom your father discussed Rawlings?"

"I am sorry. I do not recall. He was a Dutchman who came to see him on shipping business. I overheard a brief discussion about Director Rawlings knowing 'certain individuals who could gain secret information in the East.'"

"Ah. And so you went to Rawlings while you were staying at Roxbury House."

"Yes. I waited until Sir Hugo returned to India."

"Why?" he asked.

She thought he already knew, but explained again, "Sir Hugo insists that Gem is dead. I do not believe it. My situation in the family is such that turning to Director Rawlings offered my best chance of locating my son. I asked about a man I could hire to discover Gem's whereabouts. Director Rawlings was hesitant, but at last wrote out a name and handed it to me. He said I could find Javed Kasam in Calcutta, and that he was very good—for the right price." Coral's hand tightened on the beaded bag containing the Roxbury ring.

If she expected him to react to the hint of a hefty payment for his services, he did not. Coral felt a prickle of disappointment. Suppose he refused to help? Something warned her not to place all her confidence in the ring. She did not know where the Darjeeling tea plantation stood in his future plans, but the ring was worth any number of voyages he might risk on his clipper. She doubted little that he could bring himself to refuse.

"And, of course, now I know who Javed Kasam is," she continued. If Coral felt unsettled about anything, it was whether she felt more comfortable with Major Buckley, or Javed Kasam.

"And now that you know?" he repeated.

"I am even more convinced that this 'Indian mercenary'—one of the best in the East according to Director Rawlings—is the man to help me locate Gem."

She hoped he would respond to that, and her uncertainty continued to grow when he did not. If her previous suggestion of payment had not brought the response she hoped for, neither did her confidence in his abilities. He merely watched her, and as he did, she became more desperate.

Coral lapsed into an uncomfortable silence. She tried not to form opinions of the man in front of her, but they came nonetheless. *Independent, strong, and as untamable as the vast land of India.* Just what was Jace truly like beneath his many disguises? He was nothing like Ethan. *Ethan.* Suddenly she wished he were there.

"You will permit me to hire you?" she asked, breaking the uneasy silence.

He studied her for a moment in the shadows of the ghari, and answered as though he had not heard her question. "Have you mentioned Kasam to anyone? Your sisters, your aunt?"

"No. I memorized the name and the Chowringhee address while still in London, then burned the paper Director Rawlings gave me. I did not know how long it would be until I returned to India, and three years was too long to keep the paper."

"You would do well in the world of intrigue."

She gave him a side glance. . . . Certainly he was joking.

"Then no one but the boy knows you sent a message?"

"The boy? Oh, I see what you mean. Perhaps I should not have risked the two brothers, but it seemed the only way to contact you. They will say nothing, I am sure of it. You will let me hire you?"

"No."

Startled, she urged, "But I will pay you handsomely!"

"I am sorry to disappoint you over my refusal, but I am not for hire."

"If anyone can help me find out if Gem is alive, it is you. I am glad you are Javed Kasam, because you have a clear understanding of what is involved in his abduction. It was you who warned me, and it is you who can discover the truth now."

The ghari stopped, and an uneasy silence locked them in shadows. The wind buffeted the door, rocking the carriage. Coral leaned toward him.

"He is mine. I love him, I raised him, I have poured

years of my life into him, and I want him back!"

He studied her without speaking.

"Major, I will give you anything you want, anything within my authority to give. You are aware that I am a silk heiress."

Something unpleasant flickered in his eyes, but she did not accept the warning.

"That tea plantation you and Michael wanted so badly, I will buy it for you."

"Indeed?" He folded his arms across his chest and regarded her with a look that seemed to make the black in his eyes more prominent, like glowing coals.

Although she noticed the familiar set of his jaw, she took this expression for interest. "There is something I want to show you. I brought it with me."

Quickly now, believing she had won him over, she opened her beaded drawstring bag and took out the knotted handkerchief. She fumbled to untie it. A minute later she extended her palm with open handkerchief, the rubies in the Roxbury ring glimmering like fire. "Find out if Gem is alive. If he is, help me get him back and this is yours. You can retire on your plantation. You will not need to brave wind and sea on your clipper to scrimp and save, not when I can easily give it to you!"

Unexpectedly, his warm, strong hand closed over hers so tightly the jewels dug into her palm. "What do you take me for?"

Confused, she stared at him. He was angry! "But, the ring is more than enough to buy your plantation!"

"I *know* what it is worth."

Her eyes searched his and found only displeasure.

He gritted, "I do intend to own that plantation. And I shall go on scrimping and saving every miserable *rupee* until I do. And when I have accomplished what I set out to do, the plantation will be mine, not handed to me by a silk heiress. I do not want your ring. I do not want anything you have as a Kendall. I will remain forever chained to my clipper before I allow a woman to turn Jace Buckley into a 'lap dog with a diamond collar around his neck.' " He lifted her hand clutching the Roxbury heirloom. "Even if it was placed there by your pretty little hand."

He let go and opened the ghari door, prepared to leave. He looked back at her. "Give it to Ethan Boswell. I have a notion Sir Hugo's nephew will have no qualms."

Ethan? The name swirled about her brain. What did her cousin have to do with this? But she was too surprised over his reaction to find offense in his suggestion that Ethan could be bought. What did he know about her cousin?

As if to add wood to the fires of her dismay, he abruptly disembarked from the ghari despite her protests, and shouted something in Bengali to the rajput, who quickly produced his horse.

Coral was leaning out the ghari door as he swung himself onto his mount, and he looked down at her, unrelenting.

"Good day, Madam Khan." Then wheeling his horse, he rode off.

Coral sat there gripping the seat. The thud of horse hoofs disappeared, and wind struck the side of the ghari. She pondered his reaction to the ring. Had she been too glib about it? Had it seemed a bribe? Or was there something more that motivated his actions? Her brow furrowed, she fell back against the seat.

On the way back to Calcutta, weary and dejected, Coral wondered what had gone so badly.

Javed Kasam, according to Director Rawlings, was a mercenary soldier who accepted dangerous missions for precisely one reason: high pay. Then why had he been offended? She rehearsed in her mind what had happened, deciding that unlike the other men she had met in London, whose motives Granny V warned of being suspect, her position as a silk heiress was nettlesome to Jace. The ghari wheel hit a bump, and she was thrown to one side, hitting her shoulder. It was not the pain that made her wince, but a sudden realization.

"Coral Kendall! Why, you have behaved positively brutish! You have waved the ring before him as though baiting a bear! Offering to buy without difficulty the very thing Jace Buckley has struggled to attain for the last several years!"

Coral groaned at her folly. Her desperation to locate Gem had made her insensitive to Jace.

I should have known better.

But just how well did she know this man? Hardly at all. And now what?

When they arrived at Fort William, the ghari-wallah climbed down from his seat, his expression showing sullen displeasure over the afternoon. She carefully paid him, adding a tuppence.

I will not give up, thought Coral fiercely as she watched the ghari leave. *Jace Buckley is the most knowledgeable man in India. I will try again.*

Next time, she would know better than to offer him an heirloom, or flippantly promise to buy him a tea plantation from her bulging purse.

Evidently she had riled the territorial pride of a cheetah, a cheetah who staked his own prize and refused assistance from anyone—especially Coral Kendall.

3

Margaret Roxbury squared her shoulders as she paused outside the door to the suite she shared with her husband. She touched her brunette chignon, her brown eyes sober. Taking in a small breath, she opened the door.

Hugo Roxbury stood before the mirror, his broad back toward her as she shut the door.

"Good morning, Hugo."

He slipped his jacket over the watered-silk waistcoat and his black eyes met hers in the mirror. He smiled, his even teeth showing beneath his close-clipped mustache. His beard was well-groomed, and she was reminded of how striking her husband was in his outward appearance.

"You are up early after waltzing the night away," he said evenly.

She stiffened. "I waltzed little, actually. Lady Carlton had an attack of asthma and had to be rushed home. I took her place in the receiving line." She walked across the thick indigo rug and opened wide the doors to the upper verandah.

He tapped his well-manicured nails along the front of his waistcoat, and the ruby ring glinted. "I was remiss in telling you how lovely you looked at the state ball." He turned toward her. "The colonel occupied much of your time."

"I do not call a waltz or two occupying a good deal of my time. He was merely being polite." She looked at him, remembering how his appearance had first attracted her to him when she was a young girl in London. Sir Hugo Roxbury had been an exciting mystery, a distant cousin with charming manners and fair speech, convincing her that with his moral support her talent in design could be carried to the heights of success. He had won her from the attentions of the young ensign John Sebastian Warbeck, a man who was adamant about her becoming a military wife in the Company. Warbeck, in his youthful pride, had refused to bow to the pressure of the family silk dynasty and yoke himself to the will of Lord Henry and Lady Victoria Roxbury. In the end, it had been the family's disapproval of John Warbeck more than her love for Hugo that had brought about the marriage.

"What does the governor-general want to see you about today?" she asked.

Hugo's meetings at Government-House were growing more frequent. Working with the governor insured greater prestige within the confines of the Company, and so did the upcoming engagement of their daughter, Belinda, to Sir Arlen George, a relation to the governor. It was about Belinda that she wished to talk to Hugo.

"It is not about the northern frontier again, is it?" she pressed.

"I fear it is. The attack on the outpost at Jorhat was only the beginning of renewed trouble with Burma. The governor-general is keeping the incident quiet, but there was an attempt to kill the nephew of the raj at Guwahati."

"Hugo, must you get involved? It is so dangerous."

He took hold of her shoulders. "It is for the good of both England and India that I serve the governor. Do not worry. There are others in more precarious situations than I, including Hampton."

"Hampton!"

His expression turned grave. "If Hampton were wise he would change his mind about working with the Company. Kingscote is located dangerously close to Jorhat. He may soon need our help."

"Hampton Kendall is too independent to sign away control of the plantation. The Kingscote Plantation was untouched by Assam's previous trouble with Burma. Why should they be in danger now?"

"Burma's determination to possess the northern frontier, especially Assam, is not over. New fighting can break out at any time. Someday there may be a full-scale war, and we'll be fighting for the first time inside Burma!"

"Forget all this, Hugo. Let's go back to London. You have work to do there, and Victoria needs you."

His smile was faint. "Someday. There is too much to do in India now. And it affects the silk. Now that we have some manner of treaty with the king of Assam, penetration of the East India Company into the Himalayas with an objective to opening up trade with Tibet is progressing. I have expectations of working with Hampton to double, even triple, silk production."

Margaret knew there was little she could do to induce him to return to London. Year after year she waited for something to turn up that would convince him to run for Parliament.

"Opportunities in the northeast are too great to ignore," he was saying.

"Speaking of Hampton," she began casually, "I think you should speak to him about Alex and Belinda."

She saw his black eyes flicker with impatience. He was determined his daughter marry Sir George. His hands dropped from her shoulders and he turned back to the mirror, adding the finishing touches to his appearance. "We have been through this before, Margaret. Belinda's girlish infatuation with her cousin Alex will pass with maturity."

She sighed. "I am not so certain it is infatuation."

"Nonsense. She is only seventeen."

"I was only a year older when we married."

"You were different than Belinda, my dear."

"Not so different, Hugo. I see so much of myself in her these days."

He gave a short, amused laugh. "I am Arlen George, and Alex is Colonel Warbeck, is that it?"

"This has nothing to do with our past, or with the colonel. I do not want to see Belinda forced into a marriage she does not want."

"The way you were?"

"Hugo, please." She walked over to the verandah and looked out. Jay and two other servant-children were hauling buckets of water to fill the trench around the orange tree. "Hugo, she is our only child."

"Belinda is spoiled. She needs someone like Arlen George who can put up with her tantrums."

"If I have been easy, it's because you were too hard."

"Let us not get into child rearing now. It is too late to go back."

"But it is not too late where her future is concerned. Marriage is too important, and I will not have her rushed into something she is so upset about. Belinda is all I have."

"You are forgetting me, my pet."

Margaret turned her head and looked at him, feeling a throb of dull pain. "Did I ever have you, Hugo?"

His brow arched, and he eyed her curiously. "Strange remark, Mrs. Roxbury. You have always had my attention, my devotion."

Margaret looked out across the verandah. "I just left Belinda. She spent a good deal of the evening last night with Arlen. He is insisting a wedding day be set at the Christmas ball at Barrackpore. She is very upset."

"Upset? I would think she would be elated. It is not every young lady in the Company who is so sought by a man like Arlen George. Marriage to him secures her future in India."

Margaret tried to keep her exasperation veiled. "She does not want Anglo-Indian life. You know that. She wants to go back to London."

"Belinda did not seem unduly concerned last night. She looked to be enjoying herself with any number of young officers whirling her about the floor. You will admit that Arlen was mature enough not to interfere with her gaiety. He spoils her. He knows she has this infatuation with Alex Kendall, and he is willing to let her grow out of it. Arlen is the best possible husband for Belinda. Alex is temperamental. His music is his life. I doubt if he knows Belinda exists."

"He does. He wrote her while he was in Vienna."

Hugo grew still and searched her face. "This is rather sudden, is it not?"

"It is not sudden at all. They are cousins. They have corresponded since childhood."

"Alex has been writing her, and I am only now learning about it?"

"Belinda did not think it a deep, dark secret, nor did Alex. She wrote Michael, too, when he was alive."

His mouth turned grim. "I never thought Alex would lead her on this way."

"That is completely unfair. One would think Alex was

a penniless scamp. I do not understand you. You want your nephew Ethan to marry Coral, yet Alex is also an heir of Kingscote. Why not marriage to Belinda?"

"For a number of important reasons, my dear. One of them is Arlen George himself. He is an ambitious man with good sense. He'll amount to something in India. Who knows? He may one day become the governor-general himself. Now, tell me about these letters coming from Vienna."

"There were not that many from Alex."

"Has Belinda been throwing herself at him?"

"Hugo!"

"Then you did not know about the letters?"

"No. But if I had, it would not have upset me. Belinda tells me the letters had nothing to do with romance. In his last one he congratulated her on her upcoming engagement, and spent the rest of the letter discussing music and Vienna. But Belinda seems to think Alex does care, and I promised her I would speak to you about him."

"This is all sentimental nonsense, Margaret. I doubt if Alex *cares*, as she puts it. But if he did, it is surface romance. He is not the manner of man for her." Hugo came near, taking hold of her. "If Assam eventually becomes a raj state under British rule, Arlen could become commissioner. Her marriage is as important to the silk enterprise as Ethan's marriage to Coral. The Roxbury family needs them both."

"And the Kendalls?" she asked flatly. "Is it important to them?"

His face was smooth. "We are all in the silk business together, are we not? Margaret, do not look at me that way." He gave an unexpected laugh and drew her into his arms. She was so furious with him that she trembled, and she knew he felt her shaking, for his embrace tightened.

The amusement over her anger had left his voice, and it was quiet. "Darling, you are angry."

Her voice shook. "Yes, Hugo, I am angry. You are like a stubborn bear. You charge forward, trampling underfoot anything or anyone who opposes your plans."

He was silent, and she did not pull away as he held her.

"Am I to understand that you will never forgive me if I do not speak to Hampton about Alex?"

The change in his voice took her by surprise. She raised her head and searched his face. "I would like you to speak to Hampton, yes."

"Then, my dear Margaret, if it will make you happy, I will do so."

Stunned, she could not speak or move for a moment. "You mean that?"

"Yes, but I think the entire matter about Alex is a waste. You speak of my being hard on Belinda; the truth is, I would worry about her if she married Alex. He is a young man of dark moods."

"Alex?" she said with a laugh.

"I have heard—well, perhaps I should say nothing."

"About Alex? What is it?"

"I did not want to say this, but perhaps the girls were called home not only because of Elizabeth, but Alex."

"Alex, but why?"

"Do you remember back some years ago when he shut himself in his room at Kingscote? His mood was such that he refused to eat or talk to the family for days."

"Yes," she said quietly, a sense of wariness stealing over her. "He wanted to pursue his music in Vienna. Hampton wanted him to concern himself with silk. In the end, Elizabeth talked to Hampton and he relented.

Music means so much to Alex. I can understand how he was depressed."

"He was more than depressed. He tried to commit suicide."

She sucked in a quick breath. Young, handsome, sensitive Alex? "But Elizabeth never said anything; she never told me—"

"Your sister thought it best for his future that she say nothing to the family. I would not know about it if Ethan had not been acquainted with the physician treating him in Vienna. He told me about Alex when we were in London."

"He was ill again while in Vienna?"

His hands tightened on her shoulders. "He never fully recovered, even after he was encouraged to go to Vienna. Last year he collapsed during a recital and was incapacitated for months. There was a time when the physician thought he might never recover."

Margaret struggled against what she was hearing. It seemed inconceivable.

"Alex is better now. He has come home to Kingscote. But there is uncertainty over his state of mind, over what his future holds. Elizabeth does not know of this recent problem. . . . She is too ill, and Hampton kept it from her. But he thought it best that his daughters come home. He needs their help. I would have said nothing, except I cannot bear the way you looked at me now, as though I cared nothing for my daughter's happiness, or yours."

Margaret felt dazed. "If Belinda finds out, it will devastate her."

"I am sorry I had to tell you. But if you do wish to postpone Belinda's engagement to Arlen until spring, I will speak to him about a delay."

She shook her head with confusion. "I do not know! This changes everything. Poor Alex. Hugo? You are quite certain this is true? There might have been some mistake."

"I can swear to nothing, nor would I, yet Doctor Schuler is a friend of Ethan's, and neither man has cause to exaggerate the state of your nephew's mind." He sighed. "You could write to Hampton, I suppose. But you must be careful. We would not want to add to your sister's unhappiness. Elizabeth has had more than her share of sorrow. First the child—what was his name?"

Margaret's heart swelled with pain as she thought of her sister. "Ranek," she murmured dismally, thinking that she too had once lost a baby boy, but she had been only five months along when she miscarried.

"Then, there is the tragedy of the Indian boy's death, not to mention Michael."

"Hugo, hold me."

"Darling Margaret." He embraced her. "You mean everything to me. I would do nothing to hurt you. You know that? I did not want to tell you."

Margaret swallowed back the desire to cry. She was past those early days of her marriage when she had cried too much. At times she could vow that Hugo loved her; at other times he seemed as driven as Alex was with his music.

Her mind went back to her sister. Elizabeth remained strong through her emotional losses because of her confidence in the Scriptures. She relied on God's promises as her light and source of hope. *What about the foundation of my own faith?* Margaret wondered. *Is it there?* She had believed in the teachings of Christianity as a child, and yet . . . Elizabeth was able to approach God in a way that she could not, for Christ seemed far removed from her world, an impersonal force.

At the moment, the only thing that was real to Margaret was her husband's strong arms around her.

Through the twenty years of their uncertain relationship, he had not held her enough.

"I want to believe in our marriage, Hugo."

"Believe me, because it is true. Someday I will make
you happy, Margaret. I will take you back to Roxbury
House. You will see. I promise. But I have work to do here
in India that I cannot walk away from. Perhaps you can
go back to see Victoria again next year, and I will join
you as soon as I can. You would like to go back, darling?"

"Yes, you know I would."

"Victoria would be pleased if you would oversee the
Silk House for a time."

She looked at him, her breath stopping. "Hugo, do
you mean it?"

"Darling, I have felt badly taking you away, knowing
how much it means to you. Perhaps if Belinda and Arlen's
wedding day were announced this Christmas, Arlen
could take both you and Belinda to London. Your mother
would want to meet him before the wedding next year."

"Hugo, are you certain about Alex?"

"I regret the necessity of having told you. You are
right. Belinda will be hurt if she finds out. It may be more
merciful for her not to know. Perhaps if she thought that
Alex had already married the young lady in Vienna.
What was her name?"

"Katarina Fredricks," said Margaret. "But Hugo, it
would be a lie. How could we do that to our own daughter?"

"If he returns to Vienna next year, no doubt he will
end up marrying her. We must do what is best for Belinda. We must think of her children, and of the entire
family. Believe me, she will get over this girlish infatuation with her cousin. And Arlen will be good to her."

"I do not know, Hugo. . . . Maybe you are right, and
yet, I do know she wants to go back to London."

36

"And if you and Arlen went with her, I am confident matters would turn out for the best."

"Yes, perhaps. Let me think about it, Hugo."

"Take all the time you need. But the matter must be settled before the Christmas festivities at Barrackpore." He kissed her forehead. "Sir George is pressing me for a public announcement."

———

"War!" The echo of voices around the breakfast table joined Coral's alarm. If the clouds of renewed war with Burma gathered in the northeast, then she must get home before all travel was cut off!

Sir Hugo's dark eyes circled the table. "The outpost at Jorhat was attacked by Burmese soldiers. A British officer named Selwyn was taken prisoner, interrogated, then butchered."

A sick moan came from Marianna, but Hugo seemed not to notice. "The governor-general asked Colonel Warbeck to send reinforcements. He has managed to get his son back in uniform. Major Buckley will be leading a troop north."

Coral knew of Assam's past skirmishes with Burma, but an all-out war? Coral glanced about the table, and all the faces were somber.

It was Marianna who asked the question that was hovering like a ghost above Coral's head. "Then how do we get home to Kingscote?" Her light blue eyes were wide, and her delicate features were so pale that her strawberry curls seemed even brighter.

Coral reached across the table and squeezed her younger sister's hand. "We will get home. We have Seward, remember? He can hire Indian guards to join our safari."

"I am afraid not, Coral," came Sir Hugo's firm voice.

She looked at her uncle across the table. The dark eyes beneath the heavy brows were fixed upon her.

"It is too dangerous to journey now, even with Seward. I discussed this with him yesterday. For the sake of safety, it is best you and your sisters wait until the matter at Jorhat is settled." He turned to his daughter, Belinda. "I suppose you will be pleased to have your cousins here for your engagement party during the Christmas holidays?"

Belinda paled at the word engagement and said nothing. Margaret said quickly, "For a wedding gift, your father wishes Sir George to escort us to London. While your grandmother becomes acquainted with Arlen, I will be overseeing the Silk House. You will like that, will you not, Belinda?"

Belinda's sultry dark eyes came alive, and she looked from her mother's tense face to her father. "Truly, Father?"

"I thought an interval at Roxbury House with Arlen before the wedding would make you happy. You may marry in London if you wish. Your grandmother will plan an extravagant ceremony, inviting the Duke and Duchess of Sandhurst. And it is no secret how your mother has longed these years to return to her silk design."

Coral's mind remained on Sir Hugo's announcement that she could not return to Kingscote. Her stomach muscles tightened. *She had to get home!* He was her uncle, but what right did he have to order her to stay in Calcutta when her father had sent for them to come home immediately?

"Seward can handle most anything." Coral found her voice interrupting the discussion of London. "With mother so ill, I am compelled to risk the safari. There may be others at Kingscote who are ill, including the children. I want to talk to Seward. Where can I find him?"

Silence fell upon those seated around the table. She was aware of the flicker of impatience in her uncle's eyes, but it was Aunt Margaret who spoke, her voice tense but calm. "Dear, we never know what these natives will do next. Your uncle has experience in these matters. We had best listen to him. Try not to worry. You will get home to your mother as soon as it is safe to travel."

Coral pushed back her plate and stood, but Sir Hugo's voice cut through her actions. "As your guardian while away from Kingscote, I am forced to act. Hampton would expect it of me. Seward and a few hired Indian mercenaries are hardly a safe vanguard for a two-month safari. Not with the risk of fighting." He smiled. "Besides, my dear, you are in no condition to be nursing a passel of children on Kingscote. You must set aside your sensitivity and look upon these matters with the eyes of a realist. India is a mother with a million squalling children. There is little any of us can do about it. Do sit down and finish your breakfast."

She heard Margaret's cup clatter on the saucer and became aware of the awkward silence holding the others to their chairs. Margaret was hoping she would not respond. . . . Coral knew that. But if she gave in now, what possibility would there be of returning home unless Hugo permitted it?

The fear of being manipulated against her will made her react promptly. Coral's calm voice surprised even herself. "I understand, Uncle. But I know tropical fever. I know what my mother is going through, and I cannot risk a year's absence waiting for the East India Company to settle their differences with Burma." She glanced at her sisters, who stared at her with surprise. "I will not put Kathleen and Marianna at risk if they wish to stay here. I will go alone if necessary."

The silence grew heavier. *Will someone please say something?* Her heart pounded.

Sir Hugo unexpectedly gave a short laugh. She saw what seemed to be a slight flicker of respect in his eyes. "You have always been a stalwart young woman, Coral, despite your problems with illness. I do not mean to question your liberties, nor to suggest you cannot go home if your heart is set. But you must understand my concerns. A raid on the safari could mean your captivity. I blanch at the horrendous difficulty Hampton would have in bargaining for your release."

Coral found his presence overpowering, and it could intimidate her emotionally if she let it.

"Really, Hugo, I do think we should wait to discuss this," said Margaret.

"You are right." He sounded sympathetic now. "Ethan's arrival will brighten your stay in Calcutta, Coral."

Taken off guard, she sat down quickly, staring at him. "Ethan? Coming here?"

"You did not know? We discussed it before I left London. He was to catch a Dutch ship from Dover a month after we sailed. He will be here before Christmas . . . in time for Belinda's engagement."

"No. He said nothing."

"He must have assumed I had already told you."

"I did not see him for several weeks before we sailed," Coral admitted. "He was at Oxford on medical business."

"Then that accounts for the little surprise," said Hugo good-naturedly.

"It is a surprise," Margaret said brightly, obviously trying to cheer Coral. "I must say though, I am as confused by this as Coral. Was not Ethan to be elevated to some position? Research, was it not, Hugo?"

He looked intently at his wife. "You are mistaken, dear."

"I am certain he told me so. He was looking forward to the position. Pass the tea, darling."

"You know how sacrificing Ethan can be." Hugo refilled her cup. "Nothing is too great for the medical cause. Like Coral, he has a concern for the Indian people."

Caught by the turn of events, Coral tried to sort through her emotions. *Ethan is coming to India . . .*

"But he will continue his research," said Hugo. "Hampton has been in correspondence with him about setting up a lab in the jungles around Kingscote."

Margaret turned to Coral. "With Elizabeth ill, it will come at a good time."

Anxious to be alone to think, Coral rose from her chair too swiftly, and a wave of dizziness threatened her balance. Sir Hugo also stood, looking alert.

"It is nothing," murmured Coral. "I often get dizzy; it passes."

"Send for Doctor Harvey."

A doctor! "No, really, I do not need a physician," argued Coral.

Less than an hour later, Coral sat in a high-backed armchair, submitting to the lecture of the retired army physician.

"A bit of rest, and a spoonful of this before bed, and you will be up dancing again by Christmas."

"A few days in bed will do her well," added Sir Hugo.

Coral started to protest, but Doctor Harvey plucked nervously at his silver goatee. "Rightly so, Hugo, rightly so."

"I would hate to write a letter to Hampton telling him you had a relapse," said Hugo.

Coral glanced at him. Memories of her long stay at the summer house in London brought a cold feeling of

41

panic. *No, God, not that again, please.* The very thought of being placed under strong medication caused her to give in, but once in bed and alone with her sisters, she bolted upright, tossing aside the covers and confronting Kathleen.

"Why did you not stand with me against Uncle?"

Kathleen turned her back, staring out the window, but Marianna wrung her hands, and her voice quavered when she spoke. "I fear Uncle. I am sorry, Sissy."

"I was not speaking of you, Marianna, but Kathleen. She is the eldest, and she should have stood with me." Coral groaned, walked to the rattan settee by her vanity table, and sank down. "In Calcutta till after Christmas! Mama's ill and Papa needs us! I am not about to stay!" She stood again. "I know what you are thinking, Kathleen! That if we stay, you can somehow return to London with Aunt Margaret and Belinda!"

Kathleen whirled, her eyes snapping. "Yes! I am the eldest, and I have even more right to a life of my own than you. Working with Jacques at the Silk House means as much to me as the school you hope to build on Kingscote."

"Oh do, *do* stop!" cried Marianna. "I do hate for the two of you to argue! I hate it! Oh, Coral, what do you intend to do about Uncle's wishes?"

"What can I do? I am confined to bed till the picnic. Aunt Margaret will see to that. She will be watching me. They both will, just like they did in London. Five days in bed! I must get a message to Seward."

Kathleen eyed her dubiously. "What can Seward do? You heard Uncle. His 'suggestion' was more like a warning: 'Stay in bed, my dear, or you will be here till spring.' "

"Mama may be in heaven by then," sighed Marianna.

"Will you stop that!" Kathleen winced. "Uncle wants

to keep you here until Cousin Ethan arrives at Christmas," Kathleen said thoughtfully. "I was surprised you dug your heels in as long as you did."

"Uncle may be guardian, but Papa sent Seward to bring us home," said Coral. "I know Seward. He is loyal. After I explain everything, he will cooperate and arrange the safari."

"Against Uncle's concerns for safety? I am not so certain. He cannot be making it up about the danger of travel." She took a letter from her bodice. "You said I did not back you up, but I could have given Uncle more reason to delay our journey if I showed him this."

Suspicious, Coral walked toward her. "A letter?"

"From Captain McKay. It arrived from Plassey this morning by delivery boy."

"Plassey is on our way north," said Coral cautiously.

"Yes, and it is the reason Gavin was not at the ball. He was transferred to the 82nd regiment there. He wrote that they expect trouble. Not from Burma, it is too far away, but from India—the kingdom of the Maharattas."

Marianna wrinkled her nose. "Ma-ha-what?"

"A central Indian state independent of the Company. Captain McKay says they have had trouble with them for years. When we travel, we will pass near where there is fighting."

Coral was more doubtful than her determination showed. War . . . would it ever end? She thought of Major Buckley. So he, too, was back in the military and leading a troop to the outpost at Jorhat. *Jorhat!* She caught her breath.

Kathleen scowled at her, and Marianna came out of her pessimistic mood long enough to fix her with a curious stare.

"What is it?" Kathleen asked.

"I have an idea," said Coral.

"Oh, no. I do not want to hear it," said Kathleen, walking to the door. "Come, Marianna, let Coral rest."

"Wait," said Coral, her eyes gleaming. They both looked at her—Kathleen, dubious; Marianna, expectant.

Coral was thinking of Jace. How long would he be in Calcutta? A plan was blazing through her mind. What if—what if she could get Major Buckley to bring them to Kingscote? Sir Hugo's argument about the risk of danger would be annulled. English civilians often journeyed under the protection of the East India Company.

"I know what you are thinking," said Kathleen. "That we could travel under military escort. I heard what Uncle said about Major Buckley. But that still leaves the problem of Ethan. Uncle will insist we wait for his arrival so we can all travel home together."

"Coral, you will not have a relapse, will you?" asked Marianna worriedly.

Coral smiled brightly, even though she did feel tired. There was hope again. And again, like discovering information on Gem, the hope rested on Jace Buckley.

"Do not worry about me. I can survive the safari to Kingscote. And as for Ethan, he did not expect to travel with us. He will need to journey slowly to safeguard his medical equipment. Oh, I am glad he is coming! He will be able to help Mother the way he did me. See, Marianna? Everything is going to turn out well. The Lord is directing our paths."

"He is? I thought it was Uncle Hugo," said Marianna.

"Suppose Uncle discovers what you are up to?" warned Kathleen.

"He will not," said Coral with confidence, thinking of her clandestine meeting with Javed Kasam.

"Hugo is not one who enjoys being thwarted," said Kathleen. "Do you know he used to be a corsair?"

Marianna sucked in her breath. Coral stared.

"Belinda told me," said Kathleen.

"Why would Belinda say a thing like that about her father?" asked Coral.

"Because a few weeks ago she overheard him talking to an Englishman. They scuttled a Portuguese ship off the coast of Pondicherry when they were young."

Coral could believe her.

"Belinda says the man was unusual in his appearance. His eyes were pale, and his skin was unusually white-looking. Even his hair looked platinum."

"An albino?" asked Coral.

"A pale-eyed ghost," whispered Marianna.

"Nonsense," said Coral. "But whatever you do, say nothing to Aunt Margaret. Her relationship with Uncle is already strained because of Belinda and Sir George."

"I do not blame Belinda about not wanting to marry Sir George," said Kathleen. "The man is as cold and domineering as Hugo." She took hold of Marianna's arm, pulling her sister reluctantly to the door with her. "And do not repeat a word of anything I said to Aunt Margaret."

"Of course not, Sissy," Marianna replied. "What do you take me for, a silly goose?"

Kathleen smiled too sweetly, patted her sister's red curls, then shut the door behind them.

4

The next day Coral sat in the rickshaw holding on to her wide-brimmed hat, its trailing ribbons matching the yards of blue organdy of her dress worn over a layer of petticoats. The delicately puffed sleeves and tailored bodice were decorated with tiny white shell buttons.

It was the day after the picnic. And again, with the help of little Jay, she had managed to get away from the house without being noticed. Holding to the seat, Coral looked about, a little dazed by her surroundings. There were people everywhere—so many that it was inconceivable to view them as individuals with hopes and pains of their own. Shoppers and beggars ignored one another, keeping to their castes. The untouchables were at the bottom, most of them without hope, destitute of the compassion of their fellows.

Calcutta sprawled north and south along the Hooghly River. Children scampered everywhere, some of them naked except for worn loin cloths. Numerous ox-drawn carts and meandering, unattended cows blocked the movement of traffic. One old cow stood munching the fresh goods from a cart while the merchant stood by passively. Not far away beggars were chased away with

47

a ring of curses. *The paradox of Calcutta,* Coral thought.

There were various costumes among the people, each color and style belonging to different castes. Wealth and destitution met in a strange kind of coexistence, as the caste system led the majority to accept their state as divine will. Death was seen as only one more event to bring yet another reincarnation. Perhaps after ten thousand reincarnations freedom might come. Maybe. It was doubtful for most. In the meantime, to break one's caste was unthinkable.

Now, in the center of this metropolis of humanity, her own human frailty obscured spiritual vision. A multitude of faces blurred, and voices lost their distinction. She felt deluged by the need around her, and for a moment felt nothing but a sudden desire to escape it all.

How can God care for so many? she wondered. But He did. She thought of the children of Israel in bondage to Pharaoh in the book of Exodus. *I have heard their groaning,* God had told Moses.

Her eyes moistened; her palm clenched into a damp fist on her lap. *Oh, to see these as you see them, Father; to feel as you feel for their souls.*

Was it possible? Would not such love and compassion break her heart?

Then grant me but a drop of your compassion in my cup. And even then, I can only carry it by your grace.

Surely this place, however destitute of spiritual life, however miserable, is where the Lord wants me to be. In the end it will be worth every moment of sacrifice.

"And soon, I shall have a portion of Scripture in Hindi," Coral murmured with a smile. She would spread that light from one end of Kingscote to the other! She would teach the children in their own language.

Would she be able to convince Seward to proceed with the planned safari? And what would be her father's reaction to starting a mission school?

Pray, she thought. *I must pray about the school, about Kingscote, about Mother recovering from the fever.*

At times Coral felt overwhelmed at the impossibility of it all, as if she were but a tiny pebble on India's vast continent. She was not only up against Sir Hugo and the Company's displeasure, but she had no guarantee that even her parents would consent. The fire set by the sepoys at the time of Gem's abduction had frightened her father. Could she blame him? He had poured his very life into building the silk plantation into its present success. One tiny flame tossed to the caterpillar hatcheries could mean its end.

She shuddered, remembering her dream. The search for Gem among the flames was so vivid that she could almost smell the smoke.

The rickshaw found a path in the throng, and with a jolt began moving through the marketplace. Next to Government-House, Coral caught sight of St. John's Church, and it was here that she had the rickshaw boy stop. Inside, she sat in a pew and spent several minutes in silent prayer.

When she returned to the rickshaw, she heard the clatter of hoofs behind her on the stone. Turning, she saw a young man astride a Company horse. The man looked vaguely familiar. Where had she seen him before? He wore a knee-length coat and tan breeches, and as he walked the horse toward her he removed his hat and smiled.

"Why, good afternoon, Miss Kendall."

"I am sorry. The fault is mine, but . . ." her voice trailed away.

"The name is Franklin Peddington. I met you the other night at the state ball. I believe you know my brother Charles."

"Yes, of course, hello, Mr. Peddington!" She recognized the secretary to the governor-general. "Perhaps you can help me. I am looking for a friend of my father. A Mister Seward."

He glanced at the rickshaw and seemed surprised that she was without a chaperon. Coral hastened, "It is most important that I talk to him."

"By all means, Miss Kendall. I shall send someone to locate him. He is probably at the military quarters."

The court building was set back into a square, with the clerks' offices on the south and the jail on the north. There were a number of native troopers about, their scarlet coats standing out and their shakos all neatly in place upon their heads. An Indian in a blue turban stood by one of the doors. Behind him were several orientals, known unflatteringly as coolies, and these served as errand boys. He called, "*Koi hai!*" and they came running up, offering the bow of honorary greeting. "*Huzoor, huzoor, burra-sahib!*"

"Send word to find Sahib Seward at the garrison. Miss Kendall is here to see him. *Ram! Ram!* Hurry."

They ran off, and Franklin Peddington stood with her in the shade of the building, waiting for Seward. When she asked about Charles, he explained that his younger brother was still with Master Carey at Serampore, but that he would be coming to work for the Company soon after the new year.

She had not forgotten Charles's invitation to show her around William Carey's mission compound, but it would not be as easy to accomplish as slipping off for a few hours as she was doing now. Visiting Serampore meant a trip up the Hooghly by boat and would be an all-day excursion.

"I believe that is Seward now," Franklin said, politely taking his leave of her.

Seward was a giant of a man, broad-shouldered, with a full wide face to match his size. A stringy thatch of graying red hair was tied at the nape of his neck beneath his hat. At the age of fifty, he could best any man younger than himself. He had served her father on Kingscote well, arriving soon after the birth of Gem, but had left with Michael to sail on the *Madras* with Jace Buckley to Macau and Cadiz. Just how much he was involved in the Darjeeling tea project, she was not quite certain. She supposed that he had a percentage in the future plantation. Recently Seward had agreed to serve Hampton by seeing Coral and her sisters home to Kingscote.

Seward's past was a mystery, and Coral never inquired into it, but she rather suspected it might have something to do with smuggling in China. Yet she had no concern for her safety with Seward near. He was now to be her coconspirator in bringing her to meet the major and insure her safari home, although he was likely to disapprove of her plan.

His brows hunched together as he came up, his eyes searching her face. "Something wrong, lass?"

She faced him for battle, hands on hips. "Wrong? Not if Sir Hugo's attempt to keep me in Calcutta under lock and key is foiled. Where have you been?"

Seward scowled when she mentioned Sir Hugo. "Aye, I understand how ye feel, but 'twas Sir Hugo who insisted you and your sisters stay. And I've been keepin' me ear open here about any fightin' in the north. Since Sir Hugo be your uncle, there waren't very much I could do about it. His word be law now, lass."

"Trouble in Jorhat or not, I want to leave next week as scheduled."

"Now, ye wouldn't be expectin' me to risk the rage of Sir Hugo by going against his clear commands, would ye? He be an orn'ry man, and maybe he's got something about it not being wise to travel to the northern frontier. Neither Mister Hampton nor Miss Elizabeth would be wantin' me to risk their comely daughters to dangerous trekking."

She sobered, thinking more of the danger to Kingscote than to herself. "Do you think it was soldiers from Burma who made the attack on Jorhat?"

He rubbed his bearded chin and hedged. Coral's lashes narrowed suspiciously. "You do not believe Sir Hugo?"

"Not for me to say till Jace—I mean the major—looks into it."

She pressed. "Does Major Buckley think otherwise?"

"Now would he be telling me that?"

"I have a feeling he tells more than you are willing to share with me. By the way," she said cautiously, "where is the major? Is he about?"

He grinned. "He be on the *Madras*. A bit of coddling before he rides north."

"Then it is true? He will command the troop at Jorhat?"

"Aye, and not a bit pleased about exchanging the sea for the British cavalry. He be leavin' on short notice, as soon as the colonel gives the word. I be expectin' to ride with him on my way to Kingscote."

Coral offered her sweetest smile. "I thought you might intend to ride with him, Seward. That is why I'm here now. I am going with you. What safer journey could I have to the northern frontier than with you and Major Buckley's troop?"

For a moment his expression was blank. Then as he became aware of the full import of her words, the rugged lines creased above his shaggy brows. "Now look here, Jace won't be liking that, I can tell ye so right now. You're wastin' your time and breath. I be sure of it."

Coral smiled, and her eyes challenged him with good humor. "Indeed? Suppose you let him decide?"

He cocked his head and scanned her suspiciously. "I hear ye was up all night waltzing with the major at that ball."

"I could hardly refuse him. He was Michael's friend, was he not? Besides, he saved me from a batch of crows in the bazaar the day we arrived. Nevermind, I will explain later. Now, Seward, be the dear that you are, and take me to see his clipper."

He scowled and folded his muscled arms across the wide expanse of his chest. "Ain't worthy to be wastin' your eyes upon, lass. 'Tis a ship. That be all."

She gave a laugh. "Now I have heard it all. A lover of the sea telling me the *Madras* is unworthy of my inspection?"

He lowered his eyes. " 'Tis the ship we lost Michael on."

Coral had forgotten that. Her smile faded. Memory of her brother swept in like the wind across a deck. Seward's feelings for Michael were obvious, and she laid a hand on his arm. "He is with the Lord. We grieve for the loss of him, but he knows only joy."

He sighed. "Aye, that be true, little one. Sure ye be wantin' to walk aboard?"

She straightened her shoulders. "Yes, Seward. I do. And it is important I meet with the major before he leaves."

Seward gave her a wary glance as though he read the shift in her thinking. "Pardon me saying so, but I put nothin' past Sir Hugo. If he thinks you be stirring up trouble, even godly trouble, by starting some school for the little ones, Sir Hugo will swoop down on your father like a crow on a ripe mango."

She took his arm and propelled him toward the rick-

53

shaw, all the while smiling. "Let's not discuss it now. First I must get home. Now, Seward, this matter with the major is going to work out well indeed, just you wait and see."

"I don't like this. And I got a feeling Jace won't like it either."

Coral remembered her unsuccessful meeting with Javed Kasam. Would this be another cause doomed to failure? She had no doubt that the elusive captain could be difficult, but she refused to accept defeat without at least trying.

"Then if you are so certain he will refuse, there is nothing to worry about. Take me to his ship."

———

As they rode toward Diamond Point on the Calcutta harbor, Coral asked him about Jace. She learned for the first time that Seward had known Jace's father, Captain Jarred Buckley, and that he had sailed with him to China. As a boy, Jace had been raised at his father's side, sailing with him to the rich and mysterious trading ports of the East.

Seward's walnut face, creased with sun lines, settled into a scowl. " 'Tis too long a tale to embark upon now. But his father and me were traders in tea . . . and well, some other commodities that isn't fit to mention. Captain Jarred could be orn'ry at times, but he doted on Jace."

Her suspicions grew. "You mean to tell me his father was a smuggler, and you were his partner?"

Seward's hardened face reddened a bit. "Jace was but a lad at the time and he had no mother. He had nothing to do with piracy." Seward cleared his throat and glanced at her sideways. "He went wherever his father sailed. If ye feel sorry for these untouchables, lass, then you ought to feel for Jace as well. His own fate as a lad in China 'twas far worse than what may befall these untouchables. Why, after his father died, he was left alone on the beach of Whampoa and saw the Buckley ship go up in flames—taking many good men with her. Captain Jarred was beheaded by Chinese warlords before the boy's very eyes, and for a few years Jace was a child-slave. He still carries some scars on him, and they be not all on his flesh, I can tell ye that."

A child-slave . . . Coral's understanding of the captain of the *Madras* softened against her will. Jace was more vulnerable than he appeared.

"His father and me—" he paused and cleared his throat, "we owned a ship licensed by John Company."

Coral tried to recall the vague conversations that her father had engaged in with Seward when they both thought that she was not listening. Her father must already know of Seward's unscrupulous past. "John Company is like the East India Company?"

Seward let out a breath. "Aye, but John Company is merely another name for the East India Company herself. John Company handles, well, less honorable trade. They issue licenses to independent ships to haul cargo. They're better known as China traders, sailing the Eastern ports—Singapore to Pearl River in China." He glanced at her. "Most times our cargo was legitimate, as you say—tea and chinaware. But we was into dark contraband too." Seward shifted his position.

Coral felt his eyes gauging her response, to see if she was offended. She straightened her hat. "Do not forget I was born and raised in India, Seward. Father has mentioned the horrors of opium. Is that what you and Captain Jarred Buckley smuggled?"

Seward sighed. "I had nothing to do with the ugly stuff. I was against the idea of messing with it from the beginning. Jarred, too, was against it. But he got into some deep trouble, and his ship came into debt. He was afraid he'd lose her, and he got involved with the China traders."

"So he compromised."

He paused. "He did. But he was no God-fearing man, lass. He loved his son, but that was about all he did love. The opium was made here in British Bengal and sold to the Chinese mainland. We got caught in something that was dark indeed, and in the end it took his life. I escaped from the attack on the beach by swimming out to a Chinese junk. I tried to save Jace, but in the fighting I couldn't find him."

"He was left there?"

Seward's face became dark and he stared straight ahead. "Aye."

Coral digested what she was hearing about Jace's unpleasant childhood. What he must have gone through as a child-slave to angry Chinese warlords, especially as the son of an English captain! "How did he escape China?"

Seward obviously took pleasure in telling of Jace's wit. She found out that he had eventually escaped by route of the Old Silk Road across the Himalayas, a passage once used by the ancient caravan traders bringing silk from the Chinese dynasties to Persia and Baghdad. He told her that upon crossing through Sikkim and into the area of Darjeeling, he had met a so-called *munshi*— a teacher and writer—by the name of Gokul.

"But Gokul wasn't any of that, not really. He knew the ins and outs of the bazaars—the world of intrigue— and Jace learned it too."

Again, Coral remembered Javed Kasam. "Yes," she murmured. "He did learn it, and well."

By the age of fourteen, Jace had already embraced the life of an adventurer. With Gokul, they toured India and Burma. It was in Bengal that the colonel John Sebastian Warbeck had fought with a British-held outpost. A village was taken, the raja fled with his remaining soldiers, and the colonel had taken Jace with him back to Calcutta, adopting him as a son. There followed another interval when Jace entered military school in London, then returned to serve with the British forces. But he always had a love of the sea.

"Learned from Captain Jarred. He be considered by the Company to be one of the best captains about, but an interloper."

Coral vaguely recalled the word being used by her father. "Interloper?" She hoped the word did not mean anything of ill-repute.

"It means he be in business for himself."

Thinking of contraband, Coral stirred uneasily and glanced at him from beneath her hat. "How did he manage to get the *Madras*?"

Seward rubbed his beard. "I don't know. But he was hauling tea down the Pearl River from Canton, and he could have gotten the clipper that way. He's smart enough. While he's a bit of a wild one, he's not a blackguard. Least not like Captain Jarred was."

"He is going back into the military to save his ship?"

Seward unexpectedly chuckled. "The colonel be a determined man. The two of 'em butt heads at times, yet they have themselves a silent agreement of respect. The colonel, he be doin' everything to keep him in the Company. Right now Jace has got little choice in the matter. But as for the sea—well," he boasted with a grin, "there ain't an Englishman in India who knows it better. Knows the Hindu mind, too. Speaks Bengali like a native, some Marathi too, and he knows their religions like a man knows the back of his hand."

Religion. . . . Again, she wondered about Jace Buckley spending his formative years with "Gokul the munshi."

"Is he inclined . . . ah, toward the Hindu belief?"

"He knows it well, but he has books from John Newton, too, and knows the old man himself."

"He knows John Newton!"

"But that ain't to say he be a devoted Christian," he warned, looking at her.

Did her pleasure show too much?

Seward gave her a thoughtful glance. "You need to ask Jace about what he believes. He don't talk much about it. You like him, lass?"

Coral busied herself with her hat. "How can I say? He is an enigma. As adventurers go, I suppose he can mingle comfortably with the best of them, and the worst."

"There ain't no excuse when it comes to the past way of things, but a man ought not to be marked by the sins of his father. As far as Jace goes, you won't find a man with an inch more of courage, and it's my thinking that he ought to stand on his own merit, not his father's past sins."

Seward was right of course. She turned her head and cautiously scrutinized the side of his hard brown face. So this was the background of her father's most trusted friend and servant. It proved a man could change, that the grace of God was sufficient for the worst of blackguards, for Seward now claimed to adhere to the name of Christ.

When they arrived at the East India docks at Diamond Point, people of all nationalities jammed the harbor. Strange dialects mingled in Coral's ears, exotic scents floated on the light breeze that ruffled the sails of many ships, and the steps leading to the water were filled with Hindu bathers seeking religious cleansing in the holy Ganges River.

With precarious footsteps, Coral followed Seward's lead down the quay. Her eyes skimmed the ships and fell on an impressive white-masted clipper farther down the dock with the name *Madras*.

Seward stopped. "Sure ye be wantin' to do this?"

"Yes, Seward, I am certain."

"Aye, then, ye wait here a minute."

Coral watched him intercept a lean, bronzed Indian sailor known as a *karwa*, and a moment later Seward climbed the plank and disappeared. She felt a tightening in her chest. How would Jace react to seeing her aboard his ship? There was no denying that he had been upset with her offer to buy him with the Roxbury ring.

Her eyes scanned the ship. Strange. . . . He was willing to go back into the military in order to save his vessel even when the idea irked him, but he would not accept the ring from her and walk free.

She waited, rehearsing in her mind what she would say to him. Could she convince him of her desperate need to reach Kingscote? Did she dare offer to pay him for his service, this time not with the ring, but perhaps a cargo of Kingscote silk?

It seemed an endless time had crept by before she saw Seward's rugged frame walking toward her.

He hesitated and rubbed his bearded chin. "Lass, if I were you, I'd not go barging into his cabin. The captain's in a riled mood."

For a moment, she feared that he was still angry over their last meeting. "He refused to see me?"

"Nay, nothing like that. He don't know you're here, but he be a mite vexed, and nursing one black headache."

Headache. . . . Coral tensed.

From Seward's expression, she could see that he was

hoping she would turn back. Coral drew in a little breath and picked up her skirts. She had too much to gain to turn back now. She slipped past him. Riled mood or not, she was going through with the meeting. "It is all right, Seward. I want to see him."

Seward shrugged, then walked behind her as she made her way up the plank to the deck of the *Madras*.

5

Jace touched the bloody bruise on the back of his head and winced. His lack of vigilance embarrassed him. Who would have thought that after escaping harrowing expeditions from China to Sumatra, he would naively allow himself to fall prey to a common thief in Calcutta?

He had left the ship late last night with the prized Moghul sword in his scabbard when he was struck. The club must have weighed a ton, he decided sourly. His vision was blurred, his head throbbed, and he did not have a rupee left. Far worse, the magnificent sword belonging to a fifteenth century Moghul king from Agra was lost. The sword could have bought a wealth of information on what had really happened at the outpost in Jorhat.

Sprawled on his cot, donned only in worn buckskin breeches, he felt in a miserable mood when the tap on his cabin door sounded. It rattled through his head like a twelve-pound cannon. He winced again.

"No need to break it down, Seward! Just come in!" The door opened abruptly, and a shaft of bright daylight flooded the cabin. Jace turned his head away to avoid the painful glare, and snapped, "Get Jin-Soo to dig up some snake cure for this miserable headache. I am desperate. Bring the coffee?"

"The kansamah says you're out of coffee, lad. So Jin-Soo be brewin' tea." Seward cleared his throat. "You have yerself a visitor—"

"Tea! I am sick of thinking about it, smelling it, bartering for it. I must be insane to want to grow the stuff! Remind me of this if I ever get out of uniform. We will go to the West Indies for coffee beans."

"Your kansamah be ready to mutiny against his cookstove, lad. Says he needs a bag of rupees for supplies."

"I am leasing the clipper to the Company for a voyage to the Spice Islands. They can buy their own supplies."

"Aye, but the karwas are threatening to hire onto another ship. Seems the colonel didn't pay 'em when they arrived from Singapore."

"Tell them I was robbed last night. No one gets paid aboard ship until I get back from Jorhat. Here, help me with these, will you? I can't bend over." He threw the boots in the direction of Seward's voice. "Did you send men to check out the taverns?"

"Aye, nothing. No scoundrel boasting a Moghul sword."

"It is worth a fortune! I doubt if the thief even knows what it is."

"Lad, ye've got a visitor—"

"No visitors!"

———

Coral drew in a little breath, ignoring his words, and decided Seward was not doing enough to announce just *who* the captain's visitor was. Mustering her courage, she stepped through the cabin door just as the boots landed with a thud near her silk slippers. As her eyes collided with the bare-chested masculine form sprawled on the cot, she went mute and blushed.

So! He *was* a rogue, just as she had first thought at the bazaar! There was no telling where he had been during the night! And his polished manners at the state ball? Another of his masquerades!

Coral found her voice at last. "You were right, Seward. It looks as if the captain of the *Madras* is in no condition to discuss the reason for my visit. You had best take me home."

Jace abruptly turned his face toward the open doorway where she stood, and she saw him squint against the light. She stared back at him piously, hoping her blush did not show, and self-consciously touched her wide-brimmed hat.

For a moment he said nothing. "Well, Seward. Remind me to clobber you later."

Seward cleared his throat again. "Aye, Cap'n. Sorry, I'll . . . ah, wait outside. Pardon me, lass, but I'll let ye two talk this one out alone."

Coral stood with false dignity, feeling herself shaking under her armor. Nevertheless, her expression was unreadable.

A golden monkey suddenly jumped from a bookcase to swing on the lamp chain above the desk.

"Get off there, Goldfish!" Jace commanded. "You'll break it."

The monkey leaped to his cot and snatched Jace's tunic, intending to run off with it. Jace grabbed it back, and the monkey squealed and took refuge on the bookcase.

"He has no manners. I do not know why I keep him. Would you like a new pet, Madam Khan?"

Her blush deepened. *Madam Khan!*

He stood up with a slight smirk, swaying a little, and

she stared at him. He gestured with his tunic. "Would you mind?"

Her eyes widened a little at his temerity, then she quickly turned her back, arms folded.

"I assumed you would not mind, since you barged into my cabin," he said.

"I apologize. . . . I was desperate, afraid you would refuse to see me."

"Now why would I do that, my dear Madam Khan?"

"Sir, would you please stop calling me that?"

"In fact, had I known you would grace my ship with your company, I would have had dinner ready. Do you like Mughlai cuisine?" came his lightly mocking voice.

"I am not hungry, thank you." She glanced about for any signs of Hindu relics. There were none. When she turned back, he had slipped his tunic over his head, and she watched him stand unsteadily while the blood surged to his temples.

"Do you mind if I groan? It makes me feel better." He grasped the edge of the bunk and steadied himself.

Coral laughed softly. "I am usually prone to sympathy where suffering is concerned. For some reason," she said airily, "your discomfort brings me satisfaction."

"No doubt I deserve every bit of it. The natural harvest of my undisciplined appetites."

"Your description is quite appropriate."

"But your assumption is not." He made his way to an oak desk, and throwing open a drawer, rummaged through the contents. "I was robbed last night. Someone clobbered me. Nothing more."

Robbed? For a moment she was too embarrassed to answer. "Oh, I see. . . . I am terribly sorry." Coral threw off her hat and hurried toward him, taking hold of his arm to ease him into the captain's chair. "Can I . . . ah, help you find something in your desk drawer? You see, I thought—"

"Yes, I know what you thought. Well, think nothing of it. I was not exactly prepared to receive visitors. I do not care to sit down."

She dropped his arm, and he leaned against his desk. Folding his arms across his chest, he studied her intently. He seemed in no mood for compromise, so Coral walked back to her hat, picked it up, and self-consciously put it back on, tying it firmly beneath her chin.

He raised one brow but remained silent.

"I must talk to you. However, since you are in pain I can come back tomorrow."

He smiled. With relief, Coral smiled too. "I—"

"How can I help you, Miss Kendall?"

At least he had stopped saying *"Madam Khan."* She wondered how she could make amends and approach him about going home to Kingscote, and finding Gem. She felt a tug at her skirt and looked down. It was Goldfish. She stooped and picked him up, and he clung to her, his thin golden arm going around her neck.

"So you intend to open a mission school?"

His question jolted her. It was the last thing she expected him to say. "Who told you?"

"Seward."

She tried to read his thoughts, but he was inscrutable.

"William Carey, at least, would approve," he added.

That Jace would know of the missionary translator surprised her. She remembered what Seward had told her about John Newton. What books had Newton given to him?

"You know Master Carey?"

"No. Gokul told me about him." He threw open a second drawer and searched the contents.

"I am equally surprised your munshi friend would

know about the Bible translation work," she said, watching him rummage through the drawer and wondering what he was looking for.

"Carey knows a few brahmins in Serampore," said Jace. "Right now, he's looked upon as a mere oddity. They respect his interest in India, and in Sanskrit. Carey is quite a scholar for having been a shoe cobbler. But once he gains a convert to Christianity, matters will change. He will have not only the displeasure of the Company, but also the anger of the brahmins."

She was surprised Jace understood. He also knew about the Company's policy toward missionary work.

"Master Carey will never retreat in the face of opposition," she said.

"From what Gokul has said, you are right. The man is dedicated to his cause. And what of you, Miss Kendall? Are you also prepared to brave the lion's den? A mission school on Kingscote will be enough to set the ghazis on edge."

As always, her thoughts raced back to Gem's abduction. Had it been executed by Hindu religious zealots opposing his upbringing?

"The untouchables are under my father's jurisdiction," she said. "I never approved, but he bought them. And my uncle's wish to bring Kingscote under the control of the Company will be met dourly by my father. With or without the support of my uncle, I intend to help these children."

His voice was smooth. "I have little but applause for anyone who wishes to embrace orphans. But you must know that the danger to yourself is real if you ignore the ire of the Hindus. Does your father agree to the school?"

Coral was cautious. He did not yet know. Her task to convince the great Hampton Kendall would prove difficult. *The first giant to fell. . . .*

66

"I am certain that in the end I shall prevail. Father has always had a heart for the children, and I intend to convince him the school will meet a desperate need. The untouchables will learn to read and write, as well as discover a God who will not abandon them to tigers, or throw them to the river crocodiles as meaningless sacrifices."

His gaze swept her. "Well said. Noble causes are not without their sacrifices, however. Sometimes they are quite costly. I should loathe seeing you become an offering to the river. Seward seems to think you are starting the school in the memory of Gem."

At the mention of Gem she became alert, studying his face, but saw nothing to convince her that he had changed his mind about letting her hire his services. But when she remembered that he would soon become a major again, she wondered if his refusal had partly been due to his obligations to the military. She took courage and, seizing the opportunity, said with a rush, "I offended you by offering the Roxbury ring. It was not my intention." She moved to where he leaned against the desk and sought his eyes.

"That morning so long ago . . . the morning of the monsoon when I walked to the wagon carrying Jemani's son, you said something to me that I have since thought of a thousand times. In London I went to sleep with the hope of your words on my heart, and when I awoke, I was still thinking of them. Do you remember what you said to me, Captain Buckley?"

Holding her gaze, he reached over and sent Goldfish scampering away. "Suppose you tell me."

"You told me you knew Rajiv. That he had been your friend."

"He was."

"You said you knew his family. That his uncle was a raja."

"The maharaja yet lives."

Coral's heart began to pound. She sought for some flicker of hope in his eyes indicating he would reconsider.

"Since you know the maharaja, you could discover if Gem is alive. He would tell you." She waited. The moments of silence seemed long.

"A school for the untouchables is not enough to challenge your spirit, is that it? You also want to alert the maharaja."

"I want my son back."

"If he were alive, and you had him back, you could not keep him at Kingscote for long. It would demand your constant vigil. Would you have him surrounded with a bodyguard until he was man enough to carry his own sword?"

"Yes, if that is what it takes to secure his freedom. I could send him to London, even Spain. Jemani died in peace believing that her child would be taught the truth. As long as he is kept from me, and wrapped in the darkness of falsehood, the vow I made that night is but a mockery."

"Consider the idea that Rajiv was killed by his family, or someone hired by them. That should convince you of the zeal of those involved. The maharaja's nephew does not break caste without penalty. Gem would pay a high price to bear the Kendall name."

"I think he would bear that name proudly and insist on his position. And whatever price I need to pay for his return, I will pay."

"Do you think Rajiv's enemies will bargain with a woman who is dedicated to the Christ they do not own?"

"I must try. I have to know if he is alive!"

"And if he is? What makes you think he would choose to come back to you?"

Not come back to her willingly? It was unthinkable! Gem was her baby, her beloved. . . . She had held him, fed him, laughed with him, cried with him. . . .

Her thoughts were interrupted as a frail, old Chinese man with a silver braid entered with a tray and, seeing Coral, bowed at the waist.

"No evil coffee, Captain; only honorable Chinese tea."

Coral turned away to conceal her emotions. What was Jace trying to say? That Gem—if alive—had adopted his Indian ancestry to her exclusion? But he was her *son*. She had experienced Gem's devotion too long to believe he would not return to her if given the chance. Still, Jace's suggestion troubled her.

As Jin-Soo poured the tea, and bandaged the captain's bruise, Coral worked to calm her emotions by focusing on the various treasures from all the ports. There was jade from China, rice paper from Japan, and Indian ivory. A rugged but costly mahogany chest from the Spice Islands stood with a drawer open, and her eyes fell upon a glimmer of black. Absently, she picked up a miniature cheetah, noting that the piece was designed well. Its left eye was missing, but that made it more intriguing. The cheetah, the Indian panther, a symbol of freedom and strength, was in reality vulnerable. Her fevered emotions took mental solace in the cool ebony stone, and she ran her thumb over the smooth piece.

The cabin was enclosed with silence, and realizing that Jin-Soo had left, Coral turned.

Jace leaned against the desk, cup in hand, watching her.

"The Indian mercenary I met nearly two weeks ago could not be bought," she began. "But I was not trying to *buy* him."

His eyes grew remote, and she could feel the impenetrable barrier between them.

"Very well. I accept the idea that he thinks a silk heiress is a spoiled damsel demanding her way. I doubt if I shall ever see him again."

He drank his tea. Was his mood of indifference affected?

"I have not come to your ship to offer you anything, Captain, but to seek your help, to appeal to you as a friend." She walked up to him. "You are the only one left who can help me! Sir Hugo insists Gem is dead." She turned away, the pain rushing through her. "And my father accepts the same decision." She looked back at him. "But I do not. Every beat of my heart tells me he lives."

His eyes were alert. "Why did Sir Hugo insist he was dead?"

"He was there the night when Gem was abducted, and the fire—"

"He was on Kingscote?"

"Yes. It was not long after the adoption ceremony. My uncle was soon to leave for London to address Parliament."

"What exactly happened that night? Seward could not fill me in on everything. Do you remember?"

"Most of it. I was ill afterwards. It was then that my family decided to send me to London to be treated by Doctor Boswell. I told you about it at the ball."

"Yes. Go on."

"I awoke that night on Kingscote and heard horses and shouting below the verandah. I saw my father and some members of the family. There was a fire in the direction of the hatcheries. I do not know why, but I suddenly remembered what you had said to me about Gem, and I was afraid. I ran into the nursery and—" Her voice broke. "I saw a sepoy climbing over the verandah. He had Gem! And Gem kept screaming *Mummy! Mummy! Mummy!* I tried to save him but I couldn't! And ... I couldn't—"

She was sobbing, and unexpectedly, she felt the side of her face against his leather tunic, his hand on her back.

Coral stopped crying almost at once, and for an infinite moment stood there in the shelter of his arms, unable to think of anything else. He did not say a word. Slowly, awareness of his embrace crept over her. She stiffened and pulled back, turning away. Fumbling, she took a handkerchief from her purse, her face hot.

But his voice was casual. "Was Sir Hugo with your father when you noticed the fire?"

"Yes. They were all there. And my father was shouting orders, and the guards arrived on elephants."

"Why does your uncle insist Gem is no longer alive?"

A ripple of pain ran through her, and she opened up her bag, taking out the tiny cross. She brought it to him, extending her palm. "Because of this. I placed this on Gem the day of his adoption. He wore it always ... he was wearing it the night he was abducted."

He took hold of her hand, staring at the emblem. "Yes, I remember. Sir Hugo gave this to you?"

"No. My father sent it to me. My uncle and some servants found a child's body on the ghat steps. He had been attacked by—" She could not go on.

"Sit down," he said gently. "Would you like some of this tea?"

She shook her head and remained standing.

"Then Sir Hugo found the child?"

"Yes."

"And brought him and the cross to your father?"

"Yes." She looked at him, wondering if he was thinking the same thing that she had thought. "The little boy could have been someone else. An untouchable from the village, perhaps."

"Perhaps," he said.

"My ayah wrote me while I was in London. She prepared the child for burial and said there was a scar on his left heel, and that she did not recall seeing a scar on Gem."

His eyes left the cross now hidden within her knotted fist. "When I rode up to the hut where Gem was born and saw you coming out the door with an Indian baby, I thought, 'Now here is a spoiled silk heiress who wishes to collect human toys as a child collects dolls for her play nursery.' Then I saw the look on your face when you came to the wagon, holding him to your heart. You were not much more than a child yourself, but your eyes said everything that needed to be said."

For a moment she felt his look, and it seemed to contact her soul with an understanding that brought renewed tears to her eyes.

"You have not changed much," he said softly. "You still want that Indian baby. You are willing to make him a Kendall heir to a silk fortune."

"Yes, I want him . . . enough to pay any price to get him back. Enough to send him away to Europe, to hire guards if necessary until he can walk freely—as a man who knows his own heart, and is not ashamed to bear the name of his God. And if he must, he will wear a sword to protect his life. And I have every reason to believe Gem will one day stand alone. He is worth any sacrifice. So are the hundred children working in the hatcheries. You see, when I was in London I made a vow to God. If I should regain my health enough to return to India, I would seek the welfare of the children on Kingscote, and I intend to keep my promise."

She could not tell what he thought of all this, for a

breath escaped him, and he fixed his attention on the teapot and empty mug. He poured a second cup.

"I want to make sure you understand. Someone on Kingscote betrayed Gem's whereabouts to the family of the raja. Someone who silently disapproved of his up-bringing."

"That cannot be true. No one knew Gem was related to the maharaja, not even my parents."

"Someone did." He looked at her. "The same person who arranged for Rajiv's ritual killing."

"You think someone on Kingscote was to blame for that too?"

"Yes, and whoever it was is still there."

Coral masked a shiver. "Why not someone from the village who may have recognized him?"

"The two may be linked. There could have been con-tacts with any number of people in the village and else-where."

Elsewhere? What did he mean by that?

"I think I told you before," he said, "that whoever told Rajiv to meet his killer in the jungle was trusted by him. Your return home to start the school—if you convince your father—will set you up as a target."

Coral stared up into the handsome face that showed little but calm concern.

"But, Captain Buckley, you must be wrong. The In-dians who work there are like part of our family. And those serving within the house have been there since be-fore I was born. I have often wondered about Natine, but he has served my father since they were both children! He is crotchety, and he is a devout Hindu, but he would not hurt us; I cannot believe it about him. In fact, I can vouch for all the house servants. Not one of them would desire to hurt me or Gem."

He folded his arms and gave her a slanted look. "Not

all the villains in India are English, Miss Kendall. You know about the ghazis. You know their aims, do you not?"

She tensed, but tried not to show it. "Yes. They have bound themselves with an oath to rid India of every last *feringhi*."

"Foreigners, especially with English accents. It is my opinion the fire in the hatcheries was a warning to your father."

She had thought the same thing, but to blame one of their own for setting it?

"It was meant to frighten your father, to show him how easily Kingscote could be destroyed if he pursued Gem's abductors. And so he did not pursue. For he, above everyone else, knows how vulnerable Kingscote truly is."

"What! Why, you are saying my father yielded to threats, that he did not look for Gem? I know for a fact he did. He stopped because he thought they had found him."

"Oh, I am quite certain he did search, but not in the right places. You told a *certain mercenary* that your father knew Rawlings. May I suggest, he could have hired a man to track down Gem?"

Coral did not know whether she should be insulted. "Are you saying that my father deliberately—"

"I am not accusing him of anything except an understandable fear of the ghazis. And, a love for his plantation. We cannot fault him for that. By saying all this, I am trying to convince you to leave it alone. I warned you from the beginning."

"Then you will not help me?"

"I doubt if I could successfully bargain for his release, even if he is alive. Whatever the price, you can count on it exceeding anything your father or Sir Hugo is willing to pay."

"My uncle has nothing to do with it. Kingscote belongs to the Kendalls."

"Quite. But the silk enterprise is a family dynasty, is it not? The Roxburys and Kendalls are very much intertwined, as your engagement to Doctor Boswell explains."

"I am not engaged to my cousin."

"Not yet. But Sir Hugo is determined. You will have little to say about who you marry."

The idea that she would have nothing to say about it, or that she would capitulate against her will, was irksome. "Nevermind my marriage, Captain. It is the last concern I have. And it does not matter what my uncle may think, since my future is not his to bargain with."

"He will beg to differ. And if you truly intend to go your own way, you had better be wise enough, and strong enough, to walk through his traps. He is both ambitious and clever."

Coral thought of her stay in London and her experiences with her uncle. She was never quite certain whether they were traps, or merely coincidences.

She refused to show alarm, for fear it would give Jace reason to avoid looking for Gem.

"I have my father and Seward to help me avoid any traps, and my own determination. Not to mention my faith in the guidance of God. I ask only that you find out from the maharaja if Gem is alive."

He said nothing, and yet there was some change that encouraged her to think that he was beginning to relent.

"I will be leaving for the northern frontier soon," he said. "Did Sir Hugo mention the attack on the outpost?"

She recalled the second reason that had brought her to the *Madras*. Perhaps it was unwise to press him with two requests at once.

"I am commissioned to look into matters," he continued. "A friend of mine was assassinated in the attack."

"Major Selwyn?"

He was alert. "How did you know his name?"

"My uncle mentioned it. I am sorry about your friend. Did Seward know him too?"

"We all did." He massaged the back of his neck. "All right. While I am there on business, I will see what I can find out about Gem."

Coral felt so relieved that her knees went weak. "How can I ever thank you? I shall not forget your kindness, Captain Buckley."

"I am not certain my motive is kindness. I will be in touch with you here in Calcutta when I learn something."

"Ah . . . I will be at Kingscote."

He looked up from pouring another mug of black tea. "Seward said Sir Hugo arranged for you to stay here with your aunt and cousin."

"Yes, and that brings me to the other matter I wish to discuss with you." She drew in a little breath. "I do not want to stay a day longer than I must. Despite Jorhat, I intend to safari home." Aware that he watched her with veiled curiosity, she snatched up her hat and toyed with the brim. "You see, I want to ride under the protection of your military troop as far as Guwahati. From there, Seward can bring me home to Kingscote."

He did not mask his surprise. Coral hastened, "Such things are done frequently. Why, I heard of an English party traveling with British troops all the way from Bombay to the border of Burma. It is not nearly as far to Guwahati."

When he said nothing and only looked at her, she added, "I will be no trouble, Major. And I will pay you, say . . . a cargo of Kingscote silk?"

He folded his arms across his chest. "A handsome reward, but hardly acceptable since I am under military orders. As for not being any trouble—I think you will prove a good deal of trouble, Miss Kendall."

"My health will pose no problem. I am stronger than I look. I am not above riding in a howdah on the back of an elephant, or crossing rivers with crocodiles. I can handle the trek to the northern frontier as well as anyone. I am not the fainting kind."

He smiled. "Why not remain in Calcutta until the trouble in Jorhat is taken care of? While I disagree with Sir Hugo on a number of things, he is right about the journey being risky."

"And so I wish to travel with your troop and Seward. My uncle will have no reason to argue against my returning home."

"Very clever."

She smiled and put her hat on. "I thought so. With my mother ill, it is imperative I get home soon. And, I do not like to say this, but there are times when I wonder about my uncle's motives."

"About Gem, or Boswell?"

"Gem, of course. My cousin is trustworthy."

"Would your marriage to Boswell benefit Sir Hugo in any way? Say, give him greater control of Kingscote?"

Coral knew the direction of his question, and it made her uncomfortable. "My uncle might think that way, but not Ethan."

"What is the relationship between Sir Hugo and the good doctor? That is, if you do not mind explaining."

"There is nothing to hide. Ethan was my uncle's ward, a nephew, they say. He looks upon Sir Hugo as a father."

"I see."

She wondered how two simple words could suggest so much.

"What you are thinking about Ethan is not true. He is sacrificial, a man wholly devoted to medical research. His interest in Kingscote concerns a scientific lab that my father is permitting him to build in the jungle."

"If Sir Hugo wishes for you to stay in Calcutta, he is not likely to approve of your journeying north under my command. How do you expect to convince him?"

"He can hardly refuse. Not when I will be accompanied by soldiers. If you would speak to your father the colonel, I think he could alleviate my uncle's misgivings."

"I do not doubt your determination to get to Kingscote, but the journey will be hard. Are you quite certain a few more months, regardless of Sir Hugo, will not be best?"

She smiled. "I am quite certain."

He was silent, then, "As you wish. How could I turn down a young woman of such conviction? I will tell Seward to arrange your travel. We will leave in five days. Can you manage?"

"I shall be ready. Major, I do not know how I can thank you enough for your assistance."

His mouth curved slightly. "I will give that some thought, Miss Kendall."

She felt her face grow warm under his gaze. Quickly she scooped up her bag from the chair and went to the cabin door.

"Oh." She stopped, aware that she still held the ebony cheetah. She felt foolish, as though he might think that her action had been deliberate. She walked over to the half-open drawer and put the miniature back.

"Good day, Captain—I mean, Major."

He laughed. "Back to that again. Why not try Jace? It really is not that difficult to say, and less confusing."

"Yes, so it is."

He walked up, retrieved the cheetah, and turned it over. "Would you like a cheetah with a missing eye?"

"How did he lose it?"

"Right now, I cannot remember. Maybe he was born that way."

"I rather like him with a missing eye. He looks vulnerable. But, Captain, I could not take it."

"Consider him a gift from a 'certain mercenary' who was rude to leave you stranded an hour outside Calcutta in a broken-down ghari. He'll be pleased to know you got home safely. As for the cheetah, he will be happier in your custody." He pressed it into her hand with a slight smile. "He will soon be purring. Good day, Miss Kendall. I will have Seward get in touch."

Her lashes lowered, Coral slowly turned toward the door to leave. "Good day, *Jace*," she murmured softly.

6

Coral softly shut her bedroom door and leaned against it with exhaustion, closing her eyes and feeling a steady headache throb in her temples. Alone at last, she was able to release her guarded feelings without the necessity of keeping a smile of composure while affirming to Aunt Margaret that she felt "quite well, actually," and that her trip with Seward to the *Madras* had neither been tiring nor anything less than "perfectly proper." Soon she must confront the family with her decision to return to Kingscote escorted by Major Buckley's troop. But her health, already strained to its frail limits, could take no more without rest.

In the deep afternoon silence of the room with its tall windows opening onto the verandah, she absently fingered the cheetah that Jace Buckley had given her. Vaguely, she wondered if she should have accepted it.

She walked tiredly across the room and out onto the verandah, letting her wide-brimmed hat flutter to the matting as her skirts whispered with her steps. Below her, the orange garden of marigolds ended near the tangle of brush that crowded the banks of the Hooghly. The rank river masqueraded beneath rays of the sun, offering the illusion of shimmering golds, but the afternoon air was realistically harsh, housing many different sounds and smells. She saw paddle-steamers churning up the Hooghly, and the indistinguishable voices of boatmen using bamboo poles to wend their barges back down the river after a day's business at Barrackpore.

Coral sighed. It did not matter that she must yet confront Uncle Hugo with her trek to Kingscote, or that in the next several days she must find some way to travel upriver to Serampore to visit William Carey's mission station. The Scripture portion in Hindi that Master Carey might be able to give her was worth withstanding any scowl of disapproval from Hugo. She would send a message to Charles Peddington that she wished to pay Serampore a visit.

It was at this point that she thought once again of Major Jace Buckley, and was surprised that she began to make excuses to herself of why she had accepted the ebony cheetah with one missing eye, or why she felt a warm sense of satisfaction in knowing that she had won him to her side—at least in the matter of Gem. But she swiftly reminded herself that while he had agreed to look into the matter upon arriving at Jorhat, that fact did not suggest his continued involvement. Jace Buckley was puzzling; a little dangerous perhaps. His masculine appeal was indisputable, but she would not let such things turn her head. She dismissed the memory of that brief moment in his arms. She must never think of it again.

With determination, Coral went to her desk and sat down to write Charles Peddington about her wish to visit William Carey at Serampore.

———

Jace walked the path that fronted the Hooghly. In the shadow of the trees, mynahs were arguing loudly, and far in the distance pariah dogs barked. The banks of the river were crowded with narrow boats, the lean Indians in short white pants slicing their bamboo poles through the water.

His thoughts were not pleasant. Roxbury had attributed the attack on the outpost to Burma, and like the colonel, Jace nurtured his suspicions. His best source of information would be the Burmese prisoner now being held in confinement. But even interrogating the prisoner was not enough. He needed someone to wander the bazaars in Jorhat and pick up bits of information that only the watching eyes of India would see, eyes that were avid and intent, belonging to stoic faces who spoke only with Indian comrades in their mother tongue. A trusted Indian spy was needed. With the right incentive, he might convince his old friend Gokul to ride north and masquerade as a traveling merchant in the mountainous village bazaars.

He thought of the Kendall daughter, and ducked his dark head just in time to keep a mango branch from knocking off his seacap. He frowned as his boots crunched the dying grasses in his way. Whatever had possessed him to agree to help her locate the boy? He was either dead, or a eunuch. In irritation he yanked his cap lower.

He reminded himself that he had the entire journey to Assam to fill Coral Kendall's ears with shuddering tales of the ghazis. Instinctively, however, he guessed that she would not easily relent, regardless of his warnings. Behind that innocent facade, he believed there lived a woman of cool nerves. He had already discovered as much when she refused to step back from her confrontation with the guru and his crows at the bazaar. When it came to Gem and the mission school, he believed her convictions were unshakable.

Entering the bungalow that he shared with Gokul along the river, Jace drew aside the split-cane curtain that opened into his room. Outside on the courtyard the lean shadow of Gokul lay long upon the sun-warmed stone.

A strange cackle greeted him: "Major Buckley. Major Buckley. Major Buckley."

Mischief, Gokul's lime green parrot, lumbered across the rail, cocking his head and repeating the new phrase that Gokul had taught him: "Major Buckley. Major Buckley. Major Buckley."

Jace winced. In sobering agreement, the military uniform was stretched across the bed as if to salute his arrival. The black and silver was spotless, the boots were polished, and the saber gleamed.

Goldfish smacked his gums and jumped up and down.

Gokul came from the courtyard oven carrying a hot urn. His black eyes sparkled beneath thick gray brows. "Ah, sahib, time for favorite coffee!"

Jace tossed his weathered cap onto a chair, his eyes fixed on the familiar uniform. In exactly two hours he would abandon his casual buckskin and Indian tunic, and emerge as Major Buckley, the new commanding officer of the 21st Bengal Light Cavalry. And in three days he would be on his way, with twenty sowars in uniform, to Jorhat.

"How did you manage?" he asked casually of the coffee.

Gokul rolled his eyes toward the roof and smiled. "The ways and wonders of Gokul are beyond explanation." He set the urn down on the hot bricks, and rushed at Goldfish, shooing him away from the uniform. "Be gone, or I make monkey stew!" And he flicked an imaginary speck from the sleeve, and held the jacket across his chest and protruding belly for display, like some prized heirloom prepared for Jace's inspection. "Everything ready, sahib, Major!"

"Major Buckley. Major Buckley—"

Jace poured his coffee and scanned Gokul dubiously.

Gokul whipped a cloth from his tunic and gave an extra wipe across the boot, then scrutinized the shine. Jace took a swallow of coffee and looked down at his new uniform with a blank expression. The last emotion he felt was anticipation. He changed the subject, even though he began to remove his tunic and ready himself to become a major.

"Any word from your contact in the thieves' market?" His scabbard reminded him of the Moghul sword.

"Word passed. Expect news soon."

Jace continued to methodically put on the pieces of his uniform. It was an asset to Jace that Gokul not only knew a few brahmins, but also certain thieves in Calcutta, and the wealthy Chinese and Indian merchants who wittingly bought stolen booty to sell to the rich but unquestioning English. If the thief who had robbed him was from the Calcutta brotherhood, there was a chance that Gokul's contact in the bazaar would know of the sword. As though in answer to his thoughts, there came a rap on the door, and Gokul answered it.

A young sowar spotted Jace in uniform and saluted. He stepped forward and handed him an envelope. Jace read as the cavalryman waited outside the door.

Maj. J. Buckley, 21st Light Cal., B.L.C.
Sir:
The Governor-General's new Resident to the princely state of Assam in northern India, Sir Hugo Roxbury, requests that you meet with him in his office at Government-House this afternoon no later than 2 o'clock

November 11th, at Fort William, Calcutta.
Yr m.o. servant
P. Barton, Daffadar, 21st B.L.C.

Jace stared at the message. *The Governor-General's Resident!* Sir Hugo Roxbury was to represent the British government at the maharaja's palace at Guwahati!

The idea that Roxbury might want the newly vacated position had never crossed his mind. This meant that Roxbury would soon be leaving Calcutta for the northern frontier. Jace would have Sir Hugo to contend with at the outpost.

"Something wrong, sahib?"

Jace placed the letter in his sabretache, the small leather case that hung from his saber belt. Stepping to the door, he closed it on the sowar, then turned back to Gokul.

"Roxbury's been appointed ambassador to the raja at Guwahati."

Gokul gave a low whistle. "And he calls for you? The burra-sahib is interested in your new command at the Jorhat outpost. Why, I ask?" His expression was grave. "Caution, sahib. I do not trust the man."

"When will you meet with your friend at the bazaar?"

"Tonight."

"Good. There is something you must do. I need you at Jorhat. Go as a traveling merchant. Inquire about the assassination of Selwyn. More specifically, see if you can discover any connection Roxbury may have had with members of the royal family."

While Gokul stood there contemplating, Jace's mouth curved in a grim smile. He reached beneath his jacket and handed him an envelope. "Your share in the tea plantation."

Gokul smiled and placed palms together to his forehead. "Sahib most generous. I will depart before the sun rises, as soon as I negotiate meeting at the bazaar. I will bring Jin-Soo with me, and Goldfish. Yes?"

"Yes."

"You will return here tonight?"

"Yes, see that no one follows you."

"It is done."

Jace opened the door to find the sowar standing too close. Was he trying to listen? A servant of Roxbury, no doubt. The sowar turned and led the way to a waiting horse-drawn ghari.

Around Fort William a massive expanse of jungle had been cut down to give the cannons a clear line of fire, but Jace recalled that the fort had never fired a shot in battle since reclaiming Calcutta from Suraj-ud-daula in the famous Black Hole incident of 1757. Since that uprising, a massive new fort had been built with deep fortifications and trenches fronting the impregnable walls. The grounds around the fort where the jungle had been cleared were a green expanse of lawn known as the Maidan, and was bounded by the river on the west, and the bazaar to the east. The botanical gardens were in the northwest, and on any Sunday afternoon one could see a number of Company families in carriages out for a ride around the Maidan. The Company had installed a cricket field, and there were ponds, trees, and a winding strollway that led through the gardens to the banks of the Hooghly. On the bank were several ghats, landing places with stairs leading down to the river, with Indian boatmen waiting to ferry customers across, or up the river toward Barrackpore and Serampore—the Danish center for trading holdings in India.

At Government-House the sowar escorted Jace to Sir Hugo's office. Jace dismissed him, knocked, and entered. Roxbury's office turned out to be a luxurious apartment, decorated and furnished for the use of British visitors. From the window, Sir Hugo could look out across the Maidan to the river.

Upon his entry, Jace paused; Sir Hugo was not alone. Hugo sat behind a large desk, and to his right stood an Indian officer, the dark eyes measuring him with keen interest. He wore the black and silver uniform of the 21st, but Jace did not remember him from his days at the outpost. He was a rissaldar-major, second-in-command to the British officer.

He is too young, Jace was thinking when Roxbury's voice, tinged with deliberate friendliness, interrupted.

"Stand easy, Major." Roxbury pushed back his chair and stood, a large handsome figure in black. Jace noticed that the two men bore one thing in common; they both had deep-set dark eyes that observed him with the sharpness of a hunting fowl.

"Major, this is Rissaldar Sanjay from the outpost at Jorhat. He arrived a few days ago, bringing news to the colonel of the Burmese attack on the outpost."

From the taut expression on the rissaldar's face, Jace thought he appeared ill at ease, as though concerned with other matters.

"The colonel is pleased to have you back in uniform, Major," Sir Hugo was saying. "I, too, find myself in agreement with your decision to return to the honorable East India Company. Excellent soldiers are a rare breed here in India."

There followed a moment of silence in which Jace was expected to acknowledge his compliment and agree that it was also his pleasure to be back. Jace was neither pleased, nor did he find the Company altogether honorable. His gaze was hard. "A worthy captain of a ship is also a rare breed, sir. Am I to assume, then, that the death of your nephew aboard my vessel is no longer questioned?"

Sir Hugo leaned across the desk with a humorless smile. "One must never listen to rumors, Major. I see no reason why I should question Michael's death at sea."

So he wants to let the matter drop.

"If I did not have the highest regard for your abilities, I would not have spoken to the governor-general about you."

Alert, Jace noticed for the first time the official paper on the desk.

"I have heard of your reputation in the northeast. It is noteworthy that your conduct was awarded a brevet for courage and a promotion just before you left the colonel's troops."

Jace was expressionless, and the compliment made him suspicious of Sir Hugo's intentions. But Roxbury appeared not to notice the silence, although Jace believed he knew of the extreme measures used by the colonel to get him back into uniform.

Jace responded in a level tone. "There are many in India who deem themselves to be courageous and more dedicated to the cause of the English presence than I. The incident in the northeast was merely the exercise of duty."

Sir Hugo raised his brows. "I do not believe a word of it. Duty is a precious word in my ear, Major, and not a trait to ignore, and it is the reason for my request to the governor-general. Colonel Warbeck is displeased with the change in your mission, and yet I am sure he will recognize that my request to a higher authority was necessary."

Sir Hugo sucked on his pipe and seemed to be gauging his response, but Jace affected military discipline. Higher authority? A change in his orders?

"I will be truthful with you, Major. When my niece informed us that she hoped to be traveling under your protection to the northern frontier, I was prepared to forbid it, until I realized the decision was a wise one. As Rissaldar Sanjay here has informed us, anyone traveling north at this time will encounter grave risk."

Jace looked at the rissaldar, who quickly shot a glance toward Sir Hugo.

Sir Hugo stood and paced, his hands behind his back. "I will come to the point, Major. My own circumstances changed quite unexpectedly. I will not be serving the Company in Calcutta for the next few years, but the province of Assam, as the resident of the governor-general."

This position placed him in a seat of authority in rich northern territory previously independent of the Company, including the vast Kendall holdings. Jace remained silent.

"Of necessity, your orders have been changed by the governor-general. You will not command the 21st at Jorhat, but accompany me to Guwahati as commander of my security guard."

What!

"Your position is a sensitive one, Major, and it demands the best of skilled fighting men to be chosen, not only in order to protect me, but perhaps, the royal family."

Jace was furious. Outwardly he remained unreadable.

"I regret our journey cannot embark as soon as your previous orders called for," Roxbury continued. "I will need to clear up some unfinished business here in Calcutta for the Company, and then there is the matter of my family. My nephew Doctor Ethan Boswell will arrive in December and will journey with us as far as Guwahati. I would prefer to leave at once, but the first week of January must suffice. Will that suit you?"

Whether it did or not he was certain that Sir Hugo found his opinion irrelevant. Their departure was nearly two months away! Jace curbed the anger swarming over his soul like a battalion of army ants. "As you wish, sir. But what of sending reinforcements to the outpost at Jorhat? Has the governor-general decided to let the 21st sit there without a commanding officer?"

His objection was waved off by Roxbury. "Military matters are out of my jurisdiction, Major. Colonel Warbeck is looking into that now. He is expecting you on the cricket field."

The colonel had betrayed him. *Security guard for Roxbury!*

"Believe me, Major, there are valid reasons for the change in your orders," said Sir Hugo. "Rissaldar Sanjay has reason to believe the outpost at Jorhat is not the intended target of Burmese forces, but rather, Guwahati. Correct, Rissaldar?"

"Yes, sahib, that is so. I hasten to add that it is the opinion of the nephew of the maharaja that His Excellency's life may be in danger from the ghazis. They are displeased with the treaty signed with the East India Company."

The nephew of the maharaja? wondered Jace. He wanted to ask about Rajiv's brother, Prince Sunil, but did not wish to alert Sir Hugo that he knew him; nor was he certain whether Sir Hugo knew of Gem's connection with the maharaja.

Sir Hugo shot a glance at the Indian officer. "Explain."

"Since an assassination attack on Prince Sunil, the maharaja is not trusting anyone except his bodyguard."

Jace was alert. Sunil was ruthless and could not be trusted. Had he truly been attacked?

"The maharaja's nephew was fortunate. He was only wounded," continued Rissaldar Sanjay.

Roxbury turned to Jace. "It is our lone opinion that an assassination attempt will be made on the maharaja himself."

"By 'lone opinion,' are you saying Prince Sunil is the only one who agrees with you?"

Sir Hugo walked to the window. "Do not misunderstand. I mean in no way to cast your father in a dubious light. We all know his record to be above reproach. It is also true to say that the military worries too much over a handful of British soldiers at the outpost, when the palace of the raja may be the real target." He was staring in the direction of the cricket field. "I have been unsuccessful in convincing the colonel, so I was forced to go directly to the governor-general. I believe the military underestimates the danger in Assam, Major." He looked at Jace. "There is fierce determination to undermine the English presence on the northern frontier."

Jace was well acquainted with the north and knew this. Many independent nawabs and rajas feared that the East India Company would eventually try to annex all of northern India, including Darjeeling and Kashmir, by making independent treaties with the princely states as they had just done with the royal family at Guwahati. Despite any pretext of renewed hostilities with Burma, the annexation of India to British rule was a festering sore even among those native soldiers who wore the uniform of the British. There were, in fact, more Indians in English uniforms in India than there were British. The native soldiers enlisted in the Bengal ranks were commanded by British officers in regiments belonging to the East India Company. The Indians numbered in the thousands, and few of the British officers had reason to doubt their absolute loyalty. Jace had known many such sepoys and sowars. Some had enlisted for employment, others for opportunity, perhaps even to spread sedition in the army, although that possibility was unthinkable to the British officers.

"I agree," said Jace, "that the colonel is fully committed to the loyalty of Johnny Sepoy, but I am not."

The rissaldar's eyes flashed momentarily. Jace wondered if Sir Hugo was using the resentment among the sepoys and sowars for his own purposes.

"Rissaldar Sanjay has made it clear to the colonel that Prince Sunil fears worse than the recent attack on the outpost," said Sir Hugo. "We suspect the ghazis of plotting with the Burmese warlord to dispel any British presence in the north."

Jace asked smoothly, "You suspect ghazis tried to assassinate the prince?"

Sir Hugo shrugged his heavy shoulders. "Who else? What is your opinion, Rissaldar?"

"Perhaps, sahib, Major Selwyn knew something and was silenced. There may be some plot to mutiny within the ranks at the outpost itself."

Jace wondered if they were feeling him out, trying to discover what he thought. He remained silent. It remained of interest to him that the Indian officer appeared ill at ease.

Did Sir Hugo know of the Burmese prisoner taken in the raid on the outpost? Jace did not mention him.

"Your new orders were issued from the governor-general himself," Sir Hugo said. "The time may also come when you will be called upon to protect the royal family. Your task is crucial."

Jace did not trust him. What was the man up to? Why would he even want him around?

Sir Hugo lifted the paper from his desk. "Your new orders, Major."

Jace bridled his irritation. A moment passed; he took the paper. The signature of the chief representative of the English government stared up at him.

Just what had prompted Sir Hugo to go to such extremes to have the orders of Colonel Warbeck changed? Jace did not believe for a minute that his military reputation had anything to do with Roxbury's action. Jace had warned the Kendall daughter of traps, but perhaps it was *he* who needed to be on guard.

7

Jace took leave of Sir Hugo, and it was with restrained anger that he walked across the Maidan toward
the cricket field. Indian servants walked about in white
knee-length coats with polished brass buttons. The native military wore yellow, red, or blue coats, with white
crossbelts, cuffs, and collars. A few English carriages
passed on an afternoon ride toward the gardens. With
them came a rush of feminine gossip, a show of curls,
lace, and coquettish glances that Jace ignored. Ahead he
saw the colonel. He was not on the cricket field, but in a
game of croquet with several other officers, including the
portly General Basil. A dozen or so other English military and civil servants stood about in lazy discourse. Jace
stopped a few feet away.

The colonel, upon seeing his adopted son, showed neither concern for his mood nor pleasure at his presence.
He tossed his mallet to the grass and excused himself
from the game. Jace fell into step beside him, and for a
moment neither spoke. The massive walls of the fort enclosed the world of England within, while outside its
gates, India silently resented their presence.

"You knew all along I would be sent as a security guard at Guwahati."

"No. I underestimated him."

That his father would admit to being outwitted was surprising, and had a consoling effect on Jace's irritation. He turned his head to glance at the rugged face and found the colonel undisturbed by his admittance.

"The fact that Roxbury went over my head convinces me my suspicions are correct."

"He was involved in the attack?"

"And the assassination of Major Selwyn." The hard gray eyes turned to him. "I need proof. The question is, for what reason? And that is for you to find out."

Colonel Warbeck motioned toward a cluster of trees. "You may dislike the change in your orders, but it could prove the opening we need to learn what Roxbury is up to. At the maharaja's palace, you will have opportunity to pry about, and keep Roxbury in view. You are aware he asked for your service from the governor-general only because he wants to keep an eye on you? Make it mutual."

"I thought it was because of my military valor."

Only a slight twist of the colonel's mouth responded to Jace's light sarcasm.

"What of the 21st? They are sitting ducks. Roxbury will not leave until his nephew arrives in December."

"Major Packer's 34th is being sent from Plassey. You will be given men from the 17th Lancers."

"Then give me Rissaldar Nadir. He is a friend. I can trust him. Roxbury also talks of mutiny in the blood of the sepoys. I rather agree with him on that."

"Johnny Sepoy will never mutiny. Oh, yes, I know, emotions run high when it comes to their religion and dispossessed nobles, but mutiny against their British officers? Never! I have served with them too long. If there is talk, you can wager it's being propagated by men like Roxbury. They are in this for their own gain, though what it might be where he is concerned, I have no idea."

"Kingscote perhaps. But just how a mutiny would help him is unclear. Kendall himself may have ideas on that."

The colonel, seeing an Indian servant in a blue coat and turban, gestured him forward.

The servant salaamed and produced a satchel, then departed. Colonel Warbeck handed it to Jace.

Jace felt a hard, cold object meet his fingers. He slowly brought it into the light, and it sprang up like multicolored fire. The stolen idol of the Hindu god Kali!

His questioning gaze met his father's.

The colonel smiled, his gray eyes glinting with satisfaction. "Merry Christmas," he said, and chuckled.

As they strolled back across the Maidan, the colonel told Jace how he had obtained it. Sir Hugo had unexpectedly appeared at his bungalow the night before, explaining that he only recently discovered that the object had been stolen from the raja. Sir Hugo could only imagine the embarrassment over the situation if the royal family in Guwahati discovered it in his collection!

Jace would bring the statue of Kali with him to present to the raja. With it, he could gain the audience he needed.

———

Coral was startled by the news. Uncle Hugo, the resident at Guwahati? Aunt Margaret had never hinted of the possibility; had she known about it? Yet her aunt did not seem surprised.

Seward had arrived that morning with the news that Jace would take up a security post in Guwahati.

"We'll not be leaving Calcutta until January," Seward

told the small feminine gathering in the Roxbury residence that morning.

"Two months," moaned Coral, "but why so long a delay, Seward?"

"As for the major, he's all for leaving by week's end. 'Tis Doctor Boswell. Sir Hugo won't leave till he arrives."

Coral knew Seward well enough to distinguish the veiled irritation in his voice, but the others did not.

"Well, I am all for the delay," announced Aunt Margaret. "I would prefer the family to spend the holidays together. One never knows how long the separation will be." She changed the subject. "Lady Isobel's invitation arrived this morning from Barrackpore. We are to spend the holiday week there."

Barrackpore was a resort and military station to which the fashionable and affluent of the East India Company in Calcutta flocked for relaxation and entertainment, especially during the holiday season. Margaret took delight in pointing out that it was a favorite of the governor-general himself. The traditional week-long celebration would begin at their arrival in mid-December at the grand house of Lord and Lady Canterbury where they would room until after the New Year.

"There are seven absolutely wonderful balls to attend," explained her cousin Belinda. "Plus late-night suppers, house-to-house desserts, and if the weather holds, an outdoor party. You will absolutely adore Barrackpore; it is so European."

Margaret arose and, coming behind Marianna, put her arms around her neck. "Do not look so downcast, darling. A few more weeks in Calcutta will pass quickly, and you will be home to your mother soon enough. And it will be so much nicer with Ethan arriving and taking the safari with you. Elizabeth's illness will be treated, and your uncle will be only a short journey away at Gu-wahati."

Marianna raised her childish face and the wide eyes looked hopelessly up at her aunt. "Do you think so, Aunt Margaret? Will everything be all right with mother?"

"Certainly, and she would want you to enjoy the holiday festivities while you are here. I noticed that young Charles Peddington has taken quite an interest in you, Marianna."

Marianna blushed. "Oh, we are just friends. He loves to discuss Master Carey and his work."

A servant entered with a small platter in hand. On top of it lay a letter; he brought it to Coral.

"For you, missy."

Coral read the return address: Charles Peddington, Serampore. She glanced up to see the others looking at her expectantly, but was hesitant to open it in front of them.

"I suppose it is from Major Jace Buckley," teased Cousin Belinda.

"Major Buckley has no reason to write me," said Coral calmly, and ignored the little smile that passed between Belinda and Kathleen.

Coral opened the envelope and removed the contents. Her heart wanted to stop, then throb, with a surge of emotion that brought moisture to her eyes. On a sheet of paper was written in Hindi the words of Matthew 19:13–15:

> *Then were there brought unto him little children, that he should put his hands on them, and pray: and the disciples rebuked them. But Jesus said, Suffer little children, and forbid them not, to come unto me: for of such is the kingdom of heaven. And he laid his hands on them, and departed thence.*

"Coral, what is it?" asked Aunt Margaret.

Coral handed her the Scripture portion and saw written on a second piece of paper:

Dear Miss Kendall:

Master Carey and the Marshmans will be most honored to receive you at Serampore on the date you requested. A ghari will arrive at Roxbury residence at Fort William on the morning of November 14th.

Your friend in service to our Lord,

Charles Peddington

The fourteenth . . . that is today, thought Coral, and looked toward the window facing the carriageway.

Margaret was frowning at the writing. "It is Bengali, isn't it?"

"Hindi. It is a Scripture verse, from Charles Peddington," explained Coral. "Isn't it wonderful to behold? Matthew nineteen, the verse on children!"

Margaret's brow furrowed. She continued to gaze upon the verse. "Yes . . . it is nice."

"Oh, dear, I have been so taken up with Uncle's news and the change in traveling plans that I forgot I might hear from Charles today," confessed Coral. "Where is Seward?"

"He left," said Marianna.

"What does Mr. Peddington want?" asked Margaret, handing the Scripture portion back.

Belinda and Kathleen moved to the front window at the same time, drawing aside the sheer curtain. "A ghari is arriving."

"We are not expecting anyone," said Margaret.

A moment later Coral stood as a servant entered. "A ghari-wallah is here to take Miss Coral to Serampore."

Margaret turned abruptly. "Coral! Not William Carey!"

The disappointment in her aunt's voice almost made Coral feel guilty.

"You promised me you would do nothing to anger Hugo," said Margaret. "And you know how upset he gets when you mention the religious dissenter Carey."

"Aunt Margaret, that is not a fair description," said Coral. "The men and women you call dissenters have merely left the cold formality of the Anglican Church for a personal relationship with Christ and the Scriptures and—"

"Coral, please, not now." Margaret sighed. "I have never been one to argue the finer points of religion, and I would rather not get into a debate."

Coral felt the puzzled gaze of Belinda studying her. Kathleen had turned her back to look out the window, and Coral guessed that she was embarrassed. Marianna stared at her plate of cold waffles.

"I do not wish to appear rigid," said Aunt Margaret, "but a trip to Serampore would mean your absence for two or three days. Without a chaperon you cannot possibly go."

"Perhaps Seward—" began Coral, already feeling it was a lost battle.

"No, dear. Seward is involved with Major Buckley. Your uncle would be furious if I permit you to go. Try to understand. Recently Hugo has been so tense. Another of his black moods, and he may wish to cancel the holiday trip to Barrackpore."

A groan went up from Belinda, and Kathleen said crossly, "All we need is for you to spoil everyone's holidays. Do not be so selfish, Coral. A visit to Carey can wait. You know enough Hindi to do your own translation of the Scriptures anyway."

"Sissy, that is not so," defended Marianna. "Charles said you need to know Hebrew and Greek, too."

"Girls!" said Aunt Margaret.

Belinda swept up to Coral and took hold of her arms, her dark eyes pleading. "Oh, Coral, you will not ruin our holiday, will you? I shall die if I cannot go to Barrackpore! You should see the houses where the balls are held; they are huge! With crystal chandeliers! And we will dance to large orchestras, and the ballrooms are decorated with a thousand candles and green sprigs—"

"No, my sister will not ruin our Christmas," said Kathleen, hands on hips. "Because I will not let her."

Margaret moved at once to settle the matter. "Where is Pande?"

No one had noticed the servant standing near the doorway, his brown face immobile. He salaamed. "Here, sahiba."

Margaret looked across the room. "Coral?"

Coral stood with quiet dignity. She could see that her aunt wanted her to be the one to decline. Despite the unpleasant moment, Coral felt a strange peace. She desperately wanted the Scriptures in Hindi, yet somehow she felt prompted to not demand her way. *Lord, I leave the matter to you to work out.*

She walked to the desk and sat down, briefly writing a note to be delivered to Charles Peddington. A moment later she stood and handed it to Pande.

"Give this to the ghari-wallah, please. Thank you, Pande."

When he had gone, the room was quiet for a moment. They heard the wheels of the ghari, and the plop-plop of the horse's hoofs on the stone, then silence. The front door closed again behind Pande, and he passed down the hall to attend to work.

Marianna stood from her chair at the table, her expression glum, and walked out of the dining room, up the stairs.

Margaret broke the silence. "Girls, we have shopping to do for Belinda's trousseau."

When Margaret and Belinda left the room, Coral picked up the paper with the Hindi translation.

"Go ahead," said Kathleen. "Call me a traitor."

Coral glanced up at her older sister. "I do not care to argue, Kathleen. I am not upset with you, really."

"Do not be so sacrificial. That attitude makes me more upset than anything you could say."

Coral studied her, surprised. "Why, whatever are you so dour about? We are going to Barrackpore. I should think being able to dance the night away at seven balls would sweeten you."

"Oh, pooh! Sometimes you are impossible!" Kathleen snatched up her skirts and flounced out.

"I am not the only one," muttered Coral.

Calcutta had a reputation to keep up in the way of holiday gaiety, and there were party invitations arriving almost daily. These were greeted with profound glee by Belinda, who insisted to her mother that for the sake of her cousins, they *simply must* accept them all.

In the weeks following, there were not only social gaieties to attend in Calcutta but preparation for the holiday season, keeping the girls in a state of excitement over silks, satins, and brocades. The cousins also received a flattering amount of attention from the garrison, and young Marianna was overwhelmed when Mr. Charles Peddington wrote her from Serampore.

Coral had never seen Kathleen so happy since they had left Roxbury House. Young Diantha Waterman had gained her mother's permission for Kathleen to design the girl's main ball dress, even paying Kathleen several pounds, and there was great excitement when the goods arrived in four boxes carried by solemn-faced Indian servants. "For the memsahibs," they announced.

Aunt Margaret loaned Kathleen her private fitting room with a long cutting table, trestle, pins, threads, thimbles, and special cutting scissors that she had long ago ordered from Lyons, France. The excitement mounted as Diantha came to spend a week for the pinning, and careful assessment of the bust and waist design.

As departure for Barrackpore drew nearer, the preparations increased, with a great deal of shopping to do for gift-giving.

Dressed in bonnets and carrying palmetto fans to ward off troublesome insects, Aunt Margaret, Belinda, and Marianna poured excitedly into the ghari, followed by Coral. Kathleen had opted to stay behind with Diantha to work on the dress.

By afternoon the ghari was piled with boxes and packages, many of them to be toted upriver when they left for Barrackpore. Coral made a few purchases for herself and her sisters, items that they would need on the safari.

As they were returning home for afternoon tea, Coral caught a glimpse of Major Buckley coming out of the governor-general's palace in the company of two sepoys. He looked very much the disciplined officer, and his face showed no emotion when Margaret saw him and called out.

Major Buckley was the essence of propriety as he came up to the door where Lady Margaret greeted him. After bowing, he proceeded to offer all the appropriate words expected from a precise officer and gentleman, inquiring as to their well-being and to the Christmas shopping.

Margaret explained about the two weeks in Barrackpore, and insisted that he was invited to all the balls, and that she was pleased to know her husband would be in such capable hands while serving his new post in Guwahati, not to mention the safety of her nieces on the journey. And again Major Buckley made the correct reply, but with a faintly contradicting gleam in his eyes, which no one noticed but Coral. Excusing himself, he departed without so much as a second look her way.

He is quite annoyed over the turn of events. She doubted if he would bother to show up at Barrackpore.

The Dutch ship *Kron Princess Maria* docked ten days earlier than expected, and the entire household turned out for Doctor Ethan Boswell's arrival. Coral was relieved to see him, although she was not able to tell herself why that should be. She was perfectly safe in Calcutta, and the upcoming journey north was still several weeks away. She was also reminded that Ethan was a striking man. He had gotten sun aboard the ship, causing his hair to glint like ripened wheat, and his eyes were easy to look into—she felt strange that she would think of that— they were like still, gray pools. She was struck with the wide variance between Ethan and Jace Buckley, whose presence set her on guard. Despite Jace's role as the restrained and coolly observant major, she knew there lived a different man beneath that affectation.

In mid-December Coral arrived in Barrackpore by boat in the company of Ethan, and the Canterbury carriage had been waiting to bring them to the house. To her growing excitement, she discovered that Serampore was located across the river and appeared quite close. Would it be possible to visit William Carey's mission station after all?

It occurred to Coral that Ethan could meet Doctor John Thomas, who had first interested Master Carey in coming to India. Had not Charles Peddington mentioned to her that Thomas was in Serampore?

As if borne on angel's wings, an idea of how she could manage the visit to Serampore stirred within her mind. The Dutch settlement under General Bie was close enough so that a visit could be made by leaving in the morning and returning by dusk. And if Ethan accompanied her in order to see John Thomas—well, the family could hardly be upset.

As they made their way through Danish-controlled Barrackpore, Coral was reminded of a European town with fine houses situated on avenues of trees, the air from the river fresh and crisp. Coral's heart felt at peace, and she planned to enjoy the Christmas Ball in the magnificent and gaily decorated Canterbury House, now ablaze with lights.

8

Governor Bie took the elbow of the Countess of Denmark, who was a glitter of jewels and white satin, and escorted her away from the others in the direction of the stairway leading down to the ballroom. Their voices faded into the majestic strains of the waltz as they descended the circular staircase.

The small group of men who were left in the upstairs anteroom smoking expensive cheroots began to break up.

"I wish a private word with you, Arlen," stated the governor-general, who left the anteroom and walked out onto the extended railed hallway overlooking the crowded ballroom.

Sir Arlen George, an angular man with hawklike features and a flair for fashion, walked up beside him. "What is on your mind, Excellency?" asked Arlen. "You were not serious just now about me going to London to speak with His Majesty?"

The governor-general smiled at him. "Assuredly! Hugo has every confidence in you, and why shouldn't I?"

Arlen looked down on the crowded ballroom floor to

watch Belinda Roxbury waltzing with a Danish soldier in handsome uniform.

"Blasted French!" said the governor-general. "War with France will bleed the king's regiments from India! I shall be left with few white-skinned officers in a sea of native soldiers."

"I have always thought," said Sir George languidly, "that a spell of duty in India while the king's men make their colonial rounds is a curse of the English government. But I believe Governor Bie is correct. Napoleon has tasted too much defeat by Nelson and the Duke of Wellington to venture into India, although he knows breaking England commercially and industrially is the only way to defeat us."

"You may be right, Arlen. But I am serious in my decision to send you to His Majesty."

"A forthright decision. And I shall do my best to persuade the king of your concerns with France. A voyage should be safe. With Nelson's navy patrolling the sea, the French warships will soon drink their own gall."

"When can you sail?"

Sir George watched the swirling color of crinolines and uniforms beneath the glittering dazzle of chandeliers. The waltz came to him on a crescendo, and he saw Belinda standing off to one side with several young officers about her. She was laughing and talking, tossing her ebony curls like some coquettish minx he had seen in Paris. His lips narrowed. He was accused by Belinda of lacking jealousy where she was concerned, but it was a damnable lie!

"I am at your disposal. Name your convenience."

"Hugo said his wife and daughter are to voyage to London after the new year, and that you would be inclined to accompany them."

"I had not made up my mind until this night," his

eyes glittered, "but London will prove the best place for the marriage ceremony to take place."

"Ah! Then it is settled."

"By all means. Anything, Your Excellency, for the good of England."

"An honorable spirit. When you and your bride return, Hugo believes you will make a worthy commissioner for Guwahati. Between the two of you, I shall sleep more soundly in Calcutta."

————

Colorful lanterns decorated the balconies and widespread branches of the trees, casting bright festive colors through tinted glass along the front yard and entranceway. Inside the house, festoons of tropical flowers and plants decorated walls, doors, and tables, and were hung with ribbons from the chandeliers. The buffet tables were laden with delicacies fit for royalty: English and Danish pastries, huge silver platters of various smoked meats, fruits, cheeses, and a variety of drinks served from crystal bowls by richly attired servants.

Coral, dressed in a deep burgundy silk gown, left Ethan to go upstairs in search of Marianna. Her sister was not in the chamber, and Coral was returning to the ballroom when voices caused her to stop. She stood in the wide, columned hallway, with one of the private anterooms off to the side. Aunt Margaret, lovely in her personally designed amber-colored silk ball gown, stood alone facing Colonel Warbeck. He was leaning in the doorway in a stance that reminded Coral of his son, and Margaret could not pass.

"Let him accuse me. I would find it a pleasure to defend your honor."

"Please, I must go. We shall be the pinnacle of ugly gossip if you keep this up."

He laughed quietly. "I am always the topic of gossip. I shall come to London. When do you sail?"

"No. Do not come. If Hugo—"

Coral bit her lip and stepped back into the shadows. The colonel moved aside, and Margaret went past him toward the stairs. The door shut behind Colonel Warbeck. Coral stood there without moving. A minute later, she walked to the balustrade and saw Margaret below, moving off in the direction of Belinda and Kathleen.

Coral heard nothing but the waltz. How long she stood there she did not know. She walked toward the landing just as a familiar officer in the black and silver uniform of the British Cavalry was coming up the staircase. Jace appeared to have more sober contemplations on his mind than the Christmas festivities. He took the last steps two at a time, then stopped as he came upon her.

Coral wondered if her expression showed her feelings of distraction over coming upon the colonel and Aunt Margaret, for he studied her, then looked past her into the hall as if expecting to see someone else.

Coral was curious whether he had any suspicion about his father and her aunt, and found that the idea brought a tint to her cheeks. She turned away from him and walked back to the balustrade, her gaze on the dancers below.

"Hiding from someone? It must be your physician." He smiled and walked up beside her to lean against the carved stone pillar.

She smiled in spite of herself, then looked below again. A quick sweep of the dancers reminded her that Marianna was not to be seen. *Where has my little sister gone?*

"Seward said you would be too busy to come tonight," she said casually.

"And miss all this food? You do not know how I suffer from Gokul's cooking." He glanced across the room. "Your cousin?"

She followed his gaze to Ethan who stood where she had left him, but was now in conversation with several men, including Lord Canterbury.

"Yes. He arrived a week ago."

"How fortunate that he will set up his *mosquito lab* on Kingscote. When he is not busy cutting up bugs, he should be interesting company."

Her fingers tightened on the balustrade. "I gather, Major, that you do not like my cousin. Isn't this a rather hasty judgment? You have not even met him yet."

"I confess I do sound a little dour. When I was lured back into uniform, I was not informed that I would also be responsible to lead a safari of novice English civilians on a jungle trek north. Somehow, Boswell looks the sort of man who will everlastingly complain of dust and sweat."

So his dislike of Ethan has nothing to do with jealousy. "You will be surprised. Ethan labored in the jungles of Burma for several years before returning to London."

"Interesting. Perhaps I underestimate him."

She looked at him, but Jace was not watching her.

"He is not above showing his displeasure, I see."

She again followed his gaze across the room. Ethan had looked up and seen them standing there. His eyes were riveted upon the major. Even the distance could not diminish the hard expression on the usually quiet face.

Coral felt a rise of uneasiness. If Jace did not like Ethan, it was evident that the feeling was going to be mutual.

"I seem to have irritated your cousin," he said casually. "If you will excuse me, the colonel is waiting down the hall. There is something we need to discuss."

111

"Yes, of course," she murmured, and tore her eyes from Ethan to meet the major's gaze. There was a slight glimmer of amusement in the blue-black of his eyes as he made his way across the hall.

Ethan was waiting for her when she came down, but his hard gray eyes were looking behind her and up the stairs. "I must say, I am surprised to see Buckley in uniform after what happened."

"After what happened? . . . Oh, you mean Michael."

"You are a gracious woman, Coral, yet I do not think a man like Buckley deserves your slightest indulgence. I was disturbed to learn from Aunt Margaret that the man will be in command of our journey to Kingscote. I think I should appeal to the governor-general."

"Ethan, the reported incident on the *Madras* was in error. I only recently found out."

He looked at her with skepticism. "I suppose he told you that. I would not accept his version of what happened."

"He tried to save Michael's life."

"Can we expect him to admit his stupor?"

"Ethan, please, do not speak so, especially in front of him. I fear he would—"

He gave a short laugh of scorn. "Call me out as a gentleman? Then let him. It so happens, my dear, that I am a crack shot."

She did not remember seeing him in such a hostile mood while in London. Was he jealous of Jace, or did he truly dislike him because of Michael's death? "I asked Seward about what happened, and he bears witness to the major's story. He even injured himself trying to save Michael's life."

Doctor Boswell's hard expression remained. "Seward is a friend of his. Naturally he would back up his tale. I think there is more truth to what we heard than your generosity is willing to admit."

"I am not being generous. I think you best discuss this matter in private with Uncle Hugo."

"I intend to. And do not worry, Coral, I will say nothing to Buckley—yet."

"There is no need to speak to him about it at all. I have already done so and am satisfied."

His restless gray eyes met hers. "He is not a gentleman. I have heard of his reputation. There is more than the incident aboard the *Madras*. Uncle mentioned an avalanche in the Darjeeling area. It is quite curious how Buckley returned safely to the hired servants, but Michael was left for dead."

Coral's mind darted back to that night on Kingscote when Michael had mentioned his near mishap in the avalanche. He had never explained what happened, and she had never asked. She tried to ease the matter by taking Ethan's arm and leading him toward the ballroom floor. "You need not concern yourself with the major. Uncle Hugo trusts him explicitly."

"You do not mean it?"

"It was Uncle who went to the governor-general to ask him to appoint Major Buckley as commander of the security force in Guwahati."

He stopped. "Hugo arranged it?"

"He will explain his reasons to you if you ask. He will be here in Barrackpore tomorrow afternoon."

Ethan turned and looked up toward the balustrade, a thoughtful expression on his face. "Uncle did not tell me. Then perhaps I should be more cautious in my judgment."

She let out a silent breath, relaxing.

After the waltz, Coral set out to find Marianna. In the main floor hall, it was quiet. She was about to take the side stairs to the room she shared with Marianna when something caught her attention. The door into a salon that led into an enclosed garden stood ajar, and she felt a cool draft. Her suspicions were alerted. Lady Canterbury's servants would never be so remiss. Had Marianna gone into the garden? But the December night was chill, and it was no place to go without a chaperon.

Nevertheless, Coral entered the salon and found the double doors leading into the garden open. She stepped out into the shadowed evening.

For a moment she stood there on the flagstone. The chill fingers of evening ran along her shoulders and arms. She waited, letting her eyes adjust to the darkness.

The stars were a silver glimmer in the black sky, and after a minute or so she began to see the silhouettes of tropical plants and vines standing like an arsenal of soldiers guarding the red flagstone walk that wound farther into Lady Isobel's garden.

Coral took the walk, her slippers making clicking sounds on stone, and headed briskly toward the end of the far side; Marianna was not to be seen. A gate stood open. "Marianna? Are you out there?" she called.

Marianna would never wander so far alone—unless she was not alone. . . . Becoming more chilled by the minute, she hurried ahead and through the gate, discovering that it led outside the garden to a narrow stone alleyway.

Coral was on the verge of turning back when a small figure with trailing skirts came flying toward her. Marianna ran into her, gasping for breath. One glance at her face told Coral of her fear.

"Mar—" began Coral.

Marianna's trembling fingers were cold and shaking as they pressed against Coral's lips. She glanced backward over her shoulder toward the alley.

"Shh! It is Uncle Hugo!"

"He is not in Barrackpore tonight. What is wrong?"

"Yes, he is!" Marianna's nails dug into Coral's arm. "Hurry, Coral, the man he is with saw me!"

Confused, Coral saw no reason why they should run away like two thieves; nevertheless, she acted on her sister's alarm. Together they sped through the gate back into the cloistered garden.

There was not enough time to make it to the house. From behind them Coral heard running footsteps on the stone alleyway. She grabbed Marianna's arm and pulled her aside into the thick shrubs and vines, snagging her skirts and losing a slipper. She heard Marianna stifle a moan. Together they ran toward an arbor bordering a pond. Ahead there was a shed that looked to be made of split cane, and beside it a stack of baskets. Coral pushed Marianna inside and ducked in after her, pulling the door shut. The smell of moldy earth and rotting plants filled her nostrils.

9

They waited, crouching in the darkness, and Coral heard the sound of her heart pounding in her ears. A moment later they heard footsteps stop uncertainly, then start in their direction.

Lord, prayed Coral, alarm gripping her emotions like a vise. *What is this? What is going on? Do not let him come here, please!*

From behind them in the garden there were voices. The footsteps that had followed them from the alleyway stopped, then darted off into the trees.

Whoever it was had not wished to be seen, so Coral crept out of the shed looking in the runner's direction in time to catch a glimpse of a yellow turban, then he was gone.

Was Marianna right? Had he been meeting with Uncle Hugo in the alleyway?

Marianna came up behind her, grabbing her arm. "It is Cousin Ethan and Kathleen calling us. Whaa-what shall we say?"

"The truth. I came looking for you," said Coral.

"No! Say nothing, not until I explain. Please!"

"But—"

"Coral!"

"Very well. Come, they will be worried."

A few minutes later Coral stepped onto the pathway with Marianna behind her. "We are over here," she called, surprised her voice sounded calm.

Ethan hurried toward them with Kathleen. "Are you all right?"

Marianna looked embarrassed and turned her head away.

"Yes, we are just fine," answered Coral cheerfully.

"What are you doing out here without a chaperon?" Kathleen asked with a frown.

"Oh! I went for a walk," said Marianna lamely, smoothing her curls back into place.

"In this cold?" said Kathleen accusingly.

"Yes! It is cold," agreed Marianna too quickly. "Let us go inside and get some hot, mulled punch. Coming, Coral?"

"Ah . . . yes."

Coral saw Ethan's gaze flicker across her mussed hair and then to the slipper in her hand.

"What happened? Did you fall?"

"Oh, I just lost my slipper." She managed a smile.

He took her arm. "This is dreadful. Come, dear, let me get you back to the house. You might have sprained your ankle."

At the house, Coral managed to get away from Ethan, explaining that she wanted to look in on Marianna.

When Coral entered the bedroom and shut the door, her sister was sitting on a stool, the flounces of her skirt spread about her. Marianna looked up at her, white and shaking.

Kathleen stood, hands on hips. "I want the truth. What were you doing out there?"

"Kathleen, not now. Marianna is not feeling well. The

best thing you can do is go back down to the ball. I will take care of her."

"What *happened* to you, Coral?" Kathleen scanned her.

"I was in a hurry and lost a slipper."

Marianna burst into tears, covering her face with her palms. Coral rushed to her and knelt, drawing her head against her shoulder. "Kathleen, will you please let me handle this?"

Kathleen's eyes narrowed suspiciously. "Since when do you two keep things from me?"

"Trust me. I will explain later."

"Oh, very well. I could almost believe the two of you had beaus waiting out in the garden if I did not know you better, Coral. Whatever you do, do not let Aunt Margaret see you like this."

"Keep her busy for a while, will you?"

"You have a lot of explaining to do in the morning." She looked down on Marianna. Then turning abruptly, she flounced toward the door and went out, shutting it firmly behind her.

Coral let out a breath and soothed Marianna's mussed curls. "It is all right. Here, blow your nose like a good girl."

"I . . . I do not feel well, Coral. I think I am getting ill."

"Here, let me help you get out of your clothes and into bed. I will send down for something hot to drink. After you gather your wits together you can tell me what happened."

Marianna was in bed when there came a rap on the door. Her wide eyes darted to Coral. Coral found herself glancing at the door. Marianna's nervous behavior made her feel cautious. "It is just a servant," she said. "Or maybe Aunt Margaret."

"Remember your promise," she whispered. "Do not say anything until we talk first."

Coral paused before the door, her hand on the knob. She brought her features into composure before she opened it. "Yes?"

She gulped. Her stomach flipped.

Sir Hugo stood there, with a cloak over his evening clothes. His eyes were solemn, the bearded face unreadable. His stare confronted her, making Coral wish to step back. She denied being intimidated and managed a slight smile. "Oh, it is you, Uncle. Good evening. We did not expect you to arrive tonight."

"I had a change of plans. I took a shortcut through the garden. I was informed that either you or Marianna tripped and was injured."

She felt, rather than saw, his eyes taking her in.

So . . . he does not know for certain just who saw him. "Yes, I was in the garden, Uncle. I am fine."

"The servant, Piroo, was with me. He thought you might have injured yourself. He went to find you, but you had already come back to the house."

Did he come here to tell her this so she would think the man in the yellow turban was a servant? That his running after them had been out of concern? Coral suspected differently. "I was in the garden. But I did not fall."

He looked past her toward the bed where Marianna lay with the covers pulled up around her throat. Would he ask if Marianna was with her?

"Marianna is not feeling well. I noticed it early this evening. I think she may be coming down with a raw throat."

"Indeed?" He stepped inside, and Coral had no recourse but to step back. He walked up to the bedside, gazing down. Coral came up beside him, hoping Marianna would not show alarm. To her relief, her sister's eyes were shut, and she lay motionless.

Coral tensed when Hugo reached a hand to touch Marianna's forehead. Would she jump? She remained still.

"I will ask Ethan to come up. He can give her something to help her. We must have her well and happy again before your cousin's engagement party to Arlen." He stood there for a moment longer, watching Marianna, then walked to the door. Coral followed him.

"You must not wander in the garden at night, my dear. There are vipers about."

When he had gone, Coral shut the door and listened until his steps died away. She turned the key in the lock, then hurried back to Marianna. Her eyelids fluttered open, and she tried to sit up. "I do not want to see Cousin Ethan!"

"Uncle will be suspicious if you do not. Say nothing about your being in the garden, do you understand? He thinks I was alone. It is just as well." Marianna nodded, and with her teeth chattering she lay back against the pillow.

Is this a nervous reaction, or is she actually getting ill? Coral wondered, feeling edgy.

Ethan arrived a few minutes later. Coral unlocked the door and let him in. She had expected Aunt Margaret to be with him, but he was alone. As he felt Marianna's pulse and touched her forehead, Coral remained seated on the side of the bed to assure her sister.

"Well, little cousin. I see nothing to worry about," Ethan told Marianna cheerfully. "Stay in bed tomorrow for good measure. You should be up and singing for the rest of the festivities."

He handed Coral a packet of powders. "Mix this with something hot, then let her sleep."

Coral followed him to the door while the Indian servant girl entered with a hot cup of tea for Marianna.

"You know how young girls are," Coral assured Ethan, "the excitement of the ball, the holidays, and the upcoming journey home has merely proven too much."

Ethan smiled and gave her such a searching look that Coral felt her face turning warm. She was afraid he would ask again why she was in the garden, and said swiftly, "Ethan, there is a physician you should meet. Doctor John Thomas is staying at Serampore. He has worked in India for many years. If you like, we could go to Serampore in the morning. I have a friend who can bring us to see him. You remember Charles Peddington from London?"

"Your music teacher? Ah, yes, he went to work for the Company. He knows Doctor Thomas?"

"Yes. Thomas is an associate with Master William Carey."

"The minister from Kettering? The one who wrote the pamphlet?"

"He is now a Bible translator with a mission station at Serampore. They have a printing press. He also started a school. Lady Isobel has spoken well of it. A number of English and Danish here in Barrackpore send their children there."

"Marvelous. I would like to go as soon as possible. Can you arrange it with Peddington?"

"I will send word ahead. We can take a boat first thing in the morning and return before dinner at the commissioner's."

"Splendid. How good of you to have thought of this."

"Well, actually, Ethan, I do have a motive of my own. I want to see the Marshmans' school, and Charles has reason to believe that Master Carey will have some Scripture in Hindi to give to me."

He smiled. "Then, by all means, we shall go."

"I will meet you at the ghat early . . . say, around dawn?"

"Very well, dawn it is. Then we both had best turn in early."

"Good night, Ethan, thank you."

Coral shut the door behind him. As her smile faded, she frowned and walked over to the bed. The servant girl had already poured their tea. "Anything else, miss-sahiba?"

"No, that will be all. Thank you."

The girl salaamed and slipped silently from the room. When they were alone, Coral locked the door again and lit a second lamp. Quickly she was beside the bed, and Marianna sat up against the pillows.

"All right, tell me what happened."

"I went into the garden as I said, because I thought I saw Uncle through the window where I sat by the hearth. I knew he was not supposed to be here until tomorrow. I would have thought nothing about it except he looked as though he did not wish to be seen. And when Cousin Belinda also slipped away into the garden, and did not come back—well, I decided to go look for her."

"Belinda?" asked Coral surprised. "Are you certain?"

"Yes. I never did locate her."

"But Belinda was waltzing with Arlen George when I left to find you. I thought you were here in the room."

Marianna shrugged. "Then she must have come back another way. But I did not know that, and I went through the gate because I thought it led to the pond, but I found myself in an alleyway with a garden wall. There were stairs leading up to a lemon orchard. I heard two men talking. It sounded like Uncle Hugo, so I thought nothing of it and walked toward the steps. Two men were standing there. One was Uncle; the other was an Indian with a yellow turban. I started to say, 'Good evening, Uncle, where is Belinda?' when something the Indian said stopped me." Marianna's eyes grew wide, and she plucked at the coverlet.

"Yes? What did he say?" Coral urged.

Marianna gave a shiver and glanced toward the door.

"It is bolted," said Coral.

"He said to Uncle, 'An accident of one so great is not easily arranged. Not like the first time. He has many friends, even among the Hindus.' "

Coral stared into the pale face and found her own heart suddenly pounding. "You are sure, Marianna?" she whispered.

Marianna swallowed and nodded her head.

Coral tried to keep her self-control. After all, the words could mean almost anything, couldn't they?

"Anything else?"

"No. It was then that I think I made a little noise, and they both turned in my direction. I think Uncle ran up the steps and disappeared into the lemon grove, but the other man, the Indian—he started toward me, and I was afraid and ran. I could hear him chasing after me! Then I ran into you. Oh, Coral, what could it all mean? Do . . . do you think Uncle Hugo has done something wrong?"

Coral did not know what to think. "We must not rush to conclusions. But you must say nothing of this to anyone, do you understand?"

"Not even Aunt Margaret?"

"Especially her. You must promise me not to breathe a word of this until I tell you it is all right to do so, understood?"

Marianna frowned. "But if something is wrong—"

"We do not know that. Even so, all the more reason to keep quiet until I can speak to Major Buckley. We do not want anyone to know what you overheard, least of all Uncle Hugo."

"But, Coral, if that Indian man did something wrong, and he knows I heard—"

"That is why you must say nothing. Once Uncle Hugo is convinced no one overheard, it will pass."

"What if he asks me?"

"I do not think he will. I will talk to the major and see what he suggests about the matter." Coral stood, masking the alarm she felt, and prepared the medicine to add to the cup of tea.

"Oh, dear, I shall never get to sleep!"

"Try not to think about it. Here, drink this."

Marianna looked up at her with wide, frightened eyes. "What would have happened if he caught me?"

"He had no intention of catching you, or us. He could have easily outrun two women in silk slippers. I am sure he wanted to see who had overheard them talking. And you can rest secure, because he does not know."

Marianna frowned. "What makes you think so?"

"I am certain that was the reason Uncle came here to our room tonight. He wanted to find out who was in the garden. He thinks it was me."

"Oh . . ." said Marianna with a small voice. "I did not mean to get you into trouble, Coral."

Coral managed a smile. "Do not worry. Here, drink your tea."

"Coral, I wish you would not go to Serampore tomorrow."

"There is nothing to worry about. Kathleen can keep you company, and so will Aunt Margaret."

"But do you really intend to go with Cousin Ethan? Suppose Uncle Hugo finds out?"

"He will eventually. Ethan will most likely mention it to him. By then I should be back in Barrackpore. Look,

Marianna, I must get a copy of the Scriptures in Hindi. I will not get another chance soon. And it is important that I visit the Marshmans. I know so little about starting a school."

Marianna's reddish brows came together, even though her eyes began to grow sleepy from the medicine. "You are still going to start that mission school. . . . I wish you would change your mind; not because I do not think what you want to do is good, but I am afraid for you."

Coral smiled and sat down on the bed. She took the empty cup and set it aside, then covered Marianna.

"Say hello to Charles for me," her sister murmured.

"I will. Now I want you to say a verse over and over until you fall asleep. Are you willing to try to learn it?"

Marianna nodded.

" 'I will both lay me down in peace, and sleep: for thou, LORD, only makest me dwell in safety. Psalm 4:8.' " Marianna closed her eyes and repeated it softly after Coral. Within a few minutes she was asleep.

Coral lowered the lamp, having no inclination to go back down to the ball. She would be up before dawn to wait for Ethan by the river. Tomorrow night at this time, if God blessed her endeavor, a copy of the Scriptures in Hindi would be safely within her hand.

Uncle Hugo . . . and the Indian with the yellow turban . . . what had they been planning? She must inform Major Jace Buckley. But after his meeting with the colonel, he may have left. She wished to take no chances of another conversation with Sir Hugo tonight.

Coral wrote a quick note, explaining what had taken place and that she had learned something while in the garden with Marianna that might be important.

I will give the message to Seward to deliver before leaving for Serampore in the morning.

126

And just what would Jace Buckley think of her uncle's clandestine meeting in the garden?

————

As Jace came down the staircase with the colonel, he noticed that the Kendall daughter had left. Ethan Boswell, too, was gone. He sampled the dishes of food, and was about to leave, when he became aware of perfume and turned his head. Belinda Roxbury smiled.

"Why, Jace, how good of you to come. And to think my cousins have disappeared. No matter, I shall have you all to myself. I believe you owe me the next waltz."

He smiled. "My pleasure, Miss Roxbury."

She swished her fan. "Belinda." She glanced about. "I wonder where Ethan and Coral are? I saw them go off alone into the garden. . . ."

A brow arched. "Did you?"

"You do know, do you not, that they will marry at Kingscote?"

"I was not aware."

"Coral says she is madly in love."

"Did she?"

"With her health, isn't it grand she can marry a doctor! Of course, do not tell her I told you so."

"I shall be certain to keep your secret."

10

Danish-controlled Serampore stood on the banks of the Hooghly River, which flowed past the front gate of the mission house. Charles Peddington greeted Coral and Ethan warmly.

"I'm pleased you were able to come before I left for Calcutta to work at Government-House."

"Charles, you remember Doctor Boswell?"

"Most certainly. Good morning, sir. Welcome to India."

As Coral explained that he hoped to meet Doctor John Thomas, Charles brightened. "Yes! Doctor Thomas is here now. He has brought an Indian friend who wishes to inquire further of Christianity."

Coral glanced toward Ethan to see his reaction, but he seemed to be absorbed with his surroundings and the botanical garden that Carey had developed on the grounds of the mission.

"How many acres?" Boswell asked.

"At least two," said Charles. "Master Carey was able to come by it at an excellent price from a relative of Governor Bie."

Ethan looked surprised. "How fortunate for you to

129

find a friend in the Danish government."

"Indeed, sir. Had it not been for Governor Bie, we would have been sent back to London by the Company. The Lord has supplied the needs of the mission. We have a meeting hall large enough for a chapel," Charles went on, "and we all take turns preaching and holding meetings in Bengali. We have several outbuildings that we use for our residences and business needs, and of course—" he turned to Coral with a smile, "we have the Marshmans' school."

While Charles brought Ethan to meet Thomas, Coral was taken on a tour of the school by Hannah Marshman.

"How did you come to concern yourself with India?" asked Coral.

"When we heard of William's work here in India, my husband knew with a great certainty that this was his calling. He has not regretted the decision, and neither have I," Mrs. Marshman said with a smile.

Hannah Marshman was a capable woman. Her inner strength was balanced between her zeal and a practical outworking of her prudence shown in the many duties she accomplished around the mission.

Hannah had not only taken up the management of the communal affairs of the mission household, but she taught both in the school and the church, and devoted a great many hours cultivating a friendly relationship with the Hindu women who had surprisingly begun to open their doors to her.

"When I heard about your school I knew I must see it, and talk with you," said Coral, and explained her plans to start a mission school on Kingscote.

"So Charles has told us. William will be delighted to know that a young woman of your character is dedicated to making Christ known among the children," said Hannah.

"We arrive at the school at seven," Hannah told Coral as they walked along. "Classes usually run till after two each day."

"I suppose what I worry about the most is how to get the children to attend," said Coral. "How difficult was that for you?"

"Actually, our students are quite different from those you will have. Most of our boys are from English and Danish families here in Serampore and across the river in Barrackpore. We also have some from Calcutta. When the families heard of our curriculum they were immediately interested. We are noted for high instruction, and soon we had a number of students enrolled. Actually, it has become a slogan that *'everyone sends his son to Serampore.'* We can see God's working and timing. The fees we must charge and the profits from Mr. Ward's printing press are able to make the mission self-supporting. This is important to William, who does not want to burden the Mission Society in London. We board Anglo-Indian boys, and I've been able to open a school for young ladies—another extremely important task. We charge forty to fifty rupees a year, depending on whether the students receive Latin, Greek, Hebrew, Persian, or Sanskrit lessons. Of course, the school at Kingscote will not need to be so involved."

Coral smiled. "I was thinking of simple reading, writing, and Bible instruction. I also hope to feed them one hot meal a day, perhaps breakfast."

"Then I must show you the free school. We have started with the Bengali boys and have forty enrolled. At first the children were certain we were going to abduct them and send them to England, but we soon made friends. What about your supplies? I suppose you brought them with you aboard ship?"

"Not nearly enough," Coral confessed. Getting her

meager supplies shipped from London to Calcutta had proved difficult. Getting them safely home to Kingscote would prove even more troublesome. "I have one trunk of teaching materials. First I must convince my family of the need for the school."

"By God's grace you will. Come, let me show you our new supplies from London. They arrived only yesterday."

Coral went through the Marshmans' material, some of it still in shipping cartons. There was Gibbon's *Rhetoric*, Hornsey's *Grammar*, Milton's *Paradise Lost*, Cowper's *Poems*, many quills, ink made for hot climates, and a box of well-bound New Testaments in English.

"It is the Hindi New Testament that I hope to buy."

"I am sure William will present you with the Scriptures as a gift, dear. He will be so pleased with your efforts. You should also visit Mr. Ward and the printing press. William's son Felix works with him."

"I look forward to it. Charles has told me so much about it."

"Charles . . . poor boy. He was so faithful while aiding Mr. Ward. We shall miss him. But the fever takes its toll. We have lost several missionaries."

"Yes, Charles told me about John Fountain."

"Not only John. We have lost Mr. Grant, also Mr. Burson. I am afraid Mrs. Carey grows worse with the passing of time. I have enormous sympathy for her, but William carries on. He is a plodder, you know. He is not a man to let difficulties and hardship hold him back from the work."

The translation work of William Carey challenged Coral to new earnestness of purpose. She discovered that upon his arrival in India he had set out to master the languages and dialects. While he gave himself to long, arduous study, Mrs. Carey was in the very next room, sometimes wrought up to heights of great neurotic frenzy because of her mental disability, and yet he patiently handled her needs, while plodding ahead in the translation work. Coral was certain that most other servants of God in those circumstances would have given up.

Coral was graciously received by William Carey, who explained more of his work.

"My goal, as the Lord enables, is to see the Word of God in every language and dialect of India," he said.

Coral felt overwhelmed with the prospect, but Carey believed it was possible. There were others involved. Marshman, Ward, a Mr. Gilchrist, Doctor John Thomas, and at various times, native Indian munshis were engaged to assist with the finer points of the language. He had received worried criticism from the Mission Society for using the munshis, but Carey was certain of what he was doing.

"Whatever help we employ I have never yet suffered a single word or a single mode of construction without having examined it and seen through it," William Carey said. "I read every proof sheet twice or thrice myself, and correct every letter with my own hand. Brother Marshman or myself compare it with Greek or Hebrew, and Brother Ward reads every sheet. Three of the translations, mainly the Bengali, Hindustani, and the Sanskrit, I translate with my own hands, the last two immediately from the Greek and Hebrew Bible which is before me while I translate the Bengali."

Coral was delighted to discover that he intended to translate the Bible in whole or in part in the Assami language, and also in Burmese. A missionary named Chater would be sent to Rangoon, and William's son Felix intended to go with him to start a mission station.

After a full morning of touring the mission, and seeing the translation work, Coral joined the others at the dinner table where the ten missionaries and nine children, four of them Carey's sons, all ate their meals in common.

Coral quietly told Carey that she had decided to start the mission school on Kingscote after reading his pamphlet on world missions.

"Then God be the One praised, my dear child."

A prayer was offered before they ate: "May this endeavor wrought in order to share the power of the gospel with the untouchables be blessed of Him a hundredfold. Yea, let an orphanage be established as God enables."

It was now after the meal, and approaching the hour of their departure to Barrackpore, but Ethan had gone off on some excursion with Thomas. As she awaited his return, Charles led her into the chapel.

"Before you go, we have something for you," said Charles, with a warm glow in his eyes.

Coral's chest tightened with emotion as she guessed what it was. There on the communion table in the chapel, resting beside the elements that they were to share together, was a Hindi New Testament. Coral swallowed back the cramp in her throat.

William Carey led in communion, and then presented her with the Scriptures. A marker had been placed at Matthew nineteen, the portion of Scripture about Jesus and the children.

Coral stared at the words of Christ until her eyes blurred with moisture. "How can I thank you, Master Carey?"

He smiled quietly, and said: "Teach it. And when you do, never speak of William Carey, but speak of William Carey's God."

After the others left the chapel, and the last goodbyes were given, Charles walked her in the direction of the river. She stopped him, and they stood in the wide avenue of mahogany trees.

"I will meet Ethan at the boat. He may be there now waiting for me. Goodbye, Charles. I do hope your work at Government-House goes well."

He sighed. "It shall never bring the satisfaction that I received today when I saw the expression on your face." He looked at the New Testament that she held, and his face sobered. "To have experienced that moment, Coral, was worth every testing we have undergone. I shall never find at Government-House anything to bring me such joy."

His hand closed about hers as it enfolded the Scriptures in Hindi.

"I will come to see you and your sisters at Kingscote when I can. And may a school stand to His honor when I arrive."

"Goodbye, Charles, and thank you again."

With the Scriptures in her bag, Coral walked down to the ghat. The boat was there, but neither Ethan nor the river guide was waiting. She shaded her eyes and glanced about, seeing no sign of their presence.

It was still early afternoon and the December day was chill, but the sun was out, and the birds were chattering noisily in the overhanging branches. Thomas had mentioned that a Hindu temple was located not far away, and she wondered if that was where they had gone. The area was a botanist's dream, and Ethan may have wanted to take some samples back to Barrackpore to occupy his time of study.

Coral left the ghat and made her way down the tree-lined road, which soon narrowed. *A missionary must learn to do things on her own,* she told herself. *I cannot be leaning on a male chaperon all the time. Once I arrive at Kingscote I will need to depend on the Lord and take responsibility for my own actions, so why not now?*

She came to a wall and followed it. The weather was moist, and she pulled the hood of her long cloak up over her tresses.

Serampore was noted for its luxurious trees. The embankment along the Hooghly River was thick with bamboo and feathery coconut palms. There were flocks of brightly colored parakeets and the long-legged cranes that served as Calcutta's scavengers. Monkeys swung from branches, and to her dismay, poisonous snakes were abundant. As she made her way precariously in the direction of the ancient temple, she felt the familiar weakness come to sap her strength and mock her independence. Despite the moist coolness, it did not take long before she was wet with perspiration. She stopped to catch her breath. Ahead was a narrow gate and the entrance to a secondary ghat that may have belonged to the temple grounds.

Coral noticed that a number of people were gathered on the bank, and a man who looked to be a Hindu priest was speaking. Were Ethan and Doctor Thomas with them? Perhaps Thomas was engaging the priest in a discussion of the Scriptures.

Coral passed through the gate and walked along the bank toward the small crowd. She did not see Thomas, but she did get a closer view of the priest. He was a thin, older man with a shaven head and a white caste mark painted on his brown forehead. The so-called sacred thread was across his shoulder. But to Coral's horror, she realized that she had come upon a ceremony that her father had forbidden to take place on Kingscote, one that sometimes occurred in the village. It was the *suttee*—a woman who had become widowed was preparing herself to be burned alive with the body of her husband on his funeral pyre.

Why, the woman is young, no more than fifteen or sixteen.

Coral's heart thudded in her chest. She wanted to turn and run away in revulsion, but her feet would not move. The girl was throwing her life, and her soul, away.

Coral's voice surprised even herself. "Roko! Roko!" she shouted.

They turned and looked at her, wondering who would dare tell them to stop.

Coral took a hesitant step forward and confronted the immobile eyes of the priest. She walked toward the small gathering feeling as though her knees would buckle. Their expressions were indomitable, the dark eyes cool.

She floundered, wondering what to say, and her gaze fell upon the young widow standing by the pyre. There were several large bundles of wood, about two and a half feet high and four feet long. As her eyes darted to the top, she saw the body of the deceased ready for burning. Coral felt sick.

As though in a move to protect the widow, her nearest relative came to stand beside her. In the girl's hand was a basket. Coral recognized the contents as sweetmeats that were used as an offering to the god Shiva.

"W-what are you doing?" Coral managed rather weakly.

"We have come to burn our dead."

"Yes. But—but his widow is alive."

They did not reply.

Coral grew bolder. "Why, she is little more than a child!"

"This is her choice. No one forces her."

"Is this true?" Coral asked her.

The young face of the girl met hers. "It is, sahiba."

Coral tried to reason with her, then with those gathered, but they soon grew angry. Coral became desperate.

"This is no less than murder! You have forced her to this, for if she does not go through with it, her family will have broken caste, and you will denounce them! Do not do it," she told the girl, and extended a hand toward her, but several men stepped between them.

"Be gone, sahiba."

The priest stepped toward her. "You interfere in that which you do not understand. It is not your affair. You are a feringhi. You intrude where you have no right."

"I was born and raised in India; I am not a foreigner. But whether I am or not, sir, has nothing to do with the matter of life and death. The living and true God forbids human sacrifice, and it is my responsibility to speak against what you are doing. It does not please Him! He has given no such commandment."

While Coral was talking, the widow had been led six times around the pile, and now she scattered the sweetmeats while the others picked them up and ate them as a holy offering.

"Stop!" she cried. "Please! God has given His very Son as the one and only sacrifice to atone for sin. Though a Hindu be born a thousand times, and dies a thousand deaths, it is of no avail; burning is wicked in His sight—"

"Is sahiba one of those pestilent Christians from William Carey's mission?" the priest demanded of her.

"They have turned Krishna Pal into a European," said another. "He was a brahmin, yet he has eaten with them. Now they baptize others in the holy Ganges!"

"I am not of Master Carey's mission, though I would find it an honor to be one of them. For they have come in love and compassion. Is it so wrong to be concerned for the life of this girl?"

"Be gone, sahiba!" he warned, and several from the funeral group took a step in her direction. Coral refused to turn and run. She called to the girl, "Come with me.

No harm will befall you if you do. They dare not force you. They admit the decision is in your hand! Fear nothing, I will take you with me to Barrackpore. I promise to care for you for the rest of your life if you will come with me now!"

To Coral's horror, the girl suddenly climbed up onto the pile. As if to show her willingness to burn, she began to dance, her hands extended.

Coral stared with horror. "No—wait!"

The girl lay down with the deceased, placing her arms around his neck. Coral took a step backward. *Oh, God!*

The others poured dry cocoa leaves and melted butter over the two bodies, then two bamboos were pressed over the pyre and held fast.

"This is murder!" shouted Coral. "Take away the bamboo! You do it to keep her there! She cannot change her mind once you set it aflame! Murder—"

Unexpectedly, a strong hand grasped her arm and whirled her about face. Jace stood there, his eyes sparking with frustration, his jaw set. "Coral! What are you doing here!"

Before she could answer, the dry kindling crackled, then exploded into flame. "Hurree-Bol, Hurree-Bol!" The loud shout of invocation from those gathered smothered any protest that might have sounded from beneath the pyre.

Coral's hands flew to cover her ears, and her eyes shut tightly. She wanted to scream.

Almost at the same moment, Jace stepped back from the heat, swung her up into his arms, and retreated down the bank of the river. Ducking beneath the overhanging branches and avoiding the tentacles of creeper that reached to entangle them, the awful shouting was left behind as the smoke curled upward like vile incense to the Hindu god.

11

Jace did not stop until they neared the ghat where an empty boat waited. Here he set her lightly on her feet, and Coral drew away, walking weakly to the platform. Steadying herself, she sank down in a daze, sickened.

"Oh . . . I feel ill."

"Do not faint on me. I have no smelling salts."

"It is vile! It ought to be outlawed!" She looked up at him, scanning his uniform accusingly. "The East India Company should do something about such wicked practices in Calcutta."

"Ask your uncle to speak to the governor-general. He managed to change my orders," he said dryly, "perhaps he can halt widow burning. As for you, Miss Kendall, I gather you need a little more excitement in your life? A midnight excursion in the garden was not challenging enough for your rare spirit, so you must confront a Hindu priest during suttee!"

"Do not say it, Major, I do not want to hear it."

"You might have gotten yourself into a great deal of trouble! Does your father know you are wandering about Calcutta without Seward?"

No, of course he did not. And Coral knew that Major

Buckley was correct. Her father would have exploded had he come upon her just now.

"I did not go in search of this sickening experience if that is what you think."

"I hardly know *what* to think. You are certainly not the typical English girl. And I have met a few in my time."

Coral fumed. He sounded as if he had been around a generation before her entry into the world, as if she were a child who had wandered from her nursery.

She cast him a defensive glance. She said nothing and looked back at the river feeling emotionally exhausted, too weary to do anything but watch it flow past, its murky swells conjuring up fresh images of the girl dancing on the funeral pyre. The memory would long be etched upon her mind.

"A word of advice, Miss Kendall."

"I have received nothing but advice since I arrived in Calcutta. First from my aunt, then Sir Hugo. I do not particularly care to hear any more, Major."

"You have my sympathy, but I will give mine anyway since it is born from a lifetime of experience with unpleasant situations. For your own emotional well-being, Miss Kendall, learn to shield your heart with armor before you look upon a land retching with pain. You might have been born here, but you do not know the mass of humanity that is Calcutta or Bombay. Kingscote is hardly the face of the real India that I have lived and suffered with since a boy."

She found in his words something of the real Jace Buckley. When they had first encountered each other at the bazaar, he had intimated the same outlook, suggesting she not meddle with the culture of India, that she would receive nothing but trouble for her involvement. She turned her head a little in order to study his face. Beyond the obvious good looks was a resolute hardness that refused to yield to critique. Was his armor a genuine rebuff to tenderness, or a ploy to shield vulnerability?

How much pain had Jace actually experienced since seeing his father beheaded in Whampoa? And what actually was his feeling toward her willingness for personal risk? Did he think she was wide-eyed and innocent, out on a personal crusade to better India's morals? Or did he understand that her commitment went far deeper?

"You will not stop the practice of widow burning by confronting the act," he continued. "You will get nothing for your pains but spiritual exhaustion. Your revulsion means nothing to a culture rooted in religious convictions, however dark, and if you seek to interfere you will only hurt yourself, or cause a riot. Get in the boat. I intend to take you back where you belong—Canterbury House."

Coral's frustration mounted, and somehow it seemed suddenly important that he understood, that he believed as she did, that he cared for India's pain, its grievous chains of satanic bondage. She stood, her eyes searching his for some small measure of compassion that could rise to her own height for a people in anguish.

"Are you as detached from the reality of suffering as you imply? Is that how you look upon the multitudes, Major? As a mass of humanity without a face, a name, a soul? You wish to not hear the smothered wail of one girl burning in the flames, but the voice of a multitude shouting in ignorance to Shiva, an idol of death and destruction."

"Are you speaking as a follower of Christ, or as a prideful European nauseated by heathenism?"

"The gospel is not cultural, Major."

"I am pleased you are wise enough to know the difference, Miss Kendall. Many do not. The East India Company is filled with the civilized who deplore not only the Hindu rituals but also the people. I have often contemplated what Christ would do if He were on earth walking the dusty roads of India."

"He would have stopped the suttee. He would have done something, something that revealed His compassion and authority. I know He would!"

"Compassion and authority make good kinsmen, do they not? He bears them both like the sweetness of a well-watered garden. Compassion for the multitudes, authority to break the chains that bind, and His answer to Shiva? What is it, Miss Kendall?"

Somehow she knew that his question was not asked in ignorance, for his words had revealed that the person of Christ was not a stranger to his intellect. She stared at him, surprised. Why then did he probe her, sounding quiet, yet so challenging? He was not asking as a Hindu. Of that she was certain.

"I was a boy of eight when I saw my father use a scimitar to lop off the head of a pirate aboard our ship," he said matter-of-factly. "I distinctly remember being splattered with warm blood—you find that offensive, I know. I only mention it that you might understand that human suffering was part of my daily ration. But I remember something else as well, even more distinctly. Some man, I do not even remember who he was, was shouting that it was murder. 'Thou shalt not murder,' he shouted. 'God will hold your soul eternally responsible. Mercy and forgiveness of sin are found in His Son, but if you reject Him, you will surely die.'"

He looked down at her, his features unreadable. "I never forgot that. I remember washing the blood from my face in the cabin, and my father came in. He glowered down upon me, looking like some giant in a rough blue coat and hat. He grabbed me by the front of my tunic and shook me until my head snapped. 'You must never do as I have done,' he told me. 'If I go to hell, I do not want to see you there.' "

Coral felt a spasm of raw emotion, yet Jace spoke calmly, with detachment.

"It was not long after that," he continued, "that I saw my father killed. I remember retching in the sand and feeling the salt water roll over me. I could hear Seward calling me from the distance on a small boat. I knew I should swim out to him while I had a chance to escape. But I could not. I was too sick."

Coral felt the warm tears seeping from the corners of her eyes, and her throat constricted.

"I came here to India when I was around twelve; I really do not know how old I am. I watched mothers throw their infants to crocodiles on holy days, and heard their wails. I have seen men hang themselves on flesh hooks, and indulge in other self-inflicted tortures to appease Shiva's wrath. No amount of reasoning or anger on my part has ever stopped any of it."

There was silence. Coral wanted to say something, but her mouth was dry; she knew her voice would break off before she completed her sentence. She knew why his emotions were encased in armor, and she wanted to remove it and heal the wounds. The features of the man looking down at her masked what he was thinking or feeling. She sensed that beyond that hard facade was another Jace, but there would be a personal risk in discovering him.

So wrapped up was she in her own response, she did not see his, not until she felt his thumb brush the tear from her cheek. A faint smile warmed his features.

Aware that his light touch had awakened her senses, she stepped back, and gathering up her skirts, climbed down the steps of the ghat to the boat, leaving Jace standing there in silence.

A moment later he followed, frowning to himself. "I should not have said all that to you. I am not sure why I did."

Coral did not look at him. "I am glad."

The silence grew.

"Does Boswell have enough sense to get back on his own?" he asked flatly.

Thinking of Ethan brought William Carey back to mind. It was only then that Coral remembered.

"Oh, no!" she gasped, and whirled to look at him.

His brow went up. "Now what?"

"I must have set my bag down! I cannot leave without it, Major."

He folded his arms. "Most women have dozens of bags and parasols. A silk heiress can afford to lose one."

"But not this one. Master Carey gave me a copy of the Hindi New Testament. It was the reason I came today."

His eyes flickered over her with subdued impatience, and he turned his head to look down the river. "Do not tell me, Miss Kendall. Let me guess. You set it down by the funeral pyre."

She swallowed, and her voice quavered. "Well, yes."

"This is turning into one of those long, well-remembered days. Wait here. I will see if I can retrieve it from the lion's den."

"Oh, thank you, Major Buckley."

He gave a deep bow at the waist. "Your servant, Miss Kendall." And he took the steps upward.

Coral waited for him, pacing. She was confident that he could take care of himself, but as the minutes crept by, her anxiety increased.

At last she saw him coming down the steps with her bag in hand. He seemed in a hurry.

"Any trouble, Major?"

He took her arm and propelled her quickly toward the boat. "Let us just say, I would prefer a more desirable location to continue our conversation."

12

Jace assisted her onto the boat and took up the oars, then began moving swiftly down the Hooghly. For a few minutes they were silent.

"Seward delivered your message. I believe you have something else to tell me about last night," said Jace.

"Last night?"

"In the garden."

Coral tried to ease her emotions by lifting her face toward the sky and shutting her eyes. She listened to the slap of the water against the sides of the boat.

"Is that the reason you came to Serampore?" she asked finally. "Because of last night?"

"Yes and no."

"But how did you know I was here?"

"Seward warned me you were coming at Peddington's invitation."

"Is *warned* the right word, Major?"

"To my mind, yes, Miss Kendall."

"It seems I have a number of guardians keeping track of my whereabouts."

"With your eagerness for adventure, you will need them. Now, what happened last night?"

As the river swept past and monkeys chattered in the trees, Coral felt his alert gaze studying her reaction.

"Will you promise to say nothing of this to my aunt?"

"I have no reason to inform Lady Margaret, but I need to know exactly what happened."

"Marianna is quite certain that she witnessed a clandestine meeting in the garden last night between my uncle and an Indian."

He was alert. "Did she see the Indian's face?"

"No. I caught a glimpse of him running away, but I noticed nothing distinctive except a yellow turban."

"Did your sister overhear anything?"

Coral tensed. "Yes. The words, 'An accident of one so great is not as easily arranged as the first. He has many friends even among the Hindus.' "

"Who said it?"

"The Indian. I could tell that Marianna was not exaggerating. She was quite upset. Later, Sir Hugo came to my room. He said that he had been in the garden with a servant. He called him Piroo."

"Piroo," he repeated thoughtfully.

"Yes, have you heard of him before?"

"No. But if your uncle volunteered his name, it is not likely to be helpful."

"Major? You do not think this means that my uncle was involved in someone's accident?"

"You mean, what must have appeared to be an accident."

Coral's stomach tensed, but she tried to remain calm. "Who could they have been talking about?"

"One must be careful about making accusations until there is proof of wrongdoing."

His answer was too mild to convince her that he meant it. He had been willing enough to share his suspicions with her in the past. Coral had been watching him too closely to not recognize the change in his mood.

"I wish you would not keep secrets from me, Major."

He looked at her with surprise.

"Speak your mind, please," she said. "Do not forget you nearly accused him of Gem's abduction when I was on the *Madras*. There is little you could say about him that is worse than that."

"It was not my intention to hurt you, only to warn."

"I understand. I would like to know what you think."

She listened without comment while he explained about the outpost at Jorhat, of Major Selwyn, and a suspicion that Sir Hugo might be involved.

"I would not mention this at all, except it may eventually have some consequence to Kingscote. I will speak with your father after I arrive at Jorhat. So, you see, there is another reason why you must be cautious about starting that orphanage. It could be just the excuse Sir Hugo needs to bring trouble down on your father."

Coral wanted to reject his analysis of her uncle and the school, but it was difficult to do so.

"It is all so confusing," she mused. "The outpost, the talk of mutiny, and now last night. I will admit that I do not trust my uncle. But I cannot believe he would deliberately harm someone."

"Are you thinking of Major Selwyn?"

Mention of the man's death came as a start. Coral had not been thinking of him.

"I do not know—is that what you think? That he was involved? Or the man with the turban?"

"I intend to find out. As for Sir Hugo's ability to harm anyone, you must know by now that I am rather cynical. I once told you that ambition and greed can quickly become devilish masters. I think your uncle has an appetite that is not easily satisfied. You must be extremely cautious. Say nothing of our conversation to anyone."

She nodded, for words would not come. What would Aunt Margaret do if she knew her husband was suspected of being involved in a mutiny against the British at Jorhat?

"I do not know why I am telling you all this. The less you know, the better. Can Marianna be trusted to keep quiet about what she heard last night?"

"Yes, I have already spoken to her about it. You need not feel badly about speaking like this, I have long suspected my uncle of plotting to own Kingscote."

"Have you told anyone about our discussion of Gem?"

"No."

"Considering all things, do not. It may ruin any opportunity that may come my way. Sir Hugo will be watching me."

Jace rowed in silence for a while as Coral watched him from beneath her hat.

"Somehow, Major, you do not remind me of a man interested in raising tea."

"No? I suppose you think I am too unsettled to do anything but captain a ship. Maybe you are right."

"Your father must think a great deal of you to go to such difficulty to get you back in the Company. No doubt he hopes that you will one day serve willingly."

He was quiet. "I owe the colonel for my education. He did more for me than anyone else could have. But one day I shall get back to what I believe in—the *Madras*, and Darjeeling."

Coral studied him and said nothing for a moment. "Five months aboard the Red Dragon was quite enough for me. I will not miss a topsy-turvy cabin if I never see one again."

"You should sail on the *Madras*; she is quite stable."

"If that is an invitation," Coral said with a laugh, "I must decline. Only my sister Kathleen would be willing to sail to London again so soon after our return to India. She is expected to marry Captain McKay, but her heart is set on working at the Silk House."

"How did a future silk heiress get matched with a mere Company captain?"

Coral detected a slight barb. She turned away and watched the trees on the embankment slip by. "It is a long story, Major. You will find it dull. You see, Captain McKay is our cousin on my father's side of the family in Aberdeen. Father can find no wrong in any man with Scottish blood, or a fighting spirit."

"Ah . . . but of course. A relation. That explains everything."

She cast him a glance. He was scanning the embankment. "And Boswell is related to Sir Hugo. That makes for a very happy, well-knit family."

Her face felt warm. She settled her skirts to show she no longer wished to discuss the matter.

Unexpectedly he laughed softly to himself. "Gavin married to a silk heiress."

Coral felt uncomfortable. "Do you, ah . . . know him?"

"Rather well, in fact."

His smile was disarming. She could not tell what he was thinking but was reluctant to press for more information, believing that it might prove embarrassing to Kathleen. She said quickly, "Oh, look!" and pointed to the bank of the river, trying to draw his attention away from her. "A flock of parakeets," her voice trailed off. "Are they not lovely?"

He looked, and studied the familiar sight with intensity, as though he had never seen them before.

"Enchanting," he said.

13

Gokul's mission to the bazaars of Calcutta had turned up information Jace wanted on the Moghul sword. While Gokul had already departed for Guwahati to discover what he could about Sir Hugo, Jace walked the cluttered streets of Calcutta amid the noisy throng and waited for his contact. Several of the hawkers spoke to him, willing to engage in bartering, but on this day Jace was not interested.

After a time, weary of waiting, he started back to the bungalow.

A beggar approached him for alms. When close he whispered, "O Great One, what you seek is no longer in Calcutta. But the answer to many questions awaits you in Burma!"

Later, all was dark and still when he neared the bungalow he had shared with Gokul. Jace drew his blade and, entering his room, searched until he was certain of being alone; then he sat on his bed where he could not be seen and lit a candle.

Who is the man whose accident can not be easily arranged? The maharaja?—or himself?

Roxbury had gone to the governor-general to have his

155

orders changed, but Jace did not believe that Roxbury truly wanted him as security guard at Guwahati. Did he have a convenient accident planned for the long safari north?

Jace could not concentrate, and finally he lifted his mattress and removed a small black book. An ancient trader on the caravan following the Old Silk Road through the Himalayas had given it to him when he escaped China. Jace had hid under the old merchant's bundles of blankets for days, coming out only at night when the old man shared the broth he boiled over the campfire.

The old one could not read and had come across the book after rummaging through the remains of waterlogged goods left on the wharf at Pearl River. A ship from England had been captured and the cargo pirated. After the booty had been stripped of its precious contents, a second group of looters had taken everything else of value, leaving the litter for the beggars to rummage through. The old one had searched and found the book.

The pages were warped in places, and the name of its original owner, written in ink, was blotched by salt water. But some of the pages of the New Testament were readable. The gospel of John, parts of the book of Acts, Romans and the other letters of Paul. Jace had read the words many times as a boy traveling with Gokul. Life had been rough and difficult. Gokul had been acquainted with more thieves than munshis. After the battle in the village between the English and the local Muslim ruler, Jace had ceased to read it. The translation had been authorized by King James of England, and that much alone had turned him against further reading.

He could smile now over his ignorance. He had learned a great deal since the colonel had taken him in and sent him to London. There, Jace had completed his education at the East India Company's Military College at Addiscombe. He had seen many fine King James Bibles, but he had always kept the worn edition the trader had given to him on the Old Silk Road.

The next morning Jace set about making sure the arrangements for the journey to the northern frontier were in order. Two days later, the security troop he now commanded waited for him on the parade ground, standing at attention. Some distance away, Sir Hugo, the governor-general's new resident, waited with his civilian party in two gharis. Seward and a half-dozen private Indian orderlies guarded the baggage train.

Jace caught a glimpse of Coral Kendall and her two sisters in the second ghari, just behind Sir Hugo and Doctor Boswell. Jace looked away to see the colonel riding to meet him, the image of British military at its best.

Before meeting his father, Jace rode up to the troop. At once he saw that the native officer he had personally requested from the colonel, an Indian soldier whom Jace trusted with his life, had been replaced. A stranger stood at attention, his face a military mask. *No*, Jace thought. *He is not a stranger—it is that wretched Sanjay from the outpost at Jorhat.* The officer who had been in Roxbury's office!

His surprise rushed to a feeling of anger. Who had dared to replace Nadir?

For a native Indian to become a high-ranking officer in the Bengal army took many years of proven faithfulness to the British officers. One hardly ever saw a young native officer, least of all a rissaldar-major! Yet Sanjay could only be in his early thirties.

The clop of horse's hoofs drew his attention away from Sanjay. The colonel rode up to him, and Jace turned the reins of his horse to face him, saluting, his slate-blue eyes rock hard.

The colonel responded. "At ease, Major."

"I do not understand," Jace gritted. "I want Sanjay removed. Where is Nadir?"

The colonel sat rigid. "Nadir took ill last night. Severe chest pains. It is not certain if he will live. A number of other sowars are down with dysentery. Yes, I know. Very convenient. But the orders to move out this morning stand."

"Are you certain Nadir is ill? Roxbury must be behind this. I told you what the Kendall daughter overheard at Barrackpore."

"The matter is being looked into. I called on Nadir this morning. There is no question that he is ill."

Jace gripped the reins in his gloved hand.

"Colonel, I cannot be expected to lead civilians across the northern frontier with men whose loyalty is in question. Are you certain of Sanjay?"

The colonel's eyes flickered, and he retorted, "I am certain of nothing but orders from the brigadier-general himself."

"Sir! I am responsible for three women!"

The colonel's jaw set like an iron trap. He breathed between his teeth, "You have your orders, Major. I will be in touch at Guwahati. Proceed as scheduled!"

Jace crisply saluted. He turned from his father to face the troop. His eyes scanned them: their black shakos were smartly in place, their uniforms at their best, their swords gleaming. How many of them had kissed the sword of loyal oath to the British? Jace shouted brusquely for the native officer to come forth. Nadir's replacement, Rissaldar-Major Sanjay, saluted Jace precisely.

"Major-bahadur!"

Jace studied him with a cool challenge before slowly returning the salute.

"Ram, ram sidar, Rissaldar-sahib." Jace clipped the

traditional greeting of honor with a cool voice. "Your report!"

The dark eyes were muted in the bronzed face. "Huzoor, Major Buckley, sahib! The ammunition in reserve is in the baggage train with rations and medical supplies. Resident Roxbury and the other civilians wait with the civilian gharis. All is ready."

"Fall in!"

Sanjay saluted and marched to his position.

Jace shouted, "Company! Form! Right! Right wheel, quick march!"

14

The horizon was awash with a flaming sunset. Coral sat by the ghari window, masking her growing feeling of illness. In her nostrils was the all-too-familiar smell of sunbaked soil. Her skin, too, felt clogged with dust particles, and damp tendrils of her hair stuck to the back of her neck.

Was it possible that they had left Calcutta only days earlier? The long days and even longer nights crept onward like some damaged three-wheel trap led by an uncooperative mule. It would take *two months* to get home! And the more difficult part of the journey was still ahead when they entered the jungle.

Outside the window she could see the mounted sowars, with Seward riding just behind and to the side of their ghari, his tricorn in contrast to the dusty black shakos of the native cavalry. Riding some distance ahead to alleviate the dust, Coral could just catch sight of the standard-bearer, followed by six sowars, then Major Buckley. Altogether, Coral counted some twenty men riding in pairs guarding the civilians, and behind the small column, a half-dozen well-armed men hardened by travel rode to protect the military baggage train carrying food, supplies, and ammunition for the troop.

Despite her fatigue, the excitement of the journey home to Kingscote made the discomfort bearable, and she had long since failed to hear the complaints of Kathleen, who spoke endlessly of the ordeal ahead of them. Marianna appeared detached. Coral knew that her little sister had not forgotten the clandestine meeting that she had stumbled upon between Hugo and the Indian in the yellow turban. Marianna whispered to her on several occasions that she was certain Uncle *knew* that it had been she, and not Coral, who had seen him in the alleyway.

Coral was not certain what her uncle thought. For the present, she felt relief that he appeared to have forgotten the incident.

"I do not know what could possibly be worse than spending all day in this miserable coach breathing dust," groaned Kathleen. "I dare say, my skin is positively ruined. I shall never get clean again!"

"Once we arrive at Plassey, we will be able to rest a few days at the garrison," Coral reminded them, trying to bring cheer. "There may even be a ball. You will be able to see Captain McKay."

Kathleen's lips turned at the mention of Cousin Gavin, and it was not clear what she thought of seeing him after three years. Marianna, however, appeared to have something more dreadful on her mind. Coral saw her shiver in spite of the perspiration on her forehead, and she plucked at her handkerchief.

"I prefer dust to the journey we must take upriver," Marianna said. "Do you know what?" She leaned toward them, trying to keep her balance. "I overheard Seward say the crocodiles are *over twelve feet long!*"

"Oh, look at the sunset," said Coral, changing the subject to distract them. Her sisters looked westward where the twilight held the sky with shades of violet.

Crocodiles, shuddered Coral. She would not mention that tiger country also awaited them.

Ahead the dak-bungalow came into view. There would be a place to rest for the night, and the kansamah would prepare what he had available to serve the evening guests. At the two previous dak-bungalows they had stayed at since leaving Calcutta, chopped meat was served with *chuppati,* an Indian unleavened bread. At the moment, feeling nauseous and with her head throbbing, the only thing she could think of was a cup of hot, steaming tea.

The previous year's monsoon had damaged the road in places, and they bumped along for several minutes, gripping the sides of their seats. The vehicle swayed precariously, followed by a well-rehearsed complaint from the lips of the Indian driver seated on the front box. Coral's stomach did a flip. The ghari lurched to the side and off the road, throwing her against the door. Her head crashed with a sickening thud. Dazed, she became aware of the weight of Marianna and Kathleen keeping her pressed against the side of the vehicle. Then she heard voices and shouts.

Coral felt Kathleen trying to pull her to a sitting position. "Coral!"

The ghari rocked as someone climbed onto it and flung open the door. Seward's rugged frame leaned in, looking down at them. "Ye be unhurt, lassies?"

"I don't know. Coral struck her head," said Kathleen.

"I'm . . . not hurt," Coral tried to mumble, and felt the weight of her sisters pulled from her as they were lifted out of the ghari. Coral tried to sit up, and Seward leaned in and lifted her out, then gently lowered her to the dusty road. For a moment she thought her legs would go out from under her.

Jace rode up. "Get Boswell," he commanded a sowar.

"I am not hurt," Coral said, wishing to avoid the fuss, but her brain spun dizzily.

"The doctor be coming now, Sir Hugo with him," said Seward.

Coral, still holding to Seward's arm, turned her head to see the massive figure of her uncle step down from the other ghari. "Anyone injured?" he called.

"Only a bad bump, Sir Roxbury," shouted Seward.

At the same instant, Ethan stepped out of the ghari behind Hugo, medical bag in hand. The expression on his face testified to his displeasure, and his mouth creased tightly when his eyes swerved toward Jace.

"Major!" came the condescending voice. "Your driver is to blame for this. I offered a warning of the hazards of this so-called *road* when we stopped only an hour ago."

Coral glanced at Jace, who remained mounted, and she guessed what his cool response might be. Yet his outward restraint remained impeccable. Could there possibly be two men inside that now dusty uniform?

Ethan hurried forward, coming between her and Seward.

"Dear, you might have broken a bone!"

Coral ducked her head to hide her embarrassment. She wished Ethan would not publicly use words of endearment, when she had not yet given him that privilege. She said with a rush, "I am quite all right, Ethan. And the ghari-wallah handled the mishap quite well."

"I have my doubts of that."

The frustrated driver was pointing to the road in self-defense. "Mercifully all is well, sahib. There is no damage. My apology, miss-sahiba."

Ethan interrupted. "Your apology is not enough. Miss Kendall might have been seriously injured." He turned toward Jace. "Well, Major? You do agree that something must be done about your driver?"

164

"Please, it is no one's fault," said Coral. "The road is terrible. It could have happened to your own ghari."

"Hardly," said Ethan.

"The doctor is right," said Jace.

Surprised, Coral looked at him. She had not expected him to agree so easily with Ethan. He gestured to the driver to go back to the baggage train.

"For the rest of the trip you will help the kansamah." Jace turned toward one of his sowars. "Lal! I am holding you responsible to see that the Kendall daughters arrive safely to Manali."

Manali! Coral turned in Jace's direction. They were to travel to Plassey. Manali was located southeast in the area of the Ganges Delta, and more than two day's journey out of their path! Jace knew that! But he did not respond to her questioning look.

Ethan had produced a clean handkerchief to blot the small cut on Coral's temple, while Seward and several sowars, with a heave, set the vehicle back on the road.

The aftermath of the ghari incident was setting in, and she no longer cared about anything but getting off by herself.

"Do come sit down in the carriage while I treat that cut," said Ethan.

As Ethan took her arm and turned her in the direction of the ghari, she saw Rissaldar-Major Sanjay leave Uncle Hugo, who had not yet walked up. The officer rode toward Jace and saluted.

"A rider has come from Plassey, Major-sahib. There's trouble. He awaits to speak to you."

The name Plassey arrested Coral's attention, and brought her confused thinking back to why Jace had said that they must backtrack to Manali. She followed the direction that the rissaldar indicated. Near the outer rim of the secondary jungle—terrain once cleared but now marked with dense undergrowth—a troop horse, sweating and breathing hard, waited, bearing a British soldier.

Jace rode to meet him, and Coral saw the young soldier salute and hand him a letter.

Kathleen must have wondered about the trouble at Plassey where Captain Gavin McKay was stationed, for she walked to her uncle, and Coral heard her asking about the reason for their detour to Manali.

Coral heard no more, for Ethan interrupted and steered her in the direction of the ghari. "You are holding up heroically, I must say."

"Heroic?" Coral gave a small laugh. "I feel anything but that."

Ethan's face was hard. "I find the major's behavior on this journey nothing less than arrogant. The sleeping quarters in the inns, not to mention the victuals, have been dreadful. Flies, heat, the smell; this is a most unhealthy locale we must submit ourselves to, and the major seems to take a special delight in my discomfort."

Coral winced from the sting of the ointment. She could not help feeling sympathetic toward Ethan. Although a physician, and rigorous, he was not accustomed to India. She agreed, however, that Jace did seem to be hardened against showing any consideration toward him.

"Our stay at Manali shall prove welcome," he was saying.

"Then you know about Manali?" she asked quickly.

"Uncle intends for us to stay a few days at the residence of an acquaintance. The food and rest at Manali will do you good."

For a reason she could not explain, Coral found that the mention of her uncle's *acquaintance* brought her thoughts darting back to the night in the garden at Barrackpore.

"This acquaintance of Uncle's," she repeated. "Is he an Englishman?"

His gray eyes came to hers, and for a moment she felt their scrutiny.

"Quite. I believe his name is Harrington. Why do you ask?"

For a brief moment she considered telling him everything. "I wondered if I had met him during our stay in Calcutta."

"Hugo says the man retired from the Company, so you might have."

"Why does Uncle wish to go to Manali? A delay is ill advised at this time. We are in the best season for travel."

"Uncle suggested Manali only after the major requested a short delay."

"The major requested it!" she said, surprised.

"Yes, there seems to be some risk if we journey now. I thought you knew," he said. "There was fighting near Plassey."

"Fighting, here! With Burma?"

"No. I believe they were called *Maharattas*."

Coral remembered Kathleen's letter from Captain McKay warning of trouble. Coral had only a vague idea of who the Maharattas were. She knew only that the East India Company had been at war with the strong warriorlike kingdom for years.

"The major received a message last night from Captain McKay," said Ethan. "McKay informed him that a patrol from the garrison at Plassey was ambushed. None were left alive, I am told. I dare say, the ambush is the reason for the soldier speaking with the major now."

Coral's thoughts were suddenly averted. She was not thinking of Plassey, but musing over the attack on the military outpost at Jorhat near Kingscote, where Jace's friend Major Selwyn had been assassinated. "We are too far from the northern frontier to have trouble with Burma," she said. "This skirmish at Plassey would have nothing to do with the royal family at Guwahati."

"Have you met the maharaja that Uncle will represent for the Company?" he asked.

"No, that is—" she stopped.

"Kingscote is near Guwahati, is it not?"

"Yes, fairly close, but I have never met the royal family."

She said no more, unexpectedly remembering a long-forgotten incident that had occurred years earlier when she had visited Guwahati.

Her heart thudded. *No, it could not be true,* she thought.

"Ah! Seward is returning from the inn. Perhaps he was able to get you a room," Ethan said. He had turned from the ghari door to look out across the dusty road toward the dak-bungalow. Coral was absorbed in her thoughts. *I must talk to Jace about Guwahati!*

15

The dak-bungalow had extensive stables for travelers, and tonight they were not only filled with packhorses and mules but also with merchants and their coolies camping outdoors. Small fires hovered in the darkness, reminding Coral of swaying yellow ghosts. The smell of food mingled with woodsmoke.

The common room was sparsely furnished with long, low wooden tables, benches, and a few chairs made of worn cane. She was hoping to speak with the major alone. Although she knew that the sowars would remain with the horses and supplies, and sleep outdoors, she expected Jace to appear in the common room for supper.

The thought of food turned Coral's stomach queasy. Despite the open windows, the room reeked with the smell of unwashed bodies. Coral felt sympathy for an unhappy English family huddled in one corner. The haggard mother was trying to change her baby, wetting a cloth from a canteen to wash him.

"This is horrible, Sissy, I want to go home," whispered Marianna, holding her handkerchief to her nose.

Kathleen leaned toward her with a fierce little smile.

"You and Coral should have paid heed to me and stayed at Roxbury House!"

"Everyone is in the same situation as we are," said Coral. "How would you like a crying baby to attend? Think of all the underclothes you would need to wash!"

"Which reminds me," whispered Kathleen, wrinkling her nose. "I do hope the washroom has something to dry my hands on this time instead of my petticoat. I don't want to go alone. Are you two coming with me or not?"

Marianna nodded, looking dolefully about, but Coral's attention had been diverted. She looked across the packed room to where the split-cane curtain opened onto the stone courtyard, and saw the major.

Jace had entered through the courtyard with his thoughts on Captain McKay and the skirmish near Plassey. In his sabretache was the letter that had just been delivered to him by the trooper. Jace had been ordered by the commander at Plassey to join forces with McKay and track down the marauders.

The attack on Plassey compounded matters for Jace. The land routes north were presently unsafe for civilian travel. Since Roxbury had an acquaintance in Manali named Harrington, who owned and operated a large indigo plantation, he had assured Jace that he and his nieces would be well taken care of until the trek to the northern frontier was advisable.

Jace did not like the turn of events. Manali was two days out of their route. If Roxbury and his nieces must journey so far, then why not return to Calcutta? Roxbury, however, had business with Harrington and assured him the plantation was a pleasant place for Coral to recuperate. Ethan had agreed.

Jace was looking for Seward as he entered the common room through the courtyard. He had been correct in warning Coral against the journey. The incident near Plassey proved it—not that the Kendall daughter would admit it. Unruffled as ever, as an ivory blossom survives the relentless pounding of the wind, she would insist that she was "doing well enough, thank you," and nothing would alter her decision to reach Kingscote and build the school. Children. A hundred of them needed her—no, they needed her Shepherd, she said. Jace found her dedication both admirable and exasperating. She would kill herself trying to accomplish her goal.

He saw her seated on a bench across the packed room, talking to Seward. She was the outer expression of all that he had miscalculated her to be upon seeing her in the Calcutta bazaar, wearing a trail of white ribbons and silk, and smelling, he supposed, like a French perfumery. The Kendall daughter had proven to be more than mere beauty under her frail facade, but now the outer shell appeared to be in danger of shattering. She was pale and worn, her bonnet crumpled in her lap, her curls in disarray, and her expensive frock smudged with dust. The cut near her brow on the otherwise lovely face only convinced him that she was a dove stalked by a lean, hungry tiger—one that he was not in a position to stop. Under the present circumstances, he could do nothing but warn her. His lack of authority annoyed him.

Jace carefully guarded his expression as he stood in dusty black and silver, watching her. He accepted a tin of water from the barefoot boy-servant. She saw him, and he guessed that she wanted to converse. He did not wish to engage her at the moment. She would press him about the detour to Manali, and he had no answer yet. He would be riding out later that night with the 17th, leaving her and the others to be guarded by Seward and several sowars.

Jace felt restrained by military discipline to mask the annoyance he felt churning inside. If he could shed the uniform of Major Buckley to retrieve the tunic that served him on the deck of the *Madras*, he would tell her that she was too frail to be on this journey.

He handed the tin back to the boy and, looking away from Coral to Seward, gestured with his head that he should join him outdoors.

Seward looked down at Coral. "Wait here, lass. I'll be but a minute."

Coral only half heard Seward's remark as he left her side. She watched Jace leave the room and Seward follow after him by way of the split-cane curtain that led onto the court. They disappeared into the evening shadows.

The major's lack of response nettled Coral. At times his arrogance affronted her; at times she felt sympathetic toward him because of the insensitivity he had endured from others as a child. She must be cautious of being too sympathetic. She remembered a tiger cub that she and her brother Michael had supposedly rescued when they were children. Coral had felt sorry for the cub and had brought it home to the back porch of the large kitchen—until a roar from the mother had sent her father and half a dozen workers outside to turn the cub loose. The analogy between the cub and Jace Buckley might not be the same, she thought dryly, but nevertheless steeled her sympathetic inclinations from getting out of hand toward the major. *Beneath that uniform of respect and restraint there lives a man quite full of himself,* she thought. One who could not wait to retrieve his golden monkey, his Indian friend Gokul, and a clipper ship. A vessel that, like its owner, was being held unwillingly at harbor, unable to sail for ports unknown.

There were other times when she felt that beneath his outward confidence there lived a young man who was not at all sure of himself, one who was more afraid of expressing feelings, and becoming vulnerable, than he was of any outward danger. He could almost appear sensitive and caring—how else could she explain his willingness to try to locate Gem? But she had to admit that most of the time he appeared anything but that.

No matter. Wishing to ignore her or not, she would find some way to talk to him tonight, for it was essential to do so.

Aware that Ethan had joined her, she turned to him, thankfully accepting the hot cup of tea that he had brought her. He sat down beside her, and she sighed, enjoying her tea. The Hindi New Testament was beside her, and he picked it up.

"Hugo was disturbed that I brought you to William Carey's mission station."

Coral already knew as much. Thankfully, in the rush to leave Calcutta, and the weeks of hard journey, her uncle had not found time to speak to her.

Ethan frowned to himself, staring at the small book. "There is much to say about a man of William Carey's unselfish devotion."

Surprised, and even impressed by his admission, she smiled. "I am pleased you changed your mind about him."

His eyes came to hers, searching, eager to respond to the noticeable change in her voice. "Your own devotion is equally unselfish. Say nothing to Uncle, but I think your idea of a mission school for the children is noble. I shall do what I can to help you."

There was a slight pause in which her breath stopped. She stared at him, overwhelmed. "Ethan, do you mean that?"

"I do." He thumbed through the New Testament. "I, of course, am only a beginner of the language. At Kingscote I hope you will help me to learn it better. Once your school is constructed, there will also be opportunity to medically assist the children you are so concerned about."

"Ethan! How marvelous of you to think of it! I confess I've thought about your skills and what they could do. Between my school and your practice, we could do so much for the children."

He handed the Testament back to her, and when he looked at her, she read the warmth in the gray eyes. "You are right. We could do so very much together. Hugo, however, is very much set against missionary work in India, as you know. We must handle the entire matter with wisdom."

Seward strode up, ignoring Ethan. "The major's spoken to the headman. We be settin' up a shamianah for you and your sisters."

Coral was delighted. A large tent. This one, Seward told them, would have carpet and mats to sleep on, and there would be complete privacy.

Outside the shamianah, Coral talked with Seward alone while her sisters were inside delighting over the spaciousness and comfort of the tent. After two weeks of arduous outdoor travel, it did indeed seem luxurious.

"The major be ridin' out tonight," he told her quietly. "Ye'll stay at Manali until it be safe for civilian travel."

"Then the major is riding to Plassey?"

"Nay, he be meetin' Captain McKay on the way. There be word of more fighting on the road north, and they must be careful."

A chill of uncertainty enveloped her, fear of being alone. How foolish! She was not abandoned. Was not the Lord to be her vision and strength? And her father had sent Seward to escort them safely home. Yet knowing this did not remove the nagging feeling of doubt. How long would Jace be gone, leaving them at Manali?

"Does Sir Hugo know about the fighting?"

His expression darkened. "Aye," he grunted, "he does. And that be what bothers me."

She glanced at the shamianah to make sure her sisters were not listening. "You do not think he was involved!" The idea seemed incredulous.

"Pardon me sayin' so, lass, but I not be knowin' what to think of your uncle."

"Have you said anything to the major?"

He smiled. "Ye don't need to worry about him. The lad be a born cynic. He don't trust nobody. 'Twas Sir Hugo's idea to spend time in Manali while the major is gone, and that's what vexes me. Not that there's proof of anythin' going on. And Manali seems a logical choice for you and your sisters."

Coral's alarm grew. "Seward, must the major go?"

"He has his orders, lass, and he cannot ignore them. I be not likin' matters meself, but he'll join us at Manali when he can."

If there is fighting on the road north it might mean an indefinite delay, thought Coral. If they did not travel soon, the weather would turn on them, and it would become miserably hot.

"The major wouldn't like it if he knew I'd troubled you. It's rest you be needing. And the major be kind enough to have seen you get the shamianah. Took some bickering, it did."

"It is important I speak to him before he rides out tonight. Can you send him a message to come here?"

"Aye, I'll tell him."

———

What is delaying Seward? The lantern had been extinguished to discourage insects, and Coral heard the soft breathing of Kathleen and Marianna. She lay on the edge of the straw sleeping-mat wondering if she could slip out of the tent without awaking them. She was all but fully dressed except for her outer garment and shoes. Suddenly in the distance she heard the rise and fall of voices. She guessed the hour to be some time after ten. If she was to speak to Jace before he left, it must be now. She sat up and edged herself away from the straw mat.

Shafts of pale moonlight fell across the tent floor, and Coral slipped on her shoes and found her cloak on the cane stool. Her sisters' steady, deep breathing continued without interruption. She moved quietly to the edge of the shamianah, pushed back the veil, and stepped out.

The night was without a breath of wind and the black sky was sprinkled with white gems. She stood without moving, not expecting Seward to be nearby, but finding it necessary to make sure.

"Seward?" she whispered hopefully, and waited, then: "Seward!"

Silence greeted her in the stillness. A rustle of wind swept along the tops of dry elephant grass near the secondary jungle.

Lifting her hood up over her hair, she moved softly into the shadows of the bordering trees, hurrying in the direction of the camp where the troop under Jace's command was located for the night. It could be no more than four to five minutes away from the dak-bungalow. There was always the possibility of snakes, but other than that, she wasn't likely to run into trouble.

The path leading along the edge of the secondary jungle became an arcade of secretive shadows, with branches from the trees interlocking into moving silhouettes as a wind came up and played among them. Coral hurried along, instinctively casting a glance over her shoulder and keeping to the shadows, her slippers making no sound in the dust.

Ahead, beyond the supply wagons, the clearing was deserted. Jace's troop had already pulled out! She stood motionless among the shadows of the trees. And Seward? Where was he?

Several sowars were gathered near a fire. A myriad of night insects buzzed about the firelight. The men's voices were low, the words indistinct, and they came to her ears along with the odor of smoke.

Two of the sowars were seated around the fire gambling. Their backs were toward her, while the other stood watching the road in the direction of Plassey. With a throb of disappointment, Coral understood that she had been too late. Jace had left. She pushed aside her disillusionment. After all, his first responsibility was to obey military orders, and he did not need to explain them to her. He had sent Seward to tell her he was leaving; he had even managed to get them a shamianah. What more did she expect?

And yet . . . he must have known that she wanted to speak to him. Surely Seward had time to bring Jace her request before he rode out.

A vague uneasiness stirred within. She hesitated to announce her presence to the sowars and began to retrace her steps without a sound. Perhaps Seward was back at the tent by now. Perhaps he had been there all along, weary after the long day's journey, and had dozed off. And her lantern had been out; perhaps he had decided not to awaken her.

The night hovered with stillness. She could hear the unwelcome sound of someone approaching the wagon from the path behind her. Had Kathleen or Marianna found her gone and awakened Seward?

But she heard the footsteps hesitate in the shadows, then approach haltingly. Seward would not approach with such caution. His tread was purposeful, and he would be bold enough to be calling out for her whereabouts with a booming voice.

Coral's heart skipped a beat and she shrank backwards into the shadows, into the stillness of the shrubs and overhanging branches, less alarmed over the possibility of snakes than with being discovered by the owner of those cautious footsteps. . . . Marianna? No, never her. Kathleen perhaps . . . no, Kathleen, too, would be calling out. She caught her breath. *Two* people were coming, one from behind her, the other from the direction of the wagon.

A man emerged from behind the supply wagon and walked up to the fire. He said something, and the two gamblers were swiftly on their feet, then hurried off, leaving the man standing by the fire. As he turned to glance in the direction where she had stood only moments before, Coral saw his harsh face in the dancing firelight. It was Rissaldar-Major Sanjay! What was Jace's second in command doing here, when the 17th had ridden toward Plassey?

The footsteps that had stopped on the path, coming from the direction of the dak-bungalow, were now approaching. From the wagon, Rissaldar Sanjay walked forward, and waited.

Through the screen of the drooping branches, the moonlight fell upon the trodden path, and a moment later Coral was not surprised to see Sir Hugo. But the two men spoke in a pitch that was difficult for her to grasp.

" . . . Plassey . . . severed . . ."

" . . . the colonel's son?"

The wind rattled the dry leaves of the overhanging

branches. Coral took a tiny step forward, straining to hear. Sir Hugo's low voice was sharp, questioning. The rissaldar's tone was muffled, then came in sharp contrast to the strained silence.

"I am certain!"

Again Sir Hugo's words were mere sounds.

She stiffened. From behind her there came a whisper of movement like a viper slithering through the dried grasses. A quiver ran up her back. *Lord, no, please!*

16

Caught between Sir Hugo and Rissaldar Sanjay on the path, and the movement in the thick darkness behind her, Coral stood riveted in the trees.

Sir Hugo and Sanjay were still talking, but their voices lost all meaning as her mind focused on the danger of the reptile in the dry grass.

A moment later their voices fell silent as their footsteps faded into the dusty night. Stillness wrapped about her. Slowly the moments passed. Had she imagined it?

She inched forward in the direction of the path, then in a moment of blind fear she panicked and bolted toward the clearing. Her slipper gave way to a small avalanche of leaves on the embankment. A ruthless hand latched hold of her dark hood, catching her hair in a solid grip. Coral winced as she slid backwards, down the small incline into dry elephant grass. She landed hard, her breath knocked from her. She stared with wide, frightened eyes into the face of Jace, his pistol pointed at her head.

He sucked in his breath sharply and quickly released his grip on her hood, drawing his arm away. He moved back and neither of them made a sound.

Then his breath released in a rush of words. "What are you doing here! I could have struck you with my gun before I—" he stopped and shoved the pistol inside his jacket. He lifted her gently to a sitting position. "Coral, I am extremely sorry."

His voice was suddenly apologetic, and for an indulgent moment she gave in to the temptation to enjoy his self-incrimination.

"Are you hurt?"

"Yes . . . I mean, I don't know." Dazed, she stared at him in confusion. "What are *you* doing here? You are supposed to have ridden out!"

That did not seem to bother him at all.

"You haven't answered my question. I left you in the tent, and I told Seward to keep you out of trouble. And just where *is* Seward?"

"I thought he was with you."

He looked at her, alert. "I have not seen him since supper."

"I spoke with him at the shamianah when he brought us back. He explained about Plassey Junction. He went to tell you that I wished to speak to you before you left. You have not seen him?"

There was a pause. "No. I wanted to give the impression that I had ridden off with the troop. But I had no time to tell Seward. He may have—"

"Impression, but why—" She stopped short, recalling what they had just overheard between Sir Hugo and Rissaldar Sanjay. Her eyes came to his, questioning. "You suspected trouble earlier?" she whispered.

"Yes," he admitted reluctantly.

"Then you knew they were going to meet on the path?"

"My rissaldar's loyalties were in question even before leaving Calcutta."

Coral tried to digest what this could mean but still felt dizzy from her tumble. "You heard what was said a minute ago? What does it mean?"

"The fighting near Plassey has something to do with the northern frontier. I may know more after I meet with Captain McKay in the morning."

"Then you are riding to meet him now?"

"Yes. Somehow it all ties together—Plassey and the outpost at Jorhat. Here, let me help you up. You are certain you are not hurt?"

She was tender where stones had gouged her back, but she continued to sit there, her brain swirling.

"Can you walk?"

"Yes."

He glanced toward the path. "My guess is that Seward learned about the meeting. He would have ridden to warn me."

"Then he is hoping to catch up with your troop, thinking you are with them. When he discovers you are not there . . ."

"He will come back." He drew in another breath, and she guessed that he was putting a clamp on his emotions. "I sent a galloper back to Calcutta to report to the colonel."

"It appears from the meeting," she whispered, "that it is you who may face trouble at Plassey."

"Yes," he said thoughtfully, and again glanced toward the clearing. "I could almost believe . . ."

She waited. "Yes?"

He did not reply but lifted her to her feet. "Are you certain you are not hurt?"

"Perhaps you should not ride to meet Captain McKay."

"I must. My men are riding in that direction now. Let me carry you back."

"That will not be necessary," she said quickly. "Anyway, you must not be seen."

"Do not worry about me. You will be leaving for Manali in the morning. Seward should be back by then."

"Oh," Coral said, lifting her foot, "I lost my slipper."

"Here. Sit on this rock."

Coral sat there in silence, still shaken, while he searched in the brush for her slipper. She watched him in the moonlight, his dusty black and silver uniform blending into the shadows.

"Who did you think I was?" she asked.

"A guard for the rissaldar. I thought he saw me take cover here and was on his way to report."

It must have been several minutes before he returned with slipper in hand. The familiar, crooked smile was back, a smile she found disconcerting. He shook out the dirt with elaborate fanfare and wiped the slipper clean, then blew on the silver buckle, polishing it with his sleeve. "Permit me." He stooped before her.

She hesitated, then extended her foot, watching the moonlight fall on his dark head as he replaced her slipper. She stood, somewhat shakily, and he steadied her. She looked up at him to find his mood had swiftly altered. He wore a slight frown. "What were you doing here?"

"You asked me that already. I told you. I was looking for you."

He folded his arms. "Why?"

She raised her chin. "I wanted to speak to you about Gem, but when I neared the camp I realized your troop had already ridden out except for a few guards. I was going to return when I heard someone coming. I do not know why, but I felt compelled to hide."

His voice was cautious. "What about Gem?"

Coral drew in a breath. "It was something that Ethan

184

said this evening. He asked me if I had met the royal family at Guwahati. I told him no." She stopped.

"And?"

"But then something I had long forgotten came to mind. I did go to Guwahati with my father once when I was girl." She searched his face. "You once told me that Rajiv's uncle was a raja. But you did not say from which province."

He did not speak, and Coral breathed, "Is it Guwa-hati?"

Still he made no movement and only looked down at her in the pale moonlight.

Coral swallowed. "I was twelve when I visited the city with my father. There was a religious celebration going on, and I remember seeing the maharaja riding an elephant."

"Yes?" he said quietly.

"He had the members of his family with him at the time. There were two boys, perhaps sixteen years old—no more than that. Thinking back to what they looked like, I could almost insist that one of them was Rajiv."

He stood very still, and the moment seemed to stretch out.

"Tell me the truth," she whispered. "Was Rajiv the maharaja's nephew?"

His voice was quiet but even. "I warned you that you would get hurt when you took the baby. You insisted on keeping him. The fact is, the maharaja has two neph-ews—Rajiv, and a younger brother named Sunil. Sunil is ruthless."

Suddenly she wished she had not asked. "Somehow I always hoped what you said about the maharaja was a mistake. And after Gem's abduction, I told myself that if he did exist, he ruled far from Kingscote. But Guwa-hati, then it is true—Gem does have royal blood."

"Yes. But the raja does not have Gem. Coral, I do not even know if the child is alive. You must not think because I said I would help that I believe he is. Do not allow yourself to—"

"Hope?" she asked.

He said flatly, "Our hopes are often built without foundation."

Meaning that mine are. Coral felt numb. Gem, was he truly the great-nephew of the maharaja?

"I do not understand about Rajiv," she said. "What was he doing masquerading as a peasant? He told my father he came from Rajasthan."

"Rajiv was banished by the family when he broke caste and married Jemani. I do not know how he met her, or who she was. I am inclined to think she was only a girl he met and fell in love with. Rajiv was that way. He was nothing like his brother, Sunil."

"Then you think the maharaja will know where Gem is?"

"It is my guess that he will know. But I can promise you nothing, Coral."

"Yet, you will try, Jace?"

His eyes fell momentarily upon her face. "I made you a promise. I intend to keep it. I know the raja and I have something important to return to him. In exchange, I expect to be favored with the information I want. But I cannot guarantee it will be joyous—even if he is alive."

"What do you mean? Why should I not be happy?"

He turned. "Let's go back, Coral."

She let out a breath, stilling the trembling in her body with effort. He was deliberately avoiding explanation. "You are keeping something from me."

"No. I have no facts. Can we forget it? I simply would hate to disappoint you. That is all."

She did not answer him, and he said softly, "When

186

you arrive at Manali, make use of the opportunity to rest. There is a long journey ahead."

"And you? You heard what the rissaldar said to Sir Hugo."

"I am always careful. Why do you think I am still alive?" he asked lightly.

"The Lord has something to do with that."

"Agreed. I also do not fall into traps easily."

"No, I do not suppose you would."

"It is part of my ignoble character."

"It is your nature not to trust yourself to anyone."

"A profound deduction, Miss Kendall. Shall we go?"

"I will find my way back safely enough."

"Sorry. But it is also *your* nature to fall into one grave difficulty after another. Come, I will escort you."

In the shadowy premises near the tent, he paused to let her go on by herself.

"Where will you go now?" she whispered.

"To find Seward. I want him with you when you and your sisters ride to Manali."

She watched him until his silhouette disappeared into the darkened trees.

17

Manali

Sir Hugo's acquaintance was indeed English. Mr. Harrington turned out to be the owner of several large and productive indigo plantations, the smaller of which happened to be the one in Manali. When they arrived at the residence, they found a miniature estate, white with a blue roof, sitting back in the jungle.

Harrington himself was an unlikely candidate to manage his own indigo plantation at Manali, and looked anything but a farmer. His skin was the pallor of bee's wax; his pale eyes, almost a pinkish tone, reminded Coral of a lashless rabbit. He could not endure the bright sunlight nor the heat of the hot season, he had explained; therefore, he managed his Indian servants from a huge desk in the front parlor overlooking green rice fields and pools of water. He had one particular Indian servant whom he trusted to handle his important affairs, a man by the name of Zameen.

Upon seeing Zameen, Coral visibly relaxed. Her uneasiness over the possibility that he could be the Indian in the yellow turban proved unwarranted. Zameen was five feet tall, with a broad brown face that bore scars from smallpox. A glance at Marianna revealed that her sister's fears were also alleviated, and for the first time since their arrival at Manali she offered a smile. Perhaps their stay, thought Coral, would not be so terrible after all, especially since they were all given private rooms. Her own adjoined Kathleen's, and had wide double doors that opened onto the front court. In the distance she could see the rice fields, hemp, and indigo.

On the morning after their arrival, Coral watched the white-clad Indian workers flitting about their work, and the quiet plantation life brought brief reminiscences of being home on Kingscote. The memory sent Coral's prayers heavenward, upholding her mother.

"For I know the thoughts that I think toward you, saith the Lord, *thoughts of peace, and not of evil, to give you an expected end."* Coral's favorite verse emerged from the recesses of her memory, bright and vivid, like stars appearing after the wind blew away the mists.

The comfortable days of rest at Manali were passing all too swiftly without the arrival of Seward. Jace had told Coral to expect Seward the morning they had left the dak-bungalow, yet there had been no word. Without Seward to turn to, and with the major gone, Coral fretted over whom to go to with her concerns. *Ethan?* After all, he was probably the one man she should turn to before all others.

By the next morning she had decided to speak to him on the matter, only to learn from servants that he was with Sir Hugo and Mr. Harrington preparing for the up-coming tiger shoot.

Hunting for "hunt's sake" had always been revolting to Coral. She respected the magnificent jungle creatures of India, and while the cats were obviously dangerous, she saw no point in slaughtering them on a holiday just to relieve Sir Hugo's boredom.

She knew the process well. Toward dawn the *beaters*—hundreds of men on foot—would move out to encircle an area of jungle to be purged of the tigers previously held in pits or cages. By sunup, Sir Hugo, Mr. Harrington, and other hunting associates would arrive with their rifles, seated on the back of the great gray elephants, while the driver, known as a *mahout*, would guide the elephant using a long stick to prod the beast forward.

While the hunting party on elephants moved forward, the Indians would wait in the trees with ropes, to open the traps holding the tigers. From the noise of the approaching beaters, the half-starved, frightened and angry tigers would seek escape in the opposite direction, toward the line of elephants moving through the tall yellow grass.

Coral found it all quite cowardly. But she was not surprised that Mr. Harrington was staging the hunt to satisfy the appetite of her uncle.

The morning was still. The fragrance of grasses and jungle growth filled the early air. Coral shaded her eyes against the glare and walked briskly in the direction of the clearing, toward the tall elephant grass and the overhanging branches of teak.

Ethan stood with Hugo and Mr. Harrington, while Zameen went over the orders of the next morning's hunt. A handful of Indian servants in turbans and loin cloths stood by. Coral tensed when her gaze fell on Rissaldar Sanjay. It seemed inappropriate for the Indian officer to be involved in the event when his commanding officer was delayed in an area where there had been fighting. The snatches of conversation that she had overheard on the road brought unsettled feelings.

Coral paused, holding her hat, and frowned to herself. Not even Ethan appeared to be concerned about Seward. He saw her and left the others.

"I must say, you are looking fair of face today," he said, but she noted that his attempt to show a light mood appeared forced. It brought her some relief to know that he too could be concerned.

"The rest has done you good," he said.

Coral was watching the others. "Uncle Hugo appears to be in no hurry to get on with the journey."

He followed her gaze, the smile leaving his face.

"Yes. This is all a bit of a circus, I agree. Tomorrow is the hunt, and Hugo is elated."

She was bolstered in seeing his concern, hoping it was over the delay in the journey.

"I doubt if you would care to join us?" he was saying.

"No, Ethan, I am concerned about Seward. We should have heard from him by now."

"I quite agree. I was asking Hugo about the man this morning. However, he is inclined to believe that Seward decided to stay on with the major at Plassey." He looked at her, as though judging her response to the idea.

"That is not what the major told me," she assured him. "Seward was to escort us here to Manali. I was concerned when he did not show up the morning we left, but now it has been three days."

"A bit troubling. But try not to worry. Seward and the major are men who can take care of themselves. Something must have come up." He offered a smile, obviously hoping to brighten her mood. "They will arrive soon."

Coral frowned, wondering if he believed his own words. "Ethan, I am *sure* something dreadful has happened to delay Seward and the major."

"Why do you say that?"

Coral's growing doubts over her uncle nagged persistently, but her trust in Ethan had always been unwavering. She decided to take a small risk. "The night we were at the dak-bungalow, I overheard a conversation between Uncle Hugo and the Indian officer." She said nothing about Jace also being there.

"You mean Sanjay?"

"Yes, I could not hear everything that was spoken, but what I did hear brought me alarm. There was talk of fighting at Plassey, and Major Buckley's name was mentioned in terms that could only be described as threatening."

The muscles in Ethan's face tightened, and he glanced toward the others. "Did they see you?"

"No. But, Ethan—"

"Have you mentioned this to anyone else?"

"No." She felt her chest tighten at the strained look on his face. Was he frightened, or angry?

"Say nothing. Do you understand?" he said in a low, urgent voice, and when she did not answer immediately, his fingers clasped tightly about her wrist.

"Coral—"

"Yes, Ethan. I understand. I mention it to you now because I am worried."

His grip on her wrist loosened, and his face softened. He ran his fingers through his hair and tried to smile. "I do not want to add to your alarm, but I do not trust Sanjay. You must not let anyone know you saw him with Sir Hugo."

So Ethan also doubted the Indian officer even as Jace did. It made her feel better that the two men agreed.

"I will look into the matter about Seward," he said, his eyes searching her face. "Perhaps you misunderstood their conversation. Suspicions grow in darkness, my dear. Whatever the truth, let me handle this. Do not go to Hugo."

Coral had no intention of doing so but assured him that she would not. Jace had already warned her to keep silent. Snatches of conversations heard in the night were easily cloaked in mischief. Yet—neither Seward nor Jace had returned.

"I will ask Hugo to have someone ride toward Plassey," he said. "If there was more fighting, we will know soon enough."

"And if he does not agree?"

He squeezed her hand. "Trust me. I happen to be a fine horseman. I will go myself if necessary."

She believed him. His own concern was obvious.

"We have a long and difficult safari ahead of us," he told her. "You will need all of your strength. Promise that you will leave the matter to me."

Sir Hugo's voice called: "Ah, Coral, my dear, good morning. I have been wanting to talk to you."

Ethan whispered, "Say nothing," and gave her hand another squeeze before letting it go.

Sir Hugo looked cheerful as he walked up and laid a heavy hand on Ethan's shoulder, the ruby ring on his finger winking in the sunlight. "Might I suggest, dear boy, that you get some practice with that rifle? Sanjay is waiting."

Ethan looked down at Coral and smiled, his gaze reassuring. "I will see you at lunch, Coral. And do not let Uncle talk you into going on the hunt. I know how you love those golden beasts."

Ethan walked away and joined the rissaldar and Zameen, leaving Coral and Sir Hugo alone in the clearing. The warm wind tugged at the brim of her hat, and she reached up to hold it in place.

Hugo smiled down at her. "The color has come back into your cheeks. The small delay was worth every moment of frustration." He placed an arm about her shoulders and led her toward the white bungalow. "I know how worried you are about your father's good friend Seward, so I shall inform you at once that I am sending the rissaldar to Plassey in the morning."

She was surprised and pleased. Maybe she was wrong about him.

"Ah, that is better. A light has sprung up in your eyes. The major is well guarded with troops, and Seward no doubt stayed on with him."

He stopped on the road to gaze out across the field that was busy with workers, and Coral stood beside him. "My good friend Harrington tells me he wishes to sell his indigo plantations and go back to England. I am contemplating buying him out."

Coral turned her head to watch his profile. "Somehow I cannot see the Roxburys interested in anything but silk."

He laughed. "Nor can I, my dear Coral. But Harrington has made me an excellent offer. One I would lose sleep over at turning down. What do you think?"

"Are you perhaps wondering what I believe Margaret's response would be to this?"

"I was thinking of Belinda and Ethan. A string of indigo plantations might make good wedding presents. So, I was wondering what *you* thought of it."

Coral knew where his question was leading and wondered how she could avert a trek down the wedding path.

"Indigo is a most interesting product," he was saying, watching the workers bend to their task. "They gather the plant in bundles; then, I am told, it is permitted to ferment in great vats. It takes special skill to know just when the appropriate hour has come to run the green liquid into secondary vats. The coolies must beat the water until it turns a rich deep blue—much like the color of your frock. When the water has settled enough and granulated, it is drained off. The indigo dye is left on the bottom of the vats, where it is dried and pressed into bars to be shipped to England."

He turned to gaze at her. "Silk, indigo, and tea, they are the life-blood of the East India Company. When you marry Ethan, you might add this little venture to Kingscote. Who knows? The weather here is good for mulberry trees. You might even try to start a few hatcheries and expand the silk production."

Does Ethan know about this? "Ethan and I agreed in London that the test of time will not risk a relationship, if it is genuine," she said, hoping her uncle would not try to exert pressure.

Although Coral believed Ethan's Christianity was genuine, she knew that time alone would prove it. Somehow she felt compelled that the man she married must support the idea of the mission school. Yet, even she could do nothing unless her parents agreed. Was it fair to hold Ethan to the fires that burned within her own heart?

Without intending to do so, her mind wandered to Jace Buckley, and she felt an uneasy qualm. She had not meant to think about him now, but it was as if he barged into her mind without apology—much in keeping with his character, she thought grimly.

The real Jace Buckley, Coral suspected, may or may not be of genuine Christian faith, although he had intimated he believed when he had whisked her away from that dreadful suttee in Calcutta. But even if he did, she was quite certain that he did not take those beliefs seriously enough for her to feel comfortable. She wanted more. More than either he or Ethan offered. Perhaps, she thought wistfully, she was being unrealistic. But then she remembered William Carey's zeal, and Charles Peddington's sacrifice of health to serve the Christian cause in India.

When it came to Jace Buckley, she was hesitant to admit the truth: His handsome, rugged features and his energetic personality had caught her interest from the moment she had set eyes on him.

"He is falling in love with you; do you know that?"

Coral jerked her head in her uncle's direction, startled. Then she gave a short laugh. "Of that, Uncle, I am quite sure you are wrong. I do not know him well, but I am certain of one thing. He would never permit himself to be so vulnerable. He knows, as well as I, that our goals and beliefs are incompatible. He is an adventurer. He wishes to have no bonds or ties, and as soon as he can he will go back to his clipper—"

Coral stopped. Her face turned warm with the realization that Hugo had not been speaking of Jace Buckley, but of Ethan.

Sir Hugo gave her a searching look. "You speak of the major, I gather. Evidently our minds have gone their separate ways. It is Ethan who is in love with you."

Hugo's tactic of concern for her future took Coral off guard. It was far easier to resist a cold and unfeeling schemer than a fatherly confidant.

She looked away from his bright gaze, at the workers bending white amid the green, and tried to keep matters light. "Ethan has only one true love, and that is medical research."

"I fear that he was left alone too much and took solace in his studies," Hugo responded. "A lonely life, I suspect, dwarfed his ability to show much warmth to others."

"Oh, I do not think so," she said, thinking it odd her uncle would show such fatherlike concern. "Ethan has proven both thoughtful and dependable."

"I am glad to hear that much. I dare insist that he

does care for you. He will make a good husband, Coral. You are not so unlike him, after all. Illness and religious pursuits have shut you into a room of your own that few others are permitted to enter."

Coral gave an uncomfortable laugh. "I hope I am not as isolated and infertile of thought as you make me sound. I might as well cut off my hair and wear dutiful black."

"Ah, never do that, you are far too lovely for the monastic vow," he replied. "But it is true, you are a serious young woman. Thankfully lacking Belinda's frivolous nature. It is safe to say that unlike my daughter, you will not be happy in a relationship that is all emotion and no intellect. Hampton and Elizabeth realize that as well. They do want you to marry your cousin."

Yes, she thought. *My future, at least where my family is concerned, is already decided.*

"May I suggest, Coral, that you not permit sympathetic notions for the Indian children on Kingscote to turn you aside." He smiled and slipped an arm about her shoulders, walking her back toward the bungalow. "One must learn to keep religious philosophy within certain bounds. A balance is necessary for realistic judgment. Life, after all, is lived not in the sanctuary, but on the street."

"Oh, you are right. I think we are expected to live our beliefs where our feet are soiled—by walking amid the harshness of humanity. And what better place than India?"

Coral stopped and searched his bearded face. "Uncle, I want to show you something." Slowly she opened her blue lace bag, removing her Hindi New Testament. Her eyes pleaded with his to understand her joy.

"Look, Uncle! Hindi, of all languages! Who could have guessed God's plan for spreading the Scriptures, when at one time even English was outlawed."

Hugo took it and opened its pages, saying nothing. Coral fervently hoped he would be somehow touched by it. She longed for, if not his enthusiasm, his reluctant respect for men like William Carey.

His voice was quiet, and had she been less hopeful, she might have recognized the look in his eyes. "Where did you get this?"

"William Carey," she said softly. "Ethan told you of our visit to Serampore?"

"He did."

That was all. *He did.* "This translation, Uncle, is a testimony to a God too great to be confined to English, or to the small locked rooms of our lives."

He tore his eyes from the book and searched her face. "A fine work to be certain. Men like Carey have their place. But it is not every heart that wishes a god so big, or so demanding. I realize you have been taught this from childhood by Elizabeth, and even Hampton has his moments—such as when he risked Kingscote to the ghazis by allowing you to adopt Gem. But your father had the good sense to know when to stop." His black eyes stared down at her, unflinching. "I do hope you are not thinking of risking Kingscote to ashes for William Carey's translation in Hindi? Get it out of your mind, Coral. A mission school for the Hindu untouchables cannot be borne."

Her disappointment was acute. "Why must I get it out of my mind? Because the East India Company's vision is blinded to anything but its own interests? The rich are made richer, and the powerful go uncontested— is that it? What of India's greatest resource, her children?"

"Religious sentiment always sounds sweet when wrapped in the sanctimonious garb of the missionary," he scoffed. "But the premise is entirely false. The honorable East India Company was not built to propagate Christianity, but to do business. Are we to be faulted for pursuing our goals?"

"No, of course not, but—"

"Is it not reasonable? Life must go on! The Company has done much good in India. The maharajas would be the first to admit it. England has brought stability."

"That is so, Uncle, and I will be the last to fault the governor-general. Yet a higher authority also has interests in India. And I dare say that He will hold little patience for rich merchants who stand in the way."

Hugo waved a hand at her words as though they were annoying insects. "Do not misunderstand me. Religion has its place in any society, but the Company will not stand by and see an Indian uprising in order to coddle men like Carey. But enough of that. It is the family silk business I am interested in. And Hampton will agree with me that it cannot be held ransom to the torch of a mutiny. And now," he firmly took hold of her arm, looped it through his, and smiled. "One thing about you, my child. You do give your poor uncle a run for his wits."

He led her inside the house. "We will leave the greater cause of India to statesmen and maharajas. As a Kendall daughter—and a silk heiress—I have no doubt you will be practical in these matters. I might add that Hampton has already made it clear to me in a letter received at Calcutta. Your husband will either be Ethan, or you will eventually be packed off again to London to become the bride of some lord that your grandmother has in mind."

Coral said no more. She had already disclosed too much.

18

Jace drew rein, and the horse's nostrils shuddered, breaking the stillness. He peered into the darkness, where light from the silent white stars above cast an eerie glow over the road ahead. He waited, listening, but the only sounds he heard were the night creatures stirring through the jungle and the fingers of the wind rippling over dried cactus leaves.

The road that Jace had traversed for miles now opened onto a clearing sketched with clumps of dried grasses and thirsty thorn trees. Jace strained to pick out their bleak and misshapen dark forms under the stars. Somewhere out there he would meet up with his 17th and Seward, who by now had made contact with McKay and the sepoys from the outpost at Plassey.

All his instincts as well as his military experience warned him there was no time to lose. The night was oppressive, and he wished desperately for the first light of dawn. He prompted his horse forward across the padding of dust, its hooves making little sound. With caution, he saw that he was riding toward a black outcropping that loomed against the lighter skyline. A perfect trap. Then he saw him, his daffadar, a young man he had known for too long to doubt his loyalty and personal friendship.

"Hut! Sirdar-sahib! It is I!" called Jace.

The man ran toward him, saluting. "Huzoor! Major-sahib! I have been waiting!"

"Where is the jemander Rajendra?"

"He waits for you ahead. It was necessary to make camp and wait for the morning."

Jace was immediately on guard. "What happened? Where is Captain McKay and the 34th?"

"There has been a delay, Major-sahib. I do not know why. Captain McKay is still at Plassey but will show in the morning. The 34th will remain at the garrison."

"By whose orders?"

"That, Major, you will need to ask the jemander. Seward has ridden ahead to make his own inquiry."

So . . . Seward did arrive safely. Jace felt some relief, but remained tense. Something was wrong. Why would the 34th stay behind at Plassey when there was fighting between the outpost and the village?

He rode with his daffadar into the darkness. He saw no light nor smoke from the small camp belonging to his 17th, and approved of his jemander's carefulness. Automatically, Jace rested his hand on his sword hilt. "Send for the jemander," he ordered. The daffadar rode ahead and disappeared. Jace turned his horse aside toward the shrubs and waited.

A few minutes later his jemander and a sepoy rode into view with the daffadar. Jace rode to meet them, and scanned the face of the sepoy. He did not recognize the man, who wore the blue and white of the 34th.

His jemander quickly saluted. "Major-bahadur. Captain McKay will not arrive for the meeting as planned. The commissioner has sent word that you and the 17th are to report to Plassey. We have made camp for the night."

"Who delivered the message?"

"The sepoy."

Jace looked at him, and the sepoy saluted. "Under orders from the commissioner, the captain-sahib has sent me."

Jace held out his hand, and the jemander handed him the message. He could tell nothing from the jemander's face. And the sepoy from Plassey stared at him, obviously tense.

Jace could barely read it in the starlight, but he recognized Gavin McKay's handwriting.

An attack against Plassey is expected by rebel Mahar-attas. The 34th is ordered to defend the junction, the 17th with them. Report at once. Seward is with me.
Captain G. McKay, 34th Infantry, N.N.I.
Plassey Junction

"Shall I return to Plassey, Major-sahib?" the sepoy asked, seeming only too anxious to ride off.

Jace placed the message in his jacket. "No. You will ride out with the 17th at dawn."

Was he mistaken, or did the sepoy look nervous? The Indian saluted, then turned his horse out of the way.

At dawn, Jace readied the 17th to ride toward Plassey. Well into the afternoon they came to a fork in the river, where a dusty white road ran along a ruined wall of an old fortress once belonging to some forgotten raja. In the sun's glare a temple appeared to stare down at them with disdain. Jace heard dismal bells and saw priests with shaven heads moving about.

They were still some distance from Plassey when Jace saw the small rise of dust from the contingency of the 34th. He drew up and waited, watching McKay drawing nearer. Suddenly, Jace became conscious of his jemander at his right, and glanced at him, noting the man's expression. Sweat stood out on his forehead, and his gaze darted nervously toward a red fort in ruins, long abandoned since the British had come to Plassey. Jace followed the man's gaze to the trees at the left of the ruin. His breath stopped. Sepoys were waiting in ambush! And both the 17th and McKay's 34th were about to be skinned like rabbits!

He unsheathed his sword and swerved his horse toward the jemander. "Traitor! I shall have your head for this!"

The jemander looked frightened, then his face set into contempt.

Jace jerked his head toward the trees. "Who waits there? Maharattas?"

The jemander's eyes hardened into granite. He drew his sword and spat. "No, sahib. Not Maharattas. The entire 34th Native Infantry, except for those few fools who ride with McKay. You will all be food for vultures by afternoon, followed by all the British, including your stupid commissioner!"

Suddenly a rushing wall of mounted Indian sepoys and sowars, boasting the standard of the 34th, came thundering down the rocky slope.

Captain Gavin McKay, leading twenty sepoys from the regiment, had only a flash of warning. He saw that both Jace and the 17th were ahead, and the troops he had thought to be guarding the outpost were emerging from the trees near the ruin. They approached in a cloud of red dust, the sun glinting off their drawn swords and bayonets.

McKay's dark brows lowered, and his greenish brown eyes snapped. "What the devil—" McKay turned in his saddle and shouted to his rissaldar: "Mutiny! Warn the sentry! Shut the gate!"

As though in painfully slow motion, McKay was aware that his rissaldar had turned toward him, his face that of a stranger, full of something loathsome. He lifted his rifle and aimed it at McKay's heart. A shot fired, followed by a puff of white. For a moment McKay thought he was dead, yet he felt nothing. Then he saw his rissaldar fall forward in his saddle, the rifle slipping from his hand. Out of the corner of his eye, McKay saw Seward gripping a pistol still aimed at the fallen rissaldar.

McKay's sepoy was riding toward the gate to sound the warning. One of their own thrust him through with a sword. A rifle exploded. The ball smashed into the head of the British soldier bearing the company flag. McKay felt the splatter of blood on his face. Within seconds, swords, bayonets, and rifles were unleashed. The few remaining loyal sepoys drew swords against overwhelming numbers. Seward shouted at McKay, who turned to see his daffadar coming at him. McKay had a glimpse of bared white teeth just as he parried his blade, thrust and thrust again, ramming it through the daffadar's chest.

"To the 17th!" shouted Seward, racing in the direction of the river.

The jemander drove at Jace fiercely, demanding all of Jace's skill to ward off the attack. Jace smashed his sword into his attacker's blade, swerving the blow and setting him off-balance with its force. The jemander hesitated only a second, time enough for Jace to swipe a final blow against his skull. Jace glanced about. All around him fighting raged. Plunging horses, confusion, and blood. Loyal sowars of the 17th fell in the onslaught, and he caught a glimpse of his handsome young Indian standard-bearer being plunged through with a bayonet. Still he gripped the flag, refusing to let go as his other hand covered the wound in his chest.

The sight of his sowars fighting valiantly despite the inevitable tide only hardened Jace. The blue and white of the 34th crashed through their meager line of forces. His own blade crossed sword upon sword, cutting a swathe around him, and still they came. Blood ran in his eyes and seeped out from a wound in his side. Inevitably he was knocked from his horse. A wave of riders swung around him, and a sepoy on horse came at him. Jace grabbed a rifle and hurled the bayonet through the man's chest, but the rush of his horse slammed Jace back to the ground, knocking the breath from him. Struggling to rise, he glimpsed his daffadar choking in a cloud of dust, and then the daffadar threw himself against Jace, knocking him back down.

Weeping, the daffadar rasped in Bengali: "Be still, sahib!"

Smothered by the human shield of his young daffadar, Jace fought against the heat, the darkness, but instead sank deeper into the pit of unconsciousness.

———

"He still suspects it was me in the garden, Coral. I just know it," whispered Marianna. "Sometimes I look up from the dinner table to find him watching me with that probing look of his; you know the expression I mean?"

Coral said nothing. She did not want to feed her sister's uncertainties.

"It makes me feel like one of Cousin Ethan's dissected bugs," Marianna said, plucking at her handkerchief. "Like Uncle Hugo is trying to rummage through my mind. Even Mr. Harrington watches me."

Coral looked at her. "Mr. Harrington? Come, Marianna, now you *are* imagining things."

"I am not. And I overheard Mr. Harrington talking to that Indian man named Zameen. Did you know Zameen used to be the dewan at Guwahati?"

Coral tensed. "The chief minister?" she whispered.

Marianna nodded, nervously tying her handkerchief in a knot.

"And Mr. Harrington used to live there. I heard them talking about it."

"When?"

"Last night. They were below on the verandah, drinking something and smoking cheroots."

"Was Uncle with them?"

"It was only the two men."

"Did you hear them say anything about Plassey or Guwahati?"

Marianna shook her head.

Coral digested this in silence. Zameen, the maharaja's dewan! What was he doing in the subservient role of a secretary to Harrington? Was it genuine?

Kathleen poked her head in through the bedroom door. "Not dressed yet? Oh, do hurry. I am starved."

"Coming," Coral called and turned to Marianna. "Say nothing to anyone."

The dining area opened onto a wide garden with Harrington's prized tropical flowers. He was in the process of discussing them with Ethan when Coral entered with her sisters.

As evening settled over the garden and the fragrance of flowers became almost too sweet, Zameen appeared from another room to draw the drapes. Coral discreetly studied him. A retired dewan? He was dressed immaculately in a knee-length blue tunic tied at the waist with a fringed sash. She found herself mulling over Marianna's startling disclosure. Zameen did look more like an important Indian official than Harrington's personal secretary. Coral wondered why he now accepted the menial task of going about the salon shutting out the insects.

"So lovely, yet bent on her own destruction," Harrington commented.

Coral glanced up. Was he speaking of a person? Her gaze followed his pale eyes to a huge yellow and blue moth that beat its wings hopelessly against the lighted lantern.

"I shall be pleased to have little more to swat at in London than a fly," Harrington continued, looking across the table at Coral. He ran his fingers over his gold mustache. "You do not mind insects, Miss Kendall? You will find the indigo plantation most comfortable otherwise."

Before Coral could reply that she was not interested in indigo or insects, he went on: "The only thing I shall regret saying goodbye to is my collection of graceful kings and queens."

"Kings and queens?" Coral repeated.

Ethan leaned toward her with a smile. "Harrington collects spiders. You are not squeamish I hope? He has one to show us after dinner."

"Zameen, old boy, is it safely enclosed?" asked Harrington.

"It is, sahib. Right here." He held up a glass box filled with green leaves.

Coral could see only leaves, but a moan came from Marianna.

Harrington did not appear to notice. "Spiders are the most captivating creatures. My latest specimen is beautiful, velvet black with just a blush of crimson."

Marianna drew palms to her face.

"I think we better change the subject, or we shall have poor Marianna losing her appetite," said Ethan.

"Poor child, I do apologize," Harrington said. "I forget that not all look upon my hobby with equal fervor.

Away with the queen, Zameen. I shall show her to Ethan later."

Harrington turned the conversation to the jungle lab that Ethan planned to build on Kingscote. As the discussion progressed to tropical diseases, Ethan became totally absorbed in his discourse. Coral accepted the cup of tea that Uncle Hugo offered her with a smile. He had put too much honey in it. She drank it anyway, and listened to Ethan and Harrington without comment.

As time passed, Ethan's voice began to sound as wearisome as the hum of insects outside the beaded curtain in the garden. Coral felt exhausted. The meal was finished and the desert served—a fresh fruit mixture of sweet mango, bananas, and shredded coconut—but Coral had lost her appetite. She tried to stifle a yawn, and wondered what time it was. She felt relaxed, almost hypnotized by the flickering golden lantern light, the mammoth moth flapping its delicate wings, and the droning voices of Mr. Harrington and Ethan. Insects. Their voices buzzing in her ears were becoming dull and more distant as she grew more sleepy by the moment. She tried to brush a mosquito from her ear, but her hand felt heavy and wooden. Her eyes moved tiredly around the large table. Kathleen looked bored, Marianna was staring at her, and Uncle Hugo . . .

Coral's eyes sought his and they looked bright in the lantern light, almost like a cat's eyes. He leaned across the table, his heavy brows furrowing, his mouth moving as though addressing her, but she heard nothing distinguishable, only the buzzing in her ears. *These insects must be exceedingly large to drown out human voices*, she thought without feeling.

Sir Hugo was on his feet now. So was Marianna, looking pale and frightened. Kathleen frowned and spoke to Ethan. Coral did not hear what was said, but she felt

Ethan's hand take hold of her arm. Sir Hugo was standing beside her at the table, his face bent inquiringly to peer into hers. His dark eyes and brows, his meticulously clipped beard and rugged features filled her vision. His expression turned to alarm, and she responded by trying to stand to her feet. The chair fell over behind her, making no sound as it struck the polished wood floor. Coral tried uselessly to pick it up, and Ethan took hold of her shoulders. She stared up into his anxious face and heard her name, but it came as a distorted whisper: "Corrr-alll!" Her knees would not hold her up. She seemed to be in a room with grotesquely shaped shadows that loomed like the swaying heads of cobras. She tried to scream, but as she struggled, the darkness receded into a pinpoint of light until . . .

A sullen rumble sounded from the jungle, and Coral awoke, sitting up in the large bed. At once she regretted that she had moved so quickly, for a wave of nausea swept over her.

The yellow glow from a lantern on the table illuminated the bedroom at Mr. Harrington's house. Her brain felt thick. It proved tedious to think, to wade through the questions demanding answers, and she sank back to the goose-down pillow. Trying to ease the fear that wrapped its tentacles about her heart, Coral closed her eyes, allowing the fragments of what had happened to her in the last few days to filter through her mind. *Days?* Her heart pounded. How long had she been in bed? The spinning in her head had ceased, and at last the buzzing noise was gone from her eardrums. Perhaps she had been in bed for weeks!

The low tigerlike rumble echoed again in the distance beyond the house. *There cannot be any more tigers,* she thought numbly. *They shot them all. Poor tigers. Poor magnificent beasts. So strong, so free . . . like Jace. No, he was a cheetah, and he was not free. He—*

Coral started back to reality. It was all coming back now, even as her mind swam.

What had happened? There were insects filling her ears with a terrible noise. Ethan had caught her as the strength of her legs melted.

When she awoke, she was in her bed and found that Ethan had been seated in a chair beside her, his usually quiet gray eyes watching her with concern. He had tried to hide his alarm with a smile. Uncle Hugo came into the room, and she thought he looked like a giant warrior arrayed in black armor. "I've killed the enemy. . . ." he had said, lifting up a glass jar.

Through blurred vision Coral saw a dead spider.

Remembering, Coral shivered under the cover and closed her eyes. The house was quiet. If she could just regain her strength long enough to get dressed. She must find her sisters. Where was Seward? Was there news from the major? But she discovered that she was too weary to concern herself.

"Lord, you never slumber nor sleep, be our high tower, our keeper, our shield. . . ."

———

"Ethan's quick action saved your life," Sir Hugo said when she awoke again.

Ethan.

"This is the second time he has done so. First in London, and now here in Manali. Had it not been for his quick thinking, we would not have suspected a spider bite in time to treat you. He went searching under the table and found it beneath your chair."

"M-my chair? How—" she stammered weakly.

211

"A most interesting question. How the horrid thing escaped the glass box is a mystery we have all been trying to solve. Zameen swears he put the box away as Harrington ordered him to, but no one seems to distinctly remember him doing so. Zameen is upset, as you can imagine, and Harrington is threatening to destroy his entire collection. You are on the way to recovery now. You owe him your gratitude, Coral. Be kind to him, will you? He loves you so."

Be kind to him. He loves you so. Had it not been for Ethan . . .

19

For a confused minute Jace lay there in the blackness, unable to move. The weight holding him prisoner must be the piles of rock upon his grave. *No, my body feels too much pain to be dead*, he thought. He stirred and opened his swollen eyes. A tiny speck of silver shone. As he tried to focus, he realized that it was a star in the night sky, and the weight on top of him was flesh and blood—his daffadar!

Jace struggled to crawl out from under him, and as he did, he saw the bayonet in his daffadar's back. The loyalty of his sergeant had shielded him from certain death.

Lord, he thought. *How can I be worthy of this man's allegiance?*

His skull throbbed with pain. He wanted to vomit as he moved, causing the blood to surge in his temples. His fingers were swollen and stiff as he brought them to the side of his head and felt the gash. Somehow between dizzy spells he struggled to one knee and sat there in the darkness, smelling death all about him.

He squinted. On the horizon, the village of Plassey was barely visible, speckled by a few points of light. Jace

213

struggled to his feet, took a few unsteady steps, and with the last of his fading awareness, crawled toward the faint sound of a snorting horse.

He became aware of movement near him, and a harsh, low whisper. He struggled to clear his blurred eyes, wondering if the enemy had returned.

"Ye be all right, lad, just hold on," came Seward's voice.

The next time Jace awoke it was light, and the ground was moving beneath him. He was lying uncomfortably across a saddle, on his stomach. There was a cloth tied about his nose and mouth, and he immediately knew why; dust rose in clouds from beneath the slow plodding of the hoofs. Again he lost consciousness.

"He is coming around. Hand me the canteen." It was the voice of Captain McKay.

The wine was strong, and he felt it burn all the way down to his stomach. Its warmth spread through his body. He tried to shove the canteen away and turned his head, choking.

"Easy, lad, ye'll be all right now," he heard Seward say. "Drink some more. You be needing it. Take it easy! Stay put! Got yourself a severe concussion, but the gash is bandaged up nice. The village near Manali be the closest place, and Gavin and I will get you there by night. Then I'll be going for Boswell at Manali. Never thought I'd be thanking the Almighty for his being about, but I'm sure thanking Him now. All right, that's it. Nice and quiet, lad. We got to keep moving, even though it's mighty uncomfortable on that saddle. No time to camp here."

"Where—" Jace murmured.

"Say three more hours from Manali."

"17th?"

"Don't think about 'em now lad, may Christ have mercy on *them*."

"Too late," Jace whispered, and in his delirium saw the caverns of hell open wide to suck him into its jaws, to suck them all into an avalanche of burning flame. "Too late."

"Nay, lad! Don't say that," Seward choked, bending over him. But Jace could not see him, he could only feel his heavy hands patting him awkwardly, and felt something hot and wet drop onto his face. Jace blinked.

"Ye'll be all right now," Seward said. "God has His ways of mercy. I am counting on that! And I'll be getting Boswell to come and help you, even if I need to drag him all the way there!"

———————

Coral stirred from a light sleep. Something had awakened her, and she sat up, listening in the direction of the open verandah. As she strained to decipher the noise from the chirp of crickets, she caught the unmistakable echo of horses' hoofs below.

Kathleen's bedroom opened onto the same verandah, and the sound must have awakened her, too, for a moment later she hurried into Coral's room and stood in the moonlight.

"It is Seward!"

Coral threw aside the cover, the soles of her feet touching the coarse matting. She snatched up her dressing gown, putting it on as she ran toward the verandah. *Oh, thank you, Lord.* A surge of warm wind sent the leaves of a tree rustling, while somewhere in the shrubs a peacock let off with a shrill call. Coral leaned over the railing and looked down into the stone courtyard in time to see a young boy taking charge of Seward's lathered horses. Without actually seeing his face, Coral knew that Kathleen was right. In the speckled moonlight sifting its way through the leaves and branches, she recognized the broad build of Seward in his buckskin jacket and tricorn hat. She started to smile, but concern gripped her when she noted the quick, purposeful stride. And his arm was in a sling!

"Seward!" she called down breathlessly. "Seward!"

He stopped and looked up.

"You are hurt! What happened?"

"A mutiny, lass. A damnable one! The fair and honorable sowars of the 17th are dead. All of 'em!"

Coral was certain that her stomach dropped to her feet. *Jace.* Her icy hands gripped the rail.

"Lass! I be needing that cousin of yours. Can you rouse him up?"

Cousin—what cousin—?

"Lass? Are you hearing me now?"

Coral felt Kathleen's hand grip her arm as she leaned over the rail. "What is it, Seward?" Kathleen called.

"I am needing the doctor. The major be hurt and in the village."

"Yes, I will go waken him now," Kathleen cried, running through the bedroom and out the door.

Coral became alert. "Seward! Are you saying Major Buckley is not dead, but wounded?"

"He is injured, badly."

"Where is he?"

"In the village with Captain McKay."

"You should have brought him here!"

"He ought not to be moved more than be necessary. We've moved him too much already. Don't worry, lass, he's a strong one. He'll live."

"Wait for me, Seward. I am coming with you."

Coral did not stop to think. She lit the lantern with surprisingly steady fingers, dressed quickly, grabbed her hooded cloak, placed the Hindi New Testament in her bag, and ran out into the hallway.

Doctor Boswell had his bag in hand and was at the stairway. Kathleen stood near the landing and turned as Marianna poked her red head out her bedroom door. "What is it, Sissy?" she asked Kathleen.

"Go back to bed!" said Kathleen. "Coral, wait! Where are you going?"

"With Ethan," Coral called over her shoulder, rushing down the stairs after him.

The library door opened and Mr. Harrington stood there in his smoking jacket, book in hand. He looked at Ethan who had stopped near the door, then at Coral.

"What the devil is going on? Did I hear Seward?"

"There was a mutiny at Plassey," came Ethan's firm voice. "Many are dead, and there are injured to care for. I will be in the village." He threw open the door, and hurried out into the night.

Coral picked up her muslin skirts to follow after him. She cast Mr. Harrington a quick glance and said, "He needs my help. I shall be fine. We will send word tomorrow!"

She closed the heavy door behind her, hurried down the porch steps, and ran across the courtyard to where Seward waited.

As though only now aware of her, Ethan turned and scowled. "Good heavens, Coral, there is no need to wear yourself out like this. I can handle the major."

"I need to go," she stated firmly, grasping her bag. "If the major is dying, I need to speak to him."

Ethan stared down at her, and in the moonlight she could see his incredulous expression turn to thoughtful suspicion.

"It is not the way you think," she whispered.

He studied her, and she saw his mouth twist in mockery. "Are you only worried about the major's soul, my dear?"

She felt irritation well up in her chest, and whirled around just as Seward strode up with furrowed brows.

"Lass, it be best if ye stay here."

"No, Seward," she stated. "I am coming with you and Ethan." She turned to the young groom. "I will need a horse, please."

"At once, Miss-sahiba," he said and ran toward the stables.

Ethan had already mounted and was waiting in chilled silence, but she did not care. He needed to understand that she would not be treated like a child, or insulted because she insisted on seeing Major Buckley. It would do no good to tell him that she would feel this strongly about anyone else. He assumed, so she guessed from his behavior, that she was infatuated with the major, and making a fool of herself.

She turned to Seward, hoping for his support, but prepared to contend if necessary. He was staring down at her with an odd expression, stroking his mustache.

"All right, lass."

She laid a hand on his arm. He understood. A minute later the groom trotted toward them, leading a saddled mare, and Seward helped her to mount. They galloped off toward the narrow, tree-lined road, and Coral felt the wind cooling her, blowing through her hair.

"Severed to the bone," Ethan told her in a clipped, professional voice. Coral did not wince as she held the lantern close to Jace's head, nor did she look away as Doctor Boswell worked tediously to clean the area of dried blood and cut away the matted dark locks, washing the area with a strong ointment. Her eyes went to Ethan as he worked. His expression was professional, and he seemed not to be aware of who she was or, for that matter, who his patient was. He worked unceasingly, his slender fingers steady. Now and then he ordered her to hand him this strange-looking tool or that one, all of them having been boiled over the small fire that Seward kept going in the hearth.

Coral's nostrils burned from the strong smell of the ointment Ethan was using, and she now watched Jace, seeing him wince in his unconsciousness. She tried not to notice the way his hair curled near his ear, or the black lashes that she usually saw in a familiar, challenging squint over slate-blue eyes.

"That is the worst of his wounds and will do for a few days."

"Aye, and he has a wound in his side," said Seward.

There were numerous cuts and abrasions. While Ethan and Seward removed his shirt, Coral worked on his right hand. The knuckles were swollen and stiff, and discoloration had set in. She cleaned and applied the foul ointment, then wrapped his hand carefully. Ethan bound his side with strips of white cloth.

The sun was already high in the brazen sky when Coral stepped wearily outside. The village was small, consisting mostly of a few farmers and fishermen. The men were already out on the water in their barges, and the women were about their duties of washing the family clothes, or working in their gardens.

The small mud hut that Seward had brought Jace to the day before belonged to the tehsildar, the village head-man, who had obligingly moved in with his son's large family for the payment in rupees Seward had offered him. The villagers seemed to ignore their presence, and only the large, curious eyes of children stared at them.

The tehsildar's daughter-in-law, dressed in her sari

219

and carrying food, walked up to where Coral stood. "Jai ram, sahiba."

"Yes, thank you for the food. You have been very kind."

The woman smiled shyly and left, and Coral brought the basket into the hut. She proceeded to hand out the chupatti bread and pieces of vegetable root, and pour tea from the urn.

Ethan absently smiled his thanks, and Coral waited until his eyes met hers. She smiled tiredly, but hoped her gratitude showed. It must have, for he looked surprised, flushed under his growing tan, and his gray eyes brightened. She laid a hand on his.

"What would we do without you?"

He said nothing, but seemed moved by her appreciation. He walked outside with his meager breakfast and lunch combined while Coral waited on Seward.

"Only time will do the rest. And the grace of God," murmured Seward.

Coral looked over at the cot where Jace slept, and silently thanked the Lord that it appeared as though he would improve. While Seward walked outside to speak to Ethan, Coral went to the mat and stared down at Jace, studying his unguarded sleeping face for a moment. There was nothing boyish about him, for he looked just as rugged when he was unconscious as he did when he was in command, and she knew that in his unhappy childhood, he had never been permitted to be a boy. Yet, in that moment with his face relaxed, he looked far younger than she imagined. *He cannot be much older than Alex!* she concluded, surprised.

An odd feeling crept over her as she looked at him, something that wisdom warned her not to toy with. Understanding came in a flash of awareness. *He could bring me pain. As much as Gem.*

How long she stood there she did not know. Perhaps only a minute, perhaps three or four, looking at him. From outside, she heard the muffled voices of Ethan and Seward discussing the mutiny and Jace's condition.

"... at least several weeks until he will be strong enough to be about his business," came Ethan's professional voice.

Weeks, thought Coral. She must not even think of the safari to Kingscote. Her mind wandered back to Ethan, and she pondered that professional-sounding voice. Ethan did not like the major, she concluded. And yet he had come. Immediately and without question. Ethan was committed to his medical work, and with that blessed knowledge he did good. He was also kind to her, and quite satisfied with the thought of settling down. Nothing prompted him to set sail for the horizons of the world. More importantly, he was sympathetic toward her desire to reach the untouchables. He had even suggested working with her to help the children. He had attended church with her in London. . . . He had saved her life twice. What more could she want?

She scanned Jace's face.

Ethan . . . Nothing about him hinted of emotional risk.

Coral turned away and, snatching up her cloak, walked briskly out of the room, lifting her head as she went.

The sun was warm. "I am ready now, Ethan," she announced.

Something in her voice made him turn and look at her, as though she had intimated much more. Ethan walked toward her, a lean, handsome figure in his riding clothes. She noted how the sunlight on his hair made it appear golden.

"I am sorry, Coral," he said very softly, his eyes tender.

A little startled by this confession, she searched his face. "About what?"

"About not understanding the kind of woman you are."

She hesitated. "And you now understand?"

He said nothing at first. "Yes, I think I do." His smile disappeared, and he stood looking at her with a warmth in his eyes she had not seen before. "You were good to come with me, Coral. To put a friend first, even though you have been ill yourself. I was suspicious because I know my own heart. I have never known anyone to be simply *kind*. Forgive me?"

Coral felt a rush of guilt pierce through her. *Perhaps I did have other reasons*. But they would not be allowed to surface again.

She searched his gray eyes, noting that they did not make her too aware of herself as a woman. She felt more comfortable with those emotions. She smiled and nodded, allowing him to walk her to where Seward had their horses ready.

Coral was aware of Seward's eyes watching her as he assisted her into the stirrup. She avoided his eyes and turned her head to look down at him only when he took hold of her wrist, handing her the reins. His stark blue eyes were piercing.

"I'll keep you posted on how the major is doing."

"Yes, thank you, Seward. I am quite certain he will recover." She smiled. "The major will be his old self again before you know it."

A reddish brow shot up in question, and she smiled and leaned over to lay her palm against the side of his bearded face.

"Dear, faithful Seward," she said simply, but the affection of those words were not lost on him. She saw him grin beneath his mustache.

"Watch that road on the ride back. There be some dangerous holes in it. Could break a horse's leg."

As she and Ethan rode out, Coral did not look back.

———

Colonel Warbeck:
Good men of the 17th killed in ambush near Plassey. Rest of sowars have mutinied to the side of the 34th. Land travel to northern frontier may soon be cut off, leaving the Maharaja at Guwahati and the British outpost at Jorhat near Kingscote in danger. I suggest Plassey be taken at once. I am sending Captain McKay back to Calcutta for reinforcements. My Rissaldar-Major Sanjay is suspected of arranging the ambush. Intend to complete my orders to see the Governor-General's Resident to Guwahati. If I cannot journey by land through Plassey Junction, then will go by boat. I need to return the idol of Kali to the Raja. Also intend to see that Sanjay answers for death of the 17th.

J. Buckley Warbeck, Major,
17th Lan., B.N.I.
2 o'clock P.M.
February 22, near Manali

The colonel's expression was stone when he turned from the window to look at Captain Gavin McKay. He tapped the letter against his palm.

"How badly is my son injured?"

Captain Gavin McKay stood with feet apart, and hands behind him, his expression revealing none of his frustration with the military.

"That he lives at all, sir, is attributed to the death-loyalty of his young daffadar. And to the major's own determination." The greenish eyes were cool, and he said bluntly, "He intends to find Rissaldar Sanjay and see him shot for treason. When I left him three weeks ago in the care of Seward, he was flat on his back and dictated the letter to me. I suggest, Colonel, that by now he is making his plans."

The colonel said nothing and walked to his desk. He picked up a sheet of paper and handed it to him, his gaze level.

"And our plans go on, Captain. We have a treaty with the raja of Guwahati. Troops will be sent north. First, I want information on the family of Daffadar Ramon Singh. It is fitting he be properly rewarded for saving the major's life. Second, my advice to the brigadier is to send another company of cavalry and standby artillery. I have ordered Major Dalaway to lead the 13th to secure Plassey. Your orders are also changed, Captain."

Gavin McKay had been afraid of this. Like Jace, whom he had known since the unfortunate decision to attend the Company Military Academy in England, McKay also kept a calendar of his last day, hour, and minute in uniform.

"Once Plassey is secured," said the colonel, "you will proceed north to join forces with the troops at the Jorhat outpost. When Major Buckley arrives at Guwahati, you will work with him to guard the maharaja and the royal family."

Captain McKay was expressionless, but his thoughts were on Kathleen Kendall. He crisply saluted. "As you say, Colonel."

—————

The frustration that Jace felt clamped about his insides. The 17th had ridden into a death trap, the 34th had mutinied, and until Plassey could be retaken by troops from the Calcutta garrison, the land route to the northern frontier was cut off. The motives of those involved remained as misshapen shadows in Jace's mind.

Jace thought of his daffadar again, of all the sowars of the 17th. They had represented some of the best of the native troops in Bengal. They were not only men of courage, but for the most part, were men of military principle, who had been wasted in a battle for a cause promoting someone's political ambitions and greed.

Now, the 17th was food for jackal packs and insects. In his mind he could see the battlefield stretching on before him in a long profusion of fallen men. The wind seemed to carry to his hearing the indistinct sounds of the dying, and his daffadar. . . .

Jace steeled himself against the emotion trying to resurface. The realization that the native daffadar was proud to die for his British commander tore at his insides. A rush of emotion welled up within his chest, and for a moment he thought he could not stand it. *No*, he determined, clenching his jaw. *I will not allow myself to care this deeply.* He had not even wanted this ragtag band of sowars called the 17th! He did not want to belong to any part of the military. But it was not the military alone that he wanted to reject, it was emotional risk. It could hurt too much.

Jace put a clamp on his emotions as Seward came through the hut door. He raised himself to an elbow.

"Well?" Seward wore a dark scowl. "If he be anywheres about, he be a magician, that one. I ferreted about Harrington's residence for the past day and night, and there be no trace of him."

Jace looked down at his hand. He had removed the bandage days earlier, but the joints were still swollen and painful. His rissaldar-major would pay for his betrayal. If it took the rest of his days, he would track Sanjay down and bring him back to Calcutta to be shot as a traitor.

Seward was watching him. "I be thinking the same. It be months before the old fortress near Plassey be taken again, no matter how many reinforcements the colonel sends back with McKay. The temple be standing in the path, and they won't dare use the cannon. Smart move on their part, the priests be in on the mutiny, I say. Face it, lad. There be no hope of getting through to the north now. Maybe we should go back to Calcutta."

Jace watched him boil water for tea in the hearth. In Calcutta the brigadier had replaced his trusted second in command with Sanjay, but at whose orders? Who had been behind the change? Certainly not the colonel.

"Roxbury be in on this. I be sure of it," whispered Seward darkly.

Just how much had he known in advance about the ambush and mutiny of the 17th? "He wanted me dead," said Jace.

Seward's head jerked in his direction. "You, lad?"

"Yes, I think the entire motive for going to the governor-general about my orders was because he already knew about the plans for mutiny near Plassey. Sanjay was also in on it from the beginning."

Seward's eyes hardened. "I believe it. But we need proof for the colonel."

"And I intend to get it."

Seward looked at him with a granite stare. "From Roxbury?"

"Sanjay. Roxbury can wait until we reach Guwahati."

"Sanjay may still show at Harrington's," said Seward.

"Or he may come here looking for me."

"Aye," said Seward. "Let him. I'll be waiting."

20

Coral prepared for the dinner party, choosing an emerald-green satin frock with numerous flounces of matching lace. She held it up against her, and then for no particular reason she exchanged it for a white moire with small puffed sleeves, trimmed in Brussels lace.

She swept her golden tresses up and spent longer than usual fussing with the stylish side curls.

An hour later Coral took an anxious glance at herself in the mirror, wondered who would be at Harrington's dinner, and crossed the hall to the stairway, starting down.

She paused. Across the wide hall, Captain Gavin McKay was leaning against the double doors of the drawing room, back toward Coral. He was silently watching Kathleen at the other end of the hall peering cautiously out the window onto the front yard.

Not wanting to interrupt the first meeting between them, Coral pressed her palms against her skirts to keep the silk from rustling on her petticoats, and tiptoed down the remaining stairs, escaping into a small anteroom that opened onto Mr. Harrington's prized garden.

Kathleen stood on tiptoe at the window, watching Mr. Harrington greeting dinner guests who had just arrived in a ghari. She wrinkled her nose with boredom. So these were the dinner guests for the grand evening.

The man who greeted Mr. Harrington was short and portly, heavy-jowled, with ruddy cheeks and bulging eyes. *Looks like his gaudy cravat is too tight,* she thought.

Zameen assisted an elderly woman down the ghari step to the yard, her skirt descending behind her. She stood as if to sniff the atmosphere like some English hunting dog, then raised the lorgnette resting on her ample bosom to one sharp eye. She scanned Zameen, and her voice, although muffled through the windowpane, reached Kathleen. "So, Charles! You have got yourself a new man, have you?" she said, addressing Mr. Harrington. "What happened to the other? Do not tell me he died of cholera? My, but you *are* having terrible luck."

Kathleen heard a sound from the doorway behind her, and straightened.

"If you are waiting for your French couturier, Jacques Rollibard, you will be disappointed. The poor chap is still in London kissing the hands of rich widows."

The lazy voice tinged with mockery belonged to Gavin McKay. She turned her head with tilted chin and scanned him with what she hoped was indifference. He was leaning in the archway with a smile she did not like, and the green-gray eyes in the handsome face looked her over, taking in the blue ruffled dress and the cascade of chestnut-colored curls piled high on her head.

Kathleen prided herself that she did not blush the way Coral did every time a handsome gentleman looked at her; but then, she must not compare Captain McKay with a gentleman, she told herself. He was brash, spoiled, and if that was not enough, positively rude.

"Oh. It is you."

"My apology," he said dryly.

Kathleen turned her back to him and gazed out the window as if expecting someone important. The truth was, she had expected Gavin McKay to ride in with the major by way of the front drive.

Gavin came in and closed the doors behind him. "Well, do not let me stop you. The fact I nearly had my head walloped off obviously means nothing. But since I will be leaving for Calcutta in the morning, I thought I had better warn you in advance."

At that, she turned and looked at him suspiciously through her lashes. "Warn me of what?"

Gavin smiled lazily. "I am to escort you and your sisters back to Lady Margaret's. Plassey Junction is cut off. Travel to Kingscote is too dangerous. It appears as if you will be forced to delay your return home. But that should make you happy. Marianna tells me you have been wanting to go back. London, it seems, is still on your mind, or should I say heart?"

Kathleen smiled too sweetly and walked over to where he stood. "It seems little Marianna feels quite comfortable in sharing her heart with you."

"Why, Kathleen, do not tell me you are jealous?"

"Quite a presumption, Captain! Why should I be jealous of my sister? And one hardly out of braids at that."

He laughed. "Your feminine ego resents my attention on any female but yourself. Someone ought to tell you that you are too conceited. I do not suppose this Jacques would dare to presume."

Kathleen felt her quick temper ignite. She tried to swallow back the rush of words that would put him in his place. But she had lashed out at him many times before, and it only gave him the advantage, for he never appeared to be daunted by her. Instead, she smiled again, her prettiest smile, and took a moment of satisfaction when he laughed at her attempt to throw him off.

"Now, Gavin, do not be an impossible bore. After two weeks in that ghastly ghari, breathing and eating dust, the least you can do is waste a little flattery on me. The night will be horrid enough spent in the company of that old stick Mr. Harrington and his friends."

"What a nasty little tyrant you can be sometimes, Kathleen. How is it you inherited none of your baby sister's sweetness, or Coral's honor?"

Kathleen knew that he did not mean to sound malicious; she had grown used to his barbs, as he had her own, in the years they had known each other. Now, for some reason unknown to Kathleen, the words stung. Was she truly as hard-nosed and selfish as Gavin made her out to be?

Coral's honor . . . Marianna's sweetness . . .

"But for you, Kathleen, anything. Tonight I shall feed your conceit and play the charming military gentleman. You will be surprised how I can exceed your gallant but empty-headed French designer."

It must be my mood, thought Kathleen. Gavin was no more satirical with her than usual, but lacking in her customary ability to banter, tonight she felt out of step with his irony, even uncomfortable.

One would think I was the most selfish thing that ever walked in shoe leather, she thought, and for a brief moment envied both Coral and Marianna.

She realized that he was scrutinizing her. She turned away and walked over to the window. Another ghari was arriving with more of Harrington's dinner guests. Kathleen turned when she felt his hand on her shoulder, and his voice was oddly kind. "Something wrong, Kathleen?"

"No. Nothing is wrong. Why do you ask?"

"I expected you to come at me with claw and fang, and you looked instead as if you had swallowed a camel."

"You are gallant with your compliments."

He laughed. "You expect too many. But I will be generous," he said when her brows came together. "You look both charming and delectable tonight, and one would never guess you had braved the dust and insects of India to make it this far to Manali. As I said, a pity I will not be staying in Calcutta for more than a few days after I escort you there."

Kathleen's curiosity was baited, and she wanted to ask him why, but she also tried to pretend her disinterest.

"Oh, you mean your tour of duty will be over? And where will you go this time, Gavin, to London perhaps? Did you not say your aunt lived there?"

"She does. A sprightly little woman in her eighties. A friend of your dear Granny Victoria, I believe."

"I do not want to belittle your kindly old aunt, but Granny V happens to be a horrible snob. She would not hobnob with your sprightly maiden aunt from Aberdeen. Besides, she has little regard for the Scottish side of Papa's family. The Scotch," she said with a smile, "are known savages. Why, they used to be cannibals."

"They still are in the woods. I'll take you to visit them on our honeymoon."

Kathleen wrinkled her nose. "I shall never go to Scotland."

Captain McKay changed the subject. "Major Buckley hopes to gain your moral support in convincing Coral to return to Calcutta. Since it is known that you wish to return, this is your opportunity. Do you think you can do it?"

"And if I may ask, just why will you not be in Calcutta?"

"Duty is the honorable reason. The colonel transferred me to Jorhat. I cannot say that I am pleased about it. Buckley and I agree on a number of things, especially the avid desire to shed our uniforms."

"Oh, then you will be stationed at the Jorhat outpost?"

He grimaced. "Afraid so. If you were going home to Kingscote, I would be near enough to ride over and brighten your evenings. But it looks as if you will be going to Calcutta instead. Worst luck!"

Kathleen said nothing.

"Do not frown," he said. "You look so much lovelier when you laugh. Is my company that awful?"

Kathleen did smile, her dimples showing, and her curls sparkling under the light of lanterns. "After weeks of being starved of anything fun, Captain, I am not likely to complain of your company. Were you telling the truth? Did you almost get killed at Plassey?"

"Almost. But Jace was the lucky one. If it had not been for the loyalty of his daffadar, he would be dead."

In the salon, Lady Amelia's voice rang out: "Mutiny! Not one of us is safe in our beds with the natives on the loose. Gives me the vapors! I dare say, the military ought to be doing something to put a stop to this rampage."

There was a distraction in the entryway, and the clear, determined voice of Major Buckley was heard telling Zameen that he was expected by Sir Hugo and would show himself in.

Coral, who stood between Sir Hugo and Doctor Boswell in the salon, heard the small ruckus and looked toward the door to see the major enter. She paused, as did the others, taking note of both his countenance and his new spotless uniform, no doubt brought by Captain McKay from the Calcutta garrison. Except for a small bandage on the side of his head, his other wounds were inconspicuous.

"Ah, Major, good of you to show," said Sir Hugo. "Ethan has kept me informed of your progress. The news of your rissaldar-major has come as a shock. Am I to assume he is wanted for mutiny?"

"He will be tried and executed in Calcutta," replied Jace.

Coral glanced from Jace to Sir Hugo to see his response. Her uncle's expression was one of appropriate disdain for the betrayer. "A nasty business, this. Captain McKay informs me it will be sometime before we are in control of Plassey again. This loss of life is most regrettable."

Coral felt her heart thud. Would Jace call her uncle's deception now, in front of the guests? But while his expression was hard, it showed no accusation. In fact, if she had not been certain of running into Jace at the dak-bungalow that night when Hugo spoke with Sanjay, she could believe that he had heard nothing that would in the slightest way incriminate her uncle.

"Then travel through Plassey is delayed indefinitely," said Ethan. "Our journey north is out of the question. This is most disappointing."

Coral tensed. *Indefinitely!* "There is the river," she said, speaking for the first time. She noted that Jace's jaw set, as though her observation, forgotten by the others, was an unwanted intrusion.

Jace replied, not looking at her, but at Sir Hugo: "Travel by way of the river is possible but not recommended for civilians. Much of it is delta, infested with crocodiles and tigers. I advise that you send your nieces back to Calcutta."

Coral turned sharply. *He is deliberately avoiding me.*

"I do not know what your plans are, but now that Plassey is under siege, you also may wish to return," he said to Hugo.

Her uncle appeared entirely self-possessed, and he said thoughtfully, "Then do I gather, Major, that it is your intention to go on to Guwahati by river?"

"I intend to warn the outpost of another possible mutiny."

"If there is any way to continue the journey, I, too, wish to leave at once," said Sir Hugo. "My duty to the governor-general demands it."

"As you wish. Our travel will be by small boats through the delta. Eventually we will join up with the Bramaputra River."

Ethan looked skeptical. "I do hope, Major, that you will have an appropriate river guide? I should loathe getting lost in the jungle."

"Seward and I have traveled it before."

"What of boats? I have my medical supplies to consider."

"Seward is seeing to the matter now. I cannot vouch for your supplies. We will need to travel light. I would advise that you return to Calcutta with Sir Hampton's daughters. You can travel by land route as soon as the problem in Plassey is taken care of."

Coral pressed her hands tightly against her skirts. She found her voice all at once, and it came as a breathless declaration. "I beg to differ with you, Major Buckley, but I am able to survive a river journey as well as anyone."

Jace turned to look at her for the first time. Meeting the blue granite stare, she knew that he would do everything possible to see that Sir Hugo sent her back.

"I would not advise the boat trip, Miss Kendall," came the smooth voice. "I am certain Sir Hugo will agree that the risk is too great."

So. He would even go so far as to use Sir Hugo to thwart her purpose, although they both distrusted him!

She knew that he already understood her reasons for wanting to get home to Kingscote, and the formality between them was a pretext, and yet his expression was set.

Ethan interrupted, speaking to his uncle. "Coral is right, Hugo. Her heart is set upon returning home, and I, for one, cannot see her disappointed. If we continue the journey at all, then she should be permitted to travel on with us."

Surprised by his support, Coral turned and looked at him. He smiled down at her. "If you are dauntless enough to brave crocodiles and tigers, you shall hear no complaint from me. Seriously, Hugo, I quite agree with her about Elizabeth. As a physician, I can hardly turn my back and scurry to the safety of Calcutta."

Sir Hugo seemed pleased, and Coral believed his satisfaction was because she and Ethan appeared to be getting on together.

"I do not see how I can refuse the both of you. Well, Major Buckley?" he said. "It appears as if Coral shall be coming with us. I will speak to my other nieces. It may be that they will wish a military guard back to Calcutta."

Coral glanced at Jace. He said nothing more, but his gaze riveted upon her. She felt a nervous qualm and smiled, offering a little laugh. "My! Won't this be an adventure?"

"Yes," said Jace flatly. "It will."

Ethan extended his arm. "Shall we go to dinner, Coral?"

"Ah—yes, of course. Mr. Harrington is waiting for us." She walked with him across the salon toward the dining area. From behind her she heard Sir Hugo speak to Jace: "You will join us, Major?"

"Thank you, no. Good-night."

Coral glanced to see him walk past Captain McKay

and Kathleen. He did not stop to speak, but continued on, brushing past the guests. Jace paused in the entryway, looked at Zameen for a moment, and then went out. The door shut soundly behind him.

21

The morning sun dispersed rays of light along the river, while thread-legged pelicans stalked the shoreline in search of their breakfast. The boatmen, called *manjis*, had arrived from the village to load the supplies. The river safari into the northern frontier of Assam would begin that morning. Coral glanced about for Seward. Did he load her trunk of school supplies?

Coral turned in the direction of the road to see Jace with Captain McKay. Whatever they were discussing prompted a glance in her direction. Confronted with a steady stare from the major, Coral tore her eyes away and pretended to be looking for Seward. In order to thwart any new plans that he may have had to stop her from going on the journey, she had spent hours last night talking her sisters into returning with her to Kingscote, knowing that it would give Jace less justification to oppose her independent action. Evidently it had worked, and she felt rather smug to have outmaneuvered him.

"Are we trusting ourselves to those miserable little boats?" said Kathleen. "One misstep, and we will be swimming with crocodiles."

"Oh, no," moaned Marianna. "Coral, there are only

little boats—six of them. I thought we would all be on one *big* boat!"

Like her sisters, Coral had anticipated a larger river vessel. Those waiting at the ghat were the shallow-draught country boats with square sails that she was familiar with in Assam. She tried to appear confident and offered her younger sister a bright smile.

"Now, do not worry, Marianna. The boats are more secure than they look. And think of the view we will have."

Kathleen opened her pink parasol, its fringe dancing. "Maybe I *will* go to Calcutta."

Coral took firm hold of Kathleen's arm. "Oh, no. You promised me." She looked at Marianna. "Both of you did. We are going through with this. Do not look so squeamish. Major Buckley is hoping you will both faint before we leave so he can go to Uncle and tell him it is a dreadful mistake." She looked from Marianna's gloomy face to Kathleen's scowl. "We prayed together last night, remember?"

"Yes," murmured Marianna, "but you implied the Lord would give us a big boat. I thought we would have a cabin, at least. Where will we sleep at night?"

"On land, you goose," said Kathleen. "But cheer up. The major will build a fire to keep the crawling things away."

"Oh! Coral!"

"You want to get home to Mother, do you not?" Coral pressed. "And there is the mission school to start before the monsoon. If I do not arrive in time to see some kind of structure built before the ground turns to mud, I will need to wait another six months."

"You do not even know if Papa will allow the school," cautioned Kathleen.

"I shall leave that obstacle to prayer, just the way we

committed our boat trip to Him last night. Now then . . ." Coral let out a breath and smiled at them. "It is all settled. No more questions, no more fears. We must appear strong and capable before Major Buckley, or he may try to send us back with Captain McKay."

"Oh, very well," said Kathleen. "I shall never understand you, Coral, but since I do not even know my own mind sometimes, I shall go through with this."

Despite Kathleen's cynicism, Coral felt that there were times when her sister understood more than she would admit.

"Kathleen, you go say goodbye to Captain McKay. He is waiting for you. I want to talk to Seward about my school supplies."

"What about me?" said Marianna with a hopeless expression on her young face, almost as if she were an abandoned kitten.

"Wait here by the ghari until Uncle Hugo and Ethan arrive," said Coral. "I will not be long."

Kathleen looked toward the barge. "Ethan is already here. That is him squabbling with the boatmen." Coral followed her gaze to the overloaded barge where Ethan stood wearing a hat and knee-length coat, waving his arms at the manjis. She guessed that he was frustrated trying to communicate his concern over his medical supplies.

Coral made her way toward the riverbank. The morning sunshine and the feel of baked earth beneath her slippers proclaimed the beginning of another hot day. She was only occasionally aware of the weakness due to the poisonous bite at Harrington's house, and she looked a pale but pretty figure in the blue calico dress with its yards of skirts over crinolines. It was not one of her best dresses, for she knew the rigors of the safari, and yet she would have preferred a more suitable frock. She had, however, opted to omit a parasol, preferring the freedom of a wide-brimmed hat that tied beneath her chin.

The slight breeze from off the water was muggy and smelling of dead things. Already she felt her garments sticking to her flesh. Insects buzzed, and she waved her gloved hand before her eyes. Nearing the bank she saw Seward. A waft of air greeted her from off the murky water, which was stagnant in places, and dangerously low. But Jace had sailed to far distant shores, including the Spice Islands, and she did not question his ability to navigate northward toward Assam.

She walked toward the edge of the river, where pelicans prowled the oozing dark mud. Seward looked up from beneath his tricorn and saw her.

"Morning, lassie. The mud be slippery, so watch your step."

"Good morning, Seward." She smiled. "I see you have permitted Doctor Boswell to safeguard the loading of his supplies."

"Permitted?" He scowled in the direction of the ghat. "Aye, and neither me nor the major be taking the blame for 'em not arriving in one piece either. The man be smart when it comes to helping the sick but a mite lacking in river sense."

She felt uncomfortable and a little protective of Ethan. "I take it there is some trouble?"

"You take it right. The major knows these rivers. And if the doctor were as wise as he makes out, he'd listen to a man who knows the sea. The doctor be insisting on taking the big barge, but shallow water be ahead, mark it down, lass. He be in trouble."

Coral was thinking of her own trunk. "Are you saying Major Buckley will not permit us to take the baggage?"

"Nay, I didn't say that. But the doctor arrived last night with an order from Sir Hugo to the major. The doctor will haul his medical supplies on his own rented ferry barge, and he won't be taking no for an answer."

"Do not be too harsh on him, Seward. I can understand his apparent stubbornness. If we wait to have our supplies hauled, it could be close to a year before we receive them at Kingscote. The school cannot wait, and neither can his lab. We have so much work to do. And we want to build before the rains. Where is my trunk? Do you have it loaded?"

"The doctor be having it tied down now."

"Good. Then I will see how he is progressing."

Coral walked toward the ghat. As she neared the steps leading down to the boat landing, she found Ethan engaged in an ongoing dilemma of explaining his wishes to the manjis in halting English. He saw Coral and threw up his hands in helpless despair.

"Coral, thank goodness! Would you please explain to them that the crates must be handled with delicate care? They are worse than the bellicose seamen on the East India Company docks!"

Coral laughed and called down to the men in Bengali: "You must treat them gently, please. Tie them down well. When you are done, see to that blue trunk over there by the crates. It is mine, and I want it secured."

Ethan stood guard over the process like a hawk above a field of feeding mice. Coral was still smiling when she turned around to find Jace standing behind her.

In place of his uniform he wore a loose-fitting tunic and rugged jerkins. Once again he appeared the arrogant young adventurer, his hat low to keep the sun out of his eyes. The only thing missing was Goldfish.

He cocked his head and surveyed her blue dress. "Ah, I see you have already changed your mind. A wise decision, Coral, or are we back to the *Major Buckley and Miss Kendall* routine?"

"Changed my mind?" she repeated, confused.

He flashed a devastating smile. "Your ball gown."

Ball gown! She looked down at her calico, far from an elaborate dress, but obviously he wanted to pretend that it was.

"Since it is more suitable for a ball at the East India Company than a pitiless river journey, I assume," he said good-naturedly, "that you have already decided to return to Calcutta."

Coral gave him a wry smile. "Captain Buckley, do you ever give up?"

He encountered her gaze. "No."

"A commendable virtue when invested properly. However, I simply refuse to let you nettle me out of my amiable mood this morning."

"A difficult task, I can see. Are you always so angelic? You do have me curious."

He could not actually think that she was *angelic*?

She said airily, ignoring his question, "I suppose that I could try to please you and don a military uniform, if you have one to spare."

He lowered his hat and regarded her, then looked over to where Kathleen and Marianna stood beneath parasols, looking like pink and white froth on a cool summer's drink. "Do your charming sisters realize the river will be infested with smiling crocodiles?"

She folded her arms. "They were also born in India."

"But apt to swoon more often, is my guess."

"Not Kathleen. When necessary she has nerves of steel."

"Good. Because I will not have time to meander about with smelling salts."

"My, my, but you are in a nasty mood this morning, are you not? I assume the mosquitoes must have kept you awake all night. As for those crocodiles you hope to frighten me with, it will do no good. I will not go back to Calcutta. And, Major, do not forget to mention man-eating tigers and snakes."

"Pythons."

"I am sure we will run into a few of those also."

Jace folded his arms and gave her one of his familiar slanted looks. "I could say you never cease to amaze me, my dear Miss Kendall, but I will not. It is enough that I can depend on you to not swoon at the first roar of a tiger."

Swoon! She laughed. "I have never seen a Bengal tiger yet that caused me to drop into a heap of petticoats."

He smiled, and it was deliberately disbelieving. "As you wish." He lowered his voice. "But we best not tell your sisters that the tigers can swim to our little boats."

Coral refused to show alarm because she suspected that he wanted to jolt her. She also gleaned an amused hint of challenge in the slate color of his eyes. "Are you sure you are not making that part up?" she suggested.

"You might ask the several hundred fishermen in the area. However . . ." and he glanced about. "I fear that many are no longer able to explain."

Coral's stomach did a flip. "Well, I will take your word for it. The truth is, I did feel quite safe until I caught sight of those boats."

He followed her gaze. "Miserable, are they not? And to think I left the *Madras* for this." He mocked a groan. "Let us hope they stay afloat."

"With crocodiles? Indeed! Where did you get them?"

His mood changed. He looked back in the direction of the residence. "Harrington arranged for the boats. I keep thinking I have seen that man somewhere before."

"You might have."

His eyes swerved to hers. She explained quietly: "Mr. Harrington once lived in Guwahati. You may have seen him there when you served at the outpost. And Zameen was the maharaja's dewan."

"Ah! That accounts for it."

"Becoming secretary to Mr. Harrington is a humble step down from one who served as chief minister, you agree?"

"My guess," said Jace, "is that he is more than a secretary to Harrington. Interesting. I wish you had told me this sooner."

"Why? Is it important?"

"Maybe. And Zameen. It now makes sense."

"Not to me. Whatever are you suggesting?"

"I cannot prove it, but I do not think I will need to search further for the one who helped my rissaldar escape into the black of night. I also think I will find him at Guwahati."

"For that matter, we know little about Harrington," said Coral. "Except he is said to be a friend of my uncle. I hope Sir Hugo is up to nothing worse than minor disagreements with my father over Kingscote and the Company."

"In the meantime I will have McKay alert the colonel to my suspicion."

"I wondered about Zameen myself," Coral admitted. "I do not know why, but when I first learned that Uncle wished us to stay at Manali with an acquaintance, I had an odd feeling. As though Marianna and I would come face-to-face with the man we saw in the garden at Barrackpore."

He looked at her. "You are sure it was *not* Zameen?"

"Quite. The other man was tall with a yellow turban."

He smiled. "I doubt if he goes around wearing a yellow turban all the time. We will give him credit for laundering his garments and changing them."

"Regardless, the man I saw was not Zameen. And

Marianna showed no recognition when she saw him. We cannot both be wrong."

"You are quite sure he *was* an Indian?"

"Yes, well—" She stopped and bit her lip. "He wore a turban."

A brow slanted.

"And he spoke Bengali," she said with a note of defense.

"You and I both speak Bengali. Many English do. The turban and dialect could have been a deliberate disguise, just to be sure no one at Barrackpore could possibly recognize him."

Coral felt a prickle of her skin as she understood where his thoughts were leading. "Mr. Harrington?" she whispered. "Is it possible?"

"Why not?"

"Then, Uncle may have—" She paused.

"Brought you here deliberately. Just to see if either you or Marianna could identify him. And I was unwise enough to let you come."

"You could not have known."

"I should have."

For a moment they said nothing. Coral stood remembering Mr. Harrington and breathing a thankful prayer that Marianna did not perceive who Harrington was.

All those weeks at Manali without the major or Seward. She shuddered. And illness had kept her deaf and dumb to the situation around them.

"I think we have unwound the yellow turban and discovered our garden intruder. I will alert Colonel Warbeck. Say nothing to your sister about this. Sir Hugo is convinced that you are blind to Harrington's masquerade."

She glanced over her shoulder to see the arrival of a

ghari. "It is Uncle. At least he now has confidence in you. He suspects nothing."

"He is putting on an act. He does not trust me anymore than I do him. He expected me to die by the hands of my jemander near Plassey. I think it was the reason behind the change in my orders."

Coral felt sick. *No! Her uncle would never go so far in his plans!*

"Now he is stuck with me as the head of his security guard in Guwahati." He gave her a scrutinizing look. "You have not mentioned what you overheard between him and Sanjay to your sisters?"

She hesitated, thinking of Ethan. "No."

He looked relieved. "I do not want them involved. And I do not want Sir Hugo to know I overheard him and Sanjay. I can learn more of what is going on by playing his way. I only wish you did not know so much. What about Boswell? Did you tell him?"

His look evoked a feeling of guilt, and she turned defensive. "Oh, come. He is not a conniver." She rearranged the ribbon beneath her chin. Beneath his alert gaze, she turned toward Ethan, who was still inspecting the loading of his barrels and crates, as though they held the jewels of the Taj Mahal.

"Then you did tell him," he said softly.

"Why not? I trust him," she said defensively.

"I do not."

"He will not say anything to my uncle. I will ask him to remain silent."

"No. Say nothing. The less you bring up the subject, the better. What makes you so certain of your cousin?"

"He has done nothing to warrant my suspicions, and he intends to help me with the school. Besides," she reminded him, "he did doctor your wounds after the mutiny. If it is true what you think about my uncle, then

Ethan was not involved. He might have let you die. We rode to the village with Seward the moment he told us what had happened."

"We?"

She had not intended to let him know that she had felt compelled to go with Ethan and Seward. She said simply, "I went with Ethan. He needed my help."

There was silence, and she could feel his gaze. She busied herself with her hat, and when the moments continued to pass without his response, she said too abruptly, hoping to interrupt his thoughts, "Ethan's devotion to medicine is not practiced to put others in his debt. He is a man of honor."

"I can see your cousin is the embodiment of your most noble crusader."

She gave a short laugh to throw him off track. "It so happens I am a trifle more sophisticated than *that*. I hardly go about mooning and cultivating romantic notions of heroic knights sweeping me away to unknown isles aboard stolen ships."

He smiled. "A knight rode a horse, my dear; he was not a sea captain."

She turned away, glancing down the river as though impatient to be off. "I do not know how we got onto this silly subject."

"Ethan is misleading you."

"You seem to know a good deal about other people's motives."

"Regardless of the doctor's gallant intervention the other night with your uncle, I would like to insist that the man knows nothing about the dangers of the journey. You and your sisters would be better off to return to Calcutta."

"There is no need to be angry with him," she said. "I would have discovered some way to proceed with the journey without his moral support."

Her defense of Ethan seemed only to evoke Jace's impatient glance down to the ghat steps, where her cousin hovered over his crates of books.

"He is making a mistake taking the barge. Which reminds me, your contraband would be better if left to McKay than to the inexperience of Boswell. Follow his advice, and you may end up with nothing."

Coral was taken off guard. "Contraband?"

"Your *mission supplies*, being smuggled to Kingscote under the nose of Sir Hugo. McKay will see your materials are delivered when he arrives to take up his position at the outpost."

She let out a sigh of gratitude. "Why, the idea is perfect. And they will arrive in time to set up a temporary structure before the monsoon. What about Ethan's medical supplies?" she asked. "Can you ask Captain McKay to see to their safety as well?"

"I could," he said dryly. "But the doctor's great scientific mind has already rejected so simple a solution. He prefers to risk the destruction of his gear by keeping it under his own watchful eye."

She would admit Ethan's mistake to herself but not to Jace. Instead, she offered a smile of appeasement. "A lovely morning for a river trip, is it not?"

"I find nothing pleasant about the morning, nor the weeks of travel ahead. As for Boswell, you trust him too much."

She felt a slight rebuke, and turned away, watching the manjis and Ethan. "I know him better than you do. And he saved my life at Manali."

He straightened and fixed her with an alert stare. "He did *what* at Manali?"

His response took away her casual air. "I was ill, and he treated me."

He frowned and scanned her. "At Manali? You said nothing about this before."

"No, please, you misunderstand. It was not a relapse of the fever, if that is what concerns you," she hastened. "I am strong enough for the journey."

"Then would you mind explaining what you do mean?"

She absently untied the ribbon and removed her hat. "It was all rather unpleasant, actually. I was bitten by this horrid spider. Harrington kept a collection as a hobby. . . ." She glanced about the ground, feeling a desire to lift the hem of her skirts. "I was sitting at dinner."

"How soon after you arrived?"

"A day or two later. Why? What has that to do with it?"

"I know most insects around here. What did it look like?"

"Imagining the thing makes me shudder. I would rather come face-to-face with a Bengal tiger than a long-legged hairy creature with—"

"Why do you say *imagine* it? Did you not see it?"

"No. It happened too fast," she said, remembering the spell of dizziness that had overtaken her while seated at Mr. Harrington's table. She shuddered.

"And Boswell was able to bring you out of it, is that it?"

She wondered at his flat tone of voice. "Yes. Even so, I was bedridden for the entire length of time you and Seward were gone. And now that we suspect Mr. Harrington to have been the man in the garden—" she stopped.

A breath escaped his lips. "You might have told me."

Coral replaced her hat and tied it firmly under her chin. "The opportunity did not arise until now. Besides, nothing happened after all, did it? I have my strength back, and I shall do fine on the journey."

"But you did not see it?"

"I told you. It happened too fast. Why? Is it important?"

"Because I am unaware of a spider bite that is as serious as you suggest. Tell me again how it happened."

Coral began to feel uneasy. What was Jace hinting at, if anything? He did not like Ethan; the two men were opposites in nature, and that could account for his suspicions. She slapped at an insect. "I was seated at the dinner table, and the next thing I knew I felt extremely dizzy. I remember little else, except having nightmares, until some days later. Ethan can explain what kind of spider it was."

"Is that when you both became trusted friends? During your recuperation?" he asked smoothly.

"Well, yes, you could say that. But do not forget, I have known him the last few years in London. He did save my life, Jace. And this was not the first time. I am well today because of his medical expertise while at Roxbury House."

"And of course you are very grateful."

Something in his tone put her on guard. "Why should I not feel indebted to my physician?"

"That depends."

"On what?"

"On the true cause of your illness."

She blushed. "I do not know what you mean."

"I think you do."

"I think you misjudge him. He has even suggested helping me with the untouchables. The children will need medical treatment."

"And he possesses the Christian graces of faith and charity, of course. It has nothing at all to do with pleasing a silk heiress."

Her breathing felt tight. "If he is willing to risk Uncle's ire by helping with the school, I can see no reason to doubt his good intentions."

From below on the barge, Ethan's voice was heard shouting: "Wait, you there, set the crate down *gently*! It contains medical drugs."

Jace observed her from under his hat. "Did it ever occur to you that Sir Hugo may wish Doctor Boswell to appear sympathetic to your ambitions?"

"That is too complicated," she said stiffly. "Uncle disapproves of my plans."

"It is not complicated at all. What better way to drive you to the consoling support of his nephew?"

This new thorn of suspicion only frustrated her. "The trouble with you, Major, is that you do not trust *anyone*. Sometimes I am certain you must keep steel armor around your heart."

"Never mind my heart. It is you we are discussing."

"Did anyone ever suggest to you how stubborn and domineering you are, Major?"

He smiled and looked away from Doctor Boswell to a bird winging its way across the river. There followed a moment of silence. Trying to cool her emotions, Coral focused on a pelican in the mud.

"About this spider, where was the bite?"

"My ankle."

"Did it swell?"

"No! I mean—" she stopped.

"Meaning?"

"Meaning nothing at all, Major Buckley. I was asleep during that period of time. You are not suggesting Ethan put something in my tea?"

"I did not say that. But since you mention it, it must have crossed your mind."

Coral remembered back to the night she had sat at

dinner. Sir Hugo had poured her tea, not Ethan.

She turned her head. He was still watching a fowl flying through the sky. "Very well. I had tea. But it was not Ethan who gave it to me. It was Sir Hugo."

"May I suggest your *spider* was a drug?"

She refused to shudder at the thought. She remembered the drugs she had taken in London, and how ill they had seemed to make her.

"It is to your benefit that you are not good to anyone dead," he said softly but bluntly. She winced.

"If it were a drug, what would be the reason behind it? And anyway," she added with relief, "Ethan is not to blame."

"He is a physician. A good one. Do you agree?"

"But of course."

"Then why did he not recognize your symptoms were caused by an administered drug?"

Coral was growing tense as he continued to hammer away at her foundations. "You do not know for certain that it was a drug."

"No. But if you could go back and examine that bite on your ankle, you might find that it did not exist. As for a reason, Roxbury still wants you to marry his nephew?"

"The entire family wishes it, not just Uncle," she said stiffly. "He did offer to give Ethan and me Mr. Harrington's indigo plantations for a wedding gift."

"How generous," said Jace dryly, "considering his nephew will inherit the wealth of a silk heiress. What did you tell him?"

"Do you think I would marry a man for an indigo plantation?"

He turned his head, and she felt his gaze. "No. If the choice remains your own, I doubt if you would even marry to gain the Roxbury Estate and Silk House. But you *would* marry a man like Peddington and be content to live on bread and water to translate the Scriptures."

She looked at him, speechless. It made her uncomfortable to think he could analyze her so well. To cover her embarrassment, she said lightly, "I am not that saintly, Major. I will want a trifle more than that."

"Coral, please go back to Calcutta with McKay. Wait there. When this matter in Jorhat is settled, I will discover what I can about Gem. If I have something definite before then, I will send word through Gokul."

"Jace, I do appreciate your concern." His laugh told Coral he did not believe her. She looked at him evenly. "For me to turn back now is out of the question."

His eyes measured her determination. Did she see a brief hint of admiration? It happened with such haste that she was not even certain he had responded at all.

"As you wish. We will not discuss it again. Excuse me. I need to speak with McKay about your supplies before he rides out."

22

That morning the small group boarded boats and left Manali. According to what Seward told her, the delta was a marshy mangrove jungle that would demand the full attention of the armed sowars.

"We'll not be going to the extreme south into the heart of the jungle, but heading north on the delta to the Ganges. Even so, the journey be hostile."

Standing with Seward on the barge, Coral found herself looking out over the largest estuarine forest in the world. She couldn't help but feel anticipation over the journey ahead, despite the dangers.

"I suppose after this you'll be off to the tea plantation in Darjeeling?" she asked, ready to probe for some answers.

Mention of the project was all that it took to hook Seward. His eyes brightened. "The tea plantation in Darjeeling? Aye, once the major's duty to the colonel is over, we be making a success of it. Jace and me, along with Gokul and Jin-Soo—we have large plans, if God blesses. Not that I be anxious to leave Kingscote, understand," he said. "But Jace be needing me, maybe more than your father. Jace has his mind set on making it work. I don't doubt but that he can do it. He be a hard worker, and dedicated when he believes in something." He squinted at her. "What've ye got on your mind?"

The tea plantation interested her more than she cared to admit. "I've wondered about the friendship between Michael and Jace. Michael's death on the *Madras* was an accident, and yet it did get me to wondering about their past, and something Michael once told me at Kingscote. About an accident—"

"Aye, you mean the avalanche?"

"I have wanted to ask Jace about it, but the moment never seemed appropriate. Do you know what happened?"

Seward hesitated, and Coral noticed that he appeared uncomfortable.

"I know nothing about it, lass. But if there be talk about what happened on the ship, well, I be knowing exactly what happened. I be suspecting that slander came from Sir Hugo." He paused and tried to read her expression, and when she did not deny it, he grunted. "Thought so. That being true, I don't set much mind to Sir Hugo's tongue, since it can dish out anything that pleases his aims."

Coral frowned, grateful that her uncle had chosen to ride in one of the smaller boats. "I do not doubt what you and Jace say occurred on the *Madras*. But I have been curious about a number of things. Then you were not there when this incident of the avalanche happened?"

"Nay, I know nothing of it. And since Jace hasn't seen fit to talk about it with me, I don't find it my business to ask."

"Yes, of course. But if there is nothing to the story of the avalanche, then why has Jace remained silent?"

"Good question, Miss Kendall," Jace said from behind them. "But you will not find the answer with Seward. He was not in Darjeeling. It was Michael and I, and Gokul."

Coral whirled about, her cheeks turning warm.

"But perhaps you were convinced I would not tell the truth if you asked."

"No, I—" She stopped, feeling embarrassed to be caught discussing this affair behind his back.

"I suggest that any questions you have about my past be brought to me. I shall answer for my own faults."

Seward cleared his throat. "I'll be getting the kansamah to boil us up some coffee." He walked away leaving them alone.

Coral faced Jace. "I was not accusing you of wrong."

Jace said nothing, but she could see he did not believe her. "I have wanted to ask you about that avalanche ever since—"

"Ever since I was accused of losing Michael at sea?"

"No, since Michael mentioned it at Kingscote."

"But you prefer to find out about it from Seward. Perhaps you think I left Michael to die so I could latch hold of the tea plantation for myself. And when I failed the first time, I threw him overboard."

"You make it sound foolish."

"I hope so."

"I was only curious about Darjeeling."

"Then why did you not ask me?"

"I will. Would you mind telling me what happened?"

He shrugged. "We were exploring the upper mountainous region around Darjeeling years ago. I slipped and fell. There was an avalanche. It took me days to get back to the village. The truth was, I did think Michael was dead. I was surprised to find him in the village."

This, she had not expected. *Jace was the one who had slipped and fallen! What of Michael? Had he fallen also? Had he searched for Jace?*

"You said Gokul was there. He found you?"

His voice was flat. "No. He was the one who found Michael. Gokul thought I was buried under the avalanche."

"Did Michael tell Gokul that?"

"I do not remember," he said flatly. "You can ask Gokul."

In the silence that grew between them, the monkeys chattered.

There was more to the story, Coral knew that, but it was not coming from him. Perhaps Jace did not mean for it to be clear. Could it be that the story was unfavorable to Michael? If she ever met Gokul, she would ask him. It was obvious that Jace would say no more. Feeling unexpectedly tired, Coral turned away. "Excuse me, Major, but I think I will take advantage of the shade."

Jace said nothing and stepped aside.

They were five days into the river journey, and Coral sat with her sisters beneath the makeshift awning Seward had constructed for them on the river barge. The roof of palm fronds offered relief from the intense sun, and the curtains from Mr. Harrington could be drawn closed at night for privacy. Some simple deck chairs and cushions made the long hours more comfortable. While Marianna embroidered their mother a scarf and Kathleen resumed her dress designing in her prized portfolio, Coral continued her study of Hindi and the Hindu religion, hoping for ways to use the Scriptures on Kingscote.

Ethan had secured the use of the barge from a ferry owner in Manali, despite the fact that Jace had advised against it. But Ethan's enthusiasm for the exploration of fauna and insects had prompted him to use the barge not only to carry his medical supplies, but also to set up a tiny tent-lab. He had erected it at the back of the barge, on top of his crates and barrels. Seward called it a crow's nest. And at any hour, Ethan could be seen with his butterfly and fishing nets, making his way up the side of the crates with prized samples of plant life, fish, or insects.

But it was not the wide variety of small creatures that disturbed Coral. She guessed that they were nearing a dangerous area in the delta by the fact that Jace had unexpectedly, but unobtrusively, joined Seward to ride on the detested barge. And yet, from the casual manner in which he behaved, she had no proof that the motivation for his presence meant an increase in danger.

Marianna and Kathleen were busy with their projects, and Coral grew weary of her study. She placed her New Testament and some books into her bag, left them under her chair, and picked up her wide-brimmed straw hat. She would simply inquire of Jace if her suspicions were correct.

With that, she ventured forth from the shelter of shade into the sun. It was muggy. She had already exchanged her high-necked frocks and crinolines for the cooler muslins. Today her frock of pale yellow did little to ease the discomfort, and she was wishing for a breeze from off the river. The wood creaked beneath her slippers as she walked toward the back of the barge, and the rolling movement of the water made her grab the awning to steady herself.

"Easy, girl," warned Seward coming around the crates. He held her arm, his forehead furrowing beneath a waft of graying reddish brown hair. "Ye go falling into the river and it won't take long for them crocodiles to get busy."

She squinted beneath her hat and gazed across the water to the thick jungle growth on the river's bank, but saw nothing. Perhaps they were resting under the vines and shrubs covering the shore.

"I was not thinking of crocodiles, Seward."

Amid the thick emerald green, the shrill call of birds and the chatter of monkeys pierced the air.

Seward's scowl deepened as he looked away from Coral to scan the jungle. "Aye. I be knowing what ye think."

"Then I was right. We are entering tiger country."

"Aye," he admitted grudgingly.

Tigers . . . "I heard Jace talking to you last night at supper," she said quietly. "Is it true that fishermen are attacked frequently, and that these tigers can swim?"

"Ye ought to be ashamed, a daughter of Miss Elizabeth eavesdropping."

Coral smiled. "I was not holding my ear in your direction. But Jace had already mentioned tigers before we left Manali. And I could not help notice he came on the barge this morning. He usually rides in the lead boat. Tell me, Seward, is it because he thinks that we might be attacked?"

"No need to take the action of the major as sign of anything particular. The major and I be excellent shots, and it won't be the first tiger we brought low if it comes to that."

"Then it is to protect us that he chose to ride the barge?"

Seward rubbed a large hand over his beard and glanced upward. Coral whirled and followed his gaze, holding on to her hat. Jace was lounging on top of some of the crates. Had he overheard?

Coral's brows inched together. How could Jace remain so relaxed? The swoosh of the water could sound hypnotic as the Indian oarsmen dipped and sliced their poles through the river. But she remained alert. She swished an insect away with her hand, and stopped—a splash of water was followed by a cry, then a scream!

"That was Marianna!" she cried.

Seward hurled himself past her, and Coral caught up her skirts and stumbled after him. Kathleen came toward them at the same time, her face white, an arm across her stomach as if she wanted to gag. She pointed behind her. "It's Ethan, he fell! And there are crocodiles! I saw them!"

Seward ran to the rail, his eyes searching the river. Coral was beside him. Ethan's butterfly net floated past the barge. "Doctor Boswell!" Seward bellowed.

Sir Hugo was standing at the back of a small boat that was ahead of the barge. One hand cupped his mouth as he shouted: "Do something!"

Coral seized the rail, afraid of what she would witness. At first she saw only white egrets feeding. Then a movement caught her eye. Something slithered from the tall grasses on the bank and entered the water with a splash. The crocodile edged its way deeper into the river, its gray-green body sliding through the water, the small eyes protruding just above the surface.

Coral's heart thudded. A quick glance on both sides of the bank revealed more than one. Crocodiles! Everywhere.

Kathleen gripped her arm. "There! Look!"

On a mud flat along the riverbank there were a dozen creatures dozing in the sun. Their jaws were open wide displaying daggerlike teeth.

Sir Hugo was still shouting, trying to get the two sowars riding guard in his boat to save Ethan. Seward had grabbed the chairs from beneath the awning and tossed them into the river.

"Dear God!" whispered Coral, icy hands going to her mouth.

"Nay, lad!" shouted Seward.

261

Fear struck Coral's heart. *Jace! He would not!* She heard a second splash, and her heart seemed to stop. She brushed past Kathleen and ran up beside Seward.

"Shoot at anything leaving the bank!" Seward shouted to the sowars in the other boat, and had his own rifle aimed, but the uncertainty of whose movement they saw in the waters made it dangerous.

Coral's anxious gaze picked up a struggling shape some distance from the barge, and the next moment it disappeared again. Then she saw Jace swimming with strong stokes in Ethan's direction. Her eyes riveted on him as he dove beneath the water. How long? A minute? Her hands gripped the rail so tightly that her knuckles were white. *Please, Lord, protect them. Please . . .*

"Get a rope ready!" Seward was shouting to the oarsmen.

Coral saw Jace come up for air with Boswell holding on, struggling and gasping. Jace thrust him away with his foot, then grabbed the back of his collar and swam toward the barge.

"To your left!" Seward bellowed.

Coral saw the crocodile moving toward Jace. Seward raised his rifle and a shot crackled, spitting water around the head of the crocodile. Another shot pierced the water. A second and third crocodile left the banks, and the sowars riding guard in Sir Hugo's boat fired shots into the water.

A minute later Jace neared the barge with Ethan. Coral stood back to give the men room as Seward and an oarsman grabbed them by the shoulders and hauled the two of them out of the water onto the deck.

"Thank God, lad!" said Seward, thumping Jace on the shoulder. "Ye be in fine shape, but Boswell looks like a drowned rat."

Jace sat down to catch his breath, while Ethan sputtered and spat water.

"Major, I am in your debt," Ethan gasped.

Jace held up a hand. "Save your breath; we are even now." He got to his feet, swaying a little, and walked away.

Kathleen came rushing up. "Coral, come quick. Marianna's fainted. Do you have smelling salts with you?"

Coral hurried to the front of the barge where Marianna was already stirring.

"It is all right, Marianna. Ethan is alive. Major Buckley saved him from the crocodiles."

Marianna was so relieved that tears welled in her eyes. It was then that Coral saw the Hindi New Testament clutched to Marianna's heart. A wave of understanding swept over her. Marianna had turned to the Lord in the one way she knew how, by grasping His words. She could not read them, yet held them close to her heart.

Marianna looked at Coral. "Will you teach me to read Hindi? I opened the New Testament, and it was horrid! I could not read the words."

Coral smiled. "But do not forget the King James Bible Granny V gave you at Roxbury House."

Marianna looked sheepish. "I . . . I left it in the bedroom dresser drawer."

Kathleen went to her bag and pulled out a small black book edged in gold, with a bookmark made of silk, and embroidered with the Roxbury coat of arms. Her amber eyes gleamed with pride as she looked down at Marianna.

"I did not forget mine. Here," she said handing it to Marianna. "You can use it until Granny V sends yours. One of the maids is bound to find it."

"Thank you, but what will you use?"

Kathleen tilted her head and looked at her. She said nothing.

"Anyway," said Marianna to Coral. "I still would like lessons in Hindi. And so would Cousin Ethan. Maybe we could have a class. We have the time. And then I could write Mr. Peddington and tell him what I was doing."

"Charles would be pleased, indeed," said Coral.

"Count me out," said Kathleen. "I had enough difficulty with English grammar."

But Coral knew that Kathleen could speak Hindi better than she would let anyone know.

Coral looked up at the sound of bare feet on the deck to see the kansamah hurrying by. In one hand he held a pot of something steaming hot. In the other, two pewter mugs.

Coral wondered at her own action, but was on her feet and hailing him to stop. "Hot tea?"

He grinned. "No, miss-sahiba. Coffee. I made before physician fell in river. Favorite of Major-sahib."

"Yes, I know. I will take it to him. You can bring the other cup to the doctor."

How could she possibly have considered that Jace might leave Michael for dead? He had risked his life with horrible crocodiles for Ethan, a man he did not even like.

When she walked up, Jace was sprawled in the sunshine as though he had not a care in the world, his face buried in his arm, letting the heat dry him. Coral stopped, and a little breeze brushed the hem of her skirt against him. She held the coffee behind her. "Asleep already? It is not fair to the others for you to be so calm."

He moved his arm just slightly in order to peer up at her.

"I have a pleasant surprise for you," she said. "You deserve to be pampered."

He raised himself to an elbow, and a brow went up. "I am speechless."

Coral smiled and produced the mug. "Coffee. Although why you like it I cannot guess. Too bitter."

Seeing the mug, he sighed with satisfaction. "But only one cup?"

She brought the pot out from behind her.

"You are beginning to understand my weakness." He took the mug, and Coral stooped and poured, then set the pot down on the plank beside him, taking care that it not tip over. She straightened, holding her hat in place.

Jace took several gulps, then said grimly, "If you came to thank me for saving Boswell, there is no need. It was my duty."

Duty. How cool and pragmatic he deliberately made it sound. There was something else in those words. His duty on the *Madras* when Michael was lost at sea had been questioned by Sir Hugo and Ethan.

"I believe it was more than that," she said. "You would have done the same thing if you were no longer Major Jace Buckley, but captain of the *Madras*."

"If I had known there were crocodiles lurking in the waters, I would have let poor Boswell go the way of all flesh. How is he, by the way?"

Coral could not accept the glib remark. "He is fine, thanks to you. Seward is looking after him. And Sir Hugo hopes to board as soon as it is safe to do so. But Jace, you *knew* there were crocodiles."

He hesitated slightly, then finished the coffee and set the cup down. "If you see the kansamah, tell him the strength of the brew is perfect."

"The reason why I insist that you knew," said Coral, "is because you came aboard this morning knowing this is tiger country."

"Think so?"

"And, since you know that much about the area, you would know of the risk of crocodiles. It was Ethan who did not know. Marianna saw him fall in. He was trying to reach a black beetle with a red stripe, stretched too far with his net, and when he brought it down to catch it—he fell."

Jace smiled.

"Why do you wish to deliberately underestimate this deed of bravery?" probed Coral.

"You are right. Should I not wish to make myself look gallant after being accused of leaving a friend to die?"

"I do not know what happened in Darjeeling. Perhaps I no longer wish to. But I do think I know why you jumped in to save Ethan. A crisis can bring out of a man's heart what is truly there."

"Caution . . . I feel the probing fingers of a quizzical young mind. You would do best to not pry too deeply."

A strong breeze lifted her hat and sent it scuttling toward the deck. Jace reached out and caught it as it went by. He stood. "Your hat, Miss Kendall." His eyes held hers. "Perhaps you best retreat to the shade of the awning."

"You are not as cynical and pragmatic as you make out."

He said nothing and looked at her evenly.

"Are you?" she asked quietly.

He finished his coffee.

"I am beginning to think you choose the armor of a crocodile to scare people away."

"Do you have some particular person in mind?"

"It could be anyone you begin to care about."

"May I give you a word of advice?"

She smiled. "Again?"

"You might think twice before you try to remove the armor. The crocodile is even more dangerous when he doesn't want to scare away his dinner."

She felt her cheeks turning warm and took her hat from his extended hand. "Thank you for the warning, Major." She placed her hat on. "If you will excuse me."

Jace watched her walk away, the breeze catching her soft yellow skirt. *You are quite right. I would just as soon sail the Madras into battle with the French than allow your sweet fingers to meddle with my armor!* The more she thought him a risk, the more she would keep her distance.

He stood there, listening to the sounds of the jungle closing in about him. He walked over to his wet tunic and snatched it up. As he did, he felt something in the front pocket and removed it. His hand held the military medal that he had won. Gokul had placed it on his uniform jacket in Calcutta the night he became Major Jace Buckley.

"Gokul," said Jace aloud, with soft frustration, "I would not be in this predicament now if it had not been for you leasing the *Madras*." Neither would he have come up against Kendall's daughter. The sooner he got this mission in Guwahati over, the better. He would pay the colonel, board the *Madras*, and head to sea. But then there was Gem . . .

Seward approached and Jace turned, scowling.

Seward gave him a questioning look in return. "Did the lass bring you your coffee?"

"She brought it. The kansamah will do well enough next time. Where is my gun?"

"Right here, lad. Boswell be wanting to see you to offer his thanks."

"Tell him it was nothing."

23

Coral found that the days on the river—with the heat and droning insects—inched by, but the nights with thick darkness due to the trees and vines were by far the worst. With tenacity she adhered to her Hindi New Testament. The very touch of the binding, the now-familiar pages with their underlined verses brought security.

Marianna did little to help Coral's own spiritual struggle. Receiving no sympathy from Kathleen, her younger sister leaned on her for the faith that she lacked. Marianna, who feared anything that buzzed, hissed, growled, or simply spun a web, was terrified of the jungle crawling with poisonous snakes and prowling tigers.

She and Marianna read Psalm 18, memorizing the promises together.

"The Lord is my rock," Coral began. "Now it is your turn."

"And my fortress, and my deliverer." Marianna scanned the riverbank out of the corner of her eye. "My God, my strength, in whom I will trust; my buckler, and the horn of my salvation—"

"And my high tower," Coral concluded. "Stop looking for crocodiles!"

Coral knew that her words were meant not only to comfort Marianna but also to remind herself.

On an afternoon when it was safe to disembark and allow the kansamah to cook supper on land, Ethan refused to leave the barge, and Coral began to worry about him. "Your supplies are safe enough, Ethan. Do come join us by the fire. Seward says one of the sowars will stand guard."

"I shall eat here, my dear," he insisted. "Send one of the soldiers with a dish. And do make sure the victuals are well cooked. Vermin infest the waterfowl."

Was he ill? Coral wondered. She looked for Jace, but he had gone off an hour earlier on his own. Now as she walked precariously toward the trees through which he had disappeared, she frowned. Anything could happen to Ethan alone on that barge. Suppose he fell into the river again? It was not likely, of course, but they were entering tiger country. Had not Jace said that the tigers were bold enough to attack fishermen in their boats?

It was a menacing sundown that streaked the sky red, while the jungle brush reflected the shades of flame. Coral stepped with caution across the ground, with her mind on snakes. Her ears were attentive, listening for the low rumble of a tiger, but there was nothing except the quiet chortle of jungle birds settling down in the twilight for the night.

She walked under an overhang of branches, contacting a thick, sticky web that brushed against her face. Ugh! With a swift move of her hand she brushed it aside. She was about to walk on when Jace emerged through some trees, looking sweaty and hot but merrily whistling. Dirt was smudged across one side of his face, and he was carrying wild honey and several fowl, already plucked for the kansamah to roast.

He stopped when he saw her, and Coral decided that he was not pleased.

"Careful where you wander. I came across a python. It caught a wild pig," he said.

Coral envisioned the huge viper crushing the pig as it tightened its grasp about its victim's body. She shuddered, rubbing her arms, and glanced about cautiously. "It is Ethan. He refuses to leave the barge."

Jace dangled the gaunt birds by their feet, and she watched their heads flop about.

"I thought the physician was supposed to do the worrying? If you will permit the observation, you are looking frail, even if your spirit is dauntless."

His remark made her aware that the strands of her hair had come undone from the chignon. Self-consciously she brushed them away from her cheek. A safari was not exactly the environment for careful grooming.

"Tell the doctor to forget his beetles and butterflies, and do some fussing over you."

"I prefer as little fuss as possible, thank you. What do you expect to do with those scrawny birds?"

"Treat your finicky appetite to the unforgettable delights of my cooking. What else?"

"You cook?" She was not really surprised; it was like Jace to be independent.

"My dear girl, but of course! How do you think I have managed to survive all these years? On Gokul's curry and rice? Tonight I shall dismiss the kansamah, and fix roast waterfowl glazed with wild honey and mango stuffing. How does that sound?"

Coral glanced at the birds with their flopping heads, their eyes still open and staring at her. "Thank you, but perhaps rice will do."

He laughed, then scowled at the birds. "I do not

blame you for refusing the moonlight dinner. Not much to look at, are they?"

Coral followed his scowl to the scrawny plucked birds with their long, shapeless legs suspended like puppets on a string. For no apparent reason, she began to giggle.

He looked at her for a long moment, then smiled, and when Coral could not stop, he too began to laugh. He extended the birds with an elegant bow. "After you, Lady Kendall. I shall deliver my prize to the kansamah, then proceed to rescue Boswell from the barge."

Coral curtseyed. "Thank you, Major. You are kind. What would I do without you?" She cast him a glance, wondering if he would choose to make something of her words.

With concealed relief that he had let the opportunity slip by, Coral turned to walk ahead.

"Stop. Do not move," he commanded.

His voice held a note of authority that she accepted without question. She held her breath, listening, but only the buzz of a mosquito about her ear disturbed the deepening twilight. A faint rustle of leaves stirred in a breeze. What did he hear? A tiger's pant? A cobra slithering through the grasses? Jace was in tune with the jungle and experienced with danger. Her skin tingled as she waited, but only silence surrounded them.

She heard his steps come up behind her, then pause. Coral could feel his gaze, and an odd quiver inched up her back. She tensed. "Would you mind telling me why you are staring at the back of my neck?"

She waited, but he gave no answer. She was about to turn when his hand closed firmly about her forearm. "Do not move."

It was then that she felt something tickle the back of her neck. Suddenly repulsed, she sucked in her breath. *That web!* She fought an impulse to scream.

"Stay calm," came Jace's quiet voice.

A moan escaped through her lips as the slow, ticklish movement of gentle legs walked across the back of her neck and came up to a stop below her earlobe.

A spider! The imagery that jumped into her mind sent her heart pounding. A trickle of perspiration ran down her sides. It had to be huge! She could feel the hairy, spindly legs! She would faint, she would scream, she would slap at it with her palm in hysterics—

"Easy."

"No, no, no—" came her voice, ragged with fear.

His grip about her arm tightened like iron and she winced. But it brought her mind momentarily off the spider. "In a moment it will crawl up the side of your face to your hair where I can safely knock it off."

She bit her lip and wanted to cry. *Lord, please make it crawl away.*

"Jace . . . I cannot stand it," she gritted, her fingers digging into her skirts. "I can feel it *moving*!"

His short laugh came unexpectedly, and with it came a stiffening of her back.

"And this is the little girl who boasts of warding off angry Hindus to gather children under her wings? Why, in another moment you will scream and swoon into a heap of petticoats."

She caught her breath with a gasp that wanted to choke her, but his light mockery stiffened her resolve.

"Did you not tell me you feared nothing in all India? Now you can prove it."

Coral closed her eyes, squeezing them so tightly that tears oozed from the corners. She swallowed, her throat dry, and whispered, "What is it doing?"

"It has decided to get cozy. Patience."

"Do *something*!"

"I cannot. It is in the groove of your neck."

"If you do not, I will!"

"Do not move. This is not your little spider at Manali. It's deadly. Once he moves a little more to the right, I will have it."

His hand squeezed her arm again, and his voice was kind. "Concentrate on the Lord. Isn't that what you told Marianna to do? Now the Lord has given you an opportunity to trust Him. Remember your verses?"

"I c-can't think!"

Jace let out a quiet breath. "Lord, if you would just get the thing to move a few inches."

Coral felt the perspiration dampen her forehead. It was moving again, this time from beneath her ear, up the side of her face, each leg stepping slowly, cautiously touching her cheek, her temple, and now her forehead.

She did not dare open her eyes for fear she would see it. She could hear her heart thumping.

"Just another moment, Coral. Nice and steady—" His hand struck quickly, swiping it off her hair and tossing it to the jungle floor. "There. You are safe."

Relief brought a surge of weakness. She held his arm and dropped her forehead against him with a catch in her throat. She felt his fingers touch the side of her face where the spider had been, smoothing aside the damp tendrils of hair.

"It is all over now," he said softly.

She could have stayed there with his arm about her waist and basked in the hypnotic effect of his touch, but her senses came awake. Her eyes opened and she became aware of a new danger.

Her head came up to confront his close gaze, and her emotions took a tumble. If she did not resist the beckoning enticement now, it would be too late. And then what?

His arm released her. "I think," he said, "that we best get back."

Coral felt a rush of embarrassment to think that he had been the one to suggest it. She took several steps backward, her breath short. Her eyes dropped to the ground between them. The spider was cautiously stepping its way across the ground cover, and heading toward the vines that draped from the trees. The creature was the size of a mango. It was not black as she had imagined, but chocolate brown with speckles of yellow. She shuddered. If there was one spider, there must be more. She glanced up into the tree branches, rubbing her arms as her skin prickled.

Jace stepped on the spider with his boot and something spurted. Coral nearly gagged, covered her face with her palms, and turned away.

"Alas, fair maiden! The dragon has been slain! Shall we go?" He snatched up the gangly birds with a slight smile, and the intensity of the previous moment vanished.

Relieved, yet vaguely disappointed that he could shed it so easily, she quickly turned away. "Thank you for your help, Major. I think I hear Sir Hugo calling." She gathered up her skirts and walked past the squashed spider without another glance.

Sir Hugo was coming through the trees just as Coral emerged. His countenance was hard as his eyes went past her to Jace Buckley, following leisurely behind.

"I've engaged the major to see that Ethan leaves the barge," she said.

"Ethan is not a child. I suggest you allow him his own opinion and not run to Buckley with all your grievances."

She was startled by his anger. "I don't run to the major with every petty misfortune, Uncle. But since he is in command of the trek north, it is fitting he should know about Ethan."

Sir Hugo said nothing as Jace walked up. She wondered if Jace had overheard. Embarrassed, Coral brushed past them both and returned to camp. When all was quiet about the campfire, with the guards on duty, Coral tried to sleep, listening to the breathing of her sisters lying next to her. She felt ashamed of herself. There had been a brief moment when she had felt something that she was certain no decent girl should ever experience. And she had experienced that emotion not with Ethan, but the very one she knew she must avoid! And to make it all the harder to bear, *he* had been the one to calmly draw away, reminding her, as though she were a child, that they must get back to the others.

How scandalous! Had he been able to guess? Had her uncle?

No, Jace could not have known, she decided with deep relief. It had all happened too quickly, and he had glossed over it unawares, completely absorbed with the spider. If he had not stepped on it, crushing it—well, he had, and she could only guess that he had done it deliberately. It certainly had brought reality crashing between them.

24

Jace knew the route to follow and the difficulties to be encountered. Seward was in charge of camping sites, and they were few and far between. Often Coral strained her ears to hear Seward whispering to Jace that the risk was too great to disembark, for the campfire and smell of humans would attract the tigers. On many dark nights they lit fishing lanterns and remained on board the boats rather than camp on land, and always Jace saw that Coral and her sisters had more than their share of sowars guarding the barge.

During the jungle trek, Coral often found her thoughts wandering toward William Carey. His dedication to the work of the Lord encouraged her to measure her own spiritual fervor. By enabling grace, Master Carey and his family had managed to survive the suffering of life in the jungle terrain of the Sunderbans in the heart of the delta. Somehow he had managed to build a bamboo house to live in, and had even planted his garden— something that Carey did wherever he went. How long had he and his family lived in the delta, she wondered. It took courage and commitment to stay the course. Who could fault Mrs. Carey for becoming ill? She thought of herself. Did she have that measure of dedication to the One she called Lord?

"The Sunderbans is where William Carey's little boy Peter died, and Mrs. Carey became ill. She still has not recovered," Coral told Seward as they watched the sun rise over the jungle trees.

" 'Tis no wonder to me. Making a living there be hard as iron. The man had himself more than his share of courage. Would make me shudder, leaving London with a wife and children for a spot like that." He shook his head sadly.

Coral's eyes shone, and she looked out across the river. "He came, knowing the desperate need of India, knowing that there was only One who could break the chains of darkness. No sacrifice was too much to ask of himself or of his family, knowing the price the Lord willingly paid."

"Now, little lassie," he wheedled. "Ye frighten me to wit's end when ye go talking like that. 'Tis the steps of Master Carey you be willing to follow, and I don't like the looks of the way they lead."

Coral smiled up at him and looped her arm through his. "Do not worry, Seward. I could never be as brave. My steps lead to a different path. And I promise, a school on Kingscote must have Elizabeth and Hampton's approval before I ask you to lift a hand to help me build it."

His bushy brows came down, and he cocked his head, lowering his tricorn. Coral laughed at his suspicious eye.

"So ye be intending to involve poor Seward in your scheme, do you? I suspect ye intend to get a structure up before the rains. But don't go forgetting your uncle. He will have something to say to Sir Hampton about this school of yours. He be dead set against it from the start. And he won't change his mind anytime soon."

"Mother will be on my side. You wait and see. She has always had a love for the untouchables."

"Aye, that I know. And 'tis that which bothers me. She knows you grieve for Gem."

Gem. His name winged its way through her heart, bringing sweet memories. Would Jace be able to discover his whereabouts? And if he did, could she manage to retrieve him? She wanted to tell Seward, but since Jace had asked her not to mention it to anyone, she kept the secret locked within her heart. If Jace wanted to explain to Seward, he could do so himself. But she longed to share the hope with someone, and somehow Seward offered the biggest shoulder to lean on.

"What would you say if I told you Gem might come home?"

Seward's head turned, and his gaze was as sharp as a hawk's. Coral's eyes glistened, and her hand squeezed his arm.

"What's this? Gem returning home to Kingscote? Who told you such a thing? Lass, ye need be careful about dreams."

There was a movement behind them, and Coral whirled, her hand still on Seward. It was Sir Hugo. His dark handsomeness was foreboding as he stood in jungle hat and knee-length coat, a rifle in one hand and a pistol strapped about his hip.

"I think it best, my dear, you not wander the barge alone. Stay with your sisters under the awning."

"You're leaving the barge?" she asked, noting he also carried a leather satchel.

"I shall ride one of the boats in the lead. Do be cautious."

"Yes, Uncle, of course," she said, hoping her relief over his departure did not show. If he was in the lead boat, she wouldn't be under his constant eye.

"And Major Buckley?" she asked.

She felt her uncle's penetrating gaze rummage

through her mind, as though wondering about her motive in asking.

"The major will remain on the barge, not that I agree with the decision. He ought to be in the lead boat, but since he insists otherwise, I shall take the position."

From the corner of her eye, she could see Seward straighten a little with displeasure.

"The major be knowin' the river like you know the innards of the Company, Sir Roxbury. Rest assured he knows what he's about."

Hugo's mouth curved. "Your loyalty is undaunting, Seward." He turned to join the manji, who waited to bring him to a small boat, giving a last warning to Coral. "The river will soon be full of crocodiles. You best watch Marianna."

When he had gone, Seward looked after him with a scowl, lowering his hat. "Your uncle be good at intruding and imposing himself on others' business!"

"And rightly so," came Ethan's voice, but if he was offended at Seward's opinion, his expression did not show it. He appeared to be in a good mood as he walked up, and ignoring Seward, said cheerfully, "Good morning, Coral. Have you by chance read Marco Polo?"

Seward was silent, eying him, but Coral smiled. "Good morning, Ethan. No, I have not. I suppose you have, or you would not have inquired."

"I must say it was a fascinating read." He shaded his eyes with his hand and scanned the riverbanks. "He made mention of India, of course. Said he may have discovered the unicorn. I wonder if there are any about?"

Coral glanced at Seward who smirked beneath his beard. "There be none about these parts, Doctor. But if ye be wanting our opinion—that is, the major and me—'tis the one-horn rhino near Kingscote that be Mister Polo's unicorn."

"Indeed? Then we will see the brutes? Marvelous!"

Seward warmed at Doctor Boswell's interest in wild-life, and leaned his arm against the rail before launching into a discussion. "Now, if ye be interested in more than bugs and beetles, I can take you on a safari around Jor-hat."

"Kingscote is near there?"

"Aye, the plantation be running for miles along the Bramaputra River and into the jungle. If ye wish to see the rhinos, the best way is by elephant."

"I shall take you up on that, Seward, my friend. Per-haps you can suggest the best location on Kingscote for my lab as well. I should like it away from the house. My work calls for isolation. Say, a half an hour's walking distance."

"Sir Hampton be letting you do as you wish, I am sure of that much. He be grateful if you can get Lady Elizabeth back on her feet again."

"Believe me, Seward, I shall certainly try. I could not bear to see Coral going through a summer without a smile to lighten her face."

Coral turned to him with one of her loveliest smiles just as her eyes met Jace. There was a slight turn to his mouth as he walked up to the group.

Seward said, "Morning, lad. Did the kansamah bring you some coffee?"

"Yes, Seward, thanks. Morning, Miss Kendall, Doc-tor," said Jace.

"Major," said Ethan. "I understand we are nearing the worst of the delta. I find it fascinating! How is it that you and Seward know so much about it?"

"The major's been in India since he was twelve," said Seward.

"You are near to being a native yourself," said Bos-well. "There must be little you do not know of the land or of its strange assortment of religions."

"I was raised by a guru," offered Jace flatly, folding his arms. "What would you like to know, Doctor?"

Coral guessed that he enjoyed shocking Boswell. But she remembered back to that day in Calcutta when she had stumbled upon the widow burning. Jace had appeared to know something of the person and work of Christ. As she glanced at Ethan, she read his expression, and knew that the thought of being raised by one of India's strange mystic gurus did indeed shock him.

She hastened, "Oh, do tell us about the delta, Major. Do you think we will run into a tiger?"

"After our venture with the spider, are you now anticipating more excitement, Miss Kendall?"

She was about to say something when Jace turned to Ethan. "I would be interested in knowing the kind of spider that put Miss Kendall to bed for days."

There was an uncomfortable pause, and Coral's breath paused with it.

"Ah, if only I did, Major. I am afraid I can offer little information. You see, I am not acquainted with the strange species of India. Not that I am sure this one came from India, mind you. At least Sir Hugo and Mr. Harrington had never seen this particular species before in Manali."

So, thought Coral. That should answer Jace's suspicions.

She looked at Jace almost triumphantly, but he was casually studying Boswell.

"Then that explains why it took so long to get Miss Kendall back on her feet," he said smoothly. "You were not quite sure how to treat the poison?"

Ethan's smile was menacing. "Quite, Major. Mr. Harrington decided the spider may have been brought unwittingly into the house in a shipment he had sent for from the jungles near Malaysia. You have been to Malaysia, I understand?"

"Yes."

"Ah, a pity I do not have the spider with me. You might look at it and enlighten us. I kept it in a bottle for several weeks until it died."

"A pity."

"I have seen one spider too many," interrupted Coral, "so I shall not mourn its absence. If you gentleman will excuse me, I have some studying to do."

"Ah, Hindi, of course," said Ethan. "Your intelligence is a treat, Coral. So many women today would prefer to read magazines from Paris offering the latest hats."

"I imagine Miss Kendall would look enchanting in a Paris hat," came Jace's resonant voice.

Coral refused to blush, although she would not meet his eyes. She imagined he had said it to rile Ethan, yet her memory ran back to their meeting in the Calcutta bazaar, when he had asked her if they had met in Paris.

Ethan turned to him, his expression cold and challenging. "And I suppose you have been to Paris as well?"

Jace smiled. "I find travel one of my most treasured pleasures."

Coral turned, relieved, as the head boatman walked up and salaamed. She took her leave, coming up to where her sisters sat under the awning. She removed her hat and fanned herself briskly.

By afternoon, the fears that the head boatman had already delivered to Jace filtered down to Coral. The water level was low in places, and this proved difficult for the village oarsmen. She heard a second discussion in progress as the boatman and Seward tried to explain the situation to Ethan.

Jace walked up, hands on hips. "Now what?" came his flat question.

"The doctor not be agreein' about the barge and the upcoming silt beds."

"What can be done, Major?" snapped Ethan, as though Seward and the boatman were both going out of their way to be disagreeable.

"As I explained earlier, we can use the barge for perhaps another day, then we must proceed without it," said Jace.

"What! I will not consider removing my supplies from the barge!"

Jace turned to the boatman and spoke in Bengali. From where Coral stood under the awning she caught snatches of the discussion. Within several hours they would come to a bad section of the river, due to the low seasonal levels of water.

"Silt very thick, sahib," the boatman tried to explain to the infuriated Boswell. "Water very shallow! No good! Barge too big, sahib!"

"Under no circumstances will any boatman remove my supplies. I hope that is clear."

More trouble, thought Coral as she walked up. Hoping to allay matters, she smiled sweetly at Jace.

Jace folded his arms and said lazily, "Perhaps you can convince the doctor, Miss Kendall."

Coral turned to Ethan, who looked in no mood to be placated. "I fear it is all our fault, Ethan. The major warned of this in Manali."

But Ethan was still glaring at the boatman as if the matter were a conspiracy against him.

"The major sent Seward and several sowars upriver this morning to check the water level," said Coral. "We have no choice."

"But leave my supplies? Good heavens, Coral! Impossible!"

"I've already spoken to the manjis," said Jace calmly.

"They will bring the rest of your equipment back to Manali on the barge. Mr. Harrington can then prepare a careful shipment to Calcutta."

"Careful? What do novices know of medical equipment and my samples? Do you realize what pains I have taken to get samples of fauna and insects?"

"Quite aware," Jace said evenly.

Ethan caught himself, apparently remembering the crocodiles. He sighed and ran a hand over his face. "Major, you must forgive me. I am overwrought."

"As soon as Plassey is under British control, Captain McKay will be able to bring your equipment."

"The major is right, Ethan," Coral interjected. "I am relieved to have taken his advice in Manali. Your equipment can be sent on to Kingscote with my school supplies."

"Doctor, you must decide what you wish to bring with you. Baggage will be kept to what you can carry," said Jace.

"This is appalling," said Ethan. He turned stiffly and walked across the barge to survey his small mountain of crates and barrels. On the peak, the tiny tent-lab stood precariously. A black and white fowl that had landed to perch squawked and flew into the jungle.

When Coral awakened that afternoon, it was to the movement of water beneath the hard planks of the barge. She stared up at the branches that extended over the river and caught glimpses of a family of monkeys swinging from limb to limb in noisy chatter. From the position of the sun she guessed that she must have dozed off after the lunch of mangoes and coconuts.

She sat up. Kathleen and Marianna were still napping. Low voices caught her attention. Jace was again on the barge, and Seward was talking to him. Looking ahead, she saw the shallow areas coming into view. Here they would board the small boats, and several of the village boatmen would bring the barge back to Manali. Coral awoke her sisters, then gathered together their baggage.

When Seward had gone, she walked up to where Jace stood at the end of the barge. His eyes were on the thicket along the waterway, dense with jungle growth and trees. She stood next to him, saying nothing, her thoughts on the danger lurking silently beyond their line of sight.

Vines wrapped about some of the branches like pythons, reaching across the river to form a woven screen, casting deep shadows on the water. Coral knew enough of Bengal tigers to understand that they lie waiting in ambush. In the heavy thicket along the water, they could stalk the slow-moving boats for some distance without being noticed.

She glanced about at the other boats. The sowars were alert, two guarding each boat with rifles. Coral could feel the tension in the air. Vines and tree branches interlaced into an arbor above them, and birds and monkeys squawked and chattered overhead. Water slapped the side of the barge. Coral was so engrossed in staring ahead that she did not even hear the insect buzzing at her ear. The barge slid across the water, the dip and slice of the poles making a rhythmic swoosh.

The head manji glanced about the riverbank with nervous eyes. "Sahib Buckley, it is here we part. Please do not wait."

"Understood."

"Seward's boat is coming," said Coral, seeing his rugged form rowing with two sowars. Sir Hugo and his servants waited for them in a clearing in one of the other boats. Jace signaled the manji to bring the barge to the

286

bank. A minute later Seward boarded while the two so-wars kept a watchful eye on the jungle behind them. The baggage was loaded, and Kathleen and Marianna were lifted into Seward's boat.

"What about Ethan?" Coral asked, and turned to look up at the crow's nest.

Jace walked toward the supplies and shouted up. "Doctor!"

"I am coming—but I need help with the crates."

Jace said something under his breath and stood with hands on hips. Coral hurried around the supplies to the other side.

"Ethan, do hurry. It is dangerous here—"

She stopped, unable to believe her eyes. Ethan was dragging several crates behind him that he had tied together with rope. Coral's heart sank. Jace would be furious.

"You cannot take all that," she whispered.

"Nonsense," came his cryptic reply. "The boat can hold this without difficulty."

Coral turned as Jace strode up. He, too, stopped. She watched his annoyed expression.

"Will they fit?" she asked in a small voice.

Jace's cynical gaze held hers until she straightened her straw hat and glanced at Ethan's trunk. Jace turned to Ethan. "You may bring one crate and one bag. Even that is generous."

"How do you expect me to set up a lab with something so meager?"

"Your lab, sir, is the least of my concerns at the moment."

Ethan looked at him with cold anger. "No, I cannot."

Jace stepped back and gestured his arm down toward the small boat. "Allow good sense to prevail."

"Major, I—"

"If you do not move, you will take nothing. Consider that an order."

Ethan stared angrily at Jace's unrelenting features, then turned to his possessions. "Seward! If you will, I shall take this crate. Do be extraordinarily careful. And I shall carry my own bag."

As Coral waited, she glanced at Jace. A harbinger of unease crept up her spine. Her breath paused. Jace's gaze narrowed as if picking up her alarm. Suddenly he grabbed her arm and pulled her toward him. "The monkeys . . ." Jace began.

"They stopped chattering!" whispered Coral.

"What is it?" Seward called.

Coral looked up. Her throat constricted and a scream died. On the overhanging limb crouched a male Bengal tiger. Ten feet of rippling black and gold splendor tensed for the spring, his jaws partly open, his yellow eyes savage with fury. He seemed to consider his next move, lifting his head slightly, his lips drawn back, and a low rumble reverberated in his throat. The gnarl hovered above her like thunder, shaking and rattling her bones. Coral felt her body hurled to one side, and she landed on the deck, stunned, while both tiger and gun shots converged.

The shots had come from the sowars, but the beast was far from dead. One shot had missed, splintering the branch, the other grazed its shoulder, and the wound only maddened it.

The Indian manji screamed—"Save me, sahib!"—just as the tiger lunged and the splintered limb fell to the barge. A flash of yellow and black brought down the screaming boatman. Jace steadied his aim and fired. The bullet smashed into the tiger's chest. The sight nauseated Coral, and somewhere in the distance she heard Marianna's hysterical screaming.

The tiger's yellow eyes were not on her, nor on the

writing manji. It came bounding toward Jace, becoming a momentary blur of color that collided with a second blast of his gun, knocking Jace backward as they plunged into the river, sending a spray of fetid water splashing over Coral's skirt. Dazed, sickened by the moans of the manji and the smell of blood, a welcome darkness closed about her like a drawn shade upon her reason.

25

Coral awoke, aware of the anxious voices of her sisters crowded about her and a babble of men's voices in the distance. But there was something else, something stinging her nostrils as she tried to breathe . . . and she moaned, trying to turn her head. Her eyes fluttered open, and she saw Jace bending over her. Her head rested on his arm, while his other hand waved something in front of her nose.

She reached a feeble hand. "Stop—"

"She is all right now," stated Kathleen.

"I . . . w-what is that smell. . . ." murmured Coral.

"Smelling salts," said Jace. "You fainted."

She stiffened, remembering her promise to him that she would *never* faint. He obviously recalled their conversation too, for his smile was disconcertingly pleasant, and that made it worse. She pushed away the vapors and struggled to sit up.

"I am all right now, Major." It came rushing back. "The tiger! You are not hurt?"

"No."

"But the chief boatman is badly mauled," said Kathleen.

Something in her sister's tone told Coral there was cause for alarm that went beyond the unfortunate injury. Coral watched as Jace walked over to where Ethan was attending the wounded man. The rest of the hired manjis from Manali were gathered together with Sir Hugo. Jace walked up to him, and they talked in low tones.

"What is it?" asked Coral of Kathleen. "What is happening?"

"It is dreadful," whispered Kathleen. "The boatmen are blaming the misfortune on their god. Uncle Hugo insists they be allowed to placate Kali."

Kali? thought Coral, still dazed. She tried to recall what she had learned about the Hindu god. *The fiercest of gods . . . she rides a tiger and holds the weapons of destruction in her hands. . . .*

She strained to hear what Sir Hugo and Jace were saying. The manjis, along with her uncle and Seward, were preparing to leave the barge for the jungle.

Jace was reloading his gun. *What were they going to do?* Coral wondered. A terrible suspicion gripped her. She struggled to her feet.

"Coral, stay out of it," she heard Kathleen whisper, but she could not. She hurried to Jace, taking hold of his arm.

"What are they doing, Jace? Tell me."

"You're pale and shaking. Better go lie down."

"Where are my uncle and Seward going?"

"The manjis are spooked over the tiger attack. They insist on a religious ritual. They want to go ashore."

She rubbed her arms and glanced in the direction of the wounded Indian. "Kali rides the tiger because she is in control of its strength, is that it?"

"That's the idea. Kali wears a garland, but not of flowers. She adorns herself with skulls because she handles the destructive side of Hinduism and demands sacrifices." He stopped. "I think you now understand what is going on in the minds of the manjis and sowars. They spoke of it when Boswell fell into the river and the crocodiles converged on us. The fact that he was saved quieted matters down. Now there's this attack on the chief manji. Kali is vengeful."

Coral looked at him with growing alarm. "And they want to sacrifice before we go on?"

"Yes."

The thought was appalling. A sacrifice to Kali!

Jace was unreadable. She sensed, however, his veiled interest in her reaction to all of this.

But will he allow it? she wondered, recalling the incident of suttee after she had left William Carey. She also recalled that at the time he had suggested she stay out of such matters and leave the Hindu beliefs to India. Why did she expect his attitude to have changed in two months? However, he would know that in good conscience she could not leave darkness alone without trying to light a candle.

"You are not going to permit this?" she whispered.

"Believe me, Coral, I've little choice. If I do not, they will take their boats and return to Manali. That will leave us on foot in the delta. You are wise enough to know what that means."

She was. . . . Were they prepared to walk to the Bramaputra in a tiger-infested delta?

"But you have the six sowars from the troop," she argued, trying to keep her voice low. "Can you not command them to force the manjis to take us on the rest of the journey?"

"Do you think I have not thought of that? The sowars are also Hindus. After the mutiny at Plassey, I doubt very much if I can command them to do anything they find contrary to their religion. Oh, yes, they would salute, they would pretend to carry out my order. But I doubt if we could go to sleep tonight and awake with the sowars still on duty. I cannot risk the lives of you and the others."

Frustrated, Coral turned to watch her uncle and Seward rowing the small boat toward the jungle, following the manjis and sowars. They would trap a live sacrifice for Kali and offer it on a makeshift altar.

"There must be something you can do," she whispered. "Let me talk to them!"

"The way you did at the suttee back in Calcutta? I think not! You'll only make matters worse. Now go to your tent."

She stared up at him, helpless to stop it, yet knowing his course of action proved the wiser. And yet, his dismissal nettled her.

He must have noticed, for his mouth formed a wry smile. "Please."

"But, it's positively heathen to force poor Seward to attend the ritual."

"Madame, I am not forcing *poor Seward* to do anything he doesn't wish to do. I need another gun. To be frank, I don't trust Roxbury."

She drew in a breath. "What—"

"She is right, Major. We'll have none of this," Ethan's cold voice interrupted.

Oh, no! she thought, whirling around to face her cousin. Ethan's interference was the last thing they needed now!

Evidently Jace agreed, for he returned Ethan's hard stare and said flatly, "Stay out of this, Boswell; you have a wounded man to care for. No one is expecting you to involve your conscience."

"It is enough that you have asked the others to do so. And you insult the Christian sensibilities of Miss Kendall."

"That can't be helped. Interfere now, when you know nothing of what is involved, and I can guarantee that by morning you will have exceedingly more patients, and they will not all be natives."

"I will not stay out of it, *sir*. This Kali nonsense is all quite offensive to me, as well as Miss Kendall."

"I suppose you would rather see three women on foot in tiger country? Do you have any idea how far it is to Guwahati?"

"No, but I am quite certain we can find boatmen in the next village."

"The next village does not exist. It is a month till we reach Sualkashi. You will stay on the barge. You may guard the women if you can use a gun. There are still tigers in the area."

"I can use a gun, Major, and quite well as a matter of fact."

Coral saw a cold glitter in Jace's eyes that she had come to recognize as best left alone.

She said quickly, "Ethan, the major is right after all. There is nothing we can do."

Ethan stared coldly at Jace. "I fear you are quite right. There is nothing anyone with any moral sensibilities could do to convince the major of this despicable act. Perhaps he has been too long in India himself to understand those of us who are civilized and of Christian principles."

She sensed with a certain dread what was coming, but before she could act, Jace grabbed Ethan by the front of his cravat.

Jace's words came with brutal clarity. "I may take a slap across the face from a woman, but not from you. Your talk is little else but cheap hypocrisy, directed to impress Coral. It has impressed no one else. You speak of your loyalty to Christianity? You would sell your soul to marry a silk heiress!" He released him abruptly and turned to go.

Ethan said something between his teeth and grabbed Jace's shoulder, jerking him around. Ethan appeared prepared to backhand him, but Jace struck him with a savage blow, sending him crashing backward into his crates. Ethan lay sprawled, unconscious.

Coral sucked in her breath, but remained calm. Her eyes darted to Jace, and seeing his challenging expression, as if he expected her to rush to Ethan's side, her jaw set.

"That was quite uncalled for, Major," she said, surprised her voice didn't shake.

He showed no remorse, and certainly no sympathy. "He'll survive. I won't say as much for the rest of us if you insist on imposing your standards on the manjis."

She knew he was right. Jace's understanding of the Hindu people stood in stark contrast to Ethan's lack of experience. Jace had proved wiser, yet she felt irritated with both men for behaving as they had. Turning abruptly, she left him.

Jace stared after her for a moment, the blue-black of his eyes glittering; then he too turned and left for the small boat.

Coral joined Kathleen, who was kneeling beside Ethan with a wet rag, wiping his face. Her sister was pale and shaking but silent.

"Oh, I want to go home!" Marianna choked. "I hate this journey! I positively hate it!"

Coral was convinced of only one thing. If she was ever to confront India with Christianity, she would need to find another way. A gentle, loving way that did not alienate and breed confrontation. She had thought she could handle it, but she was now aware of her own weakness, failure, and fear.

"Maybe Uncle Hugo is right," said Coral wearily. "I have caused little but trouble, and no good has come from anything I have done since Jemani's baptism! Even Rajiv died—and Gem was abducted! Maybe I should forget everything! It is not worth it. Nothing is worth hate and violence!"

Surprisingly, it was Kathleen who came to her defense. "It was their angry reactions that did this. You are not to blame. It would have happened eventually anyway. And if you ask me, it had less to do with Kali or Christianity than it did with how Ethan and Jace feel about you. Besides, how can you even talk about giving up when you want to build that school for the untouchables? What do you care if others misunderstand? You cannot quit now; you have not even begun!"

Shocked, Coral looked into her sister's face, surprised at what she had heard. Kathleen's amber eyes gleamed with an emotion Coral had never seen before.

"But it is you who wish to go back to the Silk House!" said Coral.

Kathleen looked determined. "The important thing right now is that you, too, do not lose your dream. I may not go back to London—ever. I may not become a designer in the Silk House. But I shall truly be discouraged if you lose what you believe in."

"Why, Kathleen," she breathed. "I did not know; I never guessed you would come to my side like this. I thought—"

"I know what you thought. And maybe you were right. But everything that has just happened has made me think differently. I want you to win your struggle for the mission school on Kingscote, Coral. And Marianna and I are going to help."

"Oh, yes, we will, Coral," said Marianna. "We will

stand with you when you talk to Papa and Mother, and we will pray, too!"

Coral reached both arms for her sisters, hugging them to her.

Ethan was stirring. "W-what happened?"

"Some bad things worked together for good, that's what," said Marianna.

"Coming from you, Miss Pessimist, that *is* something," said Coral, laughing.

"Here, Cousin Ethan, drink some water," said Marianna. "And then you best do something about the cut on your lip. Oh, dear, you're bleeding—"

"Here, let me," said Kathleen, raising his head and bringing the canteen to his mouth.

298

26

The dawn beckoned with the first reddish hue of a new day of adventure. Coral heard the screech of a jungle cock, then the voice of Seward singing: "Amazing grace, how sweet the sound, that saved a wretch like me. . . ." She silenced her body's groan and forced herself to crawl out from under the bedroll she shared with Marianna and Kathleen. The relentless journey resumed.

The delta now lay behind them, and they continued the trek down the Ganges River. At the village, they had purchased supplies and rested for a day before resuming their journey. Coral thought she had never been so exhausted but was determined not to let anyone know. She had insisted to Jace that she was strong enough, and now she must not disappoint him or Seward by becoming an extra burden they did not need.

At the Ganges, the remainder of the manjis left them to return to Manali, and Jace and Seward hired other small boats to bring them down the wide river to the Bramaputra.

The long days marched on one by one. Coral felt as if she had ended up in the major's 21st Light Cavalry. He set a rigorous pace, but she did not complain, nor did

Kathleen and Marianna. They knew the reason, as did Sir Hugo. Having experienced the seasons, they understood the risk of the monsoon. The month delay at Manali had robbed them of important time. Coral tried to get Ethan to understand as the camp stirred to wakefulness, the campfire still burning red against the shadows.

"You have lived in Burma," she said. "You know what the monsoon means. If the major does not complete the journey before the rains start, we'll be forced to remain in one of the isolated villages for months. The entire Assam valley is usually flooded."

"I am aware of the danger, but I am also a doctor. You are near exhaustion. Can the major not see that?"

"Yes," came the cheerless reply from behind them. Coral turned, still in the process of braiding her hair, and saw Jace.

"If my memory serves me right," he said to Ethan, "I strongly advised Miss Kendall to return to Calcutta when we were at Harrington's."

What Jace did not say was what Coral and Ethan both knew. It had been Ethan who backed her up on her determination to come.

Ethan's cold stare riveted on Jace. Jace ignored him, turning his back toward Ethan to face Coral. Her eyes dropped to the mug in his hand.

"Coffee," he said, offering it to her.

Her lips turned up softly. "Thank you, Major." She took the cup from his hand, and a small smile played at the corners of his mouth before he turned and left.

"Arrogant—"

"Stop it, Ethan!" Turning abruptly away and taking her coffee with her, she strode off toward the river for her morning wash.

Coral shielded her eyes beneath her hat and glanced in the direction of the clouds. "How far to the Bramaputra?" she asked Seward, who was kneeling on the shore, splashing water on his dusty face.

" 'Tis my guess we've gone about a hundred kilometers on the Ganges. It be not far now."

As the sapping heat of May set in, building toward the rains, they arrived at a remote village near the junction of the Ganges and Bramaputra rivers.

"A bazaar," cried Marianna with excitement.

Kathleen, who had lost her bar of soap weeks earlier, clasped her hands together in delight.

While Jace and Seward found supplies, Coral went with Sir Hugo, Ethan, and her sisters. They bought dozens of personal items that would make their journey more comfortable, then visited the booths selling hot foods. Seward joined them, making much of the delicious meal.

"Where is the major?" Coral asked him, noticing that Jace had not joined them.

"Speaking to the tehsildar, the village headman, about hiring elephants farther ahead. Neither of us likes the feel of things," said Seward.

After replenishing their goods, they began the journey north up the great Bramaputra toward Guwahati. Coral grew more exhausted by the day and began masking spells of dizziness. Casting anxious glances in her small mirror, she was thankful that there were no dark circles beneath her eyes to give away her recurring illness.

I've got to get home. We are so close now.

Soon her appetite failed her. She thought no one noticed, for she was careful to throw her uneaten supper into the river.

"Feeding crocodiles?"

She turned, startled at Jace's voice. She refused to

show anything was wrong. "I wish you would not sneak up on me, Major."

"It's still some four hundred kilometers to Guwahati. Kingscote, two days more."

"I shall be all right," she insisted, and walked past him to where her sisters were gathered.

The heat continued to build. One morning, Coral awoke with a start to feel the bright sunlight. *Have I overslept? But why did they not awaken me?*

The campsite was nearly empty, her sisters no doubt having gone farther down the river to wash. She sat up and saw Sir Hugo standing with the major and Seward by the riverbank. Jace was talking in low tones. Hugo looked toward the distant cloud formations—harbingers of the monsoon.

It was unusual that the order to break camp had not come by now, thought Coral, glancing toward the position of the sun. The squeal of birds, sometimes shrill enough to pierce the ears, echoed in the trees. She dressed quickly and went to find the kansamah for a mug of hot tea, hoping to gain some strength.

When Seward gave the announcement, the news came as a pleasant surprise for Coral. The major believed he could procure elephants for a landward journey along the river toward Sualkashi. It would mean a less rigorous trek for the women, and Coral could lie down and sleep in the howdah if she wished.

"Elephants," said Coral with enthusiasm. "But where will you find them?"

"The major be friendly with the owner."

"I see." She was curious, glancing in Jace's direction.

"The trainer be not a man with liking for the British," said Seward in a low voice. "He deals with the maharaja at Guwahati, training elephants for battle. But Jace be knowing the man and is sure to get them since the trainer be a relative to Gokul."

The elephant trainer serves the maharaja. Thinking of Gem's royal blood, Coral met Jace's gaze and, for a moment, thought she saw a glimmer of anticipation in his deep blue eyes.

Coral heard the elephants trumpeting and stood, shading her eyes to gaze down the riverbank. The small cavalcade of brownish beasts were in view, their ears flapping, their feet stirring up the dust. They would ride on the backs of the elephants inside a howdah—the framework holding a seat large enough for several people, and decked with red and gold cloth. Astride the elephants' magnificent necks, close to their heads, rode the bronzed drivers, the mahouts. They were naked except for a cloth about their loins and the familiar dusty turban wrapped around their heads.

Coral smiled to herself and quickly tied on her hat. It had been years since she had ridden on an elephant, and she looked forward to the journey. The first elephant carrying Seward was followed by six more, with empty howdahs rocking on their strong backs.

Coral laughed at the moan coming from Marianna. "At least there are no more crocodiles. Come, elephants are the most wonderful animals in the world."

"Yes, like Rani?" said Kathleen with a wry suggestion in her voice.

Coral smiled at the mention of her pet elephant at Kingscote. Rani had become spoiled, trumpeting her disapproval if Coral ever forgot to have one of the boys lead her down to the river for her morning wallow.

Coral led her sisters to a young female, anxious to show that she knew something about the handling of her favorite animal. She gave a loving pat to the elephant's trunk, and a small, round eye looked down at her from under several long lashes, seeming to blink its approval.

"We will ride on this one. What is her name, mahout?"

The Indian lad smiled and stroked his hand downward across the trunk. "This is *Yakshi*, because she is a maiden who will one day be queen of the others." With a shout and a swat from his ankus, he brought the elephant down to a kneeling position. He threw down the rope ladder connected to the howdah.

Lifting her skirts, Coral climbed the ladder while the sowar held it steady. It was a long way up, and she gripped the rough rope with her gloves and tried to place her slippers into the moving rungs while the mahout leaned down to help her inside.

At last, Kathleen and Marianna were seated with her, high above the ground. Coral laughed at Marianna clinging to the side of the howdah as if the whole contraption would slide off the elephant's back.

Soon the elephant cavalcade began, with two sowars on the lead elephant followed by Yakshi. Just then, Yakshi curled her trunk, opened her mouth wide, and trumpeted her displeasure. "Behave, Yakshi!" the mahout yelled in Hindi. "You cannot be queen today!" But Yakshi's antics provoked two elephants to sidle back and offer their support. The trumpeting pierced the morning air, and the loud blast brought Marianna's hands against her ears. Coral winced at the deafening sound. But soon the elephants were on the move, and Coral focused her attention on the passing terrain. At last it seemed reasonable to dream contentedly of Kingscote. *Home!*

The days passed. The humidity continued to build toward the onset of the rains, and so did Coral's anticipation. Sunrise on the Bramaputra was rippling with golden light. Coral watched the fishermen in their small canoelike houseboats with thatched roofs. Elephant-back was the best way to view the rich and diverse wildlife, and Coral wondered how Ethan enjoyed the sight of the flock of pink flamingos. Assam was home to the native muga caterpillar, better known to Coral as the humble but glorious silkworm. There were also cheetahs, sometimes called an Indian panther, lions, tigers, and golden langur monkeys—which made her wonder if Jace missed his partner Goldfish.

On the north bank of the river, Coral was watching for something else. "There! See it?"

Kathleen and Marianna looked quickly in the direction she pointed.

The famous one-horned rhino stood dark against the tall yellow-brown elephant grass. Coral turned in the howdah and waved to Ethan, who was riding with Sir Hugo. She pointed toward the magnificent animal and heard him give a shout of exclamation: "The unicorn!" She laughed at his response, but then saw Major Buckley watching her. She averted her eyes, disturbed that his gaze could make her heart beat a little faster.

Only a grouping of chital, swift-footed spotted deer, captured their attention away from Marco Polo's unicorn.

When they arrived at Sualkashi, on the north bank of the Bramaputra, Coral's excitement mounted with her sisters'. They were perhaps no more than four days from Kingscote.

Sualkashi was noted for its fashionable silk-weaving centers, and Kingscote silk was often brought here by barge.

They arrived during the fair called a *mela*, and the bazaars were busy. Coral concentrated on the thought of the white walls and blue roof of Kingscote.

At the fair, she bought presents for the female servants of the house: silk scarves and beaded slippers. She had already purchased gifts for her parents and Alex in

London. She was pretending interest in a silver bracelet when a wave of dizziness assailed her. The low table appeared to heave, then sink, and she felt herself falling with it. A firm hand closed about her arm, holding her up.

"Thank you, Seward—I am all right. The sun is a trifle hot today."

"Deception does not become you."

Her chin jerked up, and she tried to focus on Jace. "Well, you just seem to appear out of nowhere at the oddest—"

"I think it is time I had a word with your *attentive* physician." He gazed down at her from beneath his hat.

Again she was aware of how dominant he was, and when their wills clashed, he reminded her of the walls of Jericho.

"You know quite well that my uncle will look for any excuse to delay my arrival at Kingscote."

"And that is why we are not going to give him one. You are going to bed for the next eighteen hours."

"And just how, sir, do you expect to arrange all that?"

He glanced about the bazaar. "There are some cushions over there by the shop. You can sit there like a proper young English woman and have tea with your sisters until I get back."

"Where are you going?"

"I know someone here," he said evasively. "A family."

"The man who owns the elephants?"

"Yes." He turned toward a booth. "Seward!" he called.

Seward walked up.

"Put on your best manners," said Jace. "You will be taking Miss Kendall and her sisters to tea. I will return soon."

How Jace managed it, she did not know. She and her sisters arrived by rickshaw at a private residence, where doves cooed in the mango trees. As they stepped from the rickshaw, she saw Jace speaking to a stalwart Indian man in his fifties. Some minutes later a young Indian girl arrived from the back of the house, her long, dark hair falling loosely down her back. The first thing Coral noticed was that she was quite attractive; the second thing was that her smile and eyes brightened when they fell on Jace.

Coral felt an irrational sense of annoyance with the girl. It was silly to fall all over him that way! And just *why* had the major brought her *here?* Her gaze moved from the girl's face to Jace's, saw his disarming smile, then watched him say something for her ears alone. Whatever it was brought bright, melodic laughter—*like a little bird,* thought Coral. She felt the girl's eyes turn toward her and her sisters, and then back to Jace, followed by another amused laugh. *And just what did he say about me?*

Coral felt her cheeks turning warm but did not bother to analyze the reason. The familiar look that passed between the girl and Jace brought a dart of resentment. Feeling guilty, Coral turned her head away with determination. Naturally a man like Jace would know other young women. She thought of Ethan. She must apologize to him when she next saw him for running off like this on a wild scheme of the major's. Why had she even listened to Jace?

Her heart thumped irregularly, and quite unexpectedly she found the faces of those around her becoming blurred. *If I faint now, I shall seem a silly fool. A spoiled Englishwoman who melts in the harsh reality of the world around her! It will give the girl another reason to be amused, and another reason for Jace Buckley to think of me as a fragile blossom!*

Yet the more she tried to retain her balance the more she felt ill. She became aware of a small flutter about her and the voice of Kathleen as she sank to the ground.

———

Coral stirred and sighed. . . . Her lashes fluttered open as a breath of warm wind moved the mosquito netting. The woven-grass screen on the window was wet, offering some relief from the heat. Her mind felt clear, and physically she felt more rested than she had in weeks.

She forced herself to sit up and cast aside the cover. She glanced about the room. It was small but neat, and scrubbed clean. Outside she heard the birds chittering. Kathleen and Marianna were still asleep on mats in the corner. Beside her was the empty tea cup—at least, she had thought it to be tea, and had a memory of Kathleen feeding the liquid to her a little at a time while Jace stood by. Coral remembered nothing else. Evidently she had slept through the night.

She picked up the cup and sniffed but did not recognize the faint odor. Whatever it was, she felt no harm, and in fact, she felt a good deal better. There had been no horrid hallucinations. But what had Ethan thought of the major's whisking her off like this? How had Jace managed to win over Uncle?

The door opened and the lovely Indian girl came in, carrying a breakfast tray and a jug of steaming water. Her expression was confident, with a little sly smile on her lips.

"Good morning, sahiba. You slept well?"

"Yes, thank you."

Coral made up her mind that she would not ask the girl any questions about her friendship with Jace Buckley and, thanking her in Hindi, asked, "And when will the major and Mister Seward arrive so that my sisters and I can leave?"

She pursed her lips. "I do not know when the man named Seward will come, nor when you will leave, sahiba."

"And the major? Did he say when he would come back?"

"Jace is yet asleep. Shall I go back and awaken him to ask?"

Coral stared at her. She called him *Jace*. And he had not left the day before with Seward. She turned her head away and snatched up her brush, bringing the bristles through her long tresses. "No. It does not matter."

"Sahiba? You spoke so quietly, I did not hear."

Coral met her eyes evenly. "No. Do not waken him. That is all. You may go now."

The girl smiled and left, closing the door behind her.

Coral stood. Her eyes narrowed. She realized that she was clutching the brush. She started to throw it at the door, but caught herself when Kathleen's sleepy voice broke in: "What is it, Coral? Something wrong?"

Coral sat down quickly. "No. Nothing is wrong. Everything is just as I expected from the first moment I met him."

Kathleen raised herself to an elbow and squinted at her sleepily. "W-what?"

"Do get up, both of you. I want to leave. I want to find Ethan."

Kathleen frowned. "Ethan! Whatever is the rush?"

"Yes, Ethan," repeated Coral so quietly, so insistently,

that Kathleen said nothing more and simply stared at her. Finally, she tossed aside the cover, giving Marianna a shake. "Wake up. Whatever the major put in her tea last night has cured Coral of everything but impatience."

27

On the following morning, they arrived by ferry at Guwahati, the gateway to the northeastern frontier. In a few days they would be home!

Domed temples and intricately carved white and red stone buildings were everywhere. Along the river, gondola-like boats plied up and down among the more humble barges belonging to the net fishermen. Coral recognized Peacock Island sitting in the middle of the water, housing one of the historic Hindu temples.

She commented to Ethan: "The temple of the Nine Planets was the center of the study of astrology in ancient times. And over there, on Nilachal Hill, is the important Hindu temple. It was destroyed by Muslim invaders in the 1600s but rebuilt by the Hindus. In August, pilgrims come here from all over India to keep their festival."

Ethan appeared genuinely inquisitive. "Yes, Hugo mentioned it. It is the center of energy worship, is it not?"

She looked at him sideways, unwilling to explain the rest. It was also a form of Hinduism with strong sexual and occultic undertones.

Here in Guwahati, Sir Hugo Roxbury would repre-

311

sent the East India Company; and Major Buckley, between trips to the military outpost at Jorhat, would command her uncle's security force at the British residency. They were all expected to call on the maharaja that afternoon.

The white palace with intricate stonework and inlaid marble veined with blue and gold was built near the half-circle bank overlooking the wide Bramaputra. To the north, the great Himalaya mountain range gazed back majestically. ·

Coral grew tense at the thought of seeing the maharaja face-to-face. How could she possibly remain placid when looking upon the man responsible for Gem's abduction and Rajiv's death? Was Gem alive and somewhere in the guarded palace? The possibility that he was—that Jace may soon discover the facts—set her nerves on edge. *I must trust the outcome to God*, she repeated to herself, hoping to quell her disquiet.

When they arrived at the palace, Coral glanced about for Jace, but he had disappeared without a word shortly after arriving. As Seward waited on the steps of the palace-fortress, Sir Hugo Roxbury and his family were brought by turbaned guards carrying tulwars into the Hall of the Diwan-i-Am, the hall of public audience.

Coral's heart thumped in her throat as she stood with dignity between Kathleen and Marianna. Her eyes fixed on the raised dais where the maharaja would make his lofty appearance. *I must not hate.* But only the love of God could reach through her trembling body to feel for this man.

At this very moment Gem could be a slave in the women's quarters.

A sudden dart of fear pierced her heart as a new thought mocked her faith. *Suppose they have made him a eunuch?*

Ethan glanced at her, as if aware of the change in her mood, and his hand took hold of her elbow, giving her a gentle squeeze and a reassuring smile. He leaned over, whispering in her ear, "It will all be over soon, dear. Then you can go to your room to rest."

He had mistaken what must have been a pale and tense face for weariness. As if trying to cheer her, he whispered, "Did you ever see such marvelous patterns in marble work? King George would be envious!"

She glanced about, trying to quiet her mind, trying not to think that Gem could be so near. She concentrated on two intricately carved pillars of whitish blue stone, veined with gold. A thick crimson rug near the dais was embroidered with blossoms. The walls were inlaid with tiny marble mosaics forming a mammoth peacock with ten thousand blue eyes. The domed ceiling was inlaid with veined gold marble, and there were engraved images of the Hindu idol-gods; but Coral only recognized the popular elephant-headed son of Shiva, the god of wisdom and prosperity.

A pompous voice spoke from the step of the dais: "The maharaja, His Excellency Majid Singh himself, must send his appeasement. It is with regret that we must announce that His Excellency is not well. The maharaja sends his greetings. He hopes he will be able to receive you as soon as his health improves."

The sober-faced official in yellow and purple left the step and strode toward Sir Hugo, briefly touching fingertips to his forehead, stepped backward, turned toward a beaded doorway, then clapped his palms. Several Indian guards appeared with stoic faces and black beards. The official ordered them to escort the governor-general's party to the newly constructed British residency.

"A moment please," said Sir Hugo to the official. "It

313

is with deep concern we learn of His Excellency's health. My nephew here is a respected physician of some credential in London. If the maharaja is so inclined, he will offer his opinions of the king's health."

Coral looked at her uncle, somewhat surprised by his offer. His dark eyes turned triumphantly to Ethan. Ethan's jaw tightened.

"I shall bring him your words, sahib. It may be that he will consider them to be most generous."

The English residency was a large bungalow of red stone with ten servants. They offered a salaam to Sir Hugo from the front steps as he left the ghari.

Coral could think of little but rest and sleep, and was dismayed when a gaudy-dressed Indian official informed them that there would be a state dinner in their honor the next night at the palace, hosted by the dewan, the chief Indian official in the maharaja's royal court and council. Coral remembered that Mr. Harrington's so-called secretary Zameen had been the dewan. *Just who has taken his place in the court?*

Coral's heart thumped unevenly. At the one time when she wanted to be strong and alert, she felt the weakest. *Oh, I must not get sick now!* Gem! He may be somewhere in the palace! Could it be that her child was so near, yet so far from her touch, her protection? *Lord God, if he is here, help Jace to discover his whereabouts! Please! Let me see him! Nothing is too difficult for you!*

Their bedroom chamber in the British residency seemed like paradise. There was a huge bed with room to spare for the three of them. Soft coverlets draped the bed, and thick rugs padded the floor. A private bath of marble was built into a secluded garden with flowering vines, and—

A squeal came from Marianna. "Oooh! Look!"

Coral and Kathleen whirled, expecting to find a

314

coiled cobra or a tropical spider. Instead, Coral found Marianna pointing with triumph to what the French called a *toilet*.

Kathleen took hold of Coral's elbow. "A bath, and then you are going to bed. No state dinner tomorrow night."

"But I must go, Kathleen."

Jace might have information on Gem, she thought. And where had Jace disappeared to? Despite her intentions, Coral was too fatigued to thwart Kathleen.

An hour later, bathed and comfortable within her soft peignoir, she grudgingly swallowed the medication that Ethan had left for her to take. She could hardly keep her eyes open as Kathleen pulled the covers up over her shoulders.

"I must go," she kept murmuring, "I must."

———

Jace drew the horse to a stop and peered into the gathering dusk. In the silence he heard a jackal howling as the first stars blossomed in the sky. On several occasions since he had first ridden from Guwahati that afternoon for the British outpost at Jorhat, he had nearly turned back. It was troubling that Roxbury had appeared so willing for him to interrogate the Burmese prisoner held for the assassination of Major Selwyn. After the interrogation, Jace was to gather soldiers to make up his security guard and return to his new post at Guwahati. He did not want to further deplete the meager forces at the outpost, already in short supply of fighting men, until the 13th arrived from Calcutta with McKay.

Riding his horse forward through the dried grasses, a red-necked duck was startled and with a flap of its wings flew to the other side of a swamp. Jace rode on and arrived at the gate of his old command post by early dawn.

The wall was breached in places and in the process of being rebuilt. The stone garrison wore the scars of blackened smoke. Barracks stood empty, a somber reminder of men he had served with who were now buried. Jace went with the young English ensign to the stables, where a dusty sepoy led out the black mare once belonging to Major Selwyn.

"She is a fine horse, Major," said Ensign Niles.

The sepoy handed Jace the reins, and as he did, Jace felt a piece of paper being tucked into his hand. He looked into the immobile black eyes, but the sepoy showed no response and walked away.

Jace, too, revealed nothing of his thoughts as he addressed the young ensign.

"I am under orders from Colonel Warbeck to interrogate the prisoner. I wish to see him now."

The ensign blanched. "Orders from Colonel Warbeck, sir?"

"Is something wrong, Ensign?"

"No, Major. That is, I did not know there were orders from Colonel Warbeck. The colonel is your father, is he not, Major?"

Jace said nothing for a moment and gave a pat to the neck of the friendly mare. "He is. Take me to the prisoner."

The ensign made no sound. Becoming aware of his anxiety, Jace looked at him. The ensign stood stiffly, and white showed around his mouth.

"Well, Ensign?"

"There appears to be some mistake in orders, Major."

"What do you mean—'mistake'?"

"The prisoner was brought to Guwahati several weeks ago," he hastened, "but I did not know that the colonel had expected you to interrogate him."

Jace was furious. "You *authorized* the prisoner to be sent to Guwahati?"

"I was told it was the wishes of the maharaja!"

"*He* ordered his transfer?"

"No, the dewan did, sir!"

"Since when, Ensign, does the dewan have authority over the Bengal army?"

"Yes, sir! I mean, I understand your concern."

"Concern? This is the British military! Neither the dewan nor the maharaja has authority over military matters. You are aware of that! Ensign, you will be called in question for releasing the prisoner to the dewan. The prisoner had important information on the attack. Do you understand that he may be dead by now? Obviously someone does not want him to talk."

The ensign swallowed and said nothing.

"Who is in command until the 13th arrives?"

The young English soldier shuffled his feet. "I am, Major. That is, I and the dewan. He—"

"You and the dewan! Where is the dewan? I wish to speak to him."

"He is at Guwahati, sir!"

Jace stopped. His fury with the ensign diminished as he contemplated his own folly. He had little doubt that Roxbury had known.

Jace led the black mare into the morning sunlight. Alone, he read the message that had been pressed into his hand in the stables.

Namaste. News, sahib. The bazaars in Jorhat prove full of talk. The raja may take sudden ill and die. The dewan was seen in a meeting in Darjeeling only weeks ago with the Raja Bundhu. And Burra-sahib Roxbury is a worshiper of Kali. I shall look for you in Guwahati. Gokul

317

Jace stood in silence. Roxbury a worshiper of Kali? No doubt he only wished others to think so. Ghazis, perhaps. Were these religious zealots planted within the palace of the maharaja of Guwahati? On Kingscote?

———

The next morning, Coral was unexpectedly summoned to see Sir Hugo. As Seward waited outside the door, Coral entered to find her uncle behind a desk. She felt uneasy as his pensive dark eyes fixed upon her, and her gaze dropped to a letter that lay on the desk in front of him. *Is something wrong?* she wondered.

"You called for me, Uncle?" she asked, keeping her voice calm.

He sighed, appearing troubled. "Yes, Coral. I fear there is disturbing news. Alex is missing."

"Alex!"

"He was last heard from in the mountainous regions of Darjeeling. Hampton has left Kingscote and is trekking west in order to try to find him and bring him home."

Alex, missing! "But what was he doing in Darjeeling?" she asked. "Alex has no interest in the area, or in travel—except perhaps returning to Vienna!"

"You might as well know that his mind has not been well recently. After what happened to Michael, Hampton seems to think he went to Darjeeling because it meant so much to his older brother. We think he was trying to locate the land holdings belonging to Buckley and got lost."

"How did my father learn about Alex?" she asked.

"A local from the area of Darjeeling arrived at Kingscote. Your father departed with him at once. I suppose the tension over Michael and the tea plantation weighed on his conscience. He felt he must go himself to find Alex."

Sir Hugo stood, the letter in hand. "I do not wish to alarm you further, but the journey will prove hazardous this time of year for Hampton. As for Alex, we can only hope he has been found by natives and is being cared for."

Coral's mind went in several directions, coming back to Jace. Jace *knew* Darjeeling. If anyone would know where to look, it would be he and Seward. But Jace was chained to the military in Guwahati!

"Is the letter from my father?"

"Yes, it arrived weeks ago."

Coral thought of the many delays in their travel. Her father may already be in Darjeeling searching for Alex. Had her father mentioned Mother in the letter to her uncle? "May I read the letter please?"

"Of course." He handed it to her.

Coral recognized her father's handwriting. The message was brief, making mention of his absence, of several skirmishes along the border with Burma, and of the few British soldiers patrolling the area.

The situation here near the borders is growing more dangerous with the passing weeks. Yet I have no choice but to leave matters here in the hand of the Almighty and take my leave. I have found it necessary to journey to Darjeeling to find Alex. Word arrived by courier that he is missing. I shall return to Kingscote as God enables and as soon as possible.

Coral stood looking at the letter, dazed.

"This changes matters considerably," said Sir Hugo. "Without your father or brother at Kingscote, I think it wise that you and your sisters remain here until more soldiers arrive from Calcutta."

Not return home? The thought was devastating! If Kingscote was not safe, she had more reason than ever to get home to her mother. Why, her father could be away in the Darjeeling area for several months. As for the regiment from Calcutta, they could only guess when Plassey would be retaken and troops arrive in the northeast!

"The dewan has proven most cooperative under the circumstances," he continued. "He has offered to let you and your sisters stay here at the residence. You will be guarded by the dewan's own men."

He must have seen her dismay for he walked toward her and placed his hands protectively about her shoulders. "I would stay myself, if I could. But business forces me to travel with the major to the outpost for a few weeks. I fear this nasty business with the death of Major Selwyn must be looked into. But do not be alarmed. Ethan will remain here."

Looking into his gaze, which showed nothing but concern, Coral wondered if she had just cause to feel so suspicious. Her alarm, however, had nothing to do with her uncle's departure. *I must resist his plans*, she told herself firmly. But exactly what did Uncle Hugo have in mind beyond delaying her at Guwahati? And for what possible reason?

"I am sorry to worry you, Uncle, but I cannot accept the dewan's invitation. If my father has left for Darjeeling, then Mother is not only ill but alone. There is even more reason for going home. She will be worried about Hampton and Alex, and will need me." She offered a smile. "Besides, I have Seward for protection."

"Ah, yes, Seward. A stalwart fellow. Well, I expected this response. I suppose there is little I can do to stop you. After all, I am not your legal guardian yet. But with the mutiny at Plassey delaying Captain McKay's troop,

I cannot help but be concerned as to where all this is leading."

Coral's mind stumbled over something he had said, and the words commanded her full attention. Yet Uncle Hugo did not seem to realize his mistake. She quelled the question forming on her tongue—"Not her legal guardian—yet?" But why would he even say such a thing? She had her father and mother, and Alex. Perhaps he had uttered a hopeful wish. In which case, it was best that she appeared not to have noticed.

He was frowning to himself, and Coral knew that without proof she must accept his behavior as genuine. It would be disastrous to come out and accuse him of manipulating the trouble with Major Selwyn and the mutiny at Plassey.

"It is you who faces trying times here at Guwahati," she said. "You have accepted a difficult position from the governor-general. With war looming, you will have enough concerns without your nieces here to impose."

"Major Buckley will prove of great assistance to me. I could have no one better to command the security force. And neither could the royal family."

Did he mean it? She recalled the dark accusation that Jace had made in Manali about her uncle plotting his death in the mutiny. Would the major be safe here in Guwahati? Coral's tension mounted.

He walked her toward the door. "I regret I must leave tonight after the state dinner to ride with the major to the outpost. We must delve into the matter of the attack."

Coral was cautious. She must speak to Jace. "The major will be at the dinner?"

"Yes, I believe the new dewan has especially invited him. I will contact you at Kingscote."

Coral dutifully kissed his bearded cheek goodbye and joined Seward outside the door.

"Take good care of my nieces, Seward," Hugo told him. "Unfortunately, I was unable to talk Coral into staying. See them safely to Kingscote. I will be leaving tonight with Major Buckley for Jorhat."

Seward's rugged face told Coral nothing of what he thought of the matter of her father and Alex in Darjeeling. Knowing his loyalty, he would be inclined to risk almost anything in order to be at her father's side searching for Alex.

Seward touched his hat with a salute in her uncle's direction. "Aye, Sir Hugo. I shall get them to Kingscote safely enough."

"Should you find it necessary to get in touch with me, do not hesitate to send a message to Jorhat," ordered Hugo.

Coral followed Seward out the hall and down the steps to the waiting ghari.

"Seward, something is very wrong!"

"I don't like none of what is happening. With Alex missing, and Sir Hampton taking his leave to go after him, Miss Elizabeth be alone. And things do not add up to me."

"How long will it take us to reach Kingscote?"

He squinted toward the bright sun. "If we leave in the morning, we can be there in two days."

"Oh, Seward! Do you think my father has located Alex?"

He frowned as he assisted her into the ghari seat. "As both me and the major can testify, Darjeeling is located near the Eastern Himalayas. It be rugged, mountainous trekking. It won't be easy for your father, or Alex. And that, lass, be what worries me most."

Coral's heart was heavy. First she had lost Gem, then Michael. . . .

Lord, please guide and protect my father. I cannot bear to lose him too.

28

Jace left the outpost in Jorhat and returned to Guwahati and his military quarters near the residency. A rajput guard, tough and lean, waited for him with a message from the dewan. Jace was not surprised to see the rajput here, so far from central India. Believed to be born of the warrior caste, the rajputs often served maharajas.

"His Excellency's chief minister bids that he see you before the official dinner tonight, Sirdar-Buckley."

The rajput stepped aside, allowing a lesser servant to step forward, bringing fingers to forehead. He stepped back out the door and quickly returned, holding several presents.

"The dewan requests you to accept these gifts from his hand."

Jace was skeptical of the hard look in the rajput's dark eyes. So the dewan wished to give him gifts. . . .

There was a handsome black tunic embroidered with gold, a turban, and a *tulwar*!

The sight of the curved blade strengthened his suspicions. Jace turned toward the rajput, but he was gone. He picked up the sword and tested its balance.

Arrayed in the fine clothing, Jace arrived at the palace

of the maharaja an hour before the official dinner. Two rajput guards escorted him across marble floors and up the steps between gold-embossed pillars into the Diwan-i-Khas, the hall of private audience.

Jace stopped. The dewan lounged comfortably on silk cushions, waiting. He was anything but what Jace had expected. Unlike Zameen, *this* man was young and darkly handsome, with an arrogance in his black eyes. He was lean and tough, and a deadly ruthlessness cloaked his smile, showing even white teeth. He wore the garb of wealth, his fingers winking with gems as he played with the hilt of his tulwar sheathed in a jeweled scabbard.

Caution. Jace's hand moved slightly toward his blade. The man he faced was now all too familiar.

The dewan produced what was meant to be a pleasant smile. "Greetings, friend Jace. I am surprised to see you are bold enough to come to the royal residence of my uncle. And as Roxbury's security guard!" He gave a laugh. "What I have always respected about you is your reckless humor."

Why would the nephew of the maharaja wish to be the dewan?

"We meet again, Sunil," said Jace.

"We had to meet again. It has been too long since the missing temple treasure of Kali."

"Ah. The idol of Kali. His Excellency is convinced I am a robber of temples. I often wondered who told him so."

Sunil spread his hands. "And you are assuredly innocent."

"I may acclaim merit for boldness, friend, but I am not a fool. Would I risk my head in serving the governor-general's resident to the maharaja if I were not?"

"I agree it would be most unwise."

324

"I will speak to His Excellency in private audience," said Jace. "It may be that the temple treasure will soon be returned."

Sunil gestured toward the cushions. "Sit down."

As Jace seated himself, a servant appeared with a glass of wine. Jace noticed that Sunil's gaze dropped to his sword hilt.

"You will not need that—not now," said Sunil. "As you said, you would not risk coming here unless you were innocent—or know where the treasure is."

Jace thought better than to let him know that he had the statue. He had never trusted Sunil. The young man was too ambitious, more so than his older brother, Rajiv. Sunil was likely to have a number of guards in the palace who were more loyal to him than they were to other members of the royal family.

Did he have his eyes upon a more powerful position?

Jace studied him. "So you are now the dewan of His Excellency. What happened to Zameen?"

He hoped Sunil would offer information, but the haughty young nephew of the maharaja was too cautious for that.

Sunil smiled and said easily, "You have already seen in Manali that Zameen has retired, along with Harrington."

"Who told you of Manali?"

Sunil smiled. "Roxbury. Who else?"

Jace, too, smiled. "Somehow I thought it might have been Sanjay." He watched Sunil over his glass, but the man was too clever to give himself away.

"Sanjay, Sanjay," he repeated thoughtfully. "No, I have not heard of him. A friend of yours?"

"I intend to bring him back to Calcutta to be shot for treason."

Sunil refilled Jace's glass, showing nothing.

"Sanjay planned the mutiny of the 17th near Plassey."

"Ah, yes. I have heard. A grief, a tragedy."

Is Sunil the power behind Roxbury? Or are they working together toward some compatible goal?

"His Excellency does not yet know of the mutiny at Plassey," Sunil said.

"It is not Plassey I wish to speak to him about, but the attack on the outpost at Jorhat. You have a prisoner who belongs to the British government. I would like him turned over to me at once."

Sunil smiled. "I am afraid that is out of the question. As to the attack on the British outpost, you will find that infiltrators from Burma hosted the killing of Major Selwyn. My family welcomes the English presence, do we not? His Excellency has signed a treaty with the East India Company."

Jace wondered if Sunil's own feelings corresponded with his uncle's. Rajiv had mentioned that his brother, Sunil, resented the East India Company.

"As for my position as dewan, it was the will of His Excellency."

"The raja needed a man of wisdom. One he could trust," said Jace smoothly.

"His Excellency trusts few these days."

"Was it also the raja's will that you take over the command of the British outpost?" Jace said dryly.

Sunil smiled. "No. That was my idea." He spread a hand. "It is nothing. Your English ensign was young and inexperienced in such matters, so I have been assisting him."

"The treaty between the raja and England grants the Company control over disputes that arise with neighboring states. That includes Sikkim, Bhutan, and Burma. Until troops arrive to take their positions, the ensign is in command, inexperienced or not."

"Ah, but now that you and the Resident Roxbury have arrived, I shall be most pleased to leave military matters in your hand. However, I cannot turn the prisoner over to you."

"Of course, he is dead," said Jace bluntly.

"A tragedy. Hung himself in the dungeon. He served a warlord named Zin in Burma. I understand Zin is also your friend."

Jace said nothing. Zin could not truly be called a friend. That would be like keeping a python for a pet.

"Naturally," said Sunil, "you are free to conduct your own investigations. But a private audience with the maharaja?" He dismissed the idea with a gesture. "What you wish to say to my uncle, you can say to me. He is a busy man."

As he watched Sunil, Jace became convinced that it was even more important to speak alone with the raja. He deliberately changed the subject to measure his response. "I see you carry your brother's tulwar."

Sunil touched the curved sword. "Yes. It belonged to Rajiv." His expression sobered, and he finished his glass of wine in one swallow. "My brother was a fool to marry that woman." He set the glass down harshly. "Jemani was wrong for him."

"Then you knew the peasant girl?" Jace felt his gaze and reached for a fig from the basket of fruit.

"I did not know her. She was of a lower caste. I knew that His Excellency could not accept the marriage. Caste cannot be broken."

"Then Rajiv must have told you of Jemani?"

Again he felt his granite gaze. "Yes. He told me. She worked in the silk hatchery at Kingscote."

Jace knew that Jemani had not worked in the silk hatchery. Then why did Sunil find it necessary to lie?

"A pity your brother had to die for breaking caste."

327

"You assume his death was the punishment of our uncle?"

"Who else?" said Jace smoothly.

Sunil stood. "I suppose you are right. The royal family could not accept Rajiv's marriage. Nor the son born from the untouchable."

Jace affected indifference. It was unwise to mention the abduction of Gem, or anything about the boy. He must speak first to the maharaja.

"Now that Rajiv is dead, you will reign after your uncle?"

Sunil smiled condescendingly. "No. There is another heir closer than I. At the moment I am content to be his dewan."

The question had accomplished its purpose. At the mention of power, the dark eyes came alive. If Rajiv had lived, he would have been heir. Now that right went to Sunil. But who was this heir who was closer than Sunil?

To a man like Sunil, even Gem would be seen as a threat.

"It is time," Sunil said. "The official guests arrive for the maharaja's state dinner. We will talk again."

Jace now believed the maharaja had no part in the mutiny, and that the maharaja knew nothing of his nephew's drive for power. The question was, what did Sir Hugo expect to receive by helping Sunil? Whatever was planned, it was intended to happen before British reinforcements arrived under McKay.

Jace had been able to take fifteen men with him from the outpost and still leave some measure of fighting force intact. Fifteen soldiers were not enough to protect the maharaja if it came to that. But then, that may have been someone's intention all along.

Seated on a dais, the maharaja was a glitter of jewels and silks, as were his politically powerful Indian guests and the dewan himself. Among those who were there to pay tribute to the governor-general's resident were several Portuguese representatives and some English from elsewhere in the northern frontier; men whose sharp eyes and hard faces bespoke the reason for their presence in India—the wealth of trade that reached to Calcutta in the south, and China and Burma in the east.

A lovely image in her exquisite frock designed by Jacques, Coral's gaze swept the grand hall hoping to see the major. She must discuss her father and Alex with him before she left for Kingscote in the morning. Instead, her gaze confronted the dewan, and she tensed. Rajiv appeared to be standing across the hall from her, garbed in royal Indian fashion, but that was impossible. The husband of Jemani, the father of Gem, was dead. But the dewan bore the same bronzed good looks and could easily pass for Rajiv's twin. The cool black eyes stared at her without the customary deference offered a white colonial woman. Coral turned her head away. Was this the new dewan who had taken the place of Zameen?

Coral looked about for Ethan and saw that he, too, was absent. A minute later she turned as Uncle Hugo walked up with the dewan. Coral behaved as though she were unaware of his alert appraisal.

"The Maharaja Majid Singh sends his greetings, Miss Kendall," the dewan said. "I, too, wish to assure you and your family that any infringement on Kingscote plantation by Burma will evoke my highest displeasure."

His highest displeasure?

"My family also sends good wishes to His Excellency, the Maharaja," she said.

She found the dewan's military offer disturbing but

noticed that her uncle showed no curiosity over the surprising overture.

For a century, Kingscote had been recognized by the Assam rulership to be private territory, isolated from the all-too-frequent squabbles of Hindu maharajas, Muslim nawabs, and Buddhist warlords from Sikkim and Burma. Any territorial infringements on Kingscote by warring factions were handled by her father and hired mercenaries. Sir Hampton, like his father before him, had fought to protect his holdings and had won the respect of the governing province. But now that the maharaja had signed a treaty with the East India Company, Coral suspected that her uncle would begin to insist that the mantle of Kingscote's safety fall under Company jurisdiction.

When Jace did not arrive, Coral's unease mounted. Where was he? Who knew when they would see each other again? She was certain that by now Seward would have told him about her father and Alex, but she must be positive. And what of Jace's promise to inquire of the maharaja about Gem?

Guarding her feelings, she found it uncomfortable to look at the maharaja, who had not yet descended from his dais to grace his guests with his presence. Mingled pain and bitterness welled up in her heart. Could this detached and indomitable man, glittering with jewels, have ordered his nephew killed for breaking caste?

The thought that she stood in the same room with those who had killed Rajiv and abducted Gem took away her appetite. *I cannot bear to look at him*, she thought. And Gem, where was he? Somewhere in the palace? Was he dead? Could he have been sent to some warring maharaja or nawab as a slave? Suppose . . . suppose they had tortured him, or thrown him to the tigers?

Did the dewan or the maharaja know that she was

the woman who had adopted Gem and baptized Jemani? She decided that His Excellency *must* already know. And yet his detached gaze never once glanced in her direction. Only the dewan stared at her, and Coral was becoming more concerned by the moment.

If Jace does not come soon, I must make some excuse and leave.

Perhaps he would not come. She glanced about the large room again then stopped short. Her eyes collided with a handsome Indian warrior who stood in the open arcade leading off into the garden.

Confused, she thought, *Javed Kasam! What is he doing here?* Then quickly she caught herself. Jace Buckley was not in tunic and buckskin trousers, nor in uniform, but dressed in handsome black and gold Indian garb. His steady gaze was fixed not on her, but on Dewan Sunil.

With relief, Coral picked up her skirt to cross the floor in his direction when Ethan walked up and took her elbow.

"My dear, I apologize for my tardiness. But something important came up to delay me."

At the concerned edge to his voice, she looked at him, and saw that his gray eyes were troubled.

"Uncle did not explain?" he asked.

"Explain?"

"I must talk to you alone." He glanced about, as though searching for the appropriate place, and before Coral could respond, he escorted her across the floor to an alcove screened by cascades of vine, where stone bowls were filled with floating orchids.

Ethan's expression of alarm increased her own. "What is it, Ethan?"

"A disappointment on my part. I cannot leave with you in the morning for Kingscote. Hugo needs me here at Guwahati for a time."

"I do not understand. You do not serve the Company."

"No, but the maharaja is ill. He has asked for my help."

"The maharaja?"

"Hugo agrees my cooperation will be beneficial, not only to His Excellency but to the East India Company. The king is apparently upset with his own physicians." Ethan frowned. "I cannot refuse a man of his position. And Hugo has asked me to stay on for a few months—"

"A few months, but, Ethan! What about my mother? She is very ill!"

He took hold of her shoulders and looked so unhappy that Coral restrained her disappointment.

"Believe me, Coral, this is not my wish. I have already arranged for the medicine your mother will need and sent it to your chambers by route of Seward. If you need more, you have only to send someone to me."

Coral had not noticed the maharaja looking ill, but public appearances meant little.

"It may be that I will decide to stay until the troops arrive from Calcutta," he said. "I prefer my supplies to be hauled to Kingscote under my supervision."

"As long as I have the medication for my mother, my sisters and I can manage. It is good of you to treat His Excellency. Have you any idea what is ailing him?"

"No, but I shall see him first thing in the morning. He will eat nothing tonight, so he has told me."

Coral glanced through the vines toward the dais. The maharaja had unexpectedly left the hall.

"He is gone," she said, surprised.

As Coral glanced in the direction of the dewan, she saw that he stood, unsmiling, beside Sir Hugo.

"I must say it is dreadful news about Alex," Ethan said. "Uncle, however, assures me your father is acquainted with the area of Darjeeling."

Coral wondered. No one knew the mountainous region as well as Jace. If only he were not obligated to the military, he and Seward could go in search of them! Suppose the monsoon arrived before her father found Alex? The tumultuous rivers and the mountain slides could put both their lives at risk.

"Poor Alex," murmured Ethan.

Poor Alex? Something in Ethan's voice caused her to study his face. He appeared thoughtful, and with a hint of pity, which seemed a little odd to her.

"Alex will not be the first man to lose his way in the mountains," she replied. "But he should not have gone without a guide. Losing one's way is a common problem with trekking. It could happen to most anyone, even my father."

Coral glanced toward the garden where she had last seen Jace, but he was gone and nowhere visible in the hall.

The dewan had come to stand beside her. "You will reconsider, and stay in Guwahati, Miss Kendall? Why not remain with Doctor Boswell until British troops arrive?"

"Your invitation is most generous, Dewan. But circumstances will not afford the ease. My mother is quite ill with the fever, and I am anxious to be home."

"I quite understand," he said, his handsome face too grave. "It is unceremonious of us to ask the physician to stay, yet generous on your part, Miss Kendall, and yours, Doctor Boswell."

"Have you any notion what is ailing His Excellency?" Ethan asked.

The dewan showed no expression. "Age perhaps. We trust you will do what you can, Doctor Boswell."

"I assure you, Dewan, I shall do my best."

As Ethan discussed medicine, Coral inched away until she came up beside Kathleen and whispered behind her peacock fan, "Keep the dewan and Ethan occupied. I must speak to the major alone."

"I saw him leave a minute ago."

"Which direction?"

"The garden."

Coral unobtrusively retreated across the polished floor toward the wide-open doors leading out into the parklike garden. She glanced backward and saw that everyone was occupied. She caught up her skirts of amber taffeta and, once out of sight, sped into the fragrant garden with its colored glass lanterns. He could not have gone yet, not without at least telling her goodbye.

She had not gone far into the pillared pavilion when she saw him. He was standing a short distance away by the steps that led to a lower tiered garden leading down toward the Bramaputra River. He must have heard her footsteps for he turned. Coral paused, glancing back over her shoulder. No one had followed her. She walked quickly toward him, hearing the musicians playing their *sitars* from the upper gallery. The stringed instruments played a haunting *ghazal*—music derived from poetry, always a hopeless love theme. She hurried toward Jace in a rush of slippers and silk.

29

This is not going to be pleasant, thought Jace.

The music from the sitar did not soothe but was irksome. What had come over him? Why did he let a feeling of responsibility toward her divide his mind? This was no time to let emotion come between him and the work the colonel had sent him here to do. He would pointedly tell her his concerns about Gem and say goodbye.

Coral stood before him for a moment staring at him, and he wondered what thoughts were running through her mind. He rejected what was racing through his own.

Jace believed he understood what she thought of him. He was the sometimes arrogant man who cared little about anyone or anything except completing his mission for the colonel, returning to Calcutta for the *Madras,* and disengaging himself from any emotional ties or bonds. She was more right than wrong.

"Did you hear about Alex?" she asked.

Seward had explained everything, but Jace was reluctant to tell her of his concerns, although he had shared them with Seward.

"Yes, Seward told me," he said briefly.

She came closer. The wash of moonlight fell upon her,

sending tiny shimmers through her golden tresses and lending softness to the lines of her gown.

Jace put an iron clamp about his emotions. *Not this . . .* He did not want it.

"Sir Hugo asked me to stay here until Captain McKay arrives, but I refused. I am leaving in the morning with Seward," she said.

"Yes, I know."

He saw her hesitate at his briefness, and he reinforced his action by turning away to look out at the river, as though preoccupied with more important matters.

"How long will you be in Jorhat?" she asked.

"I do not know. Longer than I first thought."

A long time, he wanted to say. *Perhaps it is best we do not see each other again.*

"There is something I want to say before I leave," Jace said.

He saw her hesitate, as though retreating emotionally. Was she misguided enough to think that he would become a romantic fool? He folded his arms. It was best that she knew who the dewan was. He had seen the way Sunil looked at her. One man knew the thoughts of another man when it came to a woman as lovely as Coral.

"Stay away from the dewan. He is the younger brother of Rajiv. He cannot be trusted."

"Then I was correct when I told you that years ago I saw two young men riding on the royal elephant with the maharaja!"

"He is ruthless. He may be the one behind the trouble at Plassey and the attack on Major Selwyn. Your father would do best not to trust him where Kingscote is concerned."

"The dewan mentioned Kingscote to me tonight. He said he would do what he could to protect the silk enterprise from Burmese soldiers."

"He wishes to appear friendly for his own reasons. I am convinced he is working with your uncle." He saw the veiled flicker of pain. "I am sorry. . . . I believe they have some plan that will benefit both of them. I have informed Seward. And when your father returns, Seward will explain."

Again she hesitated, as though wanting to avoid a decision.

"Yet there is no proof of your suspicions that my uncle is involved," she stated.

"No, but I am certain that the dewan is a man of whom to be cautious."

"My father would find the dewan's offer of protection for Kingscote suspicious," she said. "He has had a good relationship with most of the rulers here in the northeast and would not believe an attack on us likely. They call him the Burra-sahib, the *Great Man.*'"

Jace hoped that she did not notice his reaction to the description she had offered of her father. The garden at Barrackpore . . . what had Marianna overheard? *"An accident of one so great would not be as easy. He is a respected man."*

Could Sir Hampton Kendall be that man? Was the message that Alex was missing intended to be a trap?

Reluctant to alarm her, he said nothing. Whatever was happening, he could not stop it now. Sir Hampton Kendall was three weeks into his trek to Darjeeling. He must warn Seward—

"Major, is something wrong?"

He came back to awareness. "You were saying about the dewan?"

"My father has always hired mercenaries to protect the plantation. He would not accept help from the dewan."

"Yes, of course. A wise move. Sir Hampton would do

well to be suspicious, and so would you. Listen to me. I cannot prove it yet, but I think Sunil was involved with others on Kingscote to have Gem abducted."

He saw her tense, but she made no sound. He respected her for that. Her innocent appearance was an asset in confronting men like Roxbury and Prince Sunil. They underestimated her. Jace did not. Not anymore.

"But what motive would he have to abduct Gem?"

He paused, reluctant to hurt her. "You should know the answer to that."

She must have shivered, for she held her arms and glanced back toward the lighted hall.

"The ritual killing of Rajiv—you think Sunil had his own brother killed?" she whispered.

"Yes. Rajiv was a threat to his ambitions. The marriage to Jemani might have offered the excuse to destroy him. Sunil desires to be the raja after his uncle. Gem, too, could have been a threat to Sunil's royal ambitions."

"The caste system would shut Gem out," she insisted.

"You are right. Unless—" and he looked at her. "You once told me you knew very little about Jemani. Is that true?"

She hesitated. "Yes, I was only fifteen when she and Rajiv arrived. They only said they were from Rajasthan, that they were escaping a famine."

"Rajasthan," he repeated to himself. He allowed his mind to wander into a path that neither he nor Coral had ever considered. What if Jemani had not been born an untouchable? It could be true that she had come from Rajasthan, but was it also possible that she too had come from a royal line? Perhaps a faction at war with the maharaja here at Guwahati? That would explain her disguise.

That would make Gem royalty, an heir to two thrones. . . . And if peace ever came between the two warring houses he could rule either, or both. *Had Sunil somehow known this?*

Jace recalled Sunil's expression when he had asked him if he knew Jemani.

Because of Jemani's Christian baptism, and the resentment it brought to the Hindus on Kingscote, it would have been easy for Sunil to have gotten the support of someone on the plantation. That someone may have delivered the message to Rajiv to meet his brother in the jungle.

Perhaps Sunil had written a false conciliatory message from their uncle. If that were true, it would account for Rajiv's willingness to meet in secret and yet not suspect danger.

"Then Sunil may know where Gem is," Coral said.

Jace was beginning to think that Sunil did not know, not yet, but was intensely looking for the boy. Had the trail led him into Burma? Yet he did not wish to raise her hopes. Gem's danger remained real. Sunil would have no reason to leave the child alive if he found him. Jace knew he must find him first.

Perhaps he would not tell her now, not with Sunil in the palace. After she arrived at Kingscote, when her father had returned—yes, then he would send a message through Gokul.

"You must say nothing to the dewan," he demanded. "Be polite but distant. Do not mention Gem. I will first speak with the maharaja before I leave Guwahati, and learn what is possible. It is also important he understands his nephew's ambitions for the throne."

"The raja is ill. Ethan was asked to stay and treat him." She said swiftly, "Do you suppose—?"

"Poison?" Jace asked bluntly. "It is my guess. Then I must see the raja tonight."

"But how?"

"I do not know yet. . . . Who asked Boswell to stay?"
He saw her falter.

"My uncle mentioned to the maharaja that Ethan was a physician."

It did not surprise him. Did Roxbury believe he could manipulate Boswell's medicine to accomplish the raja's death? Jace did not doubt that he had used Boswell to accomplish his purposes in London with Coral, but murder? Just how far would Boswell go?

"Something else," he said. "I want you to delay your mission school until your father returns with Alex. Will you do that?"

"I . . . I will think about everything you say, and I will pray for guidance and wisdom. It is the best I can do, the wisest."

As he looked down at her, he had the disturbing notion that Coral prayed about everything. Did she ever pray for the scoundrel Jace Buckley? Thinking that she might made him uncomfortable.

"Wait until Sir Hampton returns," he repeated. She did not answer him, and the silence grew until he caught his breath with exasperation. "That I find you frustrating, yet still admire your spirit, is beyond sound reason. Nevertheless I do."

"I find your admiration a compliment, Major."
His eyes narrowed. "Will you do as I say?"

Her chin lifted slightly, and her eyes met his evenly. He read that expression and smiled for the first time. "All right. Will you 'consider' my advice?"

He saw her expression soften, and a little smile touched her lips, but it was gone as swiftly as it came.

"I always take your advice seriously, Major. After saving me from both tiger and spider, how could I not?"

His brow slanted. "And yet, you will press ahead. I will say it anyway. Take extra precaution about doing anything that would provoke the religious ire on Kings-cote. Watch your servant Natine. I think he is a ghazi." She tried to interrupt. "No, do not protest. Be cautious around him, and depend on Seward."

"You are leaving for the outpost tonight with my uncle? How long will you be there?"

"For as long as it takes to inquire into the death of Major Selwyn. The Burmese prisoner is dead. Somehow I must make a trip into Burma. How to accomplish it without Roxbury's suspicions will prove difficult."

She looked at him with surprise. "Burma?"

Jace thought of the local warlord, Zin. Did he know anything about Gem's abduction? If he did, it would prove the motive for Sunil's visit. The question was, what had the warlord been willing to tell Sunil?

Zin was a crafty man who would bargain for political favor and wealth. Jace had little to bargain with except the stolen idol of Kali, and in order to use it, he would first need to speak with the maharaja and gain his support. That would mean confiding in him about Gem.

"I expect to discover information in Burma that may prove useful," he said simply.

"And after Burma, when your duty to the colonel and my uncle is complete? Then what?"

After his military duty. . . ! He folded his arms across his chest and tilted his head to look at her. Her question was not flirtatious, he knew her too well for that. But he could almost read something into it. He knew an invitation when he heard one, even when it was disguised. Did this mean she would miss him when he disappeared out of her life once and for all? He felt some solace for his frustrations. He hoped she would think about him as much as he would remember her. He smiled to himself. The memory of Miss Coral Kendall in the bazaar of Calcutta, confronting a guru and his trained crows for a group of half-naked children, would remain with him wherever he went.

They both knew there was no possibility of a relationship. She was a *silk heiress*. He had nothing. He would not accept wealth and prestige from her hand. He must make his own success in the tea plantation in Darjeeling. Even if they admitted the attraction between them, his success could take years. Ethan, if he was smart, would not wait that long. Nor could he imagine the Kendall and Roxbury families waiting.

"After my service here," he repeated as though deep in contemplation, "I shall resume where I left off, before Gokul and the colonel trapped me back into wearing this uniform." He could have added, *And before I met a certain young woman who was out to take on the world . . .* "I shall never suddenly emerge a saint, Miss Kendall, if that is your hope."

"You misunderstand me," she said quietly. "What my expectations are for your future does not truly matter. It is not for me to choose, but what God asks of you, and what He wants to make of you. He does not make mistakes. What about you, Jace? Do you trust Him? With the *Madras*, the tea plantation, your dreams? Or do you think He wishes to destroy them, turn them into ashes?"

"A missionary to the very end. I shall keep your fair words in mind," he said with a smile. "As for your future, you will make the perfect helpmeet for the gentleman Charles Peddington. He is worth two of Boswell."

She spoke in a whisper. "I think you know the Lord better than you wish to admit. Why do you hide it?"

"Your questions have a way of backing me into a corner. I do not take well to retreating from beautiful women. It has always been the other way around."

This was unfair, he decided—a beautiful young

woman whose religion was a constant goad to his conscience.

"I think I have been honest with you about what I
believe," he said quietly. "I have never tried to mislead
you. It is Boswell's new interest in the Scriptures that
you should question."

Her confusion was evident, and her eyes searched his.
"Ethan? He has nothing to do with this—"

"I think he has quite a lot to do with this. Unlike his
glib manners, I have not pretended to be something I am
not."

"You are unfair, Major. He does have a concern for the
things of God."

"Maybe. But not in the way he has wanted you to
think. With men like Newton and Carey, Christianity is
their life. They go to sleep with God's name on their
tongue, and they awake in prayer. Boswell's consecration
is a jest. I shall let you decide why he behaves so."

"Seward said you have met John Newton?"

"In London. Seward arranged the meeting. And at
risk of dashing any new ideas you may have about Jace
Buckley, I will hasten to say that I have had no spiritual
experience like that of he or Wesley. Newton speaks of
God as though he knows Him. If I were you," he said
calmly, "I would make careful inspection of what is beneath that pious mantle Boswell is wrapping himself in."

She looked up at him, troubled, and he guessed from
her eyes that it was not over Ethan.

"Meaning, of course, that my cousin wishes to deceive
me? Major! I think it is highly inappropriate to say he is
a hypocrite."

He refused to back down and stared at her evenly.
"Nevertheless, Miss Kendall, that is what I am doing.
The dewan is not the only man of whom you need to be
cautious."

She hesitated, and her breath came quickly. "You—you would dare compare Ethan to—"

"No," Jace said flatly, feeling irritated because she insisted on defending him. "Ethan is not as cold and clever in his ambitions as Sunil or Roxbury. I suspect he merely follows his uncle's orders. As I see it, that too is a danger. He is a compromiser."

She said quickly, "I know you do not like him. And I cannot understand why it should be so. But I can assure you that Ethan can be trusted. And I will not look narrowly on his motives just because he is your opposite and—"

"I can take most any of your deductions, but I will not go so far as to let you think I envy his noble character, so opposite mine. That is not why I question his motives, and warn you to be cautious—" He caught himself from going further in his frustration and put another clamp on his emotions.

Her features showed that his words had hurt her, although she seemed to struggle to mask them. She obviously felt strongly about Boswell.

"I am sorry," he said quietly, bothered because he had brought her pain. "As you wish, we best drop the subject. I have much to do before I ride out tonight with Sir Hugo. I must see the raja. I wanted to speak to you only because of my concern about the dewan. Now that I have done so, I must go."

"Yes," said Coral, "you are right, of course, I will not keep you. As you say, you must get ready to leave."

He wanted to frown at the silence between them. It was worse than all the noisy but simple chatter of the dewan's dinner guests, and much more painful.

The music coming from the sitars filled the garden.

She spoke with a little rush. "I'd better go back before I am missed. Goodbye, Major."

He said nothing. At the moment, the word *goodbye* might have weighed as much as the *Madras*.

She turned to walk back to the lighted palace hall, then paused. Her eyes came swiftly back to his, searching one last time.

"And Gem? You will. . . . Will you speak to the maharaja?"

He said evasively, "I will speak to him."

"You will come to Kingscote to let me know?"

He felt the tension of her persistence. Did he truly want to see her again? Even if her dreams came true and he was able to rescue Gem—did he want to be the man to return him, or was it safer for his own emotions to send the child back to Kingscote through Gokul?

"I do not know," he said stiffly. "As I said, it is necessary that I visit an acquaintance in Burma. He is the friend of a 'certain Indian mercenary' you met in Calcutta, a man involved in intrigue. I think he can offer me important information on the mutiny here and at Plassey. I could be gone six months, a year, even longer."

"I see."

"But I will send Gokul with whatever news I can discover about Gem."

She stared at him, her expression strained in the pale moonlight. Hoping to ward off any further questions, he said: "You will be missed by the guests."

She stood there watching him. Suddenly, her voice tense, she whispered, "You think Gem is no longer alive."

He said nothing. He turned to lean against the garden rail, noticing the dancing glimmer of moonlight on the river. He had hoped to avoid this moment, but she persisted. He heard her hesitant steps come up behind him and felt her nearness.

"I find it painful to caution you. I wish for your hopes

and joys to come true. We both know life does not always work that way."

She paused for only a moment, and he guessed she was holding back her emotions. "You have been the only one who has understood about Gem, about how desperately I want—"

Her voice broke, and Jace knew if he did not reinforce his own feelings and remain aloof, he would be tempted to draw her into his arms and comfort her. "I will keep the promise to discover his whereabouts. But as I told you before, I cannot promise a joyful outcome. I would give anything if I could."

She did not answer him, and he saw her swallow back her disappointment. He found it difficult to bear, and looked out across the gallery rail into the shadowy garden. He was conscious of a bewildering pain that he did not want, and he tried to smother it, to reject it. His fingers clamped about the rail.

"All this time I believed that he had to be alive," she said, and her voice broke. "I was so certain. Jace—"

He felt her hand clutch his tunic in a desperate move, as if somehow he had only to say he was mistaken, and hope would rise from the ashes with a flutter of golden wings and soar. He turned to look down at her, and as he did, her eyes filled with tears, as soft as liquid jewels in the moonlight, and he became too aware of her closeness, of her touch. Despite his caution, he knew he could no longer deny the kindled flame burning in his heart. . . .

———

Coral was too surprised to react. One moment she felt pain and loss over Gem; the next, her thoughts were filled with the man who held her in his arms. The same man whom she had for so long denied access to her affections.

His voice was so soft, she wondered if she imagined the words whispered in her ear: "The game is not played fairly, Coral. I could love you so easily."

All ability to reason dwindled into something wild, sweet, and dangerous—the warmth of his lips on hers, the feel of his rugged tunic beneath her palms, the fragrance of spice as he held her tightly.

"Coral? Are you out here?" Ethan's voice shattered the stillness like the crack of a whip.

Jace breathed something in exasperation.

For Coral, reality rushed in with a flood of guilt. She wrenched free, her heart pounding in her ears, and backed away, her hands pressed hard against the sides of her skirt. She stood shaking.

Jace seemed neither intimidated by the sound of Ethan's steps approaching on the stone nor the least bit ashamed for his action.

"Coral?" Ethan called again.

She thought briefly of the perfunctory slap that society demanded of a lady on such occasions but could not bring herself to do it.

"I am waiting for my just retribution," came Jace's dry voice.

She managed a calm whisper. "I am certain it would not be worthy of either of us."

"But that cannot be said of kissing you goodbye. I found it worthy of my fondest memory."

Merely a memory? After he had *dared* to hold her in his arms and kiss her?

Her emotions took another tumble, hitting bottom with harsh cruelty. There was no doubt but that he had held other women in his arms and kissed them goodbye. How many women? What to her was the rainbow after a storm, the crown jewel of emotional commitment, meant little to a man like Jace Buckley. But of course she had known that all along and had been cautious to avoid this very moment. And he had dared to ignore her boundaries!

As though conjured up in the mocking mist, the smug young face of the beautiful Indian girl in Sualkashi flashed before her, evoking vivid scenes that lit an angry spark. Her palm was across his face before she even realized she had slapped him.

It took him by surprise, for he took a small step back.

With more dignity than she thought she possessed, Coral picked up her skirts, whipped around, and walked quickly toward the lighted banquet hall.

After she was out of his view she ran into the lighted courtyard, nearly colliding with Ethan.

He caught her by both arms, and when she looked at him, his eyes scanned her face, then hardened. He looked over her shoulder in the direction from where she had come.

"Is Buckley out there? What has he said to you, what has he done? I shall—"

"No, please, Ethan, I want to go inside. I am not feeling well."

And as Coral took an unsteady step, he led her gently toward the lighted salon.

———

The evening wore on miserably. Coral was seated at a grand table between Sir Hugo and Ethan, but she could not concentrate on either of them. Kathleen and Marianna sat beside attentive escorts. The conversation and the music from the sitar all went unnoticed by her, while she struggled to keep her frayed emotions behind a proper demeanor. The rich assortment of dishes from the maharaja's kansamah were tasteless and dry in her mouth, and she could hardly swallow. She dare not look at the dewan, for fear she would think of Gem. With every moment that dragged by she wondered what time it was, and how much longer she must stay.

One thought rekindled the smoldering flame in her heart: Tomorrow she was going home, home to Kingscote and to her mother.

From her memory, the little song she had taught Gem came back, haunting her emotions above the festive din:

Shepherd, Shepherd, where be your little lambs?
Don't you know the tiger roams the land?
Softly, little lamb, softly, I AM always here.
My rod is your protection, My arm will hold you near.

Oh, Lord, prayed Coral. *I cannot stand it. I am going to cry. Please, not here, not now, not in front of them! And Jace—*

The glass slipped from her fingers and came splashing down in her lap, soaking the lush silk skirts. "Oh!"

There was a rush by Ethan to offer her his napkin, and even the dewan stood, calling for a servant. Horrified, Coral apologized for the disturbance and murmured something about excusing herself.

Somehow she reached the stairs that led up to a public powder room. Climbing the steps, she blinked back the tears and clamped her jaw. She refused to permit her mind to find its way back to Jace.

Cold fingers of pain squeezed about her heart. She could feel, if she permitted herself to do so, an odd feeling of emptiness, a void that was left to stand stark and bare. Unsatisfied, unfulfilled. Jace was forever gone. And now?

She was certain of one thing: He had kissed her only because he thought he might not see her again. He was indeed a rogue! She had understood that he was not the manner of man to be content with the dreams of Miss

Coral Kendall. Neither her wealth nor her beauty would lure him to Kingscote. No. He had deliberately kissed her because he knew it was goodbye.

Feeling emotionally spent, Coral paused on the stairway, and looked back in the direction of the open doors that led out into the garden.

Gone. First Gem, and now this illusive man who came and went in the masquerade of three men, none of whom she truly understood. He would not remove his armor for anyone, especially her.

No, she would not think about him anymore. She forced herself to whisper aloud, "The Lord is my high tower."

Her back stiffened as her thoughts continued to be consumed with Jace. She tried futilely to erase from her memory the feel of his lips.

Maybe, yes, just maybe—I should go ahead and let Ethan know that I am ready to become his betrothed, she thought angrily. How could Jace simply say goodbye?

And just whom had she said goodbye to? Major Buckley? Javed Kasam? Or was it the captain of the *Madras*?

Coral sighed audibly, wearily, as she reached the second-floor landing and crossed to the door of her chamber.

I have work to do on Kingscote, she thought. *I have a school to open, children to teach, and Ethan . . .*

Coral straightened her shoulders, turned her back, and entered her room, shutting out the world behind her.

30

Even before the mansion's white walls and blue stone roof came into view, Coral felt the anticipation swelling within her soul. Home at last!

When Seward stepped from the boat onto the ghat steps with Coral and her sisters, a Kingscote ghari was waiting near the river. Two white-clad bearers stood to greet them, extending palms to forehead. "Welcome home, Missy Coral! Missy Kathleen! Missy Marianna!"

From the main landing on the Brahmaputra River where the elephants hauled the precious cargo down to the boats, Kings Road ran northeast through the tropical forest into the massive holdings of the Kendall silk plantation. The road, named after great-grandfather Kingston Kendall, was wide enough for four elephants to pass side by side. Although the plantation road had existed for seventy years, well-beaten by elephant feet and the wheels of wagons, the jungle creepers and ferns were in need of constant vigil to hold back their rapid growth. Tall trees arched their branches overhead, exotic leaves blocking the sunlight, while on either side of Kings Road, the dense tropical forest of northeastern Assam surrounded them.

The afternoon was hot, and Coral and her sisters swished their fans in excitement. The horses' hoofs clopped forward up the wide two-mile road toward the Kendall mansion.

"Orchids," gasped Marianna. "I'd forgotten them. Oh, stop the ghari, Mister Seward." She turned to Coral and Kathleen. "Let's pick an armful for mother!"

Coral could imagine Ethan's delight when he discovered that the orchids grew wild. The small white and lavender jewels twining about the trunks of trees reminded Coral of the decorative garlands of Christmas festoons. She offered her wide-brimmed hat, and the three of them filled it while the giant scarlet butterflies flitted from blossom to blossom. Even Kathleen was moved, and paused to look about in reverie. "I'd forgotten all this," she said simply.

Coral understood her emotion, and a melancholic hush descended upon the three of them.

Soon the ghari emerged from the steamy shadows into a wide clearing confronting the mansion that sprawled along a sloping expanse of emerald-green with sunlight gazing down upon white marble from Rajasthan. The domed roofs made of small blue mosaics glistened against the distant backdrop of the massive mulberry orchard.

Coral's heart swelled with longing. Memories of her mother seemed to rush down the wide steps. Her father, Michael, Alex, and a host of remembered family servants all seemed to move toward her in a memory-inspired homecoming. And Gem . . . Gem was always there waiting in the rose garden of her mind.

Marianna was already running toward the steps, Kathleen coming behind, but Coral stood in grateful praise to the Lord who had brought her home again.

With anticipation Coral began walking, then running, toward the verandah.

The house servants were all assembled to welcome them, and Coral smiled and called to them in greeting. But it was her mother she wished to see!

A man emerged from the others and came down the steps to greet them. He stood dressed immaculately in a blue silk three-quarter-length jacket. He wore white leggings and small woven shoes, and his turban was white cotton, embroidered on the edges with blue. His face was expressionless, but the dark eyes glinted like rippling pools as they fixed upon Coral.

"Natine," she said gently.

Then he smiled, his eyes crinkling at the corners, and he came to life. "Miss Coral, welcome, welcome!"

Looking into the eyes of Natine, Coral thought she could see her own reflection as she greeted the man she had known since she was a toddler. "*Jai ram*, friend Natine! How good to be home again."

"You look well after your sickness. You are strong again?"

"Much stronger, and delighted to be home in India."

It was Natine who ended the conversation. He brought his fingers to his forehead then turned toward the servants. He clapped his hands, and one by one the others stepped forward to greet them.

She must tell Natine not to clap at the others. He could be pretentious, but she told herself that it was his commanding way and had been for as long as she could remember. She recognized most of them and smiled her greeting to each one, speaking their names. She went out of her way to try to show respect and warmth, knowing that it was these people that she hoped to win to her cause. The Kendall family had always been informal with the workers, but to her mild surprise they remained grave, murmuring the correct response. *As though I am a stranger,* she thought. *More of Natine's rules,* she decided. She must change all of this.

She noticed a young woman standing behind the others. There was something familiar about her. Then she remembered and smiled. "Preetah?"

Natine's niece stepped forward. The girl had not been working at Kingscote when Coral left for London, but lived with relatives in the village farther north. She was pleased to see her among the house servants. Looking into the young woman's eyes, Coral thought them to be joyless.

Preetah gestured her greeting and murmured Coral's name.

"And the memsahib?" Coral asked Natine, glancing up the wide stairway. "Is she well enough to see us now?"

"Oh, we must see Mother!" cried Marianna.

Natine retained his dignity. "Memsahib is recovering but now asleep," came his faultless voice. "Her daughters are much on her mind."

"Asleep? Is that all," said Kathleen with relief. "Then we'll awaken her, won't we, Marianna? Come, Coral, let's surprise her!"

Marianna raced Kathleen to the top of the landing. Coral remembered that with her mother ill and Sir Hampton and Alex gone, she and her sisters were in command of Kingscote. Restraining the desire to run into her mother's arms, she turned and spoke quietly to Natine. "I want you to give Seward a full report of how everything on Kingscote is progressing in my father's absence. Seward will sit at the head of the table tonight in Sir Hampton's place."

"As you wish, Miss Coral."

Coral walked back to the verandah, where Seward still waited, and looped her arm through his. She smiled up at him but noticed he wore a tinge of frown. "We're home, Seward, thanks to you and Major Buckley. Learn everything you can about Father and Alex. I will speak to you alone after dinner in Hampton's office."

"Aye, lass, and give Miss Elizabeth my regards. Here be the medicine from Doctor Boswell."

With a smile Coral rushed up the stairs so swiftly she had to pause on the top landing to catch her breath. She hurried down the hall past her own room and the adjoining chamber that had once belonged to Gem, pausing only briefly to touch the door. She stopped near her parents' chambers.

The door stood wide open, and outside in the hall Jan-Lee was seated on a chair. Seeing Coral, she stood, her eyes flickering in the ageless face beneath rich black hair touched with white.

"Jan-Lee."

The Burmese woman stared at her, then her lips turned up at the corners. "Welcome home, Miss Coral." Swiftly, Coral was in her arms, and for a moment a silk heiress and a servant stood bonded in no other thought but love.

Coral pulled away. Brushing the tears from her cheeks, she looked toward her mother's bedroom. She hesitated, bringing her emotions under control; then clutching the bottle of medicine to her heart, she entered with a soft rustle of skirts.

The familiar room was rich with mahogany furniture, thick Afghan rugs, and heavy gold-braided drapes that were drawn across the verandah doors to shut out the heat. An Indian child worked the fans, her wide, curious eyes on the scene before her as Kathleen and Marianna bent over their mother beside the large bed.

Coral tiptoed to the side of the bed, and Kathleen moved away, wiping her eyes. At the sight of her mother, Coral stood transfixed, still gripping the bottle. Two black braids rested on the lace pillow-cover beside the thin face. Dark circles ringed her brown eyes, and as they came to rest upon Coral, moisture oozed from their corners and ran down her cheeks. Her fever-cracked lips quivered as she tried to speak her daughter's name. A limp hand reached out for her. In a moment Coral was in her arms.

"My Coral . . ."

Coral could not speak. Her throat cramped, and she simply clung to her.

Her mother's prolonged suffering spurred Coral to action. Bringing herself under control, she prepared Ethan's prescription, believing that God would bless the results.

"Mother," she whispered. "I've brought you medication. It will help make you stronger, just as it helped me in London."

She and her sisters stayed until the medication brought her into restful sleep, then Jan-Lee spoke. "I'll look after Miss Elizabeth now. She would want her daughters also to rest."

Her sisters showed their weariness, and they tiptoed across the polished wood floor to the door. Marianna cast a wistful glance back before reluctantly leaving.

Coral remained seated on the side of the bed, and when the sound of their steps faded, she quietly rose and stood, looking down at her mother. Despite the long battle with burning heat and hallucinations, her mother's face reflected the inner composure of her deep faith in the Scriptures. She was graying at the temples and hairline, her cheekbones prominent due to the loss of weight, but still her mother looked much like the image Coral had carried in her memory.

Jan-Lee stood at the open doors leading onto the verandah, watching Coral steadily. Her features were quiet but showed concern. Coral wearily walked up beside her. Together, they looked out into the twilight settling over the distant jungle. The smooth lawns and trees lining the drive were beginning to darken. How hushed the coming of evening was! Even the usual clamor of birds only whispered in Coral's ears. Here in this comforting interlude, she stood beside Jan-Lee, her mother's most intimate servant—her own as well. Coral laid her head against her arm and Jan-Lee held her in silence.

A peacock's shrill call pierced the oncoming shadows. Coral stirred. "How is little Emerald?"

Jan-Lee's mouth turned into a pleased smile. "She is a good child. She remembers you and the songs you teach her back then."

Back then . . . when Emerald had played with Gem. . . . Inevitably, her heart drawn down the path of warm memories, she found herself recalling the night she had brought Gem home from Jemani's hut near the silkworm hatcheries. Coral had given the tiny infant to Jan-Lee to nurse along with her own newborn daughter, Emerald. How long ago that all seemed now!

The violet dusk was losing color over the darkening jungle trees. "Tell me about Mother. Does she know that my father went to find Alex? That there is danger?"

"She knows. Each time she wakes she asks if there is word."

"The message, how did it arrive?"

The woman's eyes hardened. "It was a man of my ancestry who brought your brother's ring. The one your father gave him before Mister Alex went to study music. Said he was very ill. Your father look at ring, and his face grow sad. Then at once he gathered group of men and prepared for trek to Darjeeling. They leave the next morning while it was yet dark."

"He took men with him? From the village?"

"No, Natine was unable to find the men to go so quickly. So Mister Hampton took volunteers from the silk workers. Twelve went with him by boat, carrying guns."

"Guns?" gasped Coral, her tired mind at once alert.

Jan-Lee nodded. "For protection. There is talk of marauders from the border."

Seward would have the latest information on any infringements from the Burmese warlord, if there were any truth to the rumors from Sir Hugo, and she would speak to him later that evening.

"Has there been any trouble recently?" she asked.

Jan-Lee shook her head. "No trouble except the illness."

"Are there many sick on Kingscote?"

"Yes, women, children, the old men. Yanna and I attend them as best we can since your mother became ill."

Yanna. By now, thought Coral, the girl would be of marriageable age. She wondered how Yanna would find a Christian husband, since Coral's mother had written that Yanna had been baptized.

"Natine is displeased that his niece Preetah was helping Yanna and me with some of the sick. He threatened Preetah. Miss Elizabeth had to get up from her sickbed to speak to him. And this when she was very ill. She collapsed after that and did not come awake for many hours."

Coral felt a quiet indignation that Natine would cause her mother such trouble when she needed complete rest.

"I'll see to Natine, and to the sick," she stated. "There's little I can do about his niece, but he cannot interfere with you or Yanna. I wish to see the ill for myself. Will you take me tomorrow, Jan-Lee? I want to make a full inspection."

Jan-Lee glanced toward Elizabeth, who was moaning softly, and she leaned down to pick up the bucket of cool, scented water. She carried it to the side of the bed and Coral joined her, wringing out the cloths and handing them to Jan-Lee, who wiped down her mother. Her fever-racked body was gaunt, and Coral's heart wrenched with anxiety. Would the medicine cure her mother? And what of herself? Had she looked this bad in London? Sir Hugo insisted she had almost died. Perhaps his words had not been far from reality.

"Miss Coral, you must not take on all the burdens at Kingscote in your mother's place. If you do, you will weary yourself and get sick again. Then what?"

"Did my mother do too much, Jan-Lee?"

"She works too hard for untouchables. Mister Hampton was upset, but she would not listen. We buried three infants, and mothers, and old men, old women, all too tired to fight on. It was after that that she got very sick too. Now Yanna does what she can, and Emerald helps, but I cannot leave Miss Elizabeth for long."

"I'm feeling strong. And Kathleen and Marianna can help me."

Jan-Lee cast her a silent glance, seeming to question her sisters' willingness. Coral told herself she would send for Yanna first thing in the morning. She must also speak to Natine about his bullying ways with the other workers, but perhaps it was wiser to wait until they were home for a few days. Somehow she knew that the dignified man would not take her words as anything less than meddling. He would still see her and her sisters as mere girls who should occupy their time in frivolous activities.

Coral drew in a little breath. It was not going to be easy to put a curb on him in the absence of her father. She would also speak with Kathleen, who was the eldest.

Together, the two of them must stand shoulder to shoulder, representing the Kendall authority, until their father returned with Alex.

"Thank heaven we have Seward!" she murmured.

———————

Coral took after-dinner tea with Seward in the comfortable but overcrowded office that belonged to her father. Books lined the wall, stacked knee-high on both sides of the mahogany desk, and papers and parchments concerning the business of Kingscote were piled in disarray. The room with its many trinkets gathered haphazardly from his far-reaching travels told much of Sir Hampton Kendall's rugged personality and colorful past. Her eye fell on a carved elephant that she remembered from her childhood, for it held a special enchantment, and she had named it after her pet elephant, Rani. Somehow the miniature brought Jace to mind.

Where is he now? What is he doing? Coral stirred uneasily and tried to dismiss him from her mind.

"Like I said, lass, it's a feeling inside that bothers me. And Jace has his suspicions too."

"He said nothing of them to me!"

"He wouldn't. And he wouldn't care for me mentioning it to you now. But seeing as how I'm asking my leave to go to Darjeeling, it's only right I tell you why. But I be distressed over leavin' you and your sisters and Miss Elizabeth alone here."

"We're not alone," she hastened. "I'm sure there is little to worry about. I want you to go to my father. By now he and Alex may need you."

She leaned toward him and said quietly, "But why did Jace think the message brought to my father could be deceptive?"

Seward rubbed his bearded chin, watching her

thoughtfully, as though wondering how much he should reveal. He glanced toward the closed office door. "Jace be thinking Alex could not have the fever."

She was alert. "Why not?"

"It is very uncommon to the climate of Darjeeling. It's cool in the mountainous region."

She felt her skin prickle. "Then what could possibly lie behind the message? And who would send it? According to Jan-Lee, the messenger gave my father Alex's ring as proof."

"Aye, 'tis what bothers me."

"Did—did Jace say anything else?"

Seward frowned at her, and his eyes drifted to the elephant in her hand. She decided from his expression that Jace had said more, but Seward was sworn to silence.

"There be no proof of anything," he cautioned. "Let me worry about your father and Alex. You take care of Miss Elizabeth. So with your leave, I'd like to take out on my own."

"Go at once," she said swiftly, setting the elephant down and standing to her feet. "I wish Jace would have told me at Guwahati."

"He wanted me to see you here safely. He also expects me to stay, and he won't be liking this. But I be more worried about Sir Hampton than an attack on Kingscote. Besides, I've a few good men on Kingscote I'd trust my life to, and I know they be risking themselves to protect you and your sisters and Miss Elizabeth. They be loyal, but I can't say as much for some others," he suggested darkly.

Coral knew that he meant Natine. Somehow she could not agree. "We have Madan and Thilak, and their sons."

"Good men, all. Should you be needing any help, they

361

be at hand. And I'll be back with Sir Hampton and your brother as soon as I can."

Coral nodded, feeling suddenly jittery.

Seward stood, as if in spite of all his words to the contrary, he did feel concern about leaving them. He fingered his tricorn. "Jace not be liking this," he repeated.

"We're home, among people we've known since we were children."

She smiled, even though she was tense with mounting alarm. She knew Seward too well. If he wasn't convinced that her father could be in trouble of some sort, there would be little that could budge him from her side. She had long depended upon Seward, not only for physical protection, but in being the uncle to her that Sir Hugo was not.

If Seward was convinced, his frown did not lessen. She saw that his emotions were torn in two directions at once. "Go in peace," she said softly. "You and Jace won't tell me, but it's my father who is in danger. You must find him, Seward! If something should happen to him—" Her voice broke.

"Aye," he said huskily.

"—Uncle Hugo would become my guardian, controlling Kingscote."

"That be the part that's been eating at me . . . and Jace. So you know."

"But Sir Hugo wouldn't be involved in . . . in—" She couldn't speak the words.

Seward's eyes hardened like ice. "In harming Sir Hampton? Who knows what grows like jungle creeper in a man's heart. In the end I suppose a man could do anything if his greed is not rooted out. Mind me now, I am not saying that it's so," he hastened. "You best keep all this to yourself."

"Yes, Seward. You'll be careful on the trek?"

"Don't be worrying about me. Me and Jace been there more than a dozen times." He put his hat on and turned to leave. He smiled kindly, affection warming his eyes. "The Lord be your stay, lass."

He went out, shutting the door behind him. She was left alone.

A few minutes later she heard him mount a horse outside on the carriageway, and the sound of hoofs riding away were lost in the darkness of the night.

Coral stood without moving, wrestling with the loss. "Bring them home safely, Lord. All of them."

Coral refused to give in to a nag of doubt and fear, and instead walked behind her father's sturdy desk. She sank into the leather chair, feeling small in comparison to its size. She opened a top drawer where she knew he kept the small Bible that Elizabeth had given him one Christmas when Coral was still a child. It was gone. Her father had taken it with him before his hasty departure to search for Alex in Darjeeling. The realization brought a smile to her lips. Perhaps the difficulty facing them would end well.

Kathleen and Marianna had already gone to bed when she climbed the darkened stairs in the silent mansion. At the landing, she stopped, feeling as though she were being watched.

She turned and looked down into the Great Hall, but there was no one there.

In her room, she stood in reflective silence, trying to sweep her mind clean of everything but the satisfaction of being home where she belonged. She took a moment to drink in the familiar setting. Only the tension of the problems at hand sapped the moment of a joy-filled homecoming.

Everything appeared just as she had left it some years earlier. The four-poster bed with its mosquito netting, the brightly scattered rugs on the polished wood floor, the wide verandah that overlooked the Bramaputra River. Crossing the floor in the lantern dimness, she stepped out onto the verandah into the warm night.

There in the shadows she stood for a quiet minute and tried to calm her anxious spirit. The Lord did not slumber nor did He sleep, she repeated to herself. He knew. Whatever the future held, the promise of His strength and purpose would also be there to guide their steps.

"One day," Coral murmured, "we will understand that without the storm, there would not be the beauty of the rainbow."

Above and toward the river, the sky held a dusky hue of rose. Beneath its glow, the water appeared to sit like glass. The distant fringed tops of the palm trees stood motionless. *Home.*

"What I need is the luxury of soaking in a cool scented bath," she told herself with deliberate joy. "No crocodiles . . . no snakes . . . no spiders. . . . And after that? The feel of silk!"

31

In the days that followed, Elizabeth did not recover her strength. She spent much of her time between wakefulness and sleep, her body growing more gaunt, eaten away by fever. The medication that had helped Coral in London appeared to have no more effect than sugar-water. The sickness and hallucinations continued.

Coral decided that if any good was born from this trying time—with their father and Alex missing, and their mother slowly slipping from their grasp—it came from the effect that uncertainty and sorrow had on Kathleen. Her sister had grown sober, more reflective, and more patient with Marianna.

The three of them took their nightly vigil by their mother's bedside, while either Jan-Lee or Mera joined them. Since Coral had offered to take the late-night watch after Kathleen, she often entered their mother's room to find her sister seated in the chair reading from the worn King James Bible that rested on the bedstand. Kathleen never mentioned her new study of the Scriptures, and neither did Coral make a point to ask her, feeling it wiser to say nothing. The evidence of Kathleen's seedling faith brought the one joy to Coral's heart during this time. Indeed, God was in control, bringing His peace to Kathleen's turbulent life.

Kathleen took her by surprise one morning after tea when she announced, "I think the three of us should hold a prayer vigil for Mama. It's the one thing we haven't done. We've prayed separately but not together."

Marianna nearly spilled her tea, but Coral said smoothly, "You are right. Why didn't we think of it sooner? When should we start?"

Kathleen hesitated, accustomed to leaving such decisions to Coral.

"Well . . ." She looked from Coral to Marianna, then cleared her throat. "Tomorrow is Sunday. We could dedicate the entire day to prayer. Maybe—maybe even fast. We've so much to pray about. Not only Mother, but Father, Alex, and the mission school."

"Why Kathleen—" began Marianna in awe but stopped short when Coral nudged her beneath the table with the toe of her shoe.

With Sunday given over to prayer and Bible reading, the next weeks passed without disturbance. The answer came gradually, like the buds slowly turning into blossoms. Their mother's hallucinations grew further apart, the fever ebbed, and she became mentally alert for longer periods of time. She was able to keep warm broth down without vomiting, and within another week was eating scrambled eggs and enjoying hot tea.

As the days continued to pass, Elizabeth was able to sit up with pillows propped behind her, smiling weakly at her beaming daughters. It was during these precious times of mother-daughter fellowship that Coral became certain their mother would recover. Already there was new color in her cheeks, and though terribly thin, Elizabeth Kendall was heedful of all that was going on and able once more to pass on her commands as mistress of Kingscote.

As yet, Coral had not spoken to her about the mission school, for the opportune time did not appear to be at hand. She waited for the moment when they could speak alone.

It was ten o'clock Saturday morning when Marianna, donned in bright flounces of pink, faced Kathleen at the bottom of the stairway. "I tell you it's true. I saw the letter and asked mother."

"When! Where is it?"

Coral, hearing their excited voices, left the dining salon where she had been reading the Hindi New Testament. From the arched doorway she saw her sisters. Marianna looked pleased to have unearthed some astounding secret.

"Are you certain? Why didn't mother tell me?"

"How could she when she's been so ill? I saw the letter, I tell you. It was in Mother's sewing basket."

Kathleen groaned and raced up the stairway to her mother's room. "And to think I passed that basket every day for a month!"

"What letter?" called Coral.

Marianna whirled to follow after Kathleen, calling over her shoulder, "A letter from Granny V! She wrote Mother as soon as we left London! She's asking for both Kathleen and Mother to visit Roxbury House and settle Kathleen's future!"

"A letter! But how did it get here so soon?"

"By ship by way of Rangoon and into Assam by river," called Marianna, as though Coral should have guessed, and disappeared down the hall.

When Coral arrived at her mother's room, the door was standing open and Kathleen was speaking to her in a high state of emotional excitement. "Mother, you will let me go back to Roxbury House, won't you? You will come with me for a visit as Granny V asked?"

Elizabeth cupped her daughter's chin and looked at her sadly, as though the pleading amber eyes pricked her heart.

"Kathleen, I cannot promise now. It depends on your father and Alex."

"But Mother! I'll die if we don't go!"

Elizabeth smiled. "I don't think so; you look quite healthy to me. And you've only now come home to Kingscote. If you go running off to London so soon, what will Gavin think? Didn't you tell me he will be stationed at the Jorhat outpost as soon as he gets through Plassey? Darling, you must be fair with your cousin and not keep holding him off this way."

Kathleen kneeled beside her bed, clasping her mother's hand. "What did Granny V say to you? May I see the letter? Marianna says it arrived months ago!"

"Marianna, you should have asked my permission to tell your sister. I intended to speak to her at the proper time."

Marianna looked guilty. "Yes, Mother."

Coral watched them, saying nothing.

Elizabeth looked back at Kathleen, searching her eldest daughter's face. Evidently she saw something that disturbed her for she said quietly, "I suppose times are changing. A girl can wait until she is in her late twenties to marry, but eyebrows will be raised.

"I don't care. It is my life!"

"No," corrected Elizabeth softly. "It is God's."

Kathleen bowed her head. "Yes, I understand, and I do want His will. Only—the Silk House."

"He understands your heart."

There was a moment of silence. Coral held her breath.

"I agree, it is wise not to rush the matter with Gavin

if you're not certain. But both of you must come to some mutual agreement with your father upon his return."

"I will, I promise. Then you do understand? It's not that I don't care for him, it's just . . ." She stopped, as though her confusion made it impossible to say more. "Say you'll come with me. You know how much Granny V wishes to see you. Why it's been years since you've seen your own mother."

Coral looked at her mother and saw the wistfulness on her face.

"Yes, too long . . . I would love to see her again, and London."

"Then we'll go?" cried Kathleen with a squeal.

"We will see what happens in the coming months. First your father must approve, and we must be sure it is safe to travel, because of the fighting, and of course I'll need to regain my strength for a journey to Calcutta and a long voyage. If matters progress, and it appears as though God is leading us that way, then yes, we'll visit Roxbury House, but I cannot say when."

Kathleen threw her arms around her mother's neck. "Thank you for understanding!"

"Oh, we must write Aunt Margaret and Belinda," cried Marianna. "They'll be at Roxbury House too!"

"Yes, it would be nice," said Elizabeth. "I'll write Margaret and congratulate her on Belinda's engagement to Sir Arlen George. I am certain your grandmother will heartily approve of the choice. He comes from a good family. And that reminds me, Coral, we need to discuss Ethan."

Coral's eyes lowered, and she felt her sisters discreetly leave the room. Her heart pounding, she decided this was the moment to steer the discussion away from Ethan to the mission school.

"First, Mother, I have something to show you," Coral

369

said with a smile, her hands hidden behind her back.

Elizabeth's eyes warmed as they fixed on Coral. "A surprise?"

"One you will appreciate." She carefully handed her the Hindi New Testament and watched her mother's expression turn to awe.

"Why, it is written in Hindi. Where did you get this?"

"William Carey. He's also translating into the language of Assam, and Charles Peddington will send me a copy when it's ready."

Coral explained about William Carey, and the work he was doing in Serampore. "He will translate the Bible into six languages, imagine! And portions into many others. I've met all the missionaries laboring with him at the station—Mr. Ward and the Marshmans. It was Hannah Marshman who advised me on starting a mission school. And Master Carey is a man who loves India. I wish you could meet him, Mother! He will do more for the people in giving them the Bible in their own tongue than anything the East India Company could do! Uncle Hugo is against him. He insists I must not put Kingscote in jeopardy by wishing to follow Master Carey's vision and starting a school, but Uncle is wrong!"

Elizabeth did not appear surprised over her daughter's zeal. "I've been expecting as much," she said, holding the New Testament.

Coral knelt beside the bed. "I wrote you about the school from London. Margaret said you mentioned it to her in your letter before you became ill. Mother, the need for the children is so great."

When Elizabeth said nothing and the silence grew, Coral took heart. "We have over a hundred children working the hatcheries. Mother, we could teach them to read, to write, and tell them the stories about our Lord from the Gospels." Her eyes shone. "We could teach them in their own tongue. Think what it would mean to them to hear of Him in their own language."

Elizabeth stared at the words in Hindi. The moments dragged on, and Coral bit her lip to keep silent.

"Your uncle is right. There would be much opposition to building a mission school. And a good deal of hard work."

"But I'm willing to work hard. It's my calling, Mother. It's the main reason why I've wanted to come home. To start a school in the memory of Gem, to reach a hundred boys and girls like him with the truth of the Shepherd!"

Her mother touched the side of Coral's face.

Coral paused for a moment, then in a rush told her about Jace Buckley and the possibility that Gem could yet be alive. "The major has promised to help me discover the truth. And I feel certain the Lord is asking us to build the school. But without your support it will never happen. Only you can convince Father of the need, and we must stand together against Sir Hugo's opposition."

"I do not know, Coral . . . Hugo is right on one thing. Teaching the Scriptures so openly to the children would anger many. I've done what I could, but what you desire to do on Kingscote is far more involved."

"Have you mentioned it to Father?"

Elizabeth sighed. "Yes. He is quite concerned about the idea, but he promised to pray about it."

Coral's heart pounded. If her father promised to pray about the matter, then he was open to the suggestion, no matter how risky.

Coral wanted to press for a decision, but she knew her mother already understood her passion and was aware of the personal cost.

"Keep the Hindi New Testament, Mother. Read it and pray about what I've asked."

Elizabeth searched her face and laid a weak hand on her arm. "You are willing to accept my decision?"

Coral tensed. Her eyes searched her mother's. It was time to remove her hands from the project and depend completely upon God. "Yes."

"I'm thinking of you, too, Coral. If your father were to allow you to build the school, and teach, it could cost your best years in dedication to service."

"I've already thought that through. It is what I wish to do with my life."

Elizabeth looked pained. "What of marriage to Ethan? Children?"

"Ethan knows how I feel. He has his own work, and he will be starting his medical lab on Kingscote."

Elizabeth studied her, and Coral suddenly wanted to lower her eyes.

"I've heard the colonel's son is no longer serving the Company."

"He . . . he is in the military but serving reluctantly. The colonel managed to lure him back because of his ship."

"Seward says Jace Buckley is still determined to build the tea plantation at Darjeeling. I believe he'll be going with Major Buckley, along with an Indian friend named Gokul, and an old Chinese man," said Elizabeth.

Coral said nothing. The unexpected discussion about Jace made her feel uneasy.

"How well have you come to know the colonel's son?"

The question was simply put, not one that should have troubled Coral so deeply, nor brought warmth to her cheeks, but she stammered, "Well enough, I suppose."

"Suppose? You must know him well indeed, if he will risk so much to see if he can locate Gem."

"He has proven a friend."

"A friend," Elizabeth repeated. "Is he also a Christian?"

"He is searching, but I believe his faith in God is strong." Coral paused. "But his future plans are his own. And he remains an adventurer."

"I see."

Coral stood. "You'll let me know about the school?"

"Yes, but at the moment, it is you I shall take to heart. Are you in love with the colonel's son?"

Stunned by the blunt question, Coral blushed under her mother's gaze. "No."

Coral couldn't tell if her mother was convinced or not. She heard her sigh and look down at the Scriptures again. "How different you are from Kathleen. I'm proud of you, Coral. And pleased that the Lord means so much to you. But perhaps you are not so different from your sister." She looked up at Coral.

Coral wondered what she meant. How was she like Kathleen?

"For Kathleen it will mean another journey to the London Silk House to discover what she truly wants. Marriage to Gavin, or a career in silk. And for you it means a mission school and danger."

Coral smiled. "But I do know my heart."

Elizabeth said no more. She smiled suddenly. "I shall let you know my decision."

The decision came unexpectedly and sooner than Coral had hoped. On Sunday morning Coral was seated at the breakfast table with her sisters when, to their surprise, Elizabeth entered, dressed. Although pale and thin, she looked stronger.

They stood to their feet as she was assisted to her seat by Natine. The girls looked at one another and smiled.

"You may pour the tea, Preetah," she said brightly. "Natine, you may commence to serve."

"Yes, memsahib."

They ate cheerfully, and after breakfast Elizabeth looked across the table at Coral and smiled. "As soon as your father returns from Darjeeling, we shall discuss the building of the school. If he agrees, you may have your desire."

There was a delighted gasp from Marianna, and Kathleen looked at her. Coral sat motionless, staring at her mother.

"I can't promise you, Coral. But I think I can convince your father of the need, and the spirit which prompts you to do something so difficult. It is a noble cause, one worthy of the Kendall name."

Coral remembered little else except that she was on her feet. A moment later she was in her mother's arms as Elizabeth whispered, "In the memory of Gem, we shall build. And may God be pleased to prosper our way."

The thud of horse's hoofs sounded on the drive outside the dining-hall window, and Kathleen was the first to draw aside the curtain.

"A sepoy!"

"Natine, bring him into the sitting room and serve him refreshments," called Elizabeth.

"Yes, memsahib."

Marianna stood. "Perhaps Captain McKay has arrived at Guwahati with troops for the outpost."

"I'll see," cried Kathleen, and sped ahead of Natine to meet the Indian soldier.

Coral went to the window and looked out. Kathleen stood on the porch, and the sepoy handed her something, but Coral was thinking only of her mother's fair words.

A mission school for the children! The Lord had answered her prayer. She had little doubt that her mother would convince Hampton of the need.

A minute later Kathleen came rushing in waving a

white envelope. "It's for you, Coral. From Major Buckley."

Jace!

Coral felt her heart wrench. She tore it open and her hand shook as she read the bold, black writing:

I would not write you this brief message unless I had certain proof. Gem is alive. Gokul has discovered his whereabouts. It is not safe to say more in writing. If all goes well, I shall return him to you by Christmas.

J. Buckley

Coral stood transfixed. Gem was alive!

"Darling, what is it?" asked Elizabeth, rising to her feet but holding to the side of the table.

"Is it F-father?" Marianna stammered. "Something happened to him!"

"No, no," said Coral, her voice shaking with happiness, and she turned to her mother with a beaming smile. "Gem is alive!"

Elizabeth turned pale.

"Jace will bring him home in time for Christmas!" Coral said, embracing her mother. "Gem, and the mission school. What greater gifts could the Lord give me?"

She looked again at the message, her eyes resting on something she had not noticed before in the excitement. Jace Buckley had said that *he* would bring Gem to Kingscote.

Her heart skipped a beat. *Jace is coming.*

"This is a day of celebration," announced Elizabeth, a smile flooding her features.

"But the best is yet to come," whispered Coral.

GLOSSARY

ASSAM: Northeast India, location of Kingscote.

AYAH: A child's nurse.

BRAHMIN: Highest Hindu caste.

BURRA-SAHIB: A great man.

CHUNNI: A light head covering; a scarf.

DAFFADAR: A native cavalry sergeant.

DAK-BUNGALOW: A resting house for travelers.

DEWAN: The chief minister of an Indian ruler.

FERINGHI: A foreigner.

GHARI: A horse-drawn carriage.

GHARI-WALLAH: A carriage driver.

GHAT: Steps or a platform on the river.

GHAZI: A fanatic; usually with religious overtones, but also referring to political beliefs.

HOWDAH: A framework with a seat for carrying passengers on the back of an elephant.

HUZOOR: Your honor.

JEMANDER: A junior Indian officer promoted through the ranks.

JOHNNY SEPOY: Nickname for a common native soldier.

KANSAMAH: A cook.

KOI HAI: A call for service

MAHARAJA: A Hindu king.

MAHARATTA: A warlike central Indian kingdom.

MAHOUT: An elephant driver.

MAIDAN: A large expanse of lawn; a parade ground.

MANJI: A boatman.

MUNSHI: A teacher and writer.

NAMASTE: A respectful gesture of fingers to the forehead with palms together.

NAWAB: A Muslim ruling prince or powerful land owner.

RAJA: A king.

RAJPUTS: A warrior caste of the Hindus, a rank below the *brahmins*.

RANI: A queen.

SEPOY: A native infantry soldier.

SHAMIANAH: A large tent.

SOWAR: A cavalry trooper.

SUTTEE: The religious act of burning alive a widow on the funeral pyre of her deceased husband, based on the belief that by so doing she will attain eternal happiness and bring blessings on her family.

TEHSILDAR: The village headman.

TULWAR: A curved sword.

UNTOUCHABLE: One that is below the Hindu caste system, condemned as unclean in this life.

KINGSCOTE

KINGSCOTE

LINDA CHAIKIN

BETHANY HOUSE PUBLISHERS
MINNEAPOLIS, MINNESOTA 55438

Cover illustration by Joe Nordstrom

Published by Bethany House Publishers
A Ministry of Bethany Fellowship, Inc.
11300 Hampshire Avenue South
Minneapolis, Minnesota 55438

Printed in the United States of America

For dramatic purposes, Felix Carey, son of William, has been portrayed as several years older than he actually was in 1800. Felix was in fact born in 1785 and was ordained in 1807.

Library of Congress Cataloging-in-Publication Data

Chaikin, L. L., 1943–
    Kingscote / Linda Chaikin.
       p. cm. — (Heart of India ; 3)
   I. Title. II. Series.
PS3553.H2427K56   1994
813'.54—dc20   94–6788
ISBN 1–55661–378–4   CIP

To

Barb Lilland

"Iron sharpeneth iron;
so a man sharpeneth the
countenance of his friend."

(Proverbs 27:17)

LINDA CHAIKIN is a full-time writer and has two books published in the Christian market. She graduated from Multnomah School of the Bible and is working on a degree with Moody Bible Institute. She and her husband, Steve, are involved with a church-planting mission among Hindus in Kerala, India. They make their home in San Jose, California.

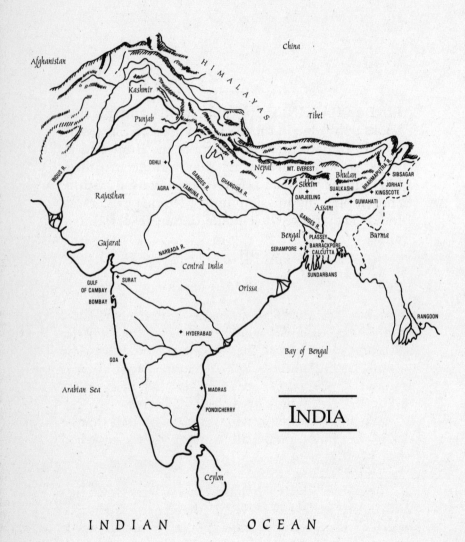

Prologue

GARDEN OF THE ROYAL PALACE, GUWAHATI, NORTHEAST INDIA

APRIL 1800

Major Jace Buckley's face was still stinging from Coral Kendall's slap. He watched the last glimmer of her silk skirts disappear as she walked quickly from view toward the maharaja's* lighted banquet hall ... and Doctor Ethan Boswell. Jace stood very still in the shadows of the garden trees, his arms folded across his chest, his blue-black eyes narrowing. He told himself that he would walk away emotionally unscathed, even as he had from other women.

Go after her.

The haunting stringed music coming from the Indian sitar as the musicians played in the upper gallery continued to throb in the fragrant night air closing in about him.

No, he decided with a stubborn determination that

---

*A glossary of Indian words is at the back of the book.

9

surprised even him. His jaw set. He would perform his duty to the colonel, learn what he could about Gem— then board the *Madras* and leave.

He turned abruptly, took the stone steps into the lower tiered garden leading down toward the Brahmaputra River, and walked the short distance to his military quarters near the British residency.

When Jace entered his chamber he tried to smother the memory of Coral and found he could not. He expressed his frustration over his emotional downfall by heaving the door shut with a bang. The windows rattled.

There came an exaggerated groan from the bunk. "Must you slam door, sahib? Ah! The treachery of romance is like goads to soul. . . ."

Jace recognized the unmistakable voice of Gokul and glanced sharply at the bunk. The presence of his old friend cheered him. He said lightly, "You are a welcome sight. Get up, you old thieving spy. Where is my coffee?"

Gokul struggled into his wrap. "Sahib, patience is the fruit of kings and wise men."

Jace walked to his wardrobe and flung open the door. "Any more news from the northeast?"

"Much. Very important."

"Why did you not come to me at once?"

A malicious glimmer showed in Gokul's black eyes as he scanned Jace.

"I fly to bring news to palace garden, but old Gokul is too much the romantic to interrupt. I see delectable English damsel in sahib's arms."

Jace turned to give him a level look. Gokul rubbed his chin. "That slap cracked silence like musket."

"Never mind. What news?"

Gokul sobered and glancing toward the open window went to close it. He drew near, his voice low and tense

10

with excitement. "I discover Gem is alive and held prisoner by Warlord Zin."

Jace's breath caught. "Zin. . . . Then my suspicions were right. But why would Zin hold Gem captive? He has made no contact with the Kendall family for ransom jewels."

"That, sabib, I could not find out. I found my contact in Jorhat with knife in back next day. Old Gokul quickly decide it is time to make hasty departure. And so here am I and will make hot coffee instead."

Zin! As Gokul went to boil water, Jace mused over the information. He grabbed his leather satchel, throwing the things on the bed that he would need to take with him to the British outpost at Jorhat.

The memory of Coral also wrapped about his heart and would not let go.

Enough, he rebuked himself. He would think of her no more.

"I must think of some way to meet with the maharaja before we ride out with Sir Hugo Roxbury. There is little time, and I have no real plan. The rajput guards are thicker than cockroaches—" He flicked one of the pesky bugs off his gold-embroidered tunic before tossing the elegant garment on the bed. He snatched a white shirt from the wardrobe.

Again he thought of Coral. He must not indulge the strange sense of loss he felt. Mulling over an idea was the first step toward acting. And if he openly admitted his feelings to her, what was left?

"Ah, sahib," sighed Gokul. "Marriage is mysterious thing, full of splendor!"

Jace turned, his eyes narrowing under his lashes as he watched Gokul brewing the coffee.

In frustration Jace unwound the turban and ran his fingers through his dark hair. . . . Commitment, sharing,

11

loving. If he admitted to Coral that he wanted her, it would mean coming into her presence without his armor. . . . Dangerous.

She would come to know his heart as she knew her own. If she should choose to do so, she could cut his heart from him and crush it in her small hand. The thought of being so vulnerable left him cold. Coral was too good to do that . . . or was she?

He stood for a moment thinking. And what of himself? Could someone so lovely and innocent trust herself to him? He would not hurt her emotionally with intention to do so, but then his moods were such that there were times when he did not even trust himself.

The great adventure of marriage: what did he know about it? Faithfulness was involved, of course. No problem there, he thought. Any man who ended up with Coral would end up with a prize for which dueling princes might fight; nor was there a problem with love, but what about commitment?

Commitment demanded his all. He must be there when she needed him emotionally, physically . . . spiritually.

Spiritually. The full-orbed meaning of the word stabbed through his soul like a dart. She belonged first of all to Christ. No man dare intrude without His permission.

Now why had he thought of that?

John Newton came to mind along with the books that the old ex-slaver had given him that rainy night in London. Jace had not planned to do so but had felt compelled to spend months aboard ship pouring over those volumes during the return voyage to Calcutta. He understood theology. In order to please Coral he could engage her in deep discussion. He believed he could even pray with her if she wanted him to.

He belted on his scabbard. He also knew that what was precious to Coral did not mean as much to him. Her will was yielded to Christ; his own remained in the hands of Jace Buckley.

First obstacle, he thought, and buttoned his shirt. The greatest obstacle. She deserved a godly hero like William Carey, or Charles Peddington. Yet . . . if he did want Coral enough to admit his feelings for her openly, could he convince her to marry him? He had never tried to convince a woman, any woman, that he truly loved her.

Gokul brought him a mug of steaming coffee, and his knowing smile caused Jace to smirk. He took the cup and turned away.

"One warning, sahib. Kendall family expect damsel to marry sahib-doctor."

Second obstacle, thought Jace. It would not be easy to convince Sir Hampton and Elizabeth Kendall to give their daughter to him instead of to Ethan. He would not allow himself to forget that Coral was a silk heiress. He had nothing to offer her but his intentions with the Darjeeling tea plantation.

Back off, Jace. Forget it.

He snapped his satchel shut and frowned. If he truly loved Coral he would stay away from her. What could he bring into her life but trouble? What of her school? Her dedication to God? She deserved Peddington.

Jace looked up at his military image in the mirror. *Yes, you might win the battle. But she would lose. Stay out of her life, Buckley. She belongs to the purposes of God, and you belong to the deck of the Madras.*

There came a rap on the door. Gokul shot him a glance. Jace slipped his pistol under his jacket, then nodded to him to answer.

An Indian servant stood there, unreadable, his turban

golden under the torchlight. "I bring a message for the major."

"Yes?" said Jace.

He salaamed. "Ambassador Roxbury regrets he cannot ride out tonight for Jorhat. The major is ordered to remain in Guwahati until further notice."

He backed away and left. Gokul shut the door and looked at Jace with caution. "The sahib-ambassador's delays smell of trap."

"Yes, but for whom, me or the maharaja?"

"Maybe both. You must be cautious, sahib. He is a clever man who knows what he is about."

"At least the delay will give me time to see the maharaja. Somehow I must gain a private audience. He must be warned of an imminent attempt on his life." He fixed a narrowed gaze on Gokul. "I need the garb of a royal bodyguard. Can you manage to produce one?"

"You turn Gokul into a thief, but yes, I manage."

When Gokul had left, Jace thought again of Coral. He snatched a piece of paper and wrote:

I would not write you this brief message unless I had certain proof. Gem is alive. Gokul has discovered his whereabouts. It is not safe to say more in writing. If all goes well, I shall return him to you by Christmas.
J. Buckley

He would have Gokul deliver the message to her . . . or . . . he might even ride to Kingscote himself once he had met with the maharaja.

He watched a large moth hopelessly beating its wings against the bright lantern.

14

If he rode there himself, his presence would inform Coral that he was only making an excuse to mend the final goodbye. Was that what he truly wished?

He watched the moth with growing irritation, then flipped it aside. It returned, beating its wings.

With a sigh Jace folded the paper and stuffed it inside his jacket. He would decide after his emotions had plenty of time to cool. He reached over and put out the lantern.

1

The night was hot and muggy as Jace left his quarters. The light wind from off the Brahmaputra River stirred the poinciana trees. He kept to the shadows as he walked across the cantonment in the direction of the Guwahati palace. What would he do when he got inside? How could he convince the guards that he must see their raja?

For weeks now, Jace's attempts to meet privately with the maharaja had been foiled. Spies were everywhere. He could trust no one in the palace, for Sunil was cunning. The prince would have worked long and hard to sow his seeds of mutinous discontent among those close to the raja before he felt the confidence to make an open move. Jace knew the assassination orders would come from Sunil. For Jace to trust any one of the royal guards or the important Indian officials meant risking his own life as well as the raja's. Who could guess who was loyal and who was not?

In these past weeks Gokul had gone into hiding, meeting with Jace late at night, and then only in disguise. Jace had long since abandoned any thought of riding to Kingscote himself. His message to Coral finally made its way there in the hands of a trusted acquaintance who had slipped away, dressed as a sepoy on route to Jorhat.

Anxiously considering his options as he neared the palace, Jace knew that this was his last chance to contact the maharaja. Roxbury's plans had forced him to risk this meeting now. Tonight Sir Hugo would join him and the small troop that was in readiness to ride to the military outpost at Jorhat. There was little time.

A whisper of sound came from behind him in the trees. Jace stepped aside, turning to face the shadows, his blade lifted from its scabbard with a glint in the moonlight.

His emotions were on edge as he confronted the same lean and tough rajput guard who weeks earlier had been waiting at Jace's military quarters near the residency. The rajput had brought him the gold-embroidered black tunic, turban, and tulwar that he'd worn to the palace that night. They had been gifts from the maharaja's dewan. The dewan had surprisingly turned out to be Prince Sunil, the king's nephew and the younger brother of Gem's father, Rajiv.

The rajput now spread his hands forward, palms showing.

"There is no need for that, Sirdar-Buckley."

"I shall decide, Rajput. Step into the moonlight."

He did so, and his expressionless face was still, his dark eyes solemn. In a small gesture of respect, he gave a low tilt to his head.

"You are summoned to the residency. Ambassador Roxbury waits to speak to you about your military papers."

Jace had already dispatched the official papers to Roxbury concerning his fact-finding mission to Jorhat. What papers did he speak of, or was it a ploy to divert him?

18

Jace glanced casually into the trees. He heard nothing. Did other guards wait? He sheathed his blade but kept his distance, and his mind shifted to Roxbury. Suddenly his own plans had become more difficult to carry out.

If Roxbury had somehow guessed his plans to seek an interview with the raja, he would resort to anything to stop him, especially if Jace was right about the new ambassador's involvement with Sunil.

For a moment he contemplated breaking with Roxbury and riding to Jorhat with Gokul, but if he did, he would be court-martialed on his return to Calcutta. As much as he chafed at the military bit binding him, he could not bear that dishonor.

As major, and commissioned by the governor-general in Calcutta to command the small security force protecting Roxbury, Jace had no choice but to serve him.

Leaving the rajput, Jace's steps made no sound on the compacted dirt that led through the avenue of shade trees. Overhead the white moon was now blotted out by clouds.

Jace's thoughts reverted to the trouble that had come to him during an earlier summons by Roxbury before they had left Calcutta. He still felt anger when he mulled the incident over in his mind, for he had been certain then, and still was, that it had been one of Roxbury's tactics to thwart his effort to discover the facts about the assassination of Major Selwyn at Jorhat. In Calcutta, Roxbury had informed Jace that his orders to command the 21st at Jorhat had been changed by the governor-general himself, and that he would become captain of Roxbury's security guard.

Jace's mouth twisted with impatience when he thought about it. The very least of his personal concerns was Roxbury's security.

He could feel the rise in tension as he walked in the darkness. Like a riled cobra, danger waited its hour to strike. But from what direction would the attack come? From Roxbury? Sunil? Would conflict explode here in Guwahati or on the quiet road northeast to Jorhat?

His instincts were on edge as he paused in the uncanny stillness of the muggy night. Ahead was the newly built British Residency House, where Roxbury would set up representation of the Company. A light burned in the lower window, and through the split-cane screen he could see a figure pacing. Roxbury?

For several minutes he studied the situation.

Roxbury had wanted him killed in the ambush near Plassey Junction. He had not truly wanted him to be captain of his security guard, and no doubt found his presence here a threat to whatever his own plans might be. Now it was too late. They found their purposes head to head in conflict. The journey they would take together inland had always been suspect to Jace, and he had wondered if a bullet might not wait somewhere out there in the darkness on the road to the outpost.

He might wish that Roxbury's summons had come because of Jace's adoptive father, Colonel John Warbeck. Had the colonel been successful in convincing the governor-general in Calcutta to release him from service to Roxbury? Captain Gavin MacKay would have arrived at Government-House in Calcutta by now to inform the military of Harrington's suspected involvement in the mutiny at Plassey Junction with Sir Hugo.

But Jace knew there was not the slightest chance of that being the cause of the summons. It would take at least two months before MacKay arrived at Guwahati with reinforcements. It might take even longer if they had trouble putting down the rebels at Plassey. Until McKay arrived, Jace would remain in the sensitive position of reporting to Roxbury, who alone had the authority to change his orders.

The residency was ahead, bone white under the brass pagoda lanterns.

From where Jace stood under a poinciana tree, the golden lantern light fell across the garden, and there on the lawn was one of the large stone idols of the Hindu religion. He recognized Kali. One of her religious feast days was drawing near, and the carved idol was wreathed with flowers.

What was it that Gokul had written him in the message received at Jorhat?

"The raja may take sudden ill and die . . . and Burra-sahib Roxbury is a worshiper of Kali. . . ."

Jace stared at the image, aware of something that had not crossed his mind until this moment. This was the British residency, and the cantonment was rarely used by Hindus, Muslims, Sikhs, and Mussulmen as a location to place religious articles. They considered all Western-ers to be "Christian," even if many British were blind and deaf to the one true and living God.

So what was the image of Kali doing in the garden of the residency?

For the first time he noticed the figures of six or seven men stooped on the grass before the idol. They were talk-ing in low, urgent voices among themselves.

Was the idol a sign that the British ambassador of the East India Company was a man to be trusted if a mutiny should break out? And would that make the res-idency safe from attack?

He heard footsteps coming from the opposite side of the road nearest the maharaja's palace. The boots rang on stone, taking no thought for the need of caution, and Jace turned his head to see who would take such small care at being seen. A moment later the figure of a man emerged from the trees. As the man hurried forward, his mind obviously on whatever had prompted him to rush to come to the residency, the moonlight shone down upon Ethan Boswell.

Ethan was the last person that Jace had expected to see. He watched the young doctor stride resolutely toward the gate, his head bent as though in deep thought. His steps alerted the small group that was gathered around the idol, and they were quick to jump to their bare feet, melting away into the darkness. All had left except one, and as he turned toward Ethan, Jace caught a glimpse of the Indian's face. He came alert. The man's long, ropelike dark hair was covered with gray ash, and he wore a rosarylike cluster of religious beads around his neck. A dark caste mark was on his forehead.

A sadhu, a religious holy man. What was he doing pretending to be the low-caste gatekeeper? Where *was* the gatekeeper? Had he melted away with the others at the sound of Ethan's steps? Had they not expected Ethan, but Jace himself?

The sadhu came forward to meet Ethan, bringing fingers to his forehead in greeting. Ethan would not know that this man was considered of high caste to his people. Jace felt that he had seen the sadhu before and tried to place him. Ethan passed through the gate, and Jace heard his steps resounding on the verandah.

It's just like Ethan to blunder his way into a situation, thought Jace.

The sadhu had disappeared when Jace neared the gate, and he suspected him to have gone into the courtyard, where he had heard a woman singing. He might follow, but it was Ethan who now commanded his attention. Wasting no time and not wishing to be seen, Jace took the path around the residency entrance and, following the wall for some distance, came to a secluded spot where the trees overhung their branches onto the dirt path. He jumped, catching hold of the wall, and pulled himself up to lie flat. Seeing that the garden below was empty, he landed softly in the soil where freshly planted bougainvillea vines were thick with crimson blossoms.

Lights blazed in the residency living quarters. Through a split-cane curtain, he looked into the drawing room, feeling no qualm at spying. Too many lives depended on learning the truth.

Ethan stood with his back toward the window, but Sir Hugo could be seen, his swarthy face showing hard and angry beneath the short-trimmed beard.

"You know better than to show up now. Buckley is due here any moment. Get out."

"Indeed, my very thoughts. I'll not stay in Guwahati. I've come to tell you I'm leaving in the morning for Kingscote."

Sir Hugo strode toward him. "I forbid it. You are needed here."

"Needed? Oh, yes, so I have discovered! But I do not take my oath as a physician lightly. Druggings are one thing; sending a maharaja to the funeral pyre is quite another."

Roxbury's hand whipped across the side of Ethan's face, jerking his head to the side.

"You fool!" came his hoarse voice. "They'll kill you in a second if you do not cooperate!"

"And you involved me knowing this?"

"I had no choice! You must go through with it, or we are both dead men. We are without sufficient troops, and left to Sunil."

"If Buckley is without adequate soldiers it was your wishes, you and Harrington—"

"Shut up, Ethan! You don't know what you're talking

about. If you don't cooperate with Sunil a dagger awaits you!"

"Yours?" came the angry sneer.

"You speak as a fool. You are my son! Do you think I want you floating down the river? I've plans for Kingscote, and for political authority here in the northeast. You've always figured highly in those plans, you and Coral."

"I want none of it." Angrily Ethan pushed past him toward the door.

"Ethan, wait," demanded Roxbury.

Ethan came out the door onto the porch, and Jace stepped back from the open window into the garden shadows. Ethan hurried down the steps and out into the night.

Jace had only a moment to decide. Follow Ethan? Force him to disclose all he knew? Or catch Roxbury now, when he was emotionally off guard?

Jace's boots rang deliberately loud as he came up the steps and entered the open door.

Sir Hugo jerked about and confronted him. There was no time to alter his expression, and for the first time Jace saw fear in Hugo's dark eyes, not because of Jace's sudden presence but because of Ethan. *So Ethan is his son, not his nephew.*

It was then that Jace understood. Sir Hugo Roxbury, despite all of his cruel ambition, did have family feelings and loyalties. Jace considered unmasking Roxbury, letting him know just how much he knew, not only about the maharaja but also the mutiny at Jorhat and Plassey; but he held back when Roxbury's agitated features swiftly composed themselves again as if by magic.

Ethan would be the man to confront, Jace decided.

Sir Hugo walked to an intricately carved black table and snatched up the decanter of wine, filling a glass.

"Ah, Major, I've been expecting you. My apology for delaying you in Guwahati these past days, but it was necessary. There's been a serious change in our plans. You may have heard by now about Hampton and Alex. Sit down, won't you? A glass of wine?"

Jace stood in a calm military stance, hands folded behind him, showing nothing. "No, thank you. I am on duty. I gather, sir, you speak of Sir Hampton's trek into the Darjeeling area?"

Roxbury turned, glass in hand, and gave him a probing stare. Jace knew that Hugo was wondering if he had seen Ethan hurrying down the path with a cut lip. Sir Hugo was a frightened man, and as such, he was even more dangerous. If he thought Jace had overheard, he would strike before he had intended to do so on the lonely road northeast to Jorhat. Not that he expected Roxbury himself to try to kill him. He would leave that to Sunil and his ghazis.

Jace stood, the image of disciplined loyalty.

Roxbury said, "Yes, Darjeeling . . . a treacherous situation, Major. The more I ponder it, the more my alarm grows. My brother-in-law is older than I and certainly no mountain climber. Nor, for that matter, is my nephew Alex. He's a musician, not an outdoorsman the way Michael was." He frowned. "I cannot for the life of me understand what prompted Alex to make the mountainous journey into Darjeeling." His dark eyes riveted on Jace.

The man has no conscience, thought Jace. *He lies without qualm. If Alex went to Darjeeling, he was lured there under pretense, even as Sir Hampton was snared into risking the trail. And Roxbury is the one who baited both traps.*

But Jace said casually, "Might he have gone there hoping to find me or Seward at the tea plantation?"

"I had not thought of that possibility, Major. Then you would know the route they would take?"

25

What a question. "I know it well. There is no house on the land yet, only a hut, but Alex knows that Michael and I were partners. I intend to see his brother's share go to Alex or one of his sisters."

"Hmm, that may account for his unexpected decision to go there. I'm worried about the weather; it will worsen with the monsoon season. Knowing they both could be lost in the rugged mountainous area near the eastern Himalayas is a matter of utmost concern to me."

"I understand, sir. You do well to have concerns. I've trekked that area several times, once with Michael, and I've experienced the terror of an avalanche."

Roxbury raised his glass and emptied it. Jace noticed a slight tremor in his hand, something unusual for the iron demeanor of Sir Hugo. So Ethan's refusal to participate in his plans concerning the maharaja had unsettled him. It was the first time Jace had seen Roxbury frightened, and watching him guzzle the liquor down was unpleasant. It brought back memories to Jace of his childhood and the drunken brawls aboard his father's ship.

Jace showed none of this, his eyes meeting Hugo's evenly. "Your concern for your brother-in-law is understood," he said briefly, observing Roxbury's reaction. "One slip, and a tumble down a mountainside would mean his end. I doubt if we could ever find him."

Hugo turned his head away and walked toward the window, but not before Jace had seen the small ugly flicker of victory in his eyes. If anything did happen to Sir Hampton and Elizabeth, Roxbury would become Coral's guardian.

"Hampton has a number of guides with him," said Sir Hugo. "In his letter he mentioned taking men from the village, but unless they are familiar with Darjeeling they are not likely to be of much assistance."

Jace knew from Seward that the guides had been pro-

cured by Natine, the headman at Kingscote, but could
these guides from the nearby village be trusted? Jace
believed Natine was serving Roxbury. All this Seward
knew as well, and Jace trusted him to keep Coral under
his watchful eye.

"You'll forgive me, Major, if the life of Hampton
weighs more heavily on my mind than does the death of
Major Selwyn and the attack on Jorhat. What is past is
already done; their deaths cannot be averted now, but
Hampton may need help."

Sir Hugo turned abruptly from the open window,
where earlier Jace had stood outside in the garden listening to the angry exchange between him and Ethan,
and looked intently at Jace.

*He has just now noticed the window is wide open. . . .
Does he suspect I was out there? That I heard?*

Sir Hugo let the cane curtain fall back into place.

"I've thought all evening about this, Major, and I've
made up my mind to send you to Darjeeling to look for
Sir Hampton."

So. . . .

"Rest assured the investigation into the death of Major Selwyn will go forward. I shall proceed as planned
to ride to Jorhat. The Burmese prisoner could have told
us what we need to know, but the dewan has informed
me that the scoundrel hung himself in his cell. Dewan
Sunil is certain that the attack on Jorhat came from
Burma."

Jace felt the conflicting emotions of anger and relief.
Any report Roxbury would send back to the governor-
general would be a cover-up of the mutiny. Colonel Warbeck would know this and not accept the report at face
value, and Captain Gavin MacKay's troop would eventually arrive to reinforce Jorhat. Unfortunately, Mac-

Kay's troop would not arrive in time to thwart a mutiny against the raja.

Jace said deliberately, "In Calcutta you believed the outpost at Jorhat was not the intended target of an 'unknown enemy,' but rather Guwahati. His Excellency's life was in danger by ghazis who were displeased with the signing of the treaty with the East India Company. If I recall, there was even an attempt made on Sunil's life. If I journey to Darjeeling, taking the security guard with me, you will be left shorthanded."

"The danger here is real, Major, and I mean not to make light of it. As I said in Calcutta, Prince Sunil suspects the ghazis of plotting with a Burmese warlord named Zin to dispel any British presence in north India. Sunil protects his uncle the maharaja, using his own guards as well as his uncle's. But you are right. We find ourselves pitifully shorthanded. It is a curse that we must wait as sitting ducks until Captain MacKay arrives with the 13th. And I'm worried about Sir Hampton. I suggest you take as few men from the security guard with you as possible. The rest, I shall keep here under my command. Perhaps the ugly matter of Jorhat should wait until Captain MacKay arrives."

Although Jace knew Roxbury was planning his demise in releasing him from duty in Guwahati, he saw opportunity in the change of orders. It was now possible to make the secret journey into Burma to speak with Warlord Zin and to discover what he could on the way northeast by stopping at Jorhat.

That Roxbury would set him free of his military obligations deserved suspicion. A shrewd man, Roxbury would know Jace's advantage in escaping his surveillance. It was a risk that he would have mulled over but had evidently found needful. No doubt he wanted him far from Guwahati when the mutiny against the maharaja took place. Had Prince Sunil advised Roxbury to send him to Darjeeling, hoping to have him ambushed on the road?

"I shall meet you and Hampton at Kingscote after MacKay arrives," said Sir Hugo. "There may be trouble ahead for Kingscote from Burma, and we'll need to work together. Sir Hampton will need to sign a protection treaty for the family holdings with the Company if the land and hatcheries are to survive."

Jace was confident that Roxbury did not expect Sir Hampton to return to Kingscote alive. He did not expect either of them to return. . . .

When Roxbury would arrive at Kingscote, it would be to announce their deaths and to coerce the ailing and grieving Elizabeth Kendall into cooperating with all he had planned for the silk holdings. And Coral would be pressured into marrying Ethan, thereby granting Sir Hugo the extra authority he needed in the family dynasty to become its sole master. With Jace having been ambushed on the road to Darjeeling, there would be no one left who was strong enough to contest Sir Hugo.

Such were his plans, or so Jace was convinced. Roxbury, however, underestimated him. He would not die by some assassin's bullet on the road to Darjeeling.

There was much to do, and he must work swiftly.

"Then I'll leave for Darjeeling tonight," said Jace easily. "I'm pleased you're sending me, since I am certain I can locate Sir Hampton. Your niece, Miss Kendall, asked me a few weeks ago to search for her father."

Sir Hugo appeared pleased, and Jace imagined him thinking that he could use Coral for a witness in backing his decision to send Jace on an emergency trek into Darjeeling. Her testimony of concern for her father and brother would lend credence to the report he would later send to the governor-general when he explained the "unfortunate assassination of the maharaja and Major J. Buckley."

Someone waited near Darjeeling to kill him. Sanjay?

"I do not blame Coral for requesting your help in locating her father, Major. I doubt if we could find a better trekking man anywhere about. You shall also be commended by the governor-general for bringing me safely on safari to Guwahati. After the mutiny at Plassey and the death of your troops, you behaved honorably. I shall mention your action in my report, and I will recommend you for a brevet."

Jace kept a straight face. "Thank you, sir."

"You are quite welcome, Major. I wish you success in Darjeeling."

Jace gave a small salute and turned to leave. At the door he paused and glanced back. Sir Hugo had his back toward him and was again staring at the open window in concern. The corner of Jace's mouth turned into a smirk. He went out, closing the door behind him.

Jace stood for a moment on the steps, thinking, his hand resting casually near his sword, his gaze fixed ahead on the open gate. The muggy night caused his shirt to cling to his skin. A whiff of breeze coming from the Brahmaputra shimmered through the flowering vines and cooled his face. First, he would locate Ethan and force him to talk. As for Roxbury's orders, they could rot. Jace would now proceed according to his own wishes. When the hour came for him to be called before the colonel on charges of desertion, Jace would have proof of Roxbury's involvement with Prince Sunil in his mutiny against British interests in Assam and its treaty with the maharaja.

From a courtyard behind one of the servant's quarters, a woman's voice could be heard singing a quavering, nasal Indian song to the accompaniment of a sitar.

He heard a subtle sound ahead of him in the garden trees lining the residency stone wall. A lone figure, telltale in white, detached itself from the trees. One of the servants, thought Jace, until the man moved out into the shaft of moonlight that fell across the carriageway. The Indian was running toward the residency gate with bare feet that made no sound on the sunbaked earth.

Jace's suspicion warned that the sadhu had overheard Ethan's argument with Roxbury and then his own conversation, and was now on his way to Prince Sunil.

"You! Halt!" commanded Jace, running down the steps after him.

The sadhu turned his head. Confronting Jace in a major's uniform, the sadhu would normally have stopped—unless he had something to hide. The sadhu ran toward the gate. The gatekeeper was in his place and arose from the ground where he sat, salaaming low.

"Stop him!" shouted Jace in Hindi.

The sadhu said something to the lower-caste gatekeeper, who stepped aside, allowing him to pass.

Jace ran past the gatekeeper into the warm road that went straight past the residency toward a ghat on the river, but the road was empty.

He ran to the ghat, but any small boats usually tied there were gone. His eyes scanned the glassy waterway and he saw no movement. He walked back to the road, which was hemmed in on one side with a long line of dark shade trees. The sadhu had escaped into their secretive embrace. Tracking him now would be as unwise as walking barefoot among a den of cobras.

Jace paused, hands on hips, turning back to the river, trying to place the religious man in his memory.

Religious? Jace straightened, staring unbelievingly toward the trees. *That face.*

"Rissaldar Sanjay!" he breathed.

The man who had betrayed the 17th had shed his uniform for the masquerade of a Hindu holy man . . . or could it also be that Sanjay *was* a sadhu and the uniform had been a disguise?

He heard soft steps on the dust behind him, and when he turned, Jace had unsheathed his blade. The gatekeeper brought fingers to forehead in a low salute.

"Sneaking up on a man may yet cost your head," stated Jace harshly in the Hindi language. "The sadhu— who is he, where has he gone, what was he doing prowling the British residency?"

"No evil, Huzoor! Holy days are nearing. He came to call upon the Hindu gods for the festival."

"You lie. There were six of you groveling around the feet of the idol when I came in. Where are the others?"

"Huzoor, I lie not. I know not where the others are now. They have left to do their duties."

Jace murmured in English, knowing the man did not understand. "You take the English for fools. Well maybe we are, seeing how we allowed ourselves to be trapped here in Guwahati with nothing but a handful of fighting men."

The gatekeeper only salaamed deeply and drew back toward his post.

Jace left and headed in the direction of the palace grounds. The sadhu, whom Jace was now certain to be Sanjay, would inform Prince Sunil of what he had overheard between Ethan and Sir Hugo, but he probably wouldn't go directly to the dewan's chambers, knowing that Jace might have recognized him and could go there to confront him. Nor would Sanjay wish to implicate the dewan in the mutiny, for he couldn't be sure that Jace knew their plans.

No, thought Jace. He would waste time if he went to search for Sanjay now. Perhaps he would find yet another disguise. Where he was now was anyone's guess, but he might have circled back to rejoin the others who had gathered at the idol of Kali. As much as Jace wished to capture Sanjay, a confrontation must wait.

It was Ethan whom he must see first. Jace frowned. Ethan did not know how much danger he was in. He was foolish to have blundered into Sir Hugo's house and boldly inform him of his refusal to cooperate. He should have known that servants would overhear, that few could be trusted when a mutiny against the British hung in the air like incense offered to Kali. Even if they did not agree with the mutiny, few would prove so loyal as to side with the British if violence struck. The English were not wanted here, and the maharaja had displeased many by signing a treaty with Company officials.

Jace slipped through the trees and walked in the direction of the royal palace, its white stone with inlaid marble reflecting in the moonlight. He frowned as he walked, thinking of Ethan. Jace was not one to suddenly develop sympathy for Boswell, but he did sense a certain unease over the man's situation in Guwahati. Not that his own was much better, he thought. Aside from Gokul, and perhaps one or two sepoys from the outpost at Jorhat, he doubted the loyalty of the guard.

But Ethan was another matter. He knew what Sir Hugo and Prince Sunil had in mind for the maharaja. If Sunil heard about the disturbance he had made tonight at the residency, he would think nothing of killing a stubborn Englishman. Sir Hugo knew this and would strive to keep his iron grip on Ethan's resolution. Jace was determined that Ethan would talk.

The night air was heavy with jungle smells. His hearing was attuned to the noises of the river lapping the bank and the piping of birds. Cautious, lest an assassin's dagger find him with unexpected accuracy, he kept close to the outer trees.

The dislike between him and Ethan would most likely cause the doctor to rebel when it came to cooperation over the maharaja. Jace had not forgotten that night at the palace when Ethan had come into the garden and found him and Coral together.

Jace quickened his stride. No matter. He would make Ethan talk. Lives depended on it, and however either of them may feel about Kendall's daughter, they must cooperate. Ethan would bring him to the maharaja. But would Maharaja Majid Singh talk of what he knew?

Jace thought of the small stolen idol of Kali. Solid gold and embedded with sapphires, emeralds, and rubies, it was worth much. Although the maharaja desired its return, Jace would need it when he met with the local warlord, Zin, on the border with Burma. Convincing the maharaja to wait would prove a bit difficult, he thought dryly. And so would retrieving it back again from Zin when the warlord left his compound.

Jace's eyes narrowed. Before this episode of intrigue was over he might get himself killed. For one moment he found himself wondering what Coral would do if Gokul did end up bringing her news that Jace Buckley was dead. He absently rubbed the side of his face, remembering her slap the night of the dinner party, then rebuked his wandering mind. If he were to stay alive he must keep alert.

Jace figured that Sunil knew him well enough to know that he had the gold idol. Jace had always suspected that Sunil had worked with Zin and his son to steal it from the temple in Burma. It might have been Sunil who had killed Zin's son, Ayub Khan.

Sunil was also looking for the jewel-studded relic.

As Jace neared his quarters he saw a faint glimmer

34

in the window. It disappeared. Was Sunil foolish enough to send the rajput guard—or even Sanjay—to search his quarters?

Jace approached the door, hearing a faint rustle of garments. He lifted his sword from its scabbard and reached for the doorknob.

2

His silhouette in the open doorway with the moon-light behind him would prove a perfect target—not for one of Sunil's warriors bearing a sword, but for a dagger, the way of assassins, thought Jace. He knew well the ways of intrigue in the dark underworld of the East.

He stood outside his quarters and coolly sheathed his sword. Instead, with deft fingers he reached beneath his jacket sleeve and drew the deadly stiletto dagger from its concealed wrist sheath.

Jace flung open the door, hit the floor rolling, and stopped in a crouched position on the other side of the room.

A glimmer of dim light from a lantern under a rattan stool cast its glow across the floor matting. His gaze searched the room.

Wearing a black turban and jacket to keep from being seen, the assassin, tough and lean, turned to face him. With a whisper, the man hurled his blade. Jace had expected it and threw his stiletto with deadly accuracy. The assassin's two hands went up to grip the hilt protruding from his chest, and he fell to his knees.

Jace remained where he was. Outside, the river

breeze brushed against a shade tree, and a bird cackled.

He made careful search of his chamber, and swiftly packed his satchel and went out into the night. There was little time to find Ethan.

———————

Ethan's nerves felt like dry thorns ready for the fire. Although he was alone in his bedroom chamber in the maharaja's palace, he continued to feel as if eyes watched him—unfriendly eyes. His chamber was on the second floor close to the king, to whom he was to give medical treatment. *Aside from a flare-up of gout, there is nothing ailing the maharaja,* he thought, his gray eyes cool.

Wearing a satin robe, Ethan sat cross-legged on a thick rug woven with blue and crimson silk. Directly in front of him there was a low marble table veined with gold. His slender hand held a feathered quill, which he dipped into a black and gold ceramic inkpot on the table beside the letter he was writing to Coral.

Again, he sensed eyes watching him and casually lifted his head, the lantern light catching the fair strands of his hair. He scanned the large chamber with its intricate stonework and inlaid marble veined with blue and gold. Woven hangings of Hindu idol-gods draped the walls. Ethan stared at them. Perhaps these were the probing eyes he felt. *Idols,* he thought, and some of the words from Psalm 135 came to mind. Coral had read a verse to him in Hindi, then translated into English while they had been standing near the great Hindu temple in Guwahati.

"Eyes have they, but they see not; they have ears, but they hear not. . . ."

He hoped the cold, lifeless eyes that stared down at him now were not peepholes for spies. The palace was large, and there were no doubt many secret chambers and passages throughout. Yet, Ethan saw nothing to validate his discomfort. He glanced to the side where an open verandah looked down on an inner court.

He set his quill down and arose, walking out on the verandah. The night was ominously still, the weather muggy. Would he ever become used to India's climate?

Beyond the inner court there was a wall with gate-towers, and torchlight reflected on a rajput guard. The palace itself was built on the half-circle bank overlooking the Brahmaputra River, and Ethan could see small lighted boats on the water belonging to fishermen or village traders.

Convinced that his feeling of apprehension was the harvest of his inability to persuade Hugo, he turned away from watching the night and went back inside his chamber to end his letter to Coral. He briefly informed her of his change of plans to not remain in Guwahati—"Matters have changed," he had written, "I will journey to Kingscote after all to set up my lab."

Ethan was signing his name when he heard a faint sound, like a groan. Silence followed. He strained his ears to hear something else, gripping the quill.

Where did the sound come from? The raja's royal chambers?

He stood, staring at the great intricately carved ivory door between his chamber and the hall leading into the raja's royal apartments. Ethan's heart pounded. His slim fingers moved slowly beneath the satin smoothness of his dressing robe to where he had concealed his pistol.

From behind him came a grating sound. He turned, pistol drawn, to face the verandah, and Major Jace Buckley climbed over the rail, casting a glance down to the inner court.

A prick of irritation stung Ethan. It was like Buckley

to slip past guards and scale the stone wall successfully.

His thin mouth tightened as he saw Buckley hesitate, a slight smile on his rugged face, his gaze dropping to the pistol in Ethan's hand.

Ethan's temper grew taut, and he deliberately kept the pistol aimed at him, his hand nice and steady. "I told you once I was a crack shot. You might have gotten a bit of your head blown off, Major."

"You've good reason to worry about your own. We need to talk."

Ethan could see a seriousness in Buckley's expression that sobered his own. He lowered the pistol.

"Keep it handy," said Jace. "You're likely to need it before this night is over."

Ethan watched as Jace glanced below in the courtyard again, made a signal, then threw a rope over the side of the railing. A moment later he hauled up a bundle. Evidently someone was below cooperating with him, but who? Surely not the rajput guard that Ethan had seen only minutes ago. . . .

Ethan walked to the desk where he had been writing the letter and sat down, picking up the quill. He said in a low voice, "Stay where you are, Major. Don't come in. I've a feeling we're being watched by a Hindu carving of an elephant mounted high on the wall. I've felt its eyes for the past hour."

Jace stopped at once and remained in the verandah shadows. "Finish your task, look as though you are going to bed, then turn out the lantern."

Ethan did so, grudgingly admiring his simple suggestion. "I heard the guard moan when you struck him. Someone else may have heard. Whoever is below aiding you had best be on the lookout."

"Gokul is an expert at deceit," came the dry retort. "You need not concern yourself. That letter—if it is to

Miss Kendall, forget it."

"I dare say!"

"Relax, old chum, it is her safety I'm thinking about. The less she knows, the better. If you intend to join her at Kingscote, simply show up."

Ethan was surprised that Buckley knew of his change in plans, but said nothing. As though he had changed his mind about what he was writing, Ethan picked up the paper and tore it into bits, then held his head in his hands.

"Good show," came Jace's quip. "Now off to bed like a good chap."

Ethan walked over to the large bed, drew back the satin covers, and climbed in. His eyes looked straight ahead to the elephant on the wall, and he felt an uneasy tingle on the back of his neck. With one hand he reached over and snuffed the lantern. Darkness swallowed up the chamber.

A moment later he heard Jace's light steps enter and cross to the other side. Ethan tossed aside the cover and was on his feet joining him.

"I was at the residency tonight when you confronted Sir Hugo," came Jace's whisper.

Ethan sucked in a breath but felt the major's iron grip on his shoulder.

"I'll have none of your self-righteous complaint at my eavesdropping. Men's lives hang in the balance—including ours. Even if I cared nothing for Sunil's assassination attempt on the raja, I care about my own neck. You'll tell me everything. Be quick about it. We haven't much time."

Ethan felt his indignation rise at the major's superior attitude, one that he had resented from the beginning, but he put a clamp on his feelings and let out a breath of resignation. "As you wish, Major," he whispered stiffly.

"As you know, it is said the maharaja has been in ill health. To the contrary, he is quite fit. I discovered that tonight."

"Was he suspicious of being poisoned by his physicians?"

"No. He said few words and seemed more intent on watching me."

"Then you were not alone with him?"

Ethan tensed as he remembered back earlier that evening. "No. The dewan was there the entire time."

"You mean Sunil?"

"Yes . . . until tonight I did not know he was the raja's nephew."

"You said the raja is fit."

"I made preliminary tests tonight. There is nothing wrong with him except a mild form of gout."

Ethan saw the major digesting the information.

"That will make it easier," said Jace.

"I do not follow you, Major."

"I think you do. I told you I overheard your words with Sir Hugo, so let's not waste time. There's to be an assassination attempt on the maharaja; we both know it. So does Roxbury. He's working with Sunil, for what reasons I've yet to discover, but I doubt if it is profound, only a matter of simple greed. You too are at serious risk now that you've refused to be the instrument of death. What did Sunil ask you to do, poison his uncle?"

Ethan flinched at his blunt questions. They came at him like hammer blows. There was no use denying what had happened. In any case, it was best he knew for the raja's sake. But Ethan refused to bring his uncle—*nay, my father*—into the quagmire of treason.

Ethan whispered tonelessly: "Sunil offered me royal treasure and authority in the palace if I would eliminate his uncle by means of a painless drug. There would be no suffering, no blood. He would die in his sleep."

"The drug being poison."

"Yes, a rare drug I came across in Burma. Sir Hugo knows of it."

"Like the one you used on Coral in London, and again at Manali?"

"If it were not that the noise would bring the guards, you'd be absent your front teeth, Major."

"Is that what you told Sunil?"

Ethan gritted, "I told him to take a swim in the river and make some hungry crocodile happy."

"Sunil, of course, insisted you participate in his plans."

"He did. Said that Sir Hugo Roxbury would see that I obliged, or we would both be dead before we ever rode out of Guwahati."

"You needn't concern yourself for Roxbury; he is in this up to his neck. It is you, old chap, who will soon be dead. I advise you to leave for Kingscote tonight. But first—bring me to the maharaja."

"Are you mad? No one is allowed in the royal chambers!"

"No one except his guards and trusted physician."

Ethan knew that he was the trusted physician, but how this helped to get the major into the royal chamber was beyond his understanding.

"It is out of the question."

"Where does that door lead?"

Ethan followed his gesture to the carved ivory door. "An antechamber. Beyond are the royal apartments—good heavens, Major! You cannot enter. What excuse could I offer for your presence? Besides, it is late and the raja will be asleep—"

Ethan halted, seeing that his argument was wasted. He watched, alert and curious, as Buckley knelt and undid the cord binding a small bundle. Ethan recognized a uniform worn by the royal guards, but this one went beyond the authority of the guard. The rich purple and black told him that this particular garb belonged to the maharaja's chief bodyguard.

"Where did you get that? Or need I ask?"

"Gokul has a degree in the clandestine."

Ethan had no notion who Gokul was, nor did he wish to meet the scoundrel. He watched Jace exchange his uniform for the royal garb and belt on his sword.

"Quick. Get dressed. And don't forget that pistol."

Ethan did so, watching as Buckley proceeded to fold the British uniform, tying it with the cord to take with him. Jace also was a master at the clandestine. Ethan remembered coming upon Coral in the palace garden, and he was certain she had come directly from the major's arms. The muscles in Ethan's jaw hardened. A man like Jace Buckley was a risk. Did Coral have feelings for him?

"I am ready, Major," he said flatly. "Let us hope your comrade Gokul did not leave a dead body lying about for the other guards to stumble across. We'll soon be amidst a swarm of tulwars," he said of the curved Indian blade.

"If we do, your repeated warning of being a crack shot had better be more than boast."

Ethan lifted his head. "You'll not be disappointed."

Jace looked at him, and Ethan thought he saw a faint grin. The major tossed him a scabbard. "How are you with the sword?"

Ethan caught it with one hand. "I'm a bit rusty on my fencing lessons, but I'll do my best should it come to that."

"Another thing. I was not the only one who overheard you tonight. Sanjay was in the garden."

Ethan was trying to notch the belt of the scabbard

around his lean hips. At the mention of Rissaldar Sanjay he paused. Buckley believed Sanjay had betrayed the 17th outside Plassey Junction.

"You do well to look worried," said Jace. "I suspect he will soon report what he heard to Sunil. When he does, Sunil will decide you are a risk to his plans. He will fear what he believes to be a nervous, uncooperative pawn. They are always a risk. Elimination is the safeguard."

Ethan tensed but said nothing. He had already suspected Sunil might feel this way about him. It was the reason for his change in plans and his decision to go on to Kingscote.

"Sir Hugo will have something to say to Prince Sunil," said Ethan after a moment.

"This is one time when even Sir Hugo is in deeper than he can swim out. He's come up against the world of Eastern assassins. He knows you are in danger; he'll do what he can, but he's likely to discover that his own sins are weights about his neck. What does the writer of Proverbs say—'A man's sins bind him in their own cord'? Roxbury's schemes have trapped even him."

"Sir Hugo is not involved in this treachery," Ethan found himself saying, but his lame excuses were hollow and he knew it.

"He was working with Harrington and Zameen in Calcutta and Manali. It was Sunil who sent Sanjay to Calcutta masquerading as a rissaldar from Jorhat, and Roxbury was in on it from the beginning. He knew about the mutiny at Plassey, and things went according to schedule—except that I survived the attack. I was meant to die with the sowars of the 17th. He wanted me dead. He still does. He and Sunil both expect me to ride out tonight for Darjeeling. I've no doubt that Sunil has another assassin waiting. This time they intend to make sure I remain lying on the road. And that goes for Sir Hampton too. He left weeks ago and I fear he's already dead."

Ethan felt the blow of his words. Coral rushed to mind. *If Sir Hampton is dead . . .*

Ethan had already guessed about Harrington and Zameen upon arrival at Manali. He had overheard Hugo talking with Harrington about a secret meeting they had undertaken at Barrackpore. Harrington had come in masquerade as an Indian to report to Sir Hugo from Prince Sunil that the ambush at Plassey was set. Harrington had been worried that he was seen by one of the Kendall daughters in the Canterbury House garden at the Christmas Ball, but Hugo assured him at Manali that he had not been identified. Ethan did not know for certain who had drugged Coral at Harrington's house, but he suspected his uncle. The drug had temporarily eliminated her from delving into matters that Sir Hugo knew would threaten them all. It had been a crude tactic, the second incident since the weeks that were spent at Roxbury House on the Strand, but his uncle often resorted to drugs in order to accomplish his plans. Ethan had gone along with the spider bite story to protect not only Coral but also her sisters. The scare had diverted them from becoming further entangled with Zameen, a man that Ethan thought to be more dangerous than even Harrington. He believed that Zameen served Prince Sunil. . . .

"Sir Hugo is like the cunning trapper who lures a den of cobras, only to fall in with them," Jace was saying. "If I were you, I'd be thinking about saving my own neck, and let him take care of his. If you don't, you'll end up bedding down with the serpents along with him."

"Rest assured, Major, I've every intention of saving my life. I have too many humanitarian plans for my medical research to see them foiled now."

"Yes, I am sure you do."

Ethan felt his frustration boil over at the smooth jab in the major's voice. He whispered harshly, "And as for your rendezvous with Coral in the garden, it will change nothing where she and I are concerned."

Jace turned his head and gave him a look that Ethan believed would have felt as sharp as a dagger.

"Get one thing straight, Ethan. Whatever there might or might not be between Coral and me is none of your business, and that includes our so-called rendezvous. Let's go."

Ethan stiffened. "When this predicament has spent itself, Major, I think there will be only one decent recourse left for both of us, and that is a duel."

Jace gave a short laugh. "You are actually serious."

"Indeed."

Jace paused, cocking his head as he scanned him. "A gentleman's way out of a sticky mess, no doubt."

"Exactly, Major. It is the decent way such matters are resolved in Europe, or have you been so long in India you have forgotten the code of honor among gentlemen?"

Jace smirked. "I've not forgotten, Doctor. But you see, India offers the easiest solution of all."

Ethan felt uncomfortable under the mocking gaze. "And what, Major, might that be?"

"I could simply leave you for Sunil. He'll lop off your head with his tulwar and save me the trouble." Jace walked to the door leading to the antechamber.

Ethan felt his face flush and was glad for the darkness. "You dare make a jest!"

"If it will make you feel better, Doctor, I promise to take you up on your offer. That is, should I decide to eliminate Coral's most vocal suitor. I've no question in my mind but that I would win."

Ethan stood in silent anger. The man's arrogance was not to be borne. "I would not count on that, Major."

"If we do not soon meet with the maharaja and leave this palace, neither of us will be around to see Miss Kendall happily married to Charles Peddington," came the jibe.

————

Jace's thoughts had already sought out every possible escape route, every stratagem, every ruse. Yet none were sure, and he wondered what information the raja would decide to give him, if any.

The door into the antechamber opened and Jace followed Ethan inside. "Be careful," Ethan said in a low voice as they neared the door into the royal chambers. "The guard is as wary as a reptile."

While Jace stood in the shadows, Ethan knocked on a second door made of heavy timber bound with straps of iron. The door opened, and a huge, powerfully muscled man stood there with a massive sword. Ethan gripped his medical bag and began to make a great fuss about the necessity of seeing the raja *immediately*.

"Be gone. His Excellency will not see you again tonight."

"I must see him. His health is at risk."

The guard began to shut the door with a scowl.

Ethan surprised even Jace by putting his foot in the door and raising his voice: "Close this door on me and you shall be called in question by Dewan Sunil! The Prince has solicited my medical knowledge to tend to his uncle and I insist you open up at once."

Jace reinforced his move by stepping forward and speaking rapidly in Hindi. "Step aside! You waste the physician's time."

The guard came alert when he saw Jace in the garb

of the chief bodyguard. "Where is Atool?" he demanded, reaching for his tulwar.

Jace drew his blade and stepped back, point lifted. "You dare threaten your new commander? I am Rajendra, appointed to be chief bodyguard by His Excellency Sunil."

The guard's cold eyes probed as if to know Jace's heart. "Where is Atool!"

"Dead," gritted Jace. "A fool who committed treason against Prince Sunil."

A noticeable twitch of surprise, then uncertainty over his own position showed in his face.

"Unlock the door *now*. If not, I shall delight to spill your innards on the floor," said Jace.

The guard warily stepped aside. "Move," ordered Jace, gesturing toward the royal ivory door veined with gold.

The guard turned a key in the lock and the door opened. Jace glanced at Ethan, who took the advantage and swiftly passed into the chambers.

"Who comes?" a tired voice called out.

The guard started to speak, but Jace's voice speaking Hindi overrode his. "A man you can trust with your life, Excellency. I bring news for your ears alone. I come in the company of the English physician Doctor Ethan Boswell."

The maharaja gestured the guard to silence. "Your name?"

Jace took a risk, but it seemed the only way to assure an audience. "Javed Kasam."

In the silence that followed, Jace suspected that he had the maharaja's alert attention, although he could not yet see him.

"Kahn, light the lantern then leave us."

The guard did so, then shut the royal door behind

him. Jace heard the key turn in the lock. Was there another exit from the chamber?

In the golden glow of ornate lanterns, Jace saw the Maharaja Majid Singh sitting on a dais. The old king was pale, but his black eyes were lively and suddenly interested in the two men. "Step forward, Javed Kasam."

Jace neared the imposing platform knowing that Singh was aware of who he was, and that the past disguise of Javed Kasam identified him as a member of the underworld of Eastern intrigue. He was quite certain that the gold idol of Kali was also much on Singh's mind.

"What is the nature of your news from Burma?"

Truth must be his guard. "I have not yet met with Zin."

"Ah?" The maharaja's fingers tapped upon his silken knee.

"I must go into Burma as quickly as time permits me, Excellency. Since Roxbury has released me from my duties as captain of his Security Guard, I shall leave tonight."

"He released you from your position? Why?"

"His motives are suspect. I would advise you to not trust him, nor your own nephew, Prince Sunil."

If his words shocked him, Singh did not blanch. He studied Jace with attention.

"The British military has sent me to discover the true motive behind the mutiny at Jorhat. While the governor-general's ambassador insists Burma was behind the attack, we have reason to suspect intrigue."

"By the use of *we*, do you mean to imply the British government at Calcutta?"

"I speak of myself and Colonel John Warbeck. Roxbury has deceived the governor-general. I believe he is working with your nephew to have you killed."

The maharaja remained calm, and only his eyes

showed his internal rage. "I see you speak the truth, Major Buckley. I believe you can be trusted. So I shall confide that such news has long been known by me. I am outnumbered by men loyal to Sunil. A power struggle goes on within the palace, and my life is in question. The struggle may go yet farther, reaching even into the palace of Raja Singh in Sibsagar."

"Your Excellency, you have a treaty with the British government. The troops assigned to me for security purposes have been killed in an ambush designed by your enemies here in Guwahati. I have no more than six or seven soldiers I would trust with plans for your protection. I suggest you do not contest your nephew, but leave the palace to him and his followers until British troops arrive in force under Captain MacKay to put down the mutiny and secure your throne. You must leave Guwahati tonight."

"I have made secret plans already to leave for Burma."

Jace showed surprise at the mention of Burma. Singh saw it and said, "He is my enemy, but I have no choice but to go there." He stood.

"Have you men in the palace loyal to your throne?"

"Not as many as I first thought. Khan, my guard, has discovered much by pretending loyalty to Sunil. I have a dozen rajputs, no more. Sunil has inflamed the ghazis against me by convincing them I have brought in the Western religion to insult the brahmins. Many of the brahmins have been quietly preparing for a mutiny under Sunil. I can do nothing to stop it."

"We must leave Guwahati tonight, Excellency. The guard at the door, can he be trusted?"

"Khan, he would die for me."

"Have him send word to those rajputs loyal to you to prepare supplies and horses. We will meet them outside the gate near the river in an hour."

51

"An hour!"

"There is no time, Excellency. A spy for Prince Sunil will soon report to him that the English physician would not cooperate in your death. Knowing Sunil, he will take no chances. He will strike at once with his assassins."

The maharaja frowned but nodded agreement. He sighed. "As your British poets declare, Major, uneasy is the head that wears the crown. An hour it shall be. I have a personal attendant I can also trust. He will prepare me for travel."

Jace thought of the gold idol of Kali. He also thought of Gem, and as he did, it was Coral's face he saw—her green eyes, and her intense pleading. He had trusted the maharaja with the truth, and in return the king had confided in him. Now he must also make good his vow to Coral, whatever the risk to himself. "One thing more, Your Excellency. Rajiv was a friend of mine. I cannot forget that someone commanded the assassin's dagger to be used on him while he took quiet refuge from your displeasure on the Kendall lands."

"You are mistaken. It was not my wrath he fled but Sunil's. I gave no order for his death, nor for the abduction of his son, Prince Adesh."

"Then I am correct in believing the child has royal blood, despite Jemani. He is not an untouchable."

"Prince Adesh is heir to my throne." The maharaja was weary and ashen as he slowly lowered himself into his seat. "It was Sunil who first loved Jemani, and he sought a wedding to take place with her, but she did not trust him and fell in love with his older brother. Sunil tried to have Rajiv killed here in Guwahati after the marriage, and it was then that both he and Jemani disappeared."

"And the family of Jemani?" asked Jace cautiously.

"I do not know. Perhaps from a brahmin guru in Rajasthan, but I cannot vow to this. After Rajiv and Jemani left Guwahati I searched for them but knew not where they were, and I suspected them both dead, that Sunil had them assassinated. It was then that news arrived to me secretly that Rajiv was masquerading as a man of low caste on the Kendall plantation near Jorhat."

Jace thought of Kingscote, of Coral, and his unease mounted. "May I ask who sent you that information, Excellency? It may be important for the lives of others involved."

The maharaja shook his gray head. "I do not know for certain. It was unsigned."

"It came by a messenger?"

"Yes. I did not speak with him, but somehow I believed the message was sent from Kendall's Kingscote, or very near the border. There are Burmese renegades hiding in the jungle who often prowl the road. It has been suggested one of these Burmese soldiers sent the message."

Jace wondered . . . *Burmese renegade? But who! Warlord Zin is far from a petty rebel living in the jungle.* And the news only heightened his concerns for Coral. Sir Hampton was not there to protect his wife and three daughters. *But Seward is there. . . .*

"Sunil must have discovered about the secret message sent to me and arranged Rajiv's death."

Jace masked his tension. If Sunil knew that Zin had Gem. . . . The question must be asked.

"Then Prince Sunil has discovered where Prince Adesh is?"

"Sunil? No! Sunil searches for him this very moment. It is the reason I must go to Burma to Warlord Zin!"

"Then you know that Zin has Prince Adesh," said Jace with masked surprise.

"Yes. It was Zin who had him abducted, perhaps with

53

the help of renegade sepoys and Burmese infiltrators who are enemies of the English on Kingscote. The warlord has held him these years as ransom. If I do not pay handsomely as he requests, he threatens to alert Sunil, to turn him over for the highest gift of rubies and emeralds. I could do nothing but capitulate." The maharaja leaned forward anxiously. "I must go to Zin. Both I and Adesh are at risk from Sunil. From the wealth of the house of Singh I will buy protection from Zin and his warriors. I am in no position to bargain my own terms. But at least I have secretly sent the best of our scholars to train little Prince Adesh to rule after me. Zin allowed this. He has grown fat on my riches."

"And Sunil? He does not suspect?"

His smile faded. "No. He thought Adesh dead until recently. I believe he received secret information that the boy is alive after all and sought by the Englishwoman. Sunil has been searching diligently. He went to Zin asking questions, offering great prizes for information, but Zin is also clever and greedy. He will continue to play us one against another until he is certain to receive the highest prize for the prince. I have been paying him well; yet my own spies have reported seeing Sunil with Zin on the Burmese border. That is why I must go there. Not only for my safety but for little Adesh."

Jace was thinking of Zin. His friendship was weak at best and easily bought for the highest bid. Gem was far from being secure. And when Sunil found out for certain that Zin had the child . . .

"This is most amazing news, Your Excellency. Gem Kendall alive and in Burma!" breathed Ethan.

Jace had nearly forgotten Ethan was in the chamber. Evidently so had the raja, for he looked sharply in the doctor's direction, his eyes cold.

"There is no such child as Gem Kendall, Doctor Boswell. Rajiv's son is Prince Adesh Singh, heir to kingship in Guwahati. Nor is my grandnephew to embrace the foreign religion of the West. I regret Sahib Kendall's daughter involved herself in matters that were none of her own, but she shall not have him back as her son."

Ethan flushed under his tan and started to protest, but Jace interrupted him with a warning stare. "The maharaja is right, Ethan. Miss Kendall was in error. She thought she was adopting an orphan, a mere untouchable, born from a humble maid and a friend . . . but Gem is royalty and as such she could not adopt him."

"I beg pardon, Major. But from what Miss Kendall has confided in me, Jemani entrusted her son to her at death. The law will have something to say about this—"

"This is not the time to protest the fate of the maharaja's grandnephew," Jace gritted, angry that Ethan would risk the raja's cooperation by throwing his allegiance to the side of Coral. "I advise you send for Khan," said Jace.

When the burly guard had received his secret orders and went to implement them, the maharaja left the chamber to ready himself for the journey to Burma. Jace turned on Ethan. "Do me a favor, Doctor. Keep your opinions to yourself in the presence of the raja. Don't you realize if Singh believes I want to find the boy for Coral's sake that he'll cease all further cooperation with me?"

"The man is obnoxious. Gem legally belongs to Coral under the laws of adoption. I'll not stand by and see her treated with scorn. If Gem is alive, then I shall go with you to rescue him."

Jace measured him, his irritation growing. Ethan was like a grain of sand in the eye. He remembered the confrontation over the sacrifice to Kali on the river safari and how it almost cost them the boats. "When it comes to risking my neck, I work alone. I advise you to get out of Guwahati while you still have your own. Leave the matter that concerns Coral to me."

"You would like it so, would you not? But when it comes to Coral, I have more to say about what concerns her than you do, Major. If Gem is alive, then I shall lend my hand to help in his rescue."

Jace's irritation grew. "You are rather late, aren't you? In London you worked with Roxbury to try to force Coral into accepting the child's death."

"Are you insinuating I deliberately tried to deceive her about his fate?"

Jace answered with a cool smile.

Ethan flushed. "I truly believed the boy was dead."

"And Coral was emotionally ill," quipped Jace.

"We've no time to waste debating. All that is in the past. I was wrong. I've asked her to understand my dilemma, and she has. I'm coming with you to Burma."

"As I said, I work alone."

"Don't be so arrogant, Major! You need another man; you're hopelessly outnumbered. I'm doing this for Coral, not for you. . . . It so happens that I proposed marriage to her after what happened between you and her in the garden."

Jace's eyes met Ethan's evenly. His jaw set.

"She accepted," said Ethan. "That was the main reason I informed Hugo tonight that I am leaving in the morning. We intend to marry immediately."

Immediately. The word left Jace stunned. Coral wouldn't marry Ethan in order to hurt him—or would she?

Pride kept him from probing, for he believed Ethan's boast just might prove true. He felt a sudden anger toward Coral. She might have at least waited until he returned from Burma, but instead she had agreed to marry Ethan on the very night he had held her in his arms and kissed her. "Congratulations," he said flatly.

"I am pleased to see you are wise enough to accept the news without calling for a duel."

"As I recall, the 'code of honor among gentlemen' already demands that we have one. Have you changed your mind?"

Ethan scanned him. "Are you saying that is what you wish?"

"If Miss Kendall wishes to spend her life helping you dissect bugs on Kingscote, far be it from me to send you to an early grave," he said flippantly. "No. Let her marry you. Sorry I won't be around for the wedding. After Burma, I have an appointment with the *Madras*."

"I'm pleased you see it that way, Major."

"A suggestion, Doctor: If you treasure winning Kendall's daughter, you had best pack your bags and ride to Kingscote tonight. It is going to get ugly before the matter of the raja and Gem is over."

Ethan smiled thinly. "You think I am unwise enough to retreat to Kingscote so you can be the hero who brings Gem home? You do not deceive me, Major. You want the accolade of victory on your own brow, hoping to change her mind about me."

"The only accolade Kendall's daughter is interested in lies within your grasp. If you were wise you'd ride out tonight. Start building her school on Kingscote and there's not a man who could turn her against you. But come to Burma and you will take on more than you're capable of handling. You are a doctor, not a mercenary soldier."

"She already knows I support the work for the children. I've promised to aid her with my medical knowledge. But since I'm to be her husband, I'll not sit back now and allow you to be the one to rescue Gem."

Jace felt a strange dart of jealousy. It angered him

that Ethan's boast could goad him like this. *She agreed to marry Ethan without so much as a second thought.* "As you wish, Doctor. But get one thing straight. My sword is committed to the survival of the others first. You are on your own."

"As I keep telling you, Major, I am well able to take care of myself."

"Yes, I know, you are a 'crack shot.' I hope you speak the truth. I should hate to leave you in some hastily dug grave between here and Burma."

Ethan's gray eyes went hard and cold. "It may be *your* unexpected fate, Major. An ironic twist to come at the end of our unhappy drama. I shall, however, comfort Coral and graciously acclaim you to be the hero after all. I could afford to do so, since I will be the one to walk back to Kingscote to her." Ethan turned his back and walked to meet the maharaja.

Jace saw that the raja was dressed for travel, wearing the rugged warrior's dress of a rajput with a belted sword. His somber attendant carried only one bag, but his grip on the handle alerted Jace to the importance of its contents.

Jewels, no doubt. He thought of the gold statue of Kali but said nothing yet. If the maharaja had too much on his mind to remember, the idol would benefit his meeting with Zin. Jace intended to use it to buy Gem's freedom.

A moment later the guard Khan arrived. Jace studied him, wondering if he could trust him. The maharaja did, but kings could be wrong about their closest guards; only they never lived long enough to tell about it.

Khan spoke low in the native tongue. "Everything is in order, Excellency. The warriors are now with the horses waiting by the river."

Jace turned to the maharaja. "Let us leave at once before Sunil has time to make plans. By morning there won't be one of us alive."

3

The maharaja trusted Khan explicitly, so Jace resigned himself to do the same. Yet he watched him carefully. The guard led them through a secret passage to a stone-flagged chamber where other warriors waited. Jace felt the penetrating eyes and immobile faces. They did not seem readily disposed toward Ethan, perhaps wondering if he could fight if it came to that.

Khan handed each of them a black cloak. He glanced at Jace's sword, noting that his hand rested there. Jace suspected he was remembering his threat at the door of the royal chamber.

Horses awaited them as promised, and a second guard of men. Jace made it a point to study each man's face. He would not be deceived again by Sanjay.

The alley down which they rode was unpaved, and the horses made no sound. As they neared a postern gate it opened, allowing them to pass, then silently closed behind them. Jace rode guard beside the maharaja, with Khan on the king's left. Jace had to respect the old king, who was willing to risk his palace and crown to Sunil during his absence in order to protect not only his own life but Gem's—or had he best begin thinking of Gem

Kendall as Prince Adesh Singh?

He imagined Coral's pain over future events. Whatever may happen in Burma, her relationship to Gem would never be the same. She could never go back to the time in the Kendall nursery when she had looked upon the baby as her own son.

Saddles creaked in the night, a breeze stirred from off the wide, dark river. The moon was setting over the Brahmaputra, and the night was still. Too still, thought Jace. He glanced into the darkness but saw nothing. Then a lone figure emerged from the trees and rode toward them. Some of the guards drew swords and reined in their horses.

Gokul came riding up, his dusty white turban showing in the moonlight. Seeing the maharaja, he salaamed, then his eyes searched the group of warriors for Jace. At last he recognized him wearing the garb of the chief bodyguard.

Jace maneuvered his horse forward from the others and rode to meet him. "It is time you finally arrived, old friend," he said in a low voice. "I was beginning to believe temptation had won the day. Did you have trouble?"

Gokul pretended an injury to his feelings. "Sahib! Would I steal gold statue of Kali and leave you in what—how do you say?—'tight spot'? Nay, Kali is safely wrapped in sacred cloth so she cannot crawl out. All set for Zin to see and drool over like a starving jackal."

"What took you so long?"

Gokul looked indignant and rested a hand on his soft belly. "Sahib, you hide treasure in a bird nest high in banyan tree. You dare ask poor Gokul with belly what takes me long? I was made to scheme, to sell goods at the bazaar, to spy, and not as you English say—'shimmy up tree'—to loot bird's nest."

Jace smiled. "Never mind. No one must see you give

it to me now. If you let anything happen to it—"

"Sahib! I guard it with my life."

Jace knew that he would. He grew sober. "Gokul . . . do not look now, but do you see the man who is the maharaja's trusty guard? His name is Khan. What do you know of him?"

Gokul reached into a cotton bag tied to his saddle and drew out a bright orange mango. He bit into it, and as he spat out the skin, his shrewd black eyes drifted casually over the fierce fighting rajputs with their long faces and dark beards, his gaze coming to rest on Khan, seated on the horse next to the maharaja. "He has served His Excellency for three years, and I can find no suspicion. He is loyal. So are all these rajputs. We have good company for the ride to the Burmese border, sahib."

Jace briefly explained about Sanjay and the danger of his reporting the conversation between Ethan and Sir Hugo to Prince Sunil. He briefly mentioned the assassin he had confronted in his quarters.

"Dark news about Sanjay. You will play hard battle to snare so slippery a fish, sahib. If you think to bring him to Calcutta to face rifles of the military for treason, it be best to kill him now, here. Sunil will—"

Jace was not listening. His tension suddenly mounted. His heart began to thud in his chest. He raised a hand to silence Gokul, all the while straining to hear off in the distance. The sound came from the royal stables . . . where the maharaja kept the war elephants. . . .

That noise. What was it? He listened in the darkness. The sound grew louder. Gokul heard too. He straightened in his saddle, his eyes darting to Jace. The others began to understand. The maharaja stirred and looked about. The captain of the rajput guard gave a shouting command. In unison they drew their mighty horn bows and reached for arrows. Jace unsheathed his sword and wished instead for cannon! A battle was about to break forth upon them. One that they could not hope to win, or even escape. Death rode the wind.

Someone had betrayed the maharaja by sending word to Sunil of his intended escape. What had first been planned as a secret assassination by poisoning the raja in his sleep had turned into open conflict. Sunil intended to have the maharaja slain before he could escape Guwahati.

The sound they heard were elephants coming, not the docile females used around the women's quarters but first-rank war elephants—mammoth size, known as "full-blooded," selected from young males who had demonstrated endurance and an even temper essential in battle.

Jace rode swiftly to the maharaja and Khan. "Make for the river. I and the rajputs will try to gain you time. You will have only minutes, so go!"

"It is too late," said the maharaja, his dark eyes calm and unafraid. Swiftly he removed huge ruby and emerald rings from his hands and pressed them toward Jace. "These must be protected! They are the royal rings and now belong to Prince Adesh. Care for his life, Major Sahib-Buckley. He is the hope of his people!"

"Khan!" the maharaja shouted. "The chest! Bring it to safety!"

Khan turned instantly to obey, but it was too late for any escape. The elephants were looming like great terrible monsters in the moonlight, their armor glinting as they came.

Jace shouted for the loyal rajputs to make an outer wall guarding the backward escape route of the raja. It would mean their death, all of them. The elephants were invincible. A well-trained war elephant could be valued at a hundred thousand rupees. Experienced commanders had been known to declare one good elephant worth five hundred horses in battle.

Jace heard Gokul ride up beside him. "Leave, Gokul! You are no soldier! Take Ethan and find Roxbury." He turned and shouted at Khan. "Bring the raja to the river! Now!"

They turned to ride, but Sunil's warriors were coming from three directions at once. Jace and the others had only a flash of warning before they heard the sound of trampling elephant feet, of earth ripping, of tulwars clashing in the moonlight, of the trumpeting of the brave warrior-beasts, which were thrilled with battle.

There was no time to reach the river in an attempt to escape. Nor was there any hope. Jace gripped the handle of his sword as a force of steel-armored elephants advanced, their armor glinting in the torchlight. Jace glanced about him, looking for an opening for the maharaja to ride through. There was none. Sunil knew exactly what he was doing, and he would show no mercy now. The rajputs guarding the maharaja could not retreat under the crushing feet of the elephants.

Then they would fight to the death. They would fight honorably for their king, but the clash of their tulwars would prove useless against the armor of the war elephants. Sunil's men were undercover. The war elephants rumbled toward them, their trunks grabbing the maharaja's rajputs and hurling them beneath their crushing feet. The screams of men mingled with the trumpeting.

The ancient rajput war cry sounded from the loyalists defending the maharaja: "RAM! RAM! RAM! RAM!"

Sunil's elephants carried steel howdahs, in which the warriors rode, with arrow slots to allow the archers to aim and shoot without standing. The maharaja's fighting rajputs fell from the screaming horses.

The maharaja, where is he? Jace looked for him but

could not see him in the chaotic attack. Had Khan somehow been able to harry him away?

Then he saw him—just as the elephant grasped him from the saddle and flung him to the ground beneath its feet.

A musket shot was fired from the long barrel of an Indian matchlock, and Jace felt a blow sear his forehead, leaving his brain ringing. Stunned, he felt himself spinning out of control into hot blackness. For a moment his ears were filled with the noise of battle, yet he could see nothing. He felt something wet and warm running into his eyes, mingling with sweat. For a moment his head felt on fire. Darkness consumed him, yet he was conscious.

"Sahib! This way!"

The muddled voice belonged to Gokul.

Into his darkened vision there sprang up tiny flames. It took a moment to understand that the flames were real; they were torches. He could see again, but the moving forms ahead of him appeared like shadows. He ran a hand across his eyes. His vision continued to clear. . . . Rajputs were fighting with two and three arrows in their bodies, their curved swords slashing as they fought on as though possessed, unaware that their maharaja was dead. In the confusion and darkness the battle raged.

Gokul was beside him, his dark eyes fierce and determined. "Sahib! There is a way! Will you die also? Flee for the sake of all tomorrows!"

Jace looked into the sweat and dust-stained face of Gokul. He could not answer him. He would not flee. Though all was useless, his fighting spirit seemed to merge with the rajputs and he could not turn his back on the warriors. One of Sunil's men rode toward them, lifting his tulwar to take the head of Gokul. For a moment Jace's emotions screamed rage, then turned heavenward in a cry of petition. *God Most High! Not Gokul—please! Do with me as you will! But do not take him! He is not ready for eternity!*

Jace's sword could not stop the slicing blow. As though the scene played out before his eyes in slow motion, his own hand reached for the pistol on his saddle. But the Indian warrior moved a second ahead of him in the attack. As he swung the curved blade for Gokul's head a pistol fired from somewhere in the hot night; a small flame leaped, landing with deadly accuracy between the eyes of the Indian warrior. He appeared to freeze, then the tulwar fell from his hand as he slid from the side of his armored horse.

Jace knew that he had not fired that shot. He turned his head and saw Ethan calmly reloading his pistol from where he had taken partial shield in a tree limb.

But as if in mockery, an arrow whizzed, striking Gokul in the back.

Jace grabbed the reins of Gokul's frightened horse, intent on making for the riverbank. It had taken the near death of Gokul, and now the arrow, to breed new sanity into his emotions. He rode beneath the tree where Ethan straddled a limb, slowed, and reached up as Ethan grabbed hold. They raced into the night, leaving the agony of the ugly ambush behind.

At the river they could hear the elephants. Jace had no recourse but to stop and take refuge in the grasses. The arrow must be removed. He and Ethan knelt in the grass, breathing heavily as they laid Gokul on his stomach. He was unconscious, and Jace feared the arrow was tipped with cobra venom, or any number of Indian drugs—which he could not survive.

"It does not look good, Major. I think your friend is in ultimate decline."

Ultimate decline . . . what a way to put it. At that

67

moment, and since the pistol shot rang out, Jace felt a grudging respect for Ethan.

"Poison?" Jace found his dull voice inquiring. His own mind was again weaving in and out of mental darkness. His head throbbed.

"I do not know . . . I cannot say for certain. We'll know soon enough." Ethan listened to the old man's heart. He frowned and slowly shook his head from side to side as though he had no answer.

All of a sudden Jace was flooded with emotions he thought no longer existed within him, emotions that had died in his youth. Now they broke within like the bursting of a dam—pain, loss, gut-wrenching loss that tasted like gall in his mouth. Death, hell, and the grave pointed a bony, accusing finger.

A voice seemed to come from far away: *Death is swallowed up in victory. The choice is yours to make. Choose life. Rebuke the harvest of death.*

Where had he heard those very words before? Had he read them? The Scriptures of course . . . where were they?

His hand, stiff from battle, fumbled under his tunic to touch Michael Kendall's Bible. No one knew he carried it everywhere he went. He touched it, but could do no more than feel the cool leather. Thoughts of Michael brought a little whiff of breeze like a summer's night in youth when friends and loved ones were gathered. Laughter seemed to ring out—

But the harsh wind blew them away. He felt sweat sting the cuts and abrasions on his face. From Guwahati, the distant sounds of death, terror, and elephants trumpeting blew toward him. Dimly, and without emotion, he was aware that other Indian guards must have joined the fighting on behalf of the maharaja, not realizing that their gray-haired king was dead. But in all the world of

India at that moment, there was only one friend his heart reached out for. Gokul. The man who had been both servant and father, peer and friend. He was losing him, losing the last person who had been in his life since childhood.

Jace stared down at him. *What will I do without you, old friend? Goldfish will miss you*, he wanted to say, giving in to a torrent of raw emotion. His vision was clouded, and he closed his eyes tightly, trying to refocus.

Gokul could never be replaced. Despite the jesting that often went on between them, despite their differences that often got Jace into tight spots—such as when Gokul had leased out the *Madras* to John Company—Gokul's loyalty was real, real enough to die for Jace, and Jace would risk his life for the old munshi who had befriended him as a boy escaping slavery in China.

Jace listened to the labored breathing that was soon to fall silent for all eternity. *Eternity.* How that word unexpectedly lashed through his heart, bringing pain. With a reality that brought tears, Jace tasted the threat of eternal separation that would come between them, realizing he had done too little for the soul of one who was a true friend.

Tears were strangers to Jace, yet they came calling, despite his struggle to hold them back. His jaw clamped, and his hand formed a fist until his nails cut into the flesh of his palm. He had not tasted salty tears since he was a child watching helplessly behind a rock as his father was beheaded on the beach by a Chinese warlord. Now that the flood of emotion had broken free, he could not stop it.

Helpless to rescue Gokul from eternal blackness, he reached out and laid a hand on his head. His gaze met Ethan's, whose face was wet with sweat, and a strange look of understanding showed in his eyes.

"Sorry, Jace."

Jace was oblivious to Ethan, to anything. He wearily leaned and rested his dark head against Gokul's, hearing his labored breathing becoming more and more weak.

Ethan stood, staring not at Gokul's still body in the dried grass, but at Jace. Then he turned and walked to the Brahmaputra River, knelt, and drew handfuls of water to splash against his face.

Strange that I would think of Coral now, thought Jace. He yearned to embrace her, to forget all the loss and ugliness.

Jace wanted to pray, not only for Gokul but for himself—to open wide his own heart to Christ in confession of his self-will, of his refusal to let go of the reins of his life to the One who had so majestically and wisely designed the universe. Too often he had chosen to back away from Him. Too often he had refused the call. A call that he knew had been unmistakable. Sometimes it had come as gentle rain in the English countryside, speaking with the voice of spring flowers, patiently wooing, patiently understanding the struggle of a carnal will that clenched fists like a child and begged to be left alone to play a little longer. Sometimes the call had come like the monsoon—fierce, overwhelming, warning of a precipice, of a fall that would leave him splattered like quivering flesh on the rocks of hell's destruction.

How could he pray? How could he plead for Gokul when his own disobedience tasted like the sweat and tears on his lips? Words from Proverbs came to mock him: *Because I have called, and ye refused . . . I will also laugh at your calamity.*

As a deadness of resignation to his own worthless state settled over him with the mugginess of the night, hope from above came on the gentle flutter of the wings of grace.

Come . . . come to Me . . . come and let us reason together, saith the Lord. . . .

As though transported back to London, to the room in John Newton's house with the fire bright and warm in the hearth, Jace could hear the rain on the windowpanes; he remembered sitting there with the Olney Hymnbook open before him while John Newton and Seward spoke of God's grace . . .

"Amazing grace, how sweet the sound that saved a wretch like me. I once was lost but now am found; was blind, but now I see. 'Twas grace that taught my heart to fear" . . .

He thought: *And grace my fears relieved!*

. . ."How precious did that grace appear the hour I first believed."

Jace opened his eyes, but he could not see clearly enough to even recognize Gokul.

4

Brahmaputra River

Jace awoke with the first chatter of birds in the branches. Strange that they were singing before the sun came up. He stirred, hearing the river lapping the bank below. His muscles were sore after the fighting in Guwahati, and for a moment he remained where he awoke.

Footsteps sounded, coming near, then stopped. "All is not dark, Major. Your Indian friend will survive." The voice belonged to Ethan.

Jace raised himself to an elbow and squinted up, expecting to see the doctor's weary smile, and was greeted instead by a blurred figure with as little color as London fog. Jace could feel dried grass brush against his hand as Ethan stooped down beside him.

"Something wrong?"

Jace ran a hand across his eyes, as if to wipe away cobwebs, slowly remembering now, recalling how they had escaped Guwahati after the assassination of the maharaja and had fled to the Brahmaputra. Gokul had been sorely wounded by an arrow containing a poisonous drug, and he himself had been grazed by gunshot—

Jace became still. The gunshot. . . . Except for a throbbing ache between his eyes, he had thought little about it when Ethan had treated the wound. He remembered that his vision had dimmed in and out like starlight obscured by clouds. He had been too worried about Gokul to make much of it at the time. He had witnessed this before in soldiers with head injuries. Sight usually returned in time, and last night before falling asleep exhausted, he had expected that by morning his vision would clear.

His brain felt bloated with pressure. He looked toward Ethan.

It is nothing, thought Jace, trying to silence the pang of fear. *It will go away. It must.*

The more he strained to clear his vision, the more the fear of being trapped like a tiger on a short chain wrapped its cold bands of iron around his heart. For a moment the thought flashed—*suppose I never see again?*

Trapped! He experienced the icy grip of fear, fear that he had never known when facing swords, guns, or wild animals. Then he had been in control, confident, free—now he was vulnerable!

He felt Ethan gripping his arm. "Good heavens, man! What is it? Do you have pain? Where?"

The urgent concern in his voice jolted Jace back to reality. He touched his head and the small bandage across his forehead. "The gunshot is all. I'll be all right."

"It's only a graze," came Ethan's voice.

Jace knew that Ethan sensed his alarm and was watching him intently.

"Unfortunately, the shot took the side of your head where you were wounded at Plassey. You have a concussion. If the pain is bad I can give you a bit of opium—"

"It's not the pain. I can't see. The idea makes me feel trapped. . . ."

Ethan went silent.

"They have a name for it, I think," said Jace.

"Yes. Can you see this?"

Ethan held something before his eyes, but Jace could barely make it out. "Your hand?"

"Good! Stay calm. Periods of dimmed vision often follow head wounds like yours. It will pass. Keep telling yourself you are in a wide open field. You can see for miles. If it helps, imagine the deck of your ship, the expanse of the ocean, the sky, the gulls soaring."

Jace envisioned it all, yet the fear that he would never *truly* see it again brought the curtain down.

He did not like the silence growing between him and Ethan, for Jace knew he watched him through the eyes of a physician, and it fed his uncertainty.

"Easy, Major."

Ethan's almost kind voice tended only to provoke him. He listened to the grass rustle around Ethan's boots as he stood, and Jace imagined him frowning down upon him as though he were a small boy with a skinned knee. The idea left him smarting.

"It's only temporary," said Ethan again. "You're not helpless. You can see well enough to distinguish objects, so you are not blind."

"How temporary?" gritted Jace impatiently. "There is Burma! Sunil will be looking for us, for Gem!"

"I do understand, Major! I do not know how long it will last. Hours, days perhaps."

Days . . . he could bear that . . . but what if it were weeks, years!

"You are a doctor, there ought to be something you can do to snap me out of it. Drugs, another impact on the head, anything."

"Don't be absurd! You touch that concussion and you may indeed go blind!"

Maybe that's what he wants, thought Jace, his hand clenching into a fist. *No . . . I'm behaving like a fool.* He let out a breath.

"You need rest, Jace. So does Gokul. Danger from Prince Sunil is real, but your condition is also real. Ignoring it will make it worse. This is one time when you must accept the fact you can do nothing but wait."

Wait. The most difficult word in any language when urgency nipped at your heels like hungry rats. Yet sanity told him Ethan spoke the obvious. He could do nothing until his vision cleared.

"We've one choice as I see it, and that is to wait at Kingscote until you can see well enough to journey to Burma," said Ethan. "Didn't you say you would need Gokul? He, too, must recover."

Jace thought of Coral. He would rather die by the tulwar of Sunil than have her see him like this. He did not want her sympathy. He would not take refuge at Kingscote. Layers of frustration mounted inside him. He pushed Coral from his mind and forced himself to think of Gokul. His friend had survived the night. Jace saw a glimmer of gratitude in his dark sky. "How did he make it? The arrow was tipped with poison."

"A question I shall never be able to answer, yet he is awake and determined to ride to Kingscote. How about you—can you get up? Can you ride?"

He would ride if it killed him, but not to the Kendall plantation. "If you wish to go to Kingscote, do so. I've friends in Sualkashi. Gokul and I will take our leave there."

Jace stood and felt Ethan's hand steady him. He resented the need of his support and wanted to pull away.

"Neither you nor Gokul are in any condition to journey alone to Sualkashi."

"We'll manage."

"Major is right," came Gokul's weak voice from somewhere in the river grass. "I am well . . . only very tired . . . I will be his eyes to reach Sualkashi. We will make it, sahib-doctor. Major and me, we face many hard places together before. This one, we will make also. The friend he speak of in Sualkashi, he is my brother."

Ethan did not argue, and Jace believed it was because he was pleased to have him away from Coral. Well, the idea also suited him just fine.

"Very well, Major. I'll saddle your horses."

Ethan returned in a short time, and Jace saw his and Gokul's shadowy figures moving about and Gokul being helped into the saddle. Ethan walked up to where Jace leaned against a tree.

"I've put medication in your saddlebag. You may find it helpful. I've included a salve and fresh bandages for both of you, and some mangoes I picked this morning before you woke. Godspeed," he said, and Jace heard him turn to leave.

"Ethan—wait."

The shadowy figure stopped.

"Coral already knows Gem is alive. I sent a message. But it is important you say nothing of what you overheard last night between me and the raja. If Coral learns the truth, that Sunil is closing in on Gem's trail, she will be prompted to act before I can reach Zin. Any blunder now will ruin the chance I have to save him from Sunil."

Ethan hesitated. Jace knew that he understood the *blunder* included anything that he and Coral might plan together.

"I hear you, Major. But if Sunil discovers where his nephew is before you are able to go to Burma, it will mean the boy's death."

"I'm aware of that. Give me time. If you do not hear

from me or Gokul—you are on your own."

"Understood. I know your friendship with this war-lord offers you the best opportunity."

"If something happens and you feel it is imperative to act, take this with you." Jace felt inside his jacket for a map of Burma and handed it toward the shadow. "If you go, proceed cautiously. The monsoon often washes away sections of the road, and avalanches are common. And whatever you do, do not journey by way of the British road. Take the route I've marked."

"But wouldn't the road be the obvious and quickest route?"

"It would," said Jace dryly. "Except Sunil and his assassins will be traveling along that road."

Ethan's response came stiffly. "Thank you for the warning."

Jace heard Ethan's steps crunch across the grass to where the horse waited. Soon the thud of hooves died away.

Jace remained leaning against the tree. In the branches a monkey jabbered. He imagined the Brahmaputra gray in the early light of dawn; he listened to the caw of mynah birds, to the whooping of long-legged cranes, and somewhere the water lapped against the bank.

His sight would come back. It had to.

But what if the worst happened to him? What if God permitted permanent blindness? What if losing his sight was God's way of teaching him important lessons he had refused to learn when strong and free?

Yet a flicker of hope shone like a singular candle in the dark empty mansion of his soul. *I am not totally blind. If the Lord wished to seal me in blackness in order to bring light to my soul, He could have already done so.*

Perhaps this experience was a warning, and God

wanted his attention—

Newton's hymn echoed and reechoed through his mind. *I once was blind, but now I see....* His fingers touched Michael's Bible inside his inner pocket next to his heart.

He heard Gokul riding toward the tree, bringing the horse. He remembered that Gokul had almost died.

Newton was right. Amazing grace.

"Well, friend, thief, and spy," Jace said. "Christ has granted you a reprieve. Last night the earth opened her jaws to swallow you inside her hellish bowels. You might have been eternally digested by now."

Jace imagined Gokul's black eyes glinting as he stopped the horses and leaned to press the reins in his hand.

"Ah, sahib, old Gokul is wiser than you think. He learns quickly. Fleshly delights only whisper, but pain shouts. He is ready to listen to words William Carey brings to Mother India."

5

Kingscote

India's hot season continued to build toward its crest, leaving those on Kingscote feeling listless, and tempers were short. Even at dawn it was wretchedly hot. Coral pushed her damp blond hair away from her face and remembered dully what her father had once said: "The hot season is the time when murders are made and suicides mount."

Once again Coral's memory strained to recount the message in her father's letter received by her uncle, Sir Hugo Roxbury, at Guwahati. What had he written?

The situation on the border with Burma grows more dangerous. . . . Yet I've no choice but to leave the matters here with God and journey to Darjeeling to find Alex. Word arrived by courier that he is missing.

The days inched by without word as they waited for the sound of horse hooves on the carriageway, while all about them the tensions of danger and war gathered like the heralding clouds of the monsoon.

Coral was anxious to move ahead with plans to complete a wooden structure for the school before the rains came and the ground turned to mud. Once the rains began they would continue until what India called "the cool" was ushered in.

Jace had pressed her to wait until her father returned, but who knew how long he would be gone? Any hope of soon hearing horses in the carriageway was unrealistic, and so she turned her energies into convincing her mother to allow her to begin the school project.

"If we delay until Father returns it will mean waiting until next year to build. When you said you'd discuss the school with him, you thought he'd be back with Alex by now."

Elizabeth's worried thoughts about Hampton and her son were visible. "Yes, I did expect them back by now."

"And planning and building will give us something to fill our hearts while we wait."

Coral could see that the thought of the school filled her mother with the same excitement. Now that Elizabeth was growing stronger from her long illness, she too needed a worthy goal in which to refocus her energies. "I suppose Hampton will not be overly upset if we begin now."

Coral was quickly out of the chair and beside her mother. "Let's take the ghari this afternoon and decide on the location. I was thinking of the clearing near the silk hatcheries. If we start today we can have a structure built before the rains."

Several days later, Coral sat at her father's big desk and began to construct on paper her idea of how the school should look. The morning was gone before she paused to scrutinize her plan. She heard the familiar sounds of the servants moving about the dining salon, preparing the table for the noon meal. The smell of baked bread wafted through the room, making Coral realize how hungry she was and that she had only taken tea for breakfast.

She frowned at her drawing. It wasn't quite what she had visualized in her mind, but then she had never claimed to be an architect. She paused, hearing a slight noise behind her.

Coral's back was toward the door and she turned, half expecting to see one of the girls announcing lunch. The door remained shut. She stood, then noticed a piece of paper had been pushed under it. Quickly she picked it up, looking to see if she could catch a glimpse of the messenger, but the hall was empty. A breeze came to rattle the cane blind on the open window.

Coral read the words in Hindi, written by a hand struggling with grammar:

Sacrifice to dread Kali. Meet me in back near smoke-house after lunch.
—A friend

On Kingscote? Who would be so bold after strict orders from her father all these years? Coral debated showing the note to her mother but changed her mind. Whoever had left the note had chosen her as a confidante instead of going openly to the memsahib, probably knowing full well that Elizabeth would be outraged.

Someone trusts me to protect their identity, she decided, heading for the dining room.

———

Seated at the large table spread with the crystal sparkling and the chinaware from Canton filled with a variety of English and Indian cuisine, Coral waited until she could make an excuse to leave. Her sisters, Kathleen and

Marianna, were discussing Cousin Belinda's marriage to Sir George and who among the nobility might be invited by Aunt Margaret and Granny V.

"Wouldn't it be grand to be able to attend the wedding in London?" said Marianna. "Or better yet, if the marriage could take place here."

"With Burmese soldiers prowling the outskirts of Kingscote?" mocked Kathleen. "Yes, how grand indeed." She looked across the table at her mother. "Is it true there was another infiltrator shot last night?"

"Yes, but before your father left he took care to assign his most trusted mercenaries to defend the plantation borders. And your father will be back soon," said Elizabeth, trying as always to ease their concerns.

Coral imagined Burmese soldiers prowling the plantation. But soon Jace would be arriving at the British outpost near Jorhat. He knew the danger; he had warned her about it that night in Guwahati. Surely he would alert the commander there to send some English troopers to check on Kingscote. Yet he believed that Seward was here, not searching for her father in Darjeeling, and he trusted him explicitly.

Kathleen was frowning thoughtfully. "About Belinda's wedding in London ... I'm surprised she didn't write Alex about her fate before leaving Calcutta."

"Yes, she did not want to marry old George, did she?" said Marianna.

"She only moaned and groaned the entire time we were in Calcutta," said Kathleen. "I wonder if Alex received a letter or a small box from her when the shipment of mail arrived with Granny V's letter."

Why is she asking that? wondered Coral. She recalled her cousin's fiery infatuation with the Kendall sons, first Michael, then Alex. With Alex, Belinda's interest had exceeded that shown in her youth for Michael.

84

"There was no letter from Belinda in the sewing box when I found the one from Granny V," said Marianna.

"I was so ill at the time I cannot say for sure," said Elizabeth. "If there was a letter Alex would have received it before going to Darjeeling. If it is important to you, Alex would not mind if you looked in his room."

Kathleen said nothing and took a second cup of tea.

Watching her, Coral came to the conclusion that something about Belinda and Alex troubled her sister. The noon meal ended, and once her mother and sisters went their separate ways, she left the back door and walked across the yard in the direction of the smokehouse.

The outbuilding, made of stone and smelling of curing meats, was nearly deserted when she arrived, and she walked around to the back entrance, where some trees formed the outer growth of the jungle. Several empty wagons were nearby, but the workers were still away eating their noon meal.

Coral stood, glancing about, smelling the odor of smoke. She waited for the approach of footsteps but there were none. "Hello?" she called out into the stillness. "Anyone here?"

A twig snapped, not from the direction of the smokehouse but the jungle. She turned quickly, her eyes searching the shadows of the trees.

The branches moved, and Preetah, Natine's niece, stepped out nervously and beckoned Coral to follow her into the jungle trees. Coral believed she could trust the young woman; after all, Natine was her father's head servant. Casting a glance over her shoulder to make certain no one had followed her from the house, Coral picked up her skirts and sped after the Indian girl.

In the cloistered shadows smelling of damp earth and ferns, they paused, breathless. Coral saw the fear in Preetah's brown eyes and felt the girl's fingers close tightly about her arm. Preetah glanced off toward a little-used trail that wound deeper into the jungle. "It was I who slipped the note beneath door."

"You must tell me everything."

"No, you must see, and hear—for your sake."

Coral felt a tingle. What was it about Kali that the girl thought so important that Coral must hear for herself? She remembered back to the river journey and the tiger attack. After the death of one of their hired guides, the others had believed a sacrifice to appease their vengeful god a necessity. She had no wish to look upon the scene now on Kingscote land, but she must learn who was involved in order to report it to her father when he returned.

Minutes later Coral followed her through the trees, uncertain of their destination. Birds twittered and a cackle of jungle noises closed in about them.

They had walked for some time. She felt insects about her face and slapped them away. Remembering when Jace had rescued her from the horrid spider that had lodged on the back of her neck, she glanced up into the overhanging branches, but saw only a bird in emerald plumage flitter away. A short time later, they stopped, and Preetah gestured for silence.

Coral saw the glow of a small fire among the distant trees. They crept up silently, the dense jungle growth shielding them. Ahead, a number of trees had been chopped down to make a small circular clearing where a fire was flickering in the breeze.

Coral stooped behind the trees and heard voices. One of them she recognized immediately. *Natine!*

There was a religious man—a sadhu—with him and two other men, none of whom she recognized. Coral saw a small altar built, and nearby a goat waited to placate Kali.

She turned her head away as the bleating of the goat died at the hand of the sadhu. Suddenly she froze with horror, hearing her name mentioned. She listened, not daring to breath, her heart pounding. The village sadhu was signaling her out as an enemy of Kali.

Preetah tugged at her arm, and they slipped cautiously away.

On the brisk walk back to the mansion, Coral was silent and Preetah was grave, clutching her long head wrap against her chest.

When they arrived back at the smokehouse, Preetah turned to face her. "The sadhu and Natine are against the presence of the English in Assam. Many in the village agree. They speak secretly of a great battle that will come, when the new maharaja in Guwahati will purify the land of all feringhis. If you seek to serve your God by building the school, I do not know what will happen on Kingscote."

Before Coral could respond, the young woman stepped around a tree and disappeared into the dense jungle. Was Prince Sunil the new maharaja the people in the village looked to in order to drive out the English?

———

Coral awoke to the sound of the punkah fan located on the wall near her bed. The bedchamber was warm and still with late-afternoon shadows, and for a drowsy moment she lay there contentedly watching the delicate flutter of the mosquito netting.

Her mind was heavy with sleep as her eyes fell on a tiny figure standing on a peacock-feather stool pulling the fan cord. The child's long ebony pigtails hung down her back like two shiny ropes. She was wearing an embroidered blue tunic that reached to her knees. Beneath, she wore tight-fitting yellow pants. It was Reena, Preetah's small sister. Both girls belonged to Natine, who was their uncle.

After what Coral had witnessed the week before with Preetah, Jace's warning about Natine set her on edge. She found her curiosity about Natine's political beliefs growing with the passing weeks.

"You do not need to keep pulling the punkah, Reena. Your arms must be tired. I am used to the heat. Why not come here and tell me about your uncle Natine. He is a respected leader, isn't he? Has he many friends in the village?"

Reena shyly climbed down from the peacock stool and, with an embarrassed smile, lifted the netting and looked at the bed. Coral beckoned her to come, and the child crawled up as if accomplishing some impossible task.

"Tell me about Natine. What does he do when he visits the priest and the other men in the village?"

Reena tensed and glanced toward the door. "I go now, Missy Coral."

Coral realized she had moved too swiftly and had set the girl on guard. "No, you need not go yet. You can help me understand about Kingscote. I've been gone from home a long time. I expect you and your sister know everything that goes on around here?"

Reena smiled and lowered her eyes. "Mostly Preetah. She is a close friend with Yanna, who works in the silk hatcheries."

Yanna . . . how long ago it seemed when the small child had come running to her with the message that Jemani had gone into labor. Yanna was now a Christian, baptized by Elizabeth Kendall.

Coral was relieved to learn the two young women

were friends. It was good that Preetah had someone like Yanna to turn to for advice.

"Do not tell our uncle they are friends. He has told my sister to stay away from Yanna because she serves another god, but she brings hot broth to Yanna for her little friends. It is a secret. If Natine finds out what Preetah does to help Yanna, he will send us both away before memsahib can stop him."

"Little friends? Why are Yanna's little friends such a secret?"

Reena glanced toward the door. "They have sweating sickness. My uncle says let them die first as sacrifice to crocodiles to stop all the sickness. Kali is angry. It is why the sickness spreads on Kingscote, even though memsahib is better now. Uncle said they would die. Maybe Sunday, maybe Monday. He does not know my sister helps Yanna bring them food. He says they will now be thrown to the river crocodiles on festival day."

"Throw them to crocodiles! Are these children from Kingscote?"

"No, the village."

So that was why Natine did not fear to offer them to the river god as a sacrifice!

"Where are they now?"

"Do not ask!"

"If children are sick they must be cared for. I need to know where they are, Reena."

"But Natine will punish Preetah for helping Yanna."

"I won't let him. Tell her I will go tonight when she brings the food to Yanna. Tell her to send me word of when and where to meet her."

When the girl had gone, Coral's thoughts raced back to the sadhu. Involving herself would be a risk, but how could she stand by and do nothing, allowing children to die?

Before going down to dinner, she opened her Bible and read Psalm 91, then prayed for those on her heart. Mentally she placed each one, along with herself, in the "secret place of the most High."

The words penetrated her mind: "There shall no evil befall thee."

6

Night softly touched the Brahmaputra River, and in the jungle perimeter around Kingscote the growl of a tiger could be heard. Coral was dressed for the secret excursion into the jungle, and her heart beat with odd little jerks as she waited expectantly in her room. She stood up quickly from her bed as the soft tap sounded.

She crossed the thick Isfahan rug and opened the door. Reena stood there with her dark eyes appearing even rounder as she put her fingers to her lips and beckoned for Coral to follow.

She sensed the urgency in the child's manner and knew that their plan must be carried out before Natine returned from his meeting in the village. Without a word, she followed her down the back stairs of the mansion to a seldom-used storage room near the cooking quarters. They could hear Rosa humming as she pounded and rolled the fresh dough for the next morning's breakfast.

Preetah met them, holding a jug of hot broth, her face tense. "I cannot go, Miss Coral. Natine did not go to the village tonight as usual. Please, you must take the broth for me. Yanna waits in the trees."

Outside in the warm night, Coral left the back porch

and walked across the dusty yard, carrying the large jug of broth. Yanna waited, a shadowy figure in her dark sari. Farther ahead and amid the thick trees surrounding the yard clearing, the two-wheeled trap called a tonga was parked.

Yanna was surprised to see her, but her delight sprang into a smile. "It is you! How glad I am!"

Coral heaved the jug into the cart, taking care not to spill its contents, then climbed in behind Yanna. The tonga creaked forward into the blackness, and the hooves of the ox lumbered over the ground, kicking up the dust. The night was sultry, and Coral raised a hand to push back damp tendrils of hair from off her neck where they'd fallen from her chignon. She glanced about, seeing jungle trees silhouetted against even blacker shadows, trying to hold down her apprehension.

She admired Yanna's courage. Elizabeth had taught her well, after the death of Jemani. Now, a silent bond formed between them as they shared the same determined spirit to save the children.

Yanna leaned close and whispered, "It was Preetah who first told me about the four children. They are untouchables from the village. She was in the ghari when Natine brought them here and left them beside the river. They were to be thrown to the crocodiles on the festival. I hid them in the jungle, since I could not bring them to the bungalows." Yanna scowled. "Natine is watching me. He has become bold since the illness of memsahib. He must not know Preetah helps me. Without your father's presence to rule Kingscote, she has no one."

"I will do what is necessary to see she and Reena are not involved. As for the children, we can't leave them out here in the jungle another night. I heard a tiger prowling."

Yanna gave a nervous glance into the trees. "I have

heard it for two nights. Angels have protected them so far. Each night I come here I feel my heart in my throat, wondering if I will find them."

"Then there is no one else involved?" Coral asked.

"No one else. If Preetah did not smuggle food from the kitchen, I would have little. Even if the other untouchables wished to help, they dare not. And the others do not want to come even if they could. Many agree with Natine." Yanna glanced at her warily. "He has spent much time in the village where the new sadhu holds meetings. He is against the English presence in Assam."

Alert, Coral asked, "When did the sadhu arrive?"

"Three years ago. He is from Sibsagar."

Sibsagar was northeast of the Jorhat outpost, and the great capital of Assam. It was strange that a sadhu would leave the ancient city for a small village. She might have told Yanna about seeing him with Natine in the Kali rite but did not wish to involve her more than she already was.

The jungle thickened. Night wrapped about them. Coral held to the seat to steady herself as the trail wound deeper into the solitude. Perspiration made her clothes stick to her, and her stomach tensed when Yanna at last brought the ox to a stop.

Coral saw the outline of a shelter built of dried branches, leaves, and dirt. "Hand me the lantern."

A moment later she was down from the seat and stooping before the opening of the small lean-to. She thrust the dull yellow light inside, and dismal sobs filled her ears. Coral's throat constricted and she swallowed hard. "Oh, Lord," she whispered, and momentarily shut her eyes against the pathetic sight that greeted her.

Four small, skinny children huddled together, naked except for the blanket Yanna had brought them. Large brown eyes stared at her with apprehension, while their breathing came in rasping chokes.

"Do not be afraid," she told them in Hindi. "I am your friend." She turned to Yanna. "It is a miracle the tiger has not come by now," she said. "My conscience will not permit me to leave them out here like this. I must do something."

Yanna knelt beside her, her eyes anxious. "But where can we bring them without Natine finding out?"

"You are right about the silk workers—who would take them in when they fear Natine? But who cared for them in the village before they became ill?"

"An old woman, Ila, but she is dead. She was sick long before they were. And no one else will bother with untouchables who have no relatives. That is why Natine brought them to the river."

"Do not fear Natine," said Coral.

"Be careful. I have heard Natine listens only to your uncle from Calcutta, Sir Hugo Roxbury."

"Who told you so? Preetah?"

Yanna looked uneasy. "Yes. Everyone whispers of war and mutiny. Preetah says she heard the sadhu mention your uncle in the village meetings."

Jace had warned her that Natine may serve Roxbury. "Sir Hugo is my uncle, but he is not the master of Kingscote, no matter what others may think," Coral assured Yanna.

While Yanna fed the children, Coral walked toward the tonga to think. If only there was someone to help her. Wearily she stood. Sounds coming from deeper in the jungle closed in about her emotions like a fort. *Fort.* . . . The word took on an image in her mind like a glimmer of hope in the thick darkness. Jorhat . . . Major Jace Buckley. . . . He would be there by now looking into the matter of the assassination of the British officer. He could not have gone to Burma yet, and Jorhat was not that far away from Kingscote.

Would he come? Could he leave his command even for a short time? Was she also searching for an excuse to get in touch with him again after their last meeting in the palace garden?

"We need a friend, Yanna. Someone strong, someone equal to Sir Hugo who can help me stand against his schemes until my father returns with Seward. I must send someone to the Jorhat outpost. Is there anyone among the workers I can trust to ride there?"

"There is Thilak. He guards the hatchery. He is a good man."

"Then I must speak with him tonight."

With that decided, Coral's heart felt a little lighter. She turned her attention back to the children. So, was this to be the fate of the untouchables—to slowly die while weakness stole the life from their bodies, or to wait until a wild beast came upon them?

If I do nothing, then what am I? thought Coral. *How can I claim to be a follower of Him?*

When they had been fed she told Yanna, "They may yet die, but if they do, they die in a warm bed with at least one person to comfort them. Help me get them in the back of the tonga. I'm taking them where I know they'll get proper care—the dispensary."

Admiration shone in Yanna's eyes. "There is no need to risk more trouble. I will do what my heart told me from the first. But I let fear stop me. I will take the children to my bungalow and care for them there. Everyone already knows I am a Christian, and if there is trouble for me among my friends, it must come. Thilak will protect me."

Coral was deeply moved. "Are you certain you wish

95

to take the risk now, Yanna? Perhaps we should wait until my father returns."

"I am certain. I live in the bungalow once belonging to Jemani and Rajiv. There is room for the four children."

"Then I will speak to my mother about it. But the children are too ill now. I must take them to the house, to the dispensary, where they can be cared for by Rosa."

"Then I shall come and help nurse them if you wish. I do not think Rosa will touch them since she is of higher caste."

Kingscote lay in sleepy stillness when they arrived near the hatcheries. Yanna jumped down from the driver's seat to return to her bungalow, and Coral took the reins. She waited until Yanna ran off into the darkness, then flapped the reins, and the ox treaded forward.

The light flooding the windows of the mansion reminded Coral of gleaming candles in St. Paul's Cathedral in London. A sense of reality flooded her heart.

There was nothing to fear. No one in earth or heaven could harm her unless God permitted it, she thought. Scripture verses memorized now winged their way across her mind. *My times are in Thy hand. If God be for us, who can be against us?*

No force could harm her here, safe in the company of her mother and sisters. And soon Jace would arrive. The petition to the idol was folly, and while Satan's power may lodge in Kali's image, the righteousness of Christ flanked her with armor.

7

Ahead, the light in the mansion burned. Coral left the ox and tonga under the trees and climbed down, lifting the blanket to cover the children. They whimpered but didn't cry aloud. Perhaps they had long ago learned that no one responded to their tears. No one at all. Dark, empty eyes stared up at her. "It is all right," she said in Hindi. "I am your friend. I will come back in a few minutes to help you." She hurried across the dusty yard, and then up the steps to the back porch. She threw open the door and walked into the brightly lit kitchen.

Piroo, the head cook, was asleep in a chair snoring loudly, the Kingscote breakfast all laid out and prepared to cook in the morning. Hearing her enter he came awake. Coral's perspiring face streaked with dust, with strands of hair hanging loose from the heavy chignon, caused the older man to struggle to his sandaled feet.

"Miss Coral! You are hurt!"

"No, no I'm quite fine, Piroo, but, I'll need hot water, milk, and sweet tea. Find Mera and tell her to awaken Jan-Lee. I'll need four more beds and blankets in the dispensary—and children's garments. Hurry."

Before he could ask questions, Coral pushed past

97

through the door into the lower hall. Her mother's health had not been strong that day, and she refused to add to her burden. She might awaken Marianna to help, but she was sleeping tonight in their mother's chamber. Coral hurried down the hall to Kathleen's room.

Her sister was asleep, the satin coverlet pulled up about her neck. Coral's mouth turned up at the corners ruefully. *She almost looks angelic,* she thought. *Let us hope she behaves as such.* She pulled the cover aside. "Kathleen, wake up, I need your help in the dispensary."

Kathleen groaned, stirred, and with her voice dulled by the pillow, mumbled, "Hmm. . . ? Coral, don't . . . bother me. . . . Leave me alone."

Kathleen burrowed down in the bed again. Coral pulled the coverlet off. "Get up, Sis, I need your help. There are four children . . . very sick. Please, Kathleen!"

Kathleen responded to the alarm in her voice. She rolled over and stared up at her. "What? Is it Mother?"

"No. Four children. They have the fever. Come, I need your help."

As though she did not hear Coral correctly, Kathleen stared up at her, scowling. "Are you daft? Children? Whose?"

"Orphans, you goose! Get up! I need your moral support. Natine will be angry."

Kathleen moaned and covered her face with her palms. "Natine! I'm beginning to wish he would mount an elephant and ride off to the Himalayas!"

"Not much chance of that—unless he returns with war elephants. Get up."

"Coral! Do you realize we're all alone here? With Mother about to have a relapse of the fever, and Father gone—"

"The major will come soon. I will send Thilak to Jorhat."

Kathleen crawled out of bed, reaching for her silk dressing gown. "Marvelous, but the message he sent about Gem said he would be gone until Christmas."

"I am hoping he is still at Jorhat. Wait for me in the dispensary sickroom, will you? I'll be there as soon as I write the major a letter. Yanna's friend will ride to the outpost tonight."

The servants watched in silence as the children were carried into a large back chamber that Elizabeth used as a dispensary. Containing beds and medicine, it had been her mother's first project as mistress, and one that had proved invaluable. As Coral went there to join Kathleen, she pretended not to notice Natine waiting at the end of the darkened hall, watching.

Mera stepped aside, troubled, as Coral entered the large room housing a number of beds. She knew that Mera feared she would ask her to help wash the children before putting them between the clean blankets.

Coral smiled at the old woman for whom she carried a deep affection. "It is all right, Mera. You best get some sleep. Kathleen and I will tend to them."

Mera's expression betrayed her relief. "I called for Jan-Lee to help you, my child. She comes now, sahiba."

If only Jace would come, thought Coral.

Deep night lay upon Kingscote. The flame on the candle burned low. Her eyes felt like sand, and she was physically and emotionally exhausted, but pleased. Already the Lord had used her to prolong the lives of four children. Instead of going up to her room, Coral rested on one of the empty beds.

Untouchables, she mused sleepily. The lepers of the caste system. Christ could touch lepers and make them whole; how much more were little ones on Kingscote precious in His sight?

Coral found her eyes closing and sleep dragging her

mind off to captivity. She dreamed of Kali, goddess of destruction. . . . The hideous four-armed idol with protruding tongue stood on a dead man and wore human skulls on her girdle like beads on a string. Coral awoke with a start.

Dawn had broken, with no relief from the draining heat. Coral looked out the window toward the dusty road, remembering that day so long ago now, when Major Jace Buckley rode in with a small troop of sowars from Jorhat to hunt the tiger. Gem had been born that night, when the monsoon broke . . . and Jemani had journeyed home to heaven. Coral felt a cloud settle over her soul as she remembered, and she desperately wished to see Jace riding now toward the house in the company of trusted sowars. The road was empty. She turned away, leaving the dispensary to take morning tea with her mother, and arrived at the door just as Preetah was coming out.

"Memsahib insists she is much better. She is dressed and taking tea on the verandah."

Elizabeth Kendall looked thin and pale, but smiled cheerily as Coral kissed her cheek and drew up a white wrought-iron chair to the table.

"You are up early, Coral." Elizabeth set her Bible aside and poured her daughter a cup of tea. "Scones? They are your favorite. Mera sent up lemon honey."

Coral shook her head no and looked across the railing toward the river, a sullen gray. To ease her mind she concentrated on the elephants being led down the road for their morning wallow. "Something must be done about Natine."

Elizabeth, in the midst of preparing her hot scone, paused and studied her daughter's face.

In low tones, Coral explained about the happenings of the night before.

"If you had awakened me I would have insisted the children be brought to the dispensary. You did the right thing, especially with a tiger roaming the perimeter. I had better see the children myself and make certain their ailment is the fever. There has been no sign of cholera this year, but we can take no chances."

"Yanna is willing to share her bungalow when they recover. She can put them to work in the hatchery, and they can be our first students in the school."

Elizabeth was calm but alert. "Natine knows better than to offer a sacrifice to the crocodiles on Kingscote property."

Coral did not tell her about the sadhu who had spoken her name to Kali. Despite her mother's determination to carry on as mistress, Elizabeth's health continued to trouble her, and Coral feared a serious relapse. Some things must wait for her father's return.

"Natine will deny everything, of course," warned Coral, "then question Preetah to see if she was involved in telling me about the children."

"I'll not mention her nor Reena. But I will need to confront him with this."

The children's fever eventually broke, and Coral knew they would live. They were emaciated and withdrawn, never smiling, never talking. They watched Coral mutely as if they were caught up in a nightmare. She tried to make friends with the four little faces staring at her with wide dark eyes, but received no response.

One morning after Coral had recounted in the Hindi language the story of Jesus touching and healing the leper, the boy named Ajay was the first to smile shyly up at her.

"Burra-sahib very good, sahiba."

Coral smiled at her success and reached a hand to the side of his face. "Jesus is more than a Burra-sahib. He is Lord of all, and just think, He loves *you*, Ajay."

Ajay covered his face with both hands and giggled shyly. His laughter provoked the other three to giggling, and soon the mattress was filled with merriment of laughter while they struggled to hide their faces under the sheet. It was hard to get them to calm down after that, and thereafter her relationship with the children was guaranteed.

"We never go back," they kept saying as if questioning her, afraid that she would return them to the village. "We never go back to Ila or hut."

"Ila dead," said Mona sadly to Ajay.

"We never go back," he repeated. "We stay with Sahiba Coral and Yanna."

8

Not long after the children's recovery, the sound of horse hooves outside the window on the carriageway brought Coral quickly to her feet. She opened the door and sped from her father's office into the large hall, her eyes expectantly on the front door as Rosa came to answer the knock.

Coral stood anxiously, her hands pressed against the sides of her skirts.

Was it Jace? Had he had arrived in answer to her request sent through Thilak?

Ethan entered the hallway, holding his familiar medical bag, and did not see Coral standing off to the side near her father's office.

"I am Doctor Ethan Boswell, a relative of the Kendall family," he told Rosa. "I've just ridden in from Guwahati."

Coral recovered from her surprise. She had been so certain it was Jace. Ignoring the twinge of disappointment, she picked up her skirts and hurried toward him across the polished wood floor. "Ethan!"

He turned quickly at the sound of her voice and, seeing her, removed his hat and set his bag on the floor.

Coral stopped short. One glimpse of his face, now soiled from sweat and dust, shouted to her of dark news. His wheat-colored hair was disheveled, his lean jaw tense. His usual formal dress was soiled and sweat stained, his jacket ripped at the shoulder seams, and there were dried bloodstains on the frilled cuffs of his shirt.

In two long strides Ethan was before her, catching up her hands into his and holding them so tightly that Coral nearly winced. She looked searchingly into his gray eyes. She had never seen him look so hard and remote.

Her eyes fell to the dried bloodstains, stark and ugly on his frilled cuffs—cuffs that belonged in the elegant parlor of Roxbury House in London, and she felt a dart of fear. "What is it, Ethan, what's happened? Are you hurt? There's blood on you. . . ."

"There has been a rebellion in Guwahati."

Coral listened, her nerves taut as he explained how he had been expected to deal treacherously with the maharaja by quietly poisoning him under the guise of medical treatment.

"A fine way to keep the British government from suspecting anything," Ethan said. "Having signed a treaty with the maharaja, the East India Company could have come to his aid."

By now Ethan's arrival was known to the rest of the house, and Elizabeth appeared on the stairs, with Kathleen and Marianna hurrying down the stairs after her.

Coral was left to her anxious thoughts as Ethan walked to meet them.

He had said nothing of the major, and Coral could hardly contain her impatience. She glanced out the front window facing the carriageway, but there was only one horse, the Indian boy now leading it to the stables to be fed and watered. She heard her mother greeting Ethan, worriedly asking of his condition and the trouble at Guwahati, yet somehow maintaining that gracious demeanor of courtesy she always displayed. She asked of Hugo's safety, and Ethan's voice went stiff.

"I am certain Prince Sunil would not dare harm the British ambassador. It would damage his relationship with the East India Company and weaken his position on the throne."

"Yet if Prince Sunil resents British incursions into Assam, would he not attack all the English presence in the north?"

Coral heard her mother's question and turned to see Ethan's response. He was tense, as though holding back feelings for Sir Hugo he did not wish on display.

"The major feels Prince Sunil is not yet strong enough militarily to risk driving the English out of northeast India, but will wait. He will first seek to rally his people around him by appealing to their religion. He may even seek to make some manner of appeasement toward Calcutta in the assassination of his uncle, as though wishing to make good the treaty signed with the Company."

"But the major thinks that Sunil will eventually attack the feringhis?" Elizabeth continued.

"Yes," said Ethan. "But before the troop under Captain MacKay arrives, Sir Hugo stands to offer the best hope of protection for Kingscote. I feel certain we'll be hearing from him soon."

"Hampton would be pleased to know of the major's presence in this dangerous situation. I do hope he felt free to make use of Kingscote on the way to the outpost at Jorhat?"

Then Jace was not injured . . . thought Coral, a sigh of relief escaping from her.

"I regret to say the major declined Kendall hospitality."

105

Coral came alert.

"Oh. I am disappointed," said Elizabeth. "He has other quarters?"

"He and an Indian friend named Gokul were both slightly wounded, nothing to be concerned about, but the major felt strongly inclined to seek the solace of a certain family in Sualkashi."

At the mention of Sualkashi, Coral's memory confronted a vision of the lovely Indian girl. Her fingers dug into her palms as she watched Ethan intently from where she stood at the window. *Inclined to seek solace elsewhere, was he? He prefers that Indian girl's company in his emotional pain instead of facing Coral Kendall again.*

"An English family?" inquired Elizabeth casually.

"No. Indian I believe."

"Sualkashi?" Marianna turned to Coral, wrinkling her pert nose. "Why, we stayed there the night you were ill. Remember, Coral? That is where you said that Indian girl was rude to you. I wonder if—"

Kathleen casually turned her head toward Marianna. Marianna looked suddenly confused, then ashamed, and her eyes darted quickly across the hall to Coral. She hastened to recover her blunder but only made it worse.

"Oh, yes . . . so it was the same family . . . but I'm sure she and Major Buckley are merely friends."

Coral made no sound. Her heart was pounding. Ethan did not look at her but said stiffly, "The girl is related to the major's Indian friend. A niece, I think, was what Gokul said. Gokul informed me that the reason the major went to Sualkashi was because he intends to marry the young woman as soon as he is relieved from his military duty. From what Gokul said, the marriage plans were rather sudden."

"Major Buckley is getting married?" gasped Marianna. "Why, I never thought he would."

The unexpected announcement caught Coral unprepared. The malicious bite of jealousy clenched its teeth into her heart before she could guard herself. Her stomach tightened into furious knots. *The knave! And after all his drivel about desiring little except his freedom and his miserable ship to take to sea again!*

The realization stung. *I couldn't influence him to give up his adventurous life, but a young Indian girl has been able to secure a marriage proposal.*

"You said the major was injured?" asked Elizabeth.

"Only a scratch."

"Well, that is some good news. Both Hampton and I thought well of the colonel's son."

"I did not realize you were acquainted with him," remarked Ethan.

"He's worked for Hampton hauling silk to the markets in Spain and England. We first met him during a tiger scare some years ago. Michael thought of him as a brother."

"A pity Michael lost his life on Buckley's ship."

"Yes. . . . I received a letter of condolence from the major while he was still at sea. It showed much insight. I was pleased to discover that the colonel's son is a Christian. But enough of this, you must be exhausted after your long ride. We've kept you far too long from the rest you need."

Elizabeth slipped her arm through his and turned him toward the stairs. "The horrid happenings at Guwahati will not be easily erased from your memory, but a good day of rest in bed will make you feel much better. This is one time, Ethan, when I shall don the role of physician."

"You are most kind, Aunt Elizabeth. I am only grieved

to have arrived in this condition and be the bearer of dark news."

Elizabeth led him slowly up the stairway. "I'll have Mera bring hot tea and something to eat. You can tell us what happened in detail when you are up to it in a few days. There is so much news, one hardly knows where to begin. I suppose Hugo received Hampton's letter about your cousin Alex in Darjeeling?"

"Yes, on arrival at Guwahati. Is there news?"

"I'm afraid not, and with the monsoon building, my concerns grow."

"If you do not hear from Hampton soon, I must insist on going there to search for them."

"We must not even consider anything so risky now. It's enough you've arrived safely, and I'm able to meet Hugo's nephew. He and Margaret have written so much, we feel we already know you. And, of course, Coral has spoken so well of you. We both are in your gratitude, Ethan. Coral seems completely recovered from the tropical fever, and I am well on my way back to good health. What a godsend to have a physician in the family, and soon a son-in-law, at that."

"Your words bring me deep satisfaction. . . ."

Their voices trailed away as they disappeared down the upstairs corridor. Coral stood stiffly looking after them. Little of their friendly discourse had sunk into her mind, for her thoughts would go no further than Ethan's announcement about Sualkashi. Not until her mother and Ethan were gone and the hall silent did she realize Kathleen and Marianna were watching her.

"I'll, ah—tell Mera to send the tea up to Cousin Ethan," said Marianna and left quickly for the cook room.

"War elephants," said Kathleen thoughtfully.

Something in her voice caused Coral to pay attention.

"The maharaja would have many," said Kathleen. "I'm surprised the fighting wasn't much worse than Ethan suggests."

Coral frowned. "The maharaja was killed. Sunil is now on the throne. How much worse could it be?"

"The major only received a 'mere scratch' is the way Ethan put it."

Coral caught the suggestion in her sister's voice. Was a mere scratch cause for Jace to seek recovery at Sualkashi? It was not like him to pamper aches and pains, and even less likely that he would set aside the secret mission into Burma, especially with the maharaja slain and Sunil as the usurper of the Guwahati throne.

Coral had a notion that Kathleen suspected her feelings about the young woman at Sualkashi, and she questioned Ethan's report in order to soothe her. The feeling of dislike between Ethan and Jace was mutual, but Ethan was not deceptive like his uncle, Sir Hugo. Ethan would not deliberately sow seeds of conflict to place Jace Buckley in an unflattering light.

Coral felt her feelings toward Jace harden into resentment. "I see no reason to think Cousin Ethan would deliberately hold back the truth as he saw it. As far as I'm concerned the matter is over."

When Kathleen made no further comment, Coral felt that her emotions had betrayed her, and she wished to get away, to be alone. She grabbed her straw hat from a stand in the corner and pulled open the front door, calling over her shoulder, "Jan-Lee says the children we rescued will recover. In a few weeks they will be on their feet. Yanna has offered to take them. I'm taking a ghari to the hatcheries to make arrangements."

The wind cooled her face as she chose to ride in the outer seat next to the ghari-wallah, but nothing cooled her emotions. Like kindled coals wanting to burst into flame, her thoughts went in all directions.

Sunil was now the self-proclaimed maharaja. A ripple of fear ran down her back. What if he came to Kingscote with Indian warriors searching for Ethan? Did Sunil know Gem was alive? And if he did, would he search for him? Had Jace abandoned his quest to bring Gem home by Christmas?

She fumed, her eyes narrowing under her lashes as the ghari bumped along the rutted road toward the silk workers' huts in the mulberry orchard. How could Jace sit in Sualkashi when there had been a mutiny in Guwahati? Would his sudden decision to marry the girl put a complete end to all other commitments?

Kathleen was in doubt, but Coral, who felt she had known him far better than anyone else, found her thoughts muddled by jealousy and a rage of which she had not known she was capable. Jace had abandoned them all for solace in the company of Gokul's smug-faced niece. Gem was at risk of being located by Prince Sunil, yet Jace did nothing to warn her.

The least he could do is tell me where Gem is so I can hire mercenaries of my own to free him, she thought bitterly.

He had led her to think she could depend on him, depend on him for honor and strength of purpose, even if he had made it clear that he would eventually leave India for the *Madras*. Now he had chosen to walk away from everyone and everything, in the darkest moment of all.

If Sir Hugo had been the bearer of the news instead of Ethan, she might have good reason to question it, for she remembered all too well the lies he had spoken about Jace in London.

Derelict in his duty. Drunk in his cabin when Michael was swept overboard.

But Ethan! Would he lie so blatantly in order to turn her against Jace? He did not like Jace, she knew that. But she could not imagine Ethan cunning enough to lie to her about Sualkashi, knowing she would one day find out.

"Unless he thinks I shall be so outraged with Jace that I'll marry him now."

She straightened her straw hat, frowning. But if it was a lie, where was Jace?

And Sir Hugo . . . where was he? Maybe Ethan was wrong and he had been killed in the fighting. Anything might have happened once the ugly torch of mutiny was lit in Guwahati. Sunil may not have planned for Hugo's death, but some enraged Indian, jealous for the worship of Kali, could strike out at any Englishman in sight.

Or was Hugo even now working with Sunil to carry out whatever plans they had in mind from the beginning?

She shaded her eyes and looked toward the clouds. Her fevered mind raced ahead to her father at Darjeeling. *What can be done to stop him from meeting whatever vile trap is set?*

Her eyes spilled over with tears of frustration as the burdens coming from so many directions at once over-whelmed her.

Rest in the Lord, wait patiently for Him.

The words scattered across her soul like seeds of new life, bringing hope. How unwise to allow herself to forget God. Soon she would be rushing about in a tizzy like some startled old hen, squawking and carrying on as though the entire safety of the coop depended on her.

Coral unexpectedly laughed at herself. The old sun-baked ghari-wallah stole a side glance at her. Coral looked off toward the silk workers' huts.

Jace marrying Gokul's niece! She lifted her chin and folded her arms tightly. He wouldn't do that. She remembered too well what had happened between them in the palace garden.

She sat up straight. *I'll write him, that's what. I'll have Thilak deliver a message to Sualkashi.*

Coral felt surprised at her decision, and at that a strange satisfaction stole over her. She would not simply retire from the scene like some scared rabbit afraid of the Indian girl. Unless—

Unless she had been right about what happened in the garden after all. Maybe Jace Buckley kissed all women goodbye that way.

Her eyes narrowed again and her fists clenched in her lap. *I'm glad I told him what I thought of his knavish ways!*

No, she would forget Jace. She would proceed with her own plans for the school, and now that Ethan was here, she would get him to help her construct the wooden structure before the rains.

Coral's mind drifted back to that night in London at the chapel when she had read William Carey's treatise on world missions. The burning desire to teach the children about Christ had come with a calling that could not be silenced. She had surrendered her future that night to the Lord. She was so sure that He had placed the burden on her heart. How then did Jace fit into all this, or did he?

The truth of her situation hit with force. She had no right to Jace until she knew that they belonged together as one. If she could not follow a man's vision, far better to be single and to pursue the cause on her own heart.

A calm came over her soul. God *was* guiding her, but not her only, He had a plan for Jace too. The thought startled her.

What was that plan? Would Jace surrender to it? She knew that his knowledge and confidence in God went much deeper than he would say. Jace would be a man worthy of any woman to follow if he ever became dedicated to the purpose of God.

Coral became still, knowing that God desired the best for them all, if only they would submit to His purpose. The one thing she could do for Jace, perhaps the greater thing, was to pray fervently for him. She would make it a daily matter of concern, then leave him with the Master Designer.

9

Despite the problems that loomed, Coral's spirits felt lighter than they had in weeks. Ethan had taken on the medical work in the dispensary, and more surprisingly, he had shown unexpected interest in the school project.

She awoke early. Her eyes took in the horizon, a hazy brown from the dust in the atmosphere on the plains of India, but sunrise on the Brahmaputra remained gold. *A perfect day for building a school,* she decided with a smile.

One of the workers walked across the lawn and Coral leaned over and called, "Send to the stables for a ghari. I will need to take a drive today. And have Rosa send someone to awaken Doctor Boswell. I want to go right away."

The boy pointed down to the riverbank. "Doctor is already awake, collecting bugs in net."

"Then tell him I wish him to come to the house at once."

As the boy ran off toward the river, Coral changed into cool muslin and came rushing down the stairs, tying her wide straw sunbonnet under her chin.

Ethan came through the front door carrying his

prized samples, and for the first time since his arrival there was a look of relaxed pleasure on his face.

She cast him a smile. "Already gathering samples for your medical lab?"

"I've never seen such a rich bounty of specimens."

Coral stepped onto the white verandah and shaded her eyes. Ethan gave his samples to the boy with strict orders for their careful handling and came up to stand beside her.

"The monsoon," she said, and started down the steps toward the waiting ghari. The driver opened the door. "Come, Ethan, don't be so slow."

"Do you expect it to break today?" he laughed, then held up his smooth hands and grimaced. "The very thought of soiling them with hammer blows and wood slivers fills me with loathing."

Coral laughed as Ethan dismissed the driver and helped her onto the open front seat. She spread her skirts, adjusted her hat to protect her from the already blazing sun, and pointed toward the other side of the plantation. "We've already chosen the location for the school, but Mother also wants your opinion."

Ethan climbed up beside her and touched the horse with the whip. The horse trotted off across the carriage-way onto the dirt road that divided the plantation. On one side were the acres of mulberry trees and hatcheries; the other side contained the workers' settlement of low buildings plastered with mud.

"Stop here, Ethan." She waved an insect away from her face.

Some of the children were bold enough to salaam to her. Coral smiled and reached down to the basket of sweet treats she had brought, when Ethan's low voice interrupted. "Wait, I believe we are about to encounter a bit of trouble."

She looked at him, wondering what he meant, then followed his gaze to the Indian foreman, who yelled in Hindi for the children to stay away from the ghari. Behind him walked a sadhu with a shaven head and a white caste mark painted on his forehead. He was the same priest Coral had seen in the jungle.

"I wonder what he is doing here?" she tried to say casually.

"The priest? I was up late last night when the butler named Natine returned from the village. He had this insufferable guru with him. I confronted him at once, demanding to know what goes. He said his niece is to be married on the plantation in a few weeks."

Coral grew uneasy. Was the wedding of Preetah a ploy to secure the sadhu's presence among the workers? He would contest her plans with the children, not publicly but in private.

Coral sat in the heat staring at the sea of faces and uselessly swatted insects. If she openly confronted the man now during the beginning of the religious festival, she would accomplish little and only alienate the workers further from her own cause.

She heard a low din of conversation break out among the elderly men as they congregated together watching, keeping their distance. The priest paused, and the foreman approached the rig and salaamed to Coral and Ethan.

"Greeting, sahib, miss-sahiba, do you wish words with me?"

Coral sensed that Ethan was about to reprimand the foreman, so she moved quickly to avert him. Her gloved hand came to rest on Ethan's wrist. "Jai ram, friend Hajo. This is Doctor Ethan Boswell from England, a cousin of mine. I'm taking him on a tour of the silk plantation. Pay us no mind. You may proceed with your work."

The Indian foreman stepped back. "Namaste, miss-sahiba, sahib."

He walked away. The priest stood like a statue in the dust and heat, and Coral watched until the foreman walked up to him and the two went away together, the workers following.

Wearily she pulled off her hat and fanned herself. Foiled, she thought. The silken strands of her hair caught the sun's rays. She turned to Ethan and he sat watching her. Coral pulled out the picnic basket she had intended to share with the children. With a rueful smile, she said, "It's not the prettiest weather for a picnic, but would you care to share some lunch?"

Ethan took up the reins, his eyes smiling with good humor. "Do you have some pleasant cove in mind with the sea breeze and a few gulls soaring above us?"

"Now you are beginning to sound like Major Buckley."

She felt Ethan's glance as if the mention of Jace's name had altered the mood.

"This is one time the major and I agree. But unlike his adventurous wanderlust, I'm not apt to mount the deck of a ship and disappear for two years. And," he added with a thin smile, "I'm willing to build your mission school."

Coral turned her head and looked at him from beneath her hat. "Yes . . . and I'll not forget."

Coral walked in the direction of the clearing, calling happily over her shoulder. "This is the location we have chosen. What do you think?"

Ethan walked to where she stood waiting for him.

She stood staring as if she could envision the completed project and hear the laughter of the children. All else was swept from her mind, as if by some refreshing heavenly breeze.

"The ground is high enough here so the rains won't wash the school into the river," Ethan commented. "We won't need to clear the ground or worry about trees."

Coral envisioned the bungalow standing with firm foundations and filled to overflowing with children singing in the Hindi language the song her mother had written:

"Saviour of all Nations,
Shepherd of young and old,
Guide us with your Words of light,
and make us all one fold. . . ."

Coral took hold of his arm. "Ethan, I can see it now, bursting with children memorizing Scripture. One large room will be sufficient to start with. Eventually we'll have several rooms, and a kitchen too, so we can serve hot meals. But now, I'll be content with a roof and four walls."

"We?" asked Ethan quietly, his hand tightening on her arm.

Jace barged into her mind, but she laid a hand on Ethan's. "I've no choice but to turn to you. Help me get the school going and I shall always be in your debt. The four children are enough to begin the class, and the priest has no jurisdiction over them. They were abandoned to death on the river, and now, what I do with them—what *we* do with them—is no concern of theirs. Soon others will see that what I teach is beneficial. When the adults see the untouchables able to read and write when they themselves cannot, and healthy and happy—they'll know the school is not cursed by Kali."

Ethan smiled ruefully and held out his hands.

Coral looked at them. They were the hands of a phy-

119

sician, smooth and slender.

"These are not quite the hands of William Carey," he said.

"At the moment they are all I need." She took them into her own and smiled up at him. "If you're willing to sacrifice them to help me start the school, I can only be grateful."

His gray eyes sobered. "You may discover my reason is not altogether sacrificial. Someone once told me the best way to win your heart is to build your school and support your interest in the untouchables. I think he knows you very well indeed."

Coral smiled. *Seward,* she thought. "Then you best listen to him."

"I intend to. And as I told him, I make no apology for whatever means brings me success."

"Success?"

"Tomorrow," he said, placing a finger over her lips, "we start the school of Coral Kendall."

————

Coral was eagerly counting the days as the mission school took shape. Daily she ventured forth in the ghari to see how Ethan was progressing with the walls and roof, sometimes in the company of her mother and sisters, and sometimes alone. She involved herself in the work and was enjoying every moment of it.

Coral became a familiar sight in the ghari and in the company of Ethan, whom the Indian men watched curiously. They knew he was a physician, and they were puzzled at his new behavior. Coral was pleased that he chose to get on well with the workers' children and with the untouchable orphans, and now that the priest had unexpectedly disappeared from sight, there were few who bothered to call the children away. The bolder children ventured forth to watch the carpentry work and to wait for sign of Coral's ghari coming down the road from Kingscote, for she began bringing them sweet cakes from Piroo's oven. The baskets were quickly emptied as she made new friends.

Ethan emptied the skin of water, then tossed it aside. "What is *my* reward for all my muscle aches and splinters besides a daily ration of lemon water?"

"Sunstroke," she teased. "Don't you know better than to work during the noon hour? You are supposed to be inside the school resting and waiting for me to bring your lunch."

"I expected you to swoon and tell me how wonderful you think I am."

"Caution. The Lord may let your roof fall in."

"I'm almost done with the roof. Splendid, is it not? Sir Hugo would be amazed if he saw me now!"

"I wonder where he is?"

"Is the physician a carpenter, or not?"

Coral shaded her eyes and looked up. Ethan stood there, his white Holland shirt glued to his skin with perspiration and wearing a huge straw hat. She laughed. He looked anything but the Ethan Boswell she had known on the safari northeast, collecting bugs and butterflies for his "crow's nest" on the wooden barge.

"I wouldn't trade your hammer for all the jewels in the Taj Mahal!"

His eyes turned a warm gray. He climbed down to meet her. "I do have jewels for you, Coral. They are at the house. I ask for your permission to give them to you tonight. It is a necklace. I have waited to give it to you . . . hoping you would wear it as a 'bond' of our growing affection. One day soon I hope you will become my betrothed."

121

Coral thought of Jace and the Indian girl at Sualkashi that he would marry.

"Yes, Ethan. One day soon. . . ."

———————

Coral's days were packed with excitement as she anticipated her success in teaching. At last the day arrived for the dedication of the school. Elizabeth, Kathleen, and Marianna sat on chairs under the shade of umbrellas held by the children Ajay, Hareesh, Mona, and Kirin. Jan-Lee and her young daughter, Emerald, were also there, and Yanna, who had long ago given up fear of Natine in order to align herself with the memsahib whom she loved so dearly.

At the conclusion of the brief ceremony, with the school now dedicated to teaching the Scriptures to the untouchables, Coral offered a praise to the Lord for His faithfulness and added: "And thank you, Lord, for Ethan in making all this humanly possible."

When the ghari returned to the house with the others, Coral remained behind with Ethan while Ajay and the children who were with Yanna bravely stepped inside to have a look at the new "shrine" that somehow was to involve them. They saw nothing exceptional, only a large bare room with woven bamboo mats for the rug. But the Bible Coral brought had been placed on the table at the front of the room, and they stared at the black holy book with awe, thinking that the words from heaven would not be read to them in the feringhi tongue, but in sweet Hindi.

"I cannot believe my first class begins on Monday," she said. "I'll bring my desk down here, too, and some cushions for the children to sit on." She walked about the room, smiling. "You've done a wonderful job, Ethan, but it does look dull in here, doesn't it? Kathleen is mak-

ing some posters, and I think the Christmas story will be
perfect to start out with."

"Christmas, Miss Coral?" asked Ajay, puzzled.

"You'll find out soon," she said with a smile.

Sualkashi

Devi made the morning tea and carried it to the salon
in her father's house, where both Gokul and Major Jace
Buckley had been staying for the past weeks. As she entered quietly, she saw that her cha-cha was still asleep
but that Jace was up and dressed and standing before
the window. She stopped. The split-cane blind had been
rolled up.

A glimmer of light from early morning fell upon the
rattan table where she had left the Bible belonging to
Michael Kendall. The other books were also there, given
to Jace in England by John Newton. His vision had not
permitted him to read them for himself, and her uncle
could barely read English and had not been able to help
him. But she had learned English well. She had sought
to please Jace Buckley from the moment that Cha-Cha
Gokul had brought him to meet his family in Sualkashi.
That had been many years ago, and Devi had still been
a girl in braids. Now she was a young woman of marriageable age, yet she had delayed her father's ambitions
to marry her off to a rajput guard at the maharaja's palace in Guwahati, hoping that Jace would at last tell her
he loved her.

He had not told her so. She had imagined his affection
all these years, she thought sadly, watching him. He
would never tell her the words she wished to hear, for
she now knew beyond all doubt that it was the young
Englishwoman who had stayed in her chamber that he

desired. He had not told her so, but she could guess. How it was that she knew this, Devi could not completely explain even to herself. Yet she was certain since his arrival here that he thought much of the Englishwoman from the silk plantation called Kingscote. He had not mentioned her; he spoke little, only asking Devi to read the holy book to him and other books about the Christian beliefs.

Not that Jace had ever given Devi any reason to think he would marry her. He had never so much as hinted he wanted a relationship with her. Once, when he had come here on his way from Kingscote to ship Kendall silk to Cadiz, she had taken it upon herself to let him know she wanted him. She had been waiting for him in his room, seated on the matting in the dim shadows when he came in. She remembered back, and now felt nothing of the shame she had felt then when he refused her and sent her away. He had never treated her as anything more than a friend, as Gokul's niece, and yet she had hoped. The hope was in vain.

During these weeks at her father's house, he had wished her presence each morning but only to read to him. Now she knew even that desire had slipped through her fingers. *He can see now.* She knew he could, because she had watched him too long, too deeply not to notice the change in his stance. She even thought she knew what was going through his mind as he watched the splendor of the sun rising over the Brahmaputra River.

Quietly she placed the tray down on the low table, but this time instead of pouring the cup of coffee she knew he always preferred instead of tea, she walked softly up behind him to also look out the window. A smile touched her lips as she looked at him and saw his expression, but his gaze remained riveted upon the glory of the golden dawn, the splashes of vermilion, of topaz on the horizon, and still farther away the great white clouds that had not yet decided to drench India.

No, he did not see her. He did not even know she stood there, so engrossed was he. *He thanks his Christian God,* Devi thought, and felt nothing. *He believes this God has done for him what no other deity could ever do . . . take the darkness from his eyes.*

Jace had told her there were no other deities, only the one true and Living God, the Creator of the universe, but she held fast to her Hindu beliefs, for it was a way of life she knew, the only one. To give up her religion was the same to her as giving up India, and how could she give up her customs, her life?

Jace thinks his God has restored his sight. Has this one named Jesus answered him? She looked away from Jace out at the new morning.

"Look—over there!"

She had pointed to the east where pink flamingoes with wings tinged with black flew in a column, their colors merging with the light of the sun breaking like a flood over the distant mountains.

"How splendid the sight," she said.

If he spoke, she did not hear his words, but rather *felt* his reaction. For that moment they stood without moving, watching the color, the light, the graceful movement of their wings soaring high into heaven's freedom.

That moment would have been complete if she had felt his hand reach over and find hers. His answer did not include her. He turned from the window as though he were a part of that freedom. His excitement seemed to grow as she turned also and watched him go to the Bible, the books, and lift them from the table and look at them. The Bible went inside his tunic—next to his heart—she noticed. The books went into his satchel. His clothes were swiftly removed from the drawer and packed. He was putting on the black and silver jacket of his British uniform. He belted on his scabbard, called out to Gokul in a calm but strong voice.

The door flew open and Gokul entered as though having waited for this moment expectantly. One look at Jace and her cha-cha's hard brown face opened into a grin. "It is time, sahib?"

"Yes, it is time, old friend. The horses?"

"They have been made ready each morning, sahib, just waiting."

"We need wait no longer. Let us ride."

Gokul laughed so jubilantly that Devi couldn't help but join in, especially when Jace looked at her and smiled. Caught up in the excitement she ran across the salon and picked up his hat.

Almost shyly now she came up softly and handed it to him. "Goodbye, Jace."

His smile slowly faded. Gently his hand reached, lifting her chin to look into her eyes. Devi told herself she would not cry. And she did not. She lifted her head proudly.

Wordlessly the blue-black of his eyes said goodbye for the last time. Then his hand fell away and she watched him leave the room.

Gokul hung back, saying something softly in Hindi. Devi nodded. "Yes, Cha-Cha, I know, I understand him. It is *her* he wishes." Her eyes hardened for a moment. "If she does not run to him when he goes to her, tell her Devi says she is a fool."

Outside the house, the doves were cooing in the mango trees, and Devi thought that the day shone bright with an expectation all its own. She watched until their horses were out of sight. Then with a dignity that was part of her Indian culture, she went to find her father. She would calmly tell him that she was ready in her heart for him to arrange the wedding with the rajput.

———

Jace paused astride his horse to read the message delivered earlier to Gokul by a rajput friend.

Danger. Sunil has discovered the whereabouts of Prince Adesh Singh—the child you call Gem. He will seek Warlord Zin himself, or send others to pay jewels to have the prince turned over to him. Sir Hugo Roxbury is also aware of Zin and is your enemy. Take heed. Roxbury left for Kingscote plantation yesterday.

Jace scowled. Sunil knew! Somehow he must reach Zin before him! How many days ahead of him was Sunil? He turned the reins of his horse to ride from Sualkashi.

"Ill news, sahib?"

"Yes. Sunil is on his way to Zin. But we must go first to Kingscote. Roxbury, too, will know. I must alert Seward to possible danger where Miss Kendall is concerned."

10

Coral felt the eyes of disapproval from the silent silk workers as she arrived in the open ghari for the first day of the mission school. They stood in small groups watching her; young boys and girls hung back, some looking at her with wide eyes from behind trees and bungalows. Coral could only imagine the words of warning to stay away from miss-sahiba that had filled their ears recently. The sadhu was nowhere in sight, nor, of course, was Natine. They were too subtle in their disapproval to confront her openly. The warnings against attending the "feringhi's shrine-school" were propagated at night behind closed doors.

The first class opened as planned, although on a much smaller scale than Coral eventually intended. For one thing, she had yet to arrange the hours of schooling to coincide with the same time periods that the children were not at their duties in the hatcheries. This was not an oversight in her planning but was due to her mother's yet frail health. Eventually, Elizabeth Kendall would call for an assembly of all the workers on Kingscote and explain not only the purpose of her daughter's school but enroll the children whose families wished them to attend. Coral was under no false impressions and knew few if any of the Hindus would immediately come forward, but she anticipated that, in time, when the parents saw the success of the other children, they would relent. There would always be the majority who turned their backs and ordered their children to stay away from miss-sahiba. Coral's main hope was for the numerous abandoned orphans who were under the Kendall family's jurisdiction, most of them untouchables.

The memsahib, as Coral's mother was called, had long ago arranged for certain women who were also untouchables according to the Hindu religion to oversee a group of ten children who had no parents or relatives. All these untouchables Coral felt certain would eventually be enrolled, and that would require an even larger structure.

But for now Coral was content. The school was built, and the first class would be held before the rains.

Yanna had arrived early, bringing the four children they had rescued from the crocodiles. They now lived with Yanna in the bungalow once belonging to Rajiv and Jemani. The children, freshly scrubbed and warned into good behavior for miss-sahiba, were bright-eyed as they anticipated a great adventure. They sat cross-legged on the floor of plain matting.

For her first lesson, Coral told the story of Jesus and the children, using colorful sketches that Kathleen had made to visualize the Bible story. The children were all eyes as Coral emphasized how the disciples of the Lord Jesus had sent away the parents with their children, scolding them, and telling them that the Lord was "too busy" with more important matters.

Coral spoke in Hindi: "But Jesus was displeased with His disciples. 'Allow the children to come to me and do not forbid them.' And he picked each child up in His arms and blessed them."

The children leaned closer to stare at Kathleen's drawing showing small children climbing happily into the arms of the Lord. Then the children looked at each other and grinned. The little girl Mona giggled, and Coral sensed her delight.

Soon Yanna passed out cups of milk and the frosted sweet breads that Marianna had struggled the night before to shape and bake in the form of children.

They sang and clapped to Elizabeth's song:

"Saviour of all Nations,
Shepherd of young and old,
Guide us with your Words of light,
and make us all one fold. . . ."

Then class ended, and Coral knew that from henceforth she would have at least four faithful students.

She left the bungalow with the children clamoring to get into the ghari for the ride back, Yanna reprimanding Ajay for shoving Mona out of the way to take first position. Coral squinted at the hot sun, tying the ribbons of her hat beneath her chin. Taking the reins, she lightly touched the horse and it moved off down the road, the inevitable layer of dust kicking up behind the wheels of the ghari.

Thank you, Lord.

The afternoon heat was sweltering; not even a light breeze afforded relief. Ajay sat beside her on the seat, still holding the remains of his child-shaped sweet bread, although only the head remained on the napkin.

"Burra-sahib say school is cursed," came the unexpected remark.

"Natine?"

"He say it, Missy Coral. He told others if they go,

much punishment will come to us all by earth and sky. Mulberry leaves will fall from trees, and a great wind will carry Kingscote Mansion into Brahmaputra River. All the Kendalls will drown."

Coral kept her tension from showing. It angered her that Natine would frighten the children this way. "Natine has no power to speak such terrible things. Pay him no mind, Ajay. The words you learned today, they are good words. They bring hope, joy, and light to our hearts. They tell of the Lord who controls the Brahmaputra River, and all rivers."

"Including the holy Ganges?" he breathed, brown eyes wide.

"He is Master over all His creation."

The little boy looked doubtful. "You mean no wind will come to destroy, no fire to burn and kill the silkworms?"

Coral felt a tightening in her spine. Fire. The night that Gem had been abducted there had been fire. Was Natine's remark a coincidence? Frowning on her school was one thing, and she might put up with the inconvenience in the hope of winning his respect if not his heart, but scaring the children with visions of destruction was quite another matter.

She might tell Ethan, but she thought better about doing so. Unlike Jace Buckley, who knew India, who understood the sometimes insurmountable differences between the Indian and English culture, Ethan was often impatient and sometimes too anxious for confrontation. If she went to him with Ajay's information he might, as Jace put it, "blunder into the situation and ruin it."

She frowned, thinking of Jace Buckley. There had been a mutiny in Guwahati resulting in the death of the maharaja. Her father should have sent some message back to the family by now. And what of the safety of Gem?

Yet the major remained with Gokul and his family in Sualkashi.

Suddenly Coral felt a desperate longing for the stalwart presence of her father. Instead she became aware of the little boy Ajay watching her, and she tried not to show alarm, for concern that he might think her fear was due to the power of Shiva, the dark god of the Hindu religion.

"The Lord Jesus is more powerful than all the idols of all the world's religions," she told him. "He can still any storm, silence any raging fire."

But what of her own faith in His authority? Did she truly have confidence that He would protect them all from the many snares that lay like hidden traps?

She did, and yet . . . she dare not presume upon the Lord, knowing that better Christians than she had faced fire, sword, and martyrdom for the honor of bearing His name. How could she complain with simple trials and testings?

"But the truth is, Ajay, the Lord does not always answer our prayers in the way we expect, or ask."

"But why, miss-sahiba?"

"Because His plans are wiser than ours. And even in what we think is failure, there is victory."

He seemed satisfied, then: "But if the Christian God is more powerful than Shiva, and also very good, then why let wind and fire come so Natine can say Shiva is better?"

Coral smiled down at him. "I see you're going to become my star pupil. Your question has provoked the thoughts of great religious men. The living God is so wise, so good, that all His ways are higher than our ways, and all His thoughts are higher than our thoughts. Whatever He allows in the lives of His children is for a wise and good purpose. Even hard and bitter things are permitted to come, not to harm and destroy us but to teach us many things."

"What things?"

"Things like having patience in all our troubles instead of complaining, trusting Him in the darkness when we cannot see our way out, learning how to wait in hard circumstances when it seems the answer to our prayers should have come yesterday."

"Even if Kingscote burns down and silkworms all die? Will you still have school for us?"

Dear God, do not let me be insincere with the child when it's so easy to be pious. . . .

For a moment she couldn't speak. As they rounded the turn in the road and the warm hush of the jungle wrapped about them, Kingscote Mansion loomed ahead of them in the distance, white and serene against the setting blaze of ruby sky, and the poignant sight of her home arose to test her words of faith. For as she looked at Kingscote she imagined it turned into charred rubble before her eyes and the blackened ashes swept away in a great wind—the wind and the fire of Natine's threats.

She could not go on. Coral stopped the ghari and sat there for a moment, staring ahead. The sun beat down upon her. For a moment it seemed to Coral that she was not only tasting what it would be like to lose her home, her family, all that she held dear and precious, but even Jace—he was not here when she secretly yearned for his strength—although she could never admit it to him.

Gone. Everything dear. Was the school worth it? Was anything worth her forging ahead, ignoring all the signs of trouble?

To speak bravely of suffering and loss with ringing words of faith when all goes well is one thing. To taste the bitter gall and swallow it is quite another.

She remembered a past vow of surrender to whatever

purpose God may have for her life, whatever the cost. In answer, she had seen Gem torn from his nursery bed and carried off screaming in terror into the darkness, to what? Death? Suffering? She had not known his outcome, and fear expected the worst.

How easy for you, Coral Kendall, to make brave speeches in the sunlight. But how realistic of you to tumble to defeat in the trial! It was too easy to feel alone, empty of His grace, in doubt of the outcome.

She thought again of her defeat when she had first lost Gem. After these years the pain was gone. Even his face had begun to slowly fade as she saw the faces of so many other children, all with needs equal to his. But at the time of the loss, the foundation of her faith in God had seemed to crumble beneath her feet. God, if He was there at all, had seemed deaf to her cries and uncaring to her pain. She had yielded to seasons of bitterness. *What would I do if everything that means so much goes up in flames?* she thought, horrified.

There was no answer, only the steady beating of her heart.

Ajay was not looking at the white mansion of Coral's birth but at her face, and his brown eyes seemed to be entranced with a lovely sight. Coral felt his sticky fingers reach out and shyly enclose her hand. She turned her head and looked down at him. Ajay was not as beautiful as Gem; he had an old scar running across his cheek to his lip.

"Miss Coral?" came the urgent question repeated. "What if all silkworms die? No more silk, no more Kingscote forever?"

Ajay squinted against the sunlight as he stared up at her, and it seemed her answer would either bring the end of the world, or secure its foundations.

Faith, like a tiny seedling, unwilling to die—that

could not die—had reemerged like new growth after a frost, unscathed by the blast, growing and green and alive forever. She smiled at him. The Lord had graciously come to her like sweet rain on the mown grass.

Ajay's hand was squeezing hers, and she looked into eyes guileless and anxious to trust something, *someone*, for the first time in his life.

"Even if Kingscote burns down and the silkworms all die, school begins tomorrow at eight A.M. sharp. And I expect you to be there."

Ajay grinned. "Yes, miss-sahiba."

As Coral turned the horse-drawn wagon into the front carriageway, the voices of the children in the back called out excitedly. She followed their gestures down to the Brahmaputra River.

"Miss Coral, dekho! Topiwallah!"

Coral looked and saw a boat docked, and baggage was stacked on the bank. A familiar Englishman with heavy shoulders and a neatly trimmed short dark beard stood in black broadcloth, a wide-brimmed Spanish-style hat covering his thick ebony locks. Around him were a dozen rajput warriors in colorful but masculine garb.

"Sir Hugo!" gasped Coral. So her conniving uncle was alive and had decided to come to Kingscote directly from the British residency in Guwahati. Her fingers closed more tightly about the horse's reins. The indomitable presence of her uncle was the last thing she now needed to add strength to the trouble she was already having with Natine!

From the looks of his trunk and baggage, she guessed that he had come for a long stay.

Coming out on the front verandah with Elizabeth Kendall, Ethan also saw his uncle. He left the steps and walked down the sloping lawn to meet him at the riverbank. From the side of the house, Natine, leading two

136

male servants in white, also walked to greet Sir Hugo.

Coral only stared off toward the river, shading her eyes to get a better view, half hoping that she was seeing a mirage in the glittering sunlight. Manjis in white loincloths were unloading still more trunks and crates containing what she guessed to be books and medical supplies belonging to Ethan. At least Ethan would be pleased at his uncle's arrival. The medicine he had been forced to leave behind in Guwahati on short notice had been a cause of vexation.

Would Uncle Hugo have brought any information on Major Jace Buckley?

She sat, too preoccupied to climb down from the wagon seat. The heavy trunk and numerous bags and crates were being loaded onto an elephant's back. She was still mulling over the untimely arrival of Sir Hugo when Natine's niece Preetah emerged from the shadowed shrubs next to the verandah and slipped up to the side of the wagon where Coral sat. She took note of her secret friend Yanna in the back with the children, then her gaze swerved anxiously to meet Coral's.

"Sahiba, is not that man, the one they call Sir Hugo Roxbury, your uncle?"

Coral could see her concern and wondered what Preetah may have heard about the new British ambassador from Calcutta.

"Yes, my uncle, and Ethan's. Sir Hugo is memsahib's brother-in-law." Coral searched her face and saw only tension. "Yes?" she encouraged. "What about my uncle?"

"I must speak to you alone, sahiba, tonight."

As Coral was about to press for more information, the girl turned and hurried back into the house. Coral turned and looked at Yanna in the back of the wagon. Yanna too was grave but shook her head. "What concerns Preetah I do not know. You must do as she asks."

Coral had every intention of meeting Preetah. But now she thought of greeting her uncle, and it gave her no pleasure. He had arrived on the same day the school opened. And what will he say when he learns it was Ethan who built it?

Sir Hugo and Ethan were walking up the lawn toward the mansion, and Elizabeth had come down the steps to greet him warmly. Hiding her frown, Coral climbed down from the wagon, and drawing in a small breath walked to meet him.

"Why, Uncle Hugo!" she cried. "What a wonderful surprise!"

That evening after the lavish dinner to welcome Sir Hugo was completed, Elizabeth gathered the family members in the large parlor that on festive occasions doubled for a ballroom. Tonight, as Natine and Preetah served refreshment from Viennese crystal, light from the chandeliers fell on the marble floors with their ivory-colored Afghan rugs. Coral sat on the divan made of polished mahogany with muted rose velvet cushions and watched Sir Hugo pace.

He had already told them what had happened in Guwahati, filling in the information that Ethan would not know about. The maharaja was dead, he stated again. Sunil was now on the throne and desired peace with the East India Company. "He claims no prior knowledge of the assassination of Majid Singh."

Coral knew that both Ethan and the major believed that Sunil was behind the entire ugly affair. She avoided looking at Ethan now for fear of giving her own feelings away and instead concentrated on Sir Hugo. He certainly appeared believable, his dark brows knitted together, his eyes somber.

"What will the Company do about the mutiny?" asked Elizabeth. "Will the treaty signed with the maharaja be honored with Prince Sunil?"

"It's my opinion they will not want to give up their foothold in Assam and will decide to work with Sunil. But until troops arrive from Calcutta we are in a precarious situation."

"You don't expect Sunil to attack Kingscote?" asked Elizabeth dubiously, and Coral wondered how much her mother actually trusted Margaret's husband. But from her poised expression Coral could tell nothing. "After all," continued Elizabeth, "we pose no threat to whatever Sunil's ambitions to rule the area may be."

"We're not out of danger yet," said Hugo. "Sunil resents the English presence, and his followers number in the thousands. Despite earlier gratitude for the Company's support when Burma had ambitions to incorporate Assam, he has changed and now wants us out of the northeast." He looked at Elizabeth pointedly. "No matter how Hampton feels about Company jurisdiction over the Kingscote silk enterprise, he would have done well to listen to me when I and Margaret were here last. Had he done so instead of demanding his independence, there would be sufficient Company soldiers here to avert any attack from Sunil or Burma."

Elizabeth's expression hardened, and Coral knew her mother resented Hugo's accusation against Hampton. It was Marianna who spoke up, her blue eyes wide. "You mean we're likely to be attacked?"

"There is no reason for undue alarm, dear," said Elizabeth. "Kingscote has always stood in the way of risk. It is the reason your father hires mercenaries to patrol our borders. We have men now."

"Thank God," said Hugo and walked to the window where a slight breeze entered. "But it is not enough, Elizabeth. I do not care to alarm you and the girls—"

"We are not alarmed," came her calm voice. "As I said, Hugo, we've faced danger many times. If it comes to an actual attack, we all know what to do. Hampton has trained us well since the girls were only children. I only wish he were here. As I said earlier, we should have heard from him and Alex by now."

Coral was watching her uncle. Her past experiences with his carefully planned schemes gave her an advantage the others did not have. Ethan, too, knew him well and undoubtedly saw behind his attempts to frighten Elizabeth into whatever cooperation he wished from her. Coral could see that Hugo was impatient with Elizabeth for remaining calm in the face of the fears he raised, but he was able to keep his irritation masked.

"I dislike to say this, Elizabeth, but Kingscote is in danger. The English military is to blame for this predicament! Even now Jorhat has less than twenty British soldiers. The rest are native sepoys and sowars!"

"Captain Gavin MacKay and Major Buckley would have arrived months ago with troops had it not been for Plassey Junction," said Kathleen, her eyes snapping with sudden temper. "If I recall, Uncle, the major's troops were all massacred in a mutiny, and he was severely wounded. We all barely got here alive!"

Coral expected her mother to speak her sister's name in a warning tone, but she did not. Coral, afraid that Sir Hugo might suspect Kathleen of knowing of his involvement in the Plassey mutiny, turned on her as though upset. "Really, Kathleen, I'm surprised at you." She stood to her feet and walked over beside Ethan, who had his back to them all, looking out the window. She laid a hand on Ethan's arm protectively. "Everyone knows that Major Buckley was to blame for Plassey. He hates the military and did little to protect his men. If we are without sufficient troops at Jorhat now, it's partly the major's fault."

Kathleen looked at her as though she had lost her mind, and even Ethan turned and stared down at her. Coral glanced at Sir Hugo. As she had hoped, he noticed how she had come to the side of Ethan, and how her hand rested possessively on his arm. "Even now the major has turned his back on the lot of us to pursue his own selfish aims," she finished.

Sir Hugo came alert, his dark eyes fixed upon her. Ethan seemed a trifle surprised, but there was a glimmer of triumph in his gray eyes.

Coral turned toward her sisters. Kathleen dropped her eyes to her lap and Marianna glanced at her mother. Elizabeth showed no expression, and Coral wondered if she guessed what she was doing.

"Well, at least Gavin will arrive soon with the 13th," spoke up Kathleen. "I'm sure the revolt at Plassey has been brought under the British control by now."

It was the first time Coral had seen Kathleen boast about Gavin MacKay. Usually she had little good to say of the military, for fear of becoming a soldier's bride and living with Gavin on one of the frontier outposts belonging to the Company.

"Yes, they should have gotten through by now," agreed Ethan.

"What is this about the major turning his back?" came Sir Hugo's voice, casual but definitely interested.

Coral felt a moment of glee. It wasn't often that she managed to divert her uncle from his own purpose. "After the maharaja and his guards were killed, the major seems to have cut all ties to his military responsibilities," said Coral.

"You mean you have not heard from him?"

Coral was about to say he was in Sualkashi, but

Ethan said casually, "He went to Darjeeling to search for Hampton. He should have been back by now."

The room went silent. *Why would Ethan say such a thing?* wondered Coral.

Sir Hugo turned to Elizabeth, who sat still and appeared rather pale. "You are wise enough to know the reasons; we all do well to worry about Hampton."

"If only he were here. With the rains coming, he and Alex will be in desperate straits," said Elizabeth.

"Yes, so I've been thinking, Elizabeth. There is little I can do here now. I'll leave you a few of the rajputs, then take the others with me. I've come to the conclusion that it's worth my risk to ride to Darjeeling to search for Hampton. I intend to leave in the morning."

The thought brought mixed feelings of joy and fear to Coral. Her eyes caught those of Preetah, who unobtrusively had brought in a tray of hot coffee and tea. Coral remembered the girl's request to speak with her tonight.

"You mustn't go alone, Uncle," Ethan protested. "I shall ride with you."

"There is no need. I have the rajputs—"

"Every extra man will help," came Ethan's cool interruption. "The journey will prove too dangerous, especially for you. You don't know India."

"And I suppose you do?"

Ethan appeared to ignore the slightly caustic tone.

"There will be mud slides and flash floods, and Darjeeling could be washed out," he said.

Coral felt a nervous qualm in her stomach. "Are you sure you should go, Ethan? Uncle does have the rajputs."

He turned to her, his gaze trying to conceal his concern. "I was going anyway, just as soon as my work here was done. I've only been waiting. Perhaps I've waited too long."

She wondered what he meant, but the answer was

not meant to be spoken aloud.

Elizabeth was quick to show her relief and gratitude. "I can spare a few extra men from the hatchery if you think they can be of help."

"You best keep them," said Sir Hugo. "Kingscote may need them far worse before this is over." Sir Hugo's expression hardened as he turned to Ethan. "Very well. Then we will leave first thing in the morning."

"I shall be ready." He turned from Hugo's cold gaze to Coral, his tension showing. "Excuse me, but I've some packing to do before I ride out in the morning. I will need a fresh supply of medicine if Alex is ill with the fever."

Coral watched Ethan cross the room and go out into the hall, then call for Natine, inquiring if the elephant had brought the baggage up from the river yet.

Elizabeth moved toward Sir Hugo, taking his arm and assuring him of her relief now that he had arrived. While they were taken up in a discourse of their own, Coral slipped from the parlor and came into the wide hallway, the lantern light shining on the red stone. She stood there, thinking. Preetah could be in the cook room, but if she went there now Natine might see them together.

As though emerging from nowhere, Preetah's small sister Reena appeared, her eyes wide and dark with the thrill of her secret mission. She glanced about, and seeing no one other than Coral, whispered, "Go down to river! Preetah wait there for you now!"

Coral gave her a pat and sent her on her way. Glancing into the parlor, she saw that Sir Hugo was occupied with her mother. Another glance up the wide stairway proved she was alone. Quickly she opened the heavy front door and stepped out into the sultry night.

11

Standing on the wide lawn looking down toward the dark water, Coral saw the slow-moving river ripple like darting silver fish in the starlight. The landing ghat appeared deserted, but she expected Preetah to be waiting there in the shadows. She lifted the hem of her billowing skirts to keep from tripping and sped down the lawn, feeling the sod sink beneath her slippers.

Nearing the bank, she listened to the soothing lap of the water. A melancholy call of a night bird echoed from the trees on the other side of the river. Soon a shadow disengaged itself from the boats, and Preetah stood nervously, her head draped in a dark chunni. Seeing Coral, she beckoned, and Coral followed her onto the ghat.

The girl appeared uneasy, glancing about as if expecting her uncle Natine to loom in the night and catch them in some conspiracy. "I fear and have affection for Natine, but I cannot keep silent, sahiba, especially now that Sahib Roxbury arrived this day. I—I must tell you what I heard in the village."

Coral tensed. "Yes?"

Preetah stepped closer, still glancing up the lawn where the mansion's windows were golden against the night. She whispered, "I fear because everyone thinks your brother Alex is somewhere in Darjeeling, perhaps lost, perhaps ill. But he is not there. I overheard Natine speak to the priest while I was in the house of a cousin. Alex Kendall is not in India but has left for England."

Coral did not move. Dazed, at first the girl's words made no impression, like falling seeds lying dormant on the cold earth. *England!* What was he doing there? When had he gone? Why didn't her father and mother know this? Why had they not seen him leave Kingscote?

Her mind raced backward to that last evening she had spent alone with Seward in her father's study. Seward was wary about the message that had been delivered to her father.

Jace and I, we be thinking Alex could not have the fever. It is very uncommon to the climate of Darjeeling.

The next deduction was obvious: If Alex was not ill, if he was not in Darjeeling, if he was in England, then the message delivered to her father was a lie to lure him away from Kingscote. But why? Was there to be some attack on Kingscote by Sunil and the ghazis opposed to the English presence in Assam? Was Sir Hugo helping them for lucrative reasons of his own?

Deliberately keeping her voice calm, so as not to frighten the girl more than she was already, Coral asked, "What exactly did you overhear Natine say when you were in the village?"

"Sahiba, I swear I did not know about your brother before your father left with the men from the village to trek east—"

"Wait, when did you hear this—when were you in the village with Natine?"

"When I went with him to see the priest about the marriage to Pravin."

"Three weeks ago!"

"Oh, sahiba, forgive, but I was so afraid, especially after I helped with the children brought to the dispensary, after what we saw in the trees! I feared to tell memsahib what I heard, feared she would go to Natine at once. He would know I overheard, that I spoke!"

Coral fought to keep her anxiety under control. And no wonder Preetah was afraid to tell Elizabeth, thought Coral. If Alex was not lost in the mountainous region as the messenger had informed her father, then both Jace and Seward were right. Someone had lied in order to lure her father away! And what of her brother's ring shown to her father as evidence?

Her father's letter to Sir Hugo at Guwahati had mentioned several skirmishes with Burmese infiltrators along the border of the Kendall holdings. Perhaps Sir Hugo was speaking the truth about an upcoming attack on Kingscote, and the enemy had wanted her father gone during the conflict. Or were there more devious plans at work?

Her heart pounded as her mind sought for answers. Could there be a plan to harm her father? Or was it Alex? Who would have sent the false message? Prince Sunil? Sir Hugo? Perhaps Hugo was working with Sunil. . . . But if that were true, why would Hugo warn them tonight of an imminent attack? His worry had appeared genuine, but then, when it came to the workings of her uncle, how could she be sure of anything?

Her meeting with Jace in the palace garden at Guwahati came to mind. At times Jace appeared preoccupied with concerns he had not been willing to share with her. Those troubling suspicions must have been about her father.

I was right to insist Seward leave Kingscote to search for Father, she thought.

But many weeks had already gone by. Anything could

have happened, and since Seward himself had gone there alone to search for her father, he too might be in danger.

Coral's first inclination was to go immediately to her mother. Yet Preetah was right. Her mother would confront Natine, perhaps even Hugo. What could she do if her own brother-in-law were involved with Sunil?

"You are right," said Coral. "My mother would confront Natine. She might go to Sir Hugo too, and he would only deny everything. He has a way of making us all appear imaginative fools driven with girlish hysteria. He would demand who his accusers were, and that would mean I must identify you."

"Natine, I do not know what he would do if he thought I told you what I heard. When he is angry, sahiba, I fear his face."

Thinking back to their excursion into the jungle trees, Coral, too, shuddered.

Ethan was the only one she could turn to now. He had insisted on going with Sir Hugo to Darjeeling. Did Ethan suspect his uncle of plotting against her father? And why did Hugo wish to journey all the way to Darjeeling to search? Was it a ruse to later convince her mother and the family that he had been worried about Hampton? If something did happen to her father, then he could be the one to return in sad spirits bringing the dark news and pretending he had gone out of his way to locate him.

"The words Natine and the priest spoke, did you hear them all? Hold back nothing."

"I was visiting relatives to make final plans for my marriage to Pravin. I had gone to the other room to sleep on the mat with the other girls, all cousins. They were soon asleep, but I could not. I heard other men from the village come quietly to talk to Natine in the next room. The priest was with them. I did not hear all they said, for they spoke in low voices, and it was this that worried me, for I heard the name of your father."

Preetah drew her chunni about her throat and glanced nervously toward the darkened lawn between them and the lighted mansion. "The priest ask Natine what will happen when the burra-sahib's son returns to Kingscote from England and memsahib learns Alex left a letter before going away. 'They will know he was never in Darjeeling,' he said. 'What then of the message? What then of the ring? How will you explain this to the mem-sahib?' Natine said the feringhi ambassador will explain everything to the memsahib. Not to worry, for by then Sahib Roxbury would be new burra-sahib of Kingscote."

Coral's hands went cold and she tightened them into fists against the sides of her skirt. Yes, Sir Hugo would be certain to have adequate answers. He always did.

Coral's mind flashed back to London to the times she had been so ill. Jace was right. She had been drugged in order to control her. And the letter she had written to the major soon after Michael's death, asking about the charges made by her uncle—there was no doubt now in her mind that Hugo had destroyed it. He feared Jace and did not want him around. And how much had her uncle been involved in Gem's abduction? Was it not he who had found the other child's body in the river? Who had helped to deceive the family into believing Gem was dead until Jan-Lee had discovered the scar on the child's foot? Hugo had been on Kingscote the night the sepoy took Gem and the fire was started in the silk hatcheries.

Coral's anger seethed. If Sir Hugo dare harm her be-loved father she would . . . she stopped, her breathing coming rapidly. Yes, she would go to Ethan. But what could he do alone?

"You did well to come to me," said Coral quietly to the girl. "Say nothing to anyone. It's important that nei-ther Natine nor Sir Hugo realize we know the truth. Perhaps Seward was able to locate my father in time . . . and if they return soon, there is hope we can stop whatever is planned."

"Yes, but what I say is not all. I have this." Preetah reached under her chunni and came out with a folded piece of paper glinting white in the starlight. "It is the letter from your brother. After I heard he left it for your father, I looked in my uncle's bungalow." Her voice shook. "It was there."

The letter! Coral could not read the words in the starlight even though she recognized Alex's handwriting. "I will not forget your loyalty, Preetah."

"I must go now quickly. They will miss me."

She watched Preetah slip away into the darkness. Coral walked back toward the lighted house, concealing the letter from Alex in her bodice. As she neared the front lawn, she became cautious.

Inside the hall, she heard voices. A brief glance through the archway into the parlor showed the family was there as she had left them earlier. Her mother and Sir Hugo were in conversation, and Marianna sat on a settee doing her embroidery, but from the stilted movement of her hands Coral could tell she was nervous around their uncle. She had never forgotten her terrifying moment in the garden at Barrackpore when she had heard the conversation between Hugo and Harrington.

What was Marianna thinking now? Did it cross her mind that the man whose demise they had spoken of might be their father?

Kathleen was not in the parlor. Coral dimly wondered where she had gone. As she climbed the stairs and went down the hall she noticed a light under the door of Alex's room. She suspected Kathleen was in there for reasons of her own, but Coral had too much on her mind now to find out. The person who could do the most good for her father now was not Kathleen but Ethan.

Ethan was in his room still packing when she tapped. He seemed surprised to see her, but Coral motioned him to silence. "Come down to my father's office after the others leave the parlor. I must talk to you alone."

He nodded, curious but alert, and Coral went past the other chamber doors to her own room to read the letter from Alex. As she stepped in, closing her door, she stopped abruptly. Her eyes confronted a large bronze urn sitting in the middle of the room. Inside, she glimpsed the charred remains of a small black book—

"No! Not the Scriptures!" She rushed forward and knelt. Despair welled within. The Hindi New Testament that she had received at William Carey's mission station in Serampore lay in ashes.

Her hands formed cold fists. *Natine!*

The bamboo rattled in a light breeze, and she looked up toward the open verandah doors. Had she not bolted them earlier?

Slowly she walked forward, and her gaze fell on the lock. *Broken.* She stepped out and looked across the lawn toward the river. Maybe not Natine. The sadhu perhaps?

She shuddered to think anyone might find her chamber so accessible. Or was the broken lock only to mislead her? Sir Hugo had arrived today. Yet she could not see her uncle staging the dramatic episode of burning her Scriptures and leaving them as an omen in the middle of her room.

She slipped out and came to the stairway. Now only a dim lantern glowed in the parlor. Her mother and sisters had retired, and she supposed that Sir Hugo had also. He and Ethan were to rise early the next morning for the ride to Darjeeling.

Coral listened tensely, then went softly down the stairs into her father's office. It was not that late, and

Mera and the other servants were still up and attending their duties.

In her father's office she shut the door and heard the gilded clock in the Long Gallery chime. She counted . . . six, seven, eight.

Outside the open window she heard a distant noise. Horses on Kings Road? She decided it must be only the elephant boys moving the beasts to their stables near the hatcheries for the night.

In the sanctuary of her father's office, she lost herself in the big leather chair, holding one of his favorite books on her lap, drawing comfort from the items that reminded her of his fatherly strength.

"If only you are safe, Father. What will the family do without you?"

She leaned her elbows on the scarred mahogany desk, resting her head in her hands, listening to the distant sounds, yet not distinguishing them in her anxiety. She must have sat there without moving for some time before she heard the office door open quietly. She was expecting Ethan, and yet felt a nervous tingle at the back of her neck. She feared to turn, almost certain she would see an angry ghazi.

"I saw the light, my dear, and thought I better look in."

At Sir Hugo's voice she stiffened. Anger flooded her chest, for she was now certain he had heaped lies upon her for the last years. Yet she must play dumb to his present workings, for if he guessed the truth were known he might implement whatever plans he had more quickly. She thought of her burned Scriptures.

"I was reading, Uncle."

"You must not worry about your father and Alex, my dear. I've confidence Ethan and I will be able to find them."

"Yes. Perhaps they have rendezvoused at the tea plantation belonging to the major and Seward," she said, forcing herself to casual conversation. "Alex may have decided to buy into the enterprise of raising tea, in memory of Michael. We know how much the Darjeeling project meant to him. I believe Seward mentioned there is a dwelling on the land now . . . they intend to build a mansion, to make the plantation into another Kingscote."

Did she sound normal?

"Then I shall find a tour of the holdings of interest."

She said nothing, hoping he would withdraw before Ethan came downstairs.

"Ethan informed me of the good news. No need to tell you how pleased I am. A pity the wedding could not be a double celebration in London with your cousin Belinda and Sir George. Grandmother Victoria would be so delighted."

Coral's heart pounded with confusion. What had Ethan told him? She stood from the chair and turned to face him for the first time.

Sir Hugo's dark eyes were alive with pleasure, but his smile teased her, forcing itself into a rueful grin. "After learning of the bungalow school, which Ethan foolishly risked the anger of the Hindus to build, news of your engagement eased my kindled displeasure."

Her lips tightened. One evening at Kingscote and he was already behaving as its new master.

"Really, Coral!" he said with a wince that came off as insulting. "I do hope your willful spirit becomes tempered with marriage. Perhaps children of your own will squelch some of your lust for excitement and daring."

She found his ugly choice of words to describe her interest in the untouchables demeaning.

"But we'll forget this dreadful mistake, my dear, and

celebrate your wiser decision to marry Ethan. I confess, I was beginning to worry over the delay. You are getting on in your twenties now, and it is past time to turn your attentions to family and home."

"Kingscote is my home," she said, holding back a look of fury that caused her voice to shake.

"Of course. And so is Roxbury House. I hear your sister Kathleen wishes to return to work in silk design. I think it a wise idea, especially with Belinda and George there now. Not to mention your aunt Margaret. I mentioned it to Ethan tonight. We should have the wedding here at Christmas, and a trip to Europe for a honeymoon—if Napoleon ends the war! It might interest you to know that I've made fruitful contact with his government, and they are enthusiastic about importing Kingscote silk into Lyons."

Coral could not speak. She tried to keep from shaking with anger over his bold audacity.

Marriage! She had not told Ethan she would marry him soon; she had only agreed to accept the necklace as a form of engagement. Whatever love she had for Ethan— if indeed it was that—was held captive in a sea of confusion by unwanted memories of Jace Buckley. She had been wrong to hint to Ethan she might marry him soon, wrong to accept the necklace; yet she had been furious with Jace and jealous at the thought of the Indian girl at Sualkashi.

She touched the ruby and diamond necklace at her throat, and when Sir Hugo came to brush his lips against her forehead, she turned hot with embarrassment, knowing she had failed miserably and had misled Ethan.

"You—you must not think we have set a date," she stammered, angry because she had backed herself into a corner.

"Nonsense, my dear. There is no reason to wait. Elizabeth is also pleased. And of course, Hampton will be as well, as soon as he knows. If all goes well, he will know soon enough. Ethan and I will leave for Darjeeling in the morning. You best not stay up late; you are looking a trifle wan. Good-night."

The door shut behind him. Coral stared at it.

A Christmas wedding, indeed! She threw the book down on the desk with a thud. How dare Ethan mislead him into thinking the matter settled!

She knew why, of course. The school. Hugo must have been furious with him at the news, and Ethan had appeased his uncle by bringing up the necklace she had accepted.

She reached behind her neck with the idea of unlatching the clasp when there came a small tap on the door, and it opened. Ethan stepped in, his face taut. "Was that Uncle talking with you?"

Coral put a clamp on her temper. "Yes," she quipped. "He's cutting the wedding cake a bit soon, is he not?"

Ethan flushed under his tan. "I am sorry about that, Coral, but—"

"Sorry? After you've announced our Christmas wedding?"

He sighed, and she folded her arms tightly, her eyes narrowing. "You'll have to disappoint him. I am not ready for that final step. I—"

"Good heavens, Coral! Will you hold me off until we have gray in our locks? Besides, I cannot tell him now," he said. "We are leaving in the morning. It must wait until we return, unless I can talk you into keeping your promise."

"I made no promise, Ethan. You are being unfair. But making me feel guilty will not force me to marry before I am ready."

"Will you ever be ready?" he snapped.

She turned away from his bright, frustrated gaze. "I do not know."

He said something under his breath and walked stiffly to the open window, pulling aside the curtain to allow in the night air, but the night was still and hot.

"Blasted India. I am sick of the heat, the dust, waiting for the monsoon."

"Ethan, I must talk to you about Alex. It was why I asked you to come here. I didn't intend to speak with Uncle, or begin an angry discourse over our future. The future must wait until matters with my father and the mutiny at Guwahati are settled. And then there is Gem. . . ."

"What about Alex? We are leaving in the morning to search."

Her heart began to race again. "Alex is not in Darjeeling."

Stunned, he stared at her. Coral produced the letter. "It's from Alex. He wrote this before leaving Kingscote weeks before my father ever went to Darjeeling. But Hampton never received it. They disagreed about his future here on Kingscote and evidently came to harsh words. Alex apologizes in the letter for the things he told my father, and informed him he was going to England to sort things out in his own mind. What 'things' he wished to sort out, Alex doesn't explain, but evidently he thought father would understand. Alex promises to return with his decision next year."

Ethan was amazed as he held out his hand for the letter. She gave it to him. "Ethan, he is not in Darjeeling. You do understand what this implies?"

"Yes. Where did you get this letter?"

She hesitated. Then told him what Preetah had overheard in the village. He showed no surprise, but she did detect a resolve of purpose that worried her.

"I'll find Hampton. Do not worry."

She took hold of his arm, her eyes searching his. "You already knew Alex was not there."

"No. But I've suspected your father may be in trouble since I left Guwahati."

"Guwahati? But how! And why! Who told you?"

She listened as Ethan explained how her uncle had altered the major's orders for the purpose of sending him to Darjeeling, but that Jace suspected that men loyal to Sunil waited in ambush.

"Is that why you stopped me from saying he was at Sualkashi tonight?"

"Yes. The major requested I say nothing. He gave me a map. If I did not hear from him in three weeks, I was to go on alone to Burma to find Gem."

She searched his eyes. "You kept it from me."

"Buckley insisted."

His flat tone alarmed her. What else had he withheld from her? Was Jace's injury worse than Ethan had earlier implied? "Why wait three weeks?"

"He has his own mission to Jorhat and Burma, but I insisted I wished to be involved in Gem's rescue."

Gem's rescue. The words brought excitement. Then Jace had not forgotten, nor changed the plans he had informed her about in the garden.

"I want the truth. Is Uncle Hugo involved in a plot with Sunil? How does it implicate my father?"

"Good heavens, Coral! Do you expect me to know the dark weavings of his mind?"

He turned away from her. *Dark weavings.* She mulled over the words, and they only provoked her alarm and suspicion.

"I think you know more about Uncle than the rest of the family," Coral ventured.

"And what is that supposed to mean?"

"It was Uncle who pressed for this marriage long before we ever met in London."

He turned, his gray eyes growing tender. He took hold of her shoulders. "Yes, but the moment I saw you, I knew I agreed. Had he been against it, I'd still desire you to be my wife."

"You know his mind. He looks on you as a son."

"Does that make me guilty of his ambitions, or that I am partner to them?"

"Where my father is concerned, no, but—"

"Had you asked me in London if Hugo was capable of planning assassinations I would have been outraged. After Guwahati I can only say I do not know."

Icy fingers of alarm gripped her and a sickening feeling settled in her stomach. Roxbury House in London . . . the time Sir Hugo had blatantly lied about Jace being negligent as captain of his ship . . . Hugo had made her think Jace was guilty of Michael's death. The drugged state that she had been kept in at the family house on the Strand until she appeared to accept his explanation that Gem was dead . . . Hugo had tried to convince her she was bordering on insanity. Only his unexpected call back to London to receive a new position as ambassador to Guwahati had caused him to voyage to Calcutta without first pressuring her into marriage with Ethan.

What was it that her uncle truly desired so badly that he schemed and lied for? To be master of the family silk dynasty? What political ambitions in Assam were included in his plans?

Whatever drove Hugo, he was willing to arrange the untimely accident of her father in the mountainous regions of Darjeeling to grasp it. Yet men murdered for far less than riches, esteem, and political power. Thieves killed on the streets of Calcutta for a handful of rupees.

What was it that Jace had once told her about Sir

Hugo? " . . . *Greed and ambition can make devilish masters. . . . I think your uncle has an appetite not easily satisfied. . . . It is his nature to disapprove of making an Indian child a silk heir. Especially if that position contests his own. . . . You must be extremely cautious."*

Her revulsion must have shown in her expression, for Ethan took her hands into his, holding them too tightly in the heat of his anxiety. "Darling, don't look like that. You must not let Hugo know you understand. Dear God, I do not know what he might plan if he thought that you and I would not marry." He swallowed and awkwardly patted the side of her face. "Please, darling, I'll find Hampton. I promise. Perhaps it is best I leave tonight ahead of him. That will give me a day's advantage. Don't worry."

His words only partially settled into her consciousness. Ethan was not involved in Hugo's plot. But what about London? What about those horrible days when he and Hugo worked together to convince her that Gem was dead?

Lies. Had Ethan obeyed Hugo and used his medical knowledge to control her for Hugo's purposes?

As she searched his eyes, she could not find malicious deceit. There was the mission school. . . . He had risked Hugo's anger to build it for her. And there was her illness, which he had successfully treated, as well as helping her mother recover. Ethan was not all dark like Uncle Hugo; he was also light, and the two natures appeared to come into constant conflict . . . perhaps because of the hold that his uncle had on his life for so long in England. He was beginning to change now, to become his own man, to resist Hugo's bidding.

She touched the rubies and diamonds around her throat. "Ethan, there is something I must know about London, about the house on the Strand."

A flicker of consternation showed in his eyes. "Coral, do not ask."

"Why?" her voice tremored, but she was calm. "I have the right to know the truth if you are to be my husband. How can you ask me to trust you in the future if you will not tell me the truth now about the past?"

"Because the past is over. It can only destroy the future if we allow it."

"I will always wonder. The time we were in London . . . when I was so ill and having those nightmares about Gem. Did you knowingly drug me in order to do as Hugo asked?"

"Do you think I would ever deliberately harm you? I am not only a physician, I cared for you even then. I have always done what I believed was for your best welfare."

"Your denial is evasive. Did you drug me to keep me from going to the director of the East India Company about Gem?"

"I tell you, no."

"What of Manali? Was Jace right about the spider bite? Was it also one of your Eastern drugs learned from your stay in Burma?"

"Darling Coral, I swear it isn't true!"

"But you have always done what Hugo wanted!"

"No! No!"

"It is he who wishes us to marry. And you agree because you have your own purposes for being here. The lab! The miserable mosquito lab! Your research means more to you than the life of my father!"

"Not anymore—"

"Not anymore? But it was true in the beginning?"

"Yes! But I tell you I love you! I would do anything for your happiness, anything! Did I not build the school?"

"For what purpose? To obligate me to marry you now

that Hugo has arrived? If my father is dead, he is my guardian, and between you and Hugo, you think you can control me. Building the school was just a way to make marriage to you more palatable. Tell me the truth, Ethan!"

"All right! I built the school for reasons of my own—to please you, to win your love. Is that so despicable a cause? I am not as religious as you are, but I approve of the work you want to do with the children. I did not deceive you for other ambitions. I meant what I said about respecting your spiritual convictions, and I'll do whatever it takes to keep my father from hurting you!"

As though struck, Coral took a step backward. She choked, "Your father?"

Ethan paled and turned his back. When he spoke his voice was dull and quiet. "Yes. Would God it were not so, but it is." He turned, his eyes blazing. "But I am not his puppet, not anymore. I'll do what is best for you, for us, for Kingscote—for Hampton. I'll find him!"

Her mind reeling, fear latched hold. "No. Do not go with him! I put nothing past him now. Nothing."

"He would never harm me," Ethan said wearily as his shoulders sagged, all energy spent. "What he does, he does for me, as well as for himself—and the family. Sometimes he truly believes he is doing the right thing. I know that's hard for you to accept, but it is so. Hampton's refusal to work with the Company, your school. Hugo has monumental dreams of greatness in Assam that will spread not only to London but Paris, Madrid, Rome. He thinks Hampton will ruin it, that his ambitions are too small and narrow. Sunil has promised Hugo a treaty for all Assam, and access to Burma, if he cooperates with his plans to rule in place of the maharaja. Hugo has been working with him. I confronted him in Guwahati; he knows how I feel about what is happening, but he would never harm me if I stood in his way. However, we have reason to fear for the others . . . Hampton and Buckley—my father will do what he must to win."

Her heart stopped. "Jace? What about him?"

Ethan shook his head as if he could not talk and walked away from her.

New suspicions fed her fears. "Hugo wishes to have Jace killed? Is that it? *That is why you stopped me tonight from saying he was in Sualkashi.*"

"Yes."

"Then he was expected to go to Darjeeling after the mutiny?"

"Yes. Jace felt certain an assassin waited for him on the road. Probably one of Sunil's rajputs. Hugo was involved in the plan. It was he who changed his orders in Guwahati at the last minute. He sent him to Darjeeling to search for Hampton."

"But he did not go!"

"No," he said flatly. "Jace is too clever to believe anything Hugo says. He came straight to me with news of the plan to kill the maharaja. We worked together to save him. We were almost out the gate when Sunil attacked with the war elephants."

Weary now, Coral walked to her father's desk and leaned against it. She heard him come up behind her, taking hold of her arms.

"I'm ashamed to be his son, but I love you. Please, Coral, do not hold me to blame for my father's sins. I'll find Hampton. I'll bring him home safely."

The depth of his anguish touched her heart with pity, and with something else—perhaps a wish to solace him. He looked so miserable.

Her lack of argument must have fed his expectations, for he grasped her, holding her tightly, burying his face in her hair. "Coral . . ."

162

Above his voice she could hear horses. "Ethan, no—"

He held her, kissing her, oblivious to all else. She tried to push him away, hearing the voice of Rosa in the outer hall. And then the door opened. Over Ethan's shoulder she faced Major Jace Buckley. He paused, his cool gaze taking them in from head to foot.

"Jace!" she breathed.

12

Ethan heard Coral's startled response and turned around. He showed no surprise, nor alarm at being caught with Coral in his arms. If anything, he seemed smugly pleased that Jace Buckley would find them together. As she sought to step back, distressed, Ethan's hard fingers grasped her waist, holding her close to his side, as though he possessed her.

"Ah, Major. Good evening. We were not expecting you."

Jace's brittle gaze held Ethan's. "Evidently not." He looked past Ethan to Coral. A familiar smirk touched his mouth, but there was no humor in it. "Miss Kendall. My apology for interrupting too soon."

Too soon? Confused by his words, she flushed with embarrassment and could say nothing. But his next statement, smooth with meaning, she did fully understand. "Had I intruded a moment later, I would have fully expected to hear a ringing slap."

Coral felt the dart pierce her heart. She turned away.

"You might as well know, Major," came Ethan's almost victorious tone. "Coral and I are betrothed. The marriage is to be held here on Kingscote this Christmas.

165

She wears the ruby and diamond necklace of engagement. And now, Major, I assume you are here on business
about Burma?"

Coral whirled, her hand going to the necklace. She
saw Jace's gaze fix upon the glimmering jewels.

"My mistake, Doctor. Congratulations," came Jace's
calm but precise voice. "I shall wait in the hall. I have
come for my map."

"The map, ah, yes, of course, Major. I shall get it at
once."

Jace stepped out into the hall; Ethan followed,
crossed the floor, and took the stairway up to his room.

Coral stood in her father's office, her heart hammer-
ing, her hands cold. If Ethan had been facing her she
might have made good the ringing slap of which Jace
had hinted. She remained without moving, hoping
against hope that Jace would come into the office. Even
a cynical remark from him would have been appreciated
at the moment.

He did not come.

She stood there, her nails digging into her palms,
waiting. The front door opened and closed, not with a
bang, but so quietly that her heart wrenched.

He was willing to leave matters as they appeared.

But of course he would. He was going to marry the
Indian girl anyway.

Before she realized it, Coral caught up her skirts and
rushed from the office into the hall. Rosa stood in the
shadows, probably wondering if she was to prepare a
room for the major. Coral drew in a breath, opened the
front door, and stepped out into the night.

The porch was empty. She glanced about for Jace and
saw him farther down the carriageway, mounting his
horse. Another man on horseback was beside him. That
would be his Indian friend Gokul.

Coral flung aside her pride and hurried down the steps. She hesitated only a second, then rushed down the cobbled drive toward Jace, who was turning his sweating horse in the direction of Kings Road, and Jorhat.

A slight look of surprise crossed his face as he reined in his slow-moving horse and half turned in the saddle to look down at her. "Miss Kendall?"

His voice spoke to a stranger, as though his eyes had never seen her before. Coral's throat tightened at his rejection and she wanted to say, *"Be as you once were, Jace, when you cared about what I did. When you felt opinionated enough to tell me I was wrong!"*

Quietly she said, "I hope you've recovered from your injury."

"Yes, thank you."

She searched his face. *There must be something left of that moment in the garden.* But he only looked down at her with eyes that refused to be searched, watching her without emotion.

"You are riding on tonight to Jorhat?"

"Yes, as soon as Ethan delivers my map."

Even the way he pronounced Ethan's name held none of the usual challenge. Coral knew she must not make a fool of herself. It was now clear that Ethan had told her the truth about Jace and the woman at Sualkashi. With as much grace as she could manage, she murmured quickly, "Goodbye, Major. A safe journey."

"Goodbye, Miss Kendall. Thank you."

Coral turned and walked back up the drive to the steps and into the house. Inside she met Ethan coming down the stairs with something in his hand. Coral said nothing to him and took the stairs up to her room.

———

Astride the black horse, Jace watched Coral walking

167

away. The sight of Coral in Ethan's arms still left him feeling cold and angry. He jammed his hat on his dark head and glanced up at a lighted window he suspected might be her bedchamber. His blue-black eyes narrowed.

"Ah, sahib," came Gokul's mock sigh. "I am disappointed in you."

Jace gave him a cold glance. "I'm in no mood, Gokul, so just keep silent."

"And sahib says he knows women," Gokul softly chuckled.

Jace flapped the horse reins across his gloved palm. Gokul continued, casually taking fruit from the cotton bag tied to his saddle. He polished the skin, held it up to the starlight to check it for its sumptuousness, then bit into it. "Is my belief, sahib, that if you let a woman like *her* escape, you received more in concussion than short loss of vision." Gokul looked at him with a smile. "I shall impart my wisdom, sahib."

Jace continued to flip the reins, growing more irritated by the moment. His eyes narrowed as he watched Gokul relishing his fruit with too much noise.

"I wager one share in tea plantation that English beauty could be had by you if sought. Yet you let her fall like ripe fruit into hand of irritating doctor." Gokul shook his head as if in disbelief. "You should not ride off tonight, sahib. Stay."

"You dream, old man. She's going to marry Boswell this Christmas."

"Yet she comes running after you. Most satisfying, I would think. Why you think she come to side of your horse all polite and pretending nothing of feelings? You too busy pretending you do not feel. But old Gokul, he took long look at young woman and see something worth fighting doctor for in eyes. Very nice eyes. Green like soft emeralds—"

"Your tongue wags too much. Silence, here comes our gallant gentleman."

Gokul chuckled and threw the core of his finished fruit into the darkness. He felt satisfied, certain he had accomplished his goal.

He was right. Gokul rubbed his face to hide a grin as he heard Jace say in an even challenge to Doctor Boswell: "I've decided my horse needs rest and food. And I'm ready for a bath and a decent bed. Tomorrow will be soon enough to be about my business."

"As you wish," came the stiff reply. "But remember, sir, we made plans to deliver the boy from Burma together."

Jace had no intention of allowing Ethan to come with him. "The map." Jace held out a gloved hand. Retrieving it from Ethan, he swung himself down from the saddle and tossed the reins to an Indian boy waiting by the side of the house. Jace was watching the lighted window and saw the verandah doors open and a woman step out into the cloistered shadows. He knew without being told that it was Coral, that she had probably wondered why the horses had not ridden away. He walked slowly toward her verandah and paused beneath it, looking up. He knew she saw him. She stepped back and went in. A moment later the door shut.

———

Perhaps the cause of her nightmare was prompted by seeing Sir Hugo again. Hurtful, frightening memories seemed to leap back into flame from smoldering embers; perhaps it was bred from the fear that lodged in her subconscious over the safety of her father. Maybe it was seeing Jace again and feeling the emptiness as he prepared to ride out of her life.

Whatever drew the dark foreboding to her mind,

Coral found herself tossing restlessly as snatches of the old nightmare that had once plagued her came stalking. . . .

Somewhere in the darkness a tiny helpless child was calling her, and she left the front steps of the porch to find him. Urgency pressed her forward toward the familiar trees. Suddenly the jungle erupted with flames; all Kingscote was on fire and the heat was unbearable, touching her skin and blackening the air with clouds of smoke. The child was trapped amid the flames and Coral was alone, trying to grasp him from certain death, but he remained ahead, just out of her grasp.

"Gem!"

Then Coral became aware that someone else was with her struggling to grasp the boy. She could not see his face, but she knew they battled together until they were ultimately torn apart by the fire. As he disappeared she saw him. Jace! Then she stood alone again with the fire everywhere. She had lost them both. She could see them receding farther and farther from her grasp as the fire of death sucked them away—

"Jace!" she called into the emptiness.

She sat up in the darkness of her room, her heart slamming in her chest, her skin wet with perspiration. She held her head in her hands, closing her eyes tightly.

As the trauma faded with reality, a flash of dry lightning streaked in the distant sky, followed by the deep rumble of thunder.

Coral looked around and realized she had not undressed for bed but had fallen asleep on top of the satin coverlet. She remembered suddenly that she had not heard Jace ride away. Earlier, she had heard Rosa talking as she had led him to a chamber in the hall not far from her own room. The idea that he had decided to stay piqued her curiosity, but after his cool reception in the carriageway she did not intend to ask questions. Perhaps the monsoon was ready to break, and he had wisely decided not to ride on.

She tried to push away any notion that she had been the cause for his unexpected change of mind. It didn't matter. In the morning they would all ride out for their various destinations, their rendezvous with time and events: Sir Hugo and Ethan, Jace and his friend Gokul.

She went to the verandah and opened the doors to see if the monsoon was arriving. The night was still and she stepped out. Not too many hours had passed since Jace had arrived, for as she scanned the sky, the location of the moon told her it was somewhere near midnight. The sky was yet clear; the rains had not yet come. And yet . . . something was wrong. . . .

The sky in the direction of the workers' bungalows glowed with a splash of crimson, etched with an unnatural haze—what was it?—black smoke! Not the silk hatcheries! Not again!

From the adjoining chamber, Jan-Lee threw open the split-cane shade and leaned out. Her young daughter, Emerald, was quickly beside her, wearing a long white nightgown, her waist-length braids showing dark against the white gown. "Missy Coral!" the girl cried. "Fire! Fire!"

Coral's fingers tightened around the verandah rail as she stared off in the distance at the billow of acrid smoke drifting from the direction of the hatcheries—no, not the hatcheries—

Her bedroom door flew open and Coral whirled to face Kathleen, whose expression of alarm mingled with sympathy. "It's the school!"

For a moment Coral wanted to weep. Her eyes met Kathleen's in wordless understanding. In a frenzy they both bolted down the hall and raced for the stairs. A bedroom door flew open but Coral did not stop. She and Kathleen ran for the kitchen. Kathleen fumbled to unbolt the door, flinging it open so wildly that it smashed into the wall. Down the steps they raced into the back garden, into the night.

Somewhere between the stairway and the back porch, Kathleen, far stronger, had surged ahead to the stables. Coral was forced to pause in the sultry night, trying to catch her breath. In the distance the red glow of fire reflected against the sky.

Too late, it's too late—the flames would swiftly consume the wood and thatch roof. All their work, gone.

Kathleen came riding on the old horse kept near the kitchen outbuilding, her skirt flaring, and her hair flying as wildly as the horse's mane. Even in that swift instant, Coral was amazed to see Kathleen's determination emerge, drawing her own up out of the pit of depression. Kathleen grabbed for Coral's arm. "Get up, hurry!"

Coral grasped the pommel with both hands, but they were sweating and slippery. She managed to swing herself up behind her sister as Kathleen slapped the reins and clapped her heels against the horse's side. With a shower of dust they galloped in the direction of the mission school.

As they rode nearer to the fire the horse became frightened and whinnied, pulling back nervously. Kathleen steadied the reins and turned the horse from facing the fire, unable to ride closer. Coral stared at the burning structure. The flames appeared to cackle mockingly and dance victoriously, casting billowing smoke and cinder about them.

Coral bit back her rage and bitter disappointment, sweat joining her tears as she dashed a hand across her face. They could never put it out—never! The hard-won mission school was dead! Years of planning, all their work and prayers, going up in smoke!

She turned her face away from the foul fumes, her throat burning from a gust of smoke that blew against them. Kathleen rode some feet away. By now a number of Indian workers appeared in silent groups, watching, no doubt believing that Kali had brought judgment on the shrine of the feringhi's religion.

Coral climbed down from behind Kathleen, her hand grasping the saddle for balance as she stared toward the burning ruin.

Kathleen's voice tensed as she leaned over her from the saddle. "If you cry, so will I, and I won't be able to stop—"

"I am not crying," said Coral. She began walking slowly across the dusty ground in the direction of the smoking rubble. Flames continued to spurt up from charred wood, bursting forth, then dying into smoke.

Coral heard another horse ride up and Jace asking Kathleen what happened.

"Someone set the mission school on fire!"

"Mission school!"

"Ethan built it. Coral has held classes for several weeks. It's gone!"

Coral heard the workers talking excitedly among themselves, then Jace's commanding voice ordering them in Hindi to leave.

Kathleen turned her horse, and seeing Major Buckley walking toward Coral, she flicked the reins and rode back toward the house. As she trotted down the road, she saw Ethan rushing to the fire, his shirt yet unbuttoned. There was a rifle in his hand. He stopped and stepped to the side of the road when Kathleen rode up.

"The school?" he asked.

"Yes, there is nothing left—no, Ethan, don't go there.

Coral wishes to be alone, and there is nothing more to be done."

"I cannot leave her out there by herself! Someone started it, and whoever it was may still be there!"

"She is not alone. And you'll receive no answers from the workers even if you threaten them. Whoever did it will be protected. Let my mother ask the questions. They respect the memsahib."

Seeing Ethan's expression harden as he began to ask further, she said firmly, "Yanna is with her."

It was true, for Kathleen had seen the girl running from her bungalow with the children to see if the fire was spreading.

Kathleen leaned toward him, extending a pleading but restraining hand. "Please. Coral wishes to be alone. We best get back. The others will have heard us leave the house and will want to know if we are all right."

"You are certain she is taking the loss well?"

"Yes. Come, I'll put water on for tea and coffee. It won't be much longer before you and Uncle Hugo will need to start out for Darjeeling."

———

Jace stood watching Coral as she faced the smoldering ruins of the small mission school. Her hair was mussed, and there were traces of smoke and ash on her dress. She had never looked more noble, more beautiful to him than she did now.

With cool determination he thought again of the reason he had stayed. Gokul's goading remarks had snapped him back into reason—he would be a fool to leave without telling her how he felt. He would contest Ethan for Coral Kendall with the same commitment he had previously given to other causes that maintained his adventurous freedom.

If necessary, in order to have her, he would pursue her across the continent of India and beyond. He would defeat Ethan. For that matter, he thought, his emotions now confident and contained, he would win over any other man who might stand in his way.

He understood what devastation she must feel over the burning school. He was not thoughtless to her pain, but there could be another school, the next one built of stone. He would see that she had it, and despite the danger, he would protect her even if he had to hire English mercenaries to guard her while she carried out her heart's purpose in serving Christ.

But there was more on his mind, which he believed to be crucial. Like the smoldering ruin that held her captive to discouragement and defeat, Jace believed that what they secretly felt for each other must be seized and secured before the kindled flame of all that was noble in love was also destroyed and left in ashes. For unlike the school, if they lost each other because of pride or fear, they could not rebuild—not if he rode away. . . .

It mattered not that she might be engaged. The engagement was wrong. The one thing that mattered to Jace was that he knew he loved her. His old friend Gokul had helped him understand the reason behind his earlier determination to ride out without contesting Ethan. Walking in and seeing her in his arms had caught him off guard, and the pain had penetrated more deeply than he had thought possible. Angry that she could hurt him, and at himself for failing to preserve his immunity, he had wanted only to protect himself. In the past he could walk away from a woman. Once at sea, or on some risky adventure, he would forget all about her. Not this time, and he felt relief, even delight. He had found a woman who could fill his life's void, who was noble, strong in godly pursuit, and pure. One that set his heart pounding, one for whom he loved enough to lay down his life.

————

Coral heard Jace walk up behind her, and turned.

The warm glow of the diminishing flames flickered against the handsome cut of his features, and the familiar blue-black eyes were intently fixed upon her. Amid the rubble he stood as the one reality that could rekindle her shattered emotions. Her cold heart began to beat again, pounding in her temples.

A familiar slight smile touched his mouth. He studied her. "I have never yet fled from a battle. When it comes to the only woman I want, I will not walk away. I've decided to stay and contest Ethan for a worthy prize."

Her breath caught in silence. For a moment their eyes held, each searching for truth, and as the realization of their need for each other became known, it drew them together at the same instant, forcing a decision that promised a love too strong to be denied any longer.

Coral moved toward him at the same moment his hands enclosed her arms, drawing her, and it seemed she belonged in his embrace, that it was home for her heart. Her head fell back to receive his kiss, and the world disappeared about her with all its ugliness and ruin.

I love you, she wanted to repeat over and over. *I love you. I love.* . . . She heard the words spoken, but not by her. Jace was breathing them as he held her.

"I once convinced myself I would never become vulnerable to any woman. I was wrong. My armor is off, and I confess I need you more than anything else this world can offer," and with those words he was kissing her again and again.

"Answer me," he whispered, looking down into her eyes.

"Yes . . . yes—"

"Yes, what?"

"You are the one I love, Jace."

It was several minutes before he released her, and all the strength had gone out of her. She clung to him desperately, oblivious to the night about them, of the smell of smoke, of sputtering wood.

He looped his finger about the necklace on her throat and lifted it, his dark eyes narrowing at the jewels. "Gaudy, and boasting of financial power. Boswell has garish taste in jewelry. I find it repugnant . . . you are much finer than this. It stands between us like the vaunted wealth of the Kendall and Roxbury family, boasting of what I do not have to give you."

Her heart pounded with expectation. "So it gets in your way, does it?" she whispered.

"It reminds me of a religious medallion to ward off an 'accident.' And I rather think that Jace Buckley is the accident."

"What would you like to do about it?" she asked softly.

His eyes held hers, then he took her shoulders and turned her around. Coral smiled as she lifted her hair and felt his fingers unclasp the latch.

A moment later she turned to face him and Jace held up the necklace to dangle in the firelight, and rubies danced like flames of their own, the diamonds flashing like starlight.

He lifted her chin and turned her eyes away from the necklace to meet his gaze. A brow went up.

"Right now there is little on the Darjeeling land except the beginning of a house and a few miserable tea plants."

She smiled at his persistent dislike of tea.

"But someday—if Seward, Gokul, Jin-Soo, and I are successful, it might be different. Notice I say 'might.' It

177

will take years before we can become as superior in tea as Kingscote is in silk. At present, I cannot offer you rubies and diamonds."

She reached a hand to his, and with her fingers, she blotted out the twinkle of the jewels, her eyes holding his, and loving the glimmer of warmth she saw in them.

"You are certain you mean this, Coral? You are the only woman to whom I would ever risk my heart."

She was thrilled, but could not resist— "What about that Indian girl?"

"What Indian girl?"

"At Sualkashi. That day you brought me there when I was ill. The next morning she was very smug. Too smug. She called you 'Jace'—and there was a gleam in her eyes when she said it. It was very intimate."

"Ah, sweet jealousy. Coming from you, I find it very satisfying. But there was never anything intimate between Devi and me. A certain damsel masquerading as Madame Khan had already filled my mind with her presence wherever I went."

Confusion and pleasure swept through her at the same time. "But Ethan said—" She stopped.

His eyes hardened. "Just what did Ethan say?"

"It does not matter now. I understand the truth."

"But you might not have. I shall demand the truth from him."

"No. Please do not."

"Is that why you accepted the necklace, because you thought I cared for Gokul's niece?"

"Yes, although I never actually told Ethan I'd marry him, but he seemed to think so."

"At Guwahati he insisted you had agreed to marry him after you left me in the palace garden. I do not know if I truly believed his boast, but I was afraid you might have agreed after that stinging rejection," he said wryly, touching the side of his face. "I guess you know you gave me something to think about when you walked away."

"I saw the Indian girl in my mind, and . . . well, became furious that you would tell me goodbye."

"I doubt if I could have stayed away. I implied as much in the message about Gem."

"Yes, and you are here now, and nothing must be allowed to come between us. But Hugo thinks I'm going to marry Ethan. They have actually been audacious enough to plan a Christmas wedding."

His mouth turned with thoughtful sarcasm. "Then I suppose he will demand his duel after all."

"Duel?"

"Never mind," he said with a smile. "It is you and me I want to discuss. I respect Elizabeth and Sir Hampton, but they are likely to favor Ethan as a son-in-law more than an adventurous sea captain. Just how deeply are you willing to commit yourself to me before I face the lions?"

She reached both hands and drew his dark head down until her lips found his, giving him all the assurance he needed.

The necklace slipped from his fingers and fell into the hot dust, and Coral felt his arm enclose her.

"Then we have a bargain, Miss Kendall."

"We do, Major."

"When?"

"Well. . . ."

"As soon as I return from Burma."

"But I will need to make plans for a grand wedding, and though I shall vow to die before I marry Ethan instead of you, I fear you will yet need to speak to my father and mother, and then there will be a wardrobe to make—"

His arms tightened about her. "Oh, no, mademoiselle,

none of that runaround you gave to Boswell for the past few years. Now that our minds are made up, I have become an impatient man. You will become Mrs. Jace Buckley as soon as I return from Burma."

She smiled. "Yes . . . just as soon as you come back to me."

"That is one thing you can be sure of—I will come back."

13

Jace took her arm and walked her away from the rubble to where his horse waited, but Coral was not anxious to get back to the house. She would never fall asleep after everything that had happened. *I am actually going to marry Jace,* she thought, and looked at him possessively. Major Buckley, the captain of the *Madras,* and Javed Kasam, all belonged to her heart. Marriage with Jace surely promised to be exciting.

"Do you still have the golden monkey?"

"Goldfish and Jin-Soo are both anxiously awaiting your arrival in Darjeeling. You do not mind if Goldfish sleeps in the same room with us?" he asked innocently. "He has a few habits that are hard to break."

She gave him an amused glance. "I suspect the captain of the *Madras* does too."

"Jin-Soo will take to you immediately," he went on smoothly. "He'll insist that his ginseng tea is just what is needed to make you strong and healthy." He held the stirrup for her foot. "Ride?"

Coral shook her head and slipped past him toward the road, calling over her shoulder, "Let's walk back. I still have so much to tell you."

She was thinking of Alex and the letter Preetah had found, but before turning to more serious matters she said innocently, "You do realize marriage to me will make you Sir Hugo's nephew?"

Jace cocked his head and looked at her.

Coral smiled and walked ahead of him. "I forgot to mention his new interest goes beyond silk to tea."

Jace grinned as he took the horse's reins and followed her on the dusty road that led the short distance to the mansion.

As Jace and Coral walked together, their mood turned as somber as the dark and silent road that hemmed them in on both sides with mulberry trees. Coral began to explain everything that had happened on Kingscote since they had parted in Guwahati, including Seward's search at her insistence and Ethan and Sir Hugo's trek the next morning with a dozen rajput warriors to Darjeeling.

"But why Alex went to England remains a curious thing," she said.

"Maybe not so curious."

"Why do you say that?"

He did not explain but asked, "Does Roxbury know you have the letter?"

"No. I only received it tonight from Preetah. I did show it to Ethan. That was the reason we met in my father's office. We had been . . . discussing matters when you arrived." She glanced at him, wondering if he understood that it had not been her intention to be in Ethan's arms. Evidently he was satisfied, for he let it pass.

"Tell me about the school. What was Roxbury's reaction?"

She thought of her uncle coming into the office earlier that evening, and shuddered. "He knows Ethan built it. The misconception Ethan gave him of an engagement has mollified him temporarily. I do not know what Uncle will do when he learns about us."

His slight frown told Coral that he was more disturbed over what Sir Hugo's reaction would be than he was over Ethan's. "Say nothing until I return from Burma. I will worry less about you that way."

"But how! Ethan will notice I've removed the necklace."

He looked thoughtful. "Roxbury is leaving at dawn with Ethan. That is not too long from now. Can you avoid them both for the rest of the night?"

"Yes, if I go in the back way I suppose I can, but eventually I will need to tell Ethan. He is likely to return before you arrive from Burma."

"When your father and Seward arrive I'll have less reason for concern." He frowned down at her. "Until tonight, I thought you were safe with Seward here guarding you."

"He felt bad about leaving, but I encouraged him. We were both so worried about my father."

"With good reason. But I have confidence in Seward. Between him and Hampton, they have a chance to survive." He stopped on the road and faced her. "It is best I do not return to the house. I'll locate Gokul and ride out tonight. Any trouble with Ethan must wait, lest Roxbury be alerted. Ethan is of the Old School and will insist on settling differences in a duel."

"You are not serious!" she said, horrified. "A duel?"

"My dear girl, are you so naive of the ways of Europe's gentlemen?"

By the tone of his voice she could not guess if he were being serious or cynical.

"Ethan will think nothing of showing up on the front lawn with pistol and sword in hand. My concern," he said dryly, "is that his temperament will prompt him to act at four in the morning. I would rather sleep by the side of the road than be rudely awakened."

"A duel is out of the question—it is absurd!"

"What! The beautiful damsel sought passionately by two men is offended by such knightly display?" He smiled and folded his arms. "You mean you do not want me to fight to win your hand? Or are you afraid Ethan will shoot me?"

His jesting nettled her. "I'm quite certain you can take care of yourself in duels, but I prefer a more civilized approach."

"Duels are a noble part of Europe's foundation, and any lord in England will tell you so. And if her ladyship required one more noble deed in order that I win her hand, you would hear my voice on the lawn calling Ethan out."

She smiled and studied him. "Would you, really?"

He lifted a brow over her seeming pleasure.

She changed the subject. "I have a notion Ethan got the necklace from Sir Hugo at Guwahati."

"Does Roxbury usually trek across India with a satchel of jewels and other bangles?" he asked dryly. He removed the necklace from his jacket. "You better take this now."

She looked up in surprise, then felt the cold jewels pressed into her palm. "I suppose I should return it to him. I will as soon as he returns from Darjeeling. He should know right away it is over between us—and, I am quite angry with him over his deception," she said, thinking of Sualkashi. Another suspicious thought entered her mind. "Ethan said you were only slightly injured in the rebellion."

"He did not explain?"

"I suppose I should have pressed him, but when he

said you had gone to Sualkashi to marry Gokul's niece, I wanted to forget—"

"That is what he told you! No wonder he sought to coerce you into a quick engagement. He thought you might just be ready. He knew I would come to Kingscote for the map within three weeks if I regained my sight."

Startled, she searched his eyes. "You lost your sight? But how?"

He touched the side of his head and said wryly, "After being struck on the skull several times, including at Calcutta when that miserable thief stole my Mogul sword, my vision was affected. I'm all right now, but I need to avoid another concussion."

Ethan had lied to her!

"Never mind me, I want to know what you've been up to while I've been at Sualkashi studying theology."

Theology? She did not take his remark seriously and let it pass, going on to tell him about the children Yanna had rescued from the crocodiles, and how she had brought them to the dispensary. "Along with Jan-Lee's daughter, Emerald, the four children were my only students. Now I've lost both the school and the Hindi Scriptures."

He regarded her. "The Scriptures from William Carey?"

"I found them in my room earlier this evening—burned."

"Natine."

Her heartbreaking loss returned with vivid clarity.

He drew her to him. She thrilled at the look of determination she saw in the blue-black eyes.

"Every end brings a new beginning," he said. "We will get new Hindi Scriptures. By now Carey may have translated them into Assamese. You can have both! We will build again, Coral. Next time in stone. It won't stop the ghazis, but it will discourage a hastily lit torch. And next time we will try building in a less confrontational spot. They see a school in their backyard as a religious shrine. It was bound to be a goad. We do not want to challenge them with an impression of superiority but in meekness instruct those who oppose the light. Next time, why not build closer to the river near the elephant walk? You'll attract more children, and being closer to the mansion will make it appear to be more of a Kendall enterprise."

She noticed he used the word "we" when speaking of rebuilding, and her heart beat with joy. "I should have thought of that—near the elephant walk. And I should have expected trouble from Natine after I witnessed the religious sacrifice to Kali."

He looked at her swiftly. "On Kingscote?"

She explained about her excursion into the jungle with Preetah.

"Are you telling me Natine and this priest from the village threatened you?"

"Not threatened exactly," she admitted cautiously. "But I heard my name mentioned."

"Which is quite the same thing, and dangerous." He took hold of her shoulders. "You never would do as I asked before, but I must insist you listen to me now, Coral, especially with the school burning down."

"Of course, Jace, anything you say," she said sweetly.

He gave her a questioning look, then went on. "What did Natine say to you about the school?"

"He was upset, but that did not surprise me. He told me the East India Company would control Kingscote if I persisted in spreading Christianity among the workers. He seemed to think the Company could stop me. I insisted they had no jurisdiction here, that neither I nor Sir Hampton would be ruled by the Company's ambitions in Calcutta. You know how they are against Wil-

liam Carey holding public meetings and distributing leaf-
lets among the people."

She did not like the gravity in his eyes, for it only
convinced her that Natine truly did serve Sir Hugo, as
Jace had already told her in the palace garden.

"So Natine appeared confident of the Company's intervention if you persisted?"

"Perhaps it is only a hope of his."

"I think not. He would not risk saying that if he didn't
have assurance from someone."

"Sir Hugo?"

"I'm sure of it. You haven't forgotten amid everything
else that Hugo wants control of the silk enterprise? His
new position as ambassador for the Company enables
him to interfere here. And with your father called away
to Darjeeling, Roxbury intends to become the new master of the Kendalls, as well as the Roxburys in London.
Except for you, there is no one left to oppose him."

"My mother will never turn Kingscote over to him,
even if something did happen to my father."

"Your mother is a strong woman. You are very much
like her. But your uncle will do what he feels he must to
gain power. I do not know what he has planned with
Prince Sunil, or for that matter with Natine, but while I
am gone you must promise me to do nothing to provoke
either one of them."

He pulled her against him. "I want you here in one
piece when I return."

His concern only awakened hers. "Ethan said you suspected an assassin on the road to Darjeeling."

"Do not worry about me; it is you who must be cautious. I'm almost tempted to take you with me."

"To Burma? I have had quite enough of crocodiles,
spiders, and tiger attacks, thank you. I'll be well enough
here. And my mother and sisters will need me with

them." She touched a palm to the side of his face. "The next journey I take with you will be to Darjeeling."

His strong hand enclosed hers. "Your father made certain to hire mercenaries to watch the borders of Kingscote?"

"Yes. We had a man killed recently. But surely they will not get through to the mansion."

He frowned. "I do not suppose you can use a pistol?"

She smiled. "I can. Father taught us all years ago. Does that surprise you?"

"Nothing surprises me about Coral Kendall. Keep it loaded—and don't get sentimental. Shoot point-blank if it ever comes to it, understood?"

She shuddered and nodded. "But it will not come to that."

He said nothing and looked down the road. "Coral . . . before I go, there is something I need to tell you about Gem."

She noted the change in his voice at once and bolstered her courage. "Yes?"

"Did Ethan say anything to you about the maharaja?"

She shifted uneasily. "He mentioned his death. The message you sent said Gokul discovered where Gem was being held."

"Yes. But it was the maharaja who shared the truth. Gem is alive, but there is more. Are you ready to hear and accept it, however it may disappoint your own plans for Gem?"

Somehow she had sensed the truth would not be what she had long hoped for since arriving home to Kingscote.

He hesitated. "Gem is heir to the throne at Guwahati. That is the reason Sunil searches for him. As long as Gem lives he is a threat to Sunil's ambition to become the maharaja."

Coral made no sound. Dazed, she listened as Jace explained the details of what he had learned in Guwahati, and of how Sunil had sought the hand of Jemani in marriage.

"And Jemani?"

"We do not know her blood. We think she came from a princely line in the south. You adopted a baby," he said softly, "but he could never be truly yours. Gem belongs to India. His title is Prince Adesh Singh."

Despite her best effort, tears welled in her eyes. She blinked them back. "Adesh—yes, I like that name."

He belonged to India. The words repeated themselves.

Jace reached inside his jacket and drew out a cloth. As he opened it in the starlight she saw gold, emeralds, and rubies.

"These rings belong to the maharaja. Sunil would kill to possess them, for they are the royal rings of the family dynasty. They belong to Prince Adesh."

His use of the Indian name was deliberate, to build a wall between her and the child she knew as Gem.

Coral remained silent, not trusting herself to speak. She watched as he folded the cloth and placed it back inside his jacket. She swallowed. "I feel proud that God allowed me to save his life. We must save him now too, Jace!"

He drew her into his arm. "Yes. I am sorry to hurt you," he whispered. "You could consider contesting his right to the throne, but I doubt if you will gain any help from the East India Company. Sunil is on the throne now, and he is no friend of the English presence in Assam. When troops arrive from Calcutta they will seek to overthrow him. The Company will see young Prince Adesh as the key to their hold in north India. Because of past ties with you, they will expect the boy to be sympathetic to the English."

Coral concentrated on the steady beat of Jace's heart beneath her ear. She had lost Gem, but she had Jace. Together they would have a new life in Darjeeling. In time she would have her own son. *Jace's son.*

And Gem? Melancholy stole over her heart. She would never forget the child of the monsoon. And as though a wind stirred, bringing back that night so long ago, her memory found its way back to Jemani and the little hut. Visions of the birth of Gem played before her with rich clarity. She could see Jemani's lovely face, hear her words as if repeated in the night wind:

"Jesus," whispered Jemani so sweetly that Coral's breath had paused. She watched Jemani's lips move softly into a sigh. Again Coral seemed to feel her fingers, hear her whispering, "Take . . . my son. His godmother— you promised—no untouchable. . . ."

"No untouchable indeed—a prince!" Coral repeated as she rested the side of her face against Jace's rough jacket. With those words she realized that Jemani had been trying to tell her that Gem did have royal blood, but she had died before she could explain.

In her memory she felt the rain, remembered carrying the baby to the ghari to bring him to the Kendall mansion. She could see Jace in the rain too, hear his smooth voice warn: "I dislike the idea of a girl ending up with a broken heart."

She came back to the moment, aware of the still night. How long they stood there she did not know. He simply held her, and she took solace in his love.

She raised her head. "Where is Prince Adesh?"

"Burma. Zin has him. Indian gurus have been schooling him for the throne."

She felt a stab. She had taught him of Christ, but how much could a small child be expected to remember? Very little. Did he even remember her?

"Listen, Coral. A rajput friend sent word to me at Sualkashi that Sunil has discovered where his nephew is. Gokul and I have little time if we are to stay ahead of him. Sunil has the loyalty of the maharaja's army, and he will try to stop us."

Suddenly she remembered the nightmare, and it brought cold fear. She held to him tightly, her eyes wide and pleading. "Do not go!"

He showed faint surprise, then smiled, but his voice was kind. "After all the zeal and prayers you have expended to locate him, and how you begged me to return him?"

"We'll hire mercenaries to find Gem. Stay with me, Jace. It was you in the awful dream!" she whispered.

"What dream?" he asked gently. "The one you had so often in London?"

"Yes, yes, only this was far worse, for *you* were in the fire with me. You disappeared. Both you and the child slipped from me into the flames and were taken away—Jace, I am afraid."

"Since when do you interpret prophecy from nightmares? Darling Coral, you've had a traumatic day, and you fell asleep disturbed. It is natural you would have a bad dream."

"No, no, you were with me helping to save Gem, just as you have been all these long months. And in the dream you had him in your grasp—only neither of you could escape. Please! Do not go. If anything happens to you I won't be able to stand it!"

"Coral!" He held her tightly, soothing her hair. "It was only a nightmare; it was not real. I will come back. Nothing can keep me from you."

"This time it was different. Both of you were in danger."

"Perhaps I was always in the dream, but you weren't

aware of it until tonight. Finding Gem has filled our subconscious thoughts. I do not believe the Lord is terrifying you with nightmares. Does not the Scripture say He speaks through His word?"

"Yes, you are right, only—what if it is a warning?"

"I am already alert to danger and the traps of Eastern intrigue. This is one time I do not need handwriting on the wall. God gave me a mind, and He expects me to use it. I'm aware Zin is a dangerous man. And Sunil will kill me if he can. But I am not going to give him the opportunity."

He lifted her face to his, and the glint of confidence in his eyes brought her courage.

"I expect to come out of this alive, and with Gem. India needs him, and I have faith enough to believe he will always think of you as his mother. He will want a relationship with you even if he does sit on the throne. Whatever happens on this excursion, the Lord is Sovereign. Is this the brave young woman who was willing to face Sir Hugo, Natine, and a host of ghazis to build a mission school? God is answering the prayers you have invested in Gem. Will you let fear steal your peace and paralyze you at the very gate of victory? I don't think so."

His knowledge and confidence in God went far deeper than she had hoped. Coral's voice quavered. "You never spoke like this before. You are right, your armor is missing, and I like it."

"I'll come back," he said again softly. "Now that He has brought us together, we will trust Him with our future."

Her eyes closed tightly, and her palm clenched. *Please, Lord. Let our lives merge into one, and with your light shining upon us.*

She raised her lips to meet his as he bent to kiss her

goodbye, and they held each other. Then he loosed her grip and turned to mount the horse while she stood watching.

He looked down at her, and Coral stared up at him, holding back her anxiety. Then he rode away, and she watched in the darkness until his shadow disappeared and the horse hooves left no sound on the wind.

Gone. She shivered, folding her arms across her chest and looking up past the tree branches toward the sky. The dark clouds were building.

She turned quickly and ran from the road onto the carriageway. There were dim lights glowing in the lower half of the house. By now Ethan and Hugo would be preparing to leave to search for her father. She must slip past them unseen, reach her room safely and bolt the door. If Ethan came and knocked, she would not answer. And when they returned with her father and Seward, she would tell him she loved Jace Buckley.

14

Except for the golden glow from the lanterns in the front hall and ends of the stairway, the house was concealed in darkness when Coral slipped through the servants' door near the cook room.

From the back of the mansion, she made her way quietly to the stairway, surprised that the family was not up waiting for her, yet relieved to be able to escape to her room.

Did Kathleen and Jan-Lee not inform the others of the fire? Had no one else heard her run from the house except Jace? Yet, if her mother was awake she would be here waiting for her with words of encouragement.

Evidently her mother's health had caused her to sleep soundly through the confusion, Coral decided, and Kathleen had not awakened her. But where were Ethan and Uncle Hugo?

She glanced cautiously about as she came to the wide stairway, then began to quietly mount the stairs. As she reached the fourth step, the door to her father's office suddenly opened. Light showered across the red stone floor. Her heart flinched as she paused, expecting to see the foreboding shadow of Sir Hugo framed against the light.

Coral let out a sigh of relief. Ethan stood there, carelessly attired in an open white shirt, his sandy hair tousled. He looked almost boyish as he walked swiftly to the stairs, but upon seeing his agitated expression, she knew his mood was far from being harmonious. She did not like the look in his usually quiet gray eyes, and as he moved closer to the bottom stair, the lantern light revealed a crafted leather holster, worn over his left shoulder, housing an ivory-handled pistol.

Jace was right, she thought with alarm. *Ethan is a man of irrational moods*. Where had she ever gotten the notion he was a gentle physician? He was a man of impatience and rash judgment when confronted by obstacles threatening his expectations.

She became aware that she was clutching his engagement necklace, and unobtrusively moved her hand into the billowing folds of her skirts.

"Are you all right, darling?"

The word of endearment came unnaturally, as though to bind her.

"Yes. Only tired and weary. I am going up to bed. Good-night, Ethan."

She mounted the stairs, feeling his overly anxious gaze.

"What were you doing so long with the major? You have been gone for two hours."

She already felt irritation toward him because of his deceit, and her voice was harsh. "Are you accusing me of impropriety?" Seeing the flicker of pain and anger, she sighed and added more kindly, "I do not wish to talk now. You too should get some rest before leaving with Uncle."

She turned, hoping to escape further confrontation, but his mood turned to frustration.

"Kathleen told me you were with the native girl. She lied to me. You were alone with the major. I suspect he sought to turn you against me."

Her nerves were taut after the evening's traumatic events. She turned sharply to look down at him, prepared to accuse him of his own lies, but bit them back. "Do lower your voice. You will awaken the household."

"They will hear soon enough of your being alone with Buckley on the dark road to the hatcheries. I know he plans to come between us. He took advantage of you in the palace garden. You must stay away from him, Coral. He is a scoundrel and no gentleman."

Her face was strained and pale, and the jewels dug into her sweating palm. She could have flung them at his feet, asking if his lies were marks of the gallantry he insisted Jace did not have.

Suddenly, Ethan no longer reminded her of the physician she had come to think well of in London. She was discovering hints of temperament that reminded her of Uncle Hugo. No, Ethan was not as dark, nor as calculating, and he was unable to remain cool the way Sir Hugo did.

She wondered why she had never noticed this before. Had she been too occupied guarding her heart against Jace? Or was it because Ethan had not yet shown his capacity for deceit? His opportunities had improved since arriving at Kingscote. He now considered her his betrothed, and he was willing to insist she had vowed. He would expect a Christmas wedding and pretend injury when refused. Jace threatened the fulfillment of what he considered to be *his*, and that provoked him to irrational behavior.

But was that so unusual? Ethan had also tended to be unreasonable on the river journey. There had been the quarrel with Jace over the sacrifice to Kali, and the insistence of taking the barge and his medical supplies against the advice of those more experienced than he.

Perhaps these quirks were small enough in themselves, but were they not typical of his temperament? Far worse was his recent threat to duel with Jace. And what of his lies to her about Sualkashi and withholding the truth from her about Jace losing his vision? These, she thought, were far more serious.

Disturbed, Coral came down the stairs and brushed past him into her father's office. At least in here, his voice would not be heard throughout the house. The last thing either of them needed was Uncle Hugo coming down.

Standing at the window, she turned as Ethan entered and shut the door. He faced her, pale and stiff, and was about to say something when his eyes reached her empty throat.

The engagement necklace—she gathered the loose strand of gems more fully into her palm.

Ethan gathered his emotions into a dignified demeanor. "The major and I shall settle this disagreement as two gentlemen. Where is he?"

Her emotions snapped. "He has left. And for your sake I am glad. You are behaving immaturely."

"I think not. I shall not be dishonored."

"Dare you speak of such injured honor when it is you who have lied to me? The major had more than a light wound in the rebellion. He lost his sight! Ethan! How could you keep anything so traumatic from me?"

Her urgent demand stripped him of his offended arrogance, and he stood without making a sound. Then, as though coming out of a daze, he turned away.

"For Jace to think he might lose his vision was a terrible dilemma," she said. "He thrives on adventure; he is a soldier, a sea captain. Had he truly gone blind he would forever remember visions of the sea he loves, the wind, the stars. . . . He would be the most miserable of men. Yet you refused to tell me."

"I had my reasons," he said dully. "When he was wounded near Plassey you insisted on going to him. Believe me, I feared for your future if the major got his way."

"I see. I am far better off with my future in your hands—and in Uncle's. It doesn't matter that you both have become adept at deceiving others."

"Do you think I wished to deceive you? I didn't plan it, but when I arrived you were so obviously concerned for him. In order to protect you I found myself resorting to methods not altogether honorable. But I knew his loss of vision was only temporary. There was no reason to alarm you when you already had enough concern with your father."

She doubted his reason for keeping silent.

"No, Ethan, you feared I would send a message to him if I knew, that I would learn how you also lied about his marriage to the Indian girl at Sualkashi—no, do not bother to explain."

"Jace has his sight back just as I knew he would! What of me? How long did you expect me to wait for your answer? Until he decided whether or not he loved you enough to ask you to marry him? I could not bear to see you running after the likes of him. You are a Kendall. It is only right you should marry me. It is the wish of Sir Hampton and Elizabeth."

Coral thrust forth her hand displaying the flashing necklace. "No, and I'll not marry you to please the family. I too was wrong, and I am sorry. I should never have accepted this from you. Now you must understand there is nothing more between us."

"Do not be hasty, I admit it was a mistake on my part, a foolish one, one I'll never make again. Do give me another chance to prove myself."

"No. I fear you find it too easy to revert to lies and deceit to manipulate people and situations for your own ends, just like Sir Hugo."

He flushed with anger and embarrassment. "But you will think nothing of throwing yourself at Buckley! A man who is nothing, who has nothing. You cheapen the Kendall name and behave like some dockside girl—and I am certain the major has known many!"

Her slap cracked the silence. The mark from her hand showed visibly on his cheek. As though shocked from his behavior, he looked stricken, defeated. He groaned, sinking with dejection into her father's chair, head in hands.

"Dear God, why did I say that. I did not mean it—I swear I didn't, Coral. Your decency and character is above reproach. I—" he stopped.

Coral could not speak.

"I am sorry," he choked.

Her rage left her as quickly as it had come, leaving her weak. She laid the necklace on the desk, then turned and opened the door.

Ethan stood in anguish. "Coral, wait—"

She felt calm now, and looking back over her shoulder said, "I am going to marry Jace Buckley as soon as he returns from Burma with Gem. And if anything happens to my father, I shall order both you and Uncle off this property, even if I must hire mercenaries to do it."

She turned and walked briskly across the hall to the stairway, determined to pay him no heed as he followed her.

"Coral—" He paused on the stair, looking after her with agony.

Coral turned, her expression without sympathy. "Enough lies. Enough deceit. I've had little else from either you or Hugo since I set foot in London. There will be no more. My mind is made up. You might as well leave Kingscote and return to London. The masquerade is over."

"Never mind Kingscote, never mind marriage! I won't have you think I'm involved in any of this rot! It is your respect I want now, nothing else."

Coral would not stop, nor did she look back as she went up the stairs, her shoulders straight.

———————

Ethan stared after her, his stomach in knots. His sweating palm balled into a fist. Hugo had provoked him to this.

Sir Hugo . . . his uncle . . . his father.

Father! What a miserable jest! Hugo had left domineering scars on Ethan's soul from the moment he had taken him away from his mother as a boy.

"The woman he pushed in the dirt," he murmured, his heart thudding in his chest so loudly he began to breathe heavily. "That was *my mother,* whether she bore me out of wedlock or not. Yet he pushed her into the dirt without a thought, the way he does everything that stands between him and what he wants. He had better plans for marriage than my mother . . . he saw an opportunity to marry Margaret Roxbury, a wealthy cousin. He has broken every rule, schemed to destroy Margaret's relationship with Colonel John Warbeck in order to marry her, not for love, but for a hefty stake in the Roxbury and Kendall silk—and he won."

Ethan stood there in an emotional daze, staring blankly up the empty stairway. Much of what she had accused him of was true. He had aided Hugo's schemes at first; his dream to possess the wealth and position to pursue his medical research had been too strong to resist. When Coral arrived in London so ill, he had cooperated with Hugo. He always did, except in Guwahati. Now he had come to love her; yet there seemed to be no hope of winning her love in return, nor even her respect. Coral was right. He was becoming like Hugo.

"Deceit learned from my father," he whispered. "I resorted to it too easily. And if I had gotten by with it, would it have bothered me? Like Hugo I could resort to other deceits to get what I wanted. I would become to Coral what Hugo was to Margaret, hating myself all the while, and lying my way through to protect myself from being unmasked. Yes . . . I have learned well from my father."

Yet Coral was too wise to be manipulated by either of them.

As he stood there thinking, he did not hear the muffled steps behind him in the darkened parlor, where the wide double doors stood open. Someone had been alerted by the arguing voices—and had come to listen.

The steps behind Ethan quietly retreated, unnoticed.

15

There came a sudden jerk to the side of her bed, and Coral awoke with a start, staring into the darkness. What time was it? Who was there, or had she only jumped in her sleep? She was surprised to find that her heart was thudding.

This is foolish. There is nothing to fear. Ethan and Hugo had ridden out with the rajputs the previous morning.

The odd sensation of alarm persisted. For a moment or two she lay still, trying to identify what had awakened her from a sound sleep, and wondered that she should feel so tense.

Another sound . . . the wind rattling the bamboo shades on the verandah doors, but she heard nothing more from the sleeping house.

The night was muggy, smothering her behind the mosquito netting that was drawn closed about her bed. Then, somewhere in her room, she heard a floorboard squeak. Every nerve in her body came alert, and she had to force herself to sit up, trying to breathe quietly so she could strain to listen.

She eased one hand out from beneath the netting,

moving cautiously, and reached to the bedstand to light the lantern. Another swoosh of wind coming from the direction of the wide, dark river made the shades snap, and also sent the netting around her bed fluttering. Coral let out a sigh of relief. It was only the wind. She must have left the verandah doors open before going to bed— *But I thought I latched the doors.*

She was certain she had done so, since the dry lightning signaling the monsoon kept her awake with its blinding flashes.

With the lantern now lit, she took her silk dressing gown from off the mahogany bedpost and wrapped it about her. The polished floorboards felt cool beneath the soles of her feet as she stood there for a moment feeling the wind. Wind was unusual at this time of year, she thought.

Again she wondered what time it was and decided that she had been asleep for several hours and that it must be nearing two in the morning. With the sheen of the lantern light illuminating the room, she walked to the verandah to shut the doors, wondering that her head felt a little odd. She recalled the lemon drink she had enjoyed with her mother and sisters before they all retired for the night, but decided that she was being overly suspicious because of past druggings. She felt a qualm, thinking of Ethan. She had been hard on him, perhaps too much so.

Coral tightened her dressing gown about her and reached to close one side of the double doors against the night, feeling a chill crawl up her back as though unfriendly eyes watched her. She turned quickly and glanced about the shadowed bedchamber and saw nothing unfamiliar.

"I'm overreacting to all the strain of these last days," she murmured to herself aloud, adding ruefully, "Dear

Uncle Hugo is gone. There will be no more druggings."
In the darkness of uncertainty, she murmured, "When
my spirit was overwhelmed within me, then thou knew-
est my path," quoting Psalm 142:3.

She paused to take a deep breath of night air, hoping
to settle the queasiness in her mind. Maybe the lemon
refreshment they drank had spoiled. Perhaps her mother
and sisters were feeling the same symptoms.

The wind had stilled as suddenly as it had risen, and
nothing moved outside the verandah on the estate
grounds. Deliberately she stood a moment longer to
squelch her unease, and looked up at the beads of white
stars that were strung across the black velvety sky. And
Jace . . . where was he now? Did he think of her as she
thought of him. . . ? Below, the silhouette of coconut
palms lined the edge of the lawn down to the river that
lay still like glass, reflecting the starlight. From somewhere in the distant jungle came the familiar sounds of
wildlife.

Sometimes the birds sound positively eerie, she
thought, listening to their cackles and hoots, almost as
if they mocked her attempt at a positive outlook on the
future.

She closed the other side of the verandah door, shutting out the jungle sounds. This time she would slide the
lock into place to make certain the wind could not blow
them open again.

She turned and something caught her attention. It
was her red and brown rattan basket where she kept
personal items: her King James Bible from Granny V, a
number of letters, some from her deceased brother, Michael, mementos belonging to Gem's baby days, and the
precious ebony cheetah that Jace Buckley had given to
her in Calcutta aboard his ship. A faint smile touched
her lips as she remembered.

She stood looking at the basket . . . strange. It was sitting on her bed, inside the mosquito netting. Had she set it there when she retired? No, it had been on the rosewood chair by her wardrobe.

She climbed into her bed and lifted the lid on the basket, setting it aside. She was about to reach inside the familiar hollow when there came a slithering movement from within. A hissing sound spat its rage, filling her ears.

Coral froze. A head lifted—the flat head of a cobra, its beady eyes immediately fixing upon her. Slowly the head moved from side to side. Coral wanted to scream but went weak with terror. Trapped! The cobra had already been riled. There was no way to climb out of bed without moving the feather mattress or pulling aside the netting. She was certain any movement from her would provoke it into striking.

Don't move, she told herself.

Then she heard it. The floor squeaked. . . .

Someone was in her room! Whoever had planted the cobra had been there all along. Had the rattan basket been placed on her bed while she stood on the verandah? But she had seen no one—

Her wardrobe, of course. No wonder she had felt unfriendly eyes! And whoever it was had come to make certain the deadly work was accomplished—

Coral screamed, but her voice sounded only a feeble protest. Drugged—the lemon drink before bed was working. . . .

The cobra's hiss filled her ears like a reverberating curse, the cold coils came unwound, the flat head darting in a momentary flash. The fangs sunk deeply into her arm and held. She gasped.

The cobra drew back, slithering across the cover and under the mosquito netting, leaving two small punctures in her arm. Her dimming vision watched in a sickening daze as its body slowly disappeared off the bed onto the floor matting.

She reached a hand to her arm. She must make a tourniquet, lance it, let the blood run to keep the poison from reaching her heart, but she could not move. Within minutes now it would all be over. . . .

Death was coming to silence her, to mock and smother her protest, to swallow her up in waves of darkness . . . no one to help . . . no one till morning. Too late then. In a few minutes she would sink into a stupor and die. . . .

She imagined herself moving from the bed, straining to toss aside the covers, to move the netting, to stagger to the door, into the darkened hall, screaming for help. But she could not—

Coral thought she was floating away. Kingscote was receding, and she was alone. She found herself in a valley, walking slowly. As she walked, the valley grew narrower and the shadow of death fell across her path. The sides of the mountains, reaching steeply toward a pale sky, closed her in, blocking out the sunlight. Yet there was no fear, only a sweetness of soul that promised the walk would not disappoint her, nor would it hurt. A gentle wind beckoned.

But unexpectedly, Coral found the sweet wind was catching her up and taking her back, back down the shadowed valley from where she had first come, and her eyes fluttered open and she heard her voice filling her mind and she was yet laughing and saying: "I saw Him, and He smiled at me . . . no, I don't want to wake up. I do not want to come back! No!"

Coral gasped, awake. She was in her bed at Kingscote again. She stared into the fearful face of Natine's niece. Preetah was sweating and breathing heavily, and her eyes were wide. Her hair was disheveled as though she had been in a fierce struggle. There was blood on the side of her face above her eyebrow, as though she had been struck, and her sari was torn.

"Coral, oh, thank your God, you are not dead!"

"I d-don't want to come back. . . ."

"It is well now, you rest in sleep. You will be very ill for many days with a great fever, but your God will help you. And memsahib is coming to you soon. She is trying to wake up now."

————

Preetah had awakened Elizabeth Kendall, shaking her by the shoulders, as she refused to respond and only moaned. It had been Preetah's words that had shocked her awake.

"Memsahib, wake up. It is your daughter Coral. She is bitten by a cobra and is dying! Wake up!"

Elizabeth was out of bed, grabbing the bedpost to support herself as Preetah ran back out calling for Kathleen.

Elizabeth lost her balance again and grabbed hold of the bedpost. Each step was laborious. She must reach Coral. . . .

I've been drugged, she thought with alarm.

She closed her eyes as her brain whirled and her stomach turned. She inched her way to the door, finding herself treading water that dipped left and right.

"Heavenly Father, help me! Help me reach Coral—"

She leaned her head against the post, drawing in deep breaths, trying to clear her mind.

Footsteps. . . .

Elizabeth opened her eyes, expecting Kathleen or Jan-Lee.

It was Natine.

Through her blurred vision she could see that his usually immaculate white jacket was soiled with something dark—blood. He was out of breath and in great agitation.

"Sahiba, we have chased the intruder away, Preetah and I. He went through verandah. A rajput, I think. I have men out searching the grounds hoping to trail him."

Elizabeth stared at him.

Natine watched her, his face strained, his hands folded tightly against his chest as though in pain. "Memsahib, can you hear me? Go back to bed. All is well. I kill the cobra with burra-sahib's military sword hanging in hall." He held up the bloody sword in proof. "Preetah has cut and already bled Miss Coral's arm. She will live, though very ill. Go back to bed, sahiba. You too are very ill."

Could she believe him? Dare she? Coral had warned her about the major's suspicions, but would Natine go so far as to attack her daughter with a cobra?

Natine may be innocent. Perhaps there had been an intruder in Coral's room who planted the cobra. The rajput that Hugo had left to guard them . . . and had there not been an intruder the night Gem was stolen from the nursery?

"Miss Elizabeth," came Jan-Lee's urgent voice as she ran into the room from the shadowed corridor. "I bring strong medicine to make you better! Drink all of it!"

Elizabeth felt a cup pressed to her lips. The odor was nauseating. She tried to push the cup away, but Jan-Lee was insistent.

"It will make you vomit, but you must. It will help. Trust me!"

"Do not listen, sahiba!" cried Natine. "She lie! It is more drugs!"

Natine was beside Jan-Lee, thrusting the cup from her hand. It fell with a clatter, spilling the contents.

209

"Vile beast!" Jan-Lee shouted at him. "What have you done?"

Elizabeth knew her faithful ayah too well. She tried to focus on Natine. "Who placed the cobra to kill my daughter!"

Natine's mouth tightened. "If sahiba thinks I would do so much evil, it is best I leave Kingscote for the village and not come back."

"You speak well, Natine. Return when Sir Hampton arrives."

Her eyes blurred, the room was spinning, and she could not see his expression. His voice was growing distant, but she thought she heard his voice unexpectedly break with emotion.

"I am innocent, sahiba! I am faithful to the Kendall family! It is not I!"

Elizabeth's brain weaved to and fro. Cobras—yes, they were everywhere now. She could see them crawling, slithering all over her floor, crawling toward her bare feet.

She clenched her teeth, shut her eyes, and her soul cried out to God. Elizabeth took a step and staggered, but Jan-Lee caught her, easing her down to the floor. Jan-Lee cradled Elizabeth in her lap as if to protect her.

"You!" she hissed at Natine. "I know the truth! Evil shall come upon your head, Natine."

"You speak like crazy old woman, Jan-Lee. Am I fool to bring a cobra to Coral's room?"

"You hate her. You knew the sepoy who stole Rajiv and Jemani's son that night. I have told Coral the baby was not Gem, because of the scar on his foot. She ask me again as soon as she come home, and we talk many hours. I take her to little grave out in the family cemetery, but she did not weep, because she knows—we both know it is not Gem."

210

Natine walked toward her, still holding Sir Hampton's sword. "You croak like a frog from the stagnant pool, words you know nothing about. I knew sepoy, yes. He served Rajkumar Sunil at Guwahati. I say nothing to Miss Coral because to search for Rajiv's son would mean death to her and many Kendalls. I knew who Rajiv was—a prince—and Jemani too has royal blood. Rajiv confided in me," he boasted. "He thought me a friend. It was I, Natine, who sent warning to maharaja that Prince Sunil would take Rajiv's son. It was I who warned him in time so he could save the boy!"

"You lie," said Jan-Lee. "And when Sir Hampton comes, I will tell him all. I was fool not to tell him everything at once. No more will I be fool."

Natine hissed at her. "It is *you* who sneak about in masquerade as faithful ayah. You have them all tricked, but not me. You are Burmese, an outsider to both English and Indians on Kingscote."

"You are insane on your own evil drugs. You drugged them tonight. You placed the cobra."

"No. And it was not I who put the dagger in Rajiv's heart, nor helped Sunil take Gem from Miss Coral, though I knew for her to take the child would only mean much trouble. I tried to warn, but no one would listen."

Jan-Lee sucked in her breath and stared at him. "No one believes your lies."

"It is Burma who fights Assam. The Burmese soldiers cross our border and fight skirmishes with English outpost! Do you not send secret messages to Burmese soldiers now attacking the borders of Kingscote? You are loyal to Burma."

Jan-Lee's face contorted with a dart of fright. "I am loyal to Miss Elizabeth, to Coral. I would give my life for them."

"No. I know your secret, woman. I know who you are.

211

You have venom in your heart for us all. Only Burmese Warlord Zin do you serve. Is he not of your family blood, Jan-Lee?"

"They will never believe you. I have deep affection for Elizabeth, for Coral—I have held her in my arms; I have wept when she was ill; it was I who nursed her when she was ill with fever after Gem was abducted. When she was in London, it was I who wrote her the truth about Gem being alive."

"If you are so loyal, then why is memsahib going into brain sickness? You fool everyone but me."

A moaning sound came from Elizabeth.

"You heard her order! She bid you go! Take your evil Kali and go from Kingscote!"

Natine turned with grave dignity and walked to the door. He glanced back over his shoulder. "I go. But I will come back. And when I do, I will have proof you are the betrayer."

Jan-Lee cringed at his threat. "You plot to destroy me to make yourself look innocent. But what proof you may bring will turn to ashes."

"I have friends in village, so think before you try to have me silenced and thrown in river. It may be I have one of your letters."

He went out, leaving the door open.

Jan-Lee followed him into the hall, her face ashen. She watched as his white turban disappeared and he went down the stairway.

She ran back into Elizabeth's bedroom and struggled to carry her back to the bed.

"What is it? What is wrong?" cried Kathleen, appearing in the doorway. She watched Jan-Lee struggle to lay her mother upon the bed. Kathleen felt drowsy, but Preetah had forced her awake, daring to dump water on her! Preetah had refused to talk and seemed to be on the verge of hysterics. "Go to memsahib," she kept repeating.

Kathleen rushed into the darkened room as her mother began to thrash about on the bed. She grabbed hold of her. "Mother!"

Kathleen crawled on top of her to hold her down by the shoulders. "Jan-Lee, go for Coral!"

"She will not come to help this time. She was bitten by cobra."

For a moment Kathleen could not think. The emotional blow felt like a dagger between her shoulder blades. Cobra! And her mother—what was going on?

"Jan-Lee! Do something!" she cried, wrestling to hold her mother down.

Jan-Lee fell to her knees, weeping, and Kathleen glanced over to see an old broken woman. The ayah's sobs mingled with the throaty noises Elizabeth was making, and Kathleen knew real fear. Through her own sweat she could see the face of her mother, white, her lips bared back and her teeth gritting together.

Kathleen wanted to faint, to go tearing from the room, screaming at the top of her voice. She would run to Coral, but Coral, always the steady one, could not help her. Their father was gone, Alex—even Jan-Lee was overwrought. Where is Marianna?

Her mother had broken from her grasp.

No one to turn to . . . alone.

"Lord, help me! I don't know what to do. Just help me!"

A logical thought came to her mind, bringing a breath of calmness. "Okay, one thing at a time," murmured Kathleen, and as if in a daze, she went to work, grabbing the top sheet and tying her mother to the mattress until the fit ceased.

While she worked, she prayed continually, but her words were only His name spoken again and again. A peace had come to guard her heart like sentinels of angels with drawn swords. *We're not alone.*

Jan-Lee lingered beside the bed, where Elizabeth was now unconscious and still, yet breathing laboriously.

Kathleen knelt on the floor, hands clasped on the bed, her head bowed.

Jan-Lee stood and, leaning over the bed, brushed her unsmiling lips across Elizabeth Kendall's forehead. Without a glance at Kathleen, she then appeared to take on swift energy. She jerked and ran toward the door. "We need doctor. I trust no one here to go with news. I go myself. I need horses for change on long ride."

"Yes, have one of the manjis take you by boat to the village tehsildar. He may know what to do about the drug."

"The village is not to be trusted. I must ride hard and overtake Doctor Boswell."

Kathleen's mind staggered at the dilemma facing them. Unless Ethan was found, there was no one to distinguish the drug used on her mother. Who would do such an evil thing? Natine? A rajput loyal to Prince Sunil? Did someone want them *all* dead?

16

Marianna's pale brows inched together above sober blue eyes. Her reddish blond hair was drawn into a smooth chignon, giving her the appearance of maturity. Her anxious gaze scanned Coral's face, flushed with high fever. Seeing the perspiration around her golden hair, she wrung out the wet cloth and proceeded to cool her face and throat.

Marianna had awakened that morning from a deep slumber, her tongue feeling thick and fuzzy, and no amount of scrubbing could take the strange taste from her mouth. . . . "Whoever planted the cobra drugged us all, to keep us from hearing Coral's scream and from coming in time to bleed the venom from her arm," she murmured. That someone had done so, and used a more potent drug on her mother, sickened her.

She thought of her mother, sometimes writhing in her bed, sometimes yelling out aimlessly, then lapsing off to sleep. Marianna shut her eyes tightly to block out the image. It would be too easy to sink into feelings of fear and despair. This time she must stand without the strength of Coral and her mother. Yet her decision to be strong rose to mock her. *Silly little Marianna, with no courage or convictions of your own.*

Her mouth set. No. She was no longer a child, but a young woman, and she must mature. She had spent the days in prayer for her mother and sister, and now she must leave them in the hand of their Master.

Yet the question demanding an answer came again. Who would do such a thing? There was no way a cobra could slither unseen into a second floor bedchamber. She glanced toward the bedroom door, but what did she expect to see? Any enemy would appear no more dangerous than the loyal servants who calmly went about their duties. How loyal were they, even those she had known since childhood?

It was Natine, of course, who else?

There was nothing more to fear, for he was no longer in the house. Her mother had ordered him off Kingscote until their father returned. Natine had gone to his relatives in the village, yet his niece Preetah had remained.

"But is it possible Natine was innocent, that he was telling the truth?"

Marianna thought of the rajput guard whom Natine had accused. Uncle Hugo had left the big, handsome, dark-bearded Indian in the house to protect the women from Burmese infiltrators or even Prince Sunil. Natine had accused the rajput, who had now disappeared . . . or was he somewhere about the estate grounds—or even in the house?

Thunder grumbled in the sky above Kingscote. Marianna left the side of Coral's bed and went to shut the verandah doors.

Uncle Hugo. . . . Marianna remembered back to the Christmas ball at Barrackpore when she had blundered into a clandestine meeting in the garden between her uncle and a mysterious Indian in a yellow turban. Coral had long since ceased to discuss the incident, and Marianna wished to forget it. Now those uncertainties about her uncle were rekindled.

A brilliant flash of dry lightning startled her. She drew the heavy velvet drapes over the split-cane shades on the doors and turned to look toward her sister to find the bedroom door ajar. Her breath caught.

"Who is it?" she demanded nervously.

Preetah stepped quietly through the door, not looking at Marianna but toward Coral, who moved restlessly in her fevered sleep. "Yanna says that Thilak has returned from the road going east without news of Jan-Lee."

There were reports that scattered Burmese infiltrators had been seen on the road, and the risk of travel was now greatly heightened. Since Thilak, the head Indian worker over the hatcheries, was a friend of Yanna's, Marianna had sent Thilak to catch up with Jan-Lee to protect her on the road.

"Thilak says she is now far ahead, but does sahiba wish for him to arm some workers and try to find her anyway?"

"No, I suppose not. As he says, Jan-Lee will be far ahead. Perhaps by now she has caught up with Doctor Boswell."

Preetah nodded hopefully and moved softly toward the bed to look at Coral. "Mera comes to take your place now, Miss Marianna. You need rest. And Yanna asks if she may come to help with memsahib."

Yanna was deeply attached to Elizabeth Kendall, and Marianna was relieved that the girl wished to come and assist Kathleen. She gave her permission, and as Preetah turned to leave, Marianna recalled how she had wanted to speak with Preetah alone about the cobra.

Images of having come into Coral's bedchamber and finding Preetah soon after the attack were recalled by Marianna with vivid horror. As she had entered through the door with her mind yet dull, Preetah had been frightened and bolted upright from the foot of Coral's bed, where she had taken vigil. Preetah's sari was torn, there were dark stains on the front, and bruises showed on her cheekbone and above her right eyebrow. Perhaps more frightening than anything to Marianna was the desperate look in Preetah's eyes, as though she might have expected someone else to return.

Marianna had then seen Coral, with her skin a sickly ashen color, twisting and turning about and muttering in her sleep, her arm bandaged.

"She has been bitten by a cobra. It was necessary to cut her arm and allow the blood to run to get rid of the poison. I used permanganate crystals in the wound. I also give a small amount of opium for pain and sleep," Preetah had told her.

The rest of the evening had seemed a nightmare. The nature of their mother's illness was bizarre. Only later did Marianna learn from Kathleen of the seriousness of Elizabeth's condition.

Now, as Marianna watched Preetah, the girl looked nervous.

"May I go now, sahiba? Yanna waits outside for permission."

It was not Marianna's nature to be confrontational. Usually she remained in the background, willing to be uninvolved. Perhaps it was best for the present if she played the silly girl everyone thought she was. *If only Major Buckley would suddenly ride up!* she thought. *He would take care of everything.* But the vain wish to hear horse hooves on the carriageway was silenced by another roll of thunder.

Marianna straightened her shoulders. "Do not go yet, Preetah. I must talk to you about last night."

Preetah's brown eyes grew remote, and Marianna recognized her tension.

"It is time you told me what happened."

"What happened?"

"Yes, the cobra. You saved my sister's life, and the family will never forget. You've not told me how it was that you came just in time. A few minutes more and—and Coral would have died from the venom."

Preetah flushed, pleased, yet her smile quickly faded as she became cautious. "Miss Coral's God watches over her. He had me come."

"Yes, I believe God has more plans for my sister, and that He did have you come. But what would your uncle say if he heard you? You are afraid of Natine."

"It is custom to fear my uncle. I have no father in the village—he died of illness. I and my mother both are grateful to Natine for family care. I must not offend Natine. It was he who spoke to your father about my position here."

Marianna took a risk and said, "Yet you did more than offend your uncle when you fought him to save my sister's life."

Preetah glanced to the door but remained dignified. "Fought against my uncle Natine? I do not understand."

"Yes, you do, Preetah. In order to lash Coral's arm and drain the venom, you had to fight off Natine."

"No, sahiba!"

"Yes, your sari was torn, there was blood on it, and those bruises on your face are from Natine."

Preetah turned pale; her fingers dug into her sari. Marianna drew in a breath and continued, surprised at her own persistence. "There was no intruder, and the rajput did not place the cobra."

"The rajput is gone, as Natine vows. He ran away! That is proof."

"The rajput serves my uncle, and I have an uneasy feeling he is yet about, watching us. Yet I do not think he placed the cobra. You were very brave to risk your life to save my sister, and she and the memsahib will reward you well, and your mother in the village. So you need not fear Natine anymore."

Preetah shook her head wildly. "Words of kindness and reward are taken with gladness, but you are wrong—it was not my uncle."

"Who then?"

Preetah's breathing came rapidly and she jumped to her feet. "You are wrong!" she said simply. "Please, I must go now."

"Did he insist you allow the venom to do its work? And when you would not, he tried to stop you from helping Coral."

Preetah stared at her, then covered her face with trembling hands. Her shoulders shook as she began to weep, holding in her sobs, and she lowered herself into a chair.

"Do not be afraid. No harm will come to you now that he has gone to the village. And soon my father will return with Seward and Alex. Tell me what happened, Preetah, I must know. It might help my mother!"

"Yes, it was my uncle. I—I was late going to bed, because I was helping in the kitchen. I—I saw him put something in the lemon water, though he did not know I saw him, and I was going to empty the pitcher outside before I brought it to the memsahib and your sisters, and was only waiting for him to leave the kitchen. But he did not leave, and Mera brought the refreshment. Later I did worry when I remembered the priest."

Marianna was shaking. "P-priest?"

"From the village. He came to Kingscote early in the morning before the doctor and Sir Roxbury left. He

220

talked with your uncle before he talked to Natine."

"Sir Hugo talked to the priest?"

Preetah nodded. "And the priest brought something to Natine in a basket. When they had all gone from our bungalow, I peek inside the container and saw the cobra. But I did not know what Natine would do! Later, after the lemon refreshment it came to me and I greatly feared! The light was on in Miss Coral's room when I came, and I heard a noise, so I knocked. Miss Coral did not answer, and so I entered and saw the cobra, saw the fang marks on her arm—then I saw Natine on the verandah. Uncle always carries a knife and I begged him for it, but he would not. I fought him for it and screamed for help and Jan-Lee come running down the hall! He heard her and was afraid and angry, and I was able to get the dagger. He ran out past Jan-Lee and I remember no more, except I flung myself onto Miss Coral's bed and tied her arm tightly with scarf, then I cut and bleed her. . . ."

Preetah looked up, her face pale and wet with tears. She stood, taking hold of Marianna. "When memsahib ordered him off Kingscote he searched for me, to make me come with him, but I hid!"

Marianna was trembling, seeing the entire ugly scene played out in her mind. She barely felt Preetah's fingers digging into her arm.

"Natine fears I will talk to your father when he returns from Darjeeling, so he had my mother send for me, saying she was ill. But I did not go to the village as she asked."

"When did you get the message?"

"This afternoon, but I will not leave Kingscote. If I do, he will never let me come back. And what I say about your God watching you, I speak with good feelings. I have learned about His way from Yanna. Natine suspected it so, and knows I helped rescue the untouchables from the crocodiles. I fear to go home to the village."

"Do not leave the house," said Marianna. "He will not dare come back now. The drug used on memsahib, think hard, Preetah! If you can tell my cousin Ethan when he arrives with Jan-Lee, he may know what to do to help her."

Preetah closed her eyes tightly and shook her head. "There are many. I have thought about what it could be. I have searched our bungalow and found nothing. Maybe he got it from the priest."

Marianna did not wish to say what frightened her. Or perhaps from Sir Hugo? He knew all about bizarre Eastern drugs.

"But I will keep thinking, keep searching to tell doctor when he comes."

There was a light knock on the door, and Mera poked her head in. "Yanna waits anxiously downstairs. She wishes to guard the memsahib, she says."

"Yes," cried Marianna with relief. "Tell her to go to my mother's room at once."

Thank God for our Indian friends, thought Marianna.

"I shall take vigil for Miss Coral now," said Mera, gently laying a hand on Marianna. "You rest, little one. You lose weight and grow pale. There is hot tea and cakes waiting in your room. You eat, then go to sleep till supper."

Marianna nodded gratefully, touching her hand to the side of Mera's wrinkled face, and turned to leave the room with a backward glance of concern toward Coral.

———

They had ridden several hours before Ethan understood that Sir Hugo had no intention of going east toward Darjeeling. Ethan had studied the map belonging

to Major Buckley well enough at Kingscote to know that
they were riding northeast.

What lay northeast? The British outpost of Jorhat?

The change in their destination came as a surprise,
although Ethan would have been the first to admit that
journeying to Darjeeling on a mission to locate Sir
Hampton was the last deed of gallantry on his mind. Yet
he had expected Hugo to go there, if only to impede any
rescue effort.

Why was his uncle riding toward Jorhat? Surely he
did not expect to find the major there? Ethan suspected
that Hugo knew of the major's mission to the borders of
Burma to meet with Warlord Zin, although he could not
guess how he had discovered it. Somehow he had known
the night of the fire that Buckley would not go to Jorhat
to inquire into the military mutiny that had taken Major
Selwyn's life.

Did he know that the Indian prince Adesh Singh was
with Warlord Zin?

As they rode, Ethan cast a side glance at his uncle.
Sir Hugo's dark eyes were preoccupied with the thick
jungle growth along the Brahmaputra River. Yet Ethan
did not think he was concerned for tigers.

He expects to meet someone.

Of perhaps even greater concern than his uncle knowing about the major's mission was whether Prince Sunil
knew of it. If he did, Sunil would have Indian warriors
prepared to stop the major, and they would kill him.

Ethan's jaw set tightly, and he refused to think about
what Jace's death might mean to Coral—and yet he did
consider. Would she forget Buckley? Would she in time
turn to him again?

Prince Sunil would also have the Indian child put to
death, thought Ethan. *No, I will have no part in the filthy
business.* He had lost respect for himself, and he had none

left for Sir Hugo. Whatever the future held, dark clouds loomed over any prospects for happiness that he might have had with Coral, or for that matter, with the Kendalls on Kingscote. His hope of a research lab on the plantation was ruined, for even if Coral proved gracious enough to permit his presence, Ethan knew he could not be content seeing her married to Buckley. If there was any hope of beginning anew, he must find it elsewhere. And when he did, he would not carry the blood of either Buckley or Gem on his conscience.

Whatever Sir Hugo was involved in, Ethan made up his mind—his own fingers would not dip into the bowl of blood.

The rajputs made primitive camp for the night. Ethan was unfamiliar with the area between Kingscote and Jorhat, but he guessed they were far from the nearest village. But if Hugo did not expect to find the major at Jorhat, what was the purpose of going there?

But perhaps Jorhat was not their destination. Where, then? He wished he had used his time at Kingscote to learn more of Assam.

Ethan kept back from the light of the campfire, and when he did not watch the rajput warriors, he watched Sir Hugo. Beneath Ethan's jacket his pistol waited, loaded, and he kept a rifle across his legs. Beside him, as though guarding a satchel of gold, sat his leather medical bag.

Sir Hugo came from the darkened trees up to the fire, and the kansamah handed him a vessel of hot broth. Ethan could not read his expression beneath the well-trimmed dark beard, but he noticed his eyes were fixed on the rajput in command of the other warriors. The rajput walked up and spoke quietly, and Sir Hugo answered in fluent Hindi.

Ethan frowned. Being a novice of the language was a

disadvantage. He watched the rajput mount his horse and quietly ride away into the darkness. The faces of the other warriors told him nothing.

How much did the rajput fighters know? He decided they were sworn to Sunil's loyalty and would carry out Hugo's orders to the death.

Ethan knew that he was alone, outnumbered, and up against some scheme that he was not capable of thwarting. Sir Hugo was not a man who easily faced defeat. Just how did Hugo look upon him since his refusal to cooperate at Guwahati? His uncle talked little, and there were times when Ethan wondered if he knew that his loyalties were no longer with him to use and shape as he wished. If he were to oppose his uncle in whatever plan might be underway, he must not let him suspect. . . . And yet Hugo had brought him on the journey knowing that the day would come when he would know they were not in Darjeeling and demand to know why and what they were doing.

He had told Coral that Sir Hugo would never harm him. Was he certain? Whatever Hugo had planned, the fact remained that he was his son.

As dawn broke, they continued riding, and by nightfall they had journeyed still deeper into the jungle frontier. The purple twilight around them was loud with the shrill call of birds and monkeys. Ethan recognized some of the wildlife he had seen on the safari to Guwahati with the major: the small spotted chital deer, monkeys, pelicans near the river, and now and then he spotted a rhino. How long could he convince Sir Hugo he did not know they traveled northeast? And if he could continue the ruse, what would he learn? So far he had discovered nothing. If the rajputs did speak English, they pretended they did not. And his uncle hardly spoke but was consumed with thoughts of his own making.

Perhaps the time had come to openly confront him as to their destination and its purpose, thought Ethan. He looked at Sir Hugo and found his dark eyes and countenance pensive.

———

Jan-Lee, her face resigned to defeat, drew the reins on the sweating horse with its heaving sides. There was no one on the road now. It lay gray and empty and deep in dust, and the silence of dawn magnified every small sound: the shudder of the horse's mouth, the startled shriek of some bird, and Jan-Lee's own uneven breathing. It seemed to her that her progress must be audible a mile away, and that her first hope of overcoming the memsahib's nephew was now impossible.

If the doctor and his uncle Sir Roxbury had traveled this way she would have come upon their tracks by now, leading to some wayside camp, for she had ridden through the night, gaining the distance while they would have stopped to eat and sleep. Her dark eyes searched the road again for fresh tracks, but she found none that convinced her that they had recently passed this way. Why she did not find what she searched for was curious, yet to go on was useless; she would kill the horses and waste precious hours. If memsahib was to be brought help from the evil of the eastern drug Natine had used, then she must look to another source, a source she did not doubt would have the knowledge, but she would risk much to contact him.

Jan-Lee's usual stoic face was lined with care. Dust and sweat left streaks, and her black eyes flickered with internal anguish as she considered her next action—for it might mean her end, and the end of her own Emerald now safely in her bed at Kingscote.

Dawn was breaking with the first pale wash that

brought the dark silhouettes of trees to green and the distant mountains to purple.

Her hand tightened on the reins. The man she must now seek had the knowledge of Eastern drugs, but in seeking his help, she unmasked her face to her own detriment and that of her daughter. It was for Emerald's sake that she had worn the mask. Yet if she must face shame and even death for the woman who had shielded her these many years, she would lift her face up to the glare of angry scowls and hisses.

But would he lay aside his sword long enough to come with her to Kingscote as a friend when he was now a secret enemy? And if he did come, would the Kendall daughters receive him into their English sanctuary? Would he not be seen as a spy who had come to search out their defenses? And if they should accuse him, or question him suspiciously, would he not see his great honor shamed and turn in anger to leave, only then to attack with great fury?

Fear showed in her face as she turned from the direction of Darjeeling and gazed behind her, seeing in her mind the shadowy borders of Kingscote plantation and the beginning of the thick jungle where Burmese infiltrators came and went unnoticed, except when they attacked in secret ambushments.

17

Burma
Fortress of Warlord Zin

The ancient map once belonging to his natural father, Captain Jarred Buckley, had again guided Jace and Gokul safely across the treacherous border into steamy Burma. The secretive trails crisscrossing the thick jungle brought them to the little-known environs of the Burmese warlord, Zin.

It was noon, and the jungle was hot and humid. Traces of sunlight filtered through thick foliage of glossy green, while overhead, the intertwining branches were vibrant with the high screeching of birds. A flash of wings showing brilliant plumage flitted among the branches, and small brown monkeys chattered excitedly.

Gokul climbed down from his horse to walk ahead, and though confident, he maintained the vigilance of a hungry tiger stalking its prey. He stooped to his haunches and studied the rich damp turf smelling of rotting leaves. There were no horse or elephant tracks, only large army ants converging on a tree beetle that had unfortunately crossed their path.

Jace unloosed his pack from the horse and lowered it to the earth, drawing out the clothing that suited the identity he was adopting. The garb had been carefully chosen, for the only way that he might enter the stronghold of Zin was as Javed Kasam.

He dressed quickly while Gokul watched the road. First came the soft undertunic next to his skin, then the English supple chain-mesh shirt carefully hidden by the Eastern outer tunic-jacket of black, worn over heavy tight-fitting trousers. Lastly came the gift from Warlord Zin. Jace knelt and untied the cloth covering. He removed the present he had not worn since his days in Burma. It was an engraved warrior's vest of leather, mounted with a silver and red dragon the size of a man's hand. The sides of the vest were looped tightly with steel rings. The other gift was a Burmese dagger in a wrist-sheath. His own blade he kept in his left boot top. Lastly came the scabbard housing a tulwar.

He picked up his silk turban and stared at it. He touched the side of his dark head and grimaced. He would prefer his old British helmet. He laid the silk aside and opted for the rajput helmet that Gokul had wisely retrieved at the last minute. Made of leather, it was held in place by a colored headband; this was dyed with indigo and embroidered with silver tigers the size of a thumbnail.

Jace walked up to Gokul, who was busily adding the finishing touches to his own masquerade as a guru. He painted the three white brahmin caste marks on his forehead and added a scholar's turban. Jace's mouth turned wryly as Gokul produced fake pearls and a large ruby, which he proceeded to mount onto the front of his turban. He turned to Jace, his dark eyes twinkling mischievously.

"Ah, sahib, you now look upon an enlightened master of India."

Jace folded his arms. "I am awed. I suppose you are at one with the rhythm of the universe."

"But indeed! I am Swami Gokul Sankar—or maybe"—he paused thoughtfully to rub his chin—"Punditji—or should I be his holiness Sri Baba of Lankali?"

"I thought you might be the incarnation of Vishnu." Jace walked to his horse and swung himself into the saddle. He smiled.

Gokul hurried after him, his hand spread across his soft belly. "Actually, I am a Vedantic scholar who has come to teach the maharaja's nephew, Prince Adesh. I shall lecture the prince on meditation to bring him deepened awareness of the divinity within."

"You are certain," said Jace, "that it is divinity, and not a greedy nature that you have discovered within?"

Gokul grinned and patted a hand on his protruding belly. "For only thousand rupees, sahib, my wisdom will deepen your awareness also."

"I am certain, Guru, that in answer to your wisdom, confusion will be rife, and chaos and anarchy will reign supreme."

The last traces of lavender twilight were giving way to a canopy of darkness when they arrived in the city. Icy stars looked down, their cold glitter soon blotched by a low-lying halo of smoke ascending from the town's cooking fires.

Jace and Gokul entered through a seldom-used packed dirt street that was inlaid with square tiles made of Burmese wood. They walked in on foot, leading their horses by the reins, keeping close to the trees.

They approached the homes of shopkeepers, clerks, and poor merchants who could not journey far for their goods and did not fare as well as rich caravan traders. Huts with walls of dried mud and roofs of palm branches lined the narrow road. Beyond, the road opened into a large square that was the noisy marketplace. Even as darkness settled, a number of slow-burning torches were lit, and the babble of hawkers, arguing women, and the merry voices of children filled the sultry air.

Old men, their narrowed eyes empty of expression, sat on their haunches, smoking opium pipes. Near the market square there were stables, and Jace noticed young girls with baskets, gathering manure cakes to use for cooking fuel.

The night breeze drifted to him, heavy with smells of food cooking over fires and the moist jungle that enclosed them.

As he and Gokul neared the center of the city, the scene was drastically altered from one of poverty to wealth and power. Structures of intricate Oriental carvings rose up like small palaces. Teakwood gates opened onto arched bridges that fanned over fountains and pools containing bright-colored fish that darted like jewels under the bronze lanterns. The air was now perfumed with the scent of flowering vines that crept over iron fences. Here the houses were two-storied, their roofs elaborately carved, and screened by wide-spreading trees.

Jace looked upon homes belonging to the wealthy commerce traders who sold to both the Dutch and English East India Companies, offering ivory, teakwood, emeralds, pearls, and Chinese tea.

The narrow streets were a maze of alleyways and avenues with the poor and the slaves performing menial tasks or errands for their rich masters.

He and Gokul were now in the heart of Zin's city, and the wide street merged under an arched bridge of ebony stone; a red dragon gazed down upon them as they passed beneath into a wide plaza with a high wall.

They arrived as the evening fires were being lit in the tall stone idols. Brown-skinned boys in loincloths shimmied up teakwood poles, carrying torches. As they thrust the torches inside to ignite the fires, flames spilled forth like lava from the gaping mouths of stone gods with fat bellies and monkey-gods with fire dancing in their empty eye sockets. Jace carefully noticed the sentries, posted atop the pagodas, looking down on the wide square. They carried the curved sword and the deadly bow with quivers of bamboo arrows. The arrows, he knew, were used more swiftly and with greater accuracy than a rifle shot.

As he casually led his horse forward through the plaza under the dancing firelight, he saw the immense pink sandstone palace-fortress with ferocious royal tigers of marble—the palace of Zin.

The Burmese guards on the steps were wearing black headbands and knee-length leather tunics over loose-fitting trousers of black, and their broad faces and almond eyes showed not a hint of congeniality.

"Getting past the guards will prove next to impossible, sahib."

Jace did not wish to publicly announce the presence of Javed Kasam, for he had enemies, and who knew how many of his old foes were now serving Zin?

"Over there, sahib . . . do you see as I?"

Jace followed Gokul's glance. Standing on the front steps inside the entranceway, a man stood turbaned, wearing conspicuous jewels that gleamed against his bronzed skin. He was an official or guard and stood blocking the inner salon. Before him, there were two plainly clothed men bowing and hastily laying out their wares for him to scrutinize with a cold eye. No doubt the man's task was to screen the valuables being offered for sale by the traveling merchants before showing them to Zin.

Jace watched as the man gestured one of the two aside impatiently. The other must have offered something of interest, for he motioned for a second guard to come and show the man and his wares inside the salon.

Several other merchants were lining up at the steps and Jace and Gokul saw their opportunity.

"Shall I go, sahib? Do we dare risk the jeweled idol of Kali?"

"Stay with our horses and our prize. We will need it, I think, before this venture is over." His eyes were fixed on the official. "I shall risk something else to his greed."

In line at the steps behind the merchants, he heard the impatient dismissal of one disappointed merchant after another.

"Nay, fool, do you think His Excellency has need of English wool here in India's heat? Return it to the miserable feringhis."

When Jace mounted the steps, the official turned to him with impatience, but it swiftly turned to wariness as he scanned him, seeing that Jace was no humble merchant to be scorned. The black eyes took in his weapons, then noticing the dragon on his leather vest, came to meet Jace's gaze.

"I wish to speak with Zin."

The man hesitated, then for reasons of his own he chose to ignore the dragon. He raised a hand sparkling with rings to gesture him aside. "Zin sees no one. I am his eyes. Have you some item worthy of His Excellency? If not, others wait."

"I must see him."

"He has canceled the daily durbar."

"Tonight, then." Jace stood there, one boot resting on

the next step. He glanced past him into the well-lighted salon.

The official's eyes turned cold and speculative. "I think that is quite impossible. His Excellency is having dinner with important guests. As for tomorrow, he will not be here then."

"He is leaving?" Jace was alert.

"His Excellency's plans are his own and not subject to idle discussion. As I said, he has given orders that no one disturb him."

"I must. It is important." Jace held out his palm. As the official's eyes dropped, Jace lifted the cloth above the royal rings of the deceased Maharaja Majid Singh, and the heavy emeralds and rubies appeared to catch fire and gleam in the torchlight coming from the fat-bellied god who sneered down from his pedestal.

"Where did you get *these*?"

"My information is for Zin alone. If he leaves tomorrow, then I will see him tonight."

"Perhaps . . . I might arrange it, however difficult, but I will need to show him the rings first."

Jace met the man's lusty eyes and smiled faintly, but his deft fingers covered the rings with the royal cloth and returned them securely inside his jacket.

The official forced a smile as he turned toward the salon and signaled for a guard. "He may wish to see you. Step this way. You may wait in the salon. Whom shall I say has come to speak?"

"Javed Kasam."

18

When Jace stepped inside the large audience hall, he found that he was one among several who waited to see the warlord. Some were French, others looked to be Portuguese, and all the merchants had something worth the time and attention of Zin. The pompous official who guarded the front steps had done well.

Bronze lanterns brilliantly illuminated the marble floor with colored stone dragons and black cheetahs, but it was the dozen muscled guards surrounding the Burmese warlord who commanded Jace's attention. Shirtless, their black trousers were loose fitting and belted with gold, and each belt supported a scabbard with an Oriental curved blade.

Would he be able to convince Zin that the maharaja had commissioned him to become Gem's new bodyguard and that Gokul was to be the child's official swami? If Zin had heard of the rebellion at Guwahati and knew that Prince Sunil was now on the throne, the cunning Burmese warlord would not willingly surrender Gem—Sunil would offer him much to eliminate the rightful heir.

Jace scanned the audience hall, looking for the warlord.

He tensed. Zin sat on a divan of teakwood covered with red silk. He was not alone. Two Indian men in white turbans conversed with him. As one turned, his face became clearly visible. *Sanjay!*

Jace's former rissaldar-major turned and stared directly into his eyes. He was not masquerading as a native sowar in the Bengal army, nor as the guru whom Jace had seen outside the British residency in Guwahati the night of the rebellion. Sanjay was dressed in the garb of a high Indian official, yet he bore a scabbard with sword.

Would he recognize him in the role of Javed Kasam?

Jace casually turned his head away, but too late. A start of confusion showed on Sanjay's face, then astonishment. Sanjay pointed with triumph. "That man! Seize him! He is an enemy!"

Zin gave some silent command to his dozen warriors, and suddenly Jace was confronted with drawn blades. The guards spanned out, crouched in striking position.

Jace stepped back, holding his weapon. The merchants withdrew to the wall, nervously clutching their wares, giving Jace a clear view of Zin on the crimson divan.

"Is this the manner of welcome you give me, Zin?" called Jace. "I am disappointed. Especially when I bring news of a certain item desirous enough to have caused the death of Ayub Khan."

At the mention of his dead son, the warlord slowly stood, his broad face hard and ruthless. His black eyes flickered over Jace, then recognition struck. He walked forward, and his warriors stepped aside to form an aisle of drawn blades glinting in the light.

"So. The *Cheetah* returns to confront Warlord Zin!"

Jace did not move as their eyes held steadily, then Zin

unexpectedly gave a short laugh. "What is this! Have you turned an honest merchant that you come into my presence in the company of such as these?" And he gave a gesture to the wary merchants who watched from the wall.

"Send them away," Zin told the official. "I will see no more of their treasures tonight. Well, Javed Kasam! What have you to say for yourself?" He grasped Jace's forearms Roman style, grinning wolfishly, his bold black eyes laughing in malicious humor over the incident.

Jace gripped Zin's shoulder with his left hand, yet retained his blade with his right and glanced toward Sanjay. "I have come for that traitor's head."

Zin looked across the audience hall at Sanjay with sudden interest, and caution.

Sanjay watched Jace, and though he did not relent, his uncertainty showed. He glanced toward the open doorway that led onto the steps, but there were guards standing there now, their weapons drawn. Sanjay then looked toward an arch leading off into another section of the palace. A big Burmese man stood there, arms folded across his oiled chest, a black cloth about his head.

"You are a man who respects daring," said Jace to Zin. "I challenge my enemy to a duel. Here, and now."

Zin's eyes glinted like a hungry wolf, for his appetite feasted on a good fight. He chuckled, then turned grim. "You came to the border of Burma to challenge this man? Why do you seek him?"

"Because he is a traitor, and many good men are dead because of him."

Sanjay stared at Jace with hatred. "He lies! His Excellency calls this man by the name of Javed, but he is a feringhi. His name is Buckley. I would remind His Excellency how the arrogant English are also his enemies here in Burma."

Zin cast Sanjay an impatient glance. "I need be reminded of nothing. But this man is no Englishman."

"He wears the uniform of the English military beneath his disguise."

"Do you think me a fool? I know his blood! But to me, he is Javed Kasam, and he will remain so until I know he is truly my enemy."

"He is a sworn enemy of the new raja of Guwahati. If His Excellency is a true ally of Sunil, then you will arrest the feringhi."

Zin, an ally of Sunil. Jace knew he must move forward in his mission with caution. The warlord must know of the rebellion at Guwahati and the assassination of the old maharaja. Had Zin somehow been involved in supporting Sunil? If so, what of Gem?

Danger loomed its deadly head like the shadow of a cobra. The warlord was watching him now with less friendliness, his look speculative.

"You know my past," said Jace. "Let it speak for itself. This traitor Sanjay will say anything to save his head."

"Whom do you now serve?" asked Zin. "The English? Another? Yourself?"

If Jace withheld the truth, Zin would soon know. His chances fared better by speaking plainly. "I am a major in the British Bengal army, but I did not willingly seek it. It was my father's plan, one I felt obliged to accept for the return of my ship."

"You come for no other reason than for this man you say is your enemy?"

"There are other reasons. I have mentioned Ayub Khan."

A tiny flame of greed sprang up in the warlord's eyes as he understood that Jace might have the long-sought-for and coveted idol. He said nothing, for it was not a matter to speak of publicly.

"I have also been sent by the Maharaja Majid Singh," said Jace. "I and the swami," he said of Gokul, who stood unobtrusively to one side.

"The maharaja is dead," said Zin with no emotion.

"Yes. Assassinated by his own nephew Sunil. As for this man," said Jace, looking at Sanjay, "he will answer to the British military in Calcutta for the mutiny at Plassey, or he may save himself a tedious journey by accepting my challenge. What will it be, Sanjay? A duel here and now with the possibility you may kill me and go free, or the firing squad at Fort William!"

Sanjay's eyes spit his hatred, and he seemed about to step forward to accept the challenge. But the second man, who had kept silent until now, stood up. He was older than Sanjay, with gray hair and a certain dignity, and he appeared to be some manner of bureaucrat. Jace did not recognize him from Guwahati but judged him to be one of the maharaja's men.

"Both I and Dewan Sanjay are here on imperial business for the new Raja of Guwahati. Who is this feringhi mercenary to threaten the dewan of Sunil?"

Dewan! Jace's eyes fixed angrily on Sanjay. "So that is the position Sunil promised you for your bloodthirsty treason at Plassey."

Zin was alert as he studied Jace, Sanjay, and the government official with him.

"A duel is unthinkable, Excellency!" warned the older man.

Zin pretended disappointment as he grinned at Jace. "So speaks the Burha Gohain of Guwahati. But—the prime minister is correct. I cannot allow harm to befall Sunil's dewan, despite my sympathy for your earnest desire to confront your enemy. My reputation as a host

241

would be ruined if either of you drew blood from the other. It is unthinkable, friend Javed."

Jace knew it was not his reputation that concerned the warlord. The fact that he was a ruthless leader to be feared was well known. He hesitated only because he was yet uncertain on which side he wished to align himself. Zin saw an opportunity for gain, and like a serpent smelling a rat he would wait; he would play one against the other for the highest gain to himself.

"Arrest him," demanded the Guwahati prime minister. "He is an enemy."

The Burmese official who had guarded the entrance unexpectedly stepped toward the warlord and whispered something.

The official must have mentioned that Jace held the royal rings of the old maharaja, for Zin seemed even more pleased at having opposing sides together under his jurisdiction. He turned toward the prime minister and Sanjay.

"You say Javed is an enemy. Whose? Mine or yours?"

"Any enemy of Sunil is yours as well, Excellency."

"It is I who shall decide, Burha Gohain, no one else." He gestured to his warriors. "Take them all away. I shall decide later who is friend and who is foe of Warlord Zin." He offered an official smile that was about as friendly as the mechanical obedience of his deadly warriors. "You are all my guests until I have wearied of your company."

The warriors moved to escort the furious prime minister and Sanjay from the audience hall.

Jace, too, felt a warrior's hand grasp his arm, but he jerked free and stepped back, his blade still in hand. The guard's eyes showed no emotion, only fanatical dedication to the Burmese warlord.

"Javed Kasam, you will go peaceably," came Zin's friendly voice, but it was absent of warmth. "Later we will speak alone without interruption." He turned to the guard. "Treat our comrade carefully. He is an old friend from the past. We have the same heartbeat—he once worked with my son to rob a Hindu temple."

Jace might have winced at that testimony. It was only half true. As the guards sheathed their blades in unison, so did Jace.

"I have come, Excellency, for the grandnephew of the maharaja."

Zin's black eyes mocked with amusement. "Which raja? Which uncle of Prince Adesh do you represent?"

Jace searched his face. Were there more than one? Certainly he did not speak of Sunil. "Maharaja Majid Singh of Guwahati has been assassinated. I seek to fulfill his dying wish. He authorized me to become the prince's bodyguard. And I bring the wisest man in the East to be his swami." Jace spread a hand and stepped aside. Gokul moved forward with all the grandeur of a king, his head slightly bent as though too holy and profound to be bothered by the mundane situation that had almost caught him up in bloodshed.

Jace managed an expression of grim dignity. "I present the Swami Gokul Sankar Punditji—his holiness Sri Baba of Lankali."

Gokul kept his eyes on the floor. With wolfish humor, the warlord scanned him. "Truly the wisest man in the East?"

Gokul did not answer. Jace stepped to the side of Zin and said in a hushed voice, "He is the Vedantic scholar who has come to lecture, to bring a deepened awareness of the divinity within."

Zin's hard, cynical gaze came to meet Jace's. Jace remained unreadable.

"And the royal rings of Guwahati? My official tells me you carry them for Prince Adesh."

"We must talk alone."

The warlord gestured a guard. "Take both Javed Kasam and his guru to a chamber." He turned to Jace. "We shall dine together, and talk."

Guards were everywhere as he and Gokul were escorted away. What could he do? How could he convince Zin to turn over Gem—and if he could not?

Inside the chamber, Jace expected trouble over his weapons, but to his surprise the Burmese made no attempt to disarm him. He was not certain how he would have reacted if they had. The door shut behind the guards, and a heavy bolt slid into place.

Gokul tossed aside his holy beads and sank wearily onto a cushion. He glanced about the chamber, watching as Jace went to the one window.

"Trapped. It is too high to escape, and if we could, Zin has posted some guards below."

"Sahib, I think we are in much trouble."

———

Zin lounged in a silk kimono against cushions at the far end of a long room whose doors were shut and guarded from the outside. A table was spread before him, and Jace and Gokul sat on either side of him. Servants brought in bowls of food, and women went about filling their glasses from bronze urns.

"In memory of my son—and your friend, speak freely," said Zin.

Jace wondered just how freely he should talk. Zin was now in control, but was there some way to gain a slight advantage? He must be alert, looking for any possibility.

"I can only imagine the lies the assassins have told you in order to have you turn over Adesh to them."

Zin waved an airy hand flashing with gems. "They spoke of a small rebellion among the Rajput Royal

Guard who favored Sunil."

"A rajput would die before becoming anything other than what caste tells him he is—a warrior. The royal guard were all loyal to the old raja and died without flinching under the feet of war elephants."

"You fought with them?"

"The maharaja knew of Sunil's treachery. He wished me to bring him here to Burma, to you."

"To me! I have been no friend to Majid Singh since I had the child abducted by traitorous sepoys from the English silk plantation near Jorhat. I have received modest payments from Guwahati with the promise I would not turn him over to Sunil."

Jace saw his opportunity to discover if he was correct about Roxbury, and Sir Hampton's headman, Natine.

"How you managed was clever. The diversionary fire in the hatcheries, the untouchable killed and thrown into the river for Natine to find—how much help did you get from the English ambassador?"

Zin's white teeth bared into a humorless smile. "There is no reason to shield the Englishman. I will tell you what happened. It was he who arranged the unfortunate accident of the untouchable, who informed me of the time to attack the plantation. He has his own ambitions."

"To control the Kendall silk."

"Yes, and a safe escort through Burma into China to open new trade routes. I will protect his future caravans passing through my territory. He is a hard man, one who bargains well. If he were not an Englishman but a warlord, I would have reason to see him as my chief enemy in Burma. He is the kind of man who eliminates his contenders."

"Yes—he works well with Sunil. Both men would use

an assassin's dagger to guarantee the success of their purposes."

"It is business between us, nothing more. What he wishes to do will also fatten my treasury, so presently we flow together smoothly down the same stream. But the future? Who knows."

"And what has Sunil promised Roxbury?"

"The protection of the plantation from the ghazis who wish the English presence out of Assam. In return for Sunil's help, the ambassador has convinced him that the Company would not interfere if he rebelled against his uncle and had him killed."

This, Jace had not expected. It did not seem wise of Roxbury to promise what he must know he could not deliver. The British military would fight to overthrow Sunil to place the maharaja's grandnephew, Gem, on the throne.

"A mistake. Roxbury will be arrested for treason against the British king, who made a treaty with the maharaja."

"Obviously the ambassador thinks he can deceive the East India Company about his own involvement. Those who know him to be involved will be dead when the English arrive. A warning to you to take to heart, Javed. You have proven to be his worst goad."

"There is one thing that bothers me. And that is why Sunil should care whether or not the Company accepts his rightful claim to the throne. He works with the ghazis, whose one aim is to rid Assam of the English. It is their wish to liberate all India of the feringhis."

Zin smiled. "I am surprised you would need ask such a question, Javed. You know the workings of intrigue. Today's friend may become tomorrow's enemy. Once on the throne with his power established, Sunil will then rid himself of the ghazis he now needs to place him there.

In the future, it will be more advantageous for Sunil to have the goodwill of the East India Company."

"By advantageous you mean that in the end, wealth and trade is the language of all races and creeds. Sunil believes he can gain more by working with the English—at least for the immediate future."

Zin waved a hand. "It is a matter of practicality."

"The ghazis would not agree," Jace said, hoping to find out about Natine. "The kotwal on the Kendall plantation has motives of his own, fired by religious fanaticism."

"You speak of Natine? That fool! He is no friend to the Burmese." Zin frowned for the first time, showing that the Indian man somehow angered him when others, more dangerous, did not. Jace wondered why, but at the moment he was more interested in Natine's workings with Roxbury. All information would be turned over to the governor-general in Calcutta.

"If he has aided Roxbury, it was not out of interest in trade," Jace prodded. "Roxbury must have promised him something important, something that would appeal to Natine's dedication to the Hindu god Shiva. Natine has helped him gain Kingscote by arranging the death of Sir Hampton Kendall in Darjeeling."

Again the warlord frowned. "I know nothing of that. But Kendall has proven a strong enemy to Burma. Even now he has mercenaries on his land to fight our infiltrators."

Jace believed him about not being involved, yet he was concerned, and stated evenly, "I plan to marry the daughter of Sir Hampton Kendall. No harm must come to them. Kingscote must remain as it always has in the past, as a separate province from either India or Burma."

There was no reply. Jace knew the silence meant that the warlord would promise him nothing. Zin changed the subject. "Why did the maharaja wish you to bring him here to the prince? We were enemies."

"He had few choices. Sunil gained the loyalty of his palace officials and the army. Prince Adesh was the old raja's last hope to stop Sunil from coming to the throne. He figured that he could offer the son of Rajiv, for Rajiv was loved." Jace was suddenly thoughtful. "I begin to doubt if those in the palace government who plotted with Sunil knew he killed his brother. They may have turned back to the maharaja had they known. As it was, the old raja could do little except wait and hope for the arrival of the English troops I was to bring. What he did not know was that Roxbury thwarted our arrival by the mutiny at Plassey. No doubt Roxbury had Sanjay stir up hatred for the English among the sepoys at Plassey."

He was certain Zin already knew all this, but the warlord behaved as though he did not. Jace was sure Zin's scheming nature was already busy at work wondering on which side to align himself.

Jace took a risk and produced the royal rings from the house of Singh.

Zin's eyes fixed upon them.

Jace realized that Zin could have his warriors take them by force, but he did not think the warlord would. Not yet. Not until he was certain in his own mind with whom he would ally himself in the battle for the throne.

"At his death, the maharaja entrusted the rings to me, along with his grandnephew." Knowing that Zin might let Sunil know he had the rings, Jace then added, "Sunil will want them to strengthen his claim."

Zin ate in silence while Jace watched him over his bronze goblet. Finally Zin spoke. "The prime minister and Sanjay bring me news that Sunil will pay much to have Adesh turned over to them."

And, of course, it was Zin who now had authority over Gem.

"Sunil will indeed pay whatever he must," said Jace. "But dealing with Sunil is like bringing starving hyenas to your table. They will eat what is there, then think nothing of eating the master who fed them. Sunil will also kill Adesh with no remorse."

"The prime minister and Sanjay speak not of his death but of his crowning."

"They lie to your face. Once in their hands, the boy will be slain. If not by them, by others waiting in Guwahati with Sunil. Come, Zin, I want the child. What is your answer?"

Zin emptied his glass, then held it out to be refilled. "What will you and the Kendall woman give me for his life?"

Jace restrained his anger. "Leave her out of this."

Zin smiled. "She must be beautiful indeed for Javed Kasam to venture into marriage. But the child can never become only her son, though he may be spared Sunil's dagger."

"I am aware of that. I will take him to a place of safety until we can place him on the Guwahati throne."

"By 'we' I assume you speak not of her but of the English in Calcutta."

"The British will not be expelled from India. Nor will they leave Assam. They will fight. They will send as many troops as are needed to secure the northeastern frontier. If you are unwise enough to align yourself with Sunil, there will also be fighting with Burma."

Zin sighed. "You are right, but Burma will not be intimidated."

"Then there could be a future war between England and Burma."

"But not between us, Javed." He smiled coolly. "Unless you insist on fighting for England. Somehow I cannot see Javed Kasam doing so."

"My only interest is a quiet departure, bringing Adesh with me. If I cannot put him on the throne, I would at least save his life. I would smuggle him to England. I leave you another thought: Sunil is untrustworthy and dangerous. Once on the throne, he would think nothing of turning against you if you get in his way. Ask yourself this, Zin. Who would you prefer on the throne of Guwahati: Sunil or Adesh?"

Jace could see by Zin's expression that he had already thought of this.

"How much will you offer for the grandnephew of Majid Singh?"

"The stolen idol of Kali."

Zin's eyes came alive. He drummed his fingers on the table, all the while staring thoughtfully at Jace. "Then you speak the truth. It is you and not Sunil who has it."

"Did he tell you otherwise?"

Zin did not answer.

Jace said, "Sunil seeks it. He had a rajput assassin in my chamber at Guwahati, hoping to find it."

"It is worth more than its gold and jewels. It will buy power from the Hindus who trouble me here in Burma."

"It is indeed worth much. It is worth the life of Adesh."

Zin's black eyes regarded him. Suddenly he smiled, slapped his palms together, and was boldly unashamed of his greed. "It is. Do you have it?"

Jace smiled and folded his arms. "Excellency! Would I, Javed Kasam, deceive such as you? Where is the son of Rajiv?"

"Safe. I shall have you and the swami visit him."

Jace remained calm but tense. "When?

Zin gestured his broad hand toward a loitering servant. "Send for the guard. My good friend Javed Kasam would see Adesh." He looked at Gokul with a condescending smile. "You too, Swami Gokul Sankar. It is good you have come from the maharaja. The royal scholar who has taught the prince has become ill and died only ten days ago. There has been sickness in the palace."

Guards entered, and Jace saw the Burmese official who had screened the merchants.

"You called, Excellency?"

"Is the prince awake?"

"He is asleep, Excellency, and his nurse is with him."

Zin nodded. "Take Javed Kasam and his swami to the chamber of Prince Adesh. They would see that he is well and safe. Prepare for his departure as well as my two noble guests," he said gesturing toward Jace and Gokul. "And the prime minister and Sanjay?"

"Bolted within their chambers, Excellency. And threatening to bring the entire army of Prince Sunil against you for treachery."

Zin sighed. "It may be that I must kill them so they do not reach Sunil." He looked at Jace. "You are certain you do not have mercenaries waiting in the jungle?" he asked with a mocking tone, for they both knew that Zin would have sent out scouts to search.

Jace smiled wryly. "You already know I have come alone. There are few I would risk my identity to as Javed Kasam. I would not wish to alert his many deadly enemies. At the moment Sunil is enough." Jace turned to follow the official out of the chamber.

Zin stood. "You have forgotten the idol, Javed."

"Excellency, would I be unwise enough to deliver before I first see the child? I will keep my side of the bargain as soon as we are safely out of the city."

Zin gave a soft chuckle. "Nor is Zin a fool. What if you

do not deliver but ride on with both Adesh and the idol of Kali?"

"You have fierce warriors and swift horses. You know I am alone except for the swami. You would overtake me before I ever crossed the border into Assam. Nor do I have reason to betray you. You must know I wish to have Adesh far more than the treasure, or I would not have risked coming to bargain."

Zin searched his face. "I shall take your word."

"And I shall take yours."

Zin gestured to the Burmese official. "Bring him to Adesh."

19

Jace followed the Burmese official to another section of the sandstone palace. They came to a door guarded by two warriors whose faces were hard masks. The official produced a key and slid back the bolt.

"Wait, I will tell Adesh Singh's nurse who you are, and to awaken him."

"We will take him at once and ride with speed. The nurse must stay."

"She will be most upset. She has been with him since he was a small child."

Jace thought of Gem being abducted from the Kendall nursery. "I can only take the prince. Tell her she may follow later to Jorhat and leave her name with the military commander. I will communicate with her when it is feasible."

The official stepped inside and returned almost at once. "Prince Adesh is awake. Come!"

Jace stepped into the chamber, Gokul behind him. He stopped short and reached for his sword, but it was too late.

Sanjay stood there with warriors holding deadly curved blades. Sanjay smiled with triumph.

"Welcome, Major-bahadur," he mocked the military term of honor. "I have been waiting. Did you truly think the warlord would betray Sunil? Ah!—do not draw your blade, Major. One flick of my finger and these warriors will attack. Not that I would not delight to see your head roll across the floor."

The door shut behind him. Jace heard it bolt. He turned toward the Burmese official, who spread his hands. "My apology, Javed Kasam. I am under orders from His Excellency. He has requested that you yield your weapons."

Jace kept his fury bridled. His voice was toneless. "Zin planned this?"

The official bowed slightly. "Would I dare lead you into a trap without his orders?"

Sanjay took a step forward, obviously impatient that the official was moving too slowly. "Kill him," he ordered the main Burmese guard standing near Jace and Gokul.

"It is like a coward to have others kill for him." Jace glanced at the guard. "Sanjay is responsible for the deaths of a hundred fighting men, each one worth ten of him. He can do nothing but plot and lie and give orders to kill."

The guard showed no emotion. Was he alive? wondered Jace dryly.

Sanjay turned angrily to the official, who stood with dignity, hands behind him.

"Stop him. Silence him now. You have your orders to kill him. Do it!"

"His Excellency will decide when and how he dies, Dewan Sanjay. There is another matter between them of which you know nothing. It will be settled first."

The idol. Was Zin mad enough to think he would turn it over to him? It would rot first! Nothing would make him talk now.

"What of Rajiv's son, Prince Adesh?" demanded Jace. "Has Zin no honor that he would lie to me and allow this piece of lice to kill a child?" he gestured to Sanjay. "At least allow the swami to see the boy, and go with him."

"The swami shall not go," said Sanjay.

"Do you also fear an old man with a soft belly?" mocked Jace.

Sanjay walked toward him as if to backhand Jace, but the guard stepped forward.

"Are these guards loyal to Sunil or not?" asked Sanjay angrily.

"Dewan Sanjay must know they are loyal first of all to His Excellency," came the official's calm voice. "As for the Swami Gokul Sankar, he cannot see Prince Adesh. The boy is ill."

"It may be that Swami Gokul Sankar can help to relieve the prince's suffering," said Jace.

"No!" snapped Sanjay. "Any man with the major is not to be trusted. He could be in disguise."

"You would know well of disguises," said Jace.

"I will look upon Adesh," said Sanjay. "He is to be prepared to ride out in the morning."

"No, while Sanjay will not fight a man, he will thrust a dagger into a child!"

"That, Javed Kasam, is none of my affair," said the Burmese official, his demeanor unchanged. "His Excellency has already agreed to release Adesh to the dewan and the prime minister in the morning. Come," he said to the smug Sanjay. "You may look in on Prince Adesh and his nurse. She will journey with him."

"Very well." Sanjay walked briskly to the door but looked back at Jace. "One day I will see you dead—I have vowed to Kali."

They went out, leaving Jace and Gokul alone. Again the door was bolted shut. He heard the sound of their feet walking away. Silence enclosed them.

Jace unleashed his emotion by kicking a stool and sending it smashing against the door. "Filthy curse! What a fool I was to trust Zin!"

"He is a cunning tiger, sahib. But Sanjay is a vicious cobra. Prince Adesh will never reach Sunil."

With frustration and anger Jace leaned his arm against the stone wall but could find no words. He uttered something beneath his breath. And Coral! How could he face her, knowing he had failed to save the child's life?

Outside in the hall, the Burmese official led Sanjay to the chamber of Prince Adesh. He unlocked the door and opened it wide, stepping aside for Sanjay to enter.

Sanjay entered boldly, his eyes sweeping the royal chamber. A Burmese nurse cringed away, frightened. "Please, mighty one! He is but a child!" She made an attempt to throw herself between Sanjay and the sick child in the bed. "Please!"

"Silence, woman! He will not die yet! Prepare him and yourself to journey at dawn."

"But Prince Adesh is ill with high fever. Moving him will—"

"If he is not ready at dawn, it is you who will die."

Pressing her fist against her mouth to silence her frightened sobs, the woman lowered her head in fearful obedience.

Sanjay turned and strode out. "Bolt the door," he ordered the official. "I want guards here."

"There is no possible route of escape. There are no windows in the chamber. Zin has been most careful. And the nurse's fear of punishment has made her fully obedient."

"Nevertheless, I want guards."

"It is done."

———

Jace could not sleep. He paced his chamber restlessly, thinking, praying, yet no ideas came to him. His call through the door to the guards went unheeded. So did his pounding, until he realized it was futile. As deep night settled over Burma, he could not sleep. Somewhere out there Sunil waited for Gem. And this time there was no one to prevent the boy's death. *No one,* he thought wearily, going to the window to look below into the torchlight, *but God.*

Had he failed because of pride? Had he not sought the Lord's blessing on his dangerous venture? But he had prayed! Why then? Why the stark, brutal face of failure?

His forehead rested against the cold iron bars. He shut his eyes. *Jesus, Son of God, perhaps you have permitted this because I have been slow to follow you. It was never a question of my not knowing who you are, or the meaning of your sacrifice for sin—it was a matter of obedience to your Lordship. . . .*

His hands closed tightly around the bars, and he felt the sweat on his forehead. "But at Sualkashi . . . I surrendered to your will. My life and my plans are meaningless without you. Your purposes are the only thing worth living for, dying for. I do not know what you may want of my life, but for whatever purpose, it is yours."

Overwhelmed, he could not think. *Lord, it is my honor to yield to you.* Dawn broke over the dark jungle, and Jace watched silently through the window as guards brought horses and a palanquin for transporting the prince. Minutes later he saw the warlord come out with his guards. Next followed the prime minister and Sanjay, followed by the Burmese nurse carrying Gem.

Jace watched as they were placed inside the covered palanquin and the others mounted horses for the ride to meet Sunil. Sanjay looked up toward the window and must have seen Jace standing there for he said something to the warlord.

Zin looked up at the window, his bronze face hard as he replied. Whatever it was pleased Sanjay, for he mounted his horse and rode off behind the palanquin without looking back.

"They are gone?" It was Gokul's sad voice.

"Yes."

"Do not grieve, sahib. We did what we could. And will not the True Master look with pity on the spirit of the child when he dies?"

"He will."

20

Northeastern Frontier

Ethan knew they were now somewhere between Jorhat and Sibsagar, the capital of Assam. They had arrived after dark at a little-used public rest house called a dak-bungalow where the tea was weak and lukewarm, and insects crawled on the walls.

The dozen rajputs belonging to Sunil, but now serving Sir Hugo, waited in the dark jungle near a narrow dirt road.

Ethan walked to the open window, where the night cloaked him in sultry heat. He turned, his nerves ready to snap, and glanced at Sir Hugo, who sat at a small table puffing on a hookah while tracing his map with an eyepiece.

Ethan had been able to discover little of his uncle's mission.

"We have journeyed miles out of our route. What can be more important than going to Darjeeling? Yet you sit for hours pouring over that wretched map!"

"You heard what the rajput told me when he arrived tonight from Kingscote."

"I saw the man, yes, but you know quite well I do not know Hindi." He jammed his hands into his trouser pockets. "I am able to pick up only a few words here and there."

Sir Hugo regarded him with a dark gaze. "Perhaps it is best you do not ask questions. The answers may prove unpleasant, to say the least."

Ethan was all too familiar with Hugo's baiting suggestions, and became cautious. "If there is dark news, Uncle, I wish to know it."

"Sit down and stop pacing like a trapped animal."

"It is Hampton, isn't it! If so, I am not entirely surprised. We have wasted weeks wandering like vagabonds while ignoring the serious matter for which we began this journey."

"It is not Hampton. The rajput arrived from Kingscote with news."

Outside in the hot darkness insects buzzed and crickets chirped. Ethan's gaze fixed on his uncle. "What ill news did the rajput bring?" he pressed.

"You might as well know what has brought us here. I have come to convince the Raja of Sibsagar to make peace with his son Sunil. If not, Sunil will go to war."

Ethan stared at him blankly. He knew nothing about Sibsagar except that it was the capital of Assam. He had heard about tension in the family dynasty between Guwahati and Sibsagar, and that squabbles had nearly led to a state of war.

"Assassinating his uncle and seizing the throne at Guwahati was not enough for Sunil, I gather?" snapped Ethan. "He wishes war with his father as well!"

"Sunil is an ambitious man. But there will be no war. Sibsagar will make peace in order to save Gem—or should I say Prince Adesh?"

"Gem!" Ethan walked toward him.

Sir Hugo stood, rolling up his map. "The boy is alive, and Sunil has discovered his whereabouts in Burma. Gem is of royal blood, not only from Rajiv but also from Jemani. She was related to the Raja of Sibsagar before she maried Rajiv."

Ethan's lips tightened, but he said nothing. So they had found out about Gem. They had located him, and now had him. Then what of the major? Had he failed in his attempt?

Ethan thought of Coral, and tension gripped his emotions. "It is a curse that Sunil has found him. He has no qualms about slaying his brother's offspring if he feels the child is a threat!"

"Your sentiment is foolish, the chatter of a woman. I am here to avert bloodshed. The death of a child is not the type of thing I would involve myself in."

"Rot! I'll have no part in this. I will not stay! Nor will I journey to Sibsagar. I am leaving in the morning." He walked toward the beaded divide. "I shall go to Kingscote."

"You will go nowhere until the matter which brought me here is complete," ordered Hugo. "Your rash behavior could ruin everything. I will have audience with the raja, promising to produce Prince Adesh, and you will journey to Sibsagar. Not because I need you, but because I do not trust you to keep silent."

Ethan turned, his face pale and taut.

Sir Hugo's black gaze glittered with wrath as he strode toward Ethan. "Do you think I do not know you informed Coral of my previous deeds in London? You might have had both her and your medical research if you had kept silent. Now it is too late for both of you."

Ethan's heart thundered in his chest. "What do you mean, both of us? What about Coral?"

"I was in the parlor the night your emotions turned

261

you into a blabbering fool, the night Buckley arrived. You destroyed in minutes what I had carefully planned for years! The entire matter of marriage was settled. I had convinced even Elizabeth to hold the wedding at Christmas. You need not have feared Buckley, but you panicked. You confessed to Coral that we drugged her in London, and that you were carrying out my wishes. It is too late now, for Coral. She is dead." Sir Hugo turned away. He went back to the table and sat down, picking up his hookah.

Ethan sucked in his breath. His stomach seemed to come up to his mouth. "Dear God—you didn't—"

"Pull yourself together, Ethan. Do you think I'd eliminate my own niece?"

"Yes! Yes!"

"You see?" said Hugo wearily. "You panic too easily. You nearly got me killed in Guwahati by your foolish outburst. That is why I cannot allow you to leave. Actually I was quite fond of Coral. . . . She outwitted me on several occasions. I should have had her as a daughter instead of Belinda. But alas, fate pulls so many ironic jests, does it not?" he scanned Ethan, his eyes mocking and malicious.

Ethan could not speak.

"She is dead," Sir Hugo repeated. "Elizabeth too. Natine has a most venomous temper when riled. He believes Kali has ordered their destruction. Shiva is a jealous god. The persistence of Coral and the sentimentality of Elizabeth in allowing the school was enough to provoke the attack by ghazis from Kingscote and the village. Did not I warn you in London?"

"Y-you allowed that fiend to kill them?"

"No! Don't you remember that I ordered a rajput to stay to protect them? Somehow Natine and the village priest arranged an accident with a cobra. The best way we can vindicate their unfortunate deaths is to see to Natine's when we return."

Sir Hugo drew on the hookah and the water gurgled. "Natine and the priest are far too risky to leave alive. I will order the rajputs to see to both of them on our return. In the meantime, you must gather your wits together. There is always Marianna . . . you might think of marriage to her. Without her parents and Coral she'll most likely have an emotional breakdown. You can be there to soothe and make her better. She will come to understand that you are her one source of strength."

Ethan stared at him. *The man is insane.* He turned swiftly and left the room. Outside, he went to the bushes to relieve his ill stomach.

How long he knelt there sick he did not know. He stared into the dark grass. He saw a mammoth bug crawl by and watched, feeling too dazed to move. He had told himself he was angry enough to break with Hugo after he had watched Coral climb the stairs and out of his life. He had thought he could cut the python from around his soul, a python that was slowly squeezing him to death. He could not. Now tormented by the death of Coral, the new plans of Hugo to marry him to Marianna left him angry. *How can I break free of Hugo?*

"God," he rasped into the tropical night, "help me. . . ."

He came alert. Horses! He scrambled to his feet, damp with sweat, and stared intently into the darkness toward the road. Armed riders were nearing, guarding a palanquin. Ethan's head turned sharply toward the dak-bungalow. Sir Hugo came out, followed by rajputs, and walked toward the road to meet them.

The entourage had stopped, and several armed men were dismounting. Ethan's trembling fingers touched the loaded pistol beneath his jacket, and he stumbled in their direction.

He arrived, stopping a few feet back to hear Sir Hugo speaking with an older Indian official. Another Indian stood near the door of the palanquin. With a start of surprise, Ethan recognized Sanjay.

"Where is the boy?" demanded Sir Hugo.

"With the nurse inside the palanquin," said the older Indian official. "He is ill."

"Turn him over to me. Once the raja realizes we have the prince, he will abdicate his throne to Sunil in order to save the child's life."

"An error, Sahib Roxbury!" came Sanjay's harsh voice. "He must die."

"Do not be a fool. The raja does not yet know of Jemani's son. If you slay him we have nothing with which to bargain."

"The house of Singh cannot be trusted. It was he who made the treaty with the feringhis—he, and the Maharaja of Guwahati. We will slay the prince now," said Sanjay.

"Slay the child and I will kill you," came Sir Hugo's voice, deadly calm.

Sanjay's eyes, hard and cold, were riveted on Sir Hugo.

Hugo gestured to the rajput guards, who stepped forward, their hands resting on their tulwars.

"You make a mistake," said Sanjay. "Letting Adesh live will mean ultimate defeat. Even if he leaves India, one day Adesh will return, as a man with a mighty army."

"Turn the boy over to the rajputs," commanded Sir Hugo. "They have been sent by Sunil to guard him until he arrives with his army."

Sanjay's angry gaze swept the others, then he turned to the palanquin. He opened the door and said something to the frightened Burmese nurse, but she would not leave the seat where the boy lay ill, covered with the royal blanket.

What happened next froze Ethan with horror. Swiftly Sanjay produced a dagger and plunged it repeatedly while the deafening screams of the nurse filled his ears. He then drew a pistol and shot the boy as the rajput guards converged on him, striking with their tulwars. He sank to the dusty ground, where they grabbed him, dragging him to the side of the road to die.

Ethan threw himself past the others into the palanquin in a desperate but futile attempt to save the child. He hesitated in confusion when he turned the boy over, ripped off the head covering, and saw his face. *He is Burmese! This cannot be Gem!*

He stared at the boy's almond-shaped eyes and lighter-hued skin. His eyes darted to the nurse, and he saw the signs of death coming upon her. Her eyes seemed to plead with him to remain silent about the boy's identity.

"Any hope?" cried Sir Hugo from outside the palanquin. "Is he alive, Ethan? Can you do anything?"

Ethan fumbled to cover the child with the blanket. His mouth was dry, and he tried to swallow.

"No. Prince Adesh is dead."

Jace heard a key turn in the lock, and the heavy bolt slid back. The Burmese official stood there, expressionless.

"His Excellency has called for you."

Jace's chill gaze swept him. "My weapons, where are they?"

A guard stepped from the hall.

"This way, Javed Kasam," he said calmly. "You also, Swami Gokul Sankar."

They followed the official into the warlord's chamber. Zin sat cross-legged on cushions, eating a sumptuous meal, and looked up when they entered. Seeing Jace's expression and brittle blue-black eyes, Zin chuckled and waved him and Gokul to join him at the table.

"Come, sit. You are my guests. But, we have made a bargain, Javed Kasam. Where is the idol of Kali?"

Jace refused to sit and stood in a military stance, his hands behind him. His even stare brought a mock wince from Zin, who looked at his official and said with wry humor, "Our guests are angry with us."

"Perhaps, Excellency, you best tell him the truth before you return his weapons."

Jace glanced from Zin to the official and saw a slight smile. He came alert. "What truth?" he demanded.

Zin finished draining his bronze goblet. His black eyes glinted. "The boy given to the Dewan Sanjay is the child of the Burmese nurse. He is expected to die from his illness. He would have been pleased to know he gave his life to save his beloved friend. Prince Adesh Singh, however, is well. This ruse of mine was necessary. But if the Burmese boy does not die, and they discover they have been tricked, they will soon return—and you had best be gone."

Stunned, Jace could not speak. His mind went back to the deceit played upon Coral. After Gem's abduction a child's body was found in the river, wearing the garments of Gem, including the gold cross.

Zin smiled, his black eyes glinting with amusement. "Adesh has been sent where they will never think to search," said Zin. "He is with a feringhi. A 'Christian' feringhi at that! His name is Felix Carey."

Felix! The son of William Carey in Serampore, thought Jace, astonished.

"The young Englishman is here in Burma translating the Christian holy writings into Burmese," said Zin. "Prince Adesh is safely held at the Carey compound. If you and the swami leave now, you will be well on your way before they return."

"Zin, I—"

"No need to tell Zin how clever he is." He smiled wolfishly and stood. "Simply produce the idol of Kali as we bargained."

Jace smiled. He glanced at Gokul, who also grinned. Jace nodded, and on cue Gokul turned his back and lifted his robe. When he turned around again, his stomach was flatter, and he presented Jace with the gold idol glimmering with precious emeralds and rubies.

"Ah. . . ." sighed Zin.

With a faint smile Jace placed it amid the tropical fruit bowls on Zin's table, adding a ripe mango for Kali's crown.

Minutes later, belting on his scabbard, and receiving a rough drawing from the Burmese official of the location of the compound, Jace turned to leave the chamber when Zin's sober voice stopped him—

"There is more we must discuss, Javed."

Caution. . . . Jace turned with a narrowed gaze.

Zin was grave and thoughtful, as though troubled, and motioned him to sit.

"There is much you do not know. Sunil's ambitions go further than Guwahati. He will war against the royal house at Sibsagar and rule both thrones."

The mention of Sibsagar brought new feelings of apprehension. Jace lowered himself to the cushions. Sibsagar's dynasty had ruled the Brahmaputra valley since the eleventh century. There had been many kings, and one of them had assumed a Sanskritic name—Singh.

His successors had also adopted the name and married with the maharajas of Guwahati. Sunil too would have his eye on the ancient city of the old Ahom kings. It was from "Ahom" that the name "Assam" had come. For Sunil to have his seat of authority in Sibsagar was in keeping with his ambition and pride.

"But why will he risk battle now? If he were wise he would wait to consolidate his rule in the south and move northeast when his military is stronger."

Zin looked at him evenly. "You do not know. Jemani is the daughter of the Raja of Sibsagar. If Sunil does not destroy the child you call Gem—then there will be one maharaja over all Assam."

For a moment Jace did not speak. He had always suspected that Jemani might have had royal blood, but somehow he had gone along with the assumption of the old Maharaja of Guwahati that she had come from some petty prince ruling a district in the south.

"Sunil will strike at Sibsagar while he has opportunity to gain military support from Burma."

Jace gave him a sharp look. It was the first mention of Burmese involvement in Sunil's plans. It all began to make sense to Jace now. The mutiny at Plassey, the massacre of his troops, even the earlier attack on Jorhat when his friend Major Selwyn was killed. Sibsagar was now isolated from military help, and Sunil and the Burmese government found it beneficial to work together.

"The British Bengal troops at Jorhat will not be enough to defeat Sunil," stated Zin. "The prime minister of Guwahati came to Burma not only about the child but to appeal to my government to join forces with Sunil. Together they will fight the king of Sibsagar to rid Assam of the English presence."

Jace thought of Coral and Kingscote. If fighting

erupted, they too would be at risk. His frustration mounted, but he must not let Zin know how weak they were. What could he do without adequate troops!

"He has come to you also?"

Zin measured him. "He has."

"And what was your answer?"

Zin looked at him gravely. "I have accepted."

In the silence, Gokul stirred uneasily, glancing from Zin to Jace. But Jace showed no expression.

"It is also true that you have informed me of your plans, and the plans of the others. You would not do so if you felt at peace in what you do."

"You give Zin more conscience than he has. I tell you only because I am a friend of Javed Kasam." His eyes were grave. "I do not wish you killed in battle by my warriors. Is it not enough I have told you where to find the child? Take him and return to Calcutta! Take the Englishwoman you love and go! The internal conflicts of the dynasty are not your burden."

"As Javed Kasam I might agree. As a major in the British military I speak for more than myself. If there is to be an attack on Sibsagar I cannot walk away. There are English soldiers at Jorhat, and I cannot desert them."

Could the gathering together of the Burmese warlords somehow be halted by convincing Zin to withdraw and to counsel the other warlords to do the same?

Zin, however, would not be easily convinced, nor did Jace think he could frighten him, yet it was his duty to stand for the Company.

"You disappoint me, Zin. I vowed in writing to the governor-general that it was not Burmese troops who attacked Jorhat and killed Major Selwyn. Colonel Warbeck did the same."

"Javed, would I be unwise enough to attack the English on my own initiative? I knew Selwyn was your

friend. The attack was Sunil's doing, along with renegade Burmese from the jungle around the Kendall lands.
It was Roxbury who approved the attack, offering important information. Selwyn, however, was not supposed
to have been killed. Roxbury knew Calcutta would look
on his death as reason to send more troops."

"And the colonel did," said Jace. "They were massacred near Plassey. Yet British reinforcements will arrive
from the south. We have a treaty with the Raja of Sibsagar to come to his aid against any attack from Burma."

"Javed, you too must know how we Burmese feel
about Assam. The territory belongs to us."

"Both India and England disagree."

"And you? Do you also disagree? Do you believe that
English blood should dictate who rules the land?"

Jace lifted the cup of strong black tea and drank to
mask any personal feelings he might have.

"I represent the British government."

"Javed Kasam is independent. He also was born
here."

"I was born on an East India ship," he said dryly. "A
pirate's vessel to be exact."

"Yet you have walked among us, as one of us. You
have been a friend to many, whether Indian or Burmese."

"Whatever I may think of the policies of the East India
Company, I am now their representative. Any attack on
Sibsagar will be deemed an attack on the good word of
His Majesty King George."

Zin sighed and shook his head. "Your honor is your
death, Javed."

Honor? Was it that? Or was it the thought of Coral
and her school on Kingscote, or perhaps all the English
yet in Assam that kept him bound to his British uniform.

"If Sunil rules Assam, there will be more at risk than
your ambitions, or even my life. I begin to see that for

the peace and well-being of Assam, Rajiv and Jemani's son must reign. Perhaps this was the reason for his survival . . . if he had not been taken by the Englishwoman, even for so short a time, Adesh would not have survived to claim his birthright."

Zin looked at him a long moment, then gave a light bow of his head to show the discourse was at an end. They had not come to agreement.

Jace stood. "I leave you with one thought. Who would you feel more secure with on the throne of Assam—Sunil or Adesh? Adesh will not come seeking you in Burma, but Sunil will never be satisfied with what he has. He will always want more."

Zin was thoughtful. Jace turned and walked out, followed by Gokul.

———

After Jace was gone, Zin pondered his words as he picked up the idol of Kali and turned it over in his hand. "What do you think?" he asked his official. "Does Javed speak wisely?"

"He does, Excellency. I too believe Assam and Burma will know better rule under Adesh. Sunil is a ruthless man."

"Ah, he is indeed." Zin removed a pearl-handled dagger from under his sleeve. "If Sunil will kill his nephew, a winsome child like Adesh, how much more easily will he put an assassin's dagger into the back of Zin!"

He threw the dagger for emphasis, and it stuck fast into the wooden table.

"Then does Your Excellency not wish me to prepare for your journey to the battle of Sibsagar?"

"I shall stay comfortable here after all. And I shall counsel the other warlords to do the same. If Sunil cannot take Sibsagar with ten thousand warriors and many elephants, he is too big a fool to reign Assam. And—send a wedding gift for Javed Kasam to Kingscote."

"Your Excellency?"

Zin beckoned to have one of his treasure chests brought to him.

Minutes later he pulled out a prized Mogul sword. His black eyes gleamed, then he sighed. "Such a sword. It is worth much. Javed will remember this delectable prize from Calcutta. A pity he had to be struck on the back of the skull. Alas! I shall make amends and send it back. We shall make him think I retrieved it from some thief at a bazaar. Who knows? I may need Javed Kasam sometime in the future."

"A wise idea, Excellency!"

———

Jace and Gokul rode from the sandstone palace and out under the arched bridge of ebony stone with its red dragon gazing down upon them.

Jace paused on the road, where the noon sun bore down on the reddish earth. Troubled, he frowned to himself, disturbed by the thought that the military at Jorhat was oblivious to the danger closing in about them. There were British and Scottish soldiers stationed there. Not many, perhaps twenty, yet they were fine soldiers.

And Kingscote was less than a day's journey from Jorhat. It would take little for the fighting to erupt beyond the walls of the outpost to ensnare the four Englishwomen alone in the mansion. . . .

And beyond Kingscote, on the road south to Guwahati, even at this minute Sunil would be preparing for war, gathering his thousands of warriors, his war elephants and war machines for the long march northeast.

"Your horse faces east, sahib, but your heart looks toward Jorhat."

Gokul faced him as Jace thoughtlessly flicked the end of the horse's reins against his palm. "Zin was right, sahib. Prince Adesh is safe with missionary Felix Carey. Each day and hour he stays, the more he knows of God. This is good. Sunil and Roxbury will not search there." He chuckled. "And if Zin's trickery went undiscovered, they will not search for him at all."

Jace agreed. Neither Sir Hugo nor Sunil would look for Gem.

"Not much time," said Gokul. "Our moments are like few raindrops caught in cup before it stops. My advice? Seize them! Is not sahib under military honor to alert the troops at Jorhat of grave danger?"

"Are you asking me to lead a death charge of some fifty men against war elephants?"

Gokul grinned. "Not with the promise of wedding to lovely English damsel."

Jace smiled faintly and turned his horse south, toward the military outpost. With only a handful of soldiers, what could he do? There was no hope of Captain MacKay arriving in time, even if his troop was near Guwahati.

"There is little to be done, Gokul. We can warn Jorhat, and see that the women on Kingscote are safe until Mackay arrives."

"It is enough, sahib."

But was it? There must be some way to stop Sunil short of storming his palace to duel him, but what?

He must alert the Raja of Sibsagar.

———

Darjeeling

The toe of his boot rested on a rock that he prayed would not dislodge from the mountainous soil; his bleeding fingers clung to another, his grip tiring. How long Hampton had clung there since the rope snapped could have been anywhere from one minute to fifteen.

Where was his Indian guide, Lal? And the Indians carrying the supplies, had they returned to camp? Why did not someone throw another rope?

Below him the mountains dropped to certain death.

Another rock fell away from under him. He heard its echo all the way to the bottom of the canyon. His body ached with weariness and was becoming slippery with sweat. Fear turned his heart into a pounding drum. If he lifted his boot from the one rock to search for a more secure handhold, his fingers might weaken.

He might yell out again to the others, but they should have heard him the first time. Had they felt the rope break—or had someone cut it?

There was no hope. Should he survive, it would be by the Almighty's help alone. As that realization struck Hampton, it eased his fears. He could not hold on like this much longer. He must move.

Cautiously he brought his boot along the rocks and felt for a wider hold, and the leg that now held him was trembling.

"Good Shepherd," he gasped hoarsely, "have mercy . . . come to the aid of this old wandering sheep . . ."

Fighting away the fear that seemed to blind him, Hampton shut his eyes and breathed deeply, concentrating on his next move, one that could bring his death.

His toe touched some obstruction, not more than several inches wide. In order to rest his weight on it he must let go of the rock his fingers clutched.

He held himself flat against the soil, gathering courage, then slid his hand across the dirt and bits of rock and weeds to grasp a mound. His legs were beginning to tremble uncontrollably, and the old familiar pain in the

274

area of his heart began to throb with spasms that brought shortness of breath.

I am going to die, he thought. *This is the end.* Elizabeth flashed into his mind, and tears mingled with his sweat. Guilt supplanted his fear as he thought of how he had never been the husband he should have been. Though he loved her dearly, he had never been the spiritual head he knew she would have wanted. And his daughters . . . what would become of them? Hugo would be their guardian until their marriages, and Kingscote . . . somehow the plantation, once all that his heart feasted upon, seemed insignificant as he stared into the face of death.

Nothing mattered as eternity opened its doors to bid him to enter, ready or not. . . . Nothing mattered as he saw his failures looming larger and larger like shadows prepared to bury him.

Sweat ran into his dimmed vision, the thatch of hair tinged with gray was glued to his forehead. He shut his eyes, feeling his strength leaving his body, as though death were saying, "Here am I."

The pain in his heart eased. He released the small mound, his fingers numb, and as his body slid down he found that his boot was on a larger rock firmly lodged into the soil. *The Lord is my Rock, my Fortress* came the words from a psalm he could not remember. He could rest now, leaning all his weight against the mountain, the side of his face feeling the pebbles dig into his skin. Slowly his heart ceased its drumbeat, and a small breeze cooled him. He was safe for the moment.

Then he heard a sound, a whisper of movement hardly detectable. Some pebbles from above rolled down over him. Who was coming? Someone from the trekking party to help, or the man who had cut the rope?

"Sahib?"

Hampton strained to distinguish the voice. It was Lal.

Should he trust him? Yet if he did not answer, and Lal had come to help. . . .

"I am here!" he called weakly into the wind. "Throw a rope!"

He waited, then heard a sound that turned his blood cold. Lal was chipping away to loosen a boulder that would come crushing down upon him.

———————

Seward lay upon a rocky slope less than sixty yards from where Hampton clung for life. Seward had been waiting nearly twenty minutes. He could have fired his rifle several times. . . . he could have killed one, perhaps more, but he waited, for they were beginning to leave. The Burmese warrior had stayed behind alone to finish the evil work of killing Sir Hampton.

Now at last . . . Seward moved.

He made no sound as he came up behind the warrior busy loosening the boulder.

Warned by some instinct, Lal turned suddenly, and Seward fired his pistol. The Burmese slumped to the ground.

Seward had little time to save Hampton. The gunfire would have alerted the others, who might come back. Seward took a rope from the dying warrior and staggered to the mountain's rim.

"Hampton!" called Seward as he quickly tied the end of the rope into a secure loop.

From below, where he clung, Hampton heard the familiar voice and would have shouted had he the strength.

"Hampton!"

"Here—" managed Hampton. It seemed an eternity passed before he saw the rope sliding down the mountain toward him. As it slid beside him, he cautiously moved his stiff hand across the rock and latched hold. He then carefully released his other handhold as he placed the loop over his head and under both arms.

Slowly he was eased up, and as the thought of safety possessed him, Hampton's energy revived, and he struggled to climb upward as Seward hauled on the rope.

Perhaps five minutes had passed before Hampton's eyes could fix on Seward straining above him on the rim. His reddish gray hair was plastered across his sweating forehead, his stark blue eyes riveted upon him.

Hampton thought he was grinning but could not be sure until he felt Seward's big hands pulling him to safety.

In a moment of relief they knelt together, gasping for air, staring up at the heavens, their minds united in offering thanksgiving.

"We best get out of here, quick. Roxbury's men be coming back, 'tis my guess."

"Roxbury!"

Seward scowled. " 'Twas naught but an evil plot to see you dead. Me and the major be thinking Roxbury and Natine worked together. We best get ourselves back to Kingscote. I've a dark feeling they be needin' us. An' I wouldn't be worrying about Alex. More chances than not, ye'll be hearing from him safe and sound, and find the lad never laid eyes on the tea plantation."

"What a fool I've been! Thank God you came, Seward. You've saved my life as you did in the past."

" 'Twas nothing, Sir Hampton. But if we don't get a move, we both may end up over the mountain."

"If Hugo has lifted a finger to harm my wife or daughters—I shall have the man sent to Newgate, brother-in-law or not."

"Are you all right? Ye be limping. . . ."

"Only an injured knee. Do you have a horse?"

"I was smart enough to bring two," said Seward with a grin. "Always did believe the Almighty would aid us."

21

Ethan heard Sir Hugo walk away from the palanquin as the others followed. Their low voices carried in the silence. He listened intently to the plan of attack. Sunil had ten thousand fighting men and many war elephants. Somehow he must locate the major and alert him. But where was he!

The Burmese nurse was dying. She sensed this as he worked to save her. Her feeble fingers reached for the front of his vest. "M-must say nothing," she rasped.

"Your secret is safe. I am a friend of Prince Adesh. An Englishman named Major Buckley went to Burma to rescue the boy. Did he arrive? Have you heard anything? I must find him!"

Her glassy eyes stared. "Zin t-tell English friend—"

"Where!" He brought his ear close to her mouth.

Her words came as a faint whisper, garbled, but they rang through—"Felix Carey . . . prince there—"

She went limp. His own breathing came more rapidly. Felix Carey? Son of William?

Ethan glanced out the palanquin door into the night and saw his uncle huddled in low conversation with the prime minister of Guwahati. The rajputs were busy watching the road again, while others had carried off Sanjay to bury him. *They must not see the child was Burmese!*

Ethan wrapped him in the blanket and climbed down to the dusty road. Sir Hugo looked over at him.

"What are you doing?"

"I will bury the child myself. Gem was deeply loved by Coral."

Sir Hugo said nothing and stood watching. Ethan felt the man's eyes on his back as he walked off the road into the trees. He stopped short, confronted by a rajput guard.

Ethan showed indignation. "I am a doctor who saves lives, yet I have witnessed the murder of an innocent boy. If you will bury a fiend like Sanjay, you must also dig a grave for the son of Prince Rajiv."

At the mention of Rajiv, the one prince beloved by the rajputs of Guwahati, Ethan saw the first flicker of emotion in the dark bearded face of the warrior.

"For the rajkumar's son," he said.

They had lain the boy to rest and were in the process of covering him with soil when dry twigs snapped. Ethan turned sharply. The dark silhouette of Sir Hugo stood silently. Ethan had the horrid notion he would hear his emotionless voice demanding to produce the child.

"We have little time. We will ride north to Sibsagar."

"Yes, of course. Give me only another minute."

He watched his uncle walk back into the darkness. The rajput had buried the child and now waited to make certain Ethan returned to Roxbury.

I must escape! I must find Jace and warn him about Sibsagar.

Ethan's mind worked swiftly now. He said firmly, "Both Rajiv and Jemani accepted the Christian belief. Leave me alone to pray and quote words from the Bible."

The rajput scowled. "Rajiv was not a Christian."

"He was. He and Jemani were baptized on Kingscote. They entrusted their child to the English Kendalls. Now leave me. I wish to pray!"

The rajput, obviously displeased, hesitated, but when Ethan began quoting the Lord's Prayer the warrior left quickly.

Ethan listened until the rajput's heavy steps died away. When he was certain the guard was gone, he darted into the trees. He must hide until his uncle and the rajputs gave up searching for him. They would sooner or later, for Hugo was anxious to reach Sibsagar. He thought of his medical bag and felt a jab of dismay.

No matter . . . as much as he hated to leave it in the dak-bungalow he could not take the chance of returning for it, even if he was certain his uncle and the rajputs had ridden on. It would be like Sir Hugo to leave a guard, knowing how much he cherished his medical supplies.

He strode swiftly forward in the darkness, trees and vines closing in about him, knowing he risked himself to poisonous serpents. He was soon drenched with sweat, and mosquitoes buzzed. Was he a fool? He could not go on this way for any length of time, and he did not know how far he must journey to reach the Burmese border. It would take weeks! And he had no notion where to find the missionary compound of Felix Carey. He might even be killed on the way by Burmese infiltrators. And where could he get supplies?

Emotionally exhausted and breathing heavily in the humid heat, he sank to the ground beneath the dark over-hang of the trees to rest a few minutes before going on. He must think!

If Sibsagar was some twenty miles to the northeast, then the British outpost of Jorhat must lie behind him to the south. Dare he go there? Would Sir Hugo send men to search for him? Yet the thought of an Englishman in uniform seemed like an oasis amid the desert of Indian and Burmese soldiers.

Jorhat—and beyond that, Kingscote . . . but no, he must not go back. He could not bring himself to enter the same house where only weeks ago Coral had lived and walked and laughed. The memory of the school came to haunt him. He could see himself working . . . and Coral coming in the ghari, so alive, so happy to see her wishes coming true. . . .

Dead. . . . He had failed her. He had risked them all because he had not stood up to Hugo sooner. No, he could not go forward to either Burma or Sibsagar, nor could he go back to Kingscote. Jorhat was his one chance, and alone on the road, with Burmese infiltrators prowling in the jungle, that chance was slim.

He must have a horse!

That noise—what was it? He scrambled to his feet. Footsteps! There was no time to rest, no time to think. He must run!

———

Coral awoke to a house wrapped in afternoon silence. The fever and loss of blood that had kept her in bed for over a week was gone. Dreary weeks since then had passed, and she wished to forget the nightmarish ordeal with the cobra.

Almost at once the old anxieties confronting her and Kingscote came crowding into her consciousness. Like frightened children, the questions clamored for answers, but she had none.

If Jan-Lee went for Ethan, why have they not returned?

Dressed in cool muslin, her hair braided and looped at the back of her neck, she came down the stairs to an empty house. She sat down on the bottom step holding her arms and staring out the front window where the carriageway was in view.

Would her mother survive? Worse yet, what if she did not regain her mind? Again she thought of what Charles Peddington had told her in Calcutta about Mrs. William Carey: *"Her mind hangs in a delicate balance."*

As Coral sat there in the empty hall she remembered back to the night that now seemed a thousand winters ago. She had newly turned sixteen and came down the stairs to speak to her mother about Jemani's baptism. Her mother and father were talking in anxious tones, and in her memory she could see them again standing there in an embrace, hearing her father say: *"Tales of abductions, of druggings permanently affecting the mind, are not exaggerations."*

Coral frowned. The mental state of her mother was not so unlike what Charles had described when he had discussed Mrs. Carey's mental aberrations. Now that she had experienced some of the fear that came with watching her mother lose her disciplined mind, she was amazed at how William Carey in the midst of such trial was able to work on the translation of Scripture in the next room. Only the grace of God could be sufficient for such ordeals, she thought.

Coral closed her eyes and tried not to imagine the worst. "Mother will get well again. She must."

But always the ugly head of doubt arose. What if she did not? What if she lived for many years deranged?

Even if Jan-Lee arrived with Ethan, could he cure her? Was her brain permanently damaged? If it was only temporary why did she not improve?

"I will not cry!" She shut her eyes tightly and kept back the tears.

When she opened them again she stared intently out the window as though expecting to see Ethan. Had Mrs.

Carey ever recovered? she wondered. Charles Peddington had implied she only grew worse.

Coral was more convinced than ever that Mrs. Carey, much maligned for her mental weakness and inability to adjust to the hardship of missionary life, had been maliciously drugged by some ghazi furious with Carey's missionary work. It could have happened when he managed the indigo plantation in Mudnabatti. When his son Peter died, he had forced several workers to break caste and bury his child—afterward, they had been angry toward him.

Natine! It is not enough that he put the cobra in my room, he had to hurt my mother too!

Her heart suddenly welled with bitterness and hate, and it frightened her more than their circumstances. "God forbids me to hate others. But where is the grace to forgive him? And Gem ... was Natine not also to blame? He and Sir Hugo!"

She buried her face in her hands. "No. I cannot forgive what you did to my mother! She will never be the same again because of you, never."

Her mother had been so gracious, so intelligent—now she was deranged! And what will we tell Father when he comes home? How will he bear the news?

Oh, Jace, if only you were here, she thought, suddenly longing for his protective embrace.

Wistfully she recalled the song of joy that had been hers only months ago when she had received the message from Jace that Gem was alive, and that he would bring him to Kingscote for the Christmas holidays. All that too was gone. There would be no Christmas. Gem did not exist—there lived instead Prince Adesh Singh, heir to a throne of India.

There was Jace. She had his love, she thought. Would this cause for happiness also die?

"I can take no more now," she murmured. It seemed that trouble had come to settle over Kingscote, like black vultures awaiting a harvest of death.

"What a dark mood I am in! *Vultures . . . harvest of death.*"

She stood up from the step and walked out onto the front verandah facing the lawn and the river. The day was hot and still; the water appeared like gray glass.

Could she not find some reasons for thankfulness among the trials allowed by God for good? For good. . . . Were they? How could the terrible things that were happening on Kingscote ever produce spiritual *good*? Yet the promises of God said they would. Coral was reminded that trouble was a part of each new day and would always be a part of life. To expect anything different was to deny the Scriptures and shipwreck one's faith. Had not the Lord said, "In the world ye shall have tribulation"? Only the presence of the One who was Life himself could sweeten the bitter, could divide the hour into minutes of joy as well as sadness.

Perhaps, she thought, *God allows these so we never lose sight that we are not citizens of time but children of eternity, where no disappointment or sorrow will ever sting.*

At least she had recovered from the cobra bite with little ill effect. She looked at her arm. The wound Preetah's knife had made was healing well.

As she looked down the carriageway toward the road lined with trees, a movement caught her eye. Her heart wanted to stop. Had she imagined it? A Burmese soldier!

She forced herself to not turn and run, screaming. She stood without moving as though watching the river but strained to see through the trees.

There was another movement, and she saw him clearly this time. A ripple of fear went up her back. She had not imagined it—Burmese soldiers on Kingscote!

Do not panic, she told herself. *They must not know you saw them lest they attack at once.*

She turned her back and walked slowly inside the house. Once inside, she slammed the heavy door, her fingers trembling as she fumbled to shove into place the several bolts her father had installed.

She whirled, racing toward the kitchen. "Mera! Rosa!"

Mera came at once, attune to the cries of alarm that seemed to constantly fill the mansion. "Yes, what is it?"

Coral held her, shaking, briefly taking solace in her arms. "Burmese soldiers! Tell Hareesh to lock the doors. Have the other servants do the same. Hurry, Mera!"

Marianna had come down the stairs, and she now clutched the banister as though she would faint. "Burmese warriors?"

"Yes! Quick! Go about the house. Warn the others. Bolt every window and every door. Then come back here!"

Marianna stared at her.

"Don't panic," gritted Coral, deliberately gripping Marianna's arm so hard that she winced. "You will need to keep your wits."

Marianna was shaking, her teeth chattering. She nodded yes, then hurried into the parlor.

As Coral raced up the stairs she heard the servants running everywhere. She threw open the door to her mother's room. Kathleen turned from her mother's bedside and hurried across the room. "What is all the noise? What's happening?"

"There are Burmese soldiers on the road. I just saw them in the trees. I doubt if they will attack the house now, since they don't know what to expect. We need to be prepared. The servants are going about locking up now."

"Father's pistol," said Kathleen. "I put it back in his desk drawer after Natine left. I'll get it." She rushed toward the door. "But we will need more than one!"

Kathleen disappeared down the hall and Coral went swiftly to the side of her mother's bed and looked at her. She was sleeping, looking peaceful. For once, the sight of her ill mother did not affect her.

Coral rushed to the wardrobe and removed her mother's pistol. There was also the rifle that she carried with her in the ghari. Coral found it leaning in one corner against the wall. There were other guns in the house which her father had kept against attack. . . . There had been many frightening times in the past.

But she had been a child then and had been sent with her sisters and the servants' children to hide with the women. Now there was no place to hide, and after the attack on herself and her mother, there were few men she would trust to be their protectors. Thilak was one, and any worker from the hatchery that Thilak trusted. There were also the mercenaries, but could they be reached in time to return to the house?

Coral was surprised at how calm she felt. Her fingers trembled as she carefully checked the pistol. When her father had insisted his wife and three daughters learn to use a gun, Coral had thought it unpleasant. Now she was glad that he had insisted. Kathleen could be depended upon too. Only Marianna was likely to faint!

Coral bolted the locks on the bedroom window and verandah doors and turned to leave the room, glancing back at her mother. She had not stirred from her sleep.

She must send a message to the hatcheries to Yanna and Thilak. Thilak must somehow get past the infiltrators to alert the armed mercenaries guarding Kingscote's border.

Out in the hall she met Preetah, her dark eyes frightened but her voice calm. "I have locked the doors and windows in the upper rooms, Miss Coral, and Reena has gone to warn Rosa in the dispensary and Yanna in the hatchery. I have told her to send for Thilak."

"Good. Can you shoot?"

Preetah raised her chin and drew in a breath. "I can."

"Come with me. My father has weapons in his office."

Thilak arrived secretly through the kitchen door, and his determined expression added to Coral's and Kathleen's courage. Yanna was with him and went immediately to take a rifle.

Coral gave weapons to Thilak as Kathleen gave him his orders.

His face turned grave. "I shall do my best to get past the infiltrators," he told them. "Then I shall go to Jorhat for more help."

"Take my horse," said Kathleen. "He is more swift than the stable horses. He's tethered by the smokehouse."

The child Reena came to cling to Preetah's skirts as Thilak hurried from the front hall.

"Godspeed," whispered Coral.

22

Jorhat Outpost

Jace waited, listening intently to the night noises: a sigh of wind rippling the tall grasses near the marsh, the lone belch of a frog, swiftly followed by the splash of a waterfowl catching its midnight delicacy.

On the far side of the marsh, he and Gokul led their horses down the well-trodden lane, hooves muffled in the powdery dust. A mile ahead, looming against the black jungle, torchlight flickered on the stone walls of the lone British outpost.

He frowned, his old irritation at the sight goading him again. He had always disapproved of allowing trees to grow so near the command post. Time and again he had requested of his commander that the outpost be surrounded by a wide clearing and cannon mounted outside the wall. Like everything in the military he disliked, the simple project of cutting down trees had been buried under mounds of mundane paperwork. And cannon, said Calcutta, was quite impossible on the frontier. It made no matter that every petty raja in the northeast had at least one—the British outpost must make do with muskets!

As they neared, Jace noticed that the ensign had at least restored the breached wall and repaired the gate. A single sepoy stood guard, the white on his uniform showing, belted with the cavalry saber. Jace unpleasantly wondered who would own the soldier's allegiance when fighting erupted. Did his allegiance belong to Sunil or to the raja at Sibsagar? Cynically, he doubted if the soldier were steadfastly loyal to the British flag that hung limp on the pole, with the colors of the 21st Bengal Light Infantry just below.

Again in the uniform of a major, Jace saluted and spoke in Hindi, and the sepoy crisply greeted him and signaled for the sentries to open the gate.

As he rode into the post with Gokul following, Jace scanned the dozen sowars who stood guard about the wall. How much did they know of what was being planned now in Guwahati?

Lights shone in the windows of the barracks and in the small residency of the officer in command—now a mere ensign—until Captain Gavin MacKay arrived. Militarily, Jace remained under orders from the governor-general as captain of Roxbury's security guard in Guwahati. A miserable jest!

He dismounted and gave the reins to Gokul to bring their horses to the stables. "See what you can discover among the ranks. I'll speak with the ensign."

He turned to walk across the yard to the residency when its door opened and a soldier stepped out. The shadows hid his rank, and Jace could not see if he were Indian or English. Jace watched the soldier nervously glance about and settle his helmet on his head, then come down the steps. The uncertain manner in which the man carried himself alerted Jace. *Something is wrong.* "Hut! You! Halt!"

The soldier hesitated, and Jace walked toward him. He should have stated his rank and name. Jace's hand reached for his pistol, but he stopped when he saw the man's face.

"Ethan!" Jace let out an exasperated breath.

Ethan recognized his voice and started with surprise, then hurried toward him, losing his hat in the process with a clatter. He stooped to pick it up, catching it by the plume.

Jace winced. "You make a lamentable sepoy."

"Abominable gadget." He shoved it back on his head, then straightened. "Good heavens, Major! I did not expect the luck of finding you here!"

"What are you doing here in masquerade? I thought that was my specialty." He added wryly, "And by the way, this is not Darjeeling."

Ethan came up, and seeing his tension, Jace sobered. "Trouble?"

"Extraordinarily so! I just left speaking with your Commander in Chief."

"The proper term is ensign," said Jace lazily, his eyes amused. "Come, I will need your report."

Inside the military office Ensign Niles was busily writing when Jace and Ethan entered. Hearing them he glanced up. "Sit down. I shall get to you in—"

Niles jumped to his feet and crisply saluted. "Major!"

"What are you writing?" Jace asked flatly.

Niles, realizing he clutched his pencil, set it down on the worn wooden desk. "A detailed report on the crucial information Doctor Boswell has given to me, sir. I intend to send one of the sepoys with the dispatch—"

"Detailed?" repeated Jace. "Crucial? You thought you would *write* it all out in flowing hand to deliver to a sepoy—is that it, Ensign?"

"Well, sir, actually—yes, that was my first thought, Major."

"Think again."

"Yes, sir!"

Jace held out his hand. The ensign snatched up his report and handed it to him.

"I had a bit more to er—fill in, sir."

"Good." Jace took the piece of paper and, meeting his eyes evenly, tore it into pieces, dropping them in the trash urn. The ensign flushed.

"Just between you and me, Ensign, we are but a handful of brave and dedicated soldiers of His Majesty amid twenty thousand heavily armed soldiers of Sunil. Let's keep the doctor's report a bit of a secret. Just in case."

"Yes, sir!"

Jace turned to Ethan. "Where is Roxbury?"

"On his way to Sibsagar."

As the ensign brewed the last of his coffee, Jace listened while Ethan quietly explained all that had occurred since Jace left Kingscote.

"You are certain Roxbury didn't suspect the child wasn't Gem?"

"He was utterly deceived."

Jace noted the look of vengeful triumph in Ethan's face. Much had changed between Ethan and his father, he thought.

Jace mused over the news Ethan brought. So Sir Hugo and Sunil had intended to use Gem for ransom in order to force the Raja Singh to abdicate his throne to Sunil. "Are you telling me the raja at Sibsagar does not know Jemani had a son?"

"He believes the infant died with her."

"And both Roxbury and Sunil thought they would be successful in using Gem for ransom," Jace said thoughtfully.

"Quite. What they truly planned for the child once the raja capitulated is anyone's guess," said Ethan distastefully.

Jace was not thinking of that but of the difference between Sunil and the raja. "Unlike Sunil, who wishes his contenders dead, Sibsagar would welcome the son of Rajkumari Jemani."

"So it seems, Major. At least Sir Hugo believed it enough to gamble on. Why do you ask? What do you have in mind?"

"Where is Roxbury now?"

"Once they gave up searching for me they must have journeyed on toward Sibsagar as planned."

"Without Gem they have lost their prized jewel with which to bargain. Sunil will now fight. How many in his army? Did you hear any discussion?"

"Ten thousand soldiers and over a hundred war elephants."

Then Zin had spoken the truth. "That is likely to be doubled. Burma has promised the individual armies of the border warlords to Sunil."

"Then there is no hope," said Ethan. "I do not know how long it will take for Sunil to move his army northeast from Guwahati, but it is obvious to me that we are all sitting like ducks in their path. After the rebellion at Guwahati and my introduction to war elephants, I've no wish for further contact."

He stood, looking uncomfortable in the uniform and anxious to mount and ride. "There is nothing we can do here, Major. You yourself informed Ensign Niles you were but a handful of English soldiers. If we stay, we will either be trampled to death or end up prisoners of Sunil."

Still, Jace lounged in the chair, thinking.

"Major!"

"I heard you, Doctor. Your coffee is getting cold." Jace

lifted his tin mug and drank. "How large of an army does Sibsagar have?" he asked the ensign.

Ensign Niles began searching through the desk drawers.

"If I recall," said Jace, "after the treaty with the Company, the raja was to reduce his standing army considerably."

"Yes, sir, since Sibsagar is under British protection, the governor-general felt a large contingency would only make the raja's neighbors worry, especially Burma, which makes no sense to me, sir, since the number of infiltrators has tripled in the last weeks. We lost Scottie only yesterday."

"Scottie?"

"McKilton. From Edinburgh. He was on patrol south of here when his squad was set upon. Only five men made it back."

Jace covered his frown. South of Jorhat, the independent lands belonging to Sir Hampton Kendall joined close to the border with Burma. It had been that tract of jungle that Jace and his troop had traversed when tracking the man-eating tiger for Sir Hampton, the time he first laid eyes on Coral. Remembering, he had to force his mind back on the problem at hand. "Near Kingscote? Sir Hampton Kendall and his dependable men are gone. We have an English family there."

"Yes, sir. I sent out another scout in that direction this morning."

"The plantation at Kingscote must be protected," Ethan said, his voice quavering.

Jace looked at Ethan and could have sworn his eyes misted. Jace scowled. *Does he truly love Coral?* The fact that he had come out the winner in the battle with Ethan for her heart caused him a twinge. The man looked positively sick!

Jace's eyes narrowed under his lashes, and he emptied his cup and stood. "Forget the official document on the size of the raja's army," he told the ensign wearily, who still searched diligently, having emptied an entire drawer.

"Major?" said Ethan.

"Yes?"

Ethan stared at him intently, then ran a defeated hand through his sandy hair. "Nothing, Major. I was going to ask if you would be riding to Kingscote."

His behavior was curious, but Jace pretended he did not notice. "No. And since you are in uniform"—he smiled slightly—"you are under orders not to do so either. I have another mission for you."

"Mission?"

"I've a plan. It may work, and most likely it will fail miserably, but in light of impossible circumstances it is the route we shall take—unless either of you unexpectedly comes up with a solution. How many trustworthy soldiers do you have, Niles?—and do not count the sepoys and sowars."

"Without the native infantry and cavalry, sir, about seventeen men."

"About? You mean you do not know?"

"Dougan is having trouble with his eyes, sir. Blackouts."

Jace was unreadable, but an illogical sense of panic swept over him. What if his own blindness reoccurred now? What would he do? "Ensign, until MacKay arrives with the 13th, I am taking command of the troops here."

The ensign showed surprise, then confusion.

Jace affected an unflinching demeanor. "Do you have reason to contest that decision, Ensign?"

"No, sir. In fact I am quite relieved."

Jace left his chair and walked behind the desk, and

Ensign Niles relinquished the chair behind the desk. Jace sat down and stretched his legs. "Your first order, Ensign."

"Yes, sir?"

"I want those seventeen soldiers—including Dougan!—placed under your command. You will ride out tonight for the Kendall plantation and stay there until you hear from me. Under no circumstances are you to venture forth on the road once you arrive there. Is that clear?"

Ensign Niles struggled not to show his emotion. "Understood, Major."

"I will give you two letters to deliver. One is to a trusty old warrior named Seward. Make certain he receives it when he arrives."

"Yes, sir."

"The other letter is to Miss Kendall."

"Major—" began Ethan softly.

"If Kingscote comes under attack you are to defend it with your lives. Go now and get your command ready to ride. Take the best of the horses. And I want the muskets brought with you."

"The muskets! But sir!"

"Load the munition wagons with all the weapons you can carry. I want to hear you riding out before dawn. Then make straight for Kingscote. That is an order, Ensign!"

"Yes, sir!" Ensign Niles hesitated. "May I speak an opposing word, sir?"

"You may, but it will do no good."

"An all-English command is most unusual. And taking the guns will leave you and the native infantry a bit short."

Jace smiled faintly. "We will manage. Anything else?"

"No, Major."

"Do this undercover with as little fanfare as possible. At the same time as you form your command, give orders to the native officer in charge to prepare his sowars for battle."

The ensign was thoroughly bewildered but saluted and went out.

Jace had made up his mind to abandon the outpost—an action that would see him called before the military court in Calcutta. At the moment, it no longer mattered. The sepoys were all a pack of traitors ready to rip open British bellies at the first order of Sunil, and if there were two or three loyal and brave men among them—and no doubt there were—they would have their opportunity to battle with honor when Sunil used his mammoth war elephants to tear down the walls of the outpost. For Jace had no question in his mind but that Sunil would destroy Jorhat. However, Jace did not plan to be around to watch, and he certainly did not intend to allow English and Scottish soldiers to be massacred for nothing. If anything was left of the outpost when MacKay arrived with the 13th, the ensign and his men could return.

There was a rap on the door, and Gokul entered.

"Any news?" asked Jace, refilling his mug with coffee.

"It smells of treachery to me, sahib. The sooner we get out of here, the happier I will be. Sunil will come sooner than we thought. He is near, perhaps a week away."

"What are our plans, Major?" Ethan asked. "Sending the English soldiers to Kingscote is a wise move. Should we not ride out with them?"

"The Raja of Sibsagar must be warned that Sunil will advance with an army, strengthened by soldiers from Burma." Leaning against the desk, he looked at Ethan. "I take it your willingness to escape Sir Hugo on the road means you've broken your ties to his plans and wishes, that you no longer intend for him to manipulate your life, and the lives of others."

"That is a blunt way to put it, but yes. I shall never return to the relationship I had with him until tonight. You might as well know, Major, that I have no desire to remain in India, least of all on Kingscote. I have thought I might return to London to Roxbury House and resume my practice. Or even travel for a time—perhaps, if war with Burma does not break out, to Rangoon. The fauna and insects available for scientific experimentation are remarkably rare indeed. I thought that I might eventually set up a lab somewhere thereabout. I—I can never go back to Kingscote again," he said. "I have many regrets."

Jace folded his arms across his chest and regarded him. "You cannot undo the past, but you may be able to help change the future of Kingscote, and Assam."

Ethan looked skeptical.

"Go back to Roxbury," said Jace.

"Go back—! Have you lost your senses?"

"I hope not. . . . You say he went to Sibsagar to seek audience with the raja. He will have one purpose on his mind: to deceive him by treachery. Go back, as though to align yourself with him. At Sibsagar warn the raja of what is planned, and tell him that Rajkumari Jemani had a son—and that son lives."

"How do you expect me to speak in the raja's ear when Sir Hugo will be there!"

"Come, Ethan! You outwitted him long enough to arrive here at Jorhat. Once there look for any opportunity—a servant girl, perhaps, one who might remember Jemani and who was loyal to her. You will think of a way."

"I have no doubt Hugo will kill me if he discovers I am your spy."

"Think not of yourself as serving me but England . . . and India. Much depends on Gem being received by his people as Prince Adesh Singh."

Ethan paced. "I don't know. The thought of going back to speak peaceably to him after he—I shall need to think about it."

"There is no time. Sunil will arrive with his army, and to survive, the Raja of Sibsagar must fight. His men are far fewer, and he will not be able to hold out for long. If he is left alone to face certain defeat, he may listen to the treachery of Sir Hugo. But if you are there to promise the arrival of Prince Adesh, I am certain the raja will fight to the death."

Ethan's eyes began to take on warmth. "Can you bring Gem in time? You heard Gokul's words."

"We can try," said Jace and wondered at his own determination. "But the fighting may begin before I arrive. That is where your persistence must come in. You must keep the raja fighting Sunil and thwart Roxbury's counsel to surrender."

"But if fighting erupts before you arrive I see no way for either the raja or the people to see their future maharaja."

"There is only one way. I will need to risk him on the raja's own royal elephant at the right moment in the battle—and hope that the rajputs fighting for Sunil might get an overwhelming dose of emotional frenzy for a change."

"Royal elephant? Good heavens, man, what do I know of such matters!"

"You don't need to. Gokul knows exactly what to do. Follow his directions. Bring that particular elephant to me at a location I will later give Gokul. If all goes well, I shall have Gem with me."

Ethan let out a breath. "I will do as you say, Major.

But so many details coming together at one time—" He shook his head. "It could mean the death of us all."

"If you will not risk yourself for the future of Assam, then do this for Coral."

Ethan's lips tightened.

"Gem is as much her son as Jemani's," said Jace. "She has invested her soul and heart in this child."

"Well said. I will go to Sibsagar and convince Sir Hugo I've had a change of mind. And somehow I will manage to warn the raja."

Jace turned to Gokul. "Go with him as far as you can. But do not let Roxbury see you with Ethan. He is clever enough to know something is in the making."

"But what of you, sahib? You will journey to the missionary alone?"

"I must. Everything depends on your getting that royal elephant."

Gokul's eyes shone. "The mammoth elephant painted black," he said with awe. "The maharaja's 'Black Royal Elephant'!"

"Yes, and if our plan works to bring Prince Adesh on his back—the eyes of the warrior rajputs will shine as yours. A cry from Gem may be our one chance of getting them to come to his side."

"A great task you give old Gokul, one he may not be able to do, sabib. The royal elephant is like a child to the raja, and the trainers, they treat the elephant as a lesser king. They eat and sleep with the royal elephant."

"You are once again the Swami Gokul Sankar Punditji—his holiness Sri Baba of Lankali," Jace told him. "You go to Sibsagar to bring your blessings to the funeral of some guru."

"Which one?"

Jace smirked. "How do I know, Gokul? There are thousands crawling about! Use your imagination. And remember, if you do not get the elephant to me, you might be scattering posies on my grave instead."

23

Burma

Jace dismounted, and taking his horse's reins he walked slowly toward the thatched-roof house surrounded by a number of smaller bungalows. He paused, glancing about the mission station. A boy stood under a wide-branched tree watching his approach. The child was dressed not in Indian garb but in white trousers cut off at the knees and a baggy white shirt. He wore a big straw hat and held a pet monkey on a rope, his gaze fixed on Jace.

Instinctively Jace knew that it was Gem. So this was the baby of the monsoon . . . the child who had brought him and Coral together in riveting emotion, the child they had all risked their lives to find again, who was yet at risk, as were those whose hearts mingled together in a long pursuit to rescue him. Did Gem understand that men wished to kill him, while others fought to save him?

Perhaps, thought Jace, it was only his emotions, but he sensed that there was a haunted, lonely spirit in this child who was starved for affection, for security—like a fawn racing from the arrows of determined hunters.

He was slim, small boned, his complexion olive, his facial features fine, almost delicate. Jace was struck by his handsome appearance, and he was drawn to the almost shy, studious expression.

Jace lowered his hat against the sun, but he did not feel its glare. In his mind he saw Coral standing in the steamy rain outside the little hut belonging to Jemani, holding the infant whom she would eventually adopt. He remembered how he had helped her into the carriage, and how she had been so protective of Rajiv and Jemani's child.

And Gem . . . did he remember anything of Coral? Or were all the childhood memories hidden in his soul?

He must. I will make him remember. Before Gem becomes Raja Adesh Singh it is essential that he knows the story of a beautiful young Englishwoman who risked her life to adopt him, to make him her own son—even only for a summer's morning in time . . . before life turned harsh and cruel.

This boy will make a fine raja, he thought.

Gem did not run away. He stood motionless, showing no fear, simply watching him. Then to Jace's surprise, Gem walked toward his horse and looked up at him, squinting beneath his lashes.

"Master Felix told me that His Excellency Zin would send a friend to bring me to my great-uncle, the maharaja. Are you the friend?"

His manners and use of the English language took Jace off guard. "I am," he said simply, and remembered that he would need to tell Gem that the old Maharaja of Guwahati was dead. Another unpleasant task, even though Gem had never met him.

"I am Prince Adesh Singh, a guest of Felix." His brown eyes unexpectedly glimmered with some excitement that brought a shy smile. "Did you know that the

God of Felix Carey speaks Hindi!"

————

Felix Carey had been eight years old when he went to India with his missionary father, William. He had learned Bengali even faster than his father did. In Calcutta, Felix had once carried the casket of an untouchable with two high-caste Indians, and the unprecedented act had begun the breakdown of the caste system among Christians in the area. At twenty-one, Felix had been commissioned by his father and the mission station at Serampore to journey to Burma as a missionary.

Although not a physician by degree, Felix was gifted in medicine, and Jace learned that he had introduced the smallpox vaccination into Burma.

The small compound was thriving, yet beset with trials and sorrows. He was impressed with Felix's tenacity; the man had already lost his wife in the missionary venture.

Many would have given up in discouragement and gone home, thought Jace. Felix remained, translating the Scriptures into Burmese.

During his brief stay with Felix, Jace wondered how he could spend time alone with Gem to begin preparing him for all that was ahead, including the battle at Sibsagar, but he need not have wondered how to win his friendship. From the beginning, Gem seemed to be drawn to him, taking keen interest in his wanderings as a youth in China and in Darjeeling. Gem was also curious about the English military and knew something of the British rule in Calcutta. He was just as interested in Jace's love of the sea, of his intentions to build a tea plantation in Darjeeling . . . and of his planned marriage to Coral Kendall, the silk heiress.

Gem's dark eyes, fringed with thick lashes, blinked

hard as he tried to take in all the adult information. He was quite intelligent and well educated, and Jace decided his years of captivity had not injured his ability to learn.

He startled Jace with his question: "The memsahib Coral Kendall—she is the Englishwoman who adopted me when my mother died giving me birth?"

"Who told you?"

Gem rarely smiled, but he did so now, almost shyly. "My Burmese nurse. She has a sister who serves the English family. Her name is Jan-Lee."

Jan-Lee? Jace remembered back to the Burmese ayah . . . was it possible? During all these years could Jan-Lee have known about Gem but kept it from Coral and the Kendall family? And just how much of a friend was the so-called faithful ayah? Had she kept silent for fear of harm to the family, or because she served Warlord Zin?

"I would like to meet my English mother," said Gem quietly, then with intensity—"I wish very much to meet her. I must thank her, not for me only but for my Indian mother and father, Rajkumar Rajiv and Rajkumari Jemani. You will take me to the plantation you call Kingscote?"

Jace saw the tender pleading in the solemn eyes and realized how the years of captivity had made him hungry for contact with those who had cared for him. The thought moved Jace. He placed his hand on the child's dark head.

"One day perhaps. Now your safety and hers are threatened by your father's brother."

"My uncle, yes. He hates me."

"His hate is born of greed and pride. He does not see you as you are but as an obstacle to keep him from fulfilling his desire to rule northern India."

Gem stirred uneasily. "Is it wrong that I do not even care if I am a raja?"

Jace picked up a twig and drew it in the dusty earth. "If you believe God rules the affairs of kingdoms, yes. You might have been born the son of an English sailor and meant to shimmy up ropes to grease the tackle." He looked at Gem and frowned when his words brought the opposite reaction than he had intended. The boy's eyes lit up.

"What is the sea like?"

Jace stood from the porch step and tossed aside the twig. "You were born a prince. You have a calling, a great and noble task to accomplish for your people. Who knows the good you might accomplish? All would be lost if you do not accept the calling of your birth."

Gem watched Jace intensely but said nothing, and as though to divert Jace, he caught sight of his pet monkey and clapped his hands to call him. The brown monkey came quickly, expecting a treat.

Jace regarded him thoughtfully, tilting his head. "Sunil will fight to keep you from the throne. He has an army of ten thousand, many of them disciplined rajputs, men who think of little but fighting and dying for the cause of their maharaja. Sunil plans to attack Sibsagar, the capital of Assam, the ancient city of kings—the home of your mother—your destined home where you can rule and bring honor to the One who gave you this earthly scepter. It is no light thing to turn away as though it is nothing, to look off toward the sunset and think you will keep running from the greed and pride of evil men.

"Your uncle Sunil is evil. If good men do nothing to stand against darkness, the darkness will swallow up the light that remains. Warriors of light battle not because they love the smell of war but because they must. Sometimes warriors must stand alone and trust that if they should die in fighting for what is the best, it was a worthy thing to do.

"We have few warriors on our side, Gem, not even the Burmese warlord—"

"You called me Gem."

"I meant to call you Prince Adesh."

"I like you to call me Gem."

"Gem—Warlord Zin will support your uncle in the battle because it is the wish of his government."

"He took much treasure from my father's uncle in Guwahati. Sometimes he was my friend, sometimes he wore a second face, an enemy."

"I told you, many men are hungry for riches and power."

"Do they ever get full?"

"No. The hunger I speak of cannot be satisfied. It is like a great pit. Not all the gold and pearls in India can fill it. Only God is big enough to fill it with himself and bring satisfaction."

Gem said nothing for a long time. He turned his monkey free and picked up the twig Jace had tossed aside. He too began to draw in the dusty earth.

"Many in India wish the English to leave, and Burma wishes to rule Assam. English soldiers from the military in Calcutta would fight to protect you, and Sibsagar, but they will not arrive in time."

"The English are my friends." He looked at Jace. "Do you fight well?"

Jace smiled a little. "Well enough. At the moment I am your bodyguard. You are my first and only responsibility."

"But I do not wish others to fight and die for me."

"You must not think so. Would you have Sunil rule?"

"No." His mouth went tight to cover a quaver. "You said he murdered my great-uncle at Guwahati with an elephant." His eyes widened. "But Sunil is also my uncle, my father's younger brother!"

It was time to let him know, thought Jace. However much it would hurt him. . . .

"Your father was a friend of mine."

Gem came alert, his eyes clinging to Jace.

"I watched him train with the war elephants at Guwahati. Sunil hired an assassin to kill your father. Because of Rajiv's death your mother Jemani gave birth to you before she was ready, and she died too. Sunil is your uncle by blood, but he is your enemy too. You must stop him. If not for yourself, for the memory of your father and mother, for Assam. You must let me and others fight, and destroy him."

Gem was pale and shaking. It wounded Jace to see the pain in his eyes, to see his small mouth tremble, but the emotional moment reinforced his own determination to bring Sunil down to defeat.

Gem threw the stick aside, and a faint color came to his cheeks. His small shoulders straightened beneath the thin white baggy shirt of a peasant.

"I know it is said that the rajputs will fight with great bravery for the true royal heir!" Jace recalled the dedication of the royal guards who fought for the old maharaja.

Quickly now the thoughts raced through his mind. He had one, possibly two friends among the rajputs at Guwahati, men who were associated with Gokul's brother at Sualkashi, men who were high in command of the warriors. Even among the dozen rajputs who were now with Roxbury there was a man, Nadir, a warrior who had alerted him at Kingscote that Sunil had discovered Gem's place of hiding with Zin. If he could get a message to these few rajputs that Rajiv's son was not

dead but heir to the ancient throne of Sibsagar, perhaps. . . .

"I have a plan. It is risky, for both of us will face a
moment when failure stares us in the face. You must be
brave and believe that what you do is worth the world.
Can you do it, Gem?"

"I am afraid!"

"All men fear. They lie if they boast they do not. It is
not fear itself but surrender to its mastery that destroys.
If a man believes his breath is in the hand of God, he
leaves his fears at the foot of the throne above all earthly
thrones. If God is for us, who can be against us? And if
He is not for us—then nothing matters."

Gem's brown eyes glistened with excitement. "I am
to be the raja. When Felix told me of the living God who
also speaks Hindi, I asked Him for a friend. I awoke at
night to see many men chasing me with tulwars. God
heard me. He sent you to be my friend. I will do as you
say. I fight for the throne of my father and mother. I will
tell Uncle Sunil that he is a bad man."

Suddenly, Gem turned and ran for the hut. "I have
something to show you, Jace!"

Troubled, Jace watched him disappear into the house.
He scowled, his eyes narrowing, as the weight of responsibility suddenly grew heavy. Placing Gem on the royal
elephant and bringing him to the battle for the rajputs
to see could bring unrest. A moment of doubt penetrated
his armor. *What if the boy's appearance as king of both
Guwahati and Sibsagar fails to rally the rajputs?* "Well,
Buckley, you spoke fine words of faith and courage. Did
you mean them?"

His blue-black eyes sought the horizon painted with
orange. "Maybe," he murmured wryly, "I can convince
myself that boarding the *Madras* with both Gem and
Coral and taking to the sea is the voice of God after all."

He was smiling as Gem returned and handed him a black book. "Felix gave it to me. He brought it from his father William Carey. It is written in Hindi, but Felix insists God can even speak these words in Assamese! Even in Bengali! I was told He was only English!"

Jace put a bridle on his emotions. He stooped until their eyes were level, then placed both hands on the small shoulders.

Gem stared at him, then suddenly the boy's eyes welled with tears. They ran down his cheeks, and he threw himself into Jace's arms, starved for affection. "You will always be my friend, Jace, promise!"

Jace held him tightly, feeling the small arms clinging desperately around his neck.

"Did I not willingly become your bodyguard? What better friend could you have than one willing to lay down his life for you?"

Gem looked up, tears wetting his cheeks. He held Jace.

Jace took the Bible and opened it to the Gospel of John, chapter fifteen. He read in Hindi: " 'Greater love hath no man than this, that a man lay down his life for his friends.'

"Christ laid down His life for us. Only He was the King of all kings dying for His subjects. He asks us to be willing to do the same for our brothers."

"B-but I do not want you to die, Jace."

Jace smiled. "I will not die—not yet. I have too much to live for. Both of us do."

"Let us both run away, Jace! Let us find your ship, the one you told me of, with big white sails that reach to the sky! We can sail to many places!"

"Do not tempt me," he said with a faint smile, and stood. "Come. We have a long way to journey, Adesh."

"To you I am Gem—and to my English mother."

"Your mother Jemani would approve of the name. Gem was the name your English mother gave you the night of the monsoon. Gem Ranek Kendall. 'Like a jewel, the one bright moment in all that has happened,' she had said."

Jace placed the book back into his hand and closed the boy's fingers about it. "Never forget. Others will seek to change your mind. But hold to it tightly."

24

Sibsagar

Where's Gokul! He should have been here waiting for me with the royal elephant!

Concealed in the jungle trees on the perimeter of the Brahmaputra valley, Jace beheld Sunil's camp some distance out on the plain that stretched before the ancient city of Sibsagar. He felt his palms sweating. As far as the eye could see, Sunil's tents, infantry, elephants, and horses filled his vision. He had spent the last day concealed with Gem, waiting for a message from Gokul, waiting for the trumpeting of the arrival of the Black Royal Elephant, debating the risk of bringing Gem into the scene of battle.

Would the mighty rajput army from Guwahati, now loyal to Sunil, break their allegiance and turn to Gem? If not, the plan that called for Raja Singh to meet Sunil in head-to-head battle would fail. Jace must produce Gem on the elephant early in the initial stage of battle, for Raja Singh could not hope to outlast the waves of warriors and war elephants that Sunil would hurl against him.

If he could not quickly produce Gem on the black elephant, Raja Singh would face certain death. His smaller rajput army and prized elephants would be slaughtered in a noble but fruitless attempt to hold Sunil back from a sweeping victory.

He must! But even then, would it work?

Where is Gokul?

A thousand things could go wrong, but everything depended upon one thing going right! The elephant!

Jace wiped his palms on the front of his rough trousers and touched his scabbard. He glanced toward Gem, who pretended to play with a bag of smooth rocks he had collected. In reality Jace knew the boy was almost sick with anxiety—waiting, wondering—and as much as Jace tried to mask his own feelings of uncertainty, he knew that Gem had picked up his tension.

I can take him and ride out, he thought. The two of us can get through Burma to Rangoon. From there we can catch a ship in the Bay of Bengal and sail up the Ganges Delta to Calcutta.

But Coral waited at Kingscote, and Sunil would easily defeat Raja Singh, and his army of victorious warriors would swarm over the area in jubilant victory. He could not take Gem and ride out leaving Coral alone at Kingscote, but then, perhaps she was not alone. He hoped that Sir Hampton and Seward had arrived by now.

Seward! Bless the old grizzly. He would take care of Coral if he had to battle all of Sunil's army single-handed.

Ensign Niles and his eighteen British soldiers, had they made it?

Jace could feel the anticipation of battle in the early morning. Seasoned warriors, elephants, and horses alike knew instinctively that this was the day, the hour, when their destiny would be decided in the roll call of war drums.

Could he hope to kill Sunil unguarded in his tent?

Disguised as a servant, Jace neared Sunil's compound. The first cluster of tents that formed the edge of the huge village-size camp met him without suspicion. His face was smeared with dust, and he wore a soiled puggari as he mingled with the untouchables who were leading elephants and horses and carrying large bundles of fodder along the lanes between the warriors' tents.

The perimeter of Sunil's royal headquarters was in the center of the camp, surrounded by a high barricade of billowing purple silk embroidered with a black border and supported with decorated poles spaced evenly apart.

Was Sunil there now?

Camped around the royal tent were the smaller tents of his officials and nobles.

An unexpected cheer erupted from a rajput, and Jace saw the warriors line the sides of the lane leading to Sunil's headquarters. Too late. Sunil was riding out on the princely horse, prepared to enter the armored howdah on the royal elephant while the rajputs beat their swords against their shields.

The elephant knelt and Sunil entered, seated beneath the wide umbrella, prepared to show himself on the battlefield as the rallying point of his army.

The captains of the rajput riders shouted staccato orders. The heavy bull elephants, their foreheads padded, began shoving the gun carriages forward as infantry marched beside them beating the kettledrums. The cannons, looped together with twisted bull hide, were rolled into fighting position on the field to target the smaller army of Raja Singh, who moved his rajputs and elephants into battle position. Jace saw a hundred cannons along the outskirts of the camp. Placed behind each cannon were the firepots, linstocks, and leather barrels of powder.

The great elephants were winding their way through Sunil's camp, waving their trunks and trumpeting proudly, knowing that they were at last being readied for the battle. Distinct from the huge war elephants, and smaller, these were tiger seizing, and considered by the trainers to be second rank, yet of admirable temperament befitting the hellish environment of battle.

How many of these animal-warriors did Sunil have with him, five hundred?

Jace admired their beauty in the murky light of dawn as they proudly marched through. Did they know they fought for kings? Somehow he thought they did.

The grand war elephants, kings in their own right, were being harnessed for battle. These would have the honor of leading the vanguard of the mighty rajput cavalry.

Fit for combat with horn bows and arrows, swords, clubs, and saddle-axes, the thousands of rajput warriors wore their unique fighting armor: a woven mesh of steel over a quilted garment, and a round shield of impenetrable rhino skin.

Was there anything he could do other than entertain the insane notion of slipping past thousands of warriors to attack Sunil in the armored howdah on the back of the royal elephant? He would have to be mad on opium to try such a stunt.

The Black Royal Elephant of the house of Singh carrying Gem was the only chance.

The sun began to climb. His tension mounted with it. He returned to the trees where he had hidden Gem. As he looked toward the walled city of Sibsagar, he saw with relief that the gate remained shut. Raja Singh had not yet decided whether to risk battle. Jace was certain

Sir Hugo was doing everything to convince him to surrender. Would Ethan be able to convince the raja to ride forth on the uncertain hope that Jemani had a son who was heir to both thrones?

The imperial forces of Raja Singh were outnumbered four to one in the foot infantry. Sunil's rajput officers were also better trained, in the pinnacle of strength, and primed for battle. Even before Sunil had his uncle assassinated, he had been secretly preparing the maharaja's army for war.

Raja Singh's elephants were also fewer. The most Raja Singh could do was to meet Sunil in a skirmish of blood and death.

That night Jace fell asleep with Gem beside him, hearing the child's quiet breathing. The stars above were shrouded by the thickening clouds.

The next morning dawned with the rumble of thunder—but no, not thunder, thought Jace, sitting up from his blanket. He stood, belting on his scabbard. Drums!

Gem jumped in his sleep and bolted up with a frightened whimper. "What is it, Jace?"

"The call for battle. Stay here on the blanket. I'm going to take a look. If the war cry is what I think, it comes not from Sunil but from your grandfather."

The solemn roll of the drums surged like waves across the darkened Brahmaputra valley. The beat spiraled into a frenzy, filling the plain with a foreboding call to the warriors to march for their maharaja in the certain face of overwhelming odds. Raja Singh, father-in-law of Jemani, grandfather of Gem, was telling Sunil he would confront him with only a few loyal men. The beat slowed into the war call of the rajputs: "Ram. Ram. Ram. Ram. Ram. Ram. . . ." Then it faded slowly. Silence.

Jace looked down at Gem with a confident smile. "This is your day, Gem. Your grandfather believes you

317

live. He sends the black elephant. It must be on its way now with his royal rajput guard."

Gem stared up at him, his teeth chattering with fear and excitement.

Jace reached down and lifted him above his head, then down to his feet. "Quickly, into your royal garb! Today you lay claim to two thrones!"

Gem groped into his bag for the gold cloth, the purple satin turban, the ruby, the small curved tulwar. His teeth continued to chatter, and his little fingers were stiff with cold. "The God who also speaks Hindi, help me! Help me! Help me!" he kept repeating.

Jace went swiftly to the edge of his position and saw a thousand winking lights from the smoldering fires in Sunil's village-camp. He too was ready. Today he hoped to kill the father of Jemani.

In the east, the first tinges of light brought a sullen hue, and in the valley where the two armies somberly converged, darkness yet clung to the dust that would turn blood red before the sun set on both victory and defeat, life and death.

As the sun advanced over the thick jungle, a chorus of battle horns cut through the morning, followed again by the awesome drums. The steady pulse beat rumbled through the ground and through the hills, erupting into a passion. The sound pulled Jace forward like a magnet as though he too must battle! It was the signal for the elite rajput cavalry in both armies to encircle their raja and fight to the death.

The drums stopped, and the Brahmaputra valley was transfixed with portentous quiet. Jace felt himself sweating even in the dawn air.

Where was the royal elephant!

In the light of day the battlefield was clearly visible now with its warriors, bull elephants, cannons, drummers, and rajputs. Like some pageant of tragedy, the act would soon commence.

The gate of Sibsagar was wide open, Raja Singh's smaller army, infantry, and elephants moving out to their death.

"I am ready," breathed Gem hoarsely, tugging at his sleeve. "Where is the elephant?"

Good question! Where was Gokul and the Black Royal Elephant!

From the edge of Sunil's camp, volleys of cannon fire exploded; the earth ripped and spat showers of debris toward the gate of Sibsagar and the raja's small but elite army. The cannons belched forth their hatred again. Rounds of slow-burning fire rained down on Raja Singh's elephants but bounced off the rhino-hide armor that straddled the mammoth beasts. The elephants trumpeted their scorn, and with their trunks encased in royal armor, they began their heavy march forward to meet Sunil's war elephants.

In Sunil's camp, the infantry standing beside the cannons pounded drums, their yellow turbans clear in the bright morning. A second volley from the cannons exploded, the impact more deadly as forty-pound shot ripped into the raja's infantry, and elephants fell and men were trampled.

Now the harsh chant from Sunil's rajputs began to echo as wave after wave of warriors moved forward toward the old raja.

But the raja's big elephants, manned by armored mahouts and carrying warriors in steel-plated howdahs, moved to encircle their king.

Jace watched, tensely gripping the handle of his sword. "Gokul! We are all dead men if you do not arrive quickly!"

Sunil's force of steel-armored elephants advanced,

their armor plate reflecting the sunlight. Five-pound cannons protruded from the armored howdahs carrying the rajputs. Other elephants carried kneeling archers who expertly shot volleys of arrows through the howdah's slits. Behind came walls of foot infantry in companies. Jace heard the ring of steel as barbs bounced off the elephants' armor.

But the faithful elephants surrounding the raja were trained to guard his particular howdah, and they reared out their magnificent trunks and snatched enemy warriors from their positions, hurling them to the ground, then crushing them.

Jace came alert as Gem tugged at his arm. He looked down, and the child's face was pale, his eyes wide and glistening. "My grandfather! He will die, Jace! Where is my black elephant?"

Jace clamped his jaw. Again his eyes searched the plain, then the perimeter of the trees. Nothing! He whistled for his horse. The stallion came and whinnied nervously, alert to the smell of battle.

"Wait here," breathed Jace. "There may be a slight chance I can get through now that the gate is open. I must find Gokul. I want you to hide in that hollowed tree, understand? Do not come out until I return. And if I do not come back, stay there. Do not go to Sibsagar. Ride your horse south to Kingscote. If you cannot find it, keep searching."

"Do not go. You too will be killed!"

"He is right," came an unexpected mocking voice.

Jace turned, sword in hand. *Sunil!*

He stood, lean and muscled in his royal garb, his dark eyes triumphant, a smile on his handsome face.

"Greetings, Javed Kasam. I would not wish you to die without first paying your greetings to me, the Maharaja of Assam." His eyes left Jace to fix on Gem. Sunil's smile faded. For one breathtaking moment Jace saw the bravado sink from his expression.

"Your brother's son," said Jace. "Your nephew, Prince Adesh."

The words, though deliberately quiet, had more effect than a shout.

"Adesh is not dead," Jace continued. "The child Sanjay murdered in the palanquin was a Burmese peasant boy too sick to know what happened. I advise you to stay back, Sunil, or I will kill you."

"Hardly, Major. Drop your sword and unbelt your scabbard. You have no hope. Take one step toward me and the twenty rajputs who have their horn bows aimed at the child will strike him down at once."

Was he lying? But no, Sunil would not come alone. Jace turned his head as the warriors stepped from the trees, their bows directed at Gem.

"I need not tell you they are expert shots," boasted Sunil.

Jace wondered what Gem would do. Would he cry, seek to hide?

Gem did not move. He stood staring at Sunil, and in his royal garb Prince Adesh never looked more noble, Jace thought with a pang of pride.

Jace scanned the rajputs, seeking some glimmer, some passion of loyalty toward Gem in their black eyes, but their rugged black-bearded faces were like flint.

He spoke to them in Hindi: "You behold the full-blooded son of Rajkumar Rajiv Singh! And Rajkumari Jemani Singh of Sibsagar! This is your future Maharaja Adesh Singh of Assam!"

Gem unexpectedly called out, pointing a small finger. "You must arrest my uncle Sunil for killing my father and mother! He is bad!"

As though lightning flashed, Jace saw the confused

expression on the warriors' faces.

"Lies!" said Sunil. "The child is an impostor brought by the English to deceive the Hindus. Kill them both!"

Jace lifted the gold chain around Gem's neck, where he had placed the royal rings of the old maharaja from Guwahati. "The boy's hand will grow strong to fit the power these rings represent. Look! They are your maharaja's!"

The rajputs recognized them and stood frozen, still uncertain of their action.

"He stole them," said Sunil with disdain.

"He entrusted them to me the night you had him assassinated."

The royal rajput guards would either bow the knee to the son of Rajiv or remain loyal to Sunil and kill them both. He acted swiftly to avert their immediate decision, fearing it would be the wrong one.

"You, Sunil! You are a coward and a murderer. You hide behind the strength of these warriors instead of fighting your own battles! Why are you not in the howdah so the warriors who die for you can see you? You break the law of your own people. A raja must be in sight at all times during a battle. Step forth. I intend to kill you for the mutiny at Plassey and for the assassination of the maharaja!"

"Kill him!" gritted Sunil to the chief rajput.

"He is my friend!" cried Gem.

A shout came from the trees, followed by a trumpeting elephant—two majestic beasts crashed forward, one carrying Gokul, the other with an empty howdah. *The Black Royal Elephant!*

In the brief moment when all eyes turned, Jace snatched Gem from the line of the archers and flung him into the bushes, retrieving his sword.

While the guards with Sunil hesitated, Gem crawled

out of sight. Six rajput guards with Gokul rode into the open, their bows taut and ready to shoot. Two were his friendly acquaintances from Sualkashi, another was Nadir, who had been among the dozen warriors riding with Sir Hugo, and who had warned Jace at Kingscote.

Nadir, a rajput captain and respected warrior, shouted to the men with Sunil, withdrawing his katar and lifting it high. "Are you of the warrior blood, but fools? Would you die for the traitor-prince who killed Rajiv? Our future maharaja lives in the blood of the son of Rajiv! Where is your love for honor? Adesh must live!"

The warriors lowered their bows.

"Adesh lives!"

Jace seized the moment. He went after Gem and returned holding the boy high overhead against the backdrop of the raging battle. The warriors removed their swords and beat them against their leather shields amid a crescendo of cheers.

Jace carried him to the royal elephant. Nadir rode up and, bowing, fist at heart, took Gem and placed him inside the howdah seat. "Prince Adesh!"

The mahout signaled the elephant to trumpet on cue, displaying all its royal beauty and power. Jace wondered if Gem would be frightened, but he was not and gazed down bravely. Jace smiled his encouragement, and Gem touched the ruby dangling below his royal turban to make certain it was in place.

Jace had never seen such a large and majestic beast. Shining with black paint, it lumbered forward, driven by a royal mahout with a red turban. The elephant's royal covering was glittering gold cloth, and its howdah was sprinkled with jewels and boasted the standard of Raja Singh. The rajputs gave another shout of allegiance. With swift precision they fell into a disciplined line, the royal entourage leading out toward the battlefield, toward danger, but toward hope—if only the thousands would hear the drums blaring, the horns sounding, and turn to see the Black Royal Elephant arriving.

Gem had turned to glance back at Jace, his eyes pleading for the major's presence. Jace went to mount his horse when suddenly he whirled. Sunil was gone!

Gokul came huffing from the jungle trees. "Over there, sahib! Behind the trees!"

Jace ran after him. He did not go far before he saw Sunil.

Alone and abandoned, he stood with rage on his face, gripping his weapon. "Do you think I run like a rat scampering for its hole? I came to don the tunic of a warrior!" Sunil stepped toward him, deadly cold. "You, Major! Come! We will do our battle here. I will kill you."

"Yes," breathed Jace. "It is fitting. Just you and I!"

25

Sunil slipped the deadly katar from his belt, and his smile was vicious. "No swords, Javed Kasam. That is too simple for warriors such as we." In contempt, he tossed him the Indian blade designed for thrusting.

"Take heed, sahib!" hissed Gokul to Jace.

Jace picked up the blade and made certain it would not fail him.

"Would I deceive you?" mocked Sunil, removing a second katar.

Gokul took position behind a rock.

Jace had used the thrusting dagger before, but he knew Sunil was far more adept. Perhaps he was a fool to give him even the slightest advantage. Sunil, however, was already unbelting his scabbard and tossing aside his sword and cumbersome turban and jewels. In minutes he was a stranger, a ruthless, deadly warrior determined to kill him.

Jace started to remove his jacket while Sunil, still wearing his terrible smile, waited with exaggerated condescension.

Jace stood within fifty feet of Sunil. He took his time, slowly removing his jacket, then his scabbard, and finally his hat, tossing it aside.

He could see the delay was getting to Sunil. "How does it feel to know that you have lost all possibility of ruling Assam, Sunil? Instead of you, your brother's son, Adesh, will sit on the throne. He looks much like the lovely Jemani, does he not? You say you loved her, but she bore Rajiv's child. It is *his* son who will reign."

"We will fight, Major. Save your words!"

Jace now matched Sunil's previous mocking smile with one of his own.

Across the plain the noise of battle continued, adding to their tension.

"Hear, Sunil? Soon your entire army will be acclaiming Prince Adesh. How that must rankle after all your meticulous scheming. Years of searching for him, foiled. You murdered your own brother . . . and your own uncle in Guwahati. The plans with Roxbury, the mutiny at Plassey—all for nothing."

At last Jace saw sweat stand out on Sunil's forehead . . . and he moved toward him.

"And now you will die. How fitting I should use the same kind of dagger that was thrust into my friend Rajiv."

His words were having their effect—he would need that emotional edge. He had no illusions about the fighting ability of Sunil, who was stronger than most of the soft and spoiled princes. Broad through the shoulders and chest, his arms and legs were powerfully muscled.

Sunil approached, and the two men circled warily.

Jace held his katar low, cutting edge up. Sunil thought he had the advantage, and Jace knew it, but his own ability rested in his fighting experience in Burma with Zin, and when he had fought for survival after escaping China on the Old Silk Road.

Sunil moved in suddenly, his blade darting with a stabbing thrust like the strike of a cobra, and the point ripped a gash in the buckskin of Jace's breeches.

Jace struck back, and they both went down, rolling over on the rocks, stabbing and thrusting. Coming up, they faced each other again. Flecks of blood spattered Jace's shirt front. He sprang suddenly, and Sunil leaped back to escape his thrust, then circling, thrusting . . . another spot of blood appeared, this time on Sunil's arm.

Sunil was incredibly swift, agile, his hard face like a mask, showing no emotion.

Jace moved, seemed to slip, and Sunil sprang in. Instantly Jace turned and swung with a chop of his left hand, catching Sunil on the side of the neck and smashing him to the ground.

Sunil, unaccustomed to Oriental fighting, seemed surprised—yet quickly recovered. He came up, lunged low, but Jace stepped aside and thrust, his katar entering Sunil's shoulder. Sunil swung around swiftly to strike back. Jace struck again with a vicious chop and Sunil fell—dazed. He stomped on his wrist and Sunil's grip on his weapon loosened. Jace viciously kicked it out of his fingers, and it landed in the brush.

"Get up."

Sunil sprang at him, knocking Jace backward, but he rolled over and came to his feet. Sunil was searching for his blade. Jace tossed his aside with disgust.

"Come, Sunil."

Sunil stood with a wide stance, staring at him.

Around them the sky churned with the monsoon clouds. Lightning flashed and rumbled above the jungle trees; below them death opened its jaws to receive the rajputs in hand-to-hand fighting.

Sunil gripped and ungripped his fists, then moved

toward him again. Jace circled to the right, causing Sunil to turn to keep in front of him. Jace feinted a move, but Sunil only watched and was not fooled. Sweat ran down their bodies and Jace's lips tasted salt.

Jace moved his left foot forward, gaining a few inches, crouching a little. Sunil feinted, then came in fast. Jace struck his hand down and, catching his wrist, swung the arm back and under, then up Sunil's back. He forced the wrist higher, toward the other shoulder. Sunil's face went white as he tried to twist out of the hold, but Jace kept his grip and heaved upward with all his strength, until he heard bone crack.

Jace released him. Sunil staggered, lost his footing, and fell. Jace turned, exhausted, and walked away, while Sunil crawled toward his horse where he had left his scabbard . . . and his pistol.

Jace sank to the earth, sweating and breathing heavily, staring up at the monsoon clouds.

A pistol shot cracked suddenly. Jace turned to see Gokul standing over the dying body of Sunil.

26

When Jace arrived near the battlefield it had become a nightmare of hand-to-hand combat. Raja Singh's loyal forces were outnumbered.

"I do not see the royal elephant," murmured Gokul worriedly.

The rajput soldiers guarding Raja Singh wore heavy leather helmets and skirts of armor. Steel netting covered their faces and necks. They fired volleys of arrows at the equally armored rajputs fighting for Sunil, whom they did not know was dead. Elephants were everywhere carrying howdahs of rajput archers; some carried two-pound swivel guns mounted on the elephants' backs.

"I fear for the raja," said Jace. "He is the focus of the fighting. Soon he will be surrounded, and there is no way to halt the battle."

Where was Nadir with the royal elephant?

Sunil's infantry massed to encircle Raja Singh. His protective wall of elephants and rajputs were coming under fierce attack. Sibsagar was on the defensive, the number of imperial forces diminishing.

"Look," breathed Gokul.

Jace watched the raja's royal war elephants with respect. Trained to protect the raja, they seemed oblivious to their own danger. The armored trunks reached and seized warrior after warrior, flinging them down to the bloody dust and crushing them beneath their feet.

"But they cannot protect him much longer, sahib."

Then Jace heard what he had longed for. The kettle-drums were rolling, swelling to a crescendo, rolling like waves over the battle scene. The battle horns pierced the morning, then the drums again, pounding the steady pulsating beat.

"Sahib! There! It is well!"

Jace had seen the Black Royal Elephant coming from the trees, led by Nadir and the rajputs sworn to Gem.

"Ram! Ram!" they cried. "Ram! Ram!"

In the center moved the mammoth black elephant, now armored and carrying Gem in a steel howdah decorated with gold. Jace caught his breath and was on his feet, intent on mounting his horse to gallop to the elephant's side. Gem was standing erect inside the howdah, beneath a huge crimson umbrella.

Gokul caught his arm. "No, sahib! No! Do not go! You will be killed in seconds!"

But he need not have worried, for Jace paused and stared. Sunil's rajputs from Guwahati saw the standard of Rajiv carried by Gem on the big black elephant. They saw the boy in royal turban and gold cloth standing erect as though to hold back the very arrows of death.

Slowly, Sibsagar's chant of "Ram! Ram!" was taken up by the rajputs of Sunil. With a swiftness that left him breathless, they turned like fierce tigers to rally to the side of their new maharaja.

Gokul looked at Jace and laughed. "It worked, sahib! God has been merciful to us, to all of us."

Jace, exhausted, let the horse's reins slip from his fingers and watched in silence as the battle turned from certain defeat to great rejoicing.

The Black Royal Elephant carrying Gem lumbered forward to the cheers of the warriors. Nadir was leading the way toward Raja Singh, who, in stunned and tearful disbelief, stood in royal garb inside his howdah to glimpse his first sight of Jemani's son, and to welcome him to the royal palace of Sibsagar.

Inside the palace of Raja Singh, Jace found Ethan. Sir Hugo, where was he? wondered Jace. It was evening in Sibsagar, and the ancient city was lit with ten thousand torches, celebrating the unexpected good fortune of getting their first glimpse of the boy who would be maharaja.

"Where is Roxbury?" demanded Jace.

"Gone," said Ethan wearily, slumping into a gilded chair in a chamber with crimson and gold hangings and black and silver-veined marble walls and floor. "I have not seen him since the battle first began. I am sure he is in hiding. He must know by now that he is defeated and his ambitions in ruin."

Jace wondered. He had no peace despite the good outcome of the battle and the homecoming of Gem. He could think of little now except reaching Kingscote. *Was all well?*

"Maybe Sahib Roxbury went to Kingscote."

Gokul's uneasy words only forced Jace onto his feet, and although exhausted, he was determined to ride out that night.

"Yes," breathed Ethan, his gray eyes coming swiftly to Jace. "He would go there first, then perhaps back to England."

"And you?" asked Jace.

"I think, Major, that I shall take advantage for a time

of His Excellency's hospitality. Then, perhaps, I will journey to Burma."

Jace reached into his jacket and drew out the soiled drawing that Zin's official had given him showing the route to the mission station of Felix Carey. Jace handed it to Ethan and smiled wearily.

"It so happens that Carey is in desperate need of a physician. He has introduced the smallpox vaccination into Burma, and he is gifted in medicine, but he is no doctor. You could be the answer to his prayers."

Ethan took the map and scanned the drawing. He said nothing for a moment. "An interesting proposition, Jace. Perhaps I shall do just that."

Ethan stood facing Jace. Their gaze met briefly, and Ethan seemed about to say something but changed his mind. "I wish you well, Major."

"Yes." Jace took his hand firmly. "You did well, Ethan. Without your help here in the palace the outcome would have been very different."

Ethan's eyes flickered with appreciation.

They stood for a moment saying nothing, then with a slight smile Jace touched his shoulder and walked out. Gokul turned to Ethan, salaamed, and followed.

Out in the hall Jace was surprised to see Gem now surrounded by muscled royal guards.

Jace smiled and bowed. "Your Excellency!"

"I have a gift for you, Jace."

Almost shy again, the boy walked forward on gold sandals and handed him a poorly wrapped present. "I wrapped it myself," he said.

Jace took the small box, turning it over in his hand. "Whatever it is, I shall cherish it."

"You will come often to see me?"

"I will come."

"And bring my English mother?"

"I am certain nothing will be able to keep her away."

Gem smiled, and Jace saw the first sign of happiness in his eyes.

"I will send a royal elephant for her—and you! My grandfather wishes to meet you both and to reward you for your bravery today."

"Your own bravery was something to behold."

"I remembered your words in Burma . . . your words about God . . . then I was no longer afraid."

The royal guards hovered over the boy, anxious to get him safely into the raja's royal chambers. Jace bowed to the young boy, and was escorted down the hall and into the courtyard, where Gokul waited with their horses.

"Kingscote shall be a welcome sight, sahib."

"You do not know how welcome. Come, our work here is done. We have exceptionally good news for Coral."

"I am sure the lovely English damsel waits, pining for you," said Gokul with glinting black eyes.

Jace arched a dark brow as he placed the wrapped present from Gem in his pocket. Then he turned the reins of his horse to ride out the gate of Sibsagar to Kingscote.

27

Kingscote

The nightmare has only begun, thought Coral, clutching the loaded pistol as she backed toward the stairway. Yanna's friend Thilak had not gotten through to warn the mercenaries her father had hired to guard the plantation—or were they all dead, including Thilak?

As night settled, the Burmese renegades were everywhere, closing in about the mansion. She heard windows breaking. The wood was splintering on the heavy front door, and she watched the bolts weakening. From behind her in the kitchen, a shot rang out as the old cook Piroo fired at an intruder, the sound followed by a woman's cry.

Rosa! thought Coral.

Out front on the lawn, she heard the Indian workers loyal to the Kendall family fighting to guard the front entrance. Old men, women, even children, had all come rushing from the hatcheries, and although outnumbered, they defended their positions with whatever weapons they had. Dazed, Coral found herself thinking of how proud she was of their heroic effort to save the feringhis.

335

Into her mind stabbed the words coming from the Indian who guarded the front door. "Run, sahiba! Run! We will try to stop them!"

"Where are Yanna and Preetah?" shouted Coral.

"We are here!" came their call from the upper hallway.

Behind her on the stairway, Kathleen stood with a pistol. Coral felt her older sister tugging at her arm, and Marianna, pale but coldly determined for one time in her life, stood staring toward the door giving way under the machetes.

"Coral!" demanded Kathleen.

Coral turned and rushed up the stairs, glancing back into the hallway. The door was caving in. Male servants converged in the hall to guard the stairway. Old Piroo stood with his gun in his hands still white with bread flour, his apron now soiled with blood. He took his stand on the lower stair to guard their retreat.

The door broke and heaved open. She saw a rugged warrior, his hand clutching a short curved blade. Piroo fired. The Burmese stumbled backward. As the servants sought to push the door in place, there were other determined footsteps rushing up the porch steps, and warriors entering through broken windows. She heard a scream from the back of the house—from her mother's room! Coral whirled toward the hallway. Someone had reached the top floor!

Her strength flowed back into her body. Her heart thudded in her ears. *Marianna!*

Coral raced up the stairs, each step too slow, hearing her sister's hysterical voice and the sound of furniture breaking. There was no one to help. The men servants were fighting in the hall, the silk workers battled on the lawn, and in the garden near the cook room door, they were trying desperately to hold the marauders back.

Coral saw the door to her mother's room standing open. Preetah was on the hall floor, unconscious; Yanna was struggling to reload her rifle, her black hair streaming wildly about her face.

"In there!" she screamed at Coral.

Coral rushed through the door, raising her pistol to see Kathleen in the grip of a renegade. But Marianna had already grabbed Sir Hampton's war saber on display in the hall. Just as Coral reached the door with the pistol, Marianna gripped the saber handle with both hands and brought it down with a whack. The man released Kathleen and stumbled onto his knees. Marianna struck him again and he fell face forward.

Kathleen stared at the unconscious warrior and slumped into a faint.

Marianna stood white-faced and still, both small hands still gripping the saber, its point resting on the carpet in front of her. Her wide eyes met Coral's.

"Quick! Get Yanna and Preetah in here! Bolt the door! I'll lock the verandah—" Coral's voice stopped abruptly. Outside in the carriageway, horse hooves pounded. There was more shouting, more gunfire, and the added sound of steel striking steel.

"Help has come!" cried Yanna from the broken verandah door. "Thilak did get through. Soldiers! No—it is not him—they look to be from Jorhat! Many of them, maybe fifty! Thank God!"

Jorhat! Was it Jace? Coral ran across her mother's room out onto the verandah and peered below, her eyes anxiously scanning the darkened lawn. In the flaring torchlight she saw men fighting, while one man in command sat astride his strong muscled horse. He looked up toward the verandah and saw her. As the glow from the firelight fell across his face, her heart paused with disappointment and alarm.

He is Burmese! These are not British soldiers from Jorhat!

Below, a woman rushed forward from the shadows and stood looking up. "Miss Coral! It is me, Jan-Lee! I bring friends!"

Friends! "Jan-Lee," cried Coral with joy. She ran from the bedchamber into the hall. Preetah was being attended by Mera while the child Reena hovered like a nervous bird, wringing her tiny hands in despair. Coral stopped long enough to draw the child into her arms. "It is all right now, Reena! Jan-Lee has come and brought friends to help us. The fighting will be over."

Coral hurried down the stairs to the ugly sight of the door hanging on broken hinges. There were dead and wounded on the hall floor and out on the porch, but the Burmese fighters Jan-Lee had brought were bringing the assault to an end.

Her knees weak, the pistol held loosely against the side of her skirt, Coral saw Jan-Lee enter through the door in a soiled hooded cloak, making her way over bodies and broken furniture.

Coral looked into the dark eyes welling with tears, a face lined with care and streaked with dust, her black hair speckled with gray hanging limp and gnarled. Jan-Lee glanced about with dismay, then looked toward Coral, her hands outstretched, and Coral met her in an embrace.

"Thank God," murmured Coral, "you came in time."

She opened her eyes to confront a strong Burmese warrior standing in the doorway, his black eyes cold, his long gray-black hair drawn back and tied with animal skin.

Jan-Lee must have felt her stiffen, for she turned toward the doorway, where the man stood motionless.

"This—this is my husband, Warrior Sun Li, nephew of Warlord Zin."

Coral held back her surprise. Zin—the man who held Gem. And Jan-Lee's husband was his nephew. But had not Jan-Lee informed them soon after Emerald was born that her husband had died in the skirmish at Jorhat defending the British? She looked at Sun Li with caution.

"He has come in peace," said Jan-Lee softly.

When Coral looked at her for explanation, Jan-Lee said quietly, "There is much to explain. My husband and I have been long separated, but when Miss Elizabeth was so sick I knew I must take a risk. I went to him in the jungle near Kingscote for help." She turned to him. "This is the daughter of the Master of Kingscote, the Kendall daughter I told you about."

Sun Li stepped forward, and with precision he lowered his head. "My humble apology for the devil renegades who trespassed your land. Those men who came once served me but were worthless dogs who acted against my wishes. My honorable soldiers are now making a quick end to their troublesome ways."

Coral rallied her strength. "Yes, thank you. Without your arrival we would all have been killed."

"It will bring you pleasure to know that the battle for Sibsagar has failed to bring Maharaja Sunil to power."

So Sibsagar had been the destination of the massive army that the mercenaries on Kingscote had seen on the road, moving northeast. She had feared Sunil was on his way to fight Warlord Zin and capture Gem. Sunil was defeated! Her thoughts raced to Sir Hugo. Where was he? Was he alive?

"And Sunil's army?" she asked worriedly.

"A courier brought us word today that Sunil's warriors have vowed loyalty to Prince Adesh Singh. The prince is safe and in loyal care."

For a moment she could think of nothing else, and her relief spiraled upward in silent thanksgiving to God. If Gem was safe, then Jace too would probably be alive.

Jan-Lee had turned to her husband and spoke in low tones. He stepped out onto the porch and gave an order in Burmese, and a man wearing a worn leather tunic with an ankle-length cloak stepped into the hall.

"I present Kung yu Tei, a wise man in the lore of Eastern drugs, both good and evil. He has come to look upon Madame Kendall."

Coral's heart leaped with joy. "Oh, yes, please, do come. This way."

The man bowed with silent dignity and followed her up the stairs.

Inside Elizabeth's chamber, Kathleen and Marianna showed surprise to see him but remained silent. Coral was about to follow him to her mother's bedside, when Jan-Lee took hold of her arm and drew her to the other side of the room.

"Jan-Lee, you risked your life to venture into the jungle for help; how can we ever thank you?"

"I did what I must to help Miss Elizabeth, who has long been a friend to me and Emerald, and to save Kingscote."

"When you did not return with Doctor Boswell we feared something had happened on the road. And Emerald has been asking for you daily!"

"I could not find your cousin or uncle on the road toward Darjeeling, so I went to the secret jungle camp of my husband. He sent a message to me only days before Natine tried to harm you both. Natine knew that my husband was not dead as I said, that I had written him several messages, and he threatened to tell your father. But I was not a spy! I wrote him pleading, asking him not to attack. I have always been loyal to you!"

Confused, Coral said, "It would take more than Na-tine's lies to turn the family against you. You need not have feared his threats. But I don't understand about your husband. You told my mother he had been killed at Jorhat."

Her haggard face turned sorrowful. "I must confess past sins to you, to Miss Elizabeth and Sir Hampton. My husband—I said he was killed when Emerald was born, but as you now see, it is not so. Sorrowfully, he served with Zin these treacherous years, and I feared to let your mother and father know. I had to think of Emerald."

Coral shook her head. "You need not have feared bearing the reputation of your husband. My parents would have understood."

"No, Miss Coral, there is—is more. My husband was a spy for Burma, for his uncle Warlord Zin. It was my husband who helped steal Gem away that ugly night."

Coral stared, stunned.

Tears showed in Jan-Lee's eyes. "I tried to stop him, but he would not listen."

"You knew?" whispered Coral, devastated.

"No, no, only when fire started in the hatcheries I guessed and feared what would happen. I rushed to the nursery to hide Gem, but the sepoy serving Zin was already there. I told him I would also go with Gem to wherever my husband waited to bring Gem to Warlord Zin, but he would not let me. He told me Zin had my sister and her child too, and that all would be killed if I said anything. Then he hit me, and I remember nothing else."

"Jan-Lee. . . ."

"My sister, she—she was Gem's nurse these years at Zin's palace. I feared not only for you and Gem but for her and her boy if you went to Zin demanding Gem's release. Sunil was also involved with my husband, promising him that the English presence in Assam would be no more, that he would give Burma the land on the border. I guessed that Sunil had an assassin kill Rajiv the night you brought Gem home from the hut, but I knew that enemies prowled in the jungle. If I said anything, all of Kingscote might have been burned."

Coral could say nothing, feeling her own dismay and seeing the pain in Jan-Lee's face.

"Tonight I learned from my husband that my sister and her son are dead. But you rejoice, Miss Coral. You be happy because Gem—Prince Adesh lives. And my husband . . . he is no longer your enemy. Sunil has lost the war, and Burma knows that with two thrones united in Gem, Assam is too strong for war now. And soon the English will arrive. My husband listened to me in the jungle as I pled for your life and Miss Elizabeth. He is a man tired of the jungle, of running and hiding. Warlord Zin sent him a message to come back, to not fight against Kingscote because of a man named Javed Kasam. Zin said you would marry this man who is his friend. That, Miss Coral, I do not understand."

Coral managed a weary smile. Javed Kasam. If only that particular warrior would walk through the door now and hold her tightly in his embrace. "Perhaps you will understand one day. I can say nothing now."

Jan-Lee nodded. "My husband will leave the jungle near Kingscote and return to his uncle. I will take Emerald and go with him."

Coral was overwhelmed with all the information, and her silence must have been mistaken by Jan-Lee for anger. "Forgive me, Miss Coral. Yet—I did tell you Gem was not dead so you would not sorrow. I told you of a scar on the child's foot."

"Oh, Jan-Lee, I am not angry. I understand the reason for your silence. You were afraid for all of us. You too were held ransom all these years. But it is over now." She took hold of the woman's shoulders. "Gem is safe. He is a prince who will rule in Guwahati."

Jan-Lee's eyes flickered with sudden emotion. "Not only Guwahati but Sibsagar."

"Sibsagar?" asked Coral curiously.

"So Sun Li tells me. You will learn soon. I know little more. I must go to Emerald now, to get her ready to ride with her father."

"Oh, but you need not go," cried Coral. "Your loyalty is not questioned. And it was you who risked your life to find your husband in the jungle camp. You saved us all. And you brought the wise man to treat my mother. I am in your debt. We all are."

Jan-Lee took hold of her. For the first time a small smile touched the ayah's lips. "It is enough that you say so. I will hold those words to my heart. But I must go. It is time for Emerald to look upon the face of her father. And now with peace coming—perhaps we will find our own peace in Burma in the house of his uncle, Warlord Zin."

"I hope so for your sake and Emerald's. And if not, remember you are always welcome to return."

"I will remember."

———

When Sun Li mounted his horse to ride out the next morning with his followers, the dead had been buried in the jungle, and the windows and doors were temporarily repaired.

Coral stood on the steps as they prepared to ride away. Jan-Lee was mounted with Emerald in front of her. It was the girl's eyes that held Coral's attention, for they shone with silent adoration as they fixed proudly upon her father.

Sun Li leaned from his horse and handed Coral a long

item wrapped in red cloth. "Zin has sent this. It is to be given to Javed Kasam on his wedding day."

Coral took the gift. It was heavy and she guessed it to be a sword.

"Tell him it is a gift from the Zin. He first thought to use it against the English at Sibsagar when he fought beside Sunil, but Zin has listened to Javed Kasam's words. My uncle now returns this gift in peace, and I also return across the border to my own place."

He turned his horse to ride, glancing at Jan-Lee and Emerald. She brought her horse beside him, the warriors following. As Jan-Lee left she turned her head, and there was a faint smile on her face. She said something to Emerald, who tore her eyes from her father to smile and lift her hand toward Coral. Then glimpsing Kathleen and Marianna on the upper verandah with Reena, she waved goodbye.

Reena brought her fingers to her forehead.

Below on the steps, Coral watched until they were out of sight behind the trees. Only a trail of dust lingered beneath the lowering sky.

Inside the house, she climbed the stairs to the upper hall and heard the excited voices of her sisters coming from her mother's chambers. Coral laid the gift from Zin on the hall table beneath her father's war saber hanging again on the wall and hurried into the room.

Kathleen and Marianna turned with the first smiles she had seen on their faces in weeks.

"Is she awake?" asked Coral expectantly.

"No, but she does seem to be moving in her sleep. And Marianna is sure she heard her whisper Father's name."

Coral came to the bedside. Though her hopes had momentarily soared with the excitement of her sisters, she saw only her mother's stillness.

"When Father arrives he may be the one able to reach her," said Kathleen.

Coral said nothing.

28

It was nearly a week later. The morning sun momentarily broke through the clouds, and peacocks strutted across the lawn, making shrill calls. Coral placed a red rose on her mother's breakfast tray held by Kathleen, while Mera looked on, smiling. Elizabeth was not well, but her condition had improved, and however feeble the ray of light, it was a cause for celebration. Suddenly, from Kings Road a company of some twenty men mounted on horses turned onto the carriageway and came riding toward the mansion. Marianna came alert and walked toward the window to look out.

As Marianna watched them, the tension in her face broke into a delighted smile. She let out a high-pitched squeal, nearly causing Kathleen to drop the tray. Coral turned to see Marianna throw open the door, and lifting her skirts, she ran down the steps to meet the riders.

Coral hurried out, scanning the riders as they approached. She caught a glimpse of the two men in front, rugged men in hats and riding cloaks. As she recognized their faces her breath paused. "It is Father and Seward!"

She ran to meet them.

"Father," Kathleen whispered and, pushing the tray toward Mera, rushed out the door.

Sir Hampton dismounted and swept Marianna into his arms, and Coral and Kathleen were quickly at his side, both trying to embrace him at the same time while Seward looked on grinning.

"Now that be a sight worth it all."

"Yes, sir," said Ensign Niles, smiling. "Makes me anxious to get home to England."

"England, he says! Nae, but Scotland it is!" said Seward good-naturedly.

The ensign and his small troop from Jorhat had met Hampton and Seward on the road toward Kingscote. The ensign, who had already given Seward the letter entrusted to him by the major, now reached into his jacket and pulled out a second letter. He waited for an appropriate lull in the exchange of tears and greetings between the Kendall daughters and their father. When he at last had an opportunity, he cleared his voice. "Miss Kendall?"

Three women turned and looked up at him. He scanned their faces and found himself growing warm. "Ah . . . Miss Coral?"

She smiled, and her eyes went to the letter. Her heart beat faster as somehow she suspected that it was from Jace. "I am Coral."

"Major Buckley asked me to give this to you before he rode to Burma."

———

In Elizabeth's dim chamber, Sir Hampton knelt beside her bed and held her thin hand between his strong ones.

"Liza?" he whispered for the third time. " 'Tis me,

Hampton." He leaned toward the pale face, and found the once-lovely features now gaunt. "Dear God," he lamented. "Liza, my love, can you hear me?" he rasped, reaching bronzed fingers to smooth away her dark hair now streaked with gray. He leaned and kissed her, then buried his head into her neck as his emotions cracked. "Liza, don't leave me. Nothing means anything without you. Not Kingscote, not all my tomorrows. Liza—"

Coral quietly shut the bedchamber door on the scene and stood in the hallway, feeling the familiar ache in her throat. The warm homecoming had quickly been shrouded by the news of Elizabeth's condition.

Her sisters stood waiting, hoping for good news. They had thought the voice of their father might bring her out of the peaceful but deep sleep. Seward hung back with a slight frown, and Coral suspected he was thinking of Natine, perhaps even blaming himself for her mother's tragedy.

"She did not respond?" asked Kathleen after seeing Coral's expression.

Coral shook her head. The gloom that hung in the hall only made her wish to get alone in her room and read Jace's letter again. At least the news of Gem was wonderful, she reminded herself.

Before going to bed she walked over to where Seward stood. "She seemed a trifle better this morning and we had hoped. . . . The Burmese doctor did what he could and left a powder. You must not feel bad, Seward. If you had stayed here instead of going to Darjeeling, Father would have been killed."

He nodded but said nothing. She laid a hand on his arm, then turned and walked to her chamber.

If only the voice of Hampton would bring Mother back to consciousness. But what if she did hear him? What if she *could not* respond?

The thought tormented her, and she clutched Jace's letter tightly, as though by doing so she received comfort. "Please, Lord, make her come out of this stupor."

Seward watched Coral walk down the hall. There was no more he could do here, he thought, depressed. What could he say to Hampton, to any of them? He turned to leave, to make his bunk with the small troop from Jorhat that was bedded down near the stables. In the hall his gaze bumped against a long object wrapped in red silk. He stopped and squinted.

That embroidered dragon! That be the sign of Warlord Zin.

And just what was it doing here?

He carefully lifted it and turned to Kathleen. "Lass, this is a sword—from Zin."

Kathleen's disinterest showed. "Oh? I've never seen it before. Maybe it belonged to Jan-Lee's husband."

Seward's suspicions were rising. "Might I look at it?"

"Why, of course, Seward."

She and Marianna turned to walk to their rooms. "Good-night," they echoed.

"Aye, lassies, good-night. I'll be with the troop near the stables if ye be needin' me."

He unwrapped the red silk and stifled a cry of jubilation. The Mogul sword!

His face broke into a smile. "Aye, Jace be happy to see this again."

He wondered that it had sat on the hall table for a week since Sun Li and his Burmese warriors had ridden back—it was worth a fortune. So it was Zin who had somehow ended up with the sword stolen from Jace in Calcutta, he thought, frowning. He hesitated as he weighed it in his sturdy hand, then his bushy brows came together. *Best be guardin' this myself until he returns.*

Wrapping it again, and still frowning, he left the mansion. He walked in the darkness in the direction of the stables, glancing up at the clouds. The monsoon would be breaking. *The lad ought to be arrivin' soon now from Sibsagar. And Roxbury, where might that conniving blackguard be lurking?*

He paused and glanced back at the mansion with the golden light burning in the upper windows, then walked on.

Seward chuckled as he imagined Jace's exuberance when he saw the prized blade. "It may be we will have us a fine mansion in Darjeeling after all."

————

Seated on the satin-covered chair, Coral listened to the grumbles of thunder announcing the monsoon. The clouds would soon open and the drenching rain would pour. Kingscote rested in stillness beneath the canopy of dense clouds. Nothing moved, nothing stirred amid the jungle. Palm fronds were etched darkly against zigzag flashes of lightning. She spread the sheet of paper to read Jace's letter again.

He wrote briefly of all that had happened since leaving Kingscote to ride to Burma in search of Gem. It came as a delightful surprise that the Lord had worked out circumstances whereby Gem had been able to spend time with Felix Carey.

Through Jace's words, she relived the tension he must have experienced when he told her of his plan to thwart Sunil in his effort to rule Sibsagar and Guwahati by introducing Gem on the Black Royal Elephant.

Coral already knew through Jan-Lee's husband that

the feat had been successful, and so she could without fear read about the risk Jace had taken. She felt pride in him as she tried to imagine how he had managed to bring Gem to Sibsagar at the right time to defeat Sunil's plot.

"Gem, an heir to two thrones. And Jemani had been the daughter of the Raja of Sibsagar!"

Coral remembered her saying at her baptism: *"My Rajiv is a prince. There is no one better among men."*

A prince! Of course! Why had she not thought of what she said before? And Jemani was a rajkumari, a princess from Sibsagar! And Gem—

"Gem is to be maharaja," whispered Coral, and laughter welled up in her heart. "God allowed Jace and me to protect him from Sunil."

She lingered again over Jace's farewell: "I shall soon return to claim Roxbury's promise of a Christmas wedding on Kingscote."

She smiled, her heart pounding; then her smile faded as feminine vanity stole over her. "Whatever will I wear? No one in the family even knows yet!"

In her own happy but disjointed thoughts tinged with nervous excitement, she did not hear the lone horse ride up in the carriageway below the open verandah. She sat in the chair holding the letter, lost in her thoughts.

———

Sir Hugo Roxbury entered the silent house. He did not know that Hampton and Seward had arrived safely from Darjeeling, nor that Coral had shared the letter from Alex with her father and sisters telling of his voyage to London.

As though a harbinger of what was to come, a blinding streak of lightning stabbed the blackness above the mansion, followed by a loud clap of thunder that rattled the broken glass in the downstairs windows. Hugo climbed the stairs to his room.

Coral heard quiet footsteps in the hall, and they seemed to slow, then abruptly stop outside her door. She wondered at the odd reaction and expected it to be followed by a knock. Her light was on and the golden glow showed beneath the door . . . but no knock sounded and the steps moved on.

Strange, she thought, and peered out her door down the hall.

Sir Hugo's chamber door was slightly ajar, and a light burned.

Her heart thudded. He was back. How dare he show his face in the house? Did he think they did not know how he had used Natine in his vile plan with the cobra and drugs? And what of the trap set for her father in Darjeeling! Did he think he could lie his way out again?

She left her room and walked quietly down the hall until she came to his door. She knocked. There was no answer. She hesitated, then pushed the door open and looked in.

Sir Hugo had his back toward her, his bags open on the bed, and he was quickly packing.

Anger filled Coral, and she said with sarcasm, "What! Uncle! You are leaving so soon? You have not yet made Kingscote your own."

At the sound of her voice he turned, startled. Coral wanted to flinch under his dark eyes.

"You," he said so quietly that she shivered. His surprise revealed that he knew about the cobra. For a moment their eyes locked, and she wanted to scream with terror and run. Perhaps because the reality struck with such awful clarity, she could only stand and meet his gaze.

"No," she whispered. "I am not dead yet, Uncle. Natine's niece Preetah was able to bleed my arm. But my mother is very ill. She may never recover the use of her mind. My father is with her now. Seward rescued him from your treachery in Darjeeling."

Sir Hugo said nothing and only looked down at her, his face and eyes too still and deep to reveal the thoughts racing through his mind.

"Where is Ethan?" she demanded. "What have you done to him? Did you try to kill him too?"

He seemed to recover from his daze and returned to his packing. "You are beginning to sound like a hysterical woman, my dear. I would have thought that emotion fitting your sisters but not you. Ethan is at Sibsagar. Do pull yourself together. As for the cobra, it was merely meant to frighten you. To keep you from stubbornly pressing ahead in your ambition with the school."

"You would know best about the ugly side of ambition. Was burning my school and my Hindi New Testament also meant to frighten me? If you think you can return to London as though nothing has happened, and simply lie your way back into Aunt Margaret's arms, you are mistaken. I shall write her of your evil. You are a wicked and dangerous man, Uncle."

He laughed softly but went on packing. "If I am so wretchedly vile and dangerous, my dear, you had best alert Seward I am here. You should not remain alone in my presence for long. I may try to make good on Natine's failure."

"More threats, dear Uncle?"

"I have no time to waste on words, Coral. I am leaving tonight, and I shall no longer hinder you or your plans. Are you not relieved?" His words held a sudden tone of sarcasm. "As for London, I have every intention

354

of returning to my wife and daughter. I advise you not to be foolish enough to write her—lest I be forced to intercept the letter." He turned, and his dark eyes were cool. "I should hate for something to happen to Margaret."

A chill ran through her. "Are you threatening Margaret or me?"

"I am telling you to be wise and keep all your wild suspicions to yourself. Hampton and I shall work this matter out together by correspondence."

"So you can think of new schemes with which to blind him? You will never give up, will you, Uncle?"

His mouth curved beneath the dark mustache. He turned away, then paused to look at her. "I admit I am relieved to see you alive. Your wit has come to be appreciated. If Margaret had half of your ability, she would have seen through me years ago."

"Maybe she found it easier to pretend that she did not."

"Yes . . . perhaps she was wise after all. And she will be both well and safe when you and Buckley show up in London—if her mind is not pained by your suspicions."

He truly believes he can get away with this, she thought. "There are British troops here from Jorhat. And if I tell either my father or Seward you are here, they will order the ensign to arrest you."

"On what charges? Your suspicions? You have no evidence."

"No. But the major has proof of your involvement in the mutiny at Plassey and the assassination at Guwahati. And he knows how Harrington and Zameem worked with you. He suspected you even at Manali and sent word to Colonel Warbeck in Calcutta."

Sir Hugo searched her face, and she hoped her fear did not show.

"Jace Buckley is dead," he said. "He was killed by Sunil at Sibsagar."

For a moment horror gripped her. Then she drew in a breath. "No, he is quite alive, and so is Gem. I am becoming accustomed to your lies. The battle at Sibsagar is over. That is the reason you are running. You know Jace will come."

He snapped his bags shut and picked them up from the bed. A smirk lingered on his face. "Goodbye, Coral."

He strode past her and walked down the hall to the stairway. Sir Hugo had never allowed anything to trap him before. Was it a mistake to let him leave Kingscote?

Coral followed. She might have alerted Seward and her father, but Hugo was not a man to apprehend at a desperate moment. It was best to let Jace bring the matter of his guilt to the governor-general in Calcutta, where he would receive a fair trial.

At the stairway she looked down into the hall, but he had already gone out the front door.

Outside on the front verandah, Sir Hugo stood in the darkness. Where was the horse he had ordered the groom to saddle? He looked down the carriageway and saw no sign of the Indian boy. Impatiently he set his two bags down. The sky churned with thick clouds. The Brahmaputra River flowed by, obscure and silent. He would travel south to Guwahati before Sunil's army returned. Was Sunil dead? It no longer mattered. All plans and schemes were now like broken pottery, fit for nothing but the dump heap. Perhaps tomorrow new plans would rise from the ashes, but now he must escape. When he returned, matters would be different. He would think of some way to start over, to rebuild his dreams.

He snapped out of his reverie. A manji was walking toward him from the river. Sir Hugo could see his white puggari.

A boat, he thought suddenly. *Yes, to Guwahati.* "You! Get the boat ready. I am going downriver. Be quick about it."

"Yes, sahib."

Sir Hugo picked up his bags and left the porch. He followed the boatman down the sloping lawn to the ghat steps.

Hugo entered the boat and settled himself on the seat, glancing back at Kingscote. The golden light in the high windows seemed to stare back at him, and for one strange moment he sensed he would never walk across the lawn again, and never mount the verandah steps to enter its hall.

"Perfect nonsense," he murmured. "Of course I shall come back. I am not yet defeated."

A movement from the manji caught his attention. He drew back in a moment of surprise as he looked into the face of Natine. "Natine, you startled me. I thought you were yet in the village."

"News has come from Sibsagar, Sahib Roxbury. Maharaja Sunil is dead. Rajiv's son is alive and will rule one day. You vowed to me it would not be so."

"Do I control the outcome of battles? If Sunil is dead, it is because he blundered badly."

"No. It is you who has made the mistake. You promised me if I help you, Gem will die. That you will be burra-sahib of Kingscote. No more feringhi religion, no more school, and Kali reigns supreme. Now Sunil is dead. I am told Gem will be the maharaja of all Assam! He will serve Miss Coral's God! Now the major comes to Kingscote. The school will be rebuilt, and more feringhis will come! It is you, Sahib Roxbury, who has done all this evil."

"Do not be a fool, Natine."

"I am a fool. I believed you. Were better that I stayed Sir Hampton's friend than listen to your lies. There will be no more lies."

Sir Hugo did not like the wild gleam in the servant's eyes. His hand moved slowly under his black coat to reach for his pistol.

Natine stood, his eyes cold. Slowly he lifted the lid from a small basket at his feet.

Hugo's eyes widened. "No, you fool—"

The cobra landed on his chest. Hugo caught only a glimpse of its flat, weaving head, its beady eyes glowing yellow. He felt the fangs sink into his throat. He cried out, trying to fling it from him into the river.

From out of the darkness the priest came, and Hugo screamed at the face of death. "Get away . . . you filthy murderer. . . ."

They lifted him from the boat and Hugo struggled to wrench free, but already the venom was working.

"God," he tried to call, but the word would go no further than his tongue. Instead he heard "Kali" chanted in his ears. Darkness was coming to swallow him up. Horror and fear seized him. Too late . . . too late. . . .

The two men threw him into the river, and Hugo felt the dark water dragging him down.

The first drops of rain began to fall and landed on the worn ghat steps as Natine and the sadhu hurried up to the lawn.

————

Coral tossed restlessly in her sleep. The familiar nightmare had returned. She was running, and the trees were on fire; the hatcheries were going up in billowing flames that reached toward the sky. *Jace!*

A brilliant streak of lightning startled her awake. She sat up and looked toward the open window, her heart pounding. Fire! She threw aside her covers, intent on reaching the verandah. The hatcheries were burning—

No! What was that odor?—smoke. The mansion was burning! She raced into the hall, banging on the other bedchamber doors as she went. "Father! Kathleen, Marianna, get up! Hurry! Fire! Get out!"

She heard them stirring in a moment of muddled confusion, but ran on. She must warn the servants downstairs. As she ran for the stairway she heard breaking glass coming from her sisters' rooms. She stopped, horrified. The parlor was burning, and her father's office. Smoke crept like evil fog ready to smother and blind its victims. Coral screamed below for the ensign, for Piroo, for Mera, Rosa, and the other servants. She heard nothing. Had they been able to get out the back door?

"Please, God, help us!"

She turned to go back down the hall to help her father with Elizabeth when a feeble wail reached her ears from somewhere downstairs in the smoke.

Reena! Why was she not with Preetah?

Cold fear gripped her stomach. Coral clutched the banister and stared below. "Reena!" she shouted. "Where are you? Can you hear me?"

Nothing. Only the crackle of fire, the stench of acrid fumes, the sputter of rich draperies going up in flames, the crystal chandelier crashing to the marble floor. The expensive family paintings from Roxbury House toppled from the parlor walls and melted in the heat.

"Miss Coral!" Reena screamed. "Here! I'm caught!"

The sound came from the ballroom.

Coral refused to think of the hopelessness of her cause. She went down the stairs holding her dressing gown over her mouth and nose. Suddenly she stopped! A man appeared in the hallway, but he did not see her, so intent was he on reaching Reena.

"Reena! It is me, Uncle Natine! Where are you!"

Coral froze. Natine stumbled through the ballroom doors.

The plantation was awake, and in the hatcheries and out on the lawn there were shouting voices looming like dying shadows in the firelight. Horses raced by, and she heard the voice of Ensign Niles shouting orders, followed by the trumpeting of elephants.

Something crashed in the direction of the ballroom. A moment later she heard Reena outside shouting: "Uncle, where are you? Are you still in there?"

There was the horrible sound of sizzling wood, and the heat was becoming unbearable. *Reena is outside safe,* thought Coral. *But Natine and I are both trapped.*

She heard his voice in the ballroom, but it seemed that it was consumed in the roar of fire. She tried to retreat in the direction of the stairs, but there was so much smoke she could not see, and her eyes and lungs burned. She crawled toward the stairs and bumped into the divan. She struggled in the direction of where she thought the front door should be. Everything was too hot to touch.

She reached her hand out. "Help me!"

———

"Sahib!" whispered Gokul, pointing.

The night air smelled of smoke, and flames were leaping into the darkness, defying the gentle rain that had begun to fall. Jace raced his horse down the carriageway, his gaze searching the crowd that was gathering on the wide lawn for a glimpse of Coral. She was not there! For a moment his emotions gave way to panic.

He maneuvered his horse through the crowd, searching. Marianna saw him and ran toward his horse, grabbing his booted leg. "Major! Coral is missing! Kathleen and I went to her room before we crawled down from the verandah, and she wasn't there! She is somewhere downstairs!"

Jace galloped the horse toward the front of the house, reining him in as the animal shied from the flames. The door was open and smoke swirled, burning his throat. *A fool's death*, he thought, but he entered.

"Coral!"

———

Sir Hampton had opened the windows in the bedchamber where Elizabeth lay moaning in her sleep. Below he saw men on horses and workers running in all directions. His daughters, had they climbed down through the verandah? He could only trust God that they had, for the hall was now dark with smoke seeping under the door.

He ran back to the bed and picked up Elizabeth, carrying her toward the verandah. Already the fire was spreading. He could see the hatcheries billowing up into clouds. Everything was aflame. Kingscote would be nothing but ashes by morning.

His heart was beating, but he felt nothing but deadness. "Elizabeth," he repeated, holding her in his arms and gazing out, numb. "Elizabeth! Kingscote is being destroyed."

The firelight fell upon them as he stood transfixed on

the verandah, staring out at what once had been his life, his pride, his passion.

Seward was shouting up at him to come down quickly. He heard the shouts of Kathleen and Marianna.

Coral. Where was his sweet Coral?

Panic gripped him. His eyes filled with tears as he looked back helplessly at the smoking door.

"She's trapped! Dear God! Coral is trapped in the fire!"

Elizabeth moaned. At the desperate wail of Hampton, she stirred, her eyes blinking. "Coral!" cried Elizabeth. "Coral!"

Hampton looked down into the drawn face of the woman in his arms and saw fear in her eyes. A surge of joy flooded through him. She understood! Her mind was not destroyed!

"Sir Hampton!" shouted Seward from below. "Aye, man, the rope, the rope! Before it burns!"

Hampton's strength of will rallied. He moved swiftly now, and holding Elizabeth with one arm, he grasped the rope that Seward had thrown to the rail.

Kingscote was on fire but his beloved was awake. All was not lost. He had her. And he had a new, more powerful love for God. Hope burned more brightly than did the flames, more enduring than a family dynasty, more lasting than brick and mortar. Casting aside all restraint he shouted upward into the cascading rain: "Almighty God! I give you thanks!"

His body was worn and hurting, but with a light heart he managed to climb down, holding on to Elizabeth. Then—rain! It was pouring!

"Beautiful monsoon!" he choked with delight, looking up at the dark clouds. "Sweet silver drops! Come!"

The lightning streaked hot white against black; thunder uttered its dominance; the huge fat drops broke in a tumultuous downpour beating against the fire in the mansion, the hatcheries, the jungle trees. Hampton laughed. Elephants trumpeted. And the fire struggled to survive. . . .

Coral heard Jace, and the sound of his strong, urgent voice shot through her like a bright arrow. She crawled in the direction of his voice, seeing nothing but the smoke that burned her lungs and parched her throat.

"Jace!" The call was feeble. Did he hear it?

She heard his steps and struggled to move in his direction.

He advanced to where she was, and Coral reached out both hands. "Jace!"

He swept her into his arms and ran back in the direction from which he had come, and soon they emerged into the drenching rain, warm and steamy. He carried her away from the house toward the cooler shrubs, where Coral coughed and gasped, filling her lungs with fresh air.

Preetah had found her sister Reena and knelt on the grass embracing her. Reena was pointing back toward the house. "Natine!"

Her cries were lost in the joy from her father and sisters as they saw Coral safely with Jace.

Only vaguely aware of the others spread out on the lawn, Coral met the penetrating blue-black eyes while the rain soaked him. "I—I thought I would never see you again."

"My dear Miss Kendall," he said with mock decorum. "Did you think I would settle for losing you to mere fire and smoke after all I've gone through to get you?"

Emotionally spent, she gave in to laughter, leaning her head against his wet chest.

The rain was pouring, soaking her through to the skin, washing the smell of smoke from her hair and face. Her head lifted, her eyes growing languid as the firelight flickered against his wet skin.

"I—I don't look or feel like a bride," she whispered, her eyes clinging to his.

"Ah! But you will!" he whispered. He smiled faintly, and she loved the glimmer of warmth in the depths of his eyes. He smoothed the wet strands of golden hair from her face and throat.

His lips met hers . . . and the moment merged with the intensity of the fire.

They were oblivious to the downpour, the trumpeting elephants, the shouting voices.

———

Across the lawn, Seward stood where Hampton knelt, Elizabeth's head on his lap. "The monsoon be putting the fire out! The Almighty be good to us this day, Hampton! Not all be lost after all."

"No, all is not lost," said Sir Hampton, cradling Elizabeth against his chest. As the rain poured upon them, Elizabeth lifted a weak hand to draw Hampton's creased face down to hers.

"You are safe."

"Yes, Liza!"

"The—the hatcheries, the house—"

"I have you, nothing else matters. But look, Liza! Seward is right!" He gestured toward the hatcheries. God has sent the monsoon for Kingscote! The blessed rains are putting the flames out. Not all is ashes! Out of what is left, we will build again!"

"C-Coral—"

"She is with the major. And Kathleen and Marianna are here—" He turned his head and held out his arm to include them. They came, kneeling, embracing their mother.

"Oh, Mama, you are all right," wept Marianna.

"Yes. . . ."

29

Convincing Sir Hampton to let him marry his daughter instead of giving her to Ethan, whom the family now knew to be with Felix Carey in Burma, had proven a simpler task than Jace had anticipated.

There was a break in the rains, and the two men stood by the banks of the Brahmaputra, looking toward the charred ruin of the Kendall mansion.

"It will take years, but we will build again," said Hampton. "The caterpillars and mulberry orchard, thank God, were not all destroyed."

Jace wrestled with his own desires. He knew Hampton wanted him to stay permanently at Kingscote. Jace was in the same position he'd been in with the colonel when it came to the expectation of having a son or daughter by his side in the family enterprise. With the colonel it was the military, with Hampton, the silk.

Jace's infatuation with Darjeeling had been too long in progress to lay it aside, yet he respected this man enough to find it difficult to take Coral and leave to chart his own course. Especially now.

He lowered his hat and looked past the sloping lawn at the Kendall ruin, but in his mind he saw another mansion, white against the backdrop of the Himalayas. The ruling rajas of Sikkim called Darjeeling *Dorje Ling*, meaning "Place of Thunderbolts." On a summit at 2123 meters, Darjeeling straddled a large ridge and was forested with lush green, offering breathtaking views of the snowy mountain peaks and down to the swollen rivers in the valley bottoms. During the monsoon season thick clouds obscured the eastern Himalaya mountain region like a crown of white, but the rest of the year the sight was majestic. His plantation would sit on soft rolling hills of tea bushes for as far as he could see, and there would be workers from Nepal, hundreds of them to cultivate and harvest, and to load the *Madras* and other ships for the voyage to Europe.

Sir Hampton studied Jace as though he recognized something akin to himself. He sighed. "I lost Michael through my stubbornness to accept what he was, what he wanted in life. I should have backed his endeavor financially. I've a feeling, Jace, you and Michael were right. Your interest in the mountainous region was farsighted. One day the East India Company may find it a crucial location."

Jace had thought he and Seward were the only ones to have thought of that. "Darjeeling could become an important pass into Nepal and Tibet. It could know rapid development as a trading center and tea-growing area along the trade route leading from Sikkim to the plains of India."

"Aye, and the climate is perfect for tea. I know a pang of regret, thinking of Michael."

"If Michael were here, I think I know what he would say."

Hampton looked at him, and it was obvious he already felt pleased that the young man would become his son-in-law. His eyes misted. "And what would my son say?"

Jace looked up the grassy slope and saw Coral walk toward them, the hem of her billowing skirts ruffling in the breeze. She stopped, one hand holding her hat. Jace thought not only of Kingscote but her school.

"He would say your dream lives on in the ashes, only waiting for you to find the strength to try again. The past bleeds with the prayers and tears of many who hold Kingscote in their heart."

Sir Hampton laid a strong hand on his shoulder and looked not at the ruin but at Jace. "Aye, he would. And he would tell you to do the same, my son. Go to Darjeeling. Take Coral, and Seward. Someday the family will have both a silk and tea dynasty in Assam."

Jace thought of Alex and said smoothly, "You may find yourself unexpectedly converged upon by a number of marriages. I can think of only one reason why Alex would go to London. A Roxbury may end up your daughter-in-law after all."

Hampton frowned. Jace tried not to smile, for he knew Belinda was looked upon as frivolous. "You might want to prepare Mrs. Kendall for the surprise. I feel certain Alex will return with Belinda as his bride."

Hampton only grunted.

"Kathleen will back me up on my suspicion. She too guessed he went to save her from Sir George. Later she found the small box she had asked Elizabeth about. It contained a ring that Alex had once secretly given to Belinda. She sent it back to Alex as a distress call. It was that ring that Natine stole and used to lure you to Darjeeling."

"Ah. . . ."

Hampton squinted toward the house, and it seemed to Jace that he was visualizing grandsons and granddaughters romping on the lawn. Jace smiled. "I think you will have a small army to carry on Kingscote in the years to come."

"And Darjeeling," Hampton was swift to add.

"The monsoon will make trekking to Darjeeling impossible for months. I have already spoken to Coral, and Seward and I would like to serve you here until Kingscote is repaired. Then, for Coral's sake, it is best she remain here until we have a residence on the Darjeeling land that can offer her what she needs," said Jace, thinking of her health. "She will also want to rebuild the school with your permission, this time in stone."

Hampton smiled his pleasure. "I shall take you up on that. It may be I shall have my first grandson born on Kingscote after all."

"Sahib," came a sober interruption.

Jace and Hampton turned to look downriver, where Gokul was returning from his walk along the banks. "What is it, Gokul?" called Jace.

"I believe the river is unhappy. It has returned the remains of Sir Hugo Roxbury."

Jace and Hampton exchanged glances. "The storm maybe," said Hampton tonelessly, his jaw hard. "His boat may have overturned."

Jace had his own suspicions. "I think Natine caught up with him. Coral said Roxbury left in haste not long before the fire."

"Aye, you may be right. Natine may have felt betrayed when their schemes did not work out."

Gokul was holding something. "This ruby ring I saw many times on his hand. The crocodiles didn't leave much, but this proves that the remains are indeed Roxbury's."

Hampton sighed as he took it between his fingers and

stared at it, remembering the many years that were forever past. "It is his ring all right. Margaret, I think, will not grieve too deeply."

—————

Amid the downpour, the task of building appropriate shelter for them all proved formidable. With the help of Jace, Seward, Ensign Niles, and the troopers, extra bungalows were constructed. Thilak and men from the hatcheries worked to put up a makeshift roof over the mansion's cook room, where Piroo morosely searched through the ashes for his precious cooking utensils, grumbling against Natine and the sadhu from morning till evening when he departed with a long face for the stables.

Nearly a month had passed since the fire. Neither Coral nor Jace had discussed the wedding. She knew why, of course.

At noon he stopped at her meager bungalow, standing in the doorway, drenching wet with a cynical lopsided smirk. "You could always run away with a derelict sea captain. At least you'll be dry in the Great Cabin. However, I cannot promise smooth sailing."

A brow arched when she said nothing. He scanned her. "Need I remind you that Christmas draweth nigh? True, we are not exactly in a merry countenance, but if I am going to live in perpetual rain, I might as well share my muddy hut with a fair damsel."

"But, Jace, a wedding here? How? I've not even a decent dress to wear and—"

He took her elbow. "Come. It is time we had a cozy gathering with your family to discuss more important matters than aching backs and sore thumbs."

"And just where, sir, do you advise we have this 'comfortable' little gathering?"

"The cook room, of course. I happen to be hungry and Piroo has baked my favorite delicacy—chupatti bread."

She smiled at his good-natured sarcasm, for their food had been as boring as their shelters. In the company of her glum sisters, she walked with Jace in the rain to the mansion shell.

They had all gathered at his request, somewhat amused, and Seward grinned as they entered. "The cook room be the most important room in the house," and his eyes twinkled as he helped himself to one of Piroo's breads.

"Indeed?" said Coral wryly. "With my wedding due on Christmas?"

"Aye, lass, but the major be willing to take you aboard the *Madras* and marry you anytime," teased Seward.

Coral heard the constant plop, plop of water splashing in the vessels Piroo and Rosa had set about the room. It was anything but romantic, thought Coral grimly.

"Christmas wedding, indeed," she said, folding her arms. "I shall stand ankle deep in water."

"We could all sail on Jace's ship for London," said Kathleen baitingly. "What a wedding you would have at Roxbury House. Granny V would think herself in heaven between you and Cousin Belinda."

"Just think," said Marianna. "Alex and Belinda. So that was why you kept asking Mother about him receiving a letter and a small box."

Coral too remembered, and had wondered, but events had kept her too occupied until now to ask about Kathleen's suspicions. It wasn't until she had produced the letter to her father and sisters that Kathleen had admitted finding an empty box in Alex's bedchamber.

"I recognized the ornate box at once as belonging to

Belinda," said Kathleen. "She showed it to me in Calcutta. Alex had given her his family ring as a token of engagement, but later changed his plans for Austria. It wasn't until she sent the letter to him telling of a forced marriage in London to Sir George that Alex decided he truly loved her."

Marianna sighed wistfully. "I wish someone would decide he loved me like that."

"You mean Charles Peddington?" teased Kathleen.

"Maybe Captain Gavin MacKay," said Marianna with a smile, and then laughed when Kathleen unexpectedly blushed.

"London, and Roxbury House," said Coral thoughtfully, and glanced sideways at Jace. She knew a grand wedding meant nothing to him. He had already remarked that waltzing his wedding night away in the stiff company of London's earls and lords at the Roxbury ballroom was the last thing he wanted. She knew, however, that if she truly wished for the wedding to be held in London he would agree. Under his even stare she smiled and pretended to be serious.

"Yes, and a wedding dress from the Silk House, created by Jacques! What more could I want?"

"It is two months from Assam to Diamond Harbor, and six months to London from Calcutta," remarked Jace smoothly. "And knowing your grandmother, it will take three more months to get ready for the wedding. Are you suggesting we wait another year to marry?"

Coral smiled at Kathleen. "Going to London for the wedding would suit me fine; however, the major is somewhat difficult to hold on to. If I delay a year he may decide to disappear again with Gokul. Or worse yet—set sail for some distant port."

She walked over to Jace and placed a protective hand on his arm. "No, I think I'd better marry you now. A girl never knows about seafarers."

He regarded her. "A wise decision, madam." He turned toward Elizabeth. "And you, Mrs. Kendall? What do you suggest for your daughter? If you would have us wait and voyage to London, both Coral and I will consider."

Coral was pleased to see the kindness in his eyes when he looked at her mother.

Elizabeth rallied and came alert. "You said something, Jace?"

He quietly repeated his question.

Every head turned toward Elizabeth. She had been silent for some time, and Coral and the others thought it trying for her to make much comment about the upcoming marriage. Although she had agreed to the wedding and was happy to welcome Jace into the family, she had offered little advice concerning the dilemma.

"Perhaps you can marry at Sibsagar. Prince Adesh would welcome the idea. I think we all would." Her brown eyes gleamed unexpectedly and a smile showed on her thin face. "I think it would prove fitting to your relationship with Gem."

Coral caught her breath and went to her, stooping beside her chair. She picked up the cool hand that rested on the shawl over her lap. "Why, Mother, what an exciting idea. It is perfect." She turned her head toward Jace, her eyes pleading.

"I think it can be arranged," he said. "Both Gem and his ruling grandfather expect to meet with you. In light of what has happened on Kingscote, a wedding in the palace isn't likely to offend Raja Singh."

Coral felt her excitement growing. A wedding in the royal palace—the home of Jemani! "Yes, that is what I want."

Jace offered a light bow. "As you wish. A royal wedding it shall be."

He left to find Gokul, and Coral turned to her mother and laughed. "No one but you would have thought of it. But a dress—why, everything in my room is either ruined by smoke or rain!"

Marianna asked dubiously, "What about an Indian wedding dress?"

Coral shook her head. "No. I want to carry on Mother's tradition and marry in white silk, with a veil and satin slippers and—"

"Maybe . . ." cried Kathleen and turned to her mother. "*Your* wedding dress! The trunk was salvaged, and if I could take the dress apart and redesign it—maybe Coral can have her white dress."

"Yes!" cried Coral, on her feet. She looked at her mother, whose brown eyes shone. "Oh, Mother, can we?"

Elizabeth smiled up at Hampton, who came and took her hand in his. "I can think of no finer use for your mother's wedding dress."

Coral and her sisters raced toward the charred remains of the back room where the goods that had been recovered were stored. Many items in the process of being sorted through by Mera and Rosa were stacked high. Coral searched for the trunk that her mother had brought from Roxbury House.

"Here it is," cried Marianna.

Coral opened the trunk, and her hopes were shattered. She groaned. She drew out various discolored objects until she came to the carefully wrapped wedding dress. She lifted it out.

"How dreadful! The cloth is scorched, and even the pearls look discolored," groaned Marianna.

"Well," said Coral, completely disheartened. "It was

silk at one time—definitely expensive and boasting that Mother was a Roxbury from London."

They stared at the remains in silence while the rain ran off the edges of the partial roof.

Coral folded it back into the trunk. "Do not say anything to Mother yet."

———————

Sibsagar

Jace sat on cushions in the royal chamber of the palace. Before him was a large display of various-size diamonds, rubies, emeralds, sapphires, and other gems. There were dozens of rings, bracelets, necklaces, nose rings, anklets, and a host of other ornaments.

Jace studied them carefully. Opposite him, Raja Singh sat cross-legged studying the Mogul sword with bright, eager eyes. Jace knew the sword's value. His primary interest at the moment was a wedding ring for Coral, but there was a residence to build at Darjeeling and many future expenses. He had intended to sell the *Madras*—his pride and joy—in order to buy her a ring, but now he would not need to. He was even pleased enough to feel kindly toward Zin. Zin had placed a short message inside the red silk cover: "A wedding gift to my friend Javed Kasam."

Jace, however, had no doubt that the "thief" he had come across in Calcutta had been one of Zin's men from the bazaars. No matter . . . he had the heirloom back—and just in time. If Seward had not taken it upon himself to safeguard it, it would have been destroyed in the fire.

Jace held up the diamond and ruby ring he wanted and a matching necklace, thinking of the one Ethan had given to Coral. This one was far more delicate, and exquisite.

"I will take these," he said. "But the sword is worth more. It is from the Mogul's palace at Agra."

"Indeed, indeed," said Raja Singh. He gestured to the servant, then smiled at Jace. "I have many gifts for you, Major Buckley. How could I ever show gratitude enough for returning Prince Adesh, son of my daughter Jemani, to his home safely? You are much in our favor!"

Servants brought in several small bags of jewels, several jewel-handled weapons, silk and satin cloaks, turbans, and all manner of ornate garb, each also adorned with jewels.

"Your generosity, Excellency, humbles me. But one thing more I do ask: I need silk cloth for a wedding dress. Would any woman in your zenana have this?"

"I feel assured we can oblige you, Major. I shall have a servant see to it at once."

"And slippers," added Jace.

"Anything you may wish."

An hour later, Jace, Seward, and Gokul gathered up the treasure, and with the wedding arranged, they departed for the humble huts of Kingscote.

"Ah, sahib," said Gokul with a grin. "This is one time silk heiress is poor, and future tea plantation master is very rich."

"Javed Kasam would be highly pleased," quipped Jace, thinking back to that moment in the ghari in Calcutta when Coral had tried to buy him with the Roxbury ring. *"I'll buy you that tea plantation,"* she had said. He would now bring her silk to make a wedding dress. He held up the diamond and ruby wedding ring to let it catch the light.

Someday the family would finish sorting through the rubble and hopefully find most of their treasures, including that Roxbury ring, but for now, the only ring Coral would own was the one Jace Buckley had placed on her finger himself.

———

Felix Carey's Mission Station
Burma

So Hugo is dead but Coral is alive.

Ethan sat on the bunk in his bamboo hut reading the letter Coral had written him explaining the death of his father. Knowing that she lived brought him joy and a new sense of freedom. Until this moment he had not understood how thoughts of her death had burdened him with false guilt. Thank God she was well— and happy in her coming marriage to the major.

Ethan's gray eyes showed no emotion, then unexpectedly he gave a laugh. "How fitting an end," he murmured.

Slowly he folded the letter and walked to his makeshift desk to file it where he might read it again when he thought of her, but he paused. The words came to mind that Felix Carey had spoke that rainy morning in chapel from the Apostle Paul's Epistle to the Philippians: ". . . forgetting those things which are behind, and reaching forth unto those things which are before . . ."

Yes, thought Ethan.

Felix would know well about forgetting yesterday and pressing toward tomorrow. A young man also, he had already lost his wife to illness here in Burma.

Ethan's decision came quietly. He would stay in Burma and dedicate himself to his medical work, aiding Felix. Someday he might wish to return to London, but for the foreseeable future he was content to lose himself in his work.

He stood in silence listening to the rain, then held the letter to the flame on the candle and watched it curl and wither into ash.

30

Coral sighed as she held up the yards of silk for Kathleen to study. "What do you think? Can you make the wedding dress?"

Kathleen held it to her cheek. "It is gorgeous."

"Oh, I want to get married too!" moaned Marianna.

"I can make a fine wedding dress—if I receive the help I will need," said Kathleen. "We haven't much time and no place to work that isn't smudged with soot."

"We will all help," said Marianna. "Preetah is good with cloth."

The girl smiled. "Oh, I would like to very much."

Preetah had not grieved over the death of her uncle Natine, whose charred body had been found in the rubble. Thinking of it now brought Coral a small shudder. What had been his reason for coming in the house once he had set the fire? Had he intended to bolt her in her room? The thought that she had come within feet of him on the stairway after she had gone down to try to find Reena was chilling. Yet Natine had performed one act of mercy in his death. He *had* saved Reena, and Coral had not been able to reach her.

The news about Sir Hugo had not been so pleasant.

Jace had informed Coral that morning that his body had been found in the river.

"Then we will begin work immediately" said Kathleen, bringing Coral's mind back to the present. Her sister frowned. "If I could only find my sewing things, but there is no chance of that. We'll do the best we can with what we have."

"Yanna said her bungalow is larger and dry," said Preetah. "You can work there. I will care for the children and let them stay with Reena."

"And I previously gave her needles and silk thread so she could make Devi a sari for Christmas," said Kathleen.

"Then I will go tell her," said Preetah and ran out.

"Christmas will not be so dreadfully disappointing after all," said Marianna.

Coral lifted her new slippers with their tiny sparkling diamonds and scrutinized them thoughtfully. More important than the slippers was the man who had thought enough of her to come back from Sibsagar with them. She was learning even more about the adventurous seafarer as the days past. Jace, she decided, was a very romantic man.

On a rainy afternoon a surprising entourage arrived at Kingscote. The 13th rode up the carriageway under Colonel John Warbeck and Captain Gavin MacKay. A lone civilian journeyed with them, Charles Peddington.

"And look at us," groaned Kathleen, staring down at her soiled Indian sari.

Marianna picked up the disfigured mirror they had found in the ash rubble and looked at herself with horror. Gone was the elaborate hairdo of curls and ribbons, and her hair was wound simply into a chignon with the strands hanging limp. Her blue eyes came tragically to

Kathleen. "Mister Peddington will never recognize me."

Kathleen was smarting under her own injured pride. The last time she had seen Gavin MacKay she had been dressed in an expensive frock at Manali, and boasting of her disinterest in anything but returning to the Silk House at London. The truth was, after all the loss and heartache they had been through recently, she was not so certain she wished to go to London. Perhaps she was ready for marriage herself.

"Well," she said wryly to Marianna, who stood disconsolately as the rain dripped through the thatch roof. "It is time we ate humble pie."

———

Jace was surprised to see his adoptive father, Colonel John Warbeck. He raced to his bungalow, where Gokul was already rushing about to produce Jace's military uniform. While Jace threw off his leather jerkins and Indian tunic, Gokul tried to polish the buttons.

"What is *he* doing here?" murmured Jace, snatching his report on the mutiny at Jorhat from a waterproof trunk under his bedroll.

"Ah, Sahib-Major, the Colonel, he will never relent until you stay in the wondrous Bengal army."

Jace cast him a wry glance as he buttoned the top collar on his jacket. "My hat."

"Here!"

Jace placed it precisely on his head, and with the report under his arm to protect it from the rain, he walked across the mud to meet Colonel John Warbeck.

Ensign Niles and the troop from Jorhat were forming a military line to receive the colonel. The colonel saw Jace and rode up, drawing his horse to a stop. The rain pelted on the colonel's hat and black raincoat, and the steely gray eyes swept Jace. "Congratulations on a mission well done," he said. "I expect a full report."

Jace saluted. "As you say, Colonel, a full report." He handed the thick volume to his father.

The colonel took the papers and glanced toward the bungalow.

Jace stepped aside. "Gokul! Send up to Piroo! Have him brew some of that coffee we brought back from the bazaar at Sibsagar!"

"At once, Sahib-Major!"

The colonel smiled for the first time, and his eyes showed a mellowed amusement as he dismounted. "Coffee, is it? What happened to your Darjeeling tea?"

Jace too smiled. "Just as soon as you release me from this uniform I shall have time enough to send plenty to your office in Calcutta."

In the bungalow the colonel leafed through the report. "I'll send this to the governor-general. You can fill me in on what has happened."

Several hours had passed while the colonel sat musing over the details and drinking the coffee that Gokul now brewed on a small fire in the corner of the hut.

"That Roxbury was involved does not surprise me. When I received your message from MacKay about Harrington and Zameen, I guessed there might be trouble against the maharaja at Guwahati. We came as quickly as we could."

"What about Harrington and Zameen?"

The colonel chuckled. "They are warming the jail at Fort William, awaiting trial. I had anticipated returning with Roxbury and Sanjay as well. It is a relief that Sanjay is dead, and I should have hated to be in attendance when Roxbury was shot."

Jace noticed an odd look in his father's eyes. Suddenly he remembered . . . Lady Margaret Roxbury—had not the colonel once been engaged to marry her?

"Roxbury's ring is the only proof the man is dead. The crocodiles got most of the rest."

"Sir Hampton has the ring?"

"He was thinking of sending it to Margaret."

Jace saw the subdued interest in the gray eyes. "She is not here?"

"She is in London at Roxbury House." He added smoothly, "You might wish to bring her the ring and the news of Hugo's unfortunate death."

The colonel smiled faintly. "Yes, a military duty, of course."

"Yes, of course. She will need words of sympathy, someone to offer a hand of encouragement. I will speak to Hampton about your upcoming voyage to London to make certain he entrusts the ring and a letter of condolence to you."

The colonel arched a brow of curiosity over Jace's influence.

Jace smiled and folded his arms. "I am going to marry his daughter Coral."

"The one with the green eyes at the ball in Calcutta?"

"You remember."

"I am certain you would also. We both have fine taste in women."

The colonel seemed to be thinking more of London than he was of military matters. "About my mission," Jace pressed. "It is complete now. Did you bring my discharge papers from the governor-general?"

The colonel smiled and reached into his pocket. "Now, Jace, would I forget anything so important?"

"I was thinking you might."

The colonel smiled and handed them to him in an official envelope. "With a marriage on the horizon and a tea plantation to make successful, I would not want to stifle you in that uniform. As of the new year you are released from the office of major."

Jace took the envelope. Their eyes met. The colonel laughed and they gripped each other by the shoulders.

"I am proud of you, Jace. I always was, even when you were off on that ship."

"I hope to keep that respect, Father."

"You will. And now . . . where is the beautiful damsel with the green eyes? I wish to meet my future daughter-in-law."

———

Coral watched Marianna and Charles Peddington huddle under the thatch roof, deep in conversation. Charles was doing all the talking and Marianna was all eyes. *She has found her hero*, thought Coral with pleasure.

But it was days later when Charles approached Sir Hampton with a breathless Marianna on his arm to ask for her hand in marriage.

"Of course we plan to wait an entire year, sir," said Charles, his face flushed under Sir Hampton's smile.

"And Charles wants to stay here permanently, Father," added Marianna.

"I hope to assist Coral with the new school. I've brought her teaching resources and the Scriptures in the Assamese language."

Sir Hampton pretended to be thoughtful. He rubbed his chin. "Of course, Charles, I will need to discuss this matter with Elizabeth."

"Yes, sir!" said Charles with a beaming smile and looked at Marianna. They both guessed they had already won.

Elizabeth, who yet had difficulty in walking, laughed when Hampton told her the news. "Well, darling, you must admit your fears about our daughters producing no heirs has proven groundless. Two marriages announced! And I am certain Kathleen and Gavin will soon come to an agreement."

"Aye, 'tis about time. And Gavin being a Scot at that."

The announcement did come. But it was not what the family expected. Coral was the first to hear about it from Jace.

"He has decided Kathleen should work at Silk House after all. While she works with your aunt Margaret and the man they call Jacques, Gavin intends to try to win Sir Hugo's old seat in Parliament. Politics seem an odd choice where Gavin is concerned, but he is adamant. He will do all he can to win the support of your grandmother."

"Granny V? She will adore him! If she has anything to say about it, he will sit in Parliament. I wonder about Alex and Belinda. . . ."

Jace scowled up at the dripping thatch roof. "How is your wedding dress coming?"

"It is nearly finished."

He looked at her. "When Alex returns with Belinda I have a suspicion he will settle down and be content to play his music in the new ballroom at Kingscote. And he should prove more of an asset to the silk than Hampton would have guessed."

"Did you hear? Colonel Warbeck will go to London with Gavin and Kathleen."

Jace smiled a little. "Yes, he wishes to return Roxbury's ring to your aunt." He stood and walked toward her. "And now, what about you and me?"

31

Sibsagar

Torchbearers marched four abreast of Jace's royal elephant. His wedding garb had been sent by Prince Adesh, no doubt carefully chosen under the scrutinizing eye of the raja himself. Jace wore immaculate black with a smoke blue sash and a jeweled tulwar. Across from him sat Seward and Gokul, also adorned for the occasion.

Seward sighed. "Well, lad, this be the best day in a long while. Never thought you'd be claiming Hampton's prized daughter, though I did suspect back in Manali that the lass was caring for you. Nothing else but love could have made her come with me and Boswell that night." He chuckled. "Darjeeling will be a bit more interesting now. Always did think some children running about would brighten the tea patch."

Jace's mouth turned. "Not a 'tea patch,' Seward—acres of tea. Containing all the miserable brew that English ladies could yearn for."

"Ah, sahib," said Gokul, settling his silk turban more carefully. "What bothers old Gokul is how we grow this

389

'miserable brew' when Sahib Hampton thinks only of silkworms."

"Don't worry, old man, I will think of something— just as soon as the Kendall mansion is livable again. We can't leave them now. But Alex is bound to arrive soon with Belinda, and that will give me a way out."

Gokul scratched his chin dubiously.

Seward's reddish gray brows came together. "Aye, we'll find us a way all right. Be anxious to turn our partnership into a rich and prosperous plantation before Burma gets new notions of trying to annex Assam. A new war will ruin everything. Be assured England will send an entire army to enter Burma if it comes to it."

"That is one war I intend to stay out of," said Jace dryly.

"Aye, if we can—and if your sons and daughters can."

Jace looked at him thoughtfully but said nothing.

"I have one thing on my mind now. And I believe we have arrived at the palace, gentlemen."

Through the flickering light emerged the vision of hundreds of spectators. Jace's elephant proceeded instinctively to the very entry, where it knelt for them to dismount. He saw the raja in royal garb and beside him, Gem—Prince Adesh Singh.

As Jace stood waiting for Coral he became aware that her elephant was coming. He watched through the myriads of bright torches lining the avenue, and another elephant slowly emerged. In the firelight he could see that it was of royal lineage and carried a golden howdah and a wide crimson silk umbrella. It came toward them, elaborately decorated, and tinkling with bells.

Jace watched as Coral's elephant neared the center of the royal court. While the rajput guards stood around him in military splendor, the elephant knelt. Several guards walked forward to help her alight. His breath paused as he saw Coral. . . .

———

Gokul wiped his eyes as he watched unobtrusively from the royal pavilion, where he had chosen the best view possible. He straddled a limb that extended out over the courtyard. Sahib would be proud of him if he could see how he had managed to "shimmy" up the tree, he thought with a smile. He glanced at little Prince Adesh. He had managed to have a big surprise waiting for sahib and sahiba, and it was he, Gokul, who had told him what would make his two friends happy.

Gokul watched now, intently.

Coral came from the torchlight, veiled and surrounded by her sisters and the memsahib herself. There was also Preetah, Yanna, and little Reena—all wearing cloth of gold. Reena carried white flowers in a woven basket.

Coral stopped and salaamed to Raja Singh and Prince Adesh, and a hush fell for a moment over the crowd. Then she turned and walked toward Jace.

He came to meet her. He stared at her for a long moment, then whispered something in her ear. She turned and looked, and from the shadows walked a young man plainly dressed and carrying a black book.

Gokul smiled. This was Prince Adesh's surprise.

Felix Carey stopped in front of them, holding open his Bible, and began to perform the marriage ceremony.

At the conclusion of the brief service, Jace reached out and lifted Coral's veil. Again he whispered something, then enfolded her in his arms.

"Ah . . ." sighed Gokul with deep satisfaction.

A cheer went up from the spectators and guests.

———

Coral stood with Jace and turned to face again the raja and Prince Adesh. Her eyes feasted on Gem. How handsome he was! How princely. He walked toward her, and Coral felt Jace's hand on the small of her back edging her forward.

Misted brown eyes looked up at her, then a shy smile. He handed her a present. "For you, Mother," he said.

Mother....

Coral swallowed back the emotion and knelt so she could meet him face-to-face. "A present for me, Excellency?"

"To you, I will be Gem. To you and to Jace. He too is my friend." He handed her the present.

Coral accepted it, the gold wrapping winking in the torchlight.

"Please open it now," urged Gem anxiously.

She gently removed the wrapping and stared. *A Bible*. She opened it and saw the words were in Hindi.

Gem smiled at her pleasure. "Jace said bad men burned your first one. I gave him this one when he left for Kingscote, but he wished me to give it to you now."

"Gem, I shall treasure it forever. It is all the more precious because it came from your hand."

"I have another gift. This one I chose when I knew you and Jace would marry here at Sibsagar."

He motioned toward the elephant. "It is yours, Mother. Jace told me about an elephant named Rani. I think I remember such an elephant. This one is now Rani too."

Coral smiled and could not speak.

The guards had come for him. The winsome child was now Prince Adesh again. His smile left, and he took on a serious expression and stepped back. They walked him back to the side of his grandfather, and Coral watched as he sat down on the dais. For a moment their eyes held;

Gem blinked, then lowered his gaze. Coral swallowed back the cramp in her throat and felt Jace's gentle hand on her elbow telling her it was time to stand to her feet and walk away.

She stood, and something in his gaze brought a smile to her lips.

"We will see Gem again," he said. "Many times. But now, Mrs. Buckley, it is *our* time."

Her eyes whispered her love, and they turned to be escorted toward the royal howdah. The wedding feast was laid out in the palace, and then a royal apartment awaited, beautifully prepared for a king and his queen. A long journey of tomorrows also waited. . . .

With one hand Coral held to Jace's arm; with the other she held the Hindi Bible from Gem. In her heart, Coral held the promise that each tomorrow would first pass through the wise and loving hand of their God.

GLOSSARY

AYAH: A child's nurse.

BRAHMIN: Highest Hindu caste.

BURRA-SAHIB: A great man.

CANTONMENT: British administrative and military area.

CHA-CHA: Uncle.

CHUNNI: A light head-covering; a scarf.

DAK-BUNGALOW: A resting house for travelers.

DEKHO: "Look."

DEWAN: The chief minister of an Indian ruler.

DURBAR: Royal public audience.

FERINGHI: A foreigner.

GHAT: Steps or a platform on the river.

GHARI: A horse-drawn vehicle; a carriage.

GHAZI: A fanatic; usually with religious overtones, but also referring to political beliefs.

HOWDAH: A framework with a seat for carrying passengers on the back of an elephant.

HOOKAH: A water pipe for tobacco.

HUZOOR: Your honor.

JAI RAM: A Hindu greeting.

KANSAMAH: A cook.

KATAR: A thrusting knife.

KOTWAL: A headman.

MAHARAJA: A Hindu king.

MAHOUT: An elephant driver.

MANJI: A boatman.

NAMASTE: A respectful gesture of fingers to the forehead with palms together.

PALANQUIN: A boxlike enclosure carried on poles.

PUGGARI: A turban.

PUNKAH: A fan made of heavy matting or canvas, sometimes wet, and pulled by a rope to make a breeze.

RAJA: A king.

RAJKUMAR: A prince.

RAJKUMARI: A princess.

RANI: A queen.

RAJPUT: A warrior cast of the Hindus, a rank below the *brahmins*.

SADHU: Hindu holy man.

SEPOY: An infantry soldier.

SOWAR: A cavalry trooper.

TEHSILDAR: The village headman.

TONGA: A two-wheel vehicle.

TOPIWALLAH: A man who wears a hat; a foreigner.

TULWAR: A curved sword.

UNTOUCHABLE: One that is below the Hindu caste system, condemned as unclean in this life.

WALLAH: A driver.

ZENANA: Women's quarters.